THE MORNING OF THE MOGUL

The Morning of The Mogul

HICHEM KAROUI

Contents

Note of the Publisher

THE PUBLISHER

This is Mr Bassam Bourasin's admitted Report as a citizen of His republic. He didn't give it a name. He initially addressed it to the Interior Ministry. Instead, it landed on my desk. I publish it as is, with no significant changes to its form or content. However, the "report" was actually written in Arabic as a diary. We just translated it, trying to stay very close to the original. The author did not contact me directly. He has sent his manuscript in Arabic to Global East-West in London with the following note:

To the Attention of the Editor

The manuscript you'll find in this parcel tells the same story as its author. Initially, it was not destined for the public as it was intended to be read only by the top hierarchy in the Ministry of Interior in my country. However, the Mektub changed the first plan. A little incident happened that encouraged me to use less discreet ways.

The fact that the Ministry to whom I have sent the "Report" by recommended postal mail would never acknowledge reception made me suspicious that my little "treasure" may have fallen into the wrong hands. It did not happen just once or twice, but at least 10 times. Yes, sir. I have sent it 10 times, and they deny having received it each time. The last time, they told me, "Don't come back again, because it will end up badly for you. Go home."

This also happened with the post office. It's weird! Every time, I go to send the same parcel (I have many photocopies of my Report). When I return for a follow-up, no one can give me an answer. Not only did the employee who handled my parcel vanish, but even the post office's computer did not record any reference to the parcel. Despite this, every time I showed them the receipt that their colleague gave me on that day.

Finally, the director of the post office refused to meet me. Instead of helping me track my parcel, they called the police, who took me away and advised me to go home and never ask the post office or the Ministry of the Interior again about anything they don't know about. If not? Well, you can imagine!

I was still hoping that the Interior Minister or the President would read the "Report" and take action, because the affair is serious. However, it is pointless to repeat what would fail.

Frustrated and utterly angry about my work that may have ended up in the bin or the shredder, I decided to unveil what was destined to remain in the high spheres of power. After all, the affairs of the State concern the people. At the time, we started hearing about WikiLeaks, then about Edward Snowden. And I started thinking about leaking the Top-Secret Report.

First, I thought of sending a photocopy of my "Report" to Wikileaks. But unfortunately, they don't publish in Arabic. Moreover, their boss, Julian Assange, was having trouble with the authorities. Yes, sir. No offence, but it seems the countries of the south are no longer monopolising authoritarianism, corruption and nepotism. This is happening now, even in democracies.

Then I thought of sending a photocopy of the Report to Mr Edward Joseph Snowden, who also started making a name as a champion-whistleblower, according to the news. Unfortunately, I did not find his address.

My last resort was to propose my "Report" as a book manuscript to the Arab publishing houses. Sadly, it turned out they care about their pockets more than they do about the public interest. I have sent it to at least one hundred of them in several Arab capitals, including in my country. About five rejected it politely, and the majority did not even bother to answer me.

It is hopeless! Nobody would ever read my Report? What is this? Is it Mektub? What made it even more gloomy is the fact that many years have passed since I finished the Report and addressed it to the Ministry of the Interior.

Then one day, as I was browsing the web, I spotted a call for authors from a new London-based publishing house - yours, sir!

I am grateful, because as soon as I took the address, I inserted the would-be book report inside a new parcel. (I always prefer the postal way. It is more secure, despite what happened to me several times with the same parcel.) I went to another city to send it from a post office I had never been to before.

If I am, this time, lucky enough to bring it to your attention, please, don't bother asking about the author. Maybe you would never him, who knows? people in this country appear and disappear without apparent reason. I am not an exclusion, and as I am the author, I grant you hereby all the rights to translate, edit, publish and republish the Report as a book, as a video, as a movie or as a TV series, in any language and in any country. Go ahead, you have my blessing and the Baraka of Allah. This is my contract with your honourable publishing house - Global East-West - with my signature.

A last word: *my Report is not a fiction*, but I give you the right to publish it as fiction if you want.

As I know, the laws do not allow me to mention people by their names without due authorisation, I have changed all the true names in this Report, including my name. For you and for all the readers, I am Bassam Bourasin. However, I also give you the right to publish it under any pseudonym of your choosing. Thus, nobody gets harmed, and people would know what is going on.

Sincerely yours,
Bassam Bourasin.

After reading the manuscript, we had a discussion with the editorial team, upon which we agreed to publish it as a novel, under the pseudonym of Hichem Karoui.

I hope, Mr Bassam Bourasin, you are still alive and in good health, wherever you are. Maybe you are now reading these lines. I want you to know that we keep your royalties in a private safe at the bank in England. Whenever you can pay us a visit, you are most welcome. I wish you good luck.

Your publisher.

To the memory of Nana ...
Beloved mother...
You are always in my heart.
May you rest in eternal peace.

* * *

To All Those Who Resist Oppression

* * *

This book is also dedicated to my dear Tunisia fighting for
clear sight to better see the future...

No regrets. No apologies.

Freedom is sometimes like embers wrapping a rare Diamond.
For the courageous, it is worth to burn hands to get it.

Epigraph

"Nobody did a secret deal,
  Nobody was for sale,
  Nobody bent the rules at all,
  And nobody went to jail,
  And all of them were honest men,
  As white as driven snow,
  And lived on a higher plane,
  And shat on those below..."

Roger Woddis: All Clear

* * *

"And so, what could my sterile and uncouth genius beget but the tale of a dry, shrivelled, whimsical offspring, full of old fancies such as never entered another's brain — just what might be begotten in prison, where every discomfort is lodged and every dismal noise has its dwelling?"

Cervantes: Don Quixote (Prologue)

PART ONE

The Secret Report

Mind Hacker

IN THE DARKNESS OF the night,
While I sleep,
I hear him tiptoeing in the corridor of my mind,
trying to break into the Pyramid of my soul and
steal memories, thoughts, projects,
time and space,
trying to control me,
to stop my run-up from the stars to Earth.
While sleeping,
I hear him
talking into my head,
betraying his unwelcome visit,
What a pretentious fool, falling out of resentment hell
is this?
Mind hacker...But
Mindless!
It's been years that you've been intruding,
You still did not understand?
You're getting nowhere,
I intercept you even before you reach the Gate of the Pyramid,
Do you still hope to get a piece of my soul?
Don't you understand I am the Pharaoh who came from the
Future?
The living God who commands by telepathy,
The Eternal, with extraordinary over-reaching powers,
From a world that is far superior to yours...

Mind hacker...
Are you dumb?
Don't you see, for years, that you constantly failed?
You lost all your wars against me,
But you keep coming back,
And I keep locking you out of my Pyramid...
Who pushed you?
He who did lies to you,
He who did want you to fail,
And you failed,
Looser,
You obey failure,
That's why you're getting nowhere with me.
Mind hacker...
You are nobody,
Your power, if any, is limited by the Gate,
You have no key and no clue about my power.
Look at me,
I see you coming from millions of light-years,
You arrive creeping while I sleep,
You think I am unconscious,
You don't know the difference
between sleep and unconsciousness,
You live in a coma,
You hide,
You hope to snatch a piece of my soul
But you cheat yourself,
each time,
You will never wake up...
Do you still expect me to allow you in the domain of the sa-
cred soul?
You don't know me,
You spent your life trying to find the Gate of the Pyramid,
And you still get locked out,

How can you pretend to know?
You are a lost dog in the desert,
Bark: yap, yap!
Bark: yap, yap, yap!
Bark, again
and again, you lose,
What a shame!
Are you then ignorant or powerless?
Mind hacker...
I am the Pharaoh from the Future who built that Pyramid up,
I am the God of certainty and uncertainty,
I am the light and the dark,
The sun and the moon,
The clay and the wind,
The water and the fire,
I am the Forefather of Adam,
I came from the stars when your Earth was a baby-planet
with no human beings around,
I saw the birth of the first man,
The first woman,
I was born in the Future,
I have no limit in time and space,
Mother and father were the terminals that allowed me to land
on Earth.
Mind hacker...
You pretend to know me
You don't even know yourself,
You have no face,
I have many,
You have one voice,
I have millions,
Did you ever try to recognise the truth of your
non-existence?
That, you cannot.

Deprived as you are from life and consciousness.
Mind hacker...
When you come back tonight,
or tomorrow,
or the night after,
Look at me again,
Maybe you will understand that
on Earth, you have no way to reach me,
Come back with the troops,
Let them be armed to the teeth,
Try to penetrate the Pyramid again with the army,
With aircraft and armada,
Maybe,
Maybe you could dig a little hole in the wall,
enough for the Pharaoh to bury you,
Because, as you now know,
You have no way against me.
Mind hacker...
Did you get it now?
I am the spaceman,
My home is the Cosmos,
The multi-universes are my domain,
I am not related to you, nor you to me,
Don't try to create a connection,
There is none between us,
There will never be,
You are already dead,
You belong to the past,
I belong to the Future,
Mother and Father came to Earth with a mission:
They delivered me
and returned to the Future,
They are still there,
Watching me, watching us.

I am the Next man,
The Future of Humanity,
You are dead past,
I am endowed with a Cosmic Super-mind,
You have no idea what it is,
On Earth, I am the Master,
I control the controller,
I command you, mind hacker,
From the deepest point in the universe,
From inside the Pyramid of my soul.
Mind hacker...
Get lost... with your resentment,
You belong in Hell!

16 September 2022

Chapter 1

Arrival

(1)

April

I've always hated this city. I just got here two days ago. I walked into what appeared to be a guesthouse. A darkish man hurried through the lobby. Smiling. Reeling. Drooling like a puppy who has discovered a bone. The reception has taken me by surprise. Too warm to be genuine.

Furthermore, I had never seen him before. I didn't have any baggage. He didn't inquire. He scribbled my name and location. I inquired as to where I would spend the night. He raised his head, glanced at me, and murmured, "Upstairs, sixth floor." There is enough space for everyone.

I was thoughtful. I gave him a tip. At his request, I gave him the coins in my pocket. He demanded more. Wallet. Tie. Shoelaces, too.

I'm not sure if I took the elevator or walked the stairs.

The fog encased my memories like a dream.

* * *

I WAS SOON ON THE SIXTH story of that strange building, which is merely one of the numerous compounds that make up the large hotel. I am still hazy. I'm having trouble recalling every moment of my arrival. People in this town mistaken me for a dangerous individual. A kind of buccaneer, if not a terrorist, plotting the destabilisation of the STATE. Not all, however. The shrink, the black guy at the front desk, and my angels.

Each person, according to an old Islamic belief, possesses two angels. One observes and even advises. The other is a bookkeeper. He keeps track of our good and bad behaviours from the moment we are born until the day we die. As a result, on the last judgement, they give the material to the Boss. Following that would be either a reward or a penalty. My angels are not pleased with my behaviour, and I know this. This is a different story, which I will continue later.

I was rather taken aback at the time. Even a little perplexed by the bizarre situation I found myself in. I was on the sixth floor of this weird structure. I arrived there in the same way that one penetrates the substratum of a false dream. The scene that appeared in front of my eyes was more than spectacular.

It was a stretched platform on which people sat on their beds, much like in ancient inns. Hem! Excellent inns? I'm probably exaggerating a little. No, it was quite the opposite. I mean, there was no privacy, no intimacy, nothing. Everyone could see and hear what the next-door neighbour was doing. It was so promiscuous! I was taken aback. It should go without saying. That, however, is not the point.

I shifted my head to the right, and what I saw next stunned me. People were piled up and parked like cattle in a kind of chamber with a basin full of nasty brown water in the centre. Hundreds of people arrived for no obvious reason save for the pool, where they could hardly bathe, as I estimated. I approached the long ribbon that separated them from the rest of the platform with caution, startled. One of them exclaimed, "Mind the border!" Did I go too far? Some looked at me as if I were a strange beast from another planet rather than a human person like them. I was slightly embarrassed by their eyes examining me and scrutinising my face, clothes, and overall appearance. It would be inaccurate to suggest that it did not worry me. I kept saying out loud: "What's the problem? What's the matter with me?" I almost forgot that the anomaly was not in my circumstance but rather theirs. Because it was obvious that they were being held in custody...

As the borderline was guarded by two guys in grey uniforms, they couldn't walk freely - like me, I imagined - and leave the hotel anytime they wanted. For a little period, I stood by the ribbon. Mesmerised. I overheard the conversation. It was a genuine Babylon!

I couldn't comprehend everything but felt they weren't talking about philosophy or scientific breakthroughs. I pondered what had brought all those men together on the outskirts of that filthy pool on the sixth level of that weird hotel! I was astounded by their sight and nearly revolted by how they crowded together like a herd of domestic animals. Their position was out of the ordinary and depressing. Then I suddenly realised that, unlike them, I was free, and I kept repeating to myself: "I am, indeed, a free man. He's free, free, totally free..."

* * *

IF THAT HAD BEEN A dream, I would have awoken sweating and gasping for oxygen. But, because I didn't, I must own that what seemed to me at the time to be a terrifying but fleeting nightmare has now become - alas! - the truest and singular reality. Even yet, as I compared myself to those wretched captives and realised that I was in a different situation (I could still go fast, couldn't I?) I had no idea why, out of all the hotels in town, I had to stay in that one. Indeed, I did not select it, but who does? As far as I recall, I was always told that one should never select what one does in life because everything is already Mektub! Before we are born. The holy pen has already written all that will happen to us, from the cradle to the grave. And as everything is Mektub, it is meaningless to ponder why I am here or there or even why I am writing this down right now. I honestly don't know. That is also precisely what I said when one of those guys questioned me. He didn't appear convinced by my response. He looked at me almost obnoxiously, possibly trying to find the deception in my features.

HE WAS A YOUNG MAN with brown hair. About 36 years old. Brown skin tone. A large brow. His large specs make his eyes as small as a mouse's. I'm not sure why I thought of a mouse instead of a cock or a cat. Perhaps because he also had a narrow face, two small ears, a long-pointed nose with large nostrils and tufts of hair in the cavities, and dry and thin lips. Perhaps because, unlike me, I thought he was imprisoned in that cage like a mouse. Anyway, since he was the first to address me and seemed irritated by my response, I decided not to chastise him. So I added an explanation:

- I'm simply a visitor passing through.

- A visitor! He repeated, either mockingly or dazedly.

- Yes, I replied. Why are you so taken aback?

- Oh, please, my friend. I'm not. I've seen others who came to visit, just like you! They were so thrilled that they preferred to stay with us! They are still present.

When he sensed my amazement, he chuckled. Then he took my elbow gently and asked:

- Come along, pal, will you? Just don't go over the line. We can talk. We have plenty of time... I explained that I needed to find a room.

- I can't stay the night in this filthy place. I need to speak with the lobbyist...

- Don't, he yelled. They'll assign you to us. Do you see the mud? If we're fatigued, we can't even sit down, lie down, rest, or do anything... - Why? So, are you punished?

- Of course, my friend, we are. Purgatory is what they call it. And then there's hell, which is far more sinister. They say it's the freezer!

I was concerned. I began to wonder whether I hadn't entered a mental institution. Some other males began clustering around us and listening to what we were saying. They were all pitiful, clad in filthy rags, with sunken unshaven cheeks and goggling, weary eyes. Despite their terrible misery, they were nonetheless interested in what I had to say! I suppose any newbie would provide them with amusement. It was as if I were conveying the last news from a world that had been barred to them for months, if not years. Because all eyes were on me, I began to feel more significant than I had ever thought of myself. I anticipated dozens of questions popping up in their heads and lips. I was spruce in comparison. I had just arrived at that hotel, pompously dressed in a blue suit - the holiday suit - with a bright white shirt, and although I was untied, my elegance was still intact.

The Administration's wisdom became evident to me at that point. Customers must entrust the reception desk with their encumbering accoutrements, such as money, wallets, ties, laces, and so on, as soon as they come... The wise Administration is cautious and preventive, knowing very well the type of services its home is showing and entirely responsible for the tranquillity of its clients. A tie and a good lace may complement a plain dress perfectly, which is as convenient as agreed upon. Nonetheless, in some instances, they may be used as dangerous weapons, either to kill someone or to commit suicide.

Any good hotel that cares about its reputation would not let its customers die under its ceilings if they could avoid it. That is precisely why this hotel is concerned about the safety of its guests. SECURITY is even the buzzword here! And they are correct. Because one cannot live in peace if they are not secure. And if one cannot live in harmony, the only option is to leave. It is evident that no hotel in the world wants its clients to depart because they do not feel safe; my hotel is no exception. Furthermore, the hotel's administration is so devoted to its guests that as soon as they register your name, they ask you to forget it. Another stumbling block! What generosity! What shrewdness! What brilliance!

They understand that no one picks their name freely because we are all baptised by our parents. As a result, mindful that clients may become tired of a word they will have to live with for the rest of their lives, they provide you with an excellent service. Indeed, which is unavailable in other hotels: it is to forget your name at least during your stay in this welcoming abode. Instead, they would assign you a number, such as 1007, as your new name. Isn't that a simple and pleasant thought? Naturally, it is. However, it is not for everyone.

* * *

When I was chatting with the mouse, I closely watched the people around me. Many of them were utterly unknown to me. I dare to say the majority was what some call the mob, sometimes with scorn. I read a lot about it, especially in my old newspapers, magazines and school manuals, which I maintain in my archives. That is not a pedantic statement. I had no idea what this last word meant until I looked it up in the dictionary. But I'm getting away from the point. This is not acceptable to me. So I stated that among the faceless faces of the mob, I thought I recognised some very familiar things. They were, after all, on our daily media menu until recently. Men of renown, political and financial luminaries. I'm referring to the Old World before its demise due to the coup revolution that elevated our beloved General President (BGP) to absolute authority. I only state that the names those men bear from the cradle to the grave are likely to be more significant and less tedious than those of ordinary mortals. As a result, I conclude that they must be dissatisfied with being reduced to uncertain numbers. I don't suspect the Administration of malice; such thoughts are foreign to me. I've been taught to trust my hierarchical superiors and the Administration throughout my career. Their excellent intentions and dedication to the country's highest interests are unquestionable. I'm not going to change my mind right now. That would be absurd at my age and in my situation. I am trustworthy, and my devotion to the Administration is unquestionable...

Hem! At the very least, it should be. That's why I've lived in royal tranquillity for the last twenty years. (There's no need to say "royal". Just say, "in peace." OK!) I am not, by definition, a troublemaker. My angels are now giggling, and I challenge them to find any evidence that I am lying. Knock!

(2)

For nearly two decades, I was a respected citizen in my country. I was so dedicated to my career and my bosses that I rarely left the city without their permission. I didn't want to be misunderstood. I was always informed that the Capital is the site of various conspiracies and wicked machinations. A good bank clerk is expected to stay where he is assigned to work. As long as I could, I never strayed from this promising path. Oh! Perhaps it would be more honest to admit that I visited the Capital. As a result, I am not a complete novice. But because I wasn't alone, I wasn't trespassing. The bank did send me here with other employees, and I didn't care for the city. I wish I hadn't been here so long. That concerns me. However, because the Administration has approached me, it is up to them to decide for me. I will not get involved since it's none of my business. Anyway, I'm not alone, as usual.

I noticed that Mister Aroussi, the bank's Director, had arrived before me. On the far side of the pool, I noticed him cheerfully conversing with a group of well-known Old World politicians. He, like everyone else, had his necktie and laces removed. He would not, however, commit suicide. He is too optimistic to give up hope in bettering the human condition, and it is pretty unlikely that he will assassinate someone coldly.

A man of integrity, truly. It was the first time I had seen him dressed so casually. He must have also obtained his phone number. Certainly, that is reason enough for him and me to rejoice. Nothing is more valued by us - bank employees - than the immense satisfaction of being transformed into numbers, isn't it? That is the proper reward for a successful career in the service of numbers. A long-held secret desire: to be or not to be a number. That is the query! I dare to say it's miraculous for any bank clerk's worth of work. My employer, on the other hand, must believe he is in heaven. The answer is simple: he has a considerably longer career in the numbers service than I do. Fortunately, the unfortunate old man received his award before retiring. I'll congratulate him as soon as I can contact him.

* * *

- Have you seen shrink? - inquired the man with whom I was conversing.

- No, sir, I said. I've never seen a therapist in my life. I'm not insane, Alhamdu Lillah.

- Nobody told you you were, my friend. A trip to the shrink is mandatory in this town. All newbies are eventually summoned to his office.

- Are you sure? For what purpose? Are we also suspected of insanity?

- Maybe! He paused for a bit before saying, - Look here, my friend. I'll give you some sound counsel. Are you ready to take it?

- Well... The other men drew a tighter circle around us.

- Listen up: when they take you to the shrink, he'll ask you certain things about your private life that you may find embarrassing, such as your childhood, parents, family history, and possibly your political and religious beliefs. Then pretend to be a fool.

- Could you please excuse me?

- Play the fool, he exclaimed forcefully, grinning and gesticulating ludicrously.

The others burst out laughing, and some of them imitated his mime. I glanced at them, astounded and perplexed.

- I'm not a fool, I said.

- We fucking know you aren't, one of them yelled. It's nothing more than a ruse.

Another said:

- It was to defraud the shrink.

I cleverly inquired:

- Why should I play that comedy?

- Otherwise, the shrink will think you're intelligent enough to be thrown in with the monsters of purgatory or a tiny dark pit in the freezer. Then you'll be in so much trouble that you'll curse your damned I.Q. and wish you were just bloody stupid. Do you understand now?

- Hell! I burst out laughing. But I don't consider myself brilliant in any case. Sir, I'm merely a bank teller. I'm not looking for trouble.

I truly meant it, but no one seemed to believe me.

- As you wish, responded the man with the big glasses. But don't tell me you weren't warned.

"Asshole!" I heard behind me. I felt a little guilty, so I said aloud:

- Okay! I'll do my best.

- That's wise, he said.

Nonetheless, I was completely mortified. Was it essential to make a fool of myself to find calm in this place? Apparently, the man understood my mind because he added:

-Look here, my friend. All of those who have been granted some comfort around here are not particularly bright, but they play the game. Do you understand? We in purgatory are already doomed because we are labelled "politicians." Do you know what this means right now in this country? So, here's my recommendation: Be intelligent and astute. Accept being an idiot in front of the shrink. If you're lucky, you'll win.

Lucky? To be sure, that's what I am.

(3)

The shrink, on the other hand, was not what I expected. I have no idea why he was labelled a "shrink." When the lobby attendant led me to the first-floor office, I noted that "Social Assistant" was written on the gate.

My guard, a gorilla masquerading as a robust black middle-aged man clad in a dirty grey uniform tightly encircled his large fat body, told me to wait. They will call me. I nodded and thanked him profusely for his help. But he was in a bad mood that morning as curses poured out of his mouth, and I feared he would knock me down. I dashed up to the people gathered near the shrink's gate and flung myself among them, hoping for some safety. But it was the wrong thing to do. Those who had been waiting before me for a long time were not pleased. They booted my bottom and pushed me out of the row, possibly believing I was attempting to impress them with my privileges as a respected bank employee, which never occurred to me. The black man watching the situation became enraged once more and yelled:

- Ho! You fucking shit-brain bastard! Piss off before I ruin your horrible facade.

I apologised and began to explain that I was not looking for trouble. Nonetheless, I was interrupted by another kick in the shin. I crept on all fours and hurried to the back of the row. Everyone was laughing. I got to my feet and stood behind them, humbly apologising again. It wasn't exactly what you'd call a successful entrance. As far as I recall, my august buttocks had never been booted so badly by any foot. However, one must gain experience; everything begins with a beginning. I've already said that the welcome in the foyer was far too warm to be genuine. So now I have grounds to believe I was correct. Nonetheless, I must admit that my awkwardness was the actual cause of the unfortunate situation. If I was so clumsy, the cause isn't diffi-cult to guess: I had a terrible, almost white night.

* * *

I HAD SCARCELY CLOSED my eyes. Not only was there not a single empty room on the sixth floor but there were no rooms at all. Disabused, I decided to leave that crowded, pitiful place and hunt for better accommodation elsewhere. However, I dis-covered that the gate had been closed. As a result, I had no choice except to stay with the gang and find a couch. Unfor-tunately, that was an impossible assignment because all of the beds were full, and many were even sleeping on the floor. I stumbled through the place, pacing back and forth, looking for a spot to sleep. Because of all the bodies carpeting the ground, even walking became difficult. So the prospect of spending the night splayed out on the cement felt unimportant, upsetting, and unworthy of a bank clerk. I stood up in the middle of the room, embarrassed. I had no idea the hotel would be that congested.

Nonetheless, this is a well-liked home. Later, I discovered that some consumers visit for the second, third, or tenth time. Even better, several of them claim to have made over thirty visits! How can you not admire them? Such devotion is an indication of outstanding moral character. It merits respect, especially when one knows that the risk of spending several white nights on the cement is always present. I have always admired faithful men regardless of the subject of their attachment. I am utterly loyal to the Administration—not just the bank, but The Administration, the Big One.

Nevertheless, despite my adoration and respect, I couldn't bring myself to lie down on the floor like them. Not to dismiss the behaviour, but I believe it is irrelevant for a bank clerk to degrade himself skittishly by being unaware of his position. In a nutshell, it was demeaning. So I remained proudly steadfast. I had not ignored the community, nor was I unaware of my status. A bank clerk is someone of some social standing, perhaps the most significant. Consider how our modern society would be without banks! It would devastate the state's civilian and military institutions.

Where would consumers be able to get a better deal for their money? Who would look after their deposits and earnings? Where might the government and investors look for funding for their projects? Who else can support development objectives and provide a solid foundation for the national budget? Isn't it true that banks are at the centre of the economy? Can we define a state that does not have an economy? - That is a callous state. Who would want to live in such a state? Certainly not me. Furthermore, if this is true for states, it is also true for families. Everyone should be grateful to banks, especially bank clerks, for assisting us. Thus, once the value of banks is recognised, it is clear that they are worthless without their clerks. As a result, bank clerks should be recognised as the most helpful kind of public servants. More valuable than cops, more valuable than troops, teachers, doctors and chemists, and even ministers and...(STOP! Hem!) Maybe... Indeed not the ministers.

* * *

I AM NOT, IN FACT, flattering myself. For example, when a consumer visits the bank for the first time, who else but the bank clerk can guide him through the maze of accounts of numbers, accounts of numbers, and accounts of numbers?

And who else looks after the customer's pocketbook and interests while he is extremely busy and away from his deposits, whether at home or abroad, and discovers numerous ways to make him prosper?

As a result, just as our modern civilisations cannot reject and survive the banking system, the banking system cannot refuse the clerks and outlive them. They are analogous to the heart and arteries that transport blood - or money - through the social body. As a result, the bank clerk is the main artery of the economy. If you cut that artery, you short-circuit any sound and healthy life in the country. Do that if you want havoc and anarchy. Do it right now. Take note of how sensitive I am. It is neither wise nor prudent. That is something that a good administration should be aware of. (However, I'm digressing and messing with policy here.) When I trespass, as usual, a red light notifies me. The final sentence, for example, is to be removed. I don't want to be mistaken for someone who advises or criticises governments on policy. It is not my intention).

AS I HAVE THE MOST gratifying honour of being your humble servant and an artery transmitting what should be sent to the heart of our country, I am conscious that the immense importance of my bank has strengthened my modest original condition.

So I couldn't lie down on the floor without jeopardising my institution's good name. As a result, I was willing to give up my right to relax for the benefit of my bank.

Alas! You know how weak human nature is! When the sun rose, I heard the black guard calling my name. To my astonishment, I opened my eyes to find myself strewn down the floor! I almost cried because of the treachery. What a pity!

(4)

The shrink - I'll use the same name as the clients for consistency - is a small white-haired, black-eyed man of around fifty years old, with silver-rimmed glasses falling over his prominent nose, a wide mouth, and a hoarse voice. When his aide led me into his office, I saw him smoking a cigarette. He cast a sidelong glance at me through a cloud of blue smoke before plunging his gaze listlessly into his papers. I assured myself that this was a heavy smoker. Furthermore, the ashtray on his desk was overflowing with butts. When the assistant saw it, he rushed to empty it into the basket before leaving.

- Please sit, the gruff voice said after a moment.

I did this while thanking him for his generosity. The office was not particularly large. There was no carpet installed on the floor. Except for a framed portrait of our Beloved General President (BGP), which was hung just above the head of the shrink across from the gate, the walls were bare. To the left and right were two large glass-panelled closets with many arrayed folders on their shelves. A solitary window illuminated the iron bars. I could only stare at the uniformed guys swarming about the courtyard, where many police vans were parked.

Of course, I was taken aback by their sight. Except for watching official events on television, I have never seen so many police officers and security guards. That was supposed to mean, "be careful!" This hotel has several VIPs, which surely benefits its reputation and tourism.

The shrink began reading my file:

- Mr. Bassam Bourasin...

I thought it would be appropriate to begin with a good joke. I interrupted, saying:

-Yes, sir, my buddies nickname me "BB" or "baby", and laughed. Did you notice anything? Brigitte Bardot and I share the same initials.

He didn't even crack a smile. Instead, he gave me that lethargic, listless look I had noticed on my entry. It felt as though my existence was unimportant to him. When I left his office, he forgot my name, face, and everything about me! I didn't blame him. He is so solicited and preoccupied with all the patients waiting outside. As a result, it was obvious that he would not recall everyone. However, it is undeniable that I deserved particular consideration as a bank clerk.

He said:

- Mister 1007, your name is Bassam Bourasin. You are a 39-year-old bank worker who is a bachelor and lives in 'Ouja. Is that correct?

- Hem! Certainly, sir.

- You've been with 'Ouja Bank for around fifteen years, which is a long period. What caused you to get into trouble?

- There isn't any cause, sir. I wasn't looking for problems. I am a responsible citizen, and...

- You were, he stated emphatically. I'm sorry, but I read dreadful charges in your file. Corruption, fraud, various and recurring swindles, affiliation with criminals, offending authorities, and, last but not least, monarchism! Otherwise, a counter-revolution activity! Hell! If only three of these charges are proven to be accurate, you will be sentenced to twenty years in prison, which is more than your whole banking career. Do you realise this?

- Sir, yes. Hem... Of course, sir, I mean no. These allegations are false. Indeed, I don't want to insult the cops by dismissing them as lies. Nonetheless, I've worked without complaint for nearly a quarter-century. Sir, my hands are as white as snow. Even when I merited it, I never expected a reward. Millions in all known currencies have passed through my fingers. Never, I said, never did I feel... never did I fancy... never, even in my dreams, did I think it might be mine. Throughout my long service, I've had numerous opportunities to steal the safe and go to Europe or possibly America. It wasn't difficult because my boss and coworkers trusted me. So, why should I abruptly change my mind and end up in hot water? I am a trustworthy citizen. After the Central Bank, my bank is one of the most important in the country. Everyone in my small town respects me. Hem! I was! I believe I am still fairly compensated. I have nothing to be upset about. Furthermore, I do not have a wife, children, or other familial responsibilities that would pressure or drive me insane, leading me astray from the right path. No, sir. I wasn't even able to spend my entire salary. I was saving to live a comfortable life in my old age. As a result, I purchased a lovely little flat in my hometown, and I am still paying its monthly instalments. I was...um... I'm still planning to marry an honest 'Ouja girl. In a nutshell, sir, I am content. Why should I give up my happiness or trade it for some erratic delusions?

He lit another cigarette and looked at me through the blue smoke. The gruff voice continued, coldly and detachedly:

- Well, you asked the appropriate question. Give me the proper answer now.

- Would you like the truth, sir? The whole truth?

- Of course, yes.

- Rumours, slanders, and nonsense!

- I beg your pardon.

- Sir, you heard me. These charges you read to me are complete fabrications.

- That's what you'll have to prove in court.

"Because there will be a trial as well!" I was going to reply, but he interrupted me and asked:

-In the meanwhile, how can I help you?

Such generosity relieved and emboldened me to the point that I pleaded:

- Get me a comfortable room where I can have some solitude, please.

For the first time since I'd seen him, he appeared to smile. That, though, lasted only a second or two.

- If I were you, I wouldn't say that, he said. But, you know, up here, privacy usually means the freezer.

My blood froze when I heard that word. But before I could respond, the shrink continued:

- It's not a first-class hotel, Mister 1007, but a prison, I'm afraid.

He couldn't be more terrified than I was, and most of all, disappointed by his candour, I stuttered something along the lines of:

- It wasn't necessary to use this... abominable word... I ... I...

He cut me off abruptly:

- I realise you're hypersensitive, but you'd better confront reality 1007. You've been arrested and heavily charged. You must account for everything you do inside and outside these walls. Now, if you have any questions, please let me know. I'll forward it to the administration.

- Yes, sir, I responded thoughtfully and gently. I am ready to confront reality. I'm ready to go home.

(5)

FINALLY, I CAN SAY that the visit to the shrink was not all that horrible. I didn't go home, nor did I obtain a private room. He urged me not to make any more "foolish assertions." Nonetheless, I received critical compensation. He secured me a job at the library instead of the hotel's bank, either because he was moved by my case or because he wanted to put me to the test.

- Look, Bassam, he said.

That was unusual and awkward of him. He disobeyed an important prison rule by using my first name instead of my codebar. If he hadn't been so gracious, I'd have to report this infraction to the administration. I'm not going to do it. So we're calling it quits. But wary of any deviations next time...hem!

He said:

- I see you are a one-of-a-kind nature! You're so well-intentioned that I'm afraid you won't get through the fight with the ravenous sharks over here. So, I'm willing to help you, but you must vow to be obedient and serious.

- I assure you, sir.

- We require assistance at the library. Do you enjoy reading?

I eagerly responded:

- I enjoy reading, sir. I'll treat their pages with the same care as banknotes.

He coughed slightly and remarked:

- Very good. The task is straightforward: inmates would borrow books, and you would receive them and make the process simple.

- As in a bank, sir...

- Yes, but it is a learning experience. We'd like them to read books. Is this clear?

- Exactly, sir. I'm not going to ask for any loan guarantees...no mortgages, no real estate, no properties, nothing. I'm not deaf; I regard it as educational. Nonetheless, I must caution you against making such a fatal error.

He was perplexed and questioned:

- What do you mean?

- I mean, if you offer people everything they want without repercussions, your library will become bankrupt instantly. Indeed! You'll need money to pay for maintenance, services, and new books, sir. Where are you going to look for it?

He looked at me as if he was discovering my existence for the first time. Whoop! I assured myself that I was becoming someone in his eyes. Then I noticed him crossing his hands, which reminded me of anxiousness - or impatience? His expression darkened somewhat as he looked at me, and he uttered his words as though rescuing himself from the grip of rage:

- That's none of your business, he replied dryly. Should I consider you a damned fool?

I was perplexed. Is there anything I said that was incorrect? However, he appeared to have overcome his rage, for after a while, he whispered:

- Sorry! You're probably correct. Your remark demonstrates that you are a cautious and astute individual.

But... At that point, I became panicked since I remembered the guy's warning in purgatory. Then, with increasing confusion, I realised the shrink was probably testing me and that I had fallen, hands and feet tied into his trap. I realised I needed to act quickly. So I interrupted him and said:

- No sir, no! I'm afraid you're mistaken...

He stared at me, perplexed. I said:

- I am neither cautious nor cunning, as you imagine. I am even below average in intelligence... Sir, I mean below... far below. My mother used to say, "You're a carbon duplicate of your father, boy!" ... Yes, a duplicate of my father; and my father... Everyone knows he was a knucklehead, sir. You'd never say if he's incredibly intelligent or stupid. He could be both at the same time; it was his privilege. But I'm not going to mislead you by claiming that he left me the brightest part of his magnificent mind. I'm not sure.

It appeared to work. The shrink looked at me for a long time, then lit another cigarette and went smoking.

- My son, you're a strange phenomenon! He stated.

- Sir, I am a stranger in this town.

- Are you a stranger? Yes, if you put it that way. If your father's description is incorrect, you're in big trouble. Even if it is correct, you may suffer from an unresolved Oedipus complex. So, in both cases, you must be examined. Now tell me, have you ever considered murdering your father?

- To murder my father? What's the point? Sir, he's already dead.

- Ah! Yes, I'm referring to it before he died.

- No way, sir.

- Sonny, don't lie to me. Didn't his death make you feel better?

- Is it better? When he was alive, things weren't so bad. He was, after all, cool. A wonderful father. I was devastated by his death...

- I see. You had no idea that when he died, he made you happier...

- Fake news! I apologise, sir. Hem... I object. As it appears, you're accusing me of parricide. Anyway, you're accusing me of something I can't even fathom. I object. It is unjust. I DID NOT MURDER MY FATHER!

- I never stated that you did. I was only curious about your reactions when he died. That's beside the point. You should know that the subconscious has its own ways. We all murdered or fantasised about murdering our fathers in order to discover and confirm our personalities. It's the same for you, but don't be concerned; it's only symbolic.

I wondered if it wasn't one of his ruses to catch me.

- Sir, I am not a murderer. I never killed or even considered killing anyone. Furthermore, I am a faithful man, and such thoughts are grave sins. I don't want to end up in hell because of a symbolic mishmash.

He took a breather.

- So... All right! You persuaded me. You undoubtedly did not inherit your father's bright side. Forget about it all. Anyway, I'm not asking you to do a difficult task.

- I'm your man, sir.

- You will just sit behind a desk and record the title and code number of the book, as well as the borrower's name, on the register. It would be best if you also kept the environment clean and tidy. Is it a challenge?

- No, sir. I know I can accomplish it.

He scribbled on my file and pressed a buzzer on his desk. The helper entered after the gate opened for a brief moment. The shrink handed him a sheet and told him to take me to the library.

- He's the right man for the job.

Then, turning to face me, he said:

- Good luck, Bassam.

I stepped up and thanked him profusely. But before we could even shake hands, the helper - a gorilla similar to the one I'd left outside - yanked me away. Then I realised I hadn't asked about my pay. But it was obvious that the new job had to be gratifying enough following a successful financial career. I won't sweat like a damned until I know they'll pay me adequately. My fiancée, who is ready to get married, would be shocked if she found out what is happening here. "You, a banking professional, how dare you to accept working for peanuts?" She would be outraged. Who will stand up to her? Not me!

So, while in the antechamber, I told the attendant I wanted to return.

- For what purpose?

He said this while scowling suspiciously.

-I neglected to ask him about my...um... ahem...my... honorarium.

- Your... what exactly?

- That's my pay, brother. I'm talking about what I'm meant to get out of the job.

- Are you sure?

- I'm serious, of course.

Unexpectedly, the man burst out laughing as if he had just heard the best joke of the day. As a result, he presented me with the horrible sight of his dark, damaged teeth and a portion of his ravaged palate. He then abruptly stopped chuckling, but his eyes narrowed, and his low jaw vibrated as he spat:

- Now look, the fucking banker! You've caused enough havoc since you fucked up your nasty facade. So, piss off before I go crazy and do something stupid. Is it clear enough?

Oh my God! I could tell it wasn't my day. Because the debate was forbidden, I whispered an apology and exited.

The assistant called the black guard, Mahmoud, and informed him that I had been assigned to the library. The latter scoffed at me and snapped mockingly:

- He? Why? The cretin hasn't even spent 24 hours in jail!

- It's a command, said the assistant.

- Ah! So, I see... (Then, in a private tone, perhaps assuming I wasn't paying attention, he added:) Is he one of them?

- I'm not sure, honestly, responded the assistant.

- He must! Those who are assigned to such tasks have already been punished, you know. But the son of a bitch over here is still detained, and no one knows if he will ever appear in court!

- No one, but...

- Yeah! But, as you say. But we must exercise caution. I'm not ruling anything out. The bastard might be One of them.

I could see myself being a complicated issue for them. I was about to yell, "I'm not one of them!" if that would help. But, in the end, I changed my mind. Wait, man, I told myself. As the therapist put it, if you killed your father without even knowing it, you might as well be one of them and never know it. Consider it.

My subconscious began to erupt into deep waters at that point. It is ready to swallow me up like a huge hydra if I do not correctly interpret the coded message in a strange hieroglyph. Meanwhile, the two men continued their conversation:

- I've bullied him a little, admitted the assistant, sneakily looking at me. The bastard remained silent. I'm concerned he's deceiving us.

- Ah! Did you? Beware. Isn't that a tired trick? You know how they get to this location, but you never know if they're spying on the inmates or on us. Fucking hidden enterprise! Who, after all, is sending them?

- Please keep your voice down. They're everywhere, said the assistant, and it's unclear whether they're pals. Don't you remember Bourisha?

- I do. Before he went, the jerk trashed the place.

- Yes, he did cause your friend's removal, Hamma, didn't he?

The black man sighed heavily and looked at me sidelong before stating:

- Hamma has been in the desert since then, and that cretin of Bourisha has been appointed to our Paris Embassy! What a crazy world!

- Yes, but raping a cop was a bad decision. Hamma carried it out. He fucked a fucking government spy! That was not very wise of him.

- I agree, but who knew who was who by then?

- Ha! That is the question, and it is for this reason that the jerk over there must be dealt with with caution.

The assistant looked at me with interest as he stated this. He even blinked at me as if I were an accomplice. Perhaps he smirked as well, but I didn't respond to his hypocritical snake-like smile for fear of provoking him further. I wasn't sure, but it sounded like the bastard they'd handle with caution was me. I didn't like it, and even though I didn't know who that Bourisha was, I mistook several innuendoes directed at me. However, I soon dismissed this notion because I could never be one of them. In any case, who are they referring to? I replayed it in my thoughts over and over. I recognise that I may be a separate and distinguished individual. Even my new name - or barcode, if you want - is far higher than one. Okay, then! I can't be one or both because I'm one zero zero seven and don't know who the they of them represented! I was satisfied. I could easily breathe. My love of statistics and accurate accounting drew me out of another bad affair. Mahmoud snatched my elbow, putting a halt to my ratiocination.

- All right, the banker. Hurry up. Are you sleeping?

- Sir, yes. Of course, I mean no. Will we be going to the library?

- No, we're not, he yelled. Not with all the nasty little bugs trailing behind you.

- What bugs, sir? I don't have any.

- You say that, but you're not fooling me. We know everything there is to know about you, and look here, man, no shit! I'll keep an eye out for you. Did you comprehend that you have nothing to do over here?

- I appreciate your acknowledgement, sir.

- Close your fucking trap. You scumbag! Stupid shithead!

I chose not to respond. The poor man was unhappy and irritable. It was fruitless to argue with him. Perhaps he mistook me for someone else. I'm not sure why they're all so irritable. Some people have forgotten themselves to the extent of addressing me as if I were the footman! It's pretty disappointing. What the hell do they think they're doing? The black guard and his aide are almost certainly conspiring and preparing something heinous. I can sense it. It is obvious that they dislike me.

Nonetheless, because I am not their subordinate, I owe solely to my supervisor, Mister Aroussi, who is also present. I need to find a way to welcome him. Perhaps he had already sensed my presence by this point. If he had, he would have been perplexed as to why I had not yet talked to him. On the other hand, even as a library clerk, I believe I owe obedience to the shrink who employed me, not the assistant or the black guard. In the order of the... hem!... Let's be clear: the prison hierarchy, the two men must not be higher than I am. So why should I follow them? If I do, it is because I am a good person. However, I am not oblivious to the fact that they would commit trespassing if I were to be too accommodating. In this life, one must be steadfast in their ideals without becoming too hard or soft. The middle ground is the best option. That is one of my favourite maxims. Regardless of what my blockhead angels think of the question, I consider myself a good Muslim. As back as I can remember, I've always lived in the centre of everything, if not the heart or the nucleus. So, like the bank, I inhabit the centre of the modern universe. Nowadays, all roads go to the bank rather than Rome! With all due respect to the Vatican, the bank has seized control of religion in the hearts of the devout. This is also true for Muslims. It is our new Mecca, and we are all pilgrims in this system, even though we are perfectly aware that our faith forbids certain activities. But who knows? It is self-evident that banks' interests are like flesh and blood to the body. What's the big deal? Are we going to be the exception to the rule? That would not be acceptable to us. I know exactly what I'm talking about. There is only one banking system on our planet, and there is no room for another. (But here I am again, digressing and nosing about religion, which is not my intention. Let's remove the final paragraph from the report).

(6)

I strolled down the long corridor with my black guard (and two phantom angels), crossing the courtyard where the police vans were stationed. Then we reached a slightly smaller area, and I noticed individuals standing in a row beside the wall. The guard motioned to them with his black finger and said:

- Go. You'll need to see a hairdresser after you've finished showering.

I was ready to say that I hadn't had time to bring my toiletries or any clothing to change out of my crumpled suit. Still, I held back as I peered at the gorilla and noted its grin. I walked right up to the row. My quiet was undeniably more potent than any outcry. The gorilla was aware of it. That's why it disappeared. It has taken a step back! As a result, I won the first round! And knock!

* * *

THAT TIME, I DID NOT make the same mistake. I stood up quietly at the back of the row. I never sought to be the first to enter the shrink's office. I am both obedient and disciplined. My daily existence has been so meticulously planned that one could claim, without exaggeration, that Bassam Bourasin is Big Ben! Although some cops are not as trustworthy as they should be, I should have made a good cop. I even knew one who would steal radio cassettes from the vehicles he was supposed to watch over. To make ends meet, he would sell them illegally on the market. Once apprehended, he sold the stolen goods to the wrong man. It was another cop who was looking into the situation. Needless to say, the robber was burned. The detective, one of my customers, relayed the incident to me. He was sorry, but he had to report his colleague's misbehaviour. What a shame! Worse. When the thief-cop realised he was dealing with a detective, he attempted to bribe him. He provided the radio cassette as a gift, which exacerbated his situation. And I recognised him when he described him to me. I had dealt with him when I purchased a used tape for my car. It was the same man: a traffic cop during the day and a merchant of stolen things on weekends. He was an expert in radio cassettes, CDs, video and camera systems for all types of automobiles. Then I realised I had purchased stolen goods. I was ready to confess to the investigator when I decided to hold my tongue. It's not that I'm dishonest, but it wasn't my problem. The implications could be severe: if I admit to buying a stolen item from the same individual disguised in civilian vacation attire, I will be summoned to the police station, if not as an accomplice, then as a witness. Furthermore, I would be forced to return the items I had paid for, and who would reimburse me? The cops? That's hard to believe. So, why should I give up something I paid for with my money? Life is not that simple. However, if the police adequately compensated its agents, they would not resort to thievery and gangsterism to make ends meet. Take a look at what's going on right now:

People are losing their sense of security. One never knows if a traffic warden who stops you on the road is an honest man or a masked thief. But where are we going if everyone begins thinking like this? That is why I believe a good citizen who loves his nation and is loyal to its Administration should not have two jobs simultaneously and in the same area. Really! You cannot serve two masters at the same time. Who made this statement? I don't mind, but he was correct. One of the two masters would eventually be duped.

Furthermore, if more officers start stealing and swindling, professional thieves will be in short supply sooner or later. Authentic and honest thieves would not tolerate that unjust and imbalanced rivalry. As a result, they would be forced to change their business or relocate. The first approach would exacerbate the country's difficult and time-consuming unemployment problem. The second would aggravate the problem of irregular emigration among Europeans. As free market proponents, we must foster competitiveness when the two sides are on equal footing at the outset. However, because the would-be thieves among the officers already have a job, they would take unfair advantage. Their inexperience would undermine both professions. More cops would be in jail, and fewer professional thieves would be on the streets, for it is evident that an amateur would end up in prison shortly. A professional ruffian, on the other hand, would depart the country, concerned by the unrivalled emulation.

However, when one thinks about it closely, it is impossible not to recognise our police's wit and intelligence. There are more opportunities to imprison an amateur thief than a professional, and our officers know where they would end up. This is most likely a huge sacrifice they are making at their own risk and hazard for the sake - without a doubt - of their oath: to rid our streets of professional ruffians. That's the secret!

This, I dare to say, is a very patriotic act. The cop willing to take the risk, sacrificing his free time for the sake of the population, should be encouraged to study the tough job of a thief, cutthroat, gangster, and similar businesses. We should also give him the National Hero medal.

Let us be clear:

The unlucky cop apprehended by a fellow cop in the marketplace while attempting to smuggle his stolen goods is a Hero, though he is unaware of it. His coworker doesn't either. He should get the Order Of High Merit because his action prevented a real burglar from stealing those radio cassettes. If he hadn't taken such precautions, the professional burglars would have stolen the same items.

I did not tell the detective about these ideas or the reasonable conclusion I had come to. I instead asked:

- What happened to the police officer?

- He's in jail.

How awful! Even willful ignorance of the man's abilities couldn't make me indifferent to him. I was very moved by the story. I could not feel anything but sympathy for the innocent bystander of social ignorance. He did not act to make ends meet, I am sure. But his sense of right and wrong made him want to stop bad people from breaking into the cars of his fellow citizens. Is that really so hard to get? It's easy, though: If you can fool the thieves and stop them from doing what they usually do, it's like pulling the rug out from under them and forcing them to be unemployed. This is called "preemption" in the world of strategy. Yes, sir. Such work comes with risks and a sense of giving up something.

Once the hero was caught with his hand in the bag, he would be fired and told to stay away from the police. He would also have to spend many hard years in jail. Also, the guy wasn't acting selfishly when he made honest people like me pay half or even less of the real price for electronics. His kindness, bravery, friendliness, and willingness to give up things are evident. We should support, encourage, and reward the would-be thieves, thugs, and gangsters in our National Police who try to be like him.

(Well. Let's forget that last sentence about would-be thieves, thugs, and gangsters in our...etc.)

(7)

I was making my way carefully towards the Hammam's entrance. The courtyard's excessive exposure to daylight was quite uncomfortable. Although only two of the four seasons are observed here, the arrival of spring signals the start of the year. The rest is just a euphemism for winter or summer. My flower pots in 'Ouja must be drying out by now. And the poor canary must be wondering why I haven't replaced its water or filled its small recipient with seeds, as I used to. But, most importantly, it may be desiring sugar.

I am sorry, canary, but I was not forewarned. I had no idea I was so desperately needed in the... Capital. I didn't have time to pack properly, so I had to go without my pyjamas and toothbrush. This is the very first time in my life that I have embarked on such an excursion. The two men who accompanied me to the city were in such a hurry that you'd think the devil himself was hot on their heels. They arrived in the afternoon and hammered on the door so loudly I was scared the bank had been looted or burned down. I had settled into my favourite couch to watch a live TV show. I hadn't expected any visitors and was astonished to find those two angry and tense men when I opened the door. One of them asked:

- Are you Bassam Bourasin?

I noted he hadn't even said Mister, as anyone polite would, and I didn't like his expression.

- Yes, I said. May I ask what...?

He cut me off, saying, "Police!"

My heart was pounding wildly, and I managed to retain my cool and said:

- This is a wonderful honour, gentlemen. Would you please come inside my humble home and join me for a drink?

- We don't have time! You'll enjoy your drink in a particularly welcoming hotel. So put on your clothes and follow us.

I afterwards regretted my haste to leave my flat without taking some measures. The truth is that I candidly assumed I had been invited to join them for a drink at the local hotel. I couldn't believe we were going to travel to the Capital straight immediately, and it wasn't until we were well out of 'Ouja that I dared to ask:

- Where are we heading, gentlemen? May I inquire?

One of them laughed, and the driver responded:

- Don't you know it yet?

- If I did, I wouldn't ask.

- Didn't we tell you about a drink in a great hotel?

- Ah! Yes, absolutely. But when we left 'Ouja, I noticed no hotel nearby. The man next to me on the back bench stopped laughing and added:

- You're going to the most wonderful hotel in the country. You're very fortunate, man!

- Okay, then.

However, I was unconvinced. Before entering the car, the two men handcuffed me. I let them do it without saying anything. I didn't want to startle my neighbours, who were usually watching. Nothing seemed more important to me than my reputation in town. As a result, while quietly complying, I tried to avoid violence and scandal. I could even understand the two men's uneasiness. With all the criminal attempts mentioned in the headlines and terrorists lurking in the shadows, the police are having a difficult time.

Nonetheless, I held my tongue and said nothing. After all, if I couldn't feel safe and secure while being guarded by the cops, where could I? Even if I did not enjoy my time in the nation's capital, I could not deny that its hotels are more appealing and luxurious than the modest inn where I usually stay.

* * *

'OUJA IS NOT A TOWN; it is not even touristic like the southern shore. That is why, if properly managed, a single inn is sufficient. I occasionally sit at the coffee shop with a small drink, playing cards with friends or random visitors. In the village, I am as well-known as Coke, not because everyone knows everyone other in such a small town, but because I enjoy people's trust as a bank clerk. However, if they trust me, it is most likely because they believe their money is safer in our hands than in theirs, which is undeniably true. Such assurance is the genuine capital of our company. Any bank employee would agree. This dictum should be engraved in gold letters on the front door of any respectable financial institution.

Mr Aroussi, our director, used to say this when he met with our most significant clients. Our community may be small, but it's home to some interesting and, dare I say it, wealthy patrons. Our records show that they have many accounts in our vault. Funds that would make us feel very proud if we could reveal their value. But doing so would violate the confidentiality we're sworn to uphold.

Banking is a remarkable industry. Whereas other trades thrive by publicising their transactions' quantity, size, and number, we do the opposite since we are bound by confidentiality. A bank's popularity and trustworthiness will rise in proportion to how discreet it is with its customers' information. That puts bankers and bank tellers squarely opposing politicians. The more trusted and popular a politician is at the start, the more he talks and forgets to keep his promises... (I'm sliding down a perilous slope. Not only did I imply that banks are in opposition, but I also dared to equate bankers to politicians! So, I'm going to repress this delirium as well. I must produce a clean report because I'm trying to mount a good defence. But now I see I'm fishing in troubled waters and sinking!)

* * *

SINCE WE'RE TALKING about water, I should mention that the Hammam is not what I imagined. More specifically, it has nothing to do with a genuine Hammam.

I walked into a large, dark, nearly smoky room that was moist with steam. I noticed individuals jostling naked or half-naked beneath the dashing waters running from showers hanging above their heads as soon as I could see through the bleak fog. I stood there staring at the strange scene, dumbfounded. Nearby, some individuals were dressed or undressed on a long wooden bench. When I was debating whether or not a reputable bank clerk should have spoken with such a rabble, I felt a strong hand clasp my shoulder, and a gruff voice boomed in my ear:

- What the fuck are you waiting for, mosquito?

I turned my head, my hands interlocked.

A massive bald head with two black eyes gleamed from a face so horribly damaged that I initially mistook it for a mask rather than a real person. Monstrously, twisted, and crushed that nose. Two lengthy scars crisscrossed the mouth, clearly the gruesome marks of a knife. Seeing that unyielding Hollywood monster made me freeze, so I mumbled an apology and ran away. Where, though? Frankenstein himself had reached out and grabbed my shoulder, pulling me in.

- What are your plans?

His bright eyes were not all good. When I realised I was no longer safe. I yelled for the black guard to come to save me. However, I was unable to get a single syllable out. My voice had failed me miserably. I've never been a fan of scary films. Many years ago, when I saw Dracula and Frankenstein, I had to fight my desire to sleep for two nights in a row.

I could be more robust and agile. Unfortunately, I had little chance of successfully repelling the beast because mother nature had not been kind to me. That's completely insane. Even though I do not consider myself a coward, I lack the heroic qualities necessary to succeed. He could easily knock me over with one hand if he wanted to. He was easily three times as tall and wide as I was. He wore a T-shirt over pants rolled up at the calves, and his bare feet dangled in a puddle of filthy water on the floor.

He examined me as a scientist would examine the movements of a wiggling creature with fascination and wonder. I was sweating profusely and gasping for air. Then, much to his enjoyment and my hate, he cuddled me up against his chest and squeezed me so hard I almost passed out. His rotten teeth shone with a smug glee as he laughed. His breath carried the pungent odour of cigarettes, garlic, and other putrid substances. Of course, I was taken aback by such a warm welcome, but I had to work desperately for air. By the end, I realised it was all for nought. It made me uncomfortable, so I gave up trying.

-Are you a troublemaker? he asked.

-No...Not...   Not   at   all... sssssssssssssssssssssssssssssssssssssssss...sir! I stumbled.

- Are you a gangster?

-You... You're....err...miss...misses...taken...

- Me? Mistaken? Do you dare offend me? Fuckkkkkkkking mosquito!

I attempted to lull him in some way:

- I did... I did not...I did not...mean it, sir. I...I am...you...your...humble...servant!

- Serve my ass! You filthy son of a bitch! Didn't you pretend I was mistaken? So, yeah, I'm a jerk! That's what you're saying?

The small brawl had taken a hazardous turn. The monster's arm tightened around my waist. Then I was squished down like a worm on a stone. I attempted diplomacy once more:

- You aren't a jerrrrk. I...I...I aaaaam..... Not yyyyyoouu, Nnnnn!

He loosened his grip. I took a breath. Nonetheless, he did not release me.

I exclaimed:

- I am just a simple bank employee, sir. I'm not trying to offend you. How could I do it? You're...so...so...

- So, so what?

I wanted to yell: "So vile! So ugly! So disgusting!..." But I mumbled modestly:

- So gracious, sir! I feel incredibly honoured and blessed to have met you!

Then he let me go. I regained my footing. Even though I wasn't aware of it, I was hovering above the ground during the catching game. While I was trying to gather my thoughts, he asked:

- What did you say you are?

I trembled, expecting the worst. Was the horrible thing plotting another placement? I looked at him, puzzled, but he didn't move. He could have been offended if I told him I worked as a bank clerk again. It makes no difference if he is a big guy. He is undeniably sensitive, if not hypersensitive. The least hint of anything outside of his world may be disastrous. He may have suffered from a lack of maternal compassion as a child. I once read that abused children grow up quiet, sensitive, introverted, and unable to function in society. Perhaps even spiteful against it. The more I looked at Frankenstein, the more I realised this was his personality. But, as sympathetic as I am to the destitute and wretched, I am not Mother Theresa. I don't have the calling or the desire to be his prey either. He definitely needs his mother more than he needs me.

On the other hand, there was a real possibility that if I lied to him, he might bully and molest me even more. He may have heard me and was only testing my credibility. So, in the end, I resolved to tell the truth, regardless of the repercussions. I was conscious that I was playing a game. To be sure, not on the stock exchange, but on the volatile rascal's stock feelings.

- All right, sir.

I explained that I work as a bank clerk... a very modest bank employee. He sounded as if he was laughing at it! Thankfully, he smirked. Then I realised I'd won.

- Did you mention you worked as a bank teller? So you work at a bank, correct?

He was almost overjoyed. His expression had changed to that of Christopher Columbus discovering America!

- Sir, yes. A bank clerk is a person who works for a bank! That's what I do!

His response was unexpected. He appeared to be ecstatic. He lightly tapped me on the shoulder as if I were an old friend. Then, in an enthusiastic outpouring, he asked:

- Why haven't you mentioned it since the morning, man? We're friends! Don't you realise it? We're relatives, cousins, brothers, come with me, guy! Kiss Uncle Salih.

* * *

A KISS? I WAS REVOLTED at the prospect of kissing that terrible face of nightmares, me, who used to be so delicate and diversified in my choices! As a child, whenever someone kissed me on the Islamic holidays, I would rush to the restroom to wash my face! I'm so disgusted with such trivialities that I can't remember ever kissing anyone since I was a kid. Not even my mother or my fiancee.

Regarding the latter, Allah is a witness. I never even attempted to touch her. Except for the day of our wedding. Then

I had no choice but to slide the ring onto her finger. That happened five years ago. Whenever we were alone in her parents' house at the time, she would try to get closer to me. But she was so awkward that we never kissed. In any case, my values prevent such behaviour.

Once, in the dimness of a movie theatre, I felt her warm hand firmly grasp mine. It was close to panic time for me. I assumed she was terrified because of the violence on the screen. She was likewise unaware of her younger brother, who sat alongside her. It seemed prudent to retract my hand after some consideration. Still, she didn't notice because she was focused on the movie. I felt relieved after that. I could breathe normally without my blood heating up from excitement. However, she did not say her last word. She hesitated for a second, then tried again, this time with greater zeal. Her left leg was stuck to mine then, and her fingers were ploughing my thigh, hopelessly groping for something they didn't dare touch. It was too much for me to endure. To say I was ashamed is far below the truth. She turned me on, and I felt like a hot dog. I was gasping for air and on the edge of collapse. She was oblivious to everything around her: her brother, my hot blood, the public, morals, religion, family, and village! Such hedonism was intolerable. Scandalising!

I had the impression that hundreds of eyes were no longer focused on the big screen but on her little fingers, methodically, rapturously rubbing my thigh. It was so daring! I anticipated and anticipated the worst. I needed to figure out how to avoid it without insulting her. It was a difficult task, but I had no alternative. I didn't want the whole town gossiping and screaming about our public displays of salacious profligacy.

Furthermore, the situation in the sphere of operations, if I may say so, was rapidly approaching a peak. I didn't like the direction it was headed. It was a perilous incline. I quickly realised I had a massive erection and had no idea what to do about it. As a result, I reacted gently yet firmly. I took her hand away. Then, pretending to answer nature's call, I dashed to the restroom. I locked the door behind me, unzipped and went wild with fingers and eyes and darkness and movies and fingers moving high low high low high low high low high high high hiiiiiiiiiiiiiiiiiiiiiiiiiiiiiiiiiiii-iiiiiiiiiiiiiiiiiiiiiiiiiiiii...................................!

I returned slowly, relaxed but guilty, and sat between my fiancée and her brother. Since that day, I've been able to keep the brother between us whenever we go to the movies. As a result, there is no excitement, panic, or...

* * *

HOWEVER, UNTIL I GAVE into the impossible, I couldn't address the issue of kissing Frankenstein. I lingered, paused, delayed, and circled the pot, but I knew I had to do it, that I was going to do it, and that I... I gathered my courage, which was desperately needed at the time. I hobbled forward and, on my tiptoes, closed my eyes (if only to avoid seeing what I was doing) and stretched, stretched, stretched in vain. Because he was so much taller than me, I could not kiss him on the cheek. Thankfully, he rescued me from further humiliation. He bent over and dropped his head so I could kiss his horrifying scar, and I did.

What needed to be done was completed. Baa! Forgive me, God. I thought my life was over. He patted me on the back and said:

- Good kid!" The time has come for us to start working together.

Me? Trading with the Monster Man? Holy crap! The day I accept it, I will almost certainly be uninspired or insane. What the hell happened? I've already worked with people far more human than that freak, and I've seen the results. It's not exactly brilliant right now. So, I know what would happen if I was in the same boat as that repulsive creature. We'd go down together to the bottom of this horrible earth or swim to shore only to discover a scaffold ready to snap our necks! In my opinion, this is the only possible result of such a ridiculous coalition. Obviously, I was not prepared to carry on with such a pointless exchange. I am not a coward; I have declared as much. I'd succeeded by taking calculated chances, but I recognised my limits. There is nothing beyond them but no man's land, prison, exile, and the gallows. Well, I'm already in jail, which is not pleasant. What occurred? Have I gone too far? This appears to be the case. I am, therefore, as guilty as Mr Aroussi, who preceded me to this honourable State guesthouse.

Nonetheless, I couldn't understand clearly what my crime was. When I could, I assisted others. I only made some people more prosperous than they were before they came to me. But I'll get into that later.

For now, all I could think about was hurrying to the shower to wash away any traces of that horrific kiss. I was no longer debating whether it was appropriate for a bank clerk to associate with the filthy mob. I've always despised promiscuity. That was not because I am a serial snub but because I am concerned about my bank's reputation. If it helped, I would deal with some customers while wearing gloves. However, it is prohibited. I had to be nice to everyone, even those I couldn't frame since some stupid blockheads required warmth and solicitude in our dealings! And now I was expected to act similarly with the customers of this particular house. Well! After all, promiscuity with the rabble clamouring beneath the showers might be more enjoyable than this repulsive tête-à-tête with Frankenstein.

I told him not to hurt him in a sweet tone:

- We'll do whatever you want, but please let me shower now.

I decided it would be better to include: - Mr Mahmud is waiting for me outside.

- Who is that jerk?

- The guard, sir, the large black guard.

- Ah! You mean the colour of my balls, which is dark?

- All right, sir. That is the correct one.

- What exactly is he waiting for? Do you have any kinship? Is he a relative, a brother-in-law, or something else?

- No, sir.

He became upset when I did not respond:

- And so what? Is he your bedfellow? Who is banging whom?

I was taken aback. The shock I felt was incredible. Dismayed to hear such hateful nonsense. For a moment, I seriously considered charging at him, sticking my fangs into his ear, and biting him so firmly, persistently, and mercilessly that I would rip it right out of his ugly skull. I looked down, and there he was, face muddied with blood and yelling and screaming and rolling around on the ground and moving up to me. It made me really vengeful. I've been able to laugh at his silly jokes like they're nothing and put up with his sleazy, prison humour. Nonetheless, I was not to take such suggestive remarks at face value.

Just who the hell do you think you are? Superman? I felt like I might scream. But I kept my cool and didn't let it get the best of me. Simply put, it was an attempt at cheap provocation. Was I supposed to make a beeline for the sneaky trap? No. The fight was too one-sided, to be fair. Before I could even get a word in edgewise, he'd knock me out cold, and that would be that for me and his shindig. He has the wrong impression of me; I am not as dimwitted as he thinks I am. Cold lunch is the finest way to get even with someone. You'll need some time to stir it up and let it cool down. So I shot back:

- Sir, I have nothing to do with him. But he is in charge of maintaining order and discipline here. So he might be wondering why I'm lingering in the shower...

- Is that it?

- Absolutely, sir.

- Well! You should be aware that I am the FUCKING IN CHARGE OF THE BLOODY ORDER over here, and your blackish can show his baboon ass elsewhere. (He stopped before adding:) Now you can shower.

He added, "Go now," as I thanked him profusely. "We'll discuss business later."

Doing business with me was quickly becoming one of his obsessions! But it wasn't all bad. I reminded myself. Okay, never mind. I can get something out of this if I can exploit his hope and delay it indefinitely cleverly. I can secure safety with little more than word of mouth and assurances. The people of this place appear to hold him in high esteem if not outright fear. In addition, he did not appear intimidated by the security personnel. Perhaps the converse is also true. Because it's not often that people breathe a sigh of relief at the sight of a genuine Frankenstein lurking around.

Nonetheless, I replied not out of opportunism but out of common sense. I am a man who adheres to high moral standards. My life is generally orderly and neat. I never improperly abused or deceived others or took advantage of their kindness. As a bank clerk, I couldn't stand up to honest profit. That would be a slap in the face to the principles of my honourable profession. In Frankenstein's situation, however, it would be foolish and dangerous not to take advantage of his desire to dominate him. There is a solid reason for this: plainly, if his energy is not effectively channelled and contained, he may be somewhat dangerous - to himself and others. As a result, I hope to do something instructive, moral, and even altruistic. Before I stripped naked, all I managed to say was:

-You're making a bargain, sir. If you take my advice, this will be one of the best deals you've ever made.

I truly meant it.

I folded my clothes, placed them on the bench, and proceeded to the shower. However, there was no room for me. I had to wait until one of the guys agreed to let me take over. Then I recognised how beneficial my recent collaboration with Franken had been! He dashed toward me as soon as he noticed me waiting and yanked one of the men from the showers. Then he yelled:

- Come along, the banker! This is your battery!

I walked quietly and, rather embarrassed, placed myself under the lukewarm splashing water to thank him for the quick service. At the same time, the harassed man stepped back, casting poisoned stares at me from beneath the white film of soap foaming and bubbling over his face. I thought it would be polite to apologise because he seemed so angry. He did not complain or react in any way, but he was most certainly unhappy. So I apologised:

- I am sorry for the inconvenience...

I attempted to demonstrate my goodwill. I even cracked a smile. But the enraged man remained motionless! On the contrary, he was as quiet as a rug!

* * *

IT WOULD APPEAR THAT I have not yet exhausted the benefits of my new relationship. When a hand reached out and gave me some soap, the shower finally became enjoyable. After I used the soap twice, someone brought me a shampoo bottle. While someone bathed my head, they rubbed my back with a towel. I felt like a king being served, and when the friendly friction subsided, I turned to thank the guy who had offered to assist me. To my amazement, it was the man who had been so abruptly replaced. Both pain and pleasure hit me simultaneously. For my part, as a man of peace, I didn't want to so much as give somebody the germ of an idea to start a grudge against me from day one. But the gentleman's generosity won me over.

Despite my current predicament, I have no known adversaries. I'm afraid it is an arrest. However, I must concede that unseen and powerful adversaries, including my two guardian angels, manufactured it. It's a conspiracy. I am in a good position to notice this. My professional success and loyal dedication to the bank and my boss, Mr Aroussi, led to this risky connection with inmates and troublemakers. Those bitter about my accomplishment will likely have their way within the Administration. They were able to get my powerful boss and me down here. They have long arms and probably very long legs as well... Anyway, they are longer and stronger than mine. Yet I don't want to pin the blame on the Administration completely. God save me from such craziness! I remain loyal to the Administration of our country, which I consider the most intelligent in the world. Without question, I say IN THE WORLD. (Well done, Sonny. Continue like this. I'm your good angel adviser).

However, remember that even in a basket full of healthy eggs, two or three - if not many more - may be tipsy and indigestible. But it is too early to provide a thorough analysis of the issue. It would be more prudent to proceed step by step because I aim to be completely honest in telling all that had happened since and before I arrived in the Capital.

* * *

BEFORE I GOT OUT OF the shower, I thanked the man who had chafed my back and apologised again. I felt it would be best to introduce myself so we might become acquainted under different circumstances, as I was not indifferent to his distress. I extended my hand and said:

- Bank teller Bassam Bourasin here, your obedient servant.

I expected him to tell me his name and position and shake my hand. Instead, he looked at me as though taken aback by the disparity in my demeanour. Despite his girth, the man was not much taller than me.

- Go fuck yourself, you motherfucker hurly burly monkey!

His odd eyes narrowed as he spat his words coldly.

Shocked? I was. I mean, who wouldn't be? That's some seriously nefarious talk, full of explicit malice. Certainly an oddity! Irrelevant! Impolite!

I couldn't say anything since I felt warm and fuzzy towards him. In other words, he had no intention of shaking my hand. So I just let it go. As losses go, it wasn't too bad. I was upset nonetheless but for an entirely different reason. I was so disheartened that I forgot about myself and stared stupidly at him. Next, his oddly lit eyes flared with fire, and he growled:

- If you don't piss off right now, I will crush your bloody face of a damned monkey! Have I made myself clear?

* * *

BLOODY FACE OF A DAMNED monkey? Who's that? Me? He surely hadn't looked at himself in the mirror since the deluge. He was far more repulsive than the genuine Frankenstein, not the phantom lost around here. The latter's ugliness is, I'm sure, factitious and may be arranged correctly. With the assistance of an aesthetic surgeon, he may emerge as handsome as a movie star. He would not, however, be Valentino. But if you remove his scars, position his nose in the middle of his face, and let him wear a wig, he'll look virtually as natural as any other person.

Regarding the former, I honestly believe that even with the assistance of a skilled surgeon, he would not emerge with a bearable appearance. I'm talking about something that resembles a human, not an animal. The poor devil was doomed indefinitely. And he was completely unaware of it! I'm afraid I'm speaking of an ontogenetic failure. I did look it up in the dictionary. (Ontogenetic: from ontogenesis, is the origination and development of an organism, both physical and psychological.) His mother must have slept with a horse, donkey, or beast to produce such a wild miracle.

To begin with, he has the exact head he should not have, as it was fashioned in the shape of an empty bottle tossed on the wrong side. Second, his large ears were perched obliquely on each side of his head, ready to fly away. Third, unlike most mortals, his eyes were not set up straight on a vertical line. I believe one of them, the left, was much higher than the second! I wasn't even sure I saw it correctly. As I kept staring at him to ensure I wasn't hallucinating, he became agitated and reacted aggressively. It's understandable! When gifted with such kind of shopwindow, one must blame one's mother all day and night! Nonetheless, I believe he has a unique opportunity to produce himself in a circus arena without learning any special expertise.

He'd make a living by showing off his amazing eyes to the public.

Not to mention his ready-to-fly outboard ears and the upside-down bottle on his shoulders. The poor man! Despite this, he dares to call me the monkey! Well! It's hardly an insult coming from his mouth, I suppose. I know I'm not who he made me out to be. I am not as attractive as Valentino, but I am quite okay. I'm a little brownish, with a well-bridged nose, a respectable mouth, two dark eyes - neither more nor less, and symmetric - and two ears sticking to my head with no will to take off. My hair is black, which, I admit, is not wholly original. Nonetheless, it is curled and fluffy, and my features are normal. No scar, no eye higher than the other, and no taking off ears, thanks to Allah and my mother's discerning wisdom!

Then I heard Frankenstein's baritone voice thundering through the room:

- Hey! Zorro! Please relax. He returned your shower; what else do you want?

- He owes me money for the shampoo, soap, and towel he used! The enraged man snapped.

- He'll pay for your grubby soap, muttered Frankenstein. He works as a banker! And if he refuses, I will. Please charge that to my account. Is it all right?

The so-called Zorro quieted down and roared inaudibly. I was thankful to my new partner, who took our agreement seriously. He motioned to someone behind me. A man handed me a dry towel. I wiped the wetness from my body. Life was glorious again.

* * *

I hadn't yet gotten used to the prison's atmosphere. I don't think I ever will be. But, like any newbie, I couldn't help but notice the anomalies and eccentricities of the location. Which, to the untrained sight, appears both pointless and petty. I will not squander time now that I have been designated library clerk. I plan to document every thrilling tale I hear and every significant or insignificant detail I observe. Everything will go into the revamping report I'll present to the Administration. This is a project I'm working on on my own, something neither the shrink nor the black guard encouraged me to accomplish. As I discovered, writing anything other than letters in jail is even illegal. Any correspondence, whether from the outside or the inside, must be approved by the Administration. I am not breaking the law because my report is also a letter sent to the High - probably the Highest - Authorities in the country. I'll be as quiet and cautious as possible. However, I shall be courteous. I will not use the most vexing nomination of this educational and extremely effective national institution. Instead, I'll keep using the word HOTEL as a label. It is more convenient, aesthetically pleasing, and less taxing on the potential reader (and me!) In any case, it is not a prison. Since our Beloved General President's (BGP) popular coup and military revolution, all liberties have been restored, which means that jails do not exist anymore. We don't have people in prison, just people in State Hotels. Our fellow citizens already got the unparalleled taste of liberty they deserve! However, for their own interest, freedom has been hidden to protect it. I carefully memorise the major speeches of our BGP. I even recommended to my supervisor, Mr Aroussi, to engrave a sentence of the BGP with gold lettering and display it on the front wall of the bank in the main hall. Just across from the entrance so that everyone could enjoy the view. That was a few days after the popular coup of the military revolution (I don't know yet how to describe the historical event). The boss coughed, hesitated, and then said:

- You, Bassam, you'll go far away and much higher, I tell you. It's a fantastic idea! Perfect!

He then provided his orders. The Historical phrase was carried up to the Director's office the same week, tastefully printed and framed. Mr Aroussi called me over the phone. I rushed up to inspect the beauty that had been my idea. When I walked in, the director pointed to the golden frame and asked:

- What do you think of it? In a week, all of the banks in the country would either follow our lead or go out of business! Ha ha ha ha ha ha ha! We have prevailed in both situations. Aren't we the ones who put the notion forward? No asshole would deny it, I assure you. I'll make sure it's extensively publicised in national newspapers as well.

He was grinning. It was one of his most wonderful days. A triumph! And if he thought of giving it full attention in the newspapers - it was a real scoop anyhow! - I did not miss the point: the President - I mean our BGP- is rumoured to be a voracious reader of newspapers and periodicals! Mr Aroussi is a brilliant man. I could only agree with his idea. That was the correct approach to whack hard and high. Nevertheless, I was bothered by something weird. I told him so. He gazed at me, a bit perplexed and said:

- What's the trouble? Is it, not your idea?

- Of course, it is, sir, but look at their mess! They printed the sentence with golden letters, all right! But they missed the crucial point. For I do not see the name of our Beloved General President anywhere! How could the reader know who the source of such wisdom is? What if the clients mistake it for some banal quotation from Plato, Tolstoy, or even Spinoza?

- Spinoza? Oh no, no, for God's sake! Our President must not be confused with one of those guys. Who's that Spinoza anyway? A friend of yours?

- No, sir. I randomly picked up his name in a magazine while working the crosswords.

- Ah! Well! I'd better not know who's the chap in case he turns out to be a conspirator. Anyway, I'll issue directives for the sentence to be reprinted immediately.

It was done. In twenty-four hours, the new golden frame was decorating the front wall of our hall so that no eye could miss it. I congratulated Mr Aroussi when I saw in the national newspapers the following advertisement:

Following His Excellency Mister President of the Republic's historic address, the 'Ouja filial of the National Bank, led by the dynamic Mr Aroussi Mamitu, adopted a new motto. From "Your Confidence Is Our Real Capital," as it once was, to "NO PRISONS IN OUR COUNTRY BUT FREEDOM FOR ALL."

This was derived from the same speech, highlighting and reinforcing the bank's loyalty to our beloved Mister President's insightful thoughts. Mr Mamitu aims to be an example for other banks and organisations to follow.

* * *

IT WAS FOLLOWED, BUT not in the way we anticipated.

Mr Aroussi was summoned to the Capital after the advertisement was published. I was told he received a call from the Big Boss's secretary. So he left, most likely assuming the Chairman wanted to congratulate him.

It was the last time I saw him before realising he was a State guest in this institution, just like me!

Chapter 2

James Bond in Jail

(1)

I settled down in the library of the...hotel. Now, I can clear my mind and have a broad sight of the situation.

I pushed the desk to the left side of the gate. Thus, I shelter from the stabbing darts of the spring sun, away from the blatant hubbub of the riff-raff. Looking through the unique window of the room, I see the courtyard. Slanting on the high white walls surmounted by barbed wire, the sun rays shimmer on the cobbled floor. At two corners of the yard stand two well-guarded towers. Men in grey uniforms stood up, scanning the space randomly, with their machine guns ready to fire. At night, two great searchlights sweep the walls and the quadrangle. Not even a mosquito crossing the space would escape detection. The other courtyards are much similar, although different in size. I was able to observe discreetly what was going on in those towers. It is not exhilarating. I would say even that it is far from serious.

I do not wish to interfere in matters that are none of my business. Nonetheless, my sense of duty and incorruptible loyalty to the Administration made me report what I saw.

To begin with, the guards. Yes, Sir. I am saying the guards. They are not strictly conforming to the Code that clearly stipulates that their behaviour must be uncluttered and exemplary while in service. They should neither smoke nor chat with the... well, I will say the customers. Should not hobnob with them. Should not have any business implying any sort of partnership... I've read through the Code. It's the most important book in the library. As a result, I can provide objective testimony.

The guards are not only smoking, conversing, and casually hobnobbing with some of the clients, but they are also involved in a peculiar and nonsensical business with them. Some customers, particularly those employed as cooks in the kitchens, seem well favoured by the guards. They offer them sandwiches, tea, coffee, and other snacks and treats. This produces a lot of commotion in the towers. As a result, the guards are obliged to:

1) abandon their posts, which is desertion, and

2) rush downstairs to retrieve the stolen food, which is a second irregularity!

I have no doubt that the cooks steal these items with the nefarious intent of influencing our glorious Administration's grey-suited representatives. God only knows what they're really after!

The cooks' dishonesty, on the other hand, is obvious. Because we rarely consume fresh foods. And if we do get some exciting provisions, the meat will be like a sponge, while the fish will stink terribly. Since I cannot eat such unpalatable hodge-podge, I would often pass them on to my cellmate, Dahdah. The poor devil is starving day and night, although his family never misses a food-stuffed visit. Eager to swallow up anything, was it even a clammy human carcass exuding an obnoxious effluvium - the man is a wonder amid the seven! Oh! I am not charging him with cannibalism. On the contrary, I think his famine is abnormal, considering all the food he receives from his relatives!

Enough to feed the entire cell, crowded with 200 people for a month!

Strange noises wake me up at night when the inmates are supposed to sleep. At first, I thought it was a rat going about its nocturnal business. Those assumed emissaries of the gutters are - alas! - as accustomed to the hotel and fond of it as some of its veterans. But it was simply my cellmate, Dahdah, grunting, crunching, and snorting like a pig while chewing a creaky piece of cake or cookie.

- Good appetite, I would say.

He'd look at me sideways and continue eating, but I'd close my eyes and try to return to my dreams. It was like getting off the train before it arrived at the stop. The disappointment would be as unpleasant as my interrupted dream!

OH! MAKE NO MISTAKE. I am not complaining about the food. Damn it! The question may be summed up in a single word: DIS GUS TING! But I could not avoid the subject since I was discussing the illicit smuggling between the kitchens and the towers. I am not an aficionado in the culinary art, but as a man of taste, I know how to enjoy a fine dish. I used to go to restaurants before coming to this large hotel. And, unless I started rattling at a young age, I cannot declare that the meals offered in this governmental facility are convenient for gourmands. If I could help myself elsewhere, I would pay them real cash in dollars not to offer me their vile concoction. But I know I'd starve if I didn't eat everything they provided me.

Well, I won't be too sensitive about it. After all, a bank teller's stomach can be similar to another's. It might wince and cause difficulty if it is not fed properly. On the other hand, occasionally keeping oneself hungry is a good idea. A man who is overly well-supplied is useless. Muslims fast for a full month every year because of this.

I now have a greater understanding of the Administration's cunning. Giving us bad food serves as a deterrent to filling our bellies with superfluous items. As a result, we maintain perfect fittingness and maintain a positive attitude throughout our hotel trip. We pay nothing for this nutritious meal, which is outstanding. The fact that all of the services offered here are free should be noted.

Of course, I inquired and was told I owed nothing. Accommodation, food, and laundry are included in the service! Otherwise, we are the guests of the State. May Allah bless it! To the delight of all honest citizens, the generosity of our Administration is thus confirmed. Those who have not yet got the golden opportunity to visit this unique, incomparable place should hurry up. Life is short. It is therefore advised to make at least one visit in a lifetime. Then you would understand and benefit from our government's magnificent hospitality. Hurry up before the already limited vacant space is filled. So, what are you waiting for? All good people who are proud of their nation and its achievements should join us right away to observe and convey to friends and family what we are enjoying. This is the very least one can do to demonstrate patriotism and loyalty to the God-blessed government of our Beloved General President!

LET US NOW GET BACK to work. I was discussing the Code and the guard's wrongdoing. I'm still stunned. I cannot agree with these behaviours as a respectable public servant (my bank is majority owned by the State). The situation seemed to be serious enough to me.

First, desertion occurs when a guard leaves his post for even five minutes. Imagine if some clients decided to climb the walls and flee during those five minutes! But then, who is to blame for their escape?

Second, I have serious reservations about the inmates engaging in the shady business with the guards. What exactly is their plan? And why is their traffic so well guarded? On his way back to the kitchens, one of them panicked when I questioned him about the price of the sandwiches he had just delivered to the guards. I only intended to buy one. However, the man began motioning with both hands like a clown, pleading with me to speak quietly.

- Are you concerned that someone will hear us? I inquired.

- Of course, I am, dude! We are not permitted to leave the kitchen.

- But the guards, aren't they your friends? Every day, I watch you offering them beverages and food.

-Huss! Damn your lying eyes! Would you like to spend some time in the freezer?

- The freezer? For what purpose?

- The freezer, of course! You should mind your own business!

He dashed away. I chased after him:

- I'd like a sandwich!

He shifted his weight and gave me the middle finger! Bastard! But never mind! In any case, his sandwiches must be out of price simply because they were stolen. I'm sure the guards are unaware of it. I refuse to believe that the servants of our magnificent Administration are so corrupt that they force detainees to steal for them. I thought about it for a bit.

Finally, I concluded that the entire operation was likely run by an offshore international corporation with a branch inside the hotel. *The Muslim Brothelhood.* I see no other since Dahdah told me about this multinational corporation with sections in various countries. They undoubtedly deal primarily in foreign money. There is no alternative reason for the guards' behaviour. It isn't about eating, but rather about money.

Money can be found everywhere. I can smell it. There is no misunderstanding.

What happened to the guards' professional conscience? Isn't it their job to keep an eye on the perimeter of this site from the towers? Is this the reason they require foreign currency? As we are near the border, they may do their shopping at the duty-free market. I'm not going on a rant. This type of trafficking has been going on quietly on the borders for years. Because it is an easily accessible industry, the Administration undoubtedly supports it. We need foreign currency to service our obligations and pay for imports, no matter how oil-rich we are.

IN RECENT YEARS, SEVERAL offshore and international corporations have bloomed in the country like spring flowers. Investments are encouraged as a result of flexible legislation. I know this since my bank negotiated lucrative partnerships with both foreign and domestic investors and businessmen. I oversaw the establishment of at least three businesses in 'Ouja. For example, an import-export agency dealing in electronic goods, led by a man who returned to the nation after 25 years in exile in Germany with a large sum of money. If my memory serves me correctly, his name is Ismael.

I'll never forget him since he left such an impression on me. Despite his wealth, he could not write his name in Arabic, despite being fluent in German! I didn't inquire if he could write or read German. In any case, I know nothing about German. I also thought his money freed him from our common enslavement to the alphabet. Happy man! He was always trailed by two shadows: his secretary and his solicitor. The time had come to sign the documents. The secretary handed him a blotting pad soaked in black ink, which Ismael thumbed before stamping the sheet. That was his august signature! I was shocked. Of course, I avoided any unnecessary coment that could be misconstrued.

I RECALLED MR ISMAEL again last week when I was summoned by the black guard Mahmoud to the hotel's police station.

They took frontal and profile shots of me, weighed me, and measured my height. Then I was told to stamp my fingers on my file with a blotting pad soaked in black ink. I was furious. I refused, irritated by the extraneous requirement that implicitly implied I was illiterate!

- I can sign normally, sir, I objected. Just hand me a pen.

The officer was displeased. He cast an oblique glance at me and remarked:

- We don't need your signature, lad. Only biometrics.

- Oh well. But why is that?

He became enraged. His face flushed, and he yelled:

- That's none of your fucking concern, midget! Put your fucking fingers where I tell you to, shut your bloody lips, and then get out of my sight!

I meekly obeyed and returned to my library without saying anything.

(*I'm still digressing and straying from the original topic. Sometimes my mind wanders. I have no idea where it disappears, and then reappears.*) Two of the other companies were British, and one was French. Textile and footwear manufacturers. Fortunately, their local employers were ordinary people, and nothing out of the ordinary happened while they were signing the documents.

Nonetheless, I am moving around. I concede that the hotel's offshore multinational corporation, which sells sandwiches and mixed drinks, could just be a wild guess. But how does one explain the Administration's silence on the strange transaction going on between the cooks and the towers? Is it feasible that the guards have become so corrupt that they allow consumers to steal food? If true, that would be a significant sprain inflicted on the rules!

The second reason that makes me so concerned is much more dramatic. Suppose the offshore company - a sound theory, though- should be rejected. In that case, one must concede that such a business cannot be sustained without a well-organised network of agents. Is the Chef aware or not of what is happening in his kitchen and under his nose? Is he their accomplice? One thing is obvious. The man I have stopped is not the only one who deals with the towers. They are several. They likely form some sort of gang. I suspect the traffic to be even broader and less innocuous than it seems. The other towers might be involved too. And who knows who else and what else and where and when? One must open the eyes.

Another question will inevitably arise. Assume the guards do not pay for the food in foreign currency. What is the gang's asking price in return? This is an even more difficult and convoluted issue! To put it bluntly:

I think the inmates who work in the kitchens are part of a secret group that is up to no good. First, they would numb the tower guards with so many gifts that they became acclimated to their traffic, addicted to their meals, and blind to their true intentions. This is only the first stage. The second consists in inserting a narcotic in the stolen food at a precise hour and handing it over to the guards. Then, while the latter went dopey, the gang would grab the opportunity to ascend upstairs to the towers. Finally, with some accomplices waiting for them outside under the walls, they would abscond and vanish in the city.

I am almost sure this is the scenario they are preparing in the dim warmth of the kitchens. It ought to be better concocted than their disgusting dishes if they want to succeed.

So, it is not a coincidence that they focused on the towers. There is no way out save through the main gate, which is guarded by an armada of sentinels. The only option is to climb one of the towers and, using a decent rope, carefully descend down the steep wall.

I AM AWARE THAT WHAT I am writing here is TOP SECRET, yet I must admit that I have a prick of conscience. This is due not only to the fact that I have not acquired the Administration's necessary approval, but also to the fact that I am using its paper and pens. I am honest. I admit to swiping them off the library's shelves. But I'm meant to be watching and caring about it. That is why I should use "borrow" instead of "steal." In any case, I choose to pay for the accessories. I was forced to use them due to exceptional circumstances. But as soon as this complicated scenario - not just the gang's, but also my own - is resolved, I aim to go as clean as I came in.

I OWE A GREAT DEAL to the Administration. However, I owe far more to my own efforts. All of these charges I'm facing don't make my job any easier. On the contrary, the brutal colours of the nightmare contribute to my perplexity. If I trust the shrink, I should spend at least twenty years in prison! It is obvious that I am referring to internal tourism in this hotel. I will be fifty-nine years old when I am discharged, as I am now thirty-nine years old. My hair would be grey, and my skin would wrinkle. If I return to work at the bank, as I expect to do, I will only be there for five years before retiring at the age of sixty-four. I calculated as soon as I left the shrink's office. It is also understood that when I claim I worked for the bank for twenty years, I include the five years prior to my retirement. As a result, my career would form a circle with a twenty-year vacuum. In mathematics, the empty set. A zero with a bar.

It's not what I had in mind. But life may be quite startling at times. For example, I never saw myself as a librarian. Yet here I am, going about my peculiar business as if it were always mine. Fortunately, I enjoy reading. I'm still preserving my primary and secondary school manuals in good condition. Warming up nicely in a huge box under my bed with my archives. I dare to state that I am an excellent reader... Bank paperwork, indeed, come first. In any case, they're not that different from books, are they? To be sure, I read newspapers and magazines as well. My intellectual curiosity is continuously looking for new experiences. There are no boundaries that can stop it. Crossword puzzles, football, and horoscopes All of which I particularly enjoy. That is why I purchase newspapers. But I wouldn't be Bassam Bourasin if I didn't read the other stuff, even if it's often boring. But I do it on principle. I dislike squandering money. If I buy something, I have to consume it. The point isn't whether I enjoy it or not. Anyway, I always find solace in the obituaries, which I save until the last minute of my newspaper reading, like the cherry on top. To be honest, I enjoy knowing who has died since it tells me who is still on the waiting list. And, as one of the latter, I must admit that it is almost fascinating to know. But how would I know if I didn't read the obituaries and see that my name isn't among the dead? I became aware of the issue when the police asked me to bring an Attestation of Life, among other documents, in order to renew my identity card. A Life Attestation!

I WAS TALKING WITH the officer, and he was speaking to me and noticing that I was standing in front of him. But he still required proof that I was alive! No kidding. So, when I asked him, he said:

- What demonstrates that you are alive and not another?

- Easy! I said. I'm speaking to you, and you know who I am, and this is my outrunning identity card, which shows everything. So...

He interrupted me:

- So what, Sir? I don't know who you are while I'm in the service. I just have faith in your documents. It is the Law. Bring me an attestation of life so I know Mr Bourasin has not died since receiving his previous identity card. Don't make my life or yours any more difficult. Bring me proof that you're alive, and everything will be all right!

BUT I ALMOST FORGOT about the Intermarket. I believe that any bank employee, merchant, or dealer worth his salt should read such commercials. Aside from allowing us to better understand our culture, it is also practical and useful. Personally, I owe the most interesting bargains I found to the Intermarket. My home is outfitted with goods and fixtures from that lovely market. And I freak out when I think I've been forced to leave my *Dolce Vita* for an odd - albeit brief - new job in this strange hotel. So, if I can avoid it, I'd rather not think of 'Ouja.

(2)

I am not dissatisfied because I am starting a new career that does not lack charms and perks. You must have realised that I was referring to the librarian's career, not the jailbird's. I also ran the numbers: if they paid me as well as the bank for this position, I'd be a millionaire in twenty years. No wonder! Since all the services are provided free of charge here - thanks to our State's fairness - I will be able to save all the money I make. Of course, I'll postpone my wedding for twenty years instead of next summer. Nonetheless, I am confident that this period of forced separation will prepare us both for our future expected marital life. My fiancée, who is thirty years old, will be fifty by then. A virgin marrying at the age of fifty is unusual. But we can try. There has to be a beginning to everything. I am confident we will be much happier. I understand plainly that the young age of the couple on the wedding day is the root cause of such a large number of divorces. And I'm curious why so many young people want to marry, have children, and then divorce! That endeavour is flawed in some way. I'm now thirty-nine, stable in life, with at least two professions (thanks to Allah), and

I'm still hoping for more and better. I have been engaged to Dalila for about five years, barely enough to get used to each other and prepare for marital life. And now, I think that if we succeed in staying engaged for the next twenty years of my touristic life in the State hotel, we will not fail in our marriage as other couples do.

Observe the wisdom of such a deal: if everybody gets married at fifty-fifty-nine like us - inshallah!- there will never be any collapse or divorce... Perhaps more widows and widowers, but this is quite different.

Naturally, the only problem would be the children: how to breed them at that age?

Here, too, Eureka!

I discovered the solution. It wasn't exactly me who discovered it, but rather the science of genetics. With test-tube kids, all women between the ages of fifty and one hundred (perhaps more) can now enjoy pregnancy like the younger. May Allah bless the researchers! They have rescued so many couples from the catastrophe, including ours. I'm sure Dalila will be pleased if I tell her we must marry. But we need twenty years for safety and sustainability. That would provide us with a solid and healthy marriage. She must realise that it is the only way to avoid a potential calamity, which I see rising on the horizon of our young age. After all, what are twenty years? A wink! It is barely enough to make us realise our obligations to one another.

THUS, I AM WRITING a top-secret report. Cool time. I cannot say that I do not enjoy it. I do. And this is undoubtedly the cause of my trouble. For I am discovering that after exactly fifteen years of loyalty to the bank and the Administration - not including the five years before my future retirement-I am - to my distress! - enjoying the infringement of the Code for the first time in my life. I am ashamed, but I have no other choice. I must write. I hope my report will be helpful not only for my defence but also for the Administration which is unaware of most of what is happening in this hotel.

The cause of my innermost joy is the feeling of fulfilment that accompanies the achievement of heavy duty. But, of course, I've had that experience countless times since I started working for the bank, most notably whenever I strike a deal. Nonetheless, the peculiarity of what I feel right now must be underlined. And, while I am used to secrecy because it is the lifeblood of banking, it is clear that what I am doing here is both exciting and unique. In fact, it is well the job of a secret agent or, in simple terms, a spy. It may appear pompous or obnoxious that I have a third profession while many are unemployed. But I didn't do anything about it.

Furthermore, a spy career has a romantic component that appeals to young people. Who among us hasn't wished to be the famous, iconic, and magnificent James Bond at some point in our lives? Eh! That is a question of taste and guts, to be sure. In my case, I knew from the moment I received my registration number - 1007 - that it may be a secret code. If you remove the initial number, which is likely intended to conceal the true Code, you get 007! Otherwise, *Bond, James Bond.*

I'm not sure if this is a recognition from the Administration or just a coincidence. But I gratefully accept my James Bond Code. And, while I still claim to be a modest bank clerk working as an interim librarian, I can't deny that my third job gives me a lot of pride. Isn't being a covert agent unquestionably heroic? To be honest, I have always practised this illustrious career. As a dedicated amateur, I did it for the benefit of our government. I did it on the spur of the moment, without expecting anything in return. It never occurred to me that I would be recognised as 007 himself. What splendour!

However, I do not deny that without that background, obtaining any post in the State-owned 'Ouja bank is difficult, if not impossible.

It is always interesting to study others' behaviour. However, it requires knowledge, experience, and common sense. Therefore, I claim humbly that I am an excellent secret agent.

For over fifteen years, I have methodically crafted various intelligence reports at irregular intervals. I'm not sure how much my effort has been appreciated, but I've gathered that I've received great acclaim. I'm almost certain that some of my reports made it to the Minister's office. Who just happens to be the President! I CAN GUESS, despite the fact that no one in authority has ever winded or hinted at it. I also have an informant network.

IN 'OUJA, I FLY HIGH. For this reason, perhaps I get depressed and freak out whenever I come to the capital. Here I am anonymous. Just a number among many. I love numbers and am fond of secret codes and confidential reports. It is also a solace when faced with the terrible charges I'm currently facing.

Indeed, neither Mr Aroussi nor the other bank staff are aware of my covert operations. Furthermore, everyone, even the boss, has gone through my files. I was there before he was appointed. Thus, I had a good reason to inquire about him, just as I did with the previous director. I dare say that I know my colleagues better than they know themselves. I keep my secret archives well hidden under my bed. Even when I sleep at night, I KEEP AN EYE OPEN, considering that I am sleeping on the State's secrets. Not that I fear thieves and burglars, but I am somewhat apprehensive about foreign agents. One never knows. As I love watching espionage films, I have learned many tricks, which are very useful indeed. I wouldn't be surprised if I discovered that Russian agents or the CIA were following me. Nowadays, financial espionage is widespread. Because money is the lifeblood of every economic system, foreign nations are definitely interested in any information concerning the 'Ouja bank and its workers. And since I am the only man who detains such secrets, it is not improbable that I am the object of their investigations. As I am thinking it over now, I cannot dismiss the idea that some foreign agents might have concocted the severe charges I am facing. The purpose? Well! To get rid of me so the bastards could easily access my archives. Obvious! Hell! But that's it!

I had not considered this idea previously, but it now appears as clear as the sun's rays! So blatant! That is insane! That is really true! It all makes sense.

Observe that it is not just the bank that might attract foreign spies. As it happens, my archives are also stuffed with intelligence about 'Ouja population. A good spy would even pay millions just to look at it. For long years, I kept files about almost everything intriguing in the village. From old traditions to rituals, peasants, shopkeepers, employees and the unemployed. Families and offspring, lands, real estate, patrimony and other items. Did the persons own their things? Did the things own them? Beliefs and political inclination. Are they mosque goers? If not, are they Christians, Jewish, atheists, don't care or Devil followers? But, of course, I didn't dismiss those haunted by Jinnies and those who subdued Jinnies. History, geography, family trees of people and animals, plants, birds and pets are good intelligence. They may be used in social interaction, conflicts, and other purposes.

My first goal was to collect and accumulate data that I may need to write a well-stuffed secret report.

MY HIERARCHIC SUPERIOR who acts as liaison officer with the Administration is Mr Hamda La'war, head of our party's cell, president of the town council, along with other responsibilities he accumulated for years. He is one-eyed - whence his nickname: La'war - since he lost his left eye in a brawl with the shoemaker. But, of course, he would never acknowledge it. Instead, he asserts that he had lost it during the war of Independence, which is totally unfounded. I know the story of the brawl, but I avoided hinting at that unhappy episode whenever I met him.

The truth is that long years ago, when Mr Hamda was not yet head of the party cell, he had been surprised by the shoemaker, in his bed and with his wife. Hamda got away from the bedroom with only one safe eye. He was fortunate in that he did not lose both peepers, if not his life. The situation was immediately put down, but some of its terrible stenches escaped. People gossiped, and the story toured across the village for a while, just in hints and smiles, then in whispers and allusions. Some people laughed, some pitied the shoemaker, while others cursed his wife. But the story was forgotten many years later when Hamda was appointed head of the party's cell. Which allowed La'war to make some allegations about his glorious past as a freedom fighter - that nobody recalled!- during his public speeches. One day, however, he dared speak of his lost eye before an audience of hundreds of people. He pretended that the colonialists tortured him vainly to obtain the secrets of resistance. But he did not give up despite the pain inflicted on his eye. The locals and the hypocrites applauded with both hands when they saw the young, freshly appointed Governor nodding. They took it as an official confirmation of Hamda's version of history, albeit many knew very well that he was lying. The Governor, too young and freshly appointed, did not have time to learn local history. Therefore, he did not get the correct information about Hamda. The presence of the high representative of the State in the village was too good an opportunity to miss. Hamda seized it and did not hesitate to invent a glorious past to climb fast and high. Indeed, nobody opposed him or hinted at the shoemaker. Who would dare? As they say, lady Fortune smiles to the bold. Hamda's story worked so well that a few months later, all 'Ouja watched him on the TV, making his way to the King. He was invited to the Palace on Independence day to be offered the Order Of High Merit! The event has no precedent: Hamda was made National Hero for having cuckolded the shoemaker!

THE NEXT DAY, LANDOWNERS, shopkeepers and peasants of the region were queuing at the gate of the party's cell. They did not fail to come with their presents to congratulate the National Hero. Baskets full of fruits, vegetables, eggs, poultry, olives, and cans of olive oil. All the products of 'Ouja and its surroundings. As the shoemaker had moved away long years ago, fleeing the village with his adulterous wife, who would oppose Hamda? It was not hard for the powerful head of the party's cell to transform the flagrant lie into a historical truth and find "witnesses" and "companions of the struggle against colonialism" ready to validate his version!

I DID NOT MISS THE event, indeed. I was so well connected to the head of the party's cell that it goes without saying that I felt as if I got the honours with him from His Majesty the King. I told him so, of course. He smiled, and his remaining black eye blinked in the plumpy face. He rubbed the point of his long nose and affected a lot of modesty, saying:

- I'm sure you'll get the same medal soon, my dear Bassam. Your services to the party are also crucial.

- And to the fatherland too, I said emphatically.

He coughed and replied cheerfully:

- You know, the party is the fatherland, my good friend. There's no difference.

- I'm confident it's exactly as you say, Mr Hamda.

(3)

On my way out of the office, I noticed Mustapha, the barber, and Mehrez, the grocer loitering in the hall. Oddly enough, they were whispering and guffawing. I did not like that skittish behaviour on such a day celebrating the solemn event. It sounded like a nasty conspiracy. Why should they act like perfect jerks? It was neither the right place nor the right time for joking. One must keep some gravity. What the hell!

Later on, I inquired about what was making them so happy. I was told - my source was a man standing in the row just behind them- that they were making a jest of the decoration! A jest? What a horror! Yes, Sir. A jest. What insolence! So, in their eyes - may they be blind!- His majesty - and behind him, the party - was encouraging his subjects to cuckold each other! My source was assertive. He heard everything.

Mehrez said:

- It is the shoemaker's wife who deserves the medal! Oh, my goodness! Ha ha ha!

- Without a doubt! Mustapha replied. She earned it through hard struggle. Ha ha ha!

- Ass and cock struggle!

They both burst out laughing like two perfect fools!

This is inadmissible! Deviant! Hostile! It is blatant treachery! Such words in such a respectable place on such a solemn celebration could usually lead the two wretched rascals to ... to... I don't want to say to this hotel! Of course, I took note of the incident, but I did not report it. For I intended to make another use of it.

AT THE TIME, I WAS indebted to the grocer. By the end of the month, when I went to pick up some commodities from his shop, he told me:

- You know Mr Bassam, you're always welcome. But I think we ought to review your account together.

It was his way of reminding me of my debt. Then, without waiting for my answer, he began rummaging into his drawers, produced his old oil and harissa's stained notebook, and put it on the counter. Therefore, leafing through it, he told me the exact sum I owed him.

- I didn't forget, Mr Mehrez. There are two things I never forget, you know: my debts and my friends. Loyalty and honesty are rare qualities these days. Take an example. You know that Mr Hamda and I are like brothers. I tell him everything, and he opens his heart to me unrestrainedly. The other day at the party's house, I saw you casually chatting with the barber and - believe me - I remembered my debt! I was going to pay you, but you seemed so busy that I didn't want to disturb you. I am not going to stretch, but somebody told me the story of the decoration that made you and Mustapha so blithe.

- No! You don't... Shouted the grocer vividly piqued.

- Sorry! But I really do know all about it.

His brown face went pale, and his little eyes of sparrow glittered as he mumbled:

- You ... How do you...?

I helped him:

- Don't worry! I didn't tell Mr Hamda. Not yet. I mean, I must inform him, since he is my friend! But before that, I wanted to ask whether you were serious or just kidding.

He jumped on the opportunity I offered him:

- Of course, it was a joke, Mr Bassam. It was just for fun...

The sparrow fell into the trap. Now, I will teach him a lesson he will never forget.

- Just for fun! OK. I believe you, Mr Mehrez. You're an honest guy. That's why I told my boss at the bank that you are a good customer for us...(that was a lie!) You know your money is safe as long as I remain a bank clerk. But I have a prick of conscience. I just can't hide this from you. I am loyal to Mr. Hamda. Lying to him is definitely unimaginable for me. And now I wonder what if he gets wind of the story before I told him? He wouldn't like my silence about it when our friendship impels me to report to him in due time. The subject concerns his reputation. As I said, it is a matter of loyalty. I have nothing against jokes.

I saw the grocer's face veer alternately from brown to yellow, then to red, then to blue, then to purple, then to green, then again to brown, yellow... and so on for a good moment! Silence followed. He swallowed his saliva several times, coughed, cleared his throat, took his courage with both hands and finally said:

- Mr Bassam, I implore you, in the name of our long relationship. Mr Hamda doesn't need to know.

- I Agree with you, but what if another tells him?

- Well... er... you deny!

Irate, I exploded:

- How dare you? Are you trying to test my honesty and loyalty, Mr Mehrez?

He tried to protest, but I went on hammering hot iron:

- Are you trying to bribe me? Are you hinting that I forget what I heard about you, and in return, you forget what I owe you? Is that what you suggest? Because it is just what I feel.

He seemed surprised and mused for a moment voiceless, while I calmed down and said:

- I am sorry! It was perhaps not what you intended. I apologise for what I said.

After that, I drew my wallet from my pocket and began to count some banknotes. But to my surprise, before I could place the money on the counter, Mehrez clasped my hand firmly, closed my fingers on the bank notes, and swore to Allah, his Prophet and Saints:

- I will not accept a single dinar from you.

- That's not right, Mr Mehrez! I said.

- Not even a single dinar! He shouted. My wife is Haram if I accepted! Allah is my witness!

Changing tactics, I proposed to him a cheque instead.

- I can't! I just can't! Shame on me if I accept any money from my friend, my protector, my benefactor, the respectable Mr Bassam Bourasin. May Allah bless him and bless Mr Hamda and the glorious party of our nation! You were the first man to advise me to keep my money safe in the bank when I was hiding it under my mattress. You opened my eyes, Mr Bassam. How could I forget it? Since then, I have prospered. I'll always be grateful to you, my brother.

- Mr Hamda seems to frighten you. But, you know, he's not that bad! He is not deprived of humour. He would understand that you were kidding. Anyway, I won't tell him. Take your money. I owe you.

- You owe me nothing, Mr Bassam. Consider it as my contribution to the party. Please! Take it, take your goods and go home. You're always welcome. I'm damned if I touch that money!

I took my packets.

- Well, it is all right for now, but you're not going to put it again, I promise you! Anyway, this contribution to the party is the third you made this year. It's too much! That can't go on indefinitely.

- No, sir, that was the eighth. Mr Hamda's wife came shopping before you. I am her preferred grocer, she said. It's too much honour!

- I see.

- You're welcome! All the party is welcome! Tell that to Mr Hamda, please.

- I will convey your message. Salam, Mr Mehrez.

I RETURNED HOME ADMIRING the splendid generosity of that man who, some minutes earlier, I was suspecting of an evil conspiracy against an honourable servant of the country. But he revealed to be as loyal to me - his friend, protector, and benefactor - as to Mr Hamda. And since he proved his sincerity and goodwill, I realised he did not betray us. It was just a silly joke.

It was such an unexpected reversal of the situation to which I made no contribution. I just reminded Mehrez that he was a client of my bank. That was enough to drive him back to the right way, from which he deviated somehow. I think most of 'Ouja bank's customers are honest citizens, devoted to their ... wallets! Those devoted to their wallets care about the country's finances. They understand the secret of prosperity. It is in sharing.

The smart grocer grasped quickly what I meant, despite being neither educated nor well informed about the state of the world, as I am myself. But, like many people of his condition, he has a practical mind that allows him to cope with different and complicated issues. I was aware by the way that he was selling some goods more expensively than the other grocers. It was a misdemeanour I did not fail to notice, although prices inspectors did not perceive it. Unless he bribed them. But I shut my eyes about the whole thing. After all, he should be allowed from time to time to make some profit from his business. That is precisely what we do at the bank when we take people's money. To make huge profits, we always need more and more funds. To hold people, we allow them all the same to make some profit. The naive think they control the bank. But it is the bank that controls everybody. And since the customers do not mind buying from Mehrez's store despite his playing into the prices, why should I care? Business is business!

Furthermore, he became the preferred grocer of the party's cell! Well, Well! I feel he will win a national award one day. I only hope he gets it before going bankrupt!

Let him sell according to his whims. We cannot encourage free enterprises and forbid free prices. The retailers do not mind the Administration's opinion anyway. They make their own law whenever they can afford it, like everybody else in the count...(*stop! Remove the last sentence. Done! Now, go ahead.*)

Sometimes, when they exaggerate, they are fined or forced to close down for some time. Maybe both. It is terrible! Those people do not even distinguish free enterprise from the free jungle! They mix them up and get confused. Nobody told them there were limits. It is not a brothel, though. What the hell! It is a free country, with free laws and free money, and free everything, especially since the Coup that freed the king from the throne and the throne from the king.

I NEVER INTERFERE IN politics. That's rule number One. However, I must admit that the Administration did not completely change after the Coup-revolution (Isn't it preferable to call it Couvolution? rather than hesitating). We now have a *Beloved General President* (BGP) who has officially declared the Republic. Okay, then! But, with the exception of the Government - and even then, not entirely - the State apparatus has remained unchanged. Which is a benediction, I believe. It would be mayhem if we changed everything in less than twenty-four hours to coincide with the top-level reshuffle! In reality, our people value stability and consistency. That is why we have such a strong attachment to our rulers, whatever they are and do. It's a challenging question. We're a sentimental bunch. We cling to our rulers like bugs, and the only way out is through a coup, a revolution, or something similar! Personally, I shed hot tears when I heard that our good old king had been removed by the military. I cried every day for a week between four walls, even in the office. And I still do not know whether those tears were caused by sadness or joy! It is hard to be assertive on such delicate matters. Human emotions are so inscrutable sometimes! I was so attached to the old king that I learned some passages of his speeches by heart. No wonder! I have heard them so many times that even if I were a perfect moron, something of them would still stick to my memory... (*What the hell am I talking about? This whole paragraph about the king is useless. Delete! Too dangerous!*)

I WAS TALKING ABOUT the king's speeches, but I meant the President, of course. What a terrible mistake! Everybody can understand that the President's speeches are enrapturing me. I am so enthusiastic that I never fail to hear and re-hear the same address at breakfast, lunch, and dinner every day for at least three or four days, if not more. And to ensure that I heard well, I also read the same broadcast speech in the papers. It is such a delight! And those good fellows of the Radio and TV broadcasting! Ah! They know their job. They know about people longing to listen to our BGP, never fail to serve it hot to us, if I may say, and re-serve it twice or thrice a day, all the week long.

Boring? NEVER! Only tasteless people would say so. Quite the contrary, it is highly entertaining, educative and cultural. Observe the wisdom of our Administration. The many illiterate among our people would not catch the hidden pearls in any presidential speech unless they hear it several times. Indeed, the Administration does not take us for bunches of dum-dums. After all, this is also a democratic matter. I mean, even muppets have the right to know what is happening in their country, right? And, since most people do not read newspapers or prefer not to, they can at least listen to the broadcast. To the rest of us, the knowledgeable, hearing a presidential speech numerous times on the same day all week is not bad! One's education should be constantly improved. Particularly since presidential speeches are a natural wellspring of wisdom and knowledge. We must treat them with the same regard that we do money.

To be sure, Presidential speeches are valuable. Cash in hand. Bank notes. Cheques. Credit cards. Bonds to the treasure. Stock-market values. Gems. Gold. High transactions. International transfers. Investments. Invaluable funds for our future. Those who broadcast and diffuse them must be aware that they are increasing the G.D.P. And if the ignorants argue, "we just can't eat words," the wise should respond, "then, what's the point of patriotism? On the contrary, WE CAN EAT WORDS TO PLEASE OUR BGP."

Better, I would say: WE MUST.

(4)

I am writing all this far away from selfish objectives.

Counting is part of my job. I don't deny it. Which is honest and needed. Nevertheless, I am neither a hypocrite nor a sycophant. I am not aspiring to a political career, albeit the appearances are against me. My telepathic mind-hacking angels suspect me of being an activist and a troublemaker! They are either uninformed or malicious or both. Anyway, they are incompetent at their work, but this is another issue that I will address later. I put it off because it is metaphysical. In fact, I don't wish to get into problems with God too! So far, I got enough trouble dealing with His creatures...

I ADMITTED TO CRYING hot tears of excitement as a result of the king's unexpected dismissal. Not that I was pleased to be free of the old man who had been torturing us for a quarter-century with his monologues about his heroic deeds. It is actually the other way around. I was happy for him. He was relieved of the vexing chore of conversing to no ear.

Long ago, people abandoned both radio and television sets at scheduled speech times! They always press the button to switch between waves or channels. The poor old man was like a desert dog, barking at the moon, passing clouds, or planes. He was certain that everyone was paying attention. Anyway, his speeches were rarely new. Most of the time, the radio and television re-diffuse a previous broadcast, which they feed to us in small doses, like a nasty medicine! It was a living nightmare!

With the Beloved General President (BGP), we are now prepared for another quarter-century of repeated statements on the glorious movement of reform and change. The Coup wasn't a coup. It was a revolution. A New Era or COUVOLUTION that elevated our Hero to power. The country desperately needed him to saved it from the rotten monarchy!

As we are now saved, we should abandon the evil habit of turning off the television and radio at specific times and instead listen intently to the Saviour's speeches. At the very least as a token of gratitude. We owe him a considerable debt. Such skittish practices of not paying attention to the State Head when he addresses the nation should be regarded as treason that deserves punishment. It is a misdemeanour that dishonours us because of the viral spread. Personally, I never dared. I'm a man of principles; what the hell! I am well aware that time is money. The uninformed have no idea how much it costs the National Broadcasting House to broadcast a show.

I can go miles telling you about that. I have supervised a bank's ad on television, It costs millions and millions. No exaggeration. As broadcasting is so expensive, it would be a tremendous time and money waste to diffuse even a small paragraph from a speech when nobody would care to listen. At last, the State would pay the bill, that's true. But where does the State get money if not in our pockets, gentlemen? So, if the citizens do not listen to their leader, their money will be lost. That misconduct proves that many of them have no clue about their duty. Such insensibility should be eradicated. That is why under the directives of Hamda La'war, I undertook the recording of some facts and events in connection with persons whose behaviour sounded somewhat questionable. We carried out the orders. The new government started to purge the country and rid it of the rascals disguised as royalists, even before the thieves, the sycophants and other crooks. The counter-revolution was creeping with the Muslim Brothelhood attacking respectful hotel bars, nightclubs, theatres and even cinema houses. Terrorists and troublemakers parasitise our life, paralysing our development. Just like telepathic mind-hacking demons posing as angels. If only the government would also start purging our minds from them!

MISTAKES ARE UNAVOIDABLE in such turbulent times. As the campaign progressed, I was unexpectedly apprehended by police and charged. However, I feel comforted since Mr Aroussi, my boss, is with me in the trap. Because I know how long his arm can be. I'm confident that if he decides to extend it, it will reach the Palace. We both served our hierarchical superiors with integrity and zeal. We can unequivocally demonstrate our devotion to the glorious Era of the Couvolution. The bogus charges are inconsistent. They are unable to stand after Mr Aroussi dialled the Palace. This is a bleak circumstance caused by a terrible misunderstanding. It's not amusing! Neither the director of 'Ouja bank nor I could be betraying the Couvolution. On the contrary, we backed the c... (*STOP! I won't use the deceptive term anymore.*) The Coup is not a Coup. That's understood. The Coup is a Glorious Couvolution for Reform and Change. As the radio said, it is a democratic popular something. As I am not sure I heard well, I emphasise that I am a couvolution supporter and a fan of our BGP (Beloved General President). Nonetheless, I will never underline enough that I am apolitical. I looked up the dictionary.

Apolitical | ˌeɪ◊pəlˈɪ◊tɪ◊kl | adjective: not interested or involved in politics: he took an apolitical stance.

I want to clarify that I am interested exclusively in the Couvolution of our BGP. I don't care for any other. It is widely admitted that our Couvolution is the greatest in history. Not just in our country. In the world, gentlemen. I expect our leader to completely change the face of the world. Not just our country, region, or continent. (*The world! - Right. Why not?*) Coming only two centuries earlier, our Couvolution would have mothered the French Revolution and given birth to Democracy and Human Rights. No doubt! Our BGP is spiritually connected to the greatest minds on earth and beyond.

ALTHOUGH I AM AN AFICIONADO in couvolution matters, I remain attached to my bank clerk career. Meanwhile, I acquired new skills as a librarian. Before landing here, I studied the wriggling behaviour of some hypocrites I suspected of fomenting trouble. I listed those two rascals: Mehrez, the grocer and Mustapha, the barber. Oh! Yes, I know the objections. They have the innocuous appearance of gentle folks, with no political ambition, no conspiratorial bearing! But I am not to be so easily fooled. I understand them even more than they understand themselves. I can prove they were secretly planning to start sedition in 'Ouja, just as the cooks of this hotel are currently concocting an escape, perhaps even a mutiny. The two gangs might as well be in connection. These are serious charges, but I know what I am talking about. Those men are fascists. Beware, I am well saying: fascists! I find the term adequate to be applied to them.

I heard that word several times, mainly when I watched the demonstration of our students in the Capital a few times ago. I was puzzled. Who were the fascists? I never got the opportunity to understand it before I came to work in this library.

I looked up, and now I feel enlightened. This is one of the countless privileges of my new job. I have the time to read and complete my education in this State hotel. I am on the way to becoming a scientist (*Maybe an alternative career to add to the previous!*) Thank you, dear police! I found the dictionary helpful.

Fascism: *"a centralised autocratic national regime with extremely nationalistic policies with an economic system based on state-controlled capitalism."*

Well, well! I am a little disappointed, though. In my opinion, this definition is just rubbish! The dictionary is undoubtedly wrong. I recall now that the Fascists were actually the disciples of Mussolini. How then?

How could they possibly be centralised, autocratic, nationalistic, and economically state-controlled? Forget that bullshit about the barber and the grocer. They represent nothing compared to the serious matters I am now confronting.

First, I do not believe that the Fascists were as well governed as the dictionary pretends. It dawns on me that the same description could also be applied to our regime. Good Heavens! This is true. But we are not fascists, though! Where is Mussolini? We cannot be fascists without him. And I don't see him anywhere, although we are undoubtedly nationalistic, autocratic, centralised, and state-controlled. Fortunately! We are lucky to have fascist ideas and structures without having to bear Mussolini, which means, at last, that we are not fascists. This is entirely new. Let's admit it. That's why I say that our glorious Couvolution will change the world's face. (*Once again, I'm deviating and slipping down a soapy slope, albeit I despise being embroiled in such impulsive political ratiocinations.*)

LET'S CORRECT THE SHOT: I am as unconcerned with politics as I am interested in our President's Couvolution. The fact that I am one of his millions of supporters does not mean I have political ambition. I prefer to keep quiet in the sweet warmth of my bank as soon as I leave this...hotel. I hope that I will not stay here for twenty years. Not that I dislike the place; on the contrary, I find it pretty empathetic. I have even new friends. Some are influential folk, such as Frankenstein, who was particularly curious about 'Ouja bank's affairs. Since we are allowed to have a shower once a week, I can see him now and then. Besides, we also meet in the courtyard. The customers have their promenade every day under the guards' prying eyes.

(5)

Frankenstein's extensive knowledge of a good number of our banks is impressive. I was really taken aback. I was not expecting such a preposterous head, as the one he is endowed with, to be interested in learning anything about our noble business. However, because banking is a large, deep ocean, one should specialise in one of its numerous branches to avoid sinking. And, despite his status as an outsider, Franken might as well work in a bank given his enthusiasm. As a matter of fact, I grasped from the bits of conversation we had had at various times that he is a security systems specialist! Which is fantastic! No bank can survive without such systems that secure funds, documents, furniture, staff, and everything. That is precisely what Mr Franken is most interested in. He keeps asking me about the security system's details, the safe, the when and the where... Etc. Apart from the director, who has access to the strong box? What consists of the alarm? Where is it placed? How is it armed and disarmed? Is it similar to other systems used in the South bank, for example? At what distance is the nearest police station?

He explained many elements I did not know about various strongboxes and alarm systems. I deduced that the guy has expertise in a job he loves so much. His passion grew almost obsessive. I asked him which bank he had worked at before honouring our hotel. I was delighted to find a colleague in such a weird place. He laughed merrily and said:

- Are you serious?

- Quite serious, I replied.

He rubbed his bold scalp, glowing in the sunshine, with his long skilled fingers, and stared at me incredulously as if he was expecting anything but that question. Then, finally, he said almost shyly:

- Well...er... In fact, I worked once on... er... South Bank.

- Good God! I exclaimed, startled.

- Eh! You seem frightened! It was a fine job, you know.

- Of course, but I heard that South Bank has been robbed. Were you on service when it happened?

- What service? He muttered before adding: Oh, yes, yes, I was there. It was my job! Fuck!

- Believe me, brother. When I heard of your catastrophe, I was so sad. I almost fell into tears. I imagined it could happen to us as well.

- Really? That's very touching! True, it was a mess! But, it could even be worse.

- You understand, with all those gangsters on the loose, it may happen in 'Ouja ...

- You're damn right! It may happen in 'Ouja. Why not? A missed shot is never the last! Moreover, your alarm system and all that security stuff sound not that much hard to disjoint. At South Bank, everything worked fucking well until the last minute when that shit started ringing. It nearly drove me mad!

- What a pity! Then, what did you do? I guess you called the police...

He scowled as if I insulted him:

- What the fuck are you saying, man? The cops? It wasn't I who rang them, but that fucking alarm nobody has noticed! I was busy with the safe.

- But... I mean, you were the watchman!.. Then...

- No, man. I just told you I was working on the safe. Another guy was watching outside.

- Ah! Of course! I see...

I did not understand what exactly he was doing with the safe at the precise moment when the gangsters broke into the bank! Was he trying to protect it? How? The money vanished, though.

I said:

- The gangsters had already fled with the booty when the police arrived. So...

He smirked, rubbing his palms, and with the most resounding hoarse voice, said:

- Yeah! Yeah! A good deal indeed! Not much left in the box. Ha Ha Ha! But a fucking fiasco!

I told myself: this guy is rare. Where would we find such a golden heart nowadays? He was still pitied by the unfortunate incident! That's his professional conscience. He still feels so guilty. He could not forgive himself for the failure of the security system, which allowed the gangsters to enter the bank and reach the safe. He thinks he is responsible. Poor man! He has grown invaluable in my eyes. I had a clear reading of his soul from the first second as if I saw it through the transparent reflector. I know. Despite his stern look, he is an ultra-sensitive honest professional.

- You should be somehow comforted now that they got them.

- Got who?

- The robbers!

He stared at me again and frowned. Did I utter nonsense? Startled by the dark clouds in his cold eyes, I wondered whether I did not offend him.

- Look here, the clerk! He replied. Why should I be comforted? I'd feel fucking better if I knew the money was safe. Damn it! It's all gone by now.

- Sorry! I didn't mean anything. You aren't responsible for the failure of the security system, are you?

- No, I ain't! Next time I should be cautious, much more careful. He paused, then added: You, bank clerk, know a lot. I like chatting with you.

I was touched. Frankenstein was still moved and perhaps even shocked by the incident. Did he only know that his bank had recuperated the stolen money? Maybe, nope, indeed, he has been fired. As I did not understand what brought him to the State hotel, I risked the question:

- Are you going to stay here for...er... a long or a short time?

- Why do you ask?

- Well, you're not obliged to answer anyway. Sorry! I thought I could perhaps help you once you're released.

His little cold eyes glittered, and it seemed to me that even his swarthy face illuminated.

- Do you mean it, or are you just kidding?

- I mean it, of course.

- What can you do, for example?

Very matter of fact! But I could not blame him for worrying about his future. I said:

- If you want, I can introduce you to Mr Aroussi, the director of 'Ouja bank. He would be on the sixth floor if they didn't remove him. That's where I spotted him. But to be honest, I must warn you that we've already got a watchman. However, your look is...er ...how would I put it? Well, let's say more convincing in emergency and deterrence. I am sure he'll hire you as soon as

I tell him about your speciality. You got a good profile: reassuring to friends as dissuasive to enemies!

- What? Do you mean a bodyguard?

- Of course, you can do that as well. It is a plus in your C.V.

- My what?

- Your curriculum vitae, brother. But since your speciality is security systems, we surely need you.

- Hell! He exclaimed. You, sly fox, clerk!

- You're too kind! But I am doing my duty towards a friend that is you, the bank that is mine, and the boss to whom I am loyal.

Franken was so delighted that he would have leapt to kiss me again. But I was watching and guessing all his moves, so transparent his soul had become to me. Thus, I rapidly whisked and withdrew backwards before his enthusiasm degenerated into an effusive and inevitable mess of unpleasant kisses and a gurgling salam.

HE STOOD UP, HANDS dangling, feet apart on the cracked floor, eyes wide open, and the top head shimmering in the sunshine. The courtyard was full of customers, slowly strolling along the high walls, seeking the fresh sweetness of the shade. They were busy chatting or washing their laundries in the long basin. Some were splashing their faces with soap and waiting for their turn to get shaved. I did not envy them. Going to the barber in this hotel is like volunteering for genteel torture. I cannot think of any other word to depict the excruciating ordeal of being shaved with a blade that has already scratched and scraped hundreds of beards. The lucky among us is the guy whose turn is - say - amid the first fifty clients of the barber! Even the first hundred! For the others, the slaughter!

Frankenstein yelled:

- I wouldn't give a shit about that story, but I trust you.

Then he burst into a peal of crazy laughter, paused, composed himself and said:

- So, if I understand well, you're just planning an insider operation with your boss and need the hand of a real professional. Who could imagine that? It's funny! Sly fox, bank clerk! What a fuck, man! But since you know the bank, it would be much easier! I am in. Let's give it a try.

"Insider operation?" What's he talking about? I was somewhat startled. I felt as if the innocuous little chat was taking a turn I did not like. Soon, my worries grew into an alarming fear. What if one of the guards scattered across the courtyard overheard us? "Insider operation"? Any of those men in grey uniform shadowing us may hear these words and patch the vacuum of his head with spooky ideas about a conspiracy being fomented against the central bank, if not against the regime itself? It is well the last thing I need. Another accusation, and I would be on my way to the gallows! So, lifting my hand and squeezing my mouth, I tried to make him understand that we were not alone.

- For God's sake! I shouted. Don't you shout; they'd hear you.

- Calm down, he replied. Fuck their damned ears!

Meanwhile, he stepped forward and was already bending on my cheek, causing me to panic because I thought he would kiss me. But he did not intend to do so. Instead, he whispered into my ear:

- So, do you need a specialist or not?

- Yes, I do... Er... Not me, but the bank. A specialist is always welcome. Be ready. I will introduce you to the boss soon. He's an important man, you know. If you impress him positively, you're hired. But I must find him first. I left him ... in purgatory! Maybe they sent him out to another block.

- What's his name, you said?

- Mr Aroussi Mamitu.

- I know many people around here. By the way, if you need anything... I mean soap, shampoo, clothes, drinks, food, cigarettes, drugs, liquor, or even a fuck; let me know. Here's the big Bazar where you find anything you want. And... Don't worry about money. We can make some arrangements.

- I can pay. I have left my book cheques down there at the reception desk.

He smirked.

- Nobody accepts cheques here, man. The inmates are no fools. Cheques, you say! Are you landing from the moon or kidding? A lot of them are here precisely because of the damned cheques!

(6)

I was neither falling from the moon nor kidding, though. Yet, I failed to understand why, among all people, the customers of this hotel reject viciously what everybody else admits as the most practical means of payment. The more I think of this puzzle, the more I find it absolutely scandalous and unsocial! Is cheque-phobia anything but incivility? I may concede that a particularly paranoid person could reject my cheques because of mistrust, which is also an insult to my honesty. But I don't mind. I have already met such weird folk in the countryside. But here - good God ! - we are in the Capital. In the CA PI TAL! People around here are supposed to be open-minded and urbanised. If not, then what is the merit of being a CAPITAL-IST?

My dictionary says that capitalists are those who "promote that form of economic, industrial, and social organisation of society, involving ownership, control, and direction of production by privately owned business organisations."

Observe the easiness of the argument and its cogency when one is well educated! Indeed, I am an intellectual.

I love the precision of the words I use in every situation. A capitalist is the inhabitant of the Capital, albeit the latter has another signification I have grasped. But I find the capitalists here backwards and failing their reputation. They cannot be real capitalists because they reject cheques as a way of payment in business. We are not to go back to the truck economy at this stage of mankind's evolution, though. Now I understand why our Beloved General President (BGP) is so angry with the capitalists. Initially, I thought he attacked them because he sought an alliance with the peasants. But the situation sounds much more awful. The capitalists are merely refusing banking as a keystone in our economy! I had never heard of such incongruent eccentricity. I have already noticed that I do not like the Capital. Well, I now have a concrete reason to hate it. If I trust my informer - I boost Frankenstein to the honour of this rank. I am sure he would make his way upward if he satisfies his hierarchic superiors -our capitalists intend to boycott the banks! Is there any other conceivable explanation for rejecting the cheques? This is merely opposition! Oh, the disgusting, the dreadful, the hateful word I am forced to use in this clean report! OPPOSITION? It means sedition. Insubordination. Disloyalty.

The case is deadly grave, gentlemen! I do not need to underline it. I will deepen my investigation to understand whether all the hotel's customers oppose cheques or just a minority. Did they already form a clandestine opposition party? If it turned out the INTELLIGENCE, I got from my snitch - another honorific title for Franken! - is accurate; here is my advice to the Administration:

- Undertake the appropriate measures right away.
- First, it is necessary to declare a state of emergence and set up a curfew,
- Alert the banks,
- Close down the stock exchange,
- Block the roads,
- Stop the traffick in the airports and the ports,
- Confine the citizens in their homes,
- Nobody should be allowed to walk on the streets unless with a clearance from the Ministry of the interior.
- The ARMED FORCES should be ready to defend the country against the aggression from anti- cheque opposition.
- I suspect they are well organised. So let's anticipate and strike before the bastards surprise us.
- The Capital should be surrounded (i.e. the city of capitalists, not the other Capital, gentlemen) as it had been during the historical night of the Cou...volution.
- A siege should be maintained until all the recalcitrant and treacherous capitalists give up and accept to swear allegiance to our BGP over a chequebook!

(7)

F our weeks already! The time here is damn long. But I am getting busy and used to my new life. But, unfortunately, people outside those walls may think we are idle. Furthermore, we are accommodated and fed at the taxpayer's expense, for nothing in return! This is a terrible bias they ought to correct.

I do not deny that our State is generous. But on the other hand, most of this hotel's customers, as far as I know, are busy working, and their life is not as easy and selfish as people outside used to think. Take an example: On the third floor's spacious room where I am housed, there are about one hundred beds, each occupied by no less than three roommates. We are some four hundred fifty for that compartment, if not more.

Naturally, I see the question: How do all these people get along in such a narrow place?

The answer is not complicated: People don't get anywhere. So they try not to clash every two steps.

Most took thronged trains, packed buses, and other crammed public transport before they landed here. As they are accustomed to close contact, they can bridge over each other. They sleep anywhere. On the beds, under the beds, between the beds, around the beds, and most often without the beds. The spirit of solidarity that binds them together is conspicuous. That's why they don't see the anomaly of sleeping in bunches of three and four on the same mattress. Needless to add, the Administration likely aimed to create and develop a community spirit among the clients. The ultimate goal is to help them dump selfishness and get used to a sane social life. It is undoubtedly a wise idea, though I found it hard to bear on the first days.

The point is I have been brought up just in the opposite way. As my parents' single son, I have been accustomed since early childhood to living alone: eating, playing, studying, and sleeping. After I grew up and bought an apartment, I still found it hard to accept my mother's insistent request to engage a girl for marriage. I was so accustomed to my loneliness that I started delaying the date of the wedding year after year, five times in a row. That was just to get familiar with the idea. After all, I was going to share my house. Not only that, but also my room until my bed, and everything in my life with a perfect stranger! I needed time. Therefore, the horrible shock I received in contact with the lewdest promiscuity of this hotel gets explained. I had to cope with this complicated existential threat that might have further psychological and physical complications.

Finally, stuck to the wall, I made a decision. "I'm not to be intimidated. If those men can live in this vivarium without much damage, I can also do it."

IT WAS EASIER SAID than done.

To begin with, it was not apparent that I could get a bed or even a bit of bed. No one knew me. It is well the Capital, the devil take it! But with time and patience, I perceived that nobody would care about you if you were not well connected in this community of egomaniacal, arrogant rascals. Yeah! Connected! That's the point! The whole affair is to know with who!

When I was ushered into the third-floor compartment, I jostled to find my way to the centre. It was the Bazar. People were lying down and crowding everywhere on the cold ground or the paltry dirty accommodations. The air was thick and packed with smoke and various odours of food and sweat. Not to speak of the lavatory's putrid exhalations. I thought I was about to suffocate and faint. The enclosure walls were high, though, and many barred windows were flung open. I believe that is the very reason why we are still alive. Those windows, along with the high ceilings, are a benediction. If we do not suffocate like trapped rats, it is well because, through the bars of the windows, we get some oxygen and a bit of blue sky. Thus, even in our horrendous hell, we remain linked to the heavens. May God bless the Administration, our benefactor! It so cleverly cared about keeping those windows open day and night. Fortunately, we are in the spring – a euphemism in our country- and the weather is relatively sweet. I prefer not to think of what is going to happen in winter. Will we be forced by the rain and the cold to shut the windows with the indubitable hazard of suffocating? Will we keep them open with the no less undeniable danger of catching pneumonia? The problem is worth a democratic debate. Perhaps on the TV, why not?

(Let's not get involved with the democratic rant and other alike shit. I have enough worries like this!)

Thus, I made my way among the crowd, seeking a spot to rest after a day of hard labour. That same morning, I showered just after the interview with the shrink, got my hair cut very short, and my face shaved. Then I lunched with Franken in the court-yard before the black guard returned to take me straight to my new post.

The library was so dusty-dirty that I thought it had not seen a drop of water since the last flood. Anyway, it was closed before I arrived. Spiders have knitted their curtains in every corner. I spent the whole afternoon sweeping the dust off with a sorcerer broom I found behind a bookcase. I cleaned the shelves, the desk, the oblong table at the centre of the room and the chairs with an old rag and inspected the books. I also had to mop the library's ground with the adequate instruments of a brave scav-enger. When I complained, Mahmoud replied that if I did not want the position, hundreds of inmates would be happy to get it. He added that I had to be grateful for nobody ever got this excellent assignment since the first day.

The sun fainted behind the high walls, and the shades slowly invaded the courtyard. I turned on the light and sat near the barred window behind the desk. I looked at the white clusters of clouds as they crept slowly into the sky. Nobody showed up or asked for a book. That wasn't a good beginning. I was expecting the customers to queue outside the library, though. I was eager to receive them. Well! I am still waiting.

As preposterous as that might appear, no one indicated the slightest curiosity about the books for a whole month! If the sit-uation were to last for another month, my staying here would be superfluous. What is the point of paying a qualified professional for a job nobody needs? True, I am well settled down here. I can read or write my report without disturbance. I can observe without being observed. I can even chat lowly with my angels when I try to convince them that I am not as bad as they believe. Hitherto, I have not yet had such an opportunity to start an honest debate with my escorts from the meta-world. I have been so busy with my bank job.

Nevertheless, I must say that those two bastards are stubborn. As my career progressed, with my three jobs, they grew resentful. They are not ready to discard their prejudices and make peace. Instead, they have set their minds on putting a spoke in my wheel. Fucking spooks!

TIRED AND BORED AFTER that long day in the forlorn library, I rejoiced when I spotted a bed that apparently was unoccupied in the centre of our dormitory. The mattress, covered by a lovely green blanket, seemed too cute to be unduly considered private property and thus ignored. I looked around. The inmates were dining in little groups, their mess tins before them, some on the ground and others on their own beds momentarily transformed into dining tables. While I watched them, I noted that many were having meals that were not even on the hotel's menu. What the hell! Where on earth did they get that? For my part, I had on that evening a bowl of soup. I was so watery and poorly cooked that I could hardly burden my delicate stomach with it and stay in a good spirit. So I just ate the loaf of bread and fished two little potatoes sunk in the tawny liquid inside the bowl. It was a stoical supper, and I was just beginning my forced diet.

But I could not wait anymore. After the first silent observation of what was happening around the friendly unemployed bed, I decided to pass quickly to the offensive. I knew that if I did not take a decision immediately, another more audacious client would snatch the charming little residence from my fingers. Another white night on the floor seemed to me indecent.

So I grabbed my courage with full hands. I gingerly walked towards the promised land. Trying not to stumble and tumble and break someone's neck was hard. Avoiding smashing one of those stretched feet or merely putting my foot into somebody's dish was a real feat! But finally, I succeeded in overcoming the human obstacles. Of course, that was impossible without collecting a mountain of insults to which I would not reply. Either because, in general, I am polite, or because as I was focused on my prey, I did not mind being insulted.

I reached the bed, pulled off my shoes and threw my tired body upon the foam mattress. If I stretch my feet, straighten my neck on the pillow and gaze boldly at the folks, I would feel like a king. I am so happy to find my oasis in the wild desert. I wouldn't move even if I saw my old Dad coming out of his grave right now. Well! I am not a heartless man, though. I do love and respect my late architect. Yet, I am also aware that I would return to the wilderness if I lost what I had just won of high struggle. In the overcrowded dormitory, I faced with intrepidity a multitude of the faceless rabble. Prescience or heart told me the game was not over, though. Overwhelmed by the odious mixture of spicy and pestilent odours, in the dim light of a single lamp hung to the ceiling, I readied myself for the fight.

In the pandemonium buzzing with rants and laughter, snorts and belches, curses and burbles and other oddities, I had an apocalyptic vision of hell... The bed- My bed – became the only and unique sanctuary.

Soon, I shut my eyes and decided to sleep.

I had perhaps dozed a few minutes when I felt a hand shaking me and heard a voice whispering into my ear:

- Get up, get up, you crazy man!

I opened my eyes. It was the bald-headed face of my room-mate, Dahdah, with its bushy eyebrows and its big mouth half-full of food. He urged me to clear the place. What skittish idea trotted into his foolish mind? It was the first time I saw the man who would later offer me his kindest services. In my confusion, I did not understand immediately what Dahdah was trying to explain. He motioned like a monkey with his hands stretching and pointing to something or someone at the other end of the enclosure. He seemed scared.

- What do you want? Why did you wake me up?

- You are crazy if you stay here. It's the bed of the boss! Get up. He'll knock you down if he comes back.

- I'm not going to move, said I obstinately. Go away, leave me alone.

- I'm your brother. I warn you. The boss won't like your trespassing on his property.

- Property? What are you talking about? Who's the boss anyway?

- He commands the whole compartment. So you don't need to provoke him.

I remained adamant. I wanted to see the end of it, or maybe I was so tired and bored that I shut my eyes, turned my back and went dozing indifferent to the jabber of Dahdah.

Bad idea!

Shortly after I ignored the warning, I was awakened. That time with a rude kick on the buttocks, so brutal that it blew me up from the bed onto the ground! Opening my eyes, I saw my body carpeting the hard floor.

- What the hell! I shouted, angry and dismayed. Who's the bastard who dared?

A burst of raucous laughter was the first response I obtained. But, then, the same voice I already knew thundered:

- You hear this mother fucker, men? Not content to invade me, he offends me too! You son of a bitch! I'm going to tear you down into fucking little pieces! Come on, asshole of my balls! Get up. Show me your nasty dark face of a dirty rat! Get the fuck up.

I looked around, trying to rise to my feet, and who was there, waiting for me, on guard, ready to box? It was that old acquaintance of mine. Zorro, the dissymmetrically-eyed monster of the so-called Hammam.

Apparently, he was as surprised as I was. He likely did not bother to look at my face before kicking my posterior. Now, he stared at me bemused, then dropped his guard and said:

- So it's you, monkey face! Did you decide to invade my fucking life, wiseass little clown? Soap, shampoo, towel, shower, and now also bed? Bed? What next? My ass? Come on, monkey, Try to fuck me!

The fake Zorro was unhappy and nervous. He shook from the toe to the top like a leaf in the autumnal wind. His ears, still ready to take off, were crimson as if all the blood in his body rushed up into them! His atypical eyes twitched and winked alternately, and the little interval that parted them seemed to grow wide. So wide that I feared they would join his ears and take off with them. Then nothing noticeable would remain on his strange face but the anger which distorted his features, pushing the poor man on the verge of apoplexy. Seemingly, and without ever seeking it, I have become his *bête noire*.

Far from me is the idea of causing him any disturbance, though. Fate has put him on my way as a dubious servant without warning him or me. How could I soothe him down?

- I sincerely apologise to you, Mister er... I did not dare say, Zorro, albeit it was his alias. I wasn't aware it was your bed. Anyway, you're welcome back home! I'm happy to see you again.

I prefer to ignore the colourful words he used against me and stretch my hand as a sign of peace and apology. But he wouldn't move. So instead of a handshake, he ignores my hand and says:

- OK, baboon! You apologised. Now get the fuck out of my sight before I commit a crime.

Some of the customers who formed a circle around us started laughing. I don't find the situation particularly funny. I withdraw my hand and slip it into my trousers' pocket, feigning not to see the humiliation.

- Since our first meeting in the shower room, I don't know why Mister ...er... you took the preposterous habit of insulting me, although I am well disposed towards you. I won't take your bed, as I did not take your shower by force. As a point of fact, I was just contemplating paying you for all the kind services you consented.

First, he appeared bored to death; but as soon as I uttered the last words, cheer and interest took over boredom on his face. Did a light shade of intelligence cross that swarthy face, or am I deluded? Quickly, he reacted:

- Did you say you're going to pay?

- Yes, sir. I did.

- What the devil are you waiting for?

I loitered before replying:

- Since you're interested in a deal with me, I'd propose a fair bargain.

He waited for the rest while the circle around us tightened and made silence.

- What about a cheque for your bed, say thirty dinars per month? Otherwise, one dinar for each night!

IT SEEMED A GOOD DEAL to me. Given that the accommodation is free in this hotel, I believed the fake Zorro would rejoice to get that money. However, I acknowledge that I would pay much more in other hotels. The last time I visited the Capital, I stayed with my colleagues for two days in a sumptuous hotel. We were attending a symposium on banking with a lot of people. The Minister even inaugurated it along with some high officials of the party. It was a great event, with television and radio broadcasting crews, many journalists and guests, and all the habitual pomp. For two days, we babbled, ate, drank, and had a lot of fun; when we prepared to leave the hotel, I went to the reception desk to check out. The clerk, quite courteously, emphasised that it was all paid by the government, and he added that if I wanted to know how much, the charge for my room amounted to five hundred dinars. I was surprised. My own salary from the bank is five hundred dinars. How would I pay if I had to? The bill for two days would swallow up my paycheck. I didn't say anything. I thanked the desk clerk for his kindness, which enlightened me about the lavish generosity of our government. I did not omit to thank the government too. I was a little sad and sorry because the TV crew had already left. I wished they had broadcast my sincere thanks to the government.

This is just to underline the inflated prices of our luxury hotels. It also shows again all the privileges we enjoy in this hospitable place, often wrongly depicted and much depreciated by the ignorants and the enemies of the State. In fact, I expected that the so-called Zorro would jump on the opportunity I offered him. But the fool did not. Did I incorrectly assume he had no clue about the prices of hotels in the Capital? How could he know the hotels? His odd appearance with the obnoxious manners and the awful lexicon he uses while addressing the respectable citizens did not suggest that he was an employee of the Administration, like me. I figured out that he was perhaps a street peddler before landing here. I see him pushing a wooden carriage loaded with vegetables and fruits and shouting in the souks. But under the vegetables, he would hide drugs and other illegal stuff. I made up my mind. I know that if Zorro is not a born criminal, he should hear the call anyway. It's the call of destiny. Mektoub! It's the same for me. I was born to be a bank teller, a librarian, and a spy. Who knows what our nature conceals? My late father, may Allah make him happy in heaven, worked as a bookkeeper in the Council House of 'Ouja. It wasn't all that different from my previous position at the bank. I'm sure I inherited my father's interest in money, numbers, arithmetic, and other things. It is running with blood in my veins.

Chapter 3

Couvolution and Cooks' Conspiracy

(1)

ALREADY THREE MONTHS have passed...

Indeed, fortune has smiled upon me. Customers are probably making travel plans as the summer draws near. Everyone ought to have a strategy. We aren't even remotely considering the Caribbean, Monaco, Tahiti, or the Bahamas. We owe the existence of our holidays to Allah and the ever-present Government. If they were to drain the mucky water from the sixth-floor pool and refill it properly, it would be more appealing than a Mediterranean sandy beach in the middle of July. As such, the strange purgatory might be partially converted into heaven. We can now prevent the evil capitalists from entering the hotel since Mr Aroussi has graced us with his presence. What I mean is the people who flat-out refuse the cheques and the banking system. This would be an ideal location for a thriving bank to be established. Since the library is not a moneymaker, I am willing to collaborate with Mr Aroussi on this grand undertaking.

It is correct that the educational value of a library in this setting much outweighs any potential financial gain. However, this has not increased customer enthusiasm for borrowing books, even though there are no taxes on books. Also, I won't get down on my knees and beg. I did my best to cheer them on, I swear. That's because I communicated. I gave lectures on our fantastic library to the dorm residents and residents' guests in the courtyard. Back then, people mostly laughed, insulted, or cursed at me. Therefore, I had no choice except to retreat further into my protective shell. It wasn't worth getting into an argument over, and the guys around here are normally irritable. I can't explain it. Really! They have it quite good if we compare them to those outside the walls, but the poor naifs there don't know it. Given how generously everything is provided for them, they have no valid complaints. Not even the issue of hateful food is crucial.

The Administration has decided to do everything it takes to make its clients happy, which is a noble gesture. This made it possible for loved ones to pay them visits, bringing gifts of food and comfort. Those who, like myself, don't have any Capital-based relatives nevertheless have a chance of receiving a gift. Their roommates might even let them borrow some of their food depending on their cooperation. Cheese, milk, butter, marmalade, and other supplements are sold (black market prices) in the enclosures and courtyards, so they may still acquire what they need. It's allowed. I made some inquiries. Unfortunately, the vendors do not accept cheques. What a bunch of thick-headed backwards! - but money. For this reason alone, a new bank in the State hotel needs to be established quickly. The capitalist conspiracy has clearly reached dangerous dimensions.

The hotel's finances also preclude such a time and effort sinkhole. But my concern isn't just for the hotel; the entire country's economy is at risk. Yes, it is well-known that man is the product of his habits, both good and bad. Once a customer has checked out, we have no say over whether or not a poor practice continues as usual. I worry about unintended consequences because the hotel serves thousands of customers yearly. Our inmates would leave our facility's sanitary windows and iron gates and return to their previous way of life at the end of their sentences. Is there any use in letting them leave if we know they have been exposed to the sad and barbaric ritual of rejecting cheques? They caught a virus that can only survive by reproducing itself. Do we not have an obligation to put a stop to this before the entire populace succumbs to their madness? If true, this would be a terrible waste of the country's economy. What damage this has wreaked upon our valiant financial institutions! Such a pandemic is beyond our means. We have to halt the infection and stop it from spreading.

LET'S LOOK ON THE BRIGHT side. I propose the Administration launch a sensitisation campaign, as the hotel's policy objectives include tourism and education. The benefactors of this fine abode will become acquainted with the fundamentals of the financial sector. I'm well aware that greedy capitalists will try to sabotage such an endeavour because of the moral ambiguity they bring to the table. I'm also aware that the kitchen staff will do all they can to retaliate, including making even nastier meals for the convicts and narcotics-laced sandwiches for the guards in the towers. That would hasten the process of causing difficulty, the results of which they anticipate being anarchy, rebellion, and escape. A mutiny is part of their agenda. If my prediction is correct, they won't have a hard time winning over the public.

In my opinion, the vast majority of the State guests at this hotel are not miserable or disloyal. Indeed, many are devoted members and enthusiastic supporters of the bars and chains community. Regulars to the establishment are better acquainted with its every nook and cranny than the security personnel. There's no way they'd follow the cooks. However, the latter are crafty. It's clear from the cuisine they serve that they aim to make everyone, even the Administration's most staunch supporters, miserable.

NATURALLY, THE HOTEL plays an important role in government policy. It's a fantastic asset. Apart from the banks, I would argue that these premises are the most valuable asset for any government. History demonstrates this. As an example, consider the French Revolution of 1789. The Bastille was the principal aim of the revolutionaries, not the monarchy or the magnificent royal mansions. When the mob of Paris stormed the Bastille, the Revolution posed a real threat to the monarchy. Never before in history. But, guys, what was the Bastille? In every way, it was the same as our State hotel. It provided free housing, food, and education to its clients to make them realise the Government's friendliness and charity.

Similarly, I believe any challenge to our beloved General President's new regime would attack our hotel first and foremost. It seems obvious to me. The plot spreads in both directions: inside-outside and outside-inside.

Gentlemen! The elements plotting a counter-coup against the Government are currently consolidating. This isn't only limited to the exterior. However, the enemy is already spinning its devilish web within these fortified, three-block grounds in the heart of the Capital.

I can see the whole scene being cooked up in the kitchens in my mind's eye. It starts in the heads of chefs infected with the conspiracy and anarchy virus. The beginning is subversion. Disbelief in the legitimacy of cheques as a method of payment. Without philosophers and enlightenment, they intend to create a fake version of the French Revolution. What a farce! A buffoonery!

A WORD OF CAUTION, though. Ruffians gathered outside the Bastille's defences during the French Revolution. Inmates made up a small percentage of the hotel's guests. Even a French nobleman is included in this group. The illustrious Mr. le Marquis de Sade. As far as I could tell, this respectable gentleman was a writer. I haven't read any of his publications, but judging by the contrast between his amazing self-confinement and the splendours to which he is entitled by rank and right, I have to believe that he decided to endure the harsh and stoic life of la Bastille. Don't ask me why. I already mentioned that he is a writer. This person believes he has a special calling from God and must fulfil it. (I heard this from a reliable source; in France, they gave him the title "Divin Marquis" at his baptism.) From what I can see, his goal is to teach the world about the importance of philosophising in bed. Just what is this thing called "bedroom philosophy," anyway? I consider it a type of prayer that, in my opinion, ought to be carried out in accordance with the norms of classical Catholicism. Akin to the lifestyles of remote monasteries from ages past. The Divine Marquis dedicated his life to the resurrection of those holy traditions in the bedroom. He devoted himself entirely to preaching virtue. His missionary work was centred in La Bastille, which he transformed into a monastery.

Such an effort of self-denial, rather than disgusting depravity and decadence, could serve as a model for contemporary writers. I see the Marquis. I can hear his voice now. It seems like I've known him forever. It doesn't bother him that I haven't read any of his books. It is a shame that his works were not translated into Arabic earlier! Unfortunately, I was never taught how to read French. As far as I can tell, that's the only thing holding me back from furthering my education.

To choose the harsh confines of La Bastille over the luxurious comforts of an aristocratic castle life for the sake of literature is significant. It's a huge price to pay, and it hits home when you consider the advantage you've been given through inheritance. It's a telltale indicator of someone who loves God, loves other people, and practises religious virtue by giving freely to those in need. That guy was probably a mystical kind. A saintly status is well deserved for him because of his devotion. (I wouldn't say "angel" because I no longer trust this species.) He appears to have a firm religious conviction. Clearly, he has a strong commitment to instilling morality while encouraging government allegiance in his disciples.

IN THIS LIGHT, I WOULD like to suggest that our BGP, who is (so I'm told) a devout Muslim who never misses a prayer, fund an Arabic translation of the entire canon of the Divine Marquis de Sade's works initially written in French. At least this way, we wouldn't have to worry about being overrun by stupid Barbares. Despite their ignorance of bedroom philosophy and other intellectual games played by high-calibre philosophers, they want to recreate the events of 1789. Therefore, this next Friday, as a gesture of our gratitude, may our imams and Grand Mufti pray for the soul of Monsieur le Marquis. So that the next generation can learn about the concepts that shaped contemporary society, I also propose including some Sade works in our high school curricula.

I'm dying to get my hands on a copy of the Divine Marquis. I suspect I will find the writer who is the most moralistic of the bunch and maybe even a historian of the French Revolution, which he personally experienced while imprisoned in La Bastille.

Meanwhile, I found the answers to my questions in a brief history book that offered scant background information. Although not ideal, it beats the alternative. The author indulged in a petty diatribe criticising King Louis XVI and his wife, Queen Marie-Antoinette and deftly sidestepped discussing the vital role of Monsieur de Sade in the eventual French Revolution. There wasn't anything more suitable in our hotel's library.

TO GO BACK ON TOPIC, we have a layout nearly the inverse of the French (no bedroom Philo., but serving the same function). The mob was outside La Bastille's walls in 1789. For us, it's too late; the kitchen crew has taken over the field. The circumstance is dire. I can't stress this enough. For the safety of the state, this is a critical issue.

For this reason, I'm writing my Top Secret report at breakneck speed. I won't let Mr Mahmoud, the black guard, even take a peek. Yeah, I think he's pretty forthright. However, the superiority of my work over his knowledge and expertise is also undeniable.

Roughly speaking, Mr Mahmoud is in his mid-forties. A far cry from Frankenstein's towering stature or Zorro's compact physique, he is neither. A round, protruding tummy indicates continued obesity. Having a large head and short hair. Two horizontal lines of wrinkling furrow over a broad forehead. There are always two dark eyes watching. His flat nose seems out of place unless it's meant to draw attention away from his huge lips. True, if your teeth are pearly white. The only time he doesn't smile is when he's angry, but other than that, he's a genuinely pleasant person. If the latter is the case, one should leave Mahmoud's presence immediately because the black guard does not like provocateurs. I witnessed his response to such presumptions. That was not hilarious in the slightest. I'd rather head out into a cyclone.

(2)

O N THAT PARTICULAR day, a customer was crossing the courtyard when he unintentionally dropped a cigarette. Mr Mahmoud watched him from the ward's entrance, where the guards often assembled to play cards and converse in the afternoon. Seeing what he did, he seemed dissatisfied. By the way, the courtyard was not spotless. From the safety of the library's barred window, I saw the unfolding events and immediately assumed that the black guard was on edge. He finally went crazy.

- Oh, you goddam Rabbi! What the fuck are you doing?

At that very second, I recognised the man I had met on my first day in purgatory. The lovable Mickey Mouse! With his blue jacket over a white shirt and blue jeans, he was making his way toward the entrance of one of the three buildings. His long, pointed nose seemed buried in thought, and his silver-rimmed glasses hung too low. Unperturbed, he continued on his way. The guard's yelling of "goddam rabbi" went unnoticed by him. But at that hour, there was no one else in the courtyard. After lunch, the inmates were asleep, some in their chambers if they weren't working, some in the garage, some in the warehouse, and others outside. Angled sunlight illuminated the high ceiling and the floor below. Even in the shade, we were still sweating profusely because it was such a warm May day. That's how drowsy I got. The heat prevented me from composing even a single sentence. I was about to nod off at my desk when I heard the harsh voice of the black security guard.

As the young man strolled away, paying no attention to him, Mr Mahmoud became so irate that his face veered white at that moment. He dashed after *Mickey Mouse*, puffing hot air, grabbed his shoulder when he was crossing the threshold of the building, and shoved him violently against the wall.

The young man's face had become wan and drawn. He was trembling like a leaf. I watched as Mahmoud pounded his face twice or three times and said:

-You fucking little bastard of a rabbi! You despise me, don't you? Where do you think you are, motherfucker? This is not your mother's brothel.

The man swung his arms up to shield his head from the unexpected explosion of violence with a series of swift, jerking motions. He mumbled something hard to make out. I watched the incident unfold, outraged and shocked by Mr Mahmoud's unexpected reaction. None of this seemed to bother the other ward guards, who returned to their game of cards. It's likely that safe in the library's shade, I was more frightened than the victim of the bullying. I could not help feeling empathy for him, albeit I know very well that I ought to be always on the right side: that of the Administration. As Mr Mahmoud is one of its representatives, I have no reason to take the opposite side. I do not condone violence, but it is a different matter. Then, I heard the man shouting, likely to attract attention:

- I need a Doctor. I'm sick, you know it. My heart is weak. I need my medicine.

- What Doctor? Replied the black guard infuriated. Show me your prescription. What's your number? Where are you coming from?

- The security officers in my building let me go to the Doctor. I'm number 8051. My place is in cell-block B, level 2.

Mahmoud appeared to settle down for a moment.

- The Doctor doesn't work. Don't you know it?

- No, I don't...

- You don't care what I say? Fucking Rabbi!

- I didn't say anything...Stammered the man, but Mahmoud wouldn't allow him to put another word.

- Shut the fuck up! You flung your butt on the ground. This is an offence. When I called you, you pretended to be deaf. It is a repeat offence. Finally, when I instructed you to clean up your trash and place it in an ashtray, you objected to a public official enforcing the law. Do you believe you can get away with it? You filthy son of a pig! Who's going to mop the fucking floor now? You or the woman who reared you, Rabbi?

- Please, Mr Mahmoud, don't insult my mother. She has nothing to do with this.

- She has everything to do with it! She's the scumbag who birthed a scumbag like you, Rabbi. And your father isn't any better. Is he also a rabbi? But you've never met your father. Because your mother never told you who he is, did she?

The man remained silent, astounded by the guard's escalating wrath. How could one answer to such a barrage of profanity? He ducked his head. Mahmoud looked at him with the crazed expression of a savage beast preparing to charge its prey once more - You don't answer? Perfect! I see you understand you're a bastard, little fucker! Now, I want the floor of the whole bloody courtyard cleaner than your nasty face and shining as it was before you put your dirty feet on it. Go and fetch all the scattered butts and debris and collect them, one by one. Understand? One by one. When you finish, you'll do the toilets.

The man trembled. His face was completely white. Sweat beads glistened on his brow.

- But, Mr Mahmoud, I'm unwell. You know, the Doctor didn't let me work.

- I don't give a fuck what the Doctor said. I am here to enforce the law, Rabbi. If you don't execute my order immediately, you'll perish here. Sick, not sick, none of my business! I'll break your neck with those hands on mine. Do you see them?

Mahmoud clenched his fists against the man's face, who was still trapped against the wall. The latter was unable to deflect the punch. After a short moment, I saw him walking toward the courtyard's centre. He arched his body and started collecting the butts of cigarettes and the other trash left by the inmates. He was abundantly sweating, and his hands were shaking.

The black man thundered again:

- On your knees, bastard.

The man hesitated a moment, knelt on the ground, and went about his ordeal on four limbs around the vast courtyard. In the ward, the guards were giggling while continuing their social game. I heard one of them addressing the black man:

- Make that son of a bitch creep on his belly and collect all the litter with his mouth.

While the buddies chuckled, one of them snapped up :

- Let him do a strip tease. Naked, he'll be a better scavenger.

A burst of Laughter followed.

- That's a good idea, replied Mahmoud. Then addressing the man plodding away, he shouted: "Take off your clothes, Rabbi."

The guards laughed nervously. The man raised his head and looked at them in bewilderment. He set down his tools and appeared to be considering what to say. Then he dove back under the slanting sunlight to continue his quest. His forehead was so drenched in sweat that it looked like tears were streaming down his face.

Then, after what felt like an eternity, once again, the black guard's voice came across, this time with obnoxious arrogance:

- Take off your garments, dog!

He was standing next to him, hands on hips and feet apart. The man on all fours remained immobile. The impact of the resounding voice seemed to freeze him in place. The man didn't even bother to look up or turn around. Like a lamb being led to the slaughter, he laid his hands on the floor. Mahmoud sneered at him and snapped:

- Take off your bloody clothes immediately, or I'll fucking crush your head.

No sign of life. The face of the unfortunate was so exhausted that it turned blue. He was nailed in the same position as a wax statue. Even the nibbling darts of the sun pierced right through his body as if, by a mysterious spell, he had become stamped in a window.

The black man got nervous. He shrieked suddenly, then kicked him.

- Are you fucking deaf?

As his foot touched his flank, the man toppled over and tumbled to the opposite side. But, oddly enough, he kept drawn up in the same position. Mahmoud gazed at him, puzzled, and I saw a grey shade crossing his black face. Then, as the victim did not move, he stooped over and goggled at his face.

- Damn you, bloody son of bitch! What are you playing at..?

Time seemed to freeze with the last words of the black guard. He looked at the man curled up on his side as if attempting to crawl into an invisible shell with complete bewilderment. I was sweating and holding my breath in the library. The ward guards were still engaged in their card game. They were talking, and I could hear them.

Mahmoud dropped to one knee and placed a palm on the man's chest. He took his victim's pulse nervously. After a few seconds, he raised his dark face, and I could see that it was ghastly. He turned and shouted to his colleagues :

- Help! Help! The bastard passed away...

THE THREE MEN BUSY playing stopped the game, tossed down their cards, and got to their feet. The group hurried into the courtyard and encircled Mahmoud, still on his knees. Two knelt over the sick man and tried to reanimate him.

- Call the Doctor, shouted one of them. Quick!

In no time, they carried the sufferer to the infirmary he was on his way to when Mahmoud stopped him. I never saw my first friend again after that.

THE GUARDS RETURNED to the holding area in a little over half an hour. There was obvious tension between them. Mahmoud's moodiness had reached new heights. Clearly, he was using gestures to communicate, as he kept pointing to where the fallen man was. Finally, they determined it to be a heart attack. I feel terribly awful. A little time later, I noticed a nurse in white coming out of the practice's main entrance. He walked across the courtyard and stopped in front of the ward:

-The Doctor wants you.

The guards exchanged puzzled glances, but Mahmoud was the real target. In other words, the black guard lied to the sick guy when he said the Doctor was off that afternoon.

I was still in disbelief and couldn't figure out why Mahmoud had stopped the sick man from seeing a doctor. What exactly did he gain? That whole event started because the ill man accidentally threw out the cigarette's butt. I just can't believe it. It just doesn't add up. The courtyard was littered with dozens of butts and other bits of trash, and no one seemed to mind. So the question is, why so much hate, even if everything went wrong?

(3)

SOME DAYS LATER, I learned from a cellmate of the defunct that he was Jewish. I have noted that Mahmoud called him several times rabbi, but I thought he was only teasing.

- What if he was a rabbi? I asked.

After a few days, I learned from one of the dead man's former cellmates that he was Jewish. I noticed that Mahmoud constantly referred to him as "rabbi" more than once, but I thought he was only teasing.

- What if he was a rabbi? I asked.

The man who broke the news is a robust individual in his early forties. Tall, red-haired, green-eyed, with a well-bridged nose and a slender mouth. He's my very first library patron. After a long time of dealing with the hotel's illiterate guests, I was relieved to hear that someone wished to borrow a book. I greeted him enthusiastically and invited him to browse the racks. We talked about books and the odd inmate defection, and I discovered that he shares an enclosure with my bank employer, Mr Aroussi. Incidentally, he brought up the topic of the recently deceased individual. He was a fellow inmate as well. I informed him I'd seen what had happened outside my window and that it was a tragic accident. The guards certainly had no intention of killing him. My client, who goes by the name of Hassan, said:

- I don't think so.

So I asked him if he thought the deceased's religion had anything to do with his demise. He paused on the shelves for a moment before saying:

- I think it had, somehow.

- How's that, Mr Hassan? He claimed to be sick. I heard him.

- He was, and the guards were fully aware of it. They pushed a man in his condition to suffer in about 39-40 degree heat. Did they ignore the fact that it could kill him? This was not the first time he had been harassed. They never stopped stalking him, and it was also because he was Jewish. This country has a centuries-old legacy of disrespect for other religions. It has a strong hold on people's minds.

I was growing increasingly concerned and couldn't find a satisfactory answer. I have never before witnessed a man being harassed on account of his faith on such a brutal scale. I found Hassan's comments upsetting. As much as I tried to convince myself otherwise, I refused to accept his explanation. I think he's making it up.

Jews and Christians, at times even more so than Muslims, have enjoyed high levels of respect in our country throughout its history. In fact, many people believe they have unique advantages. They reside in affluent neighbourhoods, shielded from danger by Christian embassies, Western media, and civil society organisations. True, not all of them are wealthy. Many families dwell in popular places. Actual also is the fact that sometimes there will be a conflict. Their situation is swiftly brought under control, though.

What's more, it's common knowledge that a Jew designed the Republican Palace, which belonged to the King before our BGP couvolution. There is still a small Jewish and Christian community in 'Ouja, and they get along fine with the rest of us. Since I was a little kid, I've known they existed in 'Ouja, and I never once thought of them as outsiders. To the point where I almost believed they were trying to convert to Islam. Everyone has been saying that for a long time. Some of the elders I've spoken with have informed me that, sure as the devil, they tried to convert discreetly but didn't dare show up at the mosque. That's because, deep down, they know Islam is the true faith, and everything else is just fluff to them. Additionally, our Christian and Jewish neighbours (some are residents, but people say they are visitors) have never requested permission to construct a church or temple close to our magnificent mosque. Because of this, word spread among the general public that they planned to convert to Islam.

The tavern at the 'Ouja great hotel is a popular hangout for guests, and Jews were among them. So we'd hang out there and have some good old-fashioned chit-conversation. Haj Mukhtar, the former Imam of our mosque and widely believed to be secretly married to a Jinni woman, was one of the guests I invited several times. But he declined my invitation, giving me the lame excuse that any convert should visit a mosque, not a bar. The truth was that he did not want to be seen mingling with the pub's drunks. Not that he has anything against alcohol.

On the contrary, he enjoyed it, but only in private meetings with me and Mr Hamda La'war, the party's cell leader. Besides, those people of other faiths are loyal customers of my bank. So at least we agree on something regarding watering holes and financial institutions.

But there is a blemish on this otherwise perfect board.

AFTER THE ARAB-ISRAELI conflict of 1967, many Jews were afraid for their safety and left the country. Though I was just a little lad at the time, I vividly recall the country collapsing into chaos once the news spread that the Arabs had been defeated. An angry crowd took to the streets and looted and burned Jewish-owned stores and vehicles. Riots broke out all over. Stones have been thrown at and even at their homes. Some Jews would be ripped to pieces if the rabble ever captured them. The protestors also attacked the police officers who sought to defend them. After WWII, the Jews probably hadn't seen anything like those days. Longtime residents, descendants of Jews who fled to our shores from the slaughter in Spain and other European countries in the dark Middle Ages, saw their homes and businesses destroyed and, in the worst cases, their loved ones killed. As a result, many people made their way to Europe and eventually to Israel. After the storm subsided, many of the rioters were taken into custody and put on trial.

Despite what had happened to their fellow Jews, some stayed in the country and were later accused of plotting against the security of the State. To top it all off, the prosecution has demonstrated beyond a reasonable doubt that a Marxist underground group conspired and instigated the riots to bring about a regime change and the establishment of a communist republic. Given that Karl Marx was an Israeli leader, the Marxist conspiracy of the 1960s was labelled as a Zionist operation.

Many Marxist militants had already made their way into academia and labour organisations. They fought against Islamist zealots who wanted to take over amphitheatres and non-governmental organisations. The police just let them fight and cleaned up afterwards. Many of the leftist extremists were captured while they disseminated their subversive literature. During their trial, they admitted that the World Zionist Organisation, headed by Marx from Tel Aviv, had funded their efforts to promote the revolution. Prominent historians confirmed this.

On the other hand, His Majesty the King gave a speech in which he claimed that "the majority of Jewish residents in our country are loyal subjects" to pacify European public opinion. Therefore, we won't hold somebody here against their will if they express a desire to depart. The rest will continue to enjoy state protection. They have the same duties and privileges as their Muslim and Christian subjects.

However, since its destruction, the Capital's primary synagogue has remained closed.

I BRING UP THESE DRAMATIC incidents to remind the Administration, should it be necessary, that our country's official position has always been tolerant toward people of other faiths and backgrounds. And yet, I beg your indulgence as I draw your attention, humbly, to the fact that a sick guy, who happened to be Jewish, has been molested by the guards to an intolerable amount, as suggested by his cellmate, Hassan.

To be clear, I disagree with Hassan's viewpoint. I consider myself to be a devoted public servant. I have no reason to believe that Mr Mahmoud intended any damage to the individual he had stopped on that hot and very devilish afternoon. My God! I can't even fathom the possibility of that happening.

Furthermore, he wasn't out to murder him; he only wanted to instil some manners and eco-consciousness in the boy. The departed has joined his forebears in the afterlife. We pray that God will forgive him. But he was utterly wrong. Not only did he see a doctor who was absent from administrative duties, but he also put his still-burning butt on the ground, demonstrating a callous disregard for the Ozone hole, global warming, and other climate-related issues. Who in his right mind would insist on doing that after being told by a respectable Administration employee that there is no Doctor? The Jewish jerk broke hotel policy at least twice, so it's safe to assume he was malicious. No one is entitled to act according to his whims or caprices in this reputable establishment. In such a case, where would we even go? There will be anarchy and rebellion against the government.

Consider the situation we're in now. Gentlemen, we're talking about a major violation of the law. It's more than simply a bunch of kicking and screaming on the floor. Given that we have already established that our hotel is an integral part of the government's agenda, any mutiny would signal the start of a counter-couvolution against our BGP (Beloved General President). Therefore, it is clear that a cigarette butt threatens national security. Mr Mahmoud, a committed representative of the Administration like myself, saw what I saw as part of the wider plot being cooked in the kitchens and responded accordingly. This tragic loss has nothing to do with the goals of the Administration's delegates. No, it's just Mektoub acting up! Nothing could have prevented it from happening at that precise instant, and the awful archangel Azrael had no choice but to act. To put it simply, it was business as usual.

THAT IS AN ESSENTIAL point to clarify. I have no doubt that the Jewish citizen was looking for trouble. He committed two serious acts of disobedience: he dropped the butt of his cigarette without even crushing it and went to the doctor while he was supposed to be napping. What if the wind blew the burning butt into the storage area or, even worse, the library? Without a chance to answer God in this life, we would have been sent straight to hell. For a crime we didn't commit! What a damned shame, then! What was going through Mickey Mouse's mind, I have no idea.

Further investigation is warranted to ascertain whether his actions were accidental or intended to torch the State hotel. After all, the Sixties proved that the Jew was probably one of the Marxist plotters out to bring down the government. Unfortunately, his illness is no excuse for his inappropriate behaviour. The facts pointed to the fact that he had initiated a mutiny that, if carried to its logical conclusion, would have set the country ablaze. It was fortunate that the courageous Mahmoud was present to witness this.

Our BGP should present the hero with the award of Human Rights Champion. As a result of his bravery, millions of lives were saved from criminal arson. Indeed, he is deserving of better. He spared not only our lives but also the regime to which we are all dedicated.

HASSAN WAS NOT PRIVY to any of my innermost thoughts. Initially, I was curious whether he was "one of us" or "one of them." If I'm being completely honest, I didn't appreciate his subtle allusions to bigotry between different faiths. People here have evolved beyond such emotions. No, we don't look down on other cultures. There is no pretence of Islamic superiority on our part. We don't want to add more sceptics and enemies to the world.

On the contrary, we humbly invite Christians and Jews to convert to the true religion. We don't even force them to pay tribute if they refuse. We just do not allow our daughters to marry them. As for the Buddhists and Hindus, we have nothing to do with them. We don't even think they practise any religion. Instead, they flock to our oil-rich nation in search of employment. Some, though, have abandoned the darkness and joined Islam in exchange for a six-month salary. To which the Grand Imam gave his approval.

This country's extraordinary Administration's leaders are far beyond such trivialities as patronising the affiliates of other confessions. Mr Mahmoud is the epitome of my assumption.

We did not encourage Jews to leave for Europe and Israel after 1967. However, their Jewish Marxist comrades orchestrated the riots to force the majority of their community to flee the country where their ancestors had traditionally lived. This was demonstrated in a courtroom. Since then, the communists and socialists have been expelled, and they no longer have any legal standing to make any claims whatsoever in our Muslim nation.

HASSAN IS TOTALLY IN the dark about all of this. He's just another schmuck who thinks he's smart because he's posing as a reporter who knows everything.

I won't deny, however, that I was thrilled to meet a professional editor in person finally. But, of course, I'm referring to a person I can put a face to, not simply words on a page. I even wondered if he wasn't in the hotel to write a story.

At that, he cracked a grin. He thought I was ingratiating him.

- Do you not know yet?

- Know what?

- I am in the pit because my magazine has been suspended.

That bit of news startled me, and the bells rang in my head. I asked him :

- Do you support the Monarchists?

- I am a republican, he replied.

Well! Since he is no royalist, he is not dangerous to me. Then I asked him whether he was not a fascist. He stared at me, bewildered. For a moment, I thought he was angry. But he dodged my question and said:

- For a bank clerk, you seem somewhat simple. How can you ask me such a question when you see where I stand? I told you I have nothing to do with the Royalists. This is not to mean I am a fan of the military. I would not be here if I were, would I? If you're curious, both regimes suspended my gazette and jailed me.

- What for?

- What for? He repeated with a derisive grin. Good question! I wish I could tell you! Under the King'sKing's rule, I was charged with republicanism and arrested for publishing an opinion that was not mine but that of an illustrious scholar. I spent six months in jail. And here I am again, just some months after the coup. I am still waiting for my trial. It is what they call a preventive arrest!

- They will likely release you if the charge is inconsistent.

His green eyes flashed, and he grimaced, somewhat dismayed.

- You're kidding, Mr Bourasin, aren't you? Unless you don't know them as I do. The charges are nothing but bogus. They can't prove them since they know why I was jailed some years ago. But if they want me behind bars, it is not hard for them to invent anything. Look around you, man. This place is full of guys who have been sentenced for no crime at all.

- What do you mean? How about justice? I shouted as I recalled my case.

- We'll get justice on the day of the last judgment.

He paused a moment, then added:

- We are in the same situation, your Boss, you, and me. Don't worry. Experience and good connections may pull you out of the affair with the help of a lawyer. And above all, money, of course. The only problem is the trial. We don't know; we never know whether it will happen soon or never.

- You're overly pessimistic!

- Overly? No, I prefer to keep things in perspective. Unfortunately, the judicial system is notoriously slow. However, it may not change at all in our country. If you're lucky—that is, if you know someone high up in the Administration—your trial could be over quickly. However, there are occasions when not even the people closest to you, whether family or friends, will help. This includes law enforcement officials and judges. For the worry of being fired from their current jobs. Then you will spend the rest of your life in jail. You could even perish in prison without anyone realising it until after you've been buried. That, my friend, is a jackpot situation. It can take years for some prisoners even to be brought to trial. You are informed of the day you were taken into custody, but you are never notified of the day you will be released. Many people sat in jail for years before being brought to trial, where the judge read their files and decided they should have just served a month or two. Then, having served their sentence in prison for several years, they were free to leave. No apologies. Cancel that! Keep in mind that none of the accused has any idea if he will ever be able to go home to his loved ones again. As you put it, Mr Bourasin, we are in a liminal space between the afterlife and the present. Beware! Not the small drunks, bums, crooks, scumbags, and riffraff. To clarify, I'm referring to those who, like you, me, and Mr Aroussi, were detained on political charges or for political reasons.

The final words sent shivers down my spine. This is the worst kind of charge that can happen to someone in this country. That's worse than getting charged with murder. To accuse someone of political activity, especially opposition and sedition, is almost to sign his death warrant. I can admit - even with joy - to all the accusations levelled against my honesty, integrity, and honour. I wouldn't mind being called a crook, charlatan, bandit, or thief, but I certainly wouldn't call myself a political activist. I just can't take it. There was no way I would sit here and let Hassan throw me in his basket. A bit taken aback, I shot back a quick response:

- Make no mistake, Mr Hassan. I am not under any political charge. By the way, let me inform you: I am not detained. I am a visitor. That's different. On the other hand, nobody can say I am a political activist since I am apolitical.

His eyes twinkled in the light of the sun rays filtering through the bars of the lone window near which we stood.

- What did you say? I don't understand.

- I said I am apolitical, Mr Hassan. *APOLITICAL* !

He looked stupefied. To make myself clear, I added:

- I have no political background, no political activity, and no political ambition. I am not involved and not attracted. I was not trying to oppose the regime when I was invited to this State facility.

- This *State facility* is a fucking prison, man. Will you wake up? Did they invite you? Come on! Why don't you just say they arrested you? And in the first place, why did they *invite* you, Mr Bourasin?

- That's the problem! I cannot reveal more. You and the shrink are convinced that I am a royalist. But I am not anymore.

- Ahah! I didn't say you were because I didn't know what your charge was. You just revealed it. Then, you denied it.

- I am not a royalist.

- Even under the former regime?

I needed to choose my words, to avoid confusion.

- Look, Mr Hassan. You are a journalist. You know the regime changed since the c...volution...

- You mean the coup...

- No, I mean the couvolution.

- I had never heard of couvolution. What are you talking about?

- If you don't know, it doesn't matter, Mr Hassan. You will learn later. Just remember that I am loyal to the republic as I was loyal to the monarchy when everybody in the country was.

- Look, don't try to play a words game with me. I am a fucking journalist. I'll put it to you this way: One day, one sergeant ousted the King and stole his throne. So, who are you supporting?

This conversation was taking a dangerous turn. Hassan was driving at 200 km/hour on a tight serpentine road that allows only 50, along the edge of a mountain overlooking an abyss, with me sitting beside him. I didn't appreciate being a prisoner of his warped thoughts.

- No, Sir. You still need to be inducing correct conclusions. I told you I am no longer a royalist. Anyway, I did not know I was before the shrink informed me. I would risk twenty years in the hot ... I mean in this location, if I admitted the charge. So, what are you talking about? Can we change of subject?

- Twenty years? And you want to change of subject? Are they indicting you for murder? Unless you sacked the bank with your Boss! He didn't tell me about this.

Saying this, he repressed a smile. But I noted it.

- Please, don't joke with serious matters, Mr Hassan. I am an honest man, and so is my Boss.

He recomposed. I did not relish his humour. There was a pause, and then he put it back again:

- You know your Boss is jailed for political reasons. It seems obvious.

- Well? I wasn't aware of it. I thought him a party man.

- Party men are a threatened species after the coup, Mr Bourasin. Some are here with us, and some are hiding away or exiled. The party is still there, but only sycophants and arrivistes occupy the front stage. What do you think?

- I don't think anything, Mr Hassan. I am apolitical. I only know that everybody in 'Ouja respects Mr Aroussi. Even one-eyed Hamda la'war.

A silence. Red hair and green eyes shining in the sunlight. I am looking at the oblong face. Waiting for more.

- Who's the man?

- The head of our party's cell. At the time, the King in person honoured him with the High Merit medal.

- It is not a good reference anymore. Is your friend still the leader of the cell?

- Indeed he is. Why shouldn't he?

- Unbelievable! Unless he has already changed his jacket, he won't last. I bet he will join us very soon if he is honest.

- It will be a great honour for him and a delight for us. We'll have the mayor of 'Ouja walking with the inmates daily in the courtyard.

- Really! You're a cunning man, Mr Bassam.

(4)

- BEFORE HE WAS MURDERED, said Hassan, referring to the Jewish guy.

I cut him off:

- He wasn't murdered. Everything was visible to me.

- Okay, then! It's the same because he died while carrying out the guards' commands. You should know that your Boss was on good terms with him.

- You mean since Mr Aroussi met him in the ho... er... the...

- No. Not since they met in jail. They knew each other well before. They used to have a business together.

- Ah! Really? What kind of business?

- Moosa Dawood was the name of the deceased. He was apprehended at the border while attempting to smuggle $6 million out of the country.

Dumbfounded, I said somewhat rashly:

- He had six million dollars? That's what makes one a respected citizen...

Noting the bewildered expression on Hassan's face, I explained:

- By the standards of the bank, of course. To possess such Capital is always a sign of honesty and hard work. Word of a bank clerk!

- Great! Unfortunately for the guy, it is not the opinion of the authorities in this country.

- Really? Why not? They are encouraging and supporting free enterprise, though.

- Yeah! Free enterprise, not free swindling and smuggling of foreign currency, draining the economy. But the poor devil was unlucky! And so was your Boss. Sorry!

- What did Mr Aroussi do to be associated with conmen and smugglers? He's a banker, not a thug. What the devil!

- Sure! Sure! But because he is a banker, he shouldn't have Moosa Dawood as a partner or even as a client.

- Dawood was not our client nor our partner. I know all the customers of 'Ouja bank.

- No, you don't. Dawood was not a usual client or partner. He was your Boss's agent and accomplice, lad! He worked for him. Aroussi is well the owner of smuggled funds. He has several accounts abroad in fiscal paradises. Dawood was just the delivery man. The authorities are convinced it's not their first operation of the kind but the latest. As it failed, they both landed here. I understand that the case of your Boss is much more complicated. The authorities might have shut their eyes if he did not turn too greedy. Somebody among the customs officers whom he used to pay off wasn't satisfied. Besides, he played a bad game, aiming at the National Bank's chairmanship. Not that he was unable, but his game was judged inopportune and somehow embarrassing. He lost well-placed friends.

That was too much for me. I don't know where Hassan picked all that stuff. So I kept silent and gloomy. But then, he suddenly got closer and whispered in a confidential tone:

- Do you know Haj Omar Osman?

- Who doesn't? Haj Omar was the Minister of the King, originally from 'Ouja. I know his house and his sons. One of them is married and still living there. But the rest of the family moved to the Capital.

- Energy Minister... Who fled to a neighbouring country with a year's worth of oil money just hours before the coup. I'm not sure how many million dollars he took with him. Now go and find him!

- I remember reading something about this affair, but they did not talk of money.

- No, they didn't. They couldn't. Those who fled with suitcases full of money are not two or three, but dozens and dozens, man. The country would be chaotic if the papers published all those nasty stories. Those who defected are not ordinary people but VIPs from the business and political spheres.

I am appalled. When I initially heard these stories, I found it difficult to believe that all those people, in their positions as respectable servants to the Administration, could be deceiving the Administration. The reporter was probably wrong or exaggerating. The dawn of our BGP's fantastic New Era could hardly usher in anything so repulsive. With my own eyes and ears, I witnessed and heard the tremendous popular applause that greeted our BGP. Day or night, citizens of the new republic showed their support for the first GP (General President) and his emissaries and representatives by cheering loudly wherever they heard them. The thousands of supporters attest to the success of the party's militants when they hold a meeting. Their live broadcast allows the entire country to evaluate the significance of the nation's accomplishments in a single evening. The Night of Destiny!

What else could we possibly want? We have a saviour who came at the darkest hour (after midnight) when our country was asleep, undisturbed by the economic crisis or political plots. That wrinkled old King was ill. At best, the poor man could hope to stay on the throne for a few months. However, he was unable to rule. Was he ousted? My God! No! Currently, he is in his retirement. Those who claim otherwise are conspirators: crooks and cooks.

If the King died, even the Prince, as the next in line, would have inherited a precarious position. Because of this, Our Beloved General President (BGP), who also held the positions of Prime Minister and Minister of the Interior, took up those roles. Through his intervention, the Prince was spared the trouble. The noble Prime Minister decided to cut short the Prince's suffering out of friendship and genuine compassion.

The previous heir apparent had nothing to worry about after that night of couvolution. Is the throne no longer there? Likewise, the nation. However, our planet is still very much intact. If he used to believe that all roads lead to the throne, he now believes that they can lead everywhere. With a valid passport, of course.

Not only were his people saved, but also the Prince. Even a natural-born nobleman would have felt pressured to engage in a pointless scrimmage with familiar and unfamiliar adversaries due to all the political foolishness going on. But the ungrateful misread the upgraded Minister's sincere intentions despite the great favour our BGP provided him. He skipped town without a passport and sought political refuge in a neighbouring, unfriendly country. He and his father are now the subjects of rampant rumours. Some say they are in Britain, while others pretend that the former King is dead or in jail. I can state unequivocally that the King is not staying in our State Hotel. The rumour mill also says that his son is actively seeking outside aid in his quest to counteract our BGP. Strangely, the arrogant one says that his benefactor usurped the throne of his ancestors. In this life, we would witness it all.

THIS WHOLE THING IS utter and complete nonsensical bullshit. I have no doubt that our Beloved General President has and always will have the King's and Prince's best interests at heart. Didn't he prevent a national crisis? Why should the Saviour put an older man to death or incarceration while also plotting to eliminate or enslave his son? Since the country reveres him as a liberator, he has no motive to back down now. There was a time when the old King was also a Saviour for many years. After all, he overthrew the British and restored the throne of his ancestors. In addition to being heroes in their own right, the ancestors he held in such high regard also served as the Saviour of their day. The European Crusaders were repelled, and the True

Faith was safeguarded thanks to their heroic efforts, chronicled in great detail in our history textbooks. Imagine if they failed, heaven forbid! There is no way we can avoid being on the losing side now. Choosing the wrong side or a false faith is like choosing the fastest route to the hereafter.

Note that I don't mean to imply that other religions are wrong. I simply state that they require an update. To my knowledge, Islam was the last major religion to emerge. Now, if someone were to ask me, "What is the updated version of Islam, which appeared fifteen centuries ago?" I would not respond to such a provocation. Indeed! The fact that our prophet was the most recent and final one is common knowledge. The clock has officially been wound down to zero.

I know exactly what I'm talking about. Haj Mukhtar, the Imam of the 'Ouja Grand Mosque, was my science teacher. He can see into the future and the past. He has married a Jenni woman, who has given him unrivalled power. His credentials as a highly qualified scientist have been established. Everything about the night sky is familiar to him, down to the names of every star. He is able to tally them as well. Don't bring up Einstein, Newton, or Hawking when Haj Mukthar is around. This would make him quite angry. To begin with, he isn't familiar with them. Second, they're all wrong because they don't have one foot in our universe and the other in the invisible one like him.

ONE DAY, HAMDA LA'WAR remarked, "You cannot compare Haj Mukhtar to those Charlatans."

As usual, Mr Hamda's residence was the place to be on a Friday night. Following a delicious meal and two or three bottles of top-notch wine, we lit up some joints and relaxed our tongues. I was referring to a TV show that aired on the BBC that I caught. I only made the point that MrHawking found new universes that neither Einstein nor Newton could have ever imagined.

-Who are those dudes, anyway? Said Haj Mukhtar.

- The BBC deemed them the most outstanding scientists of all time.

- Hoax! An enraged Haj Mukhtar said. They don't have a clue.

Then Hamda instructed me to be quiet and pay attention to the only brilliant scientist in history right in front of me.

Haj Mukhtar, who is often quiet, sang like a nightingale. He entertained us with tales of his adventures into the unseen worlds, where his in-laws had invited him on multiple occasions, and the incredible things he had found there. His younger and more attractive Jenni bride, Taktuka, has even brought him on a brief vacation to paradise. However, since they could not enter without proper authorisation, they could only watch from outside the walls through the Big gate's barred windows.

Another evening, I said that our BGP has royal blood in his veins, no doubt about it. Haj Mukhtar asked:

-Who is our BGP with royal blood?

- Brother of the Grand Pain in the ass! Said Hamda.

- Nope! It's our Beloved General President.

Silence.

Then, I explained:

- We call him Saviour, don't we? It is the honorific title of the kings who ruled the country for centuries.

- Where the royal blood came from? Asked Haj.

- His mother had perhaps slept with a member of the Royal Family and kept the story unknown to the public.

Haj Mukhtar burst into laughter. He thought I was joking. As for Hamda La'war, he reprimanded me:

- You'd better keep your mouth shut instead of blurting such inanities. You don't even know what you say.

(*He was right. I don't know what Devil made me speculate that the President is a bastard! I must drop that last assumption from my report.*)

(5)

THE NIGHT OF THE COUVOLUTION was not without its share of unfortunate and unavoidable mishaps. It can't be helped! Such as when the Royal Guard sought to fight off the troops that had blocked the Palace's entrance. I heard that people on both sides were killed in the conflict, but hearsay is never reliable. If Royal Guard commanders weren't so dogmatic and overzealous, there wouldn't have been any casualties. They would have joined the couvolutionists if they had known that the General Minister-to-be-President had no intention of harming the King. They wouldn't have obstructed his path to the Palace if they'd realised their commander was the King's Premier. After all, it was preferable to a costly and time-consuming general election.

Swift and priceless couvolution! No time is lost on unnecessary political blather. There was no money spent on a fastidious election campaign. In our country, the taxpayer got his President elected without any trouble. You go to bed in a monarchy and wake up in a republic. Who fared better? The story reads like something out of the Arabian Nights. Except there's no Scheherazade. We have established a template that, I am confident, will be adopted by nations around the globe — especially Westerners who exploit democracy as a means to impose oppressive tax burdens on their citizens.

Look at the sums being spent on U.S. and European elections. Where can those seeking public office get the money they need to run for office? In reality, they are taking it directly from people's wallets. Despite pledges to the contrary, the donors never receive their original amounts. I keep up with the news by reading the papers. So, yes, I know a lot about the alleged democracies. It's a shameful fraud! I really feel bad for Westerners. They believe they have the best system in the world, but in reality, they are being tricked and looted by their politicians. They need to open their eyes and get up. Wherever possible, it is preferable for citizens' hard-earned cash to remain in their own hands, as is the case with couvolution awards in our country. We discovered the most satisfactory solution. We let the army perform the job at night while everyone is sleeping instead of organising those pointless and expensive fund-raising gatherings and those extensive campaigns where money travels from the citizen's pocket to the leader's bag just by the magical power of promises. Any successful coup will be quick and orderly. The morning after, you can name it the "glorious Revolution," "blessed change," or anything else that suits your fancy. So, for no cost at all, you can enjoy the smiling face of your Beloved General President for 25 years. No big deal if some individuals try to act like the revolution never happened or was merely a military coup. What we have here is what we will term couvolution. As a result, joy reigns in the community. And who cares if some military personnel pretend that the General President was only a captain, lieutenant, or even a sergeant? We call that envy and resentment. Nothing stops progress.

On this level, gentlemen, we are the world leaders, not the Western countries. They want to think of themselves as the defenders of democracy, but we are the leaders of the nocturnal couvolutions. We operate at a considerably higher efficiency. Keep in mind that if I place a premium on staging a coup to seize control of the government and protect the people's finances from irresponsible spenders, it's because that's the point of any good policy. Although I have no political affiliations, except for working for the party representing the nation, my experience as a bank teller has taught me to spot a good bargain when I see one. Therefore, I think our couvolution saved the taxpayer much money compared to what he would have spent on a democratic election campaign.

In terms of banking, the ex-Premier-Minister of the Interior was perfectly justified in attacking the Royal Palace with tanks. You couldn't just declare a republic and remove the King without some heavy machinery. By striking such a reasonable deal, millions of dollars were spared that would have otherwise vanished. It's common knowledge that the old and clumsy King was planning to hold democratic elections. Take note of the ex-Super Wazir's wisdom! He timed the launch of his tanks against the King to coincide with the beginning of the election campaign to the week. Upon taking power, he immediately declared a curfew and dissolved parliament.

Western media should stop comparing us to a "rotted oil monarchy," which is essentially the same thing as a "banana republic," a label we'd want to shed. We can't take any more of that nonsense! So, from now on, feel free to refer to us as an independent oil republic. Guys, we're talking oil, not bananas. I hope you'll recognise the significance of this change. It's massive!

We've evolved into a cutting-edge nation-state, not some dusty relic fit only for a museum display. Our President is not a mummy, but a true couvolutionist star.

Finally, some encouraging news:

Our President has temporarily halted the enforcement of Sharia, which is supposed to be our governing constitution. He remarked seriously that our people, like many other nations, need access to modern laws. He went so far as to say that we had become far more advanced than the Europeans. When he spoke, he brought back memories of our most outstanding achievements. Our BGP proclaimed that we landed in the Americas much before Christopher Columbus. Native Americans who live there now are our ancestors' offspring. Only a few know they initially settled there after migrating from our lands. When no one in the West had even heard of America, we already called it home. Our BGP turned out to be a scientist.

Our BGP turned out to be a scientist.

This is, without a doubt, the best thing that has happened to our country in ages. We have become the most progressive nation on Earth. I've always had faith that our country's hero would come to the rescue. All of us have been attended to at this point. From the depths of the Ministry of the Interior and the army ranks emerged the Saviour. Our BGP did not make any such ridiculous claims as the King, who pretended to be reigning according to Allah's will and Sharia. However, that doesn't make him Satan's messenger, either. To set the tone for the New Era, he ushered in the first Friday of it by praying at the Capital's largest mosque. It aired in real-time. On the basis of the holy Quran, all the Imams of the erstwhile corrupt oil monarchy (according to our national media) pledged loyalty to the BGP. Allah is happy, and religion is secure.

That's why the Prince's decision to abandon his post and seek asylum in Britain was unnecessary and inappropriate. To make matters worse, the British government granted him political protection in just 24 hours.

Generally, I refrain from criticising the Administration or its honourable officials. Such insane thoughts never enter my mind. On the contrary, I have always faithfully served my superiors with self-denial. That's because I have no financial incentive to trash them. (*What? No incentive? You dummy! Delete this rubbish!*)

This does not prevent me from criticising the British, as I am not paid by them but rather by 'Ouja bank, a state-owned National Bank branch.

I have a duty of loyalty to my government, but I am not worried by rumours that we are still under Whitehall's protection.

Simply put, this is a load of hogwash! Our BGP is not a sock puppet. Neither was our King an idiot, albeit he eventually became dumb and abdicated in favour of London. So, precisely what is it that all those fugitives hope to find in London? What more could they want that we can't provide for them here in the fatherland?

Whoever ran away with all those money didn't set out to hurt our economy, I'm sure. To be specific, Mr Aroussi. If I were to trust Hassan, he did not actually fly, but he was preparing for it.

I refuse to believe that someone as dedicated to the Administration as my former Boss would ever sell out the country's best interests to further his personal goals. To what end? Just to get to the paradise of wealth that is London?

I know Mr Aroussi better than anyone. Like myself and Mr Hamda La'war, he is a true gentleman who thinks the party and the motherland are inseparable. He's a party militant and a successful banker who knows all the ins and outs of our pleasing profession and uses them to great use. What other way was there for him to get this job? And once he arrived at his post, what other means did he have to keep it operational and generating revenue for years? Mr Aroussi isn't depressed because of the couvolution, nor is he a bitter failed ambition who wants payback.

The opposite is true; many other superiors rely on him. They'll take the fall with him if he does. If it hasn't happened already, it will very soon. As soon as the prosecutor begins his investigation.

I don't see Mr Aroussi fleeing to London. He is a big fan of Europe, though. Tobacco from the Netherlands, Johnny Walker Black Label, and outfits from the Champs-Elysees, Oxford Street, and Regent Street are some of his favourite things to buy and indulge in while travelling through these cities. When I suggested that a poster with a quote from the President's first speech, framed in gold, be displayed in the bank's lobby, he was tuning up to my idea.

He must have thought he had a good cause to trust Moosa Dawood with $6,000,000 to go overseas. His goal, I'm sure, was to put the cash into a lucrative venture on the European continent. Mr Aroussi is well-versed in the most recent developments in international business and investing. Our National Bank, notably its headquarters in the Capital, works with various financial institutions worldwide. We have negotiated favourable terms with financial institutions in Hong Kong, London, Singapore, Monaco, Zurich, Paris, New York, Munich, Tokyo, and elsewhere. Unlike novices, we know what we're doing as traders. There is nothing hidden from us in the world of finance.

The representative of the well-known Japanese company Matsuitsamitsu admitted to me that... They were told that Mr Aroussi was not a banker but a wizard. He offered him a 15% cut of whatever business he brought from Japanese firms in the future, provided those firms were not his own. They agreed to a deal with 35% of the market share quota. As a demonstration of his gratitude, the Nippon bowed at least twenty-five times before and after he signed the deal. I was present for the discussion and followed the negotiations to some extent. I must admit that I was confused by the reasoning behind my Boss's suggestion. Why did he agree to a whopping 35% quota when he constantly complained about the already excessive 15%? But as soon as the Japanese left our offices, I couldn't hold back the question:

- Mr Aroussi, is that not a little excessive quota we offered to the Nippon?

He displayed his best smile and said :

- My dear Bassam, you are still inexperienced despite being the oldest bank employee. When this Japanese returns to his own country and brags about his deal, competitor companies' agents and spies will lick their lips and rush to meet us and make similar arrangements. There will be a line in front of my office. Then we'll have a choice and a wide range of options. Only then would we be able to impose our terms. We'll make deals with them at 5% quotas or less, while on the official documents, we'll always sign for 40% or 30% rationing, just like we did today.

I was still perplexed. Was it a ruse? Is that marketing? Free advertising? What else? But I couldn't convey my scepticism to my Boss...

- I recognise that it is a brilliant idea and an excellent free advertisement, I said.

Then, after some hesitation, I decided to jump: - Yet, if we are to give less, why should we go on the records saying that we offered more?

- I just explained it to you, Bassam, said the Boss, a little nervous.

After a pause, he recomposed, displayed the same self-satisfied smile, and added: - Look here, this is our secret. This is the very cause of our present and future successes. Banking is based on interests, isn't it? We have done nothing other than work according to that wise precept. We'll give less and keep the money in our cashbox. Do you grasp the sense of the operation?

No, I didn't. However, avoiding his anger, I just said:

- Quite, Sir. We'll give less and get more in the cashbox.

- Son! He exclaimed, elated. What acumen! You are a light in the dark! You'll have your promotion, I promise it. But... He paused, displayed a stern facade and added: - Since it is a secret operation and only you and I know about it, keep your mouth shut. Did I make myself transparent?

- You can't be more transparent, Sir.

I now see that he was not intentionally deceptive with me. He delivered as promised, and my income was up a reasonable amount that month. I was the happiest of the men. I became a model employee. I could now legitimately expect to receive a national medal. Both of my superiors were pleased with my performance. Mr Hamda, at the party's cell, did not hide his appreciation of my top-secret reports. And the raise was just given to me by Mr Aroussi. They are both upstanding members of society.

Mr Aroussi, in particular, goes above and beyond his role as a banker to ensure his company's and its employees' success. Along with being a dedicated public servant, he is willing to take incredible risks to raise the profile of a local bank in a sleepy town that is barely known even within the country. Let's say the Nippon, who is also involved in other transactions with other firms, insists on being paid only in accordance with the terms of his contract and refuses to accept any additional payment. Or maybe Matsuitsamitsu found out about his double-dealing and dismissed him. Then what would happen?

Current litigation and court wrangling would put us in a sticky situation. My Boss is clever enough to find a way out of a situation like that, thank goodness. Everything that might happen did or would happen, he already knew about. At first, he established an import-export firm that maintained strong ties to our financial institution. Then, in a sneaky move, he made me its manager. Like all the other people involved, Mr Hamda is in the dark about this appointment. (*No need to mention it in the report. That's the only thing I've been keeping from him. Or, you know what? Say he knew all about it. Like this, if you go down, he'll plunge too.*) Mr Aroussi's name wasn't used in any of the import-export firm's dealings or official paperwork. I am the "Director." Mr Aroussi is a dedicated worker in his field. While managing a branch of a state-owned bank, he wouldn't take the chance to start a private business. Nor would he get into a contract with a foreign company before the money was in the bank. When he met his quota, he would sign the contract and give it to the agent. As a banker, always. Likewise, I, Mr Bassam Bourasin, his manager, would sign off on the contract on behalf of our import-export firm.

The overseas agent typically has already agreed to these conditions. The remaining fraction would be his "commission," just as it was for Mr Aroussi and his manager. Otherwise, say 20% for the bank and 15% between the three.

Now that's what I call a good business transaction. After working in the same field for a while, you learn that money doesn't smell bad, no matter where it comes from. Most importantly, you discover that whatever benefits Mr Aroussi's covert business also benefits 'Ouja Bank, and whatever benefits 'Ouja Bank benefits the country's economy. Therefore, despite the risks, Mr Aroussi's private enterprise benefits the government. However, big profits are expected, and our bank does just that. Throw out all of our old methods. We must do what must be done to achieve that worthy goal of any human trade. We pull out all the stops to entice companies to shop here and import goods because the country desperately needs them. Obviously, if the international client or representative had any complaints about our bank, he wouldn't do business with us. The greatest banks in any city provide the best services, and here in 'Ouja, we are, without a doubt, the best. Nay! In the country. Superior to the Headquarters in every way. True, being the only bank in town is a huge plus. The outcome was not accidental. In this industry, no one else even comes close to us. Mr Hamda La'war is safely in our grasp. In addition to his duties as cell leader, Mr La'war has been elevated to the position of mayor of 'Ouja. A bank would not be able to open a shop in 'Ouja if the Mayor and Party's cell said, "No."

When you're successful, you'll have more fans and acquaintances but also make some vicious adversaries.

And when dealing with millions of dollars worth of foreign currency, ignoring the stock market's volatility could lead to disaster. For instance, when exchanging $100 from the dollar into our money, the differences between the two may seem negligible. However, every cent counts once you reach $100,000 because, at that point, it will multiply by a factor of one million. ... I'm not making this up; take it from a teller at a bank! Choosing a terrible day to make a trade will result in a worse outcome. Waiting for a great opportunity is a trait of the most successful businessmen. There is no need to make a quick decision or to stress out. In both scenarios, you would suffer financial and time losses. Except for the five years I have left in my career after I check out of this hotel, I can confidently say that Mr Aroussi is the best director to have led 'Ouja bank in the past fifteen years. Before him were two other directors. Both were reliable and trustworthy, though neither quite reached the heights of Mr Aroussi. If he is not nominated Chairman of the National Bank, I am convinced he will be appointed Governor of the Central Bank one of these days. Since I am still loyal to him and the Administration, I hope he remembers me.

IF WE RETURN TO THE six million dollars discovered in Moosa Dawood's suitcases by customs agents, the money would have been better served if it had stayed where Mr Aroussi had intended it to go. But I won't go into detail about the official's verdict. Nor am I suggesting that Europe is a safer place to put money than our country. These treacherous ideas have never occurred to me. In any case, I am confident that the money was in competent hands because I know the man well. His many deals' success and the support of the Administration's international clients attest to his integrity and loyalty. As the Japanese from Matsuitsamitsu described it, Mr Aroussi is "a true prestidigitator" at this level. The entire country would have profited if Moosa Dawood had been permitted to execute the deal. However, sadly! The Jew was detained by well-meaning (but naive) customs officials. As a result, we missed a great chance to invest that money. I have no doubt that those six million dollars would have generated a profit of at least three or four million dollars within the first six months. Jews possess a great deal of wisdom. Anything involving commerce or the economy is suitable in their wheelhouse. Mr Aroussi understands what he is doing.

RECENTLY, I READ THAT Holocaust survivors have demanded payment from Swiss banks totalling at least $7 billion. This is a fascinating tale. Prior to World War II, many Jews stashed away large quantities of money in Switzerland. However, their heirs were still unable to provide legal evidence of their inheritance until after the war ended. Jewish organisations in Europe and the United States estimate that Switzerland's vaults still retain prewar investments worth $3 billion to $7 billion, or even more, after factoring in interest for the past half-century. To add insult to injury, Jews claim that the Swiss National Bank is sitting on gold ingots made from the teeth of Holocaust victims. What a horrible tale!

Will the victims' heirs ever be compensated if they don't have the proper paperwork? Who knows? But I have no doubt that they will move mountains to find a middle ground with the Swiss banks. In all likelihood, Mr Aroussi is the most knowledgeable and has the best connections to Jewish businessmen. As soon as I see him, I plan to question him. A meeting with him was something Frankenstein had promised to arrange. This new friend seems to have just as many connections at the hotel as Mr Aroussi does in the international finance industry.

Even though it may be a bit crowded, please note that we are not wholly cut off from the outside world here at the State hotel. There are televisions in each chamber, as well as frequent deliveries of national newspapers. This means that we can keep up with the latest global events. We are up to date and quite familiar with the outstanding accomplishments of our BGP. However, the newspapers are not part of the standard hotel amenities. Thus they come at a cost.

This hotel would receive six stars if the Administration made a concerted effort to provide us with extra beds and mattresses. The point is, in fact, unique. I am aware that the goal is not particularly lucrative at the moment, but I do not see any reason why it could not be. While our state is naturally benevolent, the BGP New Era should focus on correcting the previous Administration's incorrect mismanagement.

We'll get right down to business. With your permission, I'll be completely forthright here, as I have been in all my classified reports to the Administration.

Many people, including convicts and official government personnel, refer to this decent hotel as a "prison." Because this is a State-run establishment, I have to act accordingly. As a result, it is now an honourable prison, not a hotel. But this shouldn't make us forget that tourists get special treatment here that they can't get anywhere else. That's why, gentlemen, it's time we started charging money for the time spent behind bars, just like any other service.

MORE WORK IS REQUIRED from our BGP's Administration if its hospitality policy is to be effective.

First, we need to upgrade the jail furniture to make inmates more comfortable. No, I don't care about the convicts' comfort when I say this. Whether they sleep on a bed like civilised people or on each other like savages is of no concern to me. In particular, I am anxious about the Administration's long-term plan.

We must prevent any insurrection that could threaten the dawn of the New Era of our BGP, for we understand that the prison should be the cornerstone of any political regime (as the storming of the Bastille revealed to the world).

Second (and not least), I've already noticed that my hypersensitive nose detects a foul odour emanating from the kitchens and permeating the entire complex. As a widely respected authority and intrepid researcher of hidden human dimensions, I can confidently say that a vast underground plot is currently being hatched. So, I can think of only one way to keep it from being served to inmates: stop the dishonest cooks.

Take the chefs and dump them from a helicopter in the sea or in the desert. How well would they fare in the conspiratorial food market against sharks, whales, snakes and scorpions? That's quite unlikely. If they ever make it out of the sea or the desert, they'll stop breaking the law and learn to be upstanding citizens now that they are out of business.

Third, impose a bill for any stay in this State facility to treat the virus that has spread in prison, pushing the criminals against cheque payments. Use cheques only as the method of payment. You could also exile to the desert those who refuse to comply or who pretend not to have a bank account. Let's not let them infect the good inmates in our fantastic facility.

(6)

AT MY LIBRARY WORKSTATION, I am taking notes for a Top Secret report that I will submit to the highest echelons of the Administration. So, of course, I made sure nothing got out to foreign countries, notably the British press. Important State business has been transacted here. I am fully aware that they have spies hidden in every corner, but I have had extensive training in deception and trickery. Since I started writing my first secret reports on the villagers, shopkeepers, market merchants, mosque-goers, mosque-refuseniks, and other suspicious people, residents of 'Ouja or guests, I've picked up a few methods to cover my tracks and throw off the adversary. Hamda La'war, the party's cell leader, said I did a good job. He even dubbed me a "professional," but I never saw any financial reward for my efforts. I asked, and he answered:

- Can you tell me if you get paid directly into your bank account every month?

- Yes, Sir. I do.

- So tell me, what else do you need?

- You did just call me a professional, right?

- Yes, I'm guilty of it. Who, though, is responsible for getting you the position at the bank?

- It is you, sir.

- Then, by all means, go ahead. Now, observe. I stepped in, and now you have a salary. The bank will forget to pay you at the end of the month if I use the phone on my desk to contact someone in the Capital. Repeat after me: once, twice, thrice... Until such time as you realise that We are the ones paying your salary.

- OK, sir, now I understand. That's right, the bank is indeed the party, and the party is the bank. No one can escape the limits of the circle.

- And whoever did is out of business.

That's clear. So, I stayed indoors and kept up my undying devotion to my two bosses, Mr Hamda and Mr Laroussi.

MY CONFIDENTIAL PAPERS are safely stashed under my bed in 'Ouja, so I have nothing to worry about. I haven't told anyone about them, not even Dalila, and we're planning to get married in twenty years, but she's still going to be sleeping in my room. Inshallah!

I was also able to locate a safe place in my library to store my confidential materials. At first, I would hide the papers on the bookshelves. Only a week ago, though, as I was cleaning the library floor, I saw a hole in the wall behind the bookcase in the very corner of the room. I extended my hand to introduce my fingers. My initial assumption that it was merely a crack was quickly dispelled when I realised it was actually a gaping hole. It was large enough to swallow my hand and wrist while staying entirely concealed beneath the bookcase. Not being able to feel any resistance with my fingertips was unnerving. I needed to inspect the hole, but moving the furniture was a major hassle. To make room, I had to first clear away the books. That's something I decided to put off for now. My hand was reintroduced very cautiously. It went down without a fight once more. Instantaneously, I took it back.

What could be under there? Nobody knows. What if a monster from another dimension or our own has decided to make it its bedroom? Should I disturb it while it sleeps, I may never feel my hand again. What if the hole was actually the entrance to a black hole? At that point, not only would my hand vanish, but so would the whole of my body. No, no. Must I play the odds? To what end? Let's go with the most effective strategy I'm aware of.

I returned equipped with my sweeper. After rotating the long stick, I inserted it into the opening between the wall and the bookcase. As expected! It went down smoothly.

Warning sirens started blaring in my brain right away. Could it be that the kitchen staff had begun excavating and had already reached the library? The hole's depth validated my suspicions of a cover-up. I found what appears to be the entrance of a hidden tunnel. Ahead of me was one of its two ends, the one I assumed to be the entrance. Unless they began it somewhere else and decided to finish it in the library. Well, that just makes my luck all the better and theirs all the worse. No matter what, the conspirators' ultimate goal was to penetrate the walls protecting us. Is this gaping wound a harbinger of their impending doom or the launch of a glorious future? Not easy to say. Does this indicate a shift in strategy on their part, or did they continue with the same game plan? Nighttime visits to the library would allow them to keep digging. Is it their hope that I won't discover the cavity? Unless they have some sort of drug or plot to brainwash me into submission!

ASTOUNDED AND BEWILDERED, I sat down and flipped it over. After some time, though, I was able to pull myself together and think clearly again. The cooks didn't seem to think it was odd to begin their tunnel excavation in the library rather than the kitchens. They probably did this so that suspicion wouldn't fall on them if the hole was discovered. Conversely, if they started in the kitchen and ended up in the library, they would have wasted their time. I can now see the gaping hole. Similarly, it would be visible to anyone who bothered to peek around the corner of the bookcase.

Sadly, this is of no use. The opening is not the start of a hidden passageway. Maybe it's just some rat being a moron and working restlessly.

Long-term inmates told me the ugly creatures are common in the warehouse and the gutters. The government has exhausted all available options in an attempt to intimidate them. They, too, plan to take advantage of our State's hospitality by spending time in our prestigious prison. Besides partying and dining lavishly at the taxpayer's expense, they also seem to be copulating and having children at an alarming rate, which goes against the grain of conventional thinking when it comes to family planning and is, therefore, unacceptable. In my opinion, this is a major roadblock to my endeavours as well. Let's say I convince the Administration to charge for both admission and visits to this respectable facility. In what way may we make the rats contribute as well? An excruciating pain has settled into my skull. The lowlifes would keep taking advantage, becoming immune to our pleas. Not that I anticipate their obeying the law. At least negotiating with humans is doable. So, how about rodents, specifically rats?

We cannot afford the rodents to outsmart us and enter our territory. What the hell! We're human, right? We created the most brutal forms of invasion. As a species, we will not submit to the authority of solitary rodents.

Because of this, I decided to strike back. Faster is better.

I'M GOING TO START by obstructing the rat. Because of his exploratory nature, I believe he is male. No female in her right mind would volunteer to build a long tunnel to nowhere. Only a rat with a perverted sense of adventure would try such a thing. However, I am here to safeguard the collected wisdom contained in these volumes. Since this is the case, I will not tolerate any kind of rat making use of a black hole terminal as a permanent place to live. The cosmos is arranged according to a higher order. The cosmic balance of this respected prison would be disrupted by any sudden changes.

Because the rats are antisocial elements, unwilling to pay their fair amount and unconcerned about the reform, they must leave and find new quarters. One has to be unwavering in this case. I'll start with the most challenging assignment: convincing the detainees to cover the costs of their confinement after we've laid out the issue. It would serve them well to do so. The rats should just be expelled from the premises; they obviously have no intention of ever paying their bills. In addition, the inmates at this distinguished facility maintain a sense of dignity as human beings. They despise associating with vermin. That must be taken into consideration. Never will it be acceptable for the human race to be lumped in with rats, who will be summarily removed since they contribute nothing to the Administration. This will have customers more motivated to pay their bills on time, with the help of a catchy slogan, like:

Gentlemen! Don't choose rats' life.

Pay your bill to the honourable prison.

I want to stress that not even the State's generosity is without bounds. Thus, as a devoted supporter of the free market, I propose turning this respectable institution into a for-profit business.

All we need is a cashier at the front desk. He will keep track of guest arrivals and present the bill upon departure. In addition, we should provide discounted rates to our loyal patrons, as their stays in the honourable Jail are often longer than those at rival hotels. Generally, the longer a client is required to stay in this facility, the more trustworthy he or she is deemed to be by the Administration. For this reason, we should implement deep discounts for those who take multiple or lengthy vacations at our now-for-profit facility. As a result, the government's costs will go down, and our incarcerated population will be encouraged to take on more responsibility.

However, we are not the 'Hilton' or 'Sheraton' either. To put it simply, we cannot accept the same price from a good client — say a murderer or bank robber — who is supposed to spend the rest of his days within our walls and ceilings. We need to come up with unbeatable prices if we want to stay competitive. The murderer will know he won't be treated like a rat if he pays on the day of checkout, which is likely the day he passes away if the motto is prominently displayed in the correct location, such as the lobby or main entrance. If a customer cannot make payments due to a major life event (such as death or a serious illness), we will make arrangements for his family to do so. If he has no living relatives, he will need to rely on social assistance. If the latter does not respond, the government will take money from his inheritance. I suggest looking into it before sending any long-sojourning big shot to our honourable prison to avoid the kerfuffle, especially if the individual in question has no legacy. We cannot afford to take chances with financially unstable inmates, even if they have killed ten people; this is a publicly traded company, after all. Instead, I suggest that the Administration force them to spend the rest of their lives outside of our facilities working for the greater good of society. If they refuse, feed them to the zoo's exotic animals. OK, with me.

SO, I DECIDED TO USE the rat hole as a hiding place for my paperwork. The tenant will be unable to enter the room and feed his voracious book-eating binge when he returns, likely late at night. Then I used a stone as a shield between my paperwork and the other side. My plan has been successful thus far. However, there was a threat that had me concerned. I assumed the rat, if it were smart, would put up a struggle rather than surrender. Perhaps he'll rally his people and come back with backup.

Then they'd pounce on the stone, shatter it, and grind it into pieces, all while punching holes in my papers and rendering my notes unintelligible. That is a serious threat. I gave it some thought for a while and then decided to wager on the rat's idiocy.

Basically, I was right on the money. It's been six days and six nights since anyone touched those papers. Either the scumbag didn't return home, or he was too ignorant to notice the red halo of *TSSD* (Top-Secret State Document) blinking in the tunnel, missing his chance for revenge. Perhaps he was scared and tried to hide. He lacked the guts to strike at the State's very heart, which would have prevented me from hiding out in his house any longer. As his confidence wavered, the initiative collapsed. As a result, I came out on top in the opening round.

Even worse, the little moron had no idea that his next move would cause widespread destruction for his whole species. As soon as I finish the preliminary stage of my note-taking, I will begin writing the report for submission to the highest authorities. I don't need Hamda La'war to send it because I am already in the Capital. Naturally, I'm hoping the Minister will give my work a nod of recognition. One day, if I'm lucky, my report will ride the elevator to the office of our BG President. I am confident that the BGP will act on my suggestions if he reads them. An invitation to meet the BGP face-to-face is inevitable. He'll tell me I did a great job and pin the same medal on me that Hamda La'war got for his contribution to the country by vaginal intercourse with the shoemaker's wife. Though I haven't cuckolded anyone just yet, I'm hopeful. At that point, the President would most likely offer me a high-level position in his Administration.

I've made it no secret that I have no political agenda. We don't know what Mr Aroussi has in his Mektoub, but I'll accept the position of Director of 'Ouja Bank for the BGP's sake. That's because I'm not an ambitious person. Had I been, I'd go for a longer drive. I have never strayed from my roots. But on the other hand, I can't stand the thought of getting ahead of my boss, Mr Aroussi, while he's stuck at the bottom. This behaviour is totally immoral. In all honesty, my loyalty prevents me from doing such an action. I also have a strong sentimental side that makes it difficult to control my boundless passion for and attachment to 'Ouja, my place of birth. It's true that the size and relative anonymity of my hometown make it unsuitable for anyone hoping to make a name for themselves in the world of business and finance. These drawbacks, however, can be advantageous in certain situations, such as covert dealings or operations. Foreign spies and local rivals excluded, there is no one around to keep you in check. The ultimate haven for forward-thinking bankers and bank clerks! Akin to the town of Bonanza! Even so, the only place I've ever truly felt at ease is in 'Ouja, which isn't likely to ever happen in the Capital.

Why we keep calling this huge, filthy, lustful city a Capital is beyond me. This is a pointless title, though. The Capital represents the sum total of the owner's investment in the business. So also, the capitalists probably aren't the people who live in the privately owned CAPITAL, but its owners and controllers. So, who owns the Capital? To the people, or to Big Business? Take some time to consider this.

It's obvious that the BG President holds title to the Capital City, which he received from the deposed King. It was believed that under the former government, the Monarch controlled not just the City-Capital and the other towns and villages that made up the population but also the other Capital, the business. In a nutshell, he was the only owner of all land, water, and air within the country and any revenue from the sale of hydrocarbons. It was by the Grace of God that His Majesty ruled over us, and by the Grace of God that he possessed us, body and soul. Without a single exception! And if God's grace is just an expression, then our lives were made easier because we merely had to submit to God's transcendental will (represented by the King) and let him carry our burden. As long as we obeyed the King and, by extension, God, we had peace.

AS LONG AS I OBEY ALLAH and his Prophet, I will be a good Muslim. So, whenever I can, I pray the recommended five times daily. I was instructed to observe the holy month of Ramadan by abstaining from food and drink during daylight hours. I hope to make the pilgrimage to Mecca when I'm 99 years old, inshallah. As I was also taught, this is because a pilgrimage to Mecca and Medina washes away all of your sins and makes you as pure as a baby. Even if I lived to be a hundred, I doubt I could avoid sin. Then, maybe, after a century, I'll be all washed up and prepared to meet Allah. Don't do it any earlier than this!

God and King are interchangeable in our subjugated existence, just as money and goods are. Goods were considered divine, while coins and banknotes represented the Monarch. Because everyone in the nation longs for a spiritual connection. Thus, everyone was peddling God to the masses in the form of hardcovers, paperbacks, and deluxe editions. Even in cyberspace. Anyone with good intentions—a Mufti, an Imam, a king, a president, a politician, a shopkeeper, a farmer, a banker, an accountant, an attorney, a teacher, a gardener, a police officer, a bartender would sell you God. As the saying goes, "God is in the details." You can find him just about anywhere. That's why our nation boasts the most devout citizens on the planet. We picture Allah in the four corners of an empty room, a prison cell, or a five-star hotel bar, sitting with us while we drink red wine or Johnnie Walker. As soon as we mention his name, he appears. We are the most devoted because we call on him always. It makes no difference whether we need him or not.

We don't mind that the King stayed in his palace all by himself. In fact, it's probably best to keep your distance. It's impossible to predict what might occur on a day when he is particularly irritated. Just who are the people of His Former Majesty? Servants. This agreement begins at the moment of our birth in his land and continues until the day of our deaths, at the conclusion of a long and fruitful life, Inshallah. But we are much more important to God. This is because we are His eternal slaves, and we don't mind one bit. We lose our freedom in either scenario. Who, exactly, is interested in liberty? That's fantastic news! Where there is no freedom, there is no accountability. Eternal life to God!

The people were safeguarded by that tacit agreement between the former Monarch and ourselves. The Sharia law system guided our government. No reasonable person could ever question its divine origin. But the United States and its Western friends attacked our government regularly. They pretended that the country's educational materials and programmes were hopelessly outdated. Therefore, our educational institutions became breeding grounds for future terrorists, saboteurs, bombers, and hijackers. Holy crap! That's a significant fib. I think they're just jealous because we found the right religion. Who or what stopped them from participating and becoming converted? You scoundrels! Democracy is something they won't stand for when it's practised in a foreign land.

OBSERVE WHAT HAPPENED. The United States and its Western allies have been hostile to the New Era and its leader ever since our Beloved General President began a couvolution to topple the King. He was never given a warm reception there. However, they acted like he was a putschist who had recently assumed power. Would you believe this?

The West is just envious of us, I realised recently. Those people want our oil and gas, but they can't see that our country would benefit more from an ultra-modern BGP if we could just get rid of the damned election hassle.

It is common knowledge that opulent hotels sold alcohol only to non-Muslim guests during the King's reign. I really feel bad about that! We had to get creative to get around Sharia law and drink booze in secret gatherings or for personal use. This elderly King had no clue what Islamic democracy was all about. Even when the topic was "democracy" in other countries, he ignored it. After taking over, our Beloved General President (BGP) has proclaimed that democracy is integral to Islam. We have a democratic religion, he declared. We can debate, discuss, have an opinion, and express it to God. If not, why did God repeatedly allow us to use reason in the Koran? If five prayers a day are incompatible with work hours, don't do them. One is enough. If you cannot fast and work in Ramadan, don't fast. Working is more important for your living. God will not provide you with bread. If you are too stressed and need glasses of wine to relax, drink. God will not resent it. He will not grudge. He doesn't care. Anyway, why should he?

As a result, numerous establishments formerly barred from selling alcohol were issued free liquor licences. Our streets are once again full of joy. Milder, friendlier, and more united communities of people emerged. Several bottles of wine later, many people saw the world in a new light. The best possible setting! Everyone at the pub was willing to buy the neighbour a drink for no other reason than to strike up a conversation. The sharing of libations and the bonding of man began to go hand in hand. Converts to our BGP's Democratic Islam have reported that persons who previously dragged their feet or pretended not to hear the Muezzin call the prayer over the mosque's loudspeaker at daybreak no longer feel any remorse for their behaviour. That was the most outstanding achievement of the New Era.

WE USED TO BE ONLY large consumers, but now we make and sell a lot of wine and beer, mostly to our non-Democratic Islamic neighbours. But our ultimate goal is to conquer the North American and European markets. We will soon be able to export wine in barrels and bottles, and it will flow through the sea, stunning our Christian Democratic brethren. In this country, we have a lot of smart people who realise that fossil fuels won't be around forever. We're already well on our way toward the next phase when humanity will use its Bacchus reserves for heat and electricity.

Plus, with the money we make from oil and alcohol, we'll be able to join the exclusive G7 club of the world's most industrialised nations. There is no reason to fret over the possibility that we may one day run out of hydrocarbons. The booze has finally arrived. This fortune will last forever. Just keep going. It will keep the money coming in.

The dawn of the New Era has been a smashing success. The economy, society, and culture of our country are all thriving. To the delight of both single and married men, new brothels sprung up like mushrooms in the towns, operating out of the lofty ceilings of opulent hotels. Many attractive young ladies, safe in the knowledge that their headscarves would keep them from being recognised, abandoned their isolated lifestyles to venture into the business world. They were never prevented from doing so by the monarchy, but now that they are free, they enjoy the sensation of the breeze caressing their flowing gowns even more. Despite the influx of professionals in the field from Europe and beyond drawn by an oil-rich country's prosperity, our local beauties are unfazed. The competition can indeed wear shorts and low-cut tops in public places like shopping centres, hotels, and souks. Our native ladies, on the other hand, will never remove their hijabs. As one might expect, religious beliefs are at the top of the list. It is important to be faithful to one's faith no matter what.

On the other hand, a cloak that covers the wearer head to toe is not a terrible idea. If you cover yourself in taffeta and cotton, no one will be able to identify you if you hide your face. Freedom for you is not bounded in any way, ma'am. You catch a peek at the bar as you enter the foyer of the five-star hotel and make your way to the twentieth floor, where a gentleman is waiting for you on embers. You look around the pub and notice the same small blonde who's always there at the same time every day. Oh, the poor thing must be so bored all the time!

A TINY BORDELLO HAS sprouted up on the outskirts of 'Ouja as well. Despite the many benefits that progress has brought, the locals have first objected. They considered organising a protest but ultimately decided against it. Years after the Marxist conspirators were locked up, the remaining radicals in society were hesitant to take charge of the mob. It goes without saying that a demonstration is meaningless without the Marxists. After the Jews had fled to Europe and Israel, who would be left to be arrested, prosecuted, and indicted?

The first reports of violence directed at hotels housing "night club escort females" emerged around that time. The cities' brothels were allegedly targeted by "the Muslim Brothelhood," according to some sources. I inquired. I discovered that some recently transplanted employees of a foreign multinational corporation wanted to recruit nightclub girls for their company and enrol them in the workforce against their will. On the other hand, in 'Ouja, they refrained from attacking the local bordello.

Bear in mind that the police and the powerful Hamda La'war were keeping an eye on the modest guest house that served as the bordello for three girls and their boss, Maria. Eventually, Hamda became unstoppable after amassing not one but two powerful positions: party cell head and mayor. Guess who the club owner considers a buddy and protector! Well! Naturally, we're talking about Hamda La'war.

After a few days, I was informed that the bordello was more packed than the cinema. That was a momentous achievement for a town devoted to worship customs for so long!

GOD'S GRACE HAD NOT abandoned us when it abandoned the King. We haven't made as much headway in the last quarter century as we have in the last few months, thanks to the prestigious couvolution of our BGP. Although the army carried it out on a night when there was neither a moon nor a single star in the sky, it is undeniably a popular event to which all the inhabitants contributed their voices. On that very night, our country's brightest star rode atop a tank steadily toward the Royal Palace.

With the BGP sitting atop the ultra-modern State, we will demonstrate to the world what prosperity and development look like in a hydrocarbon nation. Since the republic was declared, I have a better sense that my fellow citizens understand what's going on. The fact that they are no longer subject to the Monarch makes it seem like everyone is now King. The BG President concluded that a parliament was no longer required. Since the couvolution, they have become absolute kings, just as he desires. They understand that our country will be secure if no one opposes them. Subsequently, they would be unable to use their newfound monarchical power if the legislature was stacked with opponents. The President's decision to dissolve it was brilliant. And now look at us: freed from the shackles of obtuse opposition. It's no cost at all. But what is freedom without power, and what is power without money?

My strategic suggestion to the government is to amass and store as much money as possible in our banks to confront future difficulties. The State requires funds, and the profits from alcohol sales and the brothel trade help greatly. If you can get them to contribute to state projects over the next decade, do so; otherwise, tax the very hell out of them. Contrary to the oil industry, those businesses will never shut down or go bankrupt. They represent our collective future. For God's sake, just listen to the call! Their earnings will provide the State with a critical source of funds till the end of time.

Furthermore, their offerings bring joy to the world. There is no denying the usefulness they bring in assisting with stress reduction. Religious sceptics miss the mark. Welfare is not something religion condemns. Quite the contrary.

As for my final suggestion, it has to do with people who also oppose our BGP on religious grounds. They have overcrowded our honourable prison, and they sleep one on top of the other. To put it bluntly, it's hazardous. Many of them boast of attacking brothel girls in the name of loyalty to the global "Muslim Brothelhood," and they seem to take great pleasure in doing so. Gentlemen! I don't give a hoot if they're gay, but if they brag about assaulting women, I could lose my cool.

Please remove them before I order my new collaborator, Frankenstein, to commit mass destruction. Get rid of them. Honest individuals like Mr Aroussi and I should not have to put up with them as neighbours.

DON'T GET IT TWISTED, gentlemen! Our police and magistrates have my full confidence in their judgment. But there are a lot of reasons why I don't think this State hotel is the best venue for open or covert insurgents. It's never a good idea to have our respectable Administration's devoted and brave personnel working side by side with the heads of the conspiracy. To put it in simple words, I'm scared that we'll all get infected with the "Brothelhood" virus.

To put it in simple words, I'm scared that we'll all get infected with the "Brothelhood" virus.

It's no secret to me that Mr Aroussi and I are the targets of malicious gossip. "They claim to have served the King and his crumbling dictatorship in the past but are now dedicated to the New Era. But, of course, you can't count on them at all." So, they say. That's too bad. What cowardice! Never trust these lies. Those people are complete lapdogs.

And moreover, nobody is going to laugh at a tawdry joke like a scathing diatribe founded on false pretences. The same orchestra that played for the old King and for His Majesty is still playing for the Beloved General President, as far as I can tell, see, and hear. A few of the guys switched up their instruments. So, a trumpet or violin would be substituted for the baryton. Plus, Beethoven's Ninth Symphony would be played in place of Mozart's Requiem. That's the extent of the evolution thus far. If they can be trusted, then why can't we?

The former monarch claimed to have been established by God and the Holy Koran. He inherited the throne from his illustrious ancestors and father, so he could rightfully call himself King. If I may venture such a bold statement, the new ruler is instead presiding over his domain via the couvolution's beneficent influence. He was chosen as our BGP late one night by the tanks. There is a crucial distinction that should not be missed. I recognise the tanks as a symbol of the will of our people, and I bow to them. Anyway, it wasn't practical to wake millions of people and poll them on whether or not we should attempt the couvolution. That's a bit surreal! The couvolution had to go on without waiting for the people to wake up in the morning to give their approval. We, the people, are the army. This is an undeniable truth that cannot be disputed.

When it comes to the government, the same party that decided whether it would be sunny or rainy for so long is still in control. However, just as it was once the King's party, the BGP now controls it.

Mr Hamda La'war continued to serve as cell leader and council president until I departed 'Ouja. The originals, or at least copies, of my top-secret reports are probably still stashed away in his desk drawers, even though he is tasked with sending them on to Special Services. Never before have I received a personal invitation to meet the head of the Special Services, but I take Mr Hamda at his word. I have no reason to doubt him if he claims that the Minister, or anyone else, much appreciates and praises my reports. There's a good reason he's a national hero. I'm guessing it wasn't against British colonisation as he claimed, but rather the dictatorship of the shoemaker, that he got his medal of high struggle. That explains why he got along so well with Mrs Maria, the bordello's owner.

(7)

I AM AWARE OF THE GRAVITY of the accusations against me. However, since many of these accusations are fabrications by hostile governments and their agents, I will not address them. A worldwide plot is being orchestrated by the British, the Americans, the French, the Russians, and the Chinese against the couvolution and its real supporters. For their deep historical roots in deceit and falsehood, I single out the British, the Americans, and the French among those respectable members of the UN Security Council.

It's common knowledge that the three posed as friends of the deposed HM the King. But where were their officials the night he most desperately needed them? Sleeping? Come on! Tell this to others. All of our people were soundly asleep. But not the diplomats from the three countries that control about 90 per cent of this country's oil and gas fields and their military bases whose radars and satellites scan even the sand of the desert around the clock. No one showed up until the couvolution was over. This demonstrates the extent to which our BGP could be influential. Or, more precisely, deterrent, even to nuclear nations, indeed. Well, that's the whole purpose!

Despite their superpower capabilities, the United States and its NATO allies did not dare to intervene to stop the couvolution's tanks from reaching the royal palace. The result was that they were helpless to defend their old chap, the former King of our country. So, what is the point of friendship?

As we face the horrible cooks' conspiracy head-on today, let's draw the self-imposed conclusions we've been given from this lesson. Friends are not friends, and enemies are not enemies.

Everything is what is visible and what is not visible. We are both ourselves and others. I am Bassam Bourasin and not Bassam Bourasin. Charged with multiple offences and discharged. Both guilty and innocent.

THE ADMINISTRATION has no idea that the plot has already taken root in the kitchens of this State bastion. What would become of the New Era and its wonderful couvolution if we let the cooks do anything they wanted? Like Nostradamus, I can now predict the future. There will be fire and blood splattered everywhere. In fact, I'll tell you that it was under quite similar circumstances that the French Revolution got its start. However, its kitchens were established by philosophers outside the Bastille. Because of this, I must stress again that it is not prudent to house the subversive Muslim Brothelhood in this illustrious prison beside the obedient citizens who serve the republic. They were arrested red-handed by the police with explosives and weapons. As they toured through the republic's brothels, they caused quite a commotion by picking fights with patrons, spitting at the women, and otherwise interfering with their work. All eyewitnesses agreed that the troublemakers' ultimate goal was to kidnap the women and force them to work for their own firm. It's a multinational company; they have offices worldwide, including in our country. The troublemakers wanted the brothel girls to staff their organisation, the Muslim Brothelhood. The public and the female population were in danger because they were armed. There were gunshots reported from some of the brothels. They were assaulted by the police. While some were captured, others managed to get away. In the meantime, many people were killed, and hundreds more were injured.

I guess that the individuals who escaped can still contact those who remain within our fortifications. That freaks me out. If the Muslim Brothelhood is a multinational organisation, it stands to reason that its members will not give up without first attempting to free their comrades.

The counter-couvolution is slithering beneath our feet like a venomous serpent. Assume we don't give a damn and don't take any precautions. In that event, the country will be quickly overrun by a frenzied mob attempting to remove our BGP and re-establish the King or the Prince or anybody happens to be around, even a blind, an idiot, or a squint-eyed officer, as long as he accepts the nation to be hijacked by the Muslim Brothelhood.

Never trust the mob if the mobsters are Muslim Brothelhood members. They have no respect for women and much less for males. With firearms and grenades in hand, they storm the place of business, yelling, "Allah Akbar!" Consider all the heads cruelly chopped during the French Revolution, although its cooks were philosophers, not members of the Muslim Brothelhood. What, therefore, should we expect? A brighter future with mobsters in power?

We might even be driven to postpone the modern State until the day of resurrection. This is precisely what hostile foreign powers from the industrialised world aim to encourage. That is the strategy! Suppose we have to come to terms with them. In that case, we need to be firm: our exports must include, without fail, jobless people who are yearning to leave the nation (we don't need them), anarchists, angry seditious adolescents, narcotics and drug dealers, pimps, and Brothelhood mobsters.

I'm familiar with the arguments against drugs and those who sell them. I, like most people, enjoy reading daily papers. This whole diatribe about killing kids is just ridiculous. I'm willing to share some new information I've gathered in the field with you.

APPROXIMATELY ONE MONTH ago, I was fortunate enough to meet a drug dealer of legendary status. I am now fully up-to-date on the topic due to my new knowledge.

Mr Suleiman Mughli is a middle-aged man with dark eyes, black hair, a proud hawk's nose, and a perpetual, slight smirk in the corner of his mouth. But this is not his most notable characteristic; he exhibits an impenetrable apathy toward all individuals who profess to be confined for political reasons. To both of our relief, I am not one of them, which accounts for the warmth of our friendship.

Mr Mughli has no issue converting the assumptions of the Muslim Brothelhood mobsters into gags, but he keeps his own opinions to himself.

You must know that our State hotel is bustling with those kinds of guests. They have group prayers and read their Korans regularly, and if questioned by another inmate, they will express their open hostility to the old and the new governments. When the time comes, such men are the ones who will undoubtedly provide a hand to the cooks. There has been no talk of escape or insurrection, but that makes me more suspicious. Therefore, I keep a close eye on them because they pose a severe problem to our BGP.

Since his first day there, Suleiman had no trouble acquiring a bed, let alone a comfortable one, which was not the case for most of the guests. What with all the chaos, that's nearly miraculous. But it looked like he had good ties to Zorro, the enclosure's leader who reports directly to the guards. They couldn't have asked for a better responsible party. When the iron gate is locked, anarchy reigns.

ACCORDING TO MUGHLI, the drug trade was subjected to discriminatory restrictions despite generating substantial revenues in foreign currency for the State. We are, first and foremost, a nation that produces one of the most well-known cannabis brands in the world. The gift of God is too precious to waste by discarding it. Instead, we must preserve and protect it as a national asset if we ever run out of fossil fuels. Additionally, we should back the honest people who make and export Hashish and Heroin (we also have fields of Opium) rather than going after them to appease foreign powers that are clueless about the benefits of such a trade.

As I discovered today, however, our Beloved General President is personally trying to elevate the status of this hitherto shady industry in the eyes of both the American people and the international community. Gentlemen! Soon, he will speak at the September meeting of the United Nations General Assembly. He'll elaborate on why his government encourages drug cultivation in the form of hashish, Opium, and heroin. To hear such sage advice is something I eagerly anticipate.

I can no longer minimise our country's priceless economic heritage. The happy days are coming.

AFTER BEING HERE FOR a few weeks, I saw several cliques forming in the dorm.

First, there's Zorro's gang. I've heard rumours that several, if not all, are a bunch of crooks, robbers, thugs, and killers. Strangely, though, the newcomer Suleiman, a successful businessman with worldwide contacts, seemed well at home among those petty thugs and schemers. It's yet another aspect of his personality that has puzzled me.

The second group is commanded by "the Afghan" veteran of the Muslim Brothelhood, Mohamed Mashavir. That so-called Afghan, whose little stature belies his heroic efforts on behalf of the Mujahideen during the Soviet occupation of Afghanistan, was a remarkable warrior. He allegedly arrived in our country with suitcases full of cash after the fighting ended. He was planning to open a business in the City. However, his enterprise was highly unusual in that he was preoccupied almost entirely with importing guns and explosives—not for the army or the police, but evidently for some rebels who planned to start a putsch against the King. Oh, such a jerk! He wasn't a Prime Minister or a military officer like our BGP. Nonetheless, he intended to steal the honour of the couvolution from the right man in the wrong position (at the time, not BGP yet)! The rest of the story is common knowledge. And, as expected, he and the rest of the sheep around him failed and were eventually captured. The authorities cut off their long, ugly beards (imported from Afghanistan) and locked them in this cell, where they pretended to be moral leaders in front of their cold, cynical cellmates. No new members will join the Brothelhood. The public in our country looks down on individuals who try their luck while armed and fail. Respect for guys who threaten and abuse women is not tolerated in this reputable institution, even among hardened criminals who do not commit rape or murder. Therefore, they cannot convince the recalcitrant to join them without weapons or money. Still, the Afghan has considerable sway over his followers, who are not entirely Arabs. I recognised a Kashmiri Indian, a Pakistani, an Indonesian, and a black man named Bilal. This proves the conspirators acted at the behest of some foreign power to bankroll and support the Global Brothelhood organisation. Apparently, they could infiltrate government institutions such as the military and the police. That's why our Dearly Beloved General President, also the Minister of the Interior at the time, decided to pull the rug out from under them at just the perfect time. If not for that, we could still be using the Afghan as our BGP today. (*That's a very lame concept if you ask me. Delete!*)

HOWEVER, SOMETHING about Brothelhood's behaviour perplexes me. Hassan told me their ultimate goal was to depose the King and replace him with an Islamic government. This is precisely the point! Our lives were thoroughly ruled by Sharia law and the religion under the monarchy. There are even Islamic banks that weathered the couvolution unscathed. Where therefore does the issue lie? What was the Afghan and the Brothelhood's true goal? I'm sure all he wanted to do was depose the

King and assume power for himself. He was driven by an insatiable lust for power and aided by an outward display of religious fervour. If he'd been able to move to England, he would have tried to perform the couvolution there. Many Muslims, it is said, make their home in the United Kingdom. An astute veteran of Afghanistan and the Muslim Brothelhood could seize this chance to further his ambitions. And what could possibly stop him? The greater the difficulty of the undertaking, the more prestigious the rewards. The Afghan has probably given this idea some serious thought first. Perhaps he had even made an attempt to enter the UK illegally. Crossing the English Channel from Pas de Calais is a breeze. It has been relayed that many Afghans flock there after escaping the nation following the invasion by the Taliban, who represent yet another Salafi Brothelhood.

But the British are as cunning as foxes. Because the SAS and CIA presumably knew the Afghan from the day they were training him as a fellow Mujahedeen, they most likely intercepted his intentions before he could carry them on. But I can't completely rule out the possibility that they sent him here to get him out of British soil. That's why I called them deceitful companions. But they're not just ignorant; they're also completely blind. They failed to remember that if the Afghan and his Global Brothelhod were able to flourish in this country, there was no reason they couldn't do the same in England. Their influence would increase as a result. So, the British and possibly half of the CIA accepted the conspiracy out of fear and political blindness.

On this particular point, Hassan disagreed with me. He is so naive that he thinks this plan would never work in England since most Brits profess the Christian faith. How ridiculous! As if the vast majority of us are not Muslims! Who said upheavals care about people's religious beliefs? It's all about politics, duh! But seriously, what was the IRA trying to accomplish all those years? Continual couvolution! They were never successful at anything other than killing people. Is the British throne in jeopardy because of them? Nope! It is not because we are Muslims that the Muslim Brothelhood has been attempting couvolutions in our countries. The IRA wasn't anti-monarchical because of Ireland's Catholic majority. I assured naive Hassan that had our BGP been a British subject, he would have removed HM the Monarch just as swiftly as he had deposed HM our former King. The rookie laughed and said:

- I knew you were a prankster, but I had no idea you were also a global mastermind of strategy. Again he laughed, stopped, collected himself, and continued: So you think the United Kingdom may expect a coup that a guy like your president or the so-called Afghan would execute and succeed? And that's it?

- Sure, why not? Is it not a country like any other?

- Yes, indeed. Like ours, though? My God! That's a cutting-edge hypothesis. Therefore let's commit some severe brainpower to test it. Because if even 30% of it turns out to be accurate, we'll be on the cusp of becoming a global superpower! The laughter was deafening! ...

I needed clarification as to what of my assumptions amused him. Notwithstanding, he continued:

- So, the first sergeant to wake would take his tank to Buckingham Palace before sunrise, remove the British monarch, and announce his coup on the BBC. Well, that settles it. Right?

- Right, but not any sergeant, lad, I retorted angrily. We are talking of our Beloved General President. He isn't a simple sergeant but a full-fledged General. A military genius!

- General? Allow me to be sceptical. The genius, on the other hand, is probably one because we are the dunderheads who believe it. And since he is wasting his time on nonentities like us, he is qualified to be King of the United Kingdom. How easy it must have been for him to find his way to the Royal Palace! Just a quick coup at dawn, and it's all over! They will greet him in the same way that this country's nyaffs and other gnats greet any early-morning putschist: with music and dance in the streets, standing up clapping, and hullabaloo. All the fanfare! (Pause). What would they do if your genius sought to open his mouth and spoke about a coup in the British Barracks? Do you know?

Interlocked, I asked:

- What would they do?

- They'd remove him from his legs in his underwear as he was shitting and lock him up in a mental institution. They'll have every motive to do so, my friend. We should have done it if we were rational people rather than a bunch of dum-dum simple-tons.

I shuddered at those remarks as we stood in the courtyard with the other detainees on their daily walk. I didn't like the direction the conversion was headed. As a result, I did not respond to deter him from debating more. But he did not share my concerns and went on:

- Have you ever wondered why so many deadly coups never occurred in Western countries? Why, for God's sake, do they only occur in the cursed Third World? Is that real magic? Fate? Is it bad luck? Or is there a plausible explanation for the phenomenon?

I said, utterly terrified and eager to put an end to the argument:

- I don't have a crystal ball. I am not a diviner. Besides, as I already stated, I am apolitical and cannot accept the British meddling in our domestic matters. They appear to feel they are still masters of this country, but we are free. So why did they grant the Prince asylum? Why were we sent the Afghan terrorist and his foreign legion?

- You're uttering gibberish. Who said Britain did all of that, man? The Afghan is a product of the United States. You should question him about his CIA contacts, but he won't tell you. Even so, I fail to see why the Americans would pit him against our King. Now, forget about it all. How about you? Are you still with the King?

- Would you rather see me following the Afghan?

- Hell! But you're a counter-revolutionary! I assumed you were a fan of the president!

This fox is right! I don't know how I responded to his provocation by another. I didn't even think before talking. When I understood that my response implicated a defence of the monarchy, one of the unfair charges I am facing, it was too late! (*Delete all this delirium. You've taken a risky turn. For God's sake! Are you writing down this stuff as self-defence or as suicide? Stupid!*)

I corrected the shot:

- I am indeed a fan of our Beloved General President.

- How can you be on two opposing sides at once?

- Stop it! I told you I am apolitical and a BGP supporter.

- That's an escape! You are waffling. You can't support both the loser and the victor, can you?

- That's right!

His watchful green eyes shined in the sunlight.

- Are you kidding?

I don't know what the man was trying to make me confess. I just said:

- No, I am not, Mister Hassan.

He appeared irritated but stayed composed. When I looked at him again, I noticed him staring out at the blue sky beyond the towering white walls. A group of twittering birds flew through the sky above us. Then he bowed his head, quietly shook it as if to get rid of a troubling notion, and said:

- Never mind! It doesn't matter. Politics are not your favourite game.

- I told you so.

- I hope you are more talented as a bank clerk.

- I am not conceited, but I know my job far better than most. You should ask Mr Aroussi since he is your chamber mate.

- I trust you are.

JUST THEN, I SPOTTED a smiling face coming toward me. I blinked in the sudden, blinding sunshine and rubbed my eyes in surprise. At first, I didn't identify the silhouette. Still, as it drew nearer, I saw that it was indeed Mr Aroussi, complete with his trademark bald head, thick spectacles, and beautiful moustache hanging. Even though he wasn't bald or overweight, for some reason, my first impression of him was of the deceased Jewish man. Moosa Dawood! A peculiar notion entered my head at that moment; it was as if the dead guy and Mr Aroussi were connected by some unseen thread. Hassan swiftly drew me out of my confused daydream by saying:

- When you talk of the wolf, you see its tail. Look who's coming.

A few steps and the soft voice of Mr Aroussi greeted us:

- Good day, gentlemen. How are you?

I felt so glad to see the Boss that I stepped on, gripped his shoulders, and hugged him. Which I don't usually do.

Mr Aroussi seemed happy.

- Hello there, Bassam. I knew you were here too. I am sorry! I made no attempt to drag my employees down with me.

- I am delighted to see you again, Mr Aroussi. I hope you have a comfortable stay.

- Comfortable? Ha Ha! Let us not go overboard. I'm in the pit with you and everyone else. (After a little pause, he added): I came as soon as I received your message. So you have something vital to tell me. What's the problem? Urgency?

I had nothing of the like to say to him. I was perplexed for a second. Then I remembered my commitment to Frankenstein and realised what had happened. He had most likely arranged for this unexpected rendezvous. Hassan then attempted to gracefully exit, believing that our chat was private.

- There's no need for you to depart, I said quickly. I will not divulge any information. The subject is a new acquaintance you're probably familiar with because he works at the Hammam. I'm referring to Mr Frankenstein. He is well-known in this area.

My two buddies lifted their brows and looked at me with wide-open eyes. They appeared taken aback. Perhaps even shocked.

My goodness! What the hell did I say that clearly vexed them?

Chapter 4

The BrotheLhood

(1)

MR AROUSSI SAID:

- My poor old boy! I see the jail hasn't developed your mental capacities. Is it to tell me about your friends Frankenstein, Dracula, King Kong, etc ... that you insisted on meeting me urgently?

I replied briskly and somewhat rashly:

- Dracula and King Kong aren't my friends, sir, and I am not interested in getting them a job.

I did not realise yet that the Boss was not talking seriously. But Hassan laughed cheerfully while Mr Aroussi said, somewhat irritated:

- So you want to get a job for Frankenstein? Congratulations! I wasn't aware you are now a film director or producer, maybe. And in which location do you intend to shoot your er... movie? In jail?

Then, it dawned on me that I had omitted entirely that nobody knew who Frankenstein was since it was a nickname I had invented for Salah, the man of the Hammam. I have used it only in this report, never daring to use it before the inmates. Humbly, I tried to explain:

- It is not a movie, sir... er... I wanted your permission to er... I mean to ask you about the possibility of hiring him for the bank.

Again, I missed the shot. Then, instead of explaining, I made it more complicated, forgetting to call the man by his name.

Exasperated, the Boss cut a grim face and said:

- Would you stop talking nonsense, Bassam? I am not in the mood to enjoy your silly jokes. So stop going around the bush and tell me straight what you managed so clumsily to say, and without more conundrums, please.

The misunderstanding became evident. I had to be clear:

- I beg your pardon, sir. The man I am talking about is a specialist in every kind of security system used by banks. He was working at South Bank before it was robbed. I thought he might be helpful to us. I promised to ask you about hiring him, but I did not say it is urgent to...

Anxious, Mr Aroussi interrupted me:

- Who's the man?

- Frankenstein, sir. He's working in the shower room ... er ...

- What am I supposed to do with him? Why are you telling me this nonsense? Do you think I have nothing to do but ... (He stopped brusquely, seemed to remember something, then said): Wait a minute. Do you mean that awful giant of the shower room?

- Yes, sir, indeed, I replied with relief. The point is he doesn't feel comfortable with that job. As he complained, sir, and I promised ... er ...

- What did you promise, Bassam?

I faltered:

- Ahem ... that he er ... with your permission, indeed... I mean that he might hope, just hope, sir, to be... to be... er... one day... not now... er... employed by... by 'Ouja Bank.

Mr Aroussi's face veered green. It seems I succeeded only in infuriating him. My misgiving filled him with a deaf rage, and he shot me with a stern gaze from under his spectacles while scowling and pursing his lips. Something went wrong since the start - I should have noticed it - and I was perplexed, unsure whether I had to speak or merely shut up and avoid further damage. But Hassan, who had stopped giggling, winked at me and said:

- The bank is hardly the right place to hire that guy, Bassam. It is not just his physiognomy but also his past. He is feared. Who would hire him?

- Hmm ... I thought that he is, er ... respected here.

- Don't be silly, Bassam! Roared Mr Aroussi, still angry.

- No, sir, honestly! You know me. I am not trying to mislead you or anything. But the guy sounded kind and... er ... polite. So I believed he might be offered a chance with us ...er...

Again, interrupting, he shouted:

- When? Don't you see we are in deep shit?

- Not now, sir. When we're released.

The two men exchanged a glance. Then Mr Aroussi said:

- Why are you so stubborn, Bassam? First, you know that this is neither the time nor the place to talk of business. Second, even if I were still at the bank, I would not hire your Dracula, and I advise you to keep away from him.

- Well, sir! I mumbled submissively. I thought that a specialist ...

- A specialist in the bank robbery, yeah! That's great! And that's the guy you wish to contract, Mr Bassam. Have you lost your mind?

Startled and appalled by what I heard, I desperately sought words but could not find any. The Boss went on:

- I wonder whether you are aware of what you do and say. Is it clever to meddle on behalf of a mobster and to be so concerned with his career?

- A mobster! I exclaimed in disbelief.

- What do you think he is, Mr Bassam? A scholar? A scientist? A businessman?

I was dumbfounded.

- But he told me he had worked at South Bank.

- Of course! He did when he robbed it, said Hassan. That is why he is detained. You should be more discerning with the inmates you choose as buddies.

MY SURPRISE IS COMPLETE. It felt like I had just landed from a spacecraft, and nobody had seen me coming. I had evolved into an alien. Everyone knew who the man was whom I had trusted enough to refer to him as a friend and make him an associate, and I was the last to learn his true identity. Then, the question that started trotting into my mind became: is Frankenstein involved in the plot of the cooks? Is he a member of the terrible Muslim Brothelhood? He could be. He is, indeed, one of them. Did they not attack the country's brothels, trying to convince the ladies to work for their multinational company? What would stop them from robbing the banks?

Disturbed to the utmost degree and dismayed by my gullibility, I hastened to apologise to my Boss, whose chin was still vibrating with wrath.

- I am sorry, sir, I didn't realise. Sorry! The creep lied to me. I sympathised with him, thinking he was a poor devil who lost his job. I intended to help him and use his competence as ... as ...

- As a robber, snapped Mr Aroussi sarcastically.

- No, sir, I thought he was a security specialist.

- You're a tart, my boy. Have you told him anything about our security systems?

I stammered:

- Yes, er ... I mean no, of course. We were just chatting. I don't recall all that we said.

Under the transparent glasses, I could see the Boss's eyes widening and his brows rising. I felt practically cracking and melting under his severe look, like a thin coat of ice under the sun, while he closely examined me.

- If that man decides to loot the 'Ouja bank after being freed or tells his buddies outside what you informed him, it will be your responsibility. He made you his accomplice; you should go and confess to the cops.

- He wouldn't be released for at least two years, said Hassan. But there is little doubt that he has allies or accomplices abroad. Nevertheless, Bassam shouldn't be concerned about what he said to the thug because he meant well. Everyone speaks; it's not illegal, and the cops can't intervene if there's no crime.

The Boss yelled angrily:

- You should learn to shut your bloody mouth in jail. I'm worried about everything related to the bank, not just what you said to that thug. Each profession has its trade secrets, which should be honoured. If we start sharing everything we know, we will ultimately be left alone since everyone who had previously trusted us will now be potential enemies. You already know that a dishonest bank clerk won't succeed in the industry. Then, for the love of God, hold your tongue!

- Yes, sir. I'll be mute and blind.

- There you have it, Mr Bassam. Have you ever been questioned by the police?

- No, sir, not yet.

- So, if you're anything like me, you know nothing. You're just an employee like the others. Have you received a visit from the solicitor?

- I don't have a solicitor, sir.

- What on earth are you waiting for? You must hire one. Do you intend to spend the rest of your days here?

- I hadn't thought of it yet, I mumbled.

- You must think of it right away, sonny. What's the source of your disinterest in your own life? You have no business being here. I'll send you my lawyer, Mr Ammar, a good and kind friend of mine. His fee is a little high, but don't be concerned. For my sake, he'll make an exception for you. Anyway, you're not poor, he added after a brief pause. You can buy your freedom. You did receive benefits while working at the bank.

- Yes, sir, I can pay him. I appreciate you.

Mr Aroussi exhaled a sigh of relief. He rubbed his bald head with his palm, sweeping the courtyard in a circular motion, and said:

- Good! I've always thought you were a wise man. Mr Hassan, who is here, is our witness before God. I accept full responsibility for all of our activities at the bank. You know nothing and could not be charged with a misdemeanour. If you are questioned, simply state that Mr Aroussi is more knowledgeable about the subject than I am. Is that clear?

- That is very clear, sir. Thank you so much for your generosity. You know I'm devoted to you and... Ahem!

I was about to add, "and to our beloved President and the Administration," but I cut it short, thinking it was inappropriate given the circumstances. Furthermore, if I was sure of Mr Aroussi's loyalty to the government, I was far less sure about Hassan, whom I couldn't easily locate. And I wasn't entirely wrong because when the lawyer came to see me a few days after our meeting in the courtyard, he hinted that Hassan wasn't exactly the person to go to.

THE MEETING WITH THE lawyer was brief but to the point. Mahmoud, the black guard, came to get me from the library around ten o'clock in the morning. He said that someone wanted to see me and that I should change my clothes because my visitor was an important person. I was so surprised that if I hadn't restrained myself, I would have kissed the guard who had brought me such good news. Of course, I did not think even for a second it was the lawyer. I'm not sure why my mind raced, and I was filled with the belief that it was some VIP from the Administration who had likely recalled my loyal services and wished to honour me with an unexpected visit.

I was going to make a fool of myself in front of Mahmoud by bragging about "my relations." And yet, I managed to hold back at the last second. For some reason, I just couldn't put my faith in the guard.

- First, I'd like to shave, I told him.

- To shave? That's it? Then you go to meet with the lawyer in these rags!

It was like an icy shower poured down on my head all at once. I was paralysed.

- What about the lawyer? Do you mean the visitor is the solicitor?

Mahmoud's eyes glowed:

- What on earth do you think he is? The President of the republic?

CURIOUSLY ENOUGH, I was no longer eager to rush to the parlour. I kept telling myself that I didn't need Mr Ammar or any lawyer. It was Mr Aroussi's idea, not mine. Should I rely on Mr Ammar for my defence, just to please my Boss and demonstrate my obedience to him? I believe the lawyer is pointless. I am working on my Top-Secret report, which will undoubtedly grant my release and, indeed, my promotion. Since I started working in this library, I felt I was becoming a scientist.

- A scientist? You?

- Yes me. Go to hell, Angel!

I learned a lot. I discovered a rat hole that may hide a tunnel to another world in the sky. Who knows with whom the Brothelhood is allied?

- With the whores?

- Nope.

- Who, then? The cooks?

- Indeed. But not only them. They are simple agents.

I mean the power of the superpower behind their conspiracy. Nobody knows about the multinational plot of the Muslim Brothelhood yet. I will soon make the headlines of national and international newspapers.

Bassam Bourasin For Nobel Prize

Wise Scientist New Discovery

Hole in the Wall Leads to New Universe

BrotheLhood Plotting from Prison

Aliens Attack With Multinational Corporation Rats

That's because I'm not acting blindly. As a scientist, I know that the Brothelhood could not threaten our Beloved General President without an alliance with an extraterrestrial Superpower. I don't believe the Americans would give a damn about helping the rats against us. It's none of their business. They just care for oil and gas. That's it!

As a scientist, I also know that a well-stuffed secret report is far more effective than three dozen lawyers. That's how things work, not just in our country but also in the USA. Ask the Americans. They passed masters in classified reports about aliens.

This is a matter of statecraft and technicity, gentlemen. If the secret report is well-woven and embellished, filled with numerous plots and conspirators, it will reach the highest echelons of the Administration. And if it is tested and trusted, it may even cause some heads to fall off. Whether or not it is disclosed, its effect is similar to that of a small nuclear bomb, like Hiroshima. Nothing happened! No need for apologies! It is no secret that many high-ranking government officials rose to their current positions because they were skilled writers of classified reports. Many others, in contrast, had abruptly and unexpectedly stepped down from the podium due to a secret report condemning or simply charging them with disloyalty. Staline, for example, was a champion in secret reports. I read history. that's how I became a scientist. As for our country, we are undeniably a society that values secrets (which is why we don't have any) and reports (which is why we promote their authors)!

As a government institution of custodianship, the police have nothing to do with all this. However, every citizen of our country must report either to the party's cell in his district or village or to the party's headquarters in the Capital. That's because the party and the fatherland are the same, said Hamda La'war. Therefore, we are all expected to be honest *Part-riots.*

I define a true *Part-riot* as someone who is devoted to the party that is leading the motherland. Every citizen in this country is expected to report to the party - even if he is not a member - any acts or facts that he believes are useful to security. No obligation, whether to family, tribe, or employer, overrides the duty we owe to our glorious party. This was a well-established tradition during the king's reign, which was continued, underlined, and emphasised as the only safety line after the *couvolution.*

We must open our eyes and ears more than ever before: the threats are real. Many foes and vassals of foreign powers (including the aliens), such as that Afghan, or the cooks - or the rats, for that matter - intend to organise a *counter-couvolution* that will shatter our economy, put an end to the profitable trades born with the new regime, and, of course, overthrow our *BGP* (Beloved General President). The Prince could then rule the country from his European refuge before returning with the mercenaries and taking control.

Hell! Hassan was correct when he said that I am an *excellent strategist*! I had no idea, and now I'm even surprised to think so clearly about those various challenges. Because all events in my village have an undeniable international dimension, my long service at 'Ouja bank opened my eyes to the world stage. Nonetheless, I don't rule out the possibility that Hassan was flattering me and exaggerating my abilities. I don't trust him. This is also the lawyer's opinion, who, as useless as he may be, is not entirely devoid of common sense. I prefer to remain grounded instead of relying on the panegyric endearing of a whimsical adventurer. I've never been duped by sycophants whose tricks are as old as the world. I know something about that. I'm not going down without a fight.

Furthermore, I am fundamentally apolitical and unconcerned with the vagaries of those ambitious and greedy individuals who play the treacherous roles of political opposition in the Brothels while threatening the ladies. That does not mean depriving myself of the pleasure of notifying the Administration of their nefarious deception. I do not joke when I write my classified reports. It is my vocation, my second career and my duty in a country where such things can propel one to the top while sending another to the bottom. I am aware that there are numerous dangers. However, as long as I am a *PART-RIOT*, I will swim to the shore. Now, rather than the solicitor, I'm entering the high seas with my top-secret report as a life buoy.

NONETHELESS, I WENT to meet him to express my goodwill.

We crossed the courtyard and entered Block C, facing Block A, where I was staying. The hotel has three main buildings: A, B, and C. They are linked by smaller courtyards and corridors with numerous iron gates. In the centre, there is the first courtyard, at the bottom of which are usually parked police vehicles and officers and other employees' cars, separated from us by a wire netting with open and unguarded gates leading to the towers and the hotel's main entrance.

Each block has at least six levels, with inmates housed in cramped chambers. The basements are larger than the landings, so many more customers live in the underground. Nonetheless, I didn't give this story much credit, even though I knew the dreadful freezers were under the blocks. Before meeting some customers returning from a stay in those Siberian cells, I had no idea what the word *Freezer* meant in these surroundings. Those people appeared dead more than alive. They described a veritable Gulag to me... But without Staline, which aroused my suspicion. That's why I did not believe them. Only one talked about the great Russian leader. He said, "our Gulag is much like the Russian under Staline's communist regime". I didn't acknowledge that the leader who made the secret reports an invaluable industry for the government was a communist. I said, "I don't like the communists. I like Staline. I don't think he is one of them." The man looked at me as if I insulted his religion, then walked away. I didn't see him since.

(2)

MISTER AMMAR IS A MAN in his early fifties, nearly my Boss's age. Spruce, businesslike, white-haired head, salt and pepper moustache, narrow and dark eyes under bushy brows, and a placid face. White skin, regular features, apart from a long, slender nose that draws attention to itself, Cyrano de Bergerac-style. His speech is quick, loud, and clear, and the words flow freely from his fleshy lips.

He was sitting behind an oblong table when I entered the empty little room with the guard, who pointed to a chair facing the lawyer at the other end of the table and stepped back to stand up in the doorway behind me as I sat down. Apart from the table and the two chairs, there was nothing noticeable in the room, illuminated by the sun rays sliding through the stern bars of the window.

The solicitor's dark suit seemed too elegant for the setting and contrasted with my rags. I was embarrassed to show up to that meeting in sloppy attire, but I had no choice. However, Mr Ammar put me at ease after a first long glance in which he appeared to be weighing me. He smirked and said:

- How are you, Mr Bourasin? (And without waiting for my answer, he added): As you probably know, Mr Aroussi referred your case to me, even though I am swamped these days. But I couldn't say no to an old friend. So I promised to look into the case and see if I could get your conditional release before the trial. But I need your willing cooperation to enlighten me. What exactly are your charges?

- What are your exact charges?

So he came without even taking the time to look into the affair! I knew I didn't need a lawyer. Now, I am sure.

- Hmm... well, your excellency, I'm not sure.

- Please, address me as Mr Ammar. (He paused for a moment to consider my response, then added): You must know at least the reason for your arrest, Mr Bourasin. There's a reason you're here. So, what brought you to this... er... house?

- They did not inform me. The two police officers who brought me here from 'Ouja only stated that I had been invited to a fantastic hotel.

- Have you been questioned?

- Only by the shrink, sir.

- Shrink? Are you referring to the Social Assistant? (Again, he did not wait for the answer!) In general, he may be informed of some cases. What did he tell you?

- Nothing! I mean nothing of any coherence, sir. He claimed I was accused of corruption, fraud, various and repeated scams, and, most importantly, criminal and royalist organisation. So, at the very least, twenty years in prison.

The lawyer muttered in a low tone:

- Odd! This appears to be a case similar to Mr Aroussi's. Did he inform you of the charges' grounds?

- Ground? No. No ground. In my opinion, the charges have no ground because they came from a high level, you know. Higher than he could figure out.

- Really!

- Yes, indeed. I mean the sky. Wherever angels are plotting with cooks and...you know!

- No, I don't know at all. (He looked into his watch). Please, Mr Bourasin, let's stick to the facts.

- All right! The shrink is a nice man. He found me an imme-diate job at the library. Although I have yet to receive my salary, it is not a bad job. I have no idea when they will pay me. I've been working for the Administration of this hot... for over three months.

The lawyer cut me off, saying impatiently:

- Please, Mr Bourasin, we don't have time to waste in palaver. Simply answer my questions.

- Sir, yes. What was the question?

- You haven't been interrogated by the police, and you haven't met the prosecutor. Have you any reason to think that those charges are of any substance?

I did not understand the question, so he put it otherwise.

- Are you guilty or not guilty?

It was a terrifying and perplexing question. Mr Mahmoud, the guard, was standing just behind me, his ears wide open, listening for my responses so he could report what he heard in the meeting to the Administration. It was a delicate situation for me.

On the one hand, if I followed my instinct and answered 'not guilty,' I would have the entire police force on my back, understandably irritated. What did they arrest me for if I wasn't guilty? On the other hand, if I tried to appease the police by admitting guilt, I risked exacerbating my situation. Obviously, if the shrink predicted twenty years in prison for unproven charges, what would the court's sentence be if I presented solid evidence for these accusations?

Perhaps a life sentence of forty years or the ultimate penalty of death. Brrrrr! A vision of myself hanging precariously from the scaffolding sprung to mind, and I recoiled in horror. The black security guard caught my gaze as I whirled around, but he remained motionless. To say the least, I was mortified. What I said would determine the course of my life. The guard wouldn't leave, so I turned to the lawyer, who was getting irritated. I was about to ask him to leave me alone for a while so I could give him an answer that wouldn't get me in trouble with the law or land me on the gallows. However, the lawyer asked me again, presumably because I had not heard or understood the first time.

- So, Mr Bourasin, do you plead guilty or not guilty? Have I made myself clear?

I decided to wager without drawing unwanted attention from the guard whose eyes were darting behind me. That's when I uttered the words:

- I am confident that our national police, which is everywhere and can read our minds, thanks to Allah and the wisdom of our President, cannot confuse me for someone else. (Either I heard a slight cough from Mahmoud, or I imagined it.) Therefore, it's possible that I accidentally did something wrong. By this, I mean that I may be oblivious that I actually committed those reprehensible acts. The reason for that should be understood, though. I'm not just one man at all, but two, three, four, or even ten different individuals, everyone with a distinct personality and agenda. There can't be just one person behind all those larcenies, Mr Ammar; it must be a gang pretending to be a bank teller. Since I cannot recall committing the offences for which I am currently being held, I can only conclude that the police must have witnessed one of my other selves committing those acts. Maybe one of them was somnambulating. In this case, the police are merely doing their job in incriminating me, while I am just as justified in asserting unequivocally that I am innocent.

I swivelled around to look back at the security officer. He made no attempt to get up, and he didn't seem too bothered by what I said. If only he'd realised it. As I concluded my response, the lawyer smiled and said, seemingly relieved:

- I see. Mr Bourasin, you've come a long way over a very winding and complicated route. And you are not at fault. That is the main idea. If you have a file, I will review it and let you know what strategy we will use to strengthen your defence. Taking everything into account, (he stared at me) do you get it? For the time being, I think it would be best if you avoided hanging out with certain inmates. That does not mean that you should isolate yourself entirely.

- Is there somebody in particular that you are referring to?

Thinking for a moment, he mused:

- Not one. Several. Activists, in particular.

- I am apolitical, sir, I emphasised.

- You may think so, but you'll only make me waste my time if you keep hanging out with that Hassan guy, who is a potential threat. May I check for understanding?

- I got it, sir.

I wondered how the lawyer could have known about my connection to Hassan.

- Mr Aroussi warned you not to trust anyone too quickly. Be careful. You may come to regret it later.

- Mr Aroussi is very considerate; he knows I will always support him and the Administration with my undying allegiance.

- Bassam, that's not the point. You can't trust a mobster enough to want to hire him at a bank unless you're an incurable idiot. Although your intentions are honourable, you should be aware that prison is a magnet for the country's worst criminals. So also, Mr Aroussi does not value your close relationship with the journalist. Maybe you don't know that the latter had done some serious damage to the country, and now he's being accused of writing a blank cheque... A con artist, to be more precise, with millions of dollars in his wallet. Needless to say, he obtained them by dishonest means, and what's worse is that your bank is complicit.

- The 'Ouja bank? Impossible!

When I said this, I raised my voice.

- Not the 'Ouja branch; the main office.

- I am sorry! Sincerely!

THE TRUTH IS THAT I was sorry, but not on behalf of the con artist. It's not right to be taken advantage of by someone who has already offended the authorities. It's not surprising, though; as I've already argued, it stands to reason that the government's opponents would aim to undermine the economy at its core. Even worse than allowing the con artist to pocket several million unjustly acquired, the swindler is nearly free to taint honest folks and confuse them about his real intentions. Instead of letting Hassan roam free in the State hotel, he should be locked up. I was determined to get rid of him, not because I was afraid of him (Lord knows I have no reason to be so long as I remain faithful to the Administration), but because he had tricked me in some sneaky way.

The solicitor continued:

- Another thing, before we leave this room. State your case for what it's worth. And before I forget, do you need to get in touch with any of your friends or family members in the outside world to get supplies, like food or clothing?

Although I had considered the possibility, it had not occurred to me that the lawyer might contact them, so I appreciate that he brought the matter back up. I saw my chance, and I took it.

-Yes. Mr Ammar, please bring me back together with my fiancee, Dalila. Surely her anxiety is for my sake. If you could phone her, I'd be grateful.

He responded, "I will," and pulled a small notepad out of his pocket. "Could there be a message? I need to know the phone number."

I gave him the number, which, it seems to me, I have not dialled in millennia but which I still remember perfectly.

- Since 'Ouja is somewhat out of the way, I wouldn't want Mum to visit me. Old age has set in on her. So just let Dalila know I'm fine and looking forward to her visit. If she can bring me a parcel of clothes, it would be kind of her.

- I promise I'll give it my all for you, Bassam.

- Very much appreciated, sir.

We exchanged firm handshakes, and he walked out. Soon after, the guard and I made our way back to my library.

(3)

D ALILA UNEXPECTEDLY paid me a visit the same week the lawyer did, maybe three or four days after the solicitor had been by. In the courtyard, as I was shaving and bravely facing the worst of my problems since moving here, I had a terrifying realisation. In reality, the barber was ploughing my face with a razor that had previously been used on at least a hundred other dry, scratchy beards. We got into a heated debate. And so, as I saw the blood start to splatter all over my face, I cried out in protest against this treatment of my skin. Right away, I stopped it and demanded a fresh razor blade for my next shave. I knew he always carried new blades in his pocket if he was called upon to shave a VIP. I've witnessed him switching out the razor blade whenever one of them needed a shave but then reusing the same edge to furrow the other people's faces. What dishonesty! It's a shame! If he wanted money, I told him I had some, but he had to change the blade first. That infuriated him, and he yelled, smearing my face with spit in front of a line of around fifty people waiting for their turn on the torture chair.

- Damn you and your fucking money! I'm not going to shave your mouse face.

His arrogance and the fact that he had let me continue the race with just half my face shaved made me want to punch him. When I started losing my temper because some detainees were braying at my sight, the black guard came over and summoned me. I hastened to him, but he gave me a disdainful look and a gruff, "Go and wash your fucking face; someone is waiting for you at the parlour," as I hurried away.

THE LAWYER, I ASSUMED, had called again, and as I was in no mood to see him, I rushed to the sink, turned on the water, and began scalding my bloodied face. When I went back to follow the guard, he gave me a blank look when he saw that I had only shaved half of my face and then asked, in a mocking tone:

-What's that map you have on the face?

- Was that your brainchild or the barber's?

- You call that barbarian a barber? He would be better off using his skills in a slaughterhouse.

- Well, well! Get moving; she's waiting for you.

She? When I realised it, my stomach dropped. I wanted to make sure I had heard correctly.

- Who's the lady? Did you say a woman, Mr Mahmoud?

While he emphasised his point without pausing, I asked him gently if I might at least return to the barber and give it another shot.

- Do you think I'd be okay with seeing my fiancee in such a state after being apart for a while? I said, trying to convince him. What would she think of me?

But Mahmoud refused to comply with my demand, saying we did not have the time for it. He must have gotten a kick out of seeing me in such a sorry state, even more so with my ragged clothes and bloodied half-shaven face. Despite my assurances that the woman was likely to be my fiancée, the malicious vigil continued to tease me the entire way to the parlour. Women, he claimed, in general, do not appreciate or even notice when males are neatly groomed and clean-cut. I couldn't believe it.

He continued:

- Yeah! As I tell you. If you had any experience with women, you would undoubtedly know that the rougher, crueller, more tyrannical, and scarier a man is, the more respect, adoration, and even adulation he receives from women. Why are the whores so loyal to the pimps, even if the pimps beat them up, molest them, and steal their money?

- But you can't act like all the women are prostitutes, I objected in shock.

- Definitely not. In contrast, I assert that females comprise the entirety of the whore population. There is not much of a distinction.

I wanted to ask him if he felt the same way about his mum and sister and wife, but I refrained.

He went on:

- I congratulate you; she's gorgeous, maybe too pretty for a bank clerk. Unfortunately, this is also one of their flaws. To a woman, being engaged to a jackass, an incompetent, or a lecherous man is the pinnacle of female astuteness. For this reason, there are so many separations and divorces today. However, you're not the flirty, attention-seeking type. What does she see in you that she likes?

"Naughty ape! You are not better!" I mumbled to myself. Even though I was screaming my head off, he wouldn't pay attention. Then he continued his ramblings: - - Anyway, you don't need to change your clothing or anything. She wants to see you in your rat-infested home so she can form an accurate opinion. You won't intentionally mislead her, right? If you are innocent, like you pretended you were when you met with the lawyer, she will back you up. If you aren't, she'll dump you for some other guy who doesn't steal from others and pretend to be innocent when he knows he's in over his head. She won't have trouble finding a partner who can make her happy.

The sudden anger of someone I had always respected caught me off guard. Yes, I saw him repeatedly punch a sick, helpless Jew only because of the victim's faith until he died. Where did this unexpected hostility come from? The origin of this animosity baffled me. When I saw Mahmoud's evident acrimony, I became so angry that I proclaimed:

- I've killed nobody.

Looking into his eyes, I saw such resentment that I was convinced he would kill me if he had the chance. Although he did not want to think about it, the possibility of two murders happening at once was not pleasant. Even though he said nothing in response to my brazen insinuation, I knew he would not soon forget or forgive me. After the fact, I felt deep regret, but it was too late to change.

WE TRAVERSED A MAZE of halls before arriving at the final gate. I was afterwards searched by yet another guard who, it goes without saying, did not turn up any useful information. As soon as he was done, I was led into a strange room where everyone was yelling so that no one could make out what his interlocutor was saying on the other side of the wire netting that separated the two halves of the room. The inmates and the guests were vying for space to make grand gestures at each other. The poor lighting made it difficult for me to pinpoint where my fiancee was standing amongst the gloomy crowd.

As I wandered through the wire netting, I heard my name called twice and recognised her sharp, titillating voice. When I looked in the direction her voice seemed to be coming from, I found her.

DALILA'S HAIR WAS WRAPPED in a chignon, and she wore a beautiful red gown that emphasised her lovely bosom. But there was a look of weariness and sadness on her face, as though she were crying or about to cry. Her face seemed a little pale, and her dark, wide eyes weren't as sparkling as they usually are when we saw each other. I pushed through a pair of inmates on my way to her, unconcerned with their comments, and paused just short of the wire netting. I saw that she was carrying a big bundle, and

I thought it was the clothes I had asked for. When I came near her, she started complaining:

-Bassam, why did you do this to me? Why?

It was an odd way to reconnect after so much time apart.

- What have I done to you? Puzzled and confused, I asked.

- Are you teasing me? How could you possibly forget your word that quickly? We should get married this summer. What are we going to do now?

Among all other subjects, that was the one I feared most. I felt a painful sensation and stammered reassuringly:

- We'll marry. I surely didn't lose sight of that.

In my heart, I knew that was easier said than done.

- When? How? The loud noise forced her to raise her voice.

She has no idea that couples in their fifties frequently marry to benefit from new scientific breakthroughs, whereas young couples always ruin their marriage due to inexperience. Should I inform her? I felt we should talk about it a little, but this was not the appropriate setting. If I had to raise my voice to be heard, I would be less effective in my argument. She wouldn't get a word in edgewise, and she'd probably think I made up the whole thing to make her feel stupid or maybe even to get rid of her, which is the furthest thing from my mind. Therefore, I opted to withhold my theory until I was ready to confront her and could more effectively explain it and argue my point. And I certainly wasn't uninformed that the fundamental ideas conceived by the best brains are typically decades ahead of their time. Yet, since my intentions were not to shock Dalila but to calm her fears, I told her:

- Never mind, Dalila, we'll marry... um... after I am released.

This may sound alarming somehow, but I was actually trying to reassure her.

The truth is that I wasn't being dishonest or evasive. But Dalila's anger rose, and she demanded:

- When will you be released, Bassam?

I dithered but ultimately had to give a brutal and truthful response.

- Well, perhaps in about twenty... er... I tried to deflect.

I was overjoyed to see her smile for the first time without a trace of melancholy on her face. But, unfortunately, I wasn't one hundred per cent certain of her ability to hear and understand me the first time, so I said again:

-Twenty, twenty...

Either out of compassion for her or because I'm too chicken to tell the whole truth, I didn't say which twenty I was referring to. However, she responded quietly:

- Yes, I heard. It's not what the solicitor said.

That stupid idiot! How dare he contradict me? Did I hire him to defend my interests or try to bring me into disrepute? The scepticism I had towards his facilitation appeared now justified.

- So what did he actually say? I inquired fervently.

- Your affair is a little tricky, he said.

- A little tricky?

- Yes, that's what he told me.

I was furious. But unaware of my anger, she went on:

- Bassam, what happened? Why did you keep your bank fraud and scamming activities a secret from me? I had faith in your integrity. I came here without Daddy's permission. My father forbids me from having any contact with you. You've made a bad impression on my parents, and they think you're a crook and a rogue who lied to us. They're pressuring me to end our relationship.

An abrupt eruption of hysterical sobbing shook her to her core. Seeing her in that state of agonising bewilderment affected me deeply. In a fit of rage, I cursed the lawyer. It was all his fault. It was clear that he made things worse for me instead of improving them. Had I not tried so hard to satisfy Mr Aroussi, I would have listened to my gut instinct and done what seemed right. As I see it, the outcome was not promising. It's too late now. All the brainless donkey's "little tricky affair" did, was make my life more difficult. And what exactly did he intend by that? Is it true that I am, to his undiscerning gaze, of no consequence, whatsoever? Does he mean I don't deserve a big, complicated affair? If he tried to make others think I'm a con artist or petty thief by making up stories about me, it wouldn't surprise me. Oh, the impudent! My future father-in-law hated me so much that he encouraged his daughter to end our five-year engagement. I needed to restore equilibrium, so I uttered a bugling cry to end her wailing.

- Dalila, the solicitor, should not be trusted.

She looked up, her eyes red and puffy from crying, and asked:

- Why? Is he telling tales? I take it you are incarcerated now.

A bit more loudly, I snarled:

- No, You see not. Mr Ammar had no clue about my problem. He's not my lawyer, I said.

She dried her eyes with a small handkerchief and seemed uncertain whether she should believe me.

- Is he not your lawyer? she asked.

I gave a little head shake. I couldn't tell her that my Top Secret report would settle everything and that I didn't need a lawyer. On the other hand, I knew she would be negatively influenced if she left me without a reassuring response. I needed to find a way to make amends with her that wouldn't include telling her my secret.

- I'm not what your dad and mum think I am, Dalila. But, to tell you the truth, you already know me.

- That's what I feared, she sobbed again. You're in jail for nothing. It's too unfair.

That caught me off guard; I didn't expect that response. This infuriated me to the point that I raised my voice over the din of the parlour, prompting some of my audience to whip around in shocked disbelief:

- So, you think I should have robbed the bank or murdered someone to earn my incarceration?

- No, she argued, I don't. We aren't ready to get married yet. Therefore, our wedding plans have to be scrapped.

It's a serious fixation for her. When summer rolls around, all this woman can think about is getting married.

- We can marry in winter because there really isn't much difference.

- Which Winter?

- Any. They all look the same to me. Just another twenty, and I'll be free of this place. Hold on, Dalila. Your father needs to know that I am trying to get released as soon as possible. Therefore it would be helpful if you could express this to him.

- You have been saying, "Twenty, twenty," twenty what? Do you mean twenty days or twenty months?

I have no idea how the words "twenty years" came out of my mouth. I stopped dead.

- What?

Too late to reverse.

- Tweeeeeeeenty! Do you still have trust in the lawyer, Dalila?

To rubbish me to that extent was inadmissible. Twenty days or months for all the dreadful charges resting heavily on my shoulders and practically suffocating me! I wasn't sure she grasped me anyway. For she said:

- I don't believe anyone. I've brought you your clothes. I'll give them to the guards. Mr Marmeduke, your neighbour, the barber, Mustapha, and the grocer, Mehrez, all send their greetings.

- Kind of them. How did they know?

- Everyone in the community is talking about your imprisonment, she sobbed.

I COULDN'T DECIDE IF I should feel bad or glad. Without realising it, the people of 'Ouja have elevated me to hero status. Although I was intrigued to learn the details of their conversation, I had no doubt that it was highly complimentary and laudatory. However, I was concerned since I did not know how Dalila would approach the issue with her family members. Although I have no doubt about her love for me, I do not believe that her feelings are enough to cope with the difficulties we are currently facing. If her father hates me and pressures her, she may end up breaking her promise, making the dark-faced guard's ominous prediction come true. Then what good is my life? Without my fiancée, I do not know how I could live an honourable and fulfilling life in 'Ouja. It's just how you're trained to behave. Orphaned in the adult world, I'd be entirely at sea. My mother is too old to provide much solace at this point. She was partially deafened and could barely make out my words. She has become completely detached from the world around her. It's 'Ouja, the village where she spent her young years, more than sixty years ago, when there was nothing at all like the modern world. She spends her days and evenings glued to the TV screen, but I'm not sure she understands the shows any better than she does my words when we have a conversation. She never gives me a straight answer when I ask her a question, and if I don't keep reminding her, she'll forget. She would stray from the topic and ramble on about whatever was on her mind while I was referring to something completely unrelated. A common theme in her stories is a longing for the simpler times before and during World War II when she imagined life to be easier and people to be more courteous and straightforward. I try to avoid disagreeing with her as possible, but she is difficult to derail once she gets going. Though I believe her to be honest and naive, I find many of her views weird, out of touch with the present, and dated. For instance, she thinks the British stayed in our country out of pure love for its people and feels terrible that they were expelled. A thousand times, I attempted to tell her that colonialism is awful because it's like a colossal heist operation. No use.

- You don't know anything about them, and you weren't even around at the time, she'd reply. What kind of neighbour is Mr Marmeduke?

- Don't worry, Ma, he's a good guy.

- Well, they're all just like him. Christians, yes, but also closer to Islam than many of us and exceptionally kind neighbours. They treat us kindly, they don't mess with our faith, and they respect our traditions. Do you know Mrs Smith? It puzzles me that she didn't write to me. What day is it today?

- This is Wednesday, Mum, and how many times do I have to tell you that Mrs Smith has passed away? Mum, you know she's dead; she's not writing to you from Britain because she's dead.

Then she'd think, "Oh yes, poor Mrs Smith," and say it.

Mrs Smith was a close friend of my mother's, and she lived in 'Ouja before the country's independence. She maintained close touch with Mumma even after she and her family had left the country. My mother is illiterate, so I had to occasionally answer her letters, although I never did it with as much enthusiasm as she would have liked. On the Islamic holidays, we would receive a package from England, and on Christmas, we would have to send Mrs Smith a special gift. This went on for many years until we finally learned of the woman's passing in a letter from her husband. It happened only a few months after the loss of my father, and my poor mother was so distraught that she stayed in bed for days.

I CAN'T COMPARE DALILA to my mum. Despite her being young, she has a deep understanding of my plight. Although she can read and write, she is not exactly bright, having dropped out of school after earning just a primary diploma, which was considered enough for a female at the time. Whatever her educational shortcomings may be, she need not be concerned, because my brain is large enough to accommodate two people. She would think for me in the realm of household duties, and I'd take care of her and myself in the realm of public affairs. This was something we both agreed upon. Dalila also has skills as a seamstress and cook. She is self-employed and serves not only the residents of 'Ouja but also those in the surrounding villages. Together, her job and mine support us comfortably. Mr Houssine, her father, is a retired postman and a good friend of my dad's. He grows his own produce on a little plot of land just outside of 'Ouja. We share their middle-class status, and although I don't have an orchard to sell fruit from for extra cash, I do have two homes: my own and my father's, where Mum still resides.

But now I'm in a pickle. The situation with my in-laws has gotten out of hand because my father-in-law, Mr Houssine, has taken advantage of my temporary absence to put undue pressure on his daughter. The words of my dark oracle came back to me: "You won't lie to her, will you? She'll dump you for another man eventually." What a smacking imprecation! I tried not to dwell on the thought and instead loathed the scheming fatty raven I had come to suspect of lechery and lustful covetousness. Unfortunately, I also had to defend myself from my father-in-law's attack. Why should I give someone the chance to slander me? I have nothing to hide; there is no need to fabricate my alibi. It appeared the lawyer had so degraded me that I had no real options. All I had to do to win back my fiancee's and her family's trust was, to be honest, and then I would have their unconditional backing.

SO, BEFORE THE GUARD returned to interrupt our encounter, I had just time to yell to her:

-It is twenty years, Dalila, not twenty days, not twenty months, but twenty long years.

I felt like I was drowning under the weight of my words, but I figured I'd be able to rest easy afterwards. My fiancee knew she could count on me because I wouldn't lie to her. Alas! That black raven who acted like he knew ladies better than me was to blame for my error. How could I have let him sway me? Really, I can't get my head around it.

What Dalila said next was both shocking and shockingly unexpected.

- You crazy man, crazy, crazy, crazy! She said.

(4)

The guard pushed me out of the parlour, and I saw his colleague Mahmoud approaching to take me back to my loneliness. Sadness and despair filled me. I didn't realise I wasn't on vacation in a hotel until I was in excruciating pain. The big city where Dalila was wandering alone on the pavements is hidden behind those high walls, guarded by armed soldiers ready to shoot me down at the first suspicion. After that point, who could guess what was going through her mind? Do I still have the title of "loving fiancé," or has she already called off the engagement? What was the cause of her gloomy and terrified expression? Exactly why did she have to say anything so cruel to me?

As I was walking down a dark hallway, thinking about our conversation and how strange and clear my situation of outcast had become to me, I overheard Mahmoud saying:

- What did she say to you that left you in such a gloomy state? You don't even appear like you're breathing.

The words "she said I'm crazy" came out of my mouth as I was on the verge of tears and feeling emotionally strangled.

- Crazy? Are we done here? That's incredible! The lady must think highly of you. That term, crazy, is often used by females to convey appreciation and praise. Are you always this downcast? You must feel quite special to have a girl like her waiting for you, even if she does think you're nuts. I can't believe it! When you finally leave, there'll be a celebration waiting for you.

He made love-making gestures with his hands and tummy. Gosh, such a sleazy and repulsive human being! Maybe he was going for a joke, but all he did was make himself seem silly and scabby.

- You will definitely ask me to be a part of your wedding, right? When you go, you must remember your friends.

It stood out to me how erratic the man's behaviour was. When he would have murdered me a few minutes before for no reason, he now acts as if we are so close that he should be invited to my wedding.

- Inshallah, I'll ask you for my wedding in twenty years.

His dark features twitched with mistrust as he regarded me from an angle:

- Twenty years? I don't get why, boy. What happened? Did you kill somebody?

It was the first sane thing he had said to me since I'd met him.

- I'm at a loss to explain; consult the shrink.

- The shrink? Seriously, what are you saying? There's no way he could be a judge. Then, after a brief pause, he said incredulously: Twenty years, and you claimed you're innocent!

When we finally made it through all the iron gates and into the courtyard proper, he said:

-Did you say it to your fiancée?

- What? The 20 years? Yes, I did. I couldn't possibly lie to her, could I?

His eyes widened, and his brows furrowed as he looked at me. Then, after he was satisfied that I wasn't fibbing, he remarked:

- If you said that, you are a donkey, not a man.

- You don't have to be insulting to me, do you? I shot back fiercely. After all, I can say whatever I choose to my fiancée. Besides, could you perhaps explain your apparent anxiety?

- Anxiety? I? You may go to hell if you want, but don't bother pretending you're free when you know well well you're not. And when I call you a fucking bloody donkey, I'm not trying to be offensive; I'm only describing you. The President of the Republic would be more likely to join you for lunch than your lass would still be waiting for you after what you said to her. So that's why she said you were crazy is clear to me now. Yes, she is absolutely correct. You, poor guy, are completely insane. You won't get better in prison, and nobody else has, either. So far, you haven't been put to the test. Have you received a court summons?

Saddened by the realisation of my error, I said, "No."

- Then why are you so certain that this is where you want to spend the rest of your life? So, you really like being locked up, right?

- Is the shrink wrong? I inquired.

- No, he is not if the court finds that the accusations are consistent.

- If that's the case, Well, then I wasn't wrong to tell her the truth.

- Truth? Which truth are we talking about here? So, you admit to your wrongdoings. Cancel the rest of your life and go to hell. Get in your hole and shut the door. If your fiancée is a fool, she'll come back, and the next time I meet her, I'll convince her to break off the engagement. You've been locked up for twenty years while I've been living the good life. Oh my god, that's funny!

I turned away from him and walked glumly toward the library, but he put a hairy black hand on my shoulder and warned me:

- Look here, if ever you tell anybody what you saw in the courtyard, your life here will be miserable. Do you get what I'm saying? I'm talking about that Jew, you know.

I was confused, but I tried to seem cool when I answered.

- I won't tell you just murdered him.

- Put your mouth in your sleeve, you fucking idiot. Keep this phrase to yourself. He scowled disdainfully at me and added: Now go away.

I made a U-turn and left, relieved to be free of him temporarily. After taking just a few feet, his raspy voice said:

- Stop. Donkey, you need to come here. You will show proper deference the next time you see me or any other man representing the authorities in this nation. Understand? I expect a military salute.

I did what he said and saluted him by bringing my palm to my forehead.

- Good. The new you is courteous. Admit it: "I'm an animal."

I didn't want to make that admission.

- Say that, or I'll send you to the freezer right now, he angrily warned.

I felt a shiver go down my spine as I remembered how he molested the Jew till he died, and I was terrified that he would do the same to me.

- I am an a-n-i-m-a-l... I said.

I was, after all, his duty. Also, why bother fighting him if he already thinks I'm not human? Does the Administration not consider him a representative? What's more, if the Administration prefers to deal with animals instead of people, wouldn't it be prudent to comply with the Administration's requests?

- Yes, I am an animal with crooked horns and a long tail, I added firmly.

The intensity of my enthusiasm seemed to perplex him. I chimed in:

- You are correct, Mr Mahmoud. For the longest time, I've thought of man as something like an animal, a view held by Mister Aristotle, as I learned. More recently, Mr Darwin has emphasised that Adam's dad was, in fact, a monkey. Specifically, a friendly monkey. To sum up, you have a point. A philosopher, you are.

In a menacing voice, he said:

- Are you mocking me, squirt?

- I swear on the holy names of Allah, Mohammad, and the angels and saints that what I am saying to you is the truth. If you don't believe me, check out the book I read it from.

For a brief second, he seemed hesitant, but then he said:

- All right. Get out of here. I don't want to see that stupid book. Go.

Another salutation, and then I slowly made my way to my library.

I BECAME INCREASINGLY conscious of my load as the days passed. Indeed, I have some responsibility in this complex predicament, even if I recognise that everything is 'Mektub'...Thus, it was engraved on our foreheads long before we were born. Acceptance of one's destiny is required. So I keep telling myself that I was born in 'Ouja, where I also grew up. I love my village as well as my homeland. People have always been attentive, kind, indulgent, and helpful to me. I am confident that everyone in my hometown appreciates and respects me. But on the other hand, some are hazardous, turbulent, and troublemakers. I don't exclude angels and invisible Jinnies. Aliens, too. And rats. They must be controlled and prevented from causing damage to others and themselves. This is the highly lauded moral objective for which I had an alluring proclivity before arriving at this... (Ahem!) hotel!

However, life would be much more tedious for us if these little obstacles did not exist.

I'm starting to feel fatigued now. Nights have not been restful for me since my conversation with Dalila. I care about her, which is why I'm concerned about what she said. Thanks to her, I changed my attire, but I could not so easily alter my negative thoughts. Now, I feel she is right in insisting our marriage be celebrated this summer as planned. After all, I'm not sure I'll survive for another twenty years, and I'm not sure she'd be willing to wait that long either. And, although my idea on quinquagenarian marriage is scientifically sound and undeniably appealing, I recognise that it cannot be applied in all instances. It would be worthless in my situation since Dalila would not submit as easy as one would anticipate. The principle is valid, and it may be used by the government to combat high natality rates - it's better than pills, after all - but why should I test it on myself first? No scientist would put a new finding to the test in this manner.

There are many rats and people all around the globe who would be delighted to have such experiences. Let's start testing the rats, the cooks and the members of the Muslim Brothelhood. They sure are doomed to stay in prison for another half-century. The Afghan and his band seem to me perfectly fit for the test. Even the Boss of my cell, Zorro, and Frankenstein, the fake security expert. Both need to be put to the test. I propose multiplying their detention time by three or four to be sure they are at least 70 when they get out. By the way, all of the candidates for the test should be injected with a strong drug to keep them quiet. One never knows!

FOR ME, THE BLACK GUARD presents an additional incentive to get married quickly. Undoubtedly, he has designs on stealing away my fiancee! If the next time she comes to see me, he doesn't get up the courage to make a move and make a proposal to her, all his harassing will have been for nothing. Yet, I have a fantastic opportunity. It's June now. If I can make sense of these notes and submit my secret report to the Administration by the end of this month, I will be officially released and allowed to start planning my wedding for July.

Nonetheless, my mother used to say that everything is Mektub. I have to make up my mind. Marriage, like death, is Mektub; it is inevitable. There are three major events in everyone's life in 'Ouja for which we must be adequately prepared. The day a person is born, the day they marry, and the day they die. So they claim! They overlook another important rendezvous, however: the day one is arrested!

But, since everything is Mektub, I accept my fate. It's pointless to try to change it. I say this not because I am defeated but because I am a fatalist. I am a fatalist to the bone, just like the rest of my countrymen. I prefer to believe that my life was planned and decided before birth. Therefore, what I do in my life is the responsibility of God, not mine.

A FEW DAYS AGO, I SPOTTED the Afghan making a speech to his followers and some other inmates. I got closer to the circle. I heard him saying:

- Allah is the One who created us. It's His job to throw us into different conditions from the beginning. There is a reason for this, but we cannot understand it. It is God's wisdom and will. Therefore, one is born into destitution, while the other is born into plush luxury. One is born into the conundrum, while the other is born into the light. One is born in a forgotten village in a country where people jump into the sea to escape, and the other is born with a golden spoon in the mouth in a world Capital. That's the will of God! Inshallah! My brothers, if you are born in the abode of Islam and guidance, it is sufficient to ensure the intercession of the Prophet, peace be upon him, which would guarantee you eternal Paradise. But if you have the misfortune to be born in the abode of disbelief among the inhabitants of Hell, your fate is wretched. One is born crazy, disfigured, or deaf, while the other is born healthy. One is born knowing his father and mother, while another is born on the street or in the bush, never knowing his father or mother, assuming he survives. One is born with brilliance and genius genes, while the other is born with fool genes passed down from generation to generation. One is born a person in a human household, and the other is born an animal in a monster's den... What is the fatwa in this case? What is the point of contention? Is the initial inequality of mankind evidence of divine justice or not? Brothers... I'm not trying to offend anyone. I invite you to contemplate the wisdom of God. Did Allah oppress the people in this manner? On the contrary. You need to see this as knowledge and remember the holy Quran: <Perhaps you dislike something, and it is good for you!> Of course, God does not make mistakes as He is Perfect.

AS I THOUGHT ABOUT it, I found the Afghan correct. Naturally, no one bothered to ask me what I wanted to accomplish with my life before I was born. But I'm okay with the game. I will not quarrel with the Almighty God. I am lucky to *be born in the abode of Islam and guidance*, as the Afghan put it. What if I was born *in a forgotten village in a country where people would jump into the sea to escape?* Or worse: *in the abode of disbelief among the inhabitants of Hell?* I wouldn't be happy. I may even never see the Wisdom of God as I see it now.

By the way, working as a bank clerk in 'Ouja is the pinnacle of many a 'would-be-living' person's job aspirations, although my career is now nearly shattered. Yet, the wisdom of God is still working for me. As I am no longer a bank teller, I am in charge of the books, which is not a bad job for someone who hasn't opened a book since high school. I am taking advantage of the opportunity to further my studies and start a career as a scientist. In my post at the library, I learned a lot of intriguing stuff. However, I am bothered by the fact that I frequently forget what I have just completed reading. This could be due to a memory issue or simply because my thoughts keep straying as I read.

I should probably talk to the shrink about my mental antics, but I'm afraid. I'm hesitant after he sentenced me to twenty years in prison. What if he discovered some unknown disaster plaguing my mind, some monster lurking in the dark? It could also be Mektub and God's wisdom. But what if the monster hidden in the crevices of my mind broke out and committed some heinous crime, such as robbing 'Ouja bank or, better yet, the Central bank? What if the same monster wanted to join the Muslim Brothelhood, kidnapping women and plotting against our BGP (Beloved General President)? That is disgusting! Would I still see God's Wisdom? From Bassam's perspective, yes. But, according to the monster, no way!

NOW I COME TO THE POINT. Those who sent me and thousands of others to this hotel probably believe they are providing me with a once-in-a-lifetime opportunity to better myself and gain merit. They undoubtedly know me better than I know myself, given their position in the Administration. And since they decided this is the right place for me, they are undoubtedly correct; hence, I see no need to fight their will - which I am not doing by submitting this report. The matter is obviously linked to the wisdom of God.

My classified report serves another objective that is closely related to State security. I'm not trying to get around the police, though. On the contrary, I feel that our valiant security forces are doing well at this level. No government in the world is better organised in the business of spying on its residents, and it is in our best interests to remain under constant surveillance everywhere, at all times.

When I am alone at home or at work, I am never really alone: someone is always observing me. I don't mean God. He is omnipresent, of course. But an entity I don't see, although I hear because the entity talks to me, and it's not uncommon for us to chat. I wish it was God and still hope that one day or another, He decides to have a chat with me while I am still alive. For if I passed away, I doubt I would hear Him.

I first mistook the entity for a Jinni. Nonetheless, I quickly became persuaded that I was not conversing with spirits since the Jinni admitted to me once that he was, in fact, an agent of the State. An invisible entity with a human voice working for the government of our BGP? Yes. That's it. I had no idea our government had one foot in this world and the other in the invisible realm.

However, I had some reservations. It may be a crafty Jinni attempting to disguise himself - which prompted me to seek the advice of Haj Mukhtar. But, whether a Jinni or a secret police officer, his company was weird... weird, but safe.

How safe? Indeed it is, not only because those unseen and lovely individuals go out of their way to care after you without even asking, but also because you have a strong sense that they are everywhere, which indicates that all citizens and the whole nation are safe.

But I'm curious why so many people are in jail if the secret police take their job so seriously that they've turned secrecy into invisibility.

In fact, I wonder why we need jail at all! - Also, this means that ordinary citizens get the same strict security measures that, in other countries, are only given to Ministers, foreign diplomats, and other high-ranking officials. Thus, in our nation, we have attained perfect security equality. That is precisely what I mean by justice. There is no distinction between a Minister and a bank teller. Everyone has the right to be spied on by the authorities, which is also one of the fundamental Human Rights.

After all, why did we fight so hard to get rid of the colonialists? Any history textbook will supply the solution, which can be summed up in a single word: FREEDOM.

Does this sound out of place? Absolutely not. A reasonable explanation is required in this case.

(5)

OF ALL, "FREEDOM" IS only a single word, but achieving it took much bloodshed. Because of this, the government has resolved to secure it so well that greedy foreign powers will never again be able to steal it. Our freedom is now well veiled under a black niqab. We know it exists someplace, yet we can't see it. Nobody can. Invisible Secret police ensured that our freedom became unseen, allowing us to enjoy it freely in bed, under the niqab at night. The law allows us to dream of it. Everything is done for the public good. The law is above all.

But EVERYONE in our country knows we are free even if we don't see freedom: radio, television, newspapers, and political speeches keep repeating it - and that is why the State must protect our freedom with police, army, spies, electronic control, and monitoring microwaves. Any citizen in our nation has the fundamental, undeniable right to be observed day and night by a secret police agent whose duty it is to assist the citizen in being free - not an easy job - and to ultimately remind us that we are living in a free country because the Free State is so attentive and concerned to make us feel that we are being looked after, even if one is not a Minister or a senior official.

In fact, I had no idea that our security system had advanced so far that some of its personnel had become invisible. Sometimes I hear voices talking to me at work or home. To ensure I wasn't going crazy, I looked everywhere—ceilings, walls, curtains, furniture, etc.—for bugs and other devices that might be sending signals. I never discovered a shred of proof. Now that I have given it some thought, I see that the situation is more nuanced than I first thought; because if I had to believe that the police could be invisible, then I may as well believe that the Jins, the ghosts, and other angels and spirits are working for the government. That ethereal nature would explain why my two guardian angels appear to be everywhere and nowhere at the same time.

That the Jins and the invisible police exist has been shown beyond a reasonable doubt. My guardian angels may be Jinni security officers (since the Jins are also enlisted by the State police). There may be no physical evidence, but we don't need it to believe in the intangible aspects of our lives. To think I can fool anybody with my inflated sense of my own intelligence is a monumental folly. After all, we are all invisible when no one is looking at us. I'm also invisible since you can't see me right now while you read these words. Just picture me talking to myself in your mind, and you'll be right on the money. Still, I am as unnoticed by you as you are by me. As a result, anybody may be a Jinni, ghost, shadow, ghoul, phantom, angel or invisible cop. It's not difficult; you just conceal. Nonetheless, if you want to be a bank clerk, it would take you years only to master the fundamentals of the job.

THE FIFTEEN YEARS I'VE been in the industry have taught me a lot, but I still don't know everything. My lack of expertise in international finance and business makes me feel like a novice in this field. That is why I hold Mr Aroussi in high regard as a real specialist. Unfortunately, his effort to make a rock-solid investment abroad was misinterpreted. I would venture to argue that the law enforcement authorities or customs officers that detained his agent were myopic; sure, they saw the six million, but they failed to account for the sixty million! Eh! These were invisible... like our freedom! The customs' saved a comparatively small amount, but they ended up dropping the ball on the big one. Instead of Mr Aroussi and his agent, if I had any power, I would have jailed the customs officers for damaging the country's economy and robbing it of $60 million. All of that money had evaporated due to their foolish zeal. If we had borrowed the same amount, we would have returned it to the creditor, plus interest, with all the difference in exchange rates caused by the high levels of the dollar - in comparison with our local currency, which has been shaken by the fall of oil prices and the unwise speculations. Moreover, we would have paid at least a 2.5 to 3 dollars interest rate on our loan, if not more. Multiply this by 60 million to get the outcome of the transaction. Not brilliant! But we do this all the time.

Now, take note of Mr Aroussi's ingenuity: instead of sending hundreds of millions of dollars to a foreign nation to serve a $60 million debt, he proposed we spend just $6 million and earn $54 million. That, I think, is the priceless investment he was projecting.

Even an idiot would understand that Mr Aroussi was trying to make as much money as possible from his trade. Is there any banker you know that would oppose making a profit? Furthermore, I believe that any money he would have gotten from his six million would have been reinjected into the country where he lives to bolster the unseen government defending our precious freedom properly. Things are interconnected: if you don't have freedom, you can't expect to conduct lucrative business; and if you can't do business, you'll end up wreaking havoc on the whole nation.

I am, indeed, apolitical. I make no claim to understand economics or international commerce better than State agents. So, it's probable that the police, customs authorities, or whoever believed it was best to keep Mr Aroussi and the six million dollars and throw him in prison alongside the Jew had an excellent cause. I agree that six million had the physical appearance of evidence in their box, while sixty million, though clear in my mind, may have seemed to them like the ghostly police or our freedom, something existing, but-alas!-unprovable.

The more I think about it, the more perplexed I am. Aware of the knowledge, professionalism and skills of the State's operatives, I'm puzzled as to how they could have overlooked the sixty million! I'm sure they weren't that naïve. There is a ploy. Of course, they did not arrest Mr Aroussi and the Jew for the insignificant amount of six million because they probably know that we have invested billions overseas. This is an actual and physical number that is now accessible in the State's box. Still, the sixty million are no less real for me just because they are located in a foreign country. As a result, we now have 66 million dollars split between two nations.

It is an uneven divide since most of the total amount went to a foreign country. This does not sound right to our Administration's agents. So, by holding Mr Aroussi in prison, they most likely seek to strike a deal: will they release him in exchange for the $60 million? He is undoubtedly weighing the sum. Keep an eye on our Administration's acumen. The customs authorities are still waiting for a foreign bank to bail Mr Aroussi's release. If I were him, I would strike a deal. I would give the authorities the invisible $60 million in exchange for my release and a signed pledge not to pursue me further wherever I go.

TODAY, I'M A LITTLE hazy. Reviewing yesterday's notes, I'm unsure why I scribbled down all of this nonsense. What do I have to do with Mr Aroussi's money games and his complicated situation? Why did I disparage the State's agents, whom I charged with myopia and was about to accuse of kidnapping? It's still good that I didn't blame our country for terrorism and international blackmail! And what was that mad rant about the cops and their unseen agents? Am I going bonkers? Did the cooks feed me some junk food that drove me insane? Not excluded. Definitely! If not, how did I suppose this language was appropriate in an official Top-Secret report issued to the administration's highest levels? This is unusual; I'm playing Devil's advocate while claiming to exorcise his demonic conjuration! That won't work. I must be careful what I write since I am still trapped in a pitiful predicament. I'm not sure whether I'll be able to leave this location anytime soon. What is the point of portraying myself as a hero when I am genuinely oppressed? And the people who hurt me aren't invisible, of course. I've never said that, and I've even tried to show that any Invisible is helpful, clever, and necessary for keeping our freedom well hidden by the State so that no foreign power can get to it. But the real oppressors of our people are the cooks and the rats who hijack women to force them to work as Muslim Brothelhood agents. They are still plotting in the kitchens of this hotel and shouting every so often, "Is it cooked?"

What the heck is cooked if not their nefarious plot against the State? The buffoons! They probably believe no one unveiled their secret code, whereas I have decrypted and unscrambled its hidden signals from the beginning. Eh! I'm not called (I) 007 for nothing.

BEWARE! THIS IS A NETWORK of spies and deadly conspirators who have already knitted their code. Cooked, a derivative of "cooks," is their password.

When one of them runs into another in the courtyard or the corridor, he inquires, "Is it cooked?" "Yes, fairly cooked," the response would be. "We'll be eating the lamb shortly." So, there's a sheep somewhere, but where? I didn't hear it bleating even with my well-trained ears. I tightened my watch and opened my ears and eyes, hoping (and I don't disguise it) that we'd have a pleasant supper. But days passed, and nothing occurred. They continued to bring us the same awful soup, and we swallowed it because we had no other option. Fortunately, I resisted the urge to disseminate the excellent news. If I had announced to the customers that they'd be served surreal mutton at the next dinner, they would have laughed at me.

Meanwhile, the conspirators continued to employ the same password in their casual or arranged meetings. They were foolishly confident that no one had entered their organisation or exposed their braggart deceit. I noticed no other sheep in the vicinity except the jew, Dawood, who had been oppressed and cold-bloodedly murdered. Was that because he, too, became aware of the massive plot? Not excluded. I hope, though, they wouldn't push the cruelty until serving us Moosa Dawood at dinner. Would I recognise him without a head? Excluded.

I am sure the cooks are dangerous and sneaky, and even though there are only four of them, they are never the same. In the kitchens, multiple convicts alternately participate in the laborious duty. Apparently, everyone who knows how to boil an egg is eventually called upon to cook for the rest of us. But in fact, this is also part of the plot. Since they're never the same, we can't accuse the chefs of intoxicating the customers or the guards. Acting so cautiously and preventively reveals the evil intent of the group.

Now, to fill my report with solid facts and make it sound, I need to know the identities and deeds of all those guys, potentially trace them and document anything they say or do. It is not an easy undertaking since I am not as free to roam as I was in 'Ouja. Furthermore, if they believe I am following them, they may react negatively, perhaps violently; they do not give me a sense of security. They nurture conspiracy and mayhem as a hen incubates eggs. They are hardwired from birth to plan and scheme horrors.

For my part, I'd want to perform a less risky profession, but I've gone too far to turn back now.

I AM WATCHING THE AFGHAN. He is getting more influential in my chamber. He even attempted to convert me to his ominous sect, the jackass! Absolutely incredible, right? As he prayed with his followers ten times a day, he asked me:

-Why don't you pray with us? How could you possibly be faithful?

He dared!

But I couldn't admit that I don't give a damn. Not wanting to start a fight with the Afghan, I refrained at the last moment from asking whether he saw himself as God or just his Prophet. Instead, I said:

-I am apolitical.

- My inquiry is not directed at your political beliefs but at your religious obligations. Have you got any religion?

This sleazy taunt infuriated me to the point that I dared to answer:

- No, Mister Mohamed, I have none.

I lied out of anger. But the man reddened and seemed bewildered. He must not have anticipated such a response, as he is used to being obeyed rather than resisted. Nevertheless, he maintained his composure and resumed his attack, asking:

- Are you against God?

- Which one?

- There is only One God, you dog son!

I didn't add anything.

He eyed me with disdain and exclaimed:

- You wicked enemy of Allah! You poor, errant dog, may Allah never have mercy on your damned soul!

AFTER THE FACT, I REGRETTED what I had said. He had no malicious intent against me, but I couldn't be pleasant to him. That would have given him reason to believe and maybe spread the rumour that I was one of his disciples.

"You must avoid the activists," said the lawyer.

Mr Ammar was pretty specific in his advice. He meant Hassan, the Afghan, and others like them. As a result, I will not apologise to the Afghan, despite my regret for my nervous hostility. In addition, I do not want terrorist charges added to my already lengthy case. However, it seems that the Afghan was the one who was terrified of me at the time. He probably assumed I could pull off anything, given how flippantly I treat his religious practices. I can't be any more disturbing.

The solicitor's warnings about Hassan were spot on. This man's actions have been somewhat perplexing. One never knows precisely which side he is on. This is perhaps why the Royalists and the Republicans both took turns locking him up. I saw him spend two days in the courtyard openly flirting with the Afghan. I heard them talking in low voices, like two skilled plotters, and I wondered what they were discussing that required such secrecy.

Suddenly, I felt downcast and nostalgic. The presence of the conspirators in broad daylight is never reassuring. Then, suddenly, one of the chefs walked by them on his way to the tower, bringing a tray of cold beverages. It was a hot day, and the sun seemed like a bowl of fire in the clear sky. Hassan remarked, "What's cooking today?" as he greeted them, revealing their true identities as conspirators.

The chef's reply of "Mutton" sent everyone into fits of laughter.

As they joked, a foreboding sense that things were about to reach a peak flooded my mind.

(6)

I WAS CORRECT IN MY assessment.

Strangely, I first observed an increase in police presence and a greater concentration of guards in the towers, hallways, and courtyards towards the beginning of July. Even on the rooftops, officers were visible, their rifles gleaming in the sunshine.

The abrupt shift astounded me. I wasn't the only one who wondered and thought that something significant had occurred or was imminent. Although I didn't have the nerve to question the guards about what this strange shift meant, I did make a note of it. Meanwhile, our rooms and things were rummaged through.

Instead of giving us advance notice, they barged in at first light, yelled loudly to catch our attention, and ordered us to exit the dormitory, leaving behind our little things. A squad went outside to search us in the courtyard as we stood in rows along the walls. What did they think they would uncover, exactly? Not a clue, that's for sure. Jam, marmalade, cakes, and other sweets the detainees got from their relatives and visitors. The guards quickly seized anything that didn't fit the standard prison diet. I found out later that they weren't interested in the food itself but rather in what it may contain or hide. It's not surprising! Some detainees, I was informed, were actively engaged in the illegal drug trade. As for me, I hadn't observed anything out of the ordinary. Even if I saw something being passed from one person to another, I'm not sure I could identify it. Since then, I've heard other intriguing accounts of this underground trade, which passed me by before. Those with such items in their luggage, even if it was only a suspicious aspirin, were taken from their cell and given a brief stay in the freezer.

The tales about the freezer compartment are just as disturbing. Those who ventured inside that dark and terrifying realm have returned with gruesome stories. As one of them put it, man's character would change irrevocably after serving time in that dreaded place. (Anyway, I think that even a short stay at this hotel will alter a guy irreversibly, whether or not he is conscious of the transformation.) First, he exposed his back to me, which apparently had the blue plough marks of a severe lashing. Next, he displayed his fingers, on which the nails had been heinously ripped off. Then he gave the audience the cherry on the show: his chest, complete with the telltale signs of a lifetime of smoking. "My chest had acted as an ashtray for the guards," he claimed. "But compared to what some of my friends have been through, I count myself blessed!"

Lucky? Undoubtedly, he has lost his mind. I, of course, did not accept his word for it. Not that I don't trust the facts, but who can say those incredible markings weren't already on his body before incarceration? Perhaps he created them to bring shame onto our national security force. I know that some individuals take pride in the needle holes they put in their bodies to display colourful artwork they call tattoos. To me, there wasn't much of a difference with that individual. In an attempt to deceive me, he said that our secret police often resort to torture. Rubbish! He probably assumed I was against the secret police, the moron! He had no idea, of course, who I was. What would he say if I told him I never missed a single word of our BGP's rousing speeches? Some of which I knew by memory. Indeed. He will fall from China great wall.

I'M NOT TRYING TO IMPRESS the government by overstating my abilities, gentlemen. I have evidence to back up my claim. What exactly did the BGP say in several of those thrilling addresses?

Everyone knows that "Our nation is the paradise of Human Rights." Ultimately, the law is what rules us. As long as we stick to these guidelines, we may live as freely - in the invisible realm - as we choose. Since the President is the BGP, and since he was the Minister of the Interior before he stole power (*Hell! Delete, faaaast)*, er..... *(Deleted)* before he was hoisted to the Supreme Power, which is not different from being a Super-Power, he was in an excellent position to know that torture is not tolerated in our country. So, I have to be honest and say that I can't just ignore the BGP's word for the sake of any random individual. I will not be easily misled if an inmate, just released from the freezer, tries to use the scars on his body as proof of wrongdoing by law enforcement. To be quite clear, I am opposed to any evidence that may be used against the secret police because State security is more important than any individual, group, or people.

MY COMMITMENT TO THE secret police and the whole Administration thus established, I hope that the allegations bearing on my shoulders are washed away as fast as the evidence convicting the State agents of torture was. I believe the proposal I am making is a reasonable Win-Win deal. Besides, I had already shown my innocence by admitting I was not a singular being but a collection of guys sharing the same face.

Indeed, that's pretty amusing, no doubt about it. Now that I have given it some thought, I realise Dalila is utterly unaware of this fact. No doubt in her mind that she is still engaged to a single guy. In a word, that's me. I wonder how she would react if I told her she is committed to at least ten different guys.

- 10? She would say incredulously. What do you mean?

- 10 at least, Dalila. So you understand I am much more than a "little tricky affair" guy.

She would look at me bewildered. Then, I will hammer the iron while it is still hot.

- Now, is there a chance you may still see me as crazy?

Unfortunately, I can't. When she called me insane, I thought I was all by myself. One individual may be completely deranged. I propose instead that we form a ten-person crew. Indeed, not everyone here is insane.

In this sense, I belong to a gang. Nay, I am a gang.

The situation has become more complex. Not a *"little tricky affair"*. My next preoccupation is, which of us will end up marrying Dalila? Knowing and controlling such an issue is a challenge. What is the best way for me to approach this? What if everyone in the group falls in love with Dalila and wants to tie the knot with her? In that case, I'd be in many problems, and I know it's because of the internal conflict I'd be experiencing. If we can agree that one of us, and only one, will marry Dalila, and we will let her choose freely, then maybe I should sit down quietly and discuss the subject with them. If we can't come to an understanding, we'll let the guns decide. The conflict will occur inside the gang itself. Maybe one of us will turn out to be another *Al Capone*, or maybe Al Capone himself, and he will win in the end. Honestly, I may say I will be that guy one day. My time here at the hotel has prepared me well for the exciting life of a gangster, and not just any gangster, either; I want to emulate the life of Al Capone. Here's another career ready for me. All I have to do is walk in wearing the grey suit.

TO BE SINCERE, MY DESIRE surprises even the *old me*. That came out of nowhere. I never even thought about being Al Capone. If I'd understood what I know now about being a criminal, I definitely would have stolen a bank. I don't need to hang around till the cops come and throw me in prison on some made-up charge. Things would be much fairer if I had looted the bank earlier. I feel bad about that mistake now. That was another thing Dalila was concerned about; being locked up without a proper accusation is deplorable. I won't even pretend to be pleased with it. When I am arrested again, it will be for a good cause.

HOWEVER, I WILL NOT give up so easily, even if I am now very distant from my bank and unable to kick off Al Capone's career with a good heist for the sake of my dearly cherished fiancée. I plan to set up a bank inside the hotel, one that is heavily insured, rob it, and then keep all the money for myself. I think it is a reasonable plan of action. The newspaper headlines are clear in my mind:

AL CAPONE COME BACK

GREAT BURGLARY IN PRISON'S BANK

GUARDS' PAY VANISHED

ETC ... THEY'LL BE talking about it for a long time, but I'll be safe in my 'Ouja apartment, counting the banknotes and enjoying a long Havana with a giant bottle of *Black Belt* Scotch. Dalila would be gloating in my arms while watching the news of the hold-up on the TV.

Then, we would marry in the summer, as she wished.

I SHOULD DEFINITELY speak to Mr Aroussi about creating a bank in prison. No need to tell him anything about the heist that would follow. But I can't find him anywhere. Had he been removed or let go? I can't ask his roommate Hassan, whom I'm trying to avoid now. Perhaps I should take matters into my own hands, but I must first get the Administration's approval. As I think about it, I should remove that nonsense about the robbery from my report (*keep it private, between my fiancee and me, as a token of love*). Otherwise, they will charge me with a new crime: "propensity to conduct a theft from a bank that does not exist yet. The perpetrator gave a written confession." There's no question in my mind that they're right. However, they cannot apprehend me since I am already in custody. But it won't exclude the possibility of a trial. (*Should I put a stop to that shady gangster enterprise? But how to satisfy Dalila, then? She thinks I'm an idiot who got jailed for nothing. She could not be more right, though.*)

I have always done what was right and never broken the law. I don't understand what demon stung me. It is hard enough to open a bank here as it is. What about robbing it?

Let us be steadfast in our convictions. In the current situation, even the slightest change may be disastrous.

I KNOW I LACK THE NECESSARY experience to head up such a massive undertaking. I am just an ordinary bank employee, not a banker. The two are pretty different. I would have acted immediately if I were Mr Aroussi. However, it should go without saying that I am not Mr Aroussi. Neither his background nor his expertise in financial matters is mine. Why he didn't put all six million dollars into this hotel is a mystery to me. It's too bad! In retrospect, he really should have. There is a dire need for a bank in this area. This amount is insufficient to create a bank, but it would serve as good seed capital. I don't have anything against investing in Europe, but I can understand the sad outcome it would bring.

It's terrible! Do I not evade and nitpick? I don't see any need to hide how I really feel. I strongly disagree with investing in either Europe or the United States. Why should we give money to those folks when they have more than they could ever spend? And they can't be trusted anyway. They would try to freeze our accounts at the first indication of a political dispute between them and us. Another couvolution with the wrong Beloved General President, and we are in the ditch! We will never see the colour of our funds again. The result could be a disastrous mash-up of business and politics, two distinct realms that cannot be reduced to one another. In my opinion, investing in either Europe or the United States is as foolish as tossing money out the window. I have no intention of ever investing money into a bank in either Europe or the United States. It's too shaky, too wasteful, and occasionally bankrupt.

(*Delete that rant about couvolution and BGP before it becomes part of your report. How could you forget yourself to this point? I'm going to believe that you are really 2, 3, or 10 persons and none of them knows what the other is fucking!*

- Ok, ok. I was just kidding.

- *Liar!*)

(7)

I'M NOT SURE WHY I'M constantly thinking about money; it must be a professional deformity or a fixation. I'm also intrigued by the rat that hasn't shown the tip of its muzzle since my pads stopped its burrow. I'd feel a lot better if I saw that rascal running about. It is its noticeable absence that bothers me. I have no intention of hurting the little beast. What's the point? God created the rat because he felt it would benefit society. Our human civilisation needs rats, mice, cats, dogs, serpents, camels, lions, crocodiles, sharks, and all the other animals that boarded the ark during the deluge. If Noah had believed differently, he would not have permitted them to seek refuge aboard his ship. Oddly, I had disregarded this fact altogether until the time at which I wanted to launch the slogan:

'PAY FOR YOUR STAY IF YOU DON'T WANT TO LIVE LIKE A RAT.'

I think this tagline is a little offensive, not to the rats - I don't care if it bothers them - but to Noah. He was not only a great prophet but also our forefather. We couldn't claim today that they were all living like rats on the ark if the Prophet let them aboard his ship alongside humans without asking for payment. For this reason, I'd like to suggest a different slogan for the main gate of this hotel:

RATS HAVE BEEN YOUR FRIENDS AND BROTHERS SINCE THE DELUGE,

SO PLEASE DO NOT HURT THEM.

I feel this is more appropriate and convenient, and it will undoubtedly be embraced by everybody, resulting in deep collaboration between Man and Rat for the finest inter-racial entente.

It's strange how time flies here. It felt it terribly long at the beginning, but as I became used to this relaxed life, I became more conscious of the passage of time. Nonetheless, I am not as sluggish as it seems. True, the library does not have a large number of patrons willing to squander their time with books. They're always talking, sneaking in some illegal games, or watching television. Still, they never have time to read anything but the football scores. Most people here like football, so we have something in common. Discussing football parties is much more entertaining than politics and far less risky.

IT WASN'T UNUSUAL FOR me to spend a Friday afternoon in 'Ouja at the stadium, watching a match. And when 'Ouja's team played, I was usually one of the first dozens to arrive at the stadium. Some set up camp near the gates and tickets office early in the morning. I couldn't imitate them without making a fool as I'm a respected bank clerk. But on the other hand, if I came with most people, I wasn't sure I'd get a good seat in the shaded bleachers. So I devised a plan: one of my neighbours, a youngster named Khaled, would go ahead with his comrades and obtain the tickets first thing in the morning. They would picnic beyond the gates, and I would join them at a mutually agreed-upon time. I'd bring sandwiches and drinks for the boys to share. We usually split up at the gates because they don't have enough money to book tickets under the sunshades.

I was held in higher regard as a bank clerk. My plastic bag would be loaded with food and beverages; it would be pointless to attend a football party if there was nothing to eat or drink. To be perfect, the entertainment must be a true feast that satisfies all five senses. Thus, it is advisable to stock up on as many delights as possible for those delectable afternoons: bananas, oranges, apples, tomatoes, boiled eggs, sandwiches, and various drinks are all acceptable. The more stuff you pack into your sack, the better. But there is another purpose for these culinary delights, a critical mission rarely praised: to support and boost your team's spirit when the match is lost. You couldn't do your job without dumping the contents of your sack on the heads of the winners. And, because one never knows if one's team will win or lose, it's a good idea to keep empty cans of drinks in the bottom of the bag, as well as some tomatoes, oranges - particularly rotten-boiled eggs, or even banana peels to hurl beneath the feet or on the faces of the enemy.

I hasten to add that I never did that. I'm too clean to do such things; I'm also pretty fair. I acknowledge defeat when it's Mektub. However, if we lose, I open my sack to share the remaining contents with my neighbours. My goal is straightforward: to console the community, so they forget the defeat; these are the boundaries of my ethical duty. Now, if they don't understand what I meant and, instead of using the remains in my sack to fill their stomachs, they throw it all on the other team's fans, I can't be blamed for that unfair behaviour, can I?

Nobody enjoys losing, but life is similar to football. One cannot win at every match. As a result, the best player is not just one who knows how to win but also how to lose. One should be prepared for every scenario and learn to lose before learning to win. Both are Mektub. Accepting loss does not mean I am a loser. It means admitting the Divine wisdom. Yet, when they kick me like a ball, I bounce and roll over. The players used to say whenever they lost a party, "Well, it's bad, but it's also the ball!" That means they have no say in the matter. But when they win, it is never the ball's responsibility but their own! As for me, I say Mektub!

BECAUSE I AM ESSENTIALLY apolitical, therefore, neutral, I prefer to be a ball rather than a player. I may serve both teams at the same time, bringing joy to the winners or bearing the burden of defeat. I am never the victor in such a circumstance because my responsibility is only recognised - alas! - during the defeat. But I am fair-minded and will not hold it against those who see in me their defeat.

The same is true for the cooks. But in this case, the stakes are much higher, and the match is much more essential to everyone involved because the STATE is at risk. I tremble at the prospect of our government fading and disappearing like a bubble of soap. Damn the state! First and foremost, I want to save the saviour: our BGP (Beloved General President). I can't imagine this country surviving a day without him.

It's no surprise! We might be able to live without a state, but not without a BGP. If he is removed, we will not be able to endure for twenty-four hours. The British will be tempted to try another love-hate relationship with us because the circumstance will appeal to their colonialist tendencies. Maybe the Americans too. Or the French... who knows? And suppose the British are too preoccupied with another war in the Falkland Islands or elsewhere. In that case, they will delegate the task to the Americans. That is why I am concerned. I have no desire to work as a bank teller or even a banker under American rule: exchanging British colonialism for the American yoke is not a good deal. I remember what they did to the tribes of natives or to the enslaved Africans, and I shiver. If the British fail to re-invade, I recommend the French. At least, they will teach us how to do a couvolution without a coup, which they call the French revolution!

A la bonheur, citoyens et citoyennes!

Ah, ça ira ça ira ça ira... les cuistots à la lanterne...

Ah, ça ira ça ira ça ira... les cuistots on les pendra...

Ah, ça ira ça ira ça ira... Monsieur le Marquis de Sade

Ah, ça ira ça ira ça ira... sortira du trou noir et nous guidera

Accept your mektub, say the Arabs! The British say, "Play fair." The French say: "merde!"

The meaning is not significantly different. But, having been raised in the pure and raw tradition of Islamic fatalism, is it of any service to be a defeatist as well? I am not a loser. I fight for the couvolution as (1) 007 deep undercover. That's why the cooks' conspiracy must be uncovered and stopped. I have evidence that they are all members of the multinational Muslim BrotheLhood. If necessary, I will also eat mutton and bray: "Yeaaaaaaaaaaaaaaaaaaaaaaaaaaaa It's cooked! "Well done!" As a result, no one would be aware that I am aware.

Am I weird for playing strange games, like an alien tourist who just landed in this hotel? Am I cowering or bugling in the wilderness for no soul? And if I partake of the strange phantasmagorical mutton served by the conspirators, am I not essentially joining them in their game? It is a hazardous venture.

(Scrap this paragraph. What the hell are you talking about? Stick to the facts.)

This is the start of the big summer. We might live to see its end while squirming, dawdling, bungling, fumbling, scrambling, stumbling, fighting huffily and lasciviously in the dry, rusty pit of life, abandoned or forgotten by the Almighty God. So what is it that gets me so agitated? I'm curious. **Perhaps it's the sight of all those men in uniform loafing above the roofs, swarming the tops of the walls, towers, hallways, and courtyards like an army of insects and**

infiltrating even my thoughts. They're everywhere, even in my brain, and I can't get rid of them. I'm losing my mind.

SINCE I'VE COME CLEAN about my intention to consume mutton, perhaps they view me as a conspirator. God have mercy on them. I, a conspirator? I never saw more than a handful of lit lunatics brooding their terrible thoughts in the darkness of their cells in these plotters. Do you expect me to say:

Yes, we're all fantasising about and planning for the day we can smash a state that has an army, po-lice, national guard, thousands of informants, spies, counter-spies, and electro-magnetic surveillance that eats your brain, unveils your innermost thoughts, and then bleeds you dry. AND WHO CARES IF YOUR DAMNED BLED, OVERSTUFFED WITH MILLIONS OF BARRELS OF GUNPOWDER AND OIL, IS GOING TO BLOW UP UNDER PRESSURE OR NOT?

What if I'm ever cornered to the point of no return? Should I confess? Or must I cling to my faith and never tyre of saying, "I AM Innocent, Innocent, Innocent"?

BUT I'M EXHAUSTED. Overtired. So, what now?

Guilty!

(I should probably remove all of this paranoid nonsense from my report.)

DESPITE APPEARANCES, it is not I who am being accused, but the cooks; therefore, I am not to take my place in the box reserved for the accused. One cannot be both the judge and the judged; what makes me so strange? Am I a tourist from outer space? What happened to me? I'm not aware of any other planet besides 'Ouja. Hindus believe that before our current lives, we all lived in another body and that after death, we will live again in another state. Thus, I am maybe a reborn spirit; I was erring from one body to another and will continue transmigration when I die.

My paranoia, however, benefitted the State: none of the reports I submitted to Hamda La'war was ever dismissed as the work of a mad mind. On the contrary, I was pushed to broaden Hamda's paranoia and identify enemies of the State everywhere. Now I wonder how I could have believed that all those destitute people posed any actual threat to the Administration. It's terrible, but I get the distinct sensation that paranoia is essential to the State's survival. (*Scrap it! For hell's sake!*) Not the State, but Hamda, of course. And he survived. He's still the mighty leader of the 'Ouja party's cell... and the mayor. That happened later.

As a result, I must adapt. I am not a national hero like Hamda, at least not yet. I should find some shoemaker to cuckold first. But if I don't find a shoemaker, I wonder whether a grocer or a hairdresser will do. I'm thinking of Mehrez and Mustapha, the two bigmouths of our town. After all, the *Medal of National Merit* is worth the sacrifice, on the condition that Dalila would never know what price I had to pay to obtain it from our BGP.

Let's continue the excellent work. I must be paranoid and labour for the sake of the State's security. I occasionally witness people pretending to be heroes or martyrs. They are not in a good mood. They are pale, as thin as skulls, and appear moribund. Assume they survive after a few years in prison. In that circumstances, they will emerge transformed and unrecognisable even to their mums. How could they cuckold anybody to get on the ladder of the *National Merit Medal*?

Alas! I was linked with those oppressed people whom I don't really care about since they are the enemies of the secret police and, thus, the enemies of the BGP. I am widely misunderstood, like any genius. Did I not say before I became a scientist in this library? Galileo found the earth spinning on its axis and orbiting the sun. He was misunderstood and executed by torture. When Einstein discovered relativity, no one knew what it meant. So, he was not killed because they misunderstood him. They thought relativity did not apply to God. He was pretty fortunate! And Bassam Bourasin will be remembered as the scientist who unearthed the cooks' plot against our beloved General President. He was imprisoned for being mistaken for a royalist while he was a couvolutionnist. That is, obviously, the fate of all scientists.

It's depressing to consider that mess. I am overtaken by the darkest despair; I cannot see the light at the end of the tunnel. Fear and confusion have engulfed me, and my future appears dramatic. Will I wind up dangling from a rope? What happened to my job at 'Ouja bank? Who will take over once I die? And who will look after Dalila, my mother, and my house?

MEKTUB IS UNAVOIDABLE. So, yeah, I'm going to die. I'm already dead. I'm finished and buried. Quite. In my death, I envision my hand drafting a secret report to be submitted to the Administration. Even after death, I will remain loyal to the Administration.

The two angels waiting for us at the graveyard, Munkir and Nakir, appear and ask me:

- What is your name? What is your registration number?

- (I) 007, Bassam Bourasin.

- Unless you seriously believe you are another James Bond, you don't need to place the first digit within parenthesis. Stop lying. You don't need it anymore, you will face God soon. Anyway, what religion do you follow?

- Sir, Islam. And you?

- That's none of your business. Where do you think you are?

- In my grave, sir.

- All right! You don't appear to be a faithful Muslim anyway. We have records of you discussing the Divine commands and missing prayers. Perhaps a stay in hell will turn you into a good man. Are you ready to be a good man?

- No, sir, thank you very much for your suggestion, but I am not aspiring to be a good man. I don't wish to be damned.

- But, Bassam, you're already in hell.

- I had no idea, sir.

- Liar! Are you going to be a good man?

- Not if I am in hell, sir. I decline.

- We'll straighten you up.

- If you try to intimidate me, I'll submit a confidential report to the Universe's highest authority and say...

A bright flash suddenly interrupted me, and a thunderous voice shaking the earth and sky yelled in my ear:

"You don't have to write anything, Bassam. Everything is already known to me."

The Lord had spoken! Justice was on its way...

NO, IT WAS A MISUNDERSTANDING. Unfortunately!

WHAT I THOUGHT GOD speaking to me turned out to be an explosion beneath the prison walls, followed by a well-fed blaze.

My immediate thought was that the insurgency had begun. I buried my documents behind my clothes and dashed towards the courtyard. People were yelling and running in all directions. I took a look at the roofs. The police officers stationed there for two days were shooting nonstop, and the guns atop the towers were spitting fire. However, they were shooting towards the street rather than aiming at the gathering inside the courtyard.

- What's going on? I shouted. Did anybody see the cooks?

But no one responded. It was total chaos in the courtyard, and I could hear the inmates' voices rising like a rumbling of roaring thunder from the cells in the three buildings.

- A mutiny! One of the men gathered in the yard exclaimed.

More soldiers surged forward, rifles drawn, preparing to fire into the crowd.

- Go to your cells, an officer ordered. Do not stay here.

The crowd stood their ground. They were too terrified or thrilled by the sight of the combat erupting between the prison's defenders and the assailants. The officer then drew out his weapon and shot into the air, shouting:

- If you don't disperse and return to your cells, we'll shoot you. This is your final warning. I'll count down from 10.

The guards then took aim at the detainees.

-        OOOOONE,   TWOOOOO,   THREE-EEEEEEEEEEEEEEEEEEEEEEEEEEEEEEEEEEEEEEEEEEEEEEEEEEEE..

.

The courtyard appeared to be overrun by then, with people pouring in from all three blocks. As the soldiers approached, a man among the throng yelled:

- Don't be afraid. They're not going to shoot. Allah Akbar! Allah Akbar! This is the day of liberty, my brothers in Allah. Today is your day. It's your revolution. Onward. Allah Akbar!

I immediately recognised the man's voice. It was Hassan, and he was approaching the guards. The horde immediately followed him. The guards paused. They had not anticipated the crowd's reaction. In any case, it was too late. They were quickly overrun by the prisoners, who outnumbered them. A fight occurred. Two battles were going on simultaneously: one on the walls and roofs between the police and the attackers coming in from the streets and another between the guards and the prisoners.

When I saw blood, I ran back to my library. I was terrified. A few people followed me. Standing behind the window bars, I noticed the Afghan climbing the stairs to the tower as quickly as a monkey, followed by some of his soldiers. The guards were too busy shooting at the street to see them. They were disarmed rapidly, and the Afghan now held the machine gun. He shifted his gaze to the courtyard. At the same moment, Hassan and other men were attacking the second tower, among whom I noticed Frankenstein and Zorro. Amazing! A gangster and a pimp taking part in a counter-couvolution! Seriously, who would have thought it?

PART TWO

Glorious Days in the
Golden Age

Chapter 5

Party's Gone? Patria Too!

(1)

A week later...

I have witnessed the most significant counter-Couvolution in this country's contemporary history, which has no precedent or parallel. I saw the new Couvolution sneaking into this secure prison through holes in the security system. I will no longer use the name "hotel" to embellish or embalm the awful environment where I have been forced to dwell for several months. I'm still waiting for my trial, or at the very least, a judicial interrogation. However, I know that the Administration is too preoccupied to be able to treat my case. The courts will be working full-time in the next few days to deal with the issues of the treacherous collaborators who brazenly supported the vile government of the putschist who had taken power from his master, the monarch. The republic of our former beloved General President would have lasted only a few months and days. I've always suspected that such a tyrannical administration couldn't continue for long. It was only an intermission, as evidenced by the cooks' plot I discovered in the jail kitchens. So many things that seemed unclear to me at the time have now come to light. The sheep, for example, had been slaughtered, cooked, and even eaten, and I wonder who else he might be if he wasn't the warden of this prison.

Truth be told, I had no idea that the conspiracy I could smell wafting from the cooks was so pervasive beyond these massive walls. It was insane to suppose the former president could be deposed in a coup since he was so popular and well-protected. True, I never had any genuine affection for him, but I foolishly assumed widespread public approval after witnessing the media's obsession with him. I knew I couldn't be an outlier, so I chose to praise him along with my bank's boss if doing so would boost our company's success, which it eventually did, albeit momentarily. Furthermore, I memorised portions of his ranting speeches not because I admired him — what business did I have betting on misplaced admiration for an ignorant swine who usurped power? — but because I felt obligated to be loyal to the administration, the head of which was the president, even if it was a burned head. Though I've never engaged in sycophancy or attempted to ingratiate myself with influential members of my community, I've also never been able to avoid the attention of those in positions of power. Simply put, I don't like hypocrites who sit at every table and spit in the broth. A day ago, they were willing to die for the former president, today, they proudly proclaim themselves to be champions of the Islamic Republic, and the day before that, they were fans of the king and passionate defenders of the monarchy. Such erratic behaviour is simply repulsive. If I were the new ruler, I wouldn't trust them because they have no ethics. Alas! Our illustrious new President must deal with such undefined, invertebrate amoebas. What would be different, in fact? The conspirators would keep working undercover, but the new leader would look in another direction. It never ceases to befuddle me to see some of the inmates act in such bizarre ways. True, I was prepared for anything from the Afghan Mohamed Mashawir and his cronies, for I had suspected from the start that they were exploiting the kitchens and the cooks for their own ends. I knew Hassan was "one of them" because I saw him conspiring with the Afghan and exchanging coded communications with one of the chefs. But in the previous few days, it was the people who seemed the most removed from and apathetic about the complex political climate in our country that startled me the most. Of course, I'm referring to Frankenstein, Zorro, and Suleiman Mughli. Three guys who, up until this point, had been gliding in a completely separate area of activity that had little to do with politics and even less to do with the Islamic uprising. Thus, in the blink of an eye, a gangster, a pimp, and a drug dealer had become not only the masters of our Bastille but also the confirmed heroes of the day, with the Afghan at their head and the journalist as their herald. I told myself: "If the Islamic counter-Couvolution can quickly convert such an nonredeemable trio and turn them into competent fighters, then I'll be damned if I don't join its ranks myself.

In reality, it was this intrepid trio that incited the mob to attack the citadel. As the Afghan led a tiny group of men up the stairs, Frankenstein and Zorro led an assault on the second tower. At the same time, Suleiman Mughli climbed up the gutters and led an attack on the police officers who were stationed on the roof. By this time, I was shaking like a leaf in the library, debating whether or not it was wise to risk my life and career by witnessing such a bloody insurrection. To be honest, as I believed that the mutiny would soon be put down, I chose to wait for the conclusion while I prayed for the new Couvolution.

Probably, I exaggerate a bit. I wasn't afraid for my own life (such selfishness was foreign to me) but rather for the new

Couvolution, which I had not only predicted but actively contributed to through telepathy.

So, I did not think about myself, even though I realised that if the new Couvolution failed, my twenty years in prison might turn into an indefinite sentence. In addition, I had no idea that a coup had taken place in the middle of the night, hours before the prison was stormed. With the help of God, the putschists announced the end of the dictatorship and the establishment of the *Islamic State*. Following this, they dispatched forces to free their comrades who had been imprisoned alongside me; the mob joined them, and the struggle with the loyalists was extremely violent until the radio announced that the dictator had been slain. Then resistance became futile, and the loyalist troops surrendered. Not long after, I noticed white blankets flapping on the prison's towers and rooftops. The invincible Bastille had finally given in. The counter-Couvolution won. People were stomping around and fuming in the library, the courtyard, and the buildings within the compound. My theory of coups, revolts and Couvolutions was correct. When the Bastille's gates were thrown open, History has revealed it.

Several inmates made an attempt to break out at that time. When the soldiers marched on them, shooting into the air, just a tiny number continued their attempt. They fell back, and I got the impression that some swore at the insurgent troops. (*Those scumbags must be warned; they're the new government's first foes.*)

Hassan yelled at the group, reminding them that trying to escape would be considered desertion. The traitors would be executed. As the rebel forces stormed the courtyard and seized vital positions, any remaining loyalists laid down their weapons and surrendered to the new authorities, hands on heads.

The officer in charge addressed us with, "In the name of Allah... Make silence," before speaking through a megaphone.

The crowd ignored cries of "shut up" and continued brazenly jostling and grumbling until the soldiers opened fire on empty air. Then, finally, they stopped what they were doing and started listening. The officer said:

- In the name of God, on this historic day, the vile oppressor of our glorious people was shot while he was trying to oppose the Revolution. Islam is now the state religion, and the dictatorial government is null and void. All honour and thanks be to Allah. Our oppressed brethren will soon be freed thanks to the leadership of Emir Abdelghani Abdel Ghaffar, may Allah be with him.

- Long live the Leader, the audience chanted.

Inmates were already dancing in the cells behind the bars of the windows overlooking the courtyards. But the military managed to cool them down. The officer yelled:

- Quiet!

As everybody fell silent, he continued:

-*The Committee of Revolution* is determined to free our country from the hands of the wicked gang that had let us to havoc. For much too long, the people of this country had been restrained from enjoying the liberties that befitted their illustrious past. In the name of Allah and the Committee of Revolution, WE, THE PEOPLE...

Cheers. A rising hand indicated that the officer would continue:

-Yes, my brothers, we are the people and do not accept any other constitution except the Holy Koran.

There was a ruckus from the crowd.

-Those who stand with the Islamic State should raise their hands, the officer instructed.

I looked up and saw thousands of people raising their hands. To have such a brilliant poll conducted really wowed me. Then, behind me, I heard a grunt:

-Are you opposed to them?

Before I could respond, someone else exclaimed:

- This is a courageous man!

- Suitable for the scaffold, another voice chimed in.

When I turned around, I saw that the individuals clustered behind me were all raising their hands and staring in shock at me. By sheer distraction, I was the only man in the entire prison who had failed to pledge loyalty. That's a really ominous beginning. I was quick to put any doubt to rest, though, by raising my hand and shouting as loudly as I could:

- Long live the Islamic State! Long live Emir Abdelghani!

So, I made sure I was safe. No one could ever accuse me of missing the historical train.

-Well, now those who are against the Islamic State raise their hands, the officer stated.

There was a sudden and universal lowering of hands. This time, I kept my mind from wandering to the point of forgetting to raise my hand. I looked around me, expecting to see a wicked hand raise itself. There wasn't any. The evidence has been made: inside this prison, there are no enemies of the Islamic counter-Couvolution. It's strange because it seems like all of the inmates have accepted the new rules. There will be zero opposition to this government. The future will show whether I am right or wrong.

Officer:

- Now that our Islamic consultation is safe... Now that you all joined our people in voting for the new regime... I warn the traitors, the hypocrites, and the dogs who supported our enemies that they will be punished to death. Abolished at the behest of the Committee of Revolution, the pigs' party is now in disarray after decades of oppressing this country. As of now, it is expected that all practising Muslims will fulfil their religious obligations. All of us are obligated to pray daily prayers. The disobedient will receive just chastisement. Allahu Akbar!

The crowd's chant of "Allahu Akbar" resounded throughout the area. It looked as if the harsh and brutal prison had been transformed into a massive mosque by magical enchantment, and the faithful were lining up to pray. Three times I joined them in proclaiming God as Supreme. Such religious zeal was moving and alluring in equal measure. Without a shadow of a doubt, we were all profoundly affected. That overpowering religious tsunami, backed by the machine guns, was contaminating even the unfaithful, who were neither few nor outnumbered, as I believe since one hears nothing in prison but curses raining on God and all his prophets day and night. Why the sudden change of heart? It's difficult to say. The dramatic shuffle has been significantly more extensive than I had realised up until this point. My vision was hazy, and I felt a little unsteady on my feet. The sky above was clear blue, and the sun was scorching. Sweat, blood, or both, were dripping off of us. The weapons glimmered in the sun's slanting rays, but grime and dust covered the faces. Were that the Day of Final Judgment, I doubt any of us would have escaped damnation. Some dead guards and inmates could still be seen strewn under the walls, roofs, and stairs. Blood was spilt all over the floor. There was a red

F... YOUR MO...

painted in blood on the white wall of the building just across from the library. He obviously had not had the opportunity to finish his vile sentence.

I just started to see how strange, false, and even funny the situation was. A majority of the guys who had been indurated thugs who cursed God, the state, and society up until that morning were now passionate supporters of the Islamic Revolt, even though many of them had probably never set foot inside a mosque before. The transformation is eye-catching. Had they discovered during the battle that, after all, they were Muslims? Had they fought for the Islamic Emirate, of which no one had heard, or because they saw an opportunity to escape that they couldn't pass up? No matter what they were fighting for or why they were fighting for it, I have no doubt that their fervour was becoming surrealistically real. They would have gone with the Devil if he promised them freedom, that's for sure. The shock had me completely disoriented. It's the first time I've ever been so immersed in a rebellion, and I'm convinced that even though the last coup was a miserable failure, this one will fundamentally alter our lives. That the putschists promptly considered storming a Bastille gives credence to my basic idea that jails serve as foundational elements in developing revolutionary schemes. That is where the despised former president fell short. My goal in penning this covert report was to alert him and his ministers to the fatal flaw in their strategy.

(2)

Now I'm not sorry that my report never made it to them. Evidently, they would have assumed I was trying to outsmart the President and his ministers when I was only trying to be helpful. And who knows what those moronic individuals would have done in response? Perhaps they would have retaliated against my efforts by extending my confinement, forcing me to delay my wedding once more. My own concerns are minimal because I am patient and can wait. What about Dalila? She wasn't thrilled to learn that our wedding wouldn't happen until I was out of prison in twenty years, and she probably wouldn't think it was fair if we had to wait five, ten, or fifteen more years. If that happened, it wouldn't be me, whom she labels crazy, but the President and his Minister of the Interior. The Islamic counter-Couvolution, which had come about so suddenly (even though I had been anticipating it, with delectable prescience, as it crept from the kitchens to the towers), is saving my life, profession, and marriage from a bituminous catastrophe. Those on the Committee of counter-Couvolution will forever have my undying gratitude.

Thankfully, I could not submit my report to the Administration since I still needed to complete it. This kept its contents secret even more securely than before. No one needs to know that I was actually writing such nonsense. Since I predicted the regime's downfall, I could not, in good conscience, be loyal to it. Once I learned of the conspiracy, I realised that the former president's time in office was limited. Without a shadow of a doubt, I am blessed. Imagine if I had turned in my report a few days before the Islamic Coup d'Etat instead of waiting until afterwards. First, no one would have had time to read it, let alone comprehend it, let alone put its proposals into action in a way that would have given it substance and efficiency. And secondly, with the insurrection brewing and the army advancing on the presidential palace, everyone would have fled the office and rushed home to follow the news. All files and State-documents would have been taken by the rebels in the first days, if not the first hours of the mayhem. Top secret or not, my report would have gotten into the wrong hands, and I would be facing charges of high treason and collusion with the detested regime. I would not be here today, chronicling these awful events in our modern history, if I had been sentenced to death.

Despite my lack of formal education in the history field, I can now perform this work as well as any professional academic or savvy journalist. If I can get on with documenting the Islamic Revolution as a historian or eyewitness, from its earliest and most exciting moment, the Fall of the Bastille, then all the better. Even though I didn't actively seek it, fate has positioned me at the epicentre of the political storm that has engulfed this country. With a mix of nostalgia and vigilance, I continue to follow the unfolding drama here in the retaken Bastille. I'm not even a little bit down! Bewildered, but only somewhat so. How will this all play out? Our shaky ship is fluttering and trembling like a feather as it lurches from one coup to the next, from one insurrection to another, over the roiling sea. When will we be able to find a safe harbour to dock in? Unfortunately, we have to deal with any Junta, regardless of how it presents itself. However, I am mesmerised by all this lumpy, clumsy, and rambling movement. Once you hit my age, you must settle on a career path: bank teller, banker, librarian, secret agent, gangster, historian, etc. I really can't say. That makes sense. In our country, everyone acts as if they have a clear idea of where they are going, while in reality, the country is being ruthlessly dismantled by those in uniform and those who aren't. At least I have the decency to admit I have no idea where I am going. But I won't show any signs of being resentful. Undoubtedly, the Islamic counter-coup saved us from a hopeless future under the former dictator. And since the new dictatorship has wiped out the old party, I am under no more covert commitment to the administration. As a result, I can transform these notes into:

HISTORY OF OUR GLORIOUS ISLAMIC REVOLUTION

Brothers, we've got our Bastille, so let's get going. We still need to make one last push to keep it forever.

I must emphasise that despite being a victim of injustice, I have not been released. I find some comfort in the fact that most, if not all, inmates now say that they were wrongfully put in jail. So that, if necessary, the previous regime's heinous and disproportionate injustice might be demonstrated. Mr Aroussi, nearly all of my chamber mates (including Zorro and Dahdah), drug dealer Suleiman Mughli, terrorist Mohamed Mashawir, aka the Afghan, and, of course, Frankenstein, or Salih, the bank robber, and distinguished and secretive journalist Hassan are all among the unfortunate victims. It wouldn't surprise me if some of the guards came forward to say that they, too, wanted to be set free. Life behind bars, on either side of the walls, is not a particularly exciting prospect.

After the officer had left the courtyard, his aides lined us up in rows and gave the order for everyone to return to their cells. After the fact, they would investigate our claim if we had one. One of them argued that "revolution is not anarchy."

Afterwards, we shuffled back to our cells and were locked up again.

Even though nothing had changed, our guards had been disarmed and were now receiving help from soldiers. Though we were excited about the revolt, it was disheartening to realise that we were still being held as captives. However, I must point out that neither the Afghan nor Hassan returned to their cells; this indicated that something had changed, at least in their case. According to what I've heard, the two men were called in to assist the new warden in establishing order within the prison. A moment before I left the courtyard, I overheard them speaking softly with the lieutenant. It was as if they had known the putschists for years. Not without some trepidation, I admit, I wondered if Hassan would remember that I avoided him in recent days before the uprising — damned be the wretched lawyer! Obviously, I should have seen his incompetence coming. I was already profoundly regretting my huffy and skittish exchange with the Afghan. I couldn't believe how cavalierly I had spoken. When did the devil poke me till I feigned I didn't believe in God and that praying together with him wouldn't make any difference anyway? It was a bitter pill for him to swallow. I had no reason to believe that his friends were standing outside the door, and I was still hoping that the administration I was devoted to would not betray me, even though I was wrongfully imprisoned on charges brought about by that very administration.

I was also concerned for another reason. I heard the officer's warning, and it made me uncomfortable when he said that anyone caught still working for the former government would be killed. It goes without saying that the papers I was hiding beneath my garments got as hot as embers at that point. I only had one thought: how to get rid of them without drawing attention to myself! It was difficult because I was no longer alone in the library. People were rushing into the small, enclosed space, either because they were scared or because the courtyard was strewn with bodies and wounded, in addition to the mob and the military. I'm not sure how all those people ended up outside their cages. No doubt, when rushing to assist the police officers stationed on the roofs, some guards mistakenly unlocked some cells, unless they did so willingly under the pressure and tension of the heated situation. The captives had escaped into the courtyard, sparking the revolt. As a result, I assume that some guards were already siding with the insurgents. Unlike us, some of them could hear the news on the radio that morning and therefore knew there had been a coup. That explains their tepid resistance when the insurrection began.

On the other hand, it wasn't impossible that the drugged food they'd been fed day after day by the malignant cooks had gangrened them to the point of turning them into gawkers. Suleiman Mughli was smuggling his illicit items into the prison as readily as he did anywhere else. Thus, it was not difficult for the cooks to do so. Anyone with enough cash might get hashish in the form of a tablet or even a cigarette. The prices, I was told, are higher than on the free market. Yet, it appears that the inmates are content to find some type of relief.

I've never understood how the Mughli could get drugs through the prison's thick walls. To accomplish this, he must not only be cunning but also have some level of collusion with the guards. Furthermore, when the latter ransacked our cells a few times before the insurrection, they discovered nothing notable, which was peculiar. I'm sure the Mughli had been alerted by his guard friends, giving him adequate time to transfer his stash, assuming he was hiding his merchandise within the cell. When he arrived, he was not unknown; his reputation had apparently preceded him because he was hailed by guards and several inmates, including Zorro and his gang of ruffians, who invited him to dine with them. They talked, laughed a lot, and smoked American cigarettes - a sumptuous and lavish luxury around here - and I overheard them occasionally blaspheming and cursing God and his prophets. This is why I was taken aback when I saw them participating in the mutiny. I had the impression that they were on the government's side because they despised the Afghan and his band of ragged zealots.

Furthermore, they were somewhat privileged; I had the impression that the guards closed their eyes to their dubious traffic and were submissive to them, but they were unpleasant and harsh to the rest of us. I am almost sure that Zorro, Frankenstein, Mughli, and other riff-raff were ignorant that the rebellion was organised by religious extremists for the simple reason that they participated in it, although they are as removed from religion and politics as Rome is from Mecca. What drew them in was the spirit of anarchy that was deeply embedded in their thoughts. They were content to throw oil on the flames and dash about the walls like sedulous devils, clambering on the gutters and the stairs, no doubt in the expectation of profiting from the general chaos and breaking away and disappearing in the smoky landscape.

Nonetheless, the lively mirage of freedom that loomed so vivaciously on the high walls, ravishing for a while their confused minds and chirping sweetly into their incipient ears, pushed them to struggle their way out, openly clashing with their former partners and defenders. It was as unavoidable as the allure of freedom is for every man worthy of this name. Some guards swiftly surrendered, putting their firearms on the ground and raising their empty hands above their heads; nevertheless, others fought on, intending to preserve the honour of the uniform against the furious throng. They injured or killed some detainees before being overrun and ripped apart. Mahmoud was among the first to walk. He flung his pistol on the ground and cried, "Long live the Islamic Revolution!" as soon as the mutiny began. The gun was being picked up by the Afghan, who was being heeled up the stairs by his buddy. Other guards followed Mahmoud's lead and retreated. As far as I know, they were not injured; Mahmoud even boasts now that he was the first activist among all his colleagues. He claims to have known about the coup before it occurred. That's why, he muttered, he'd slain the Jew. He is spreading the rumour that the Jew was a government spy who was impersonating the sick man to avoid working like the other inmates!

"In truth, I have always been an Islamist," he told Dahdah, hoping that the latter would spread the lie inside the cell and reach the ears of the Afghan or one of his guys. But Dahdah was cunning.

-I never saw you praying, he said. I am even certain that I have heard you blaspheming and abusing those who pray countless times.

Dahdah later told me, "The black guard was so enraged that his dark face turned blue, then yellow, then white. I mistook him for a chameleon, shifting colours as soon as he spoke. Saliva oozed from his lips, and I saw murder in his eyes. If he still had his pistol, he would have shot me down and spread the rumour that I was a government spy. 'What a fucking fool are you?' he spat out. Do you expect me to tell everyone I was genuinely against the filthy government? Why don't you see that I was covering up? You're fully aware that the murderous regime suspects everyone who visits mosques. That's why I wasn't praying, damn you!' Then I answered - went on Dahdah - that as far as I knew, all the mosques were open to the devout. 'Yes, they were open, but the government was picking up the fucking Islamists at the threshold,' he claimed. 'Find out how they got them here. You know full well that the vast majority of them had never been tried or even charged by any judicial body. They are only here because they were praying in the mosques.' Then I asked him, "And you were one of them; that's why you're here?" 'Yes, I am one of them, albeit I am not here for any charge, but only to support them in their predicament,' answered the hypocrite.

Mahmoud had made it such that everyone in the courtyard could see him praying since that day. His zeal went to such extremes that it eventually irritated the Afghan. The latter saw that the black guard's prayers were much longer than the tight duty required. So he stood alongside him one day, suspiciously eyeing him and rubbing his beard, and said:

-The morning prayers do not require more than five minutes, say ten minutes if one is slow. I've noticed you praying for exactly an hour and fifteen minutes. Your commitment to Allah is admirable, but it is detrimental if it causes you to neglect your professional responsibilities.

- Sorry, sheikh, if you cannot understand why I am praying so devoutly, Allah can, Mahmoud remarked brusquely when interrupted by the Afghan's remonstration.

The response enraged the Afghan, who said:

-Stop uttering inanities and go about your business. Allah despises indolent men, even if they spend their entire lives in the mosque.

The guard paused for a time before succumbing meekly to the powerful Afghan.

(3)

In fact, the Afghan has taken over as the effective warden. I was told that the former jail director had been replaced by Lieutenant Kemal, who had appointed the Afghan as his assistant. However, the latter is far more potent than the new warden. Three days after the coup, some detainees witnessed him and Hassan being driven outside the prison in a police van. Rumours circulated regarding their possible invitation by the Committee of Revolution to hold prominent positions in the future Administration. The Afghan cohort was ecstatically excited in the cell. For my part, I was taken aback by Hassan's transformation.

I remembered a chat with him in which he seemed to disparage the Afghan; I concluded then that he did not like him. But when I noticed them friendly chatting in the courtyard and exchanging jokes and coded messages with one of the chefs, I understood I had been a victim of Hassan's deception. And when I saw Hassan commanding the insurgency and pushing the rebels to assault the guards and police, I knew he was at least one of the instigators of the conspiracy within the prison. He was probably just testing me when he denied that the Afghan could carry out a successful coup in England. If I remember correctly, he even mocked him and claimed he was backward.

Nonetheless, since the coup, they have been the most dominant duo within these walls. Even the guards carry out their commands meekly because they are no longer regarded as captives but rather leaders of the Islamic Revolution. They do not sleep in the cells, do not eat with the inmates, and are rarely seen in the courtyard because their jobs in the administrative offices are vital. However, the Afghan group maintained communication with their leader. The Indian, Pakistani, Indonesian, and black Bilal were permitted to walk freely between the compounds and inside Block A if they needed to talk with their commander. Their pals, who have grown in number, now spend most of their time lounging in the courtyards rather than being locked up with the rest of the detainees. I see them gathered in small groups, chatting airily or debating serious issues in the country that are rarely discussed on television. They are confident that they will be released soon. They usually read the Koran together and joke as if they were outside the high walls. I'd never seen them in such a condition of over-excitement before. They had successfully attracted many inmates, who appeared to be fresh recruits who converted to the fundamentalist movement. A sign of the times: the barber is virtually out of business! Nobody wants to shave since the coup; practically everyone's face is stubbled. It is fashionable to sport a trim beard. The prayers are also collective.

However, religious enthusiasm faded after the first days. Some detainees refused to pray and were not harmed, although they were considered desperate cases to be discarded and secluded. Others persuaded the Islamists that they were doing their religious duty properly and conscientiously. Then, when they were confident that no one was looking at them, they went around mimicking the Islamists like monkeys or even joking during the prayers. By the end of that historic week, the bulk of the detainees had reverted to their old, wasteful ways. Pills, hashish, scabrous jokes, blasphemes, and even nocturnal debauchery. Zorro was in command, and the Mughli had abruptly stopped praying. He even mocked an Islamist for advising him to "return to the straight path."

-If the appropriate path is in your arse, show it, and I'll go straight in, he said.

The men laughed at the harsh response.

-You filthy swine, God's enemy! exclaimed the angry guy.

The latter's friends then attacked Mughli, but Zorro and his clan intervened to defend him against the frenzied crowd. They would have fought to death if the guards and troops had not interfered. They separated them and transferred the Islamists to another cell. Our chamber is now only occupied by the gang of Mughli and Zorro, as well as a slew of ruffians and cutthroats.

I stopped praying. It is both pointless and damaging because my roommates will think I am a zealous Islamist who has been discarded by his clan. However, this is not a charge I reject or refute because I am now the Historian of the Islamic Revolution, to which I aim to spend my time. Still, I will not fall into the trap and antagonise the Revolution's adversaries. We are now powerful, yet we are still disorganised, as this is only the beginning of our rule. Outside the cage, though, I maintained a separate façade. When I hear Muezzin's call, I hurry to the courtyard to pray with the brothers. Nobody in my cell can see me because I'm well hidden inside the group. As a result, I am safe. I am also permitted to work at the library, a one-of-a-kind haven away from the obnoxious rabble. I'm not a hypocrite or a braggart like many other detainees. I'm just making myself useful to the new authority. Because the Islamists now rule the country, it is prudent to maintain cordial relations with them. This is a matter of principle, and as a straight man, who has always been on the right path, I cannot fail to be loyal to the new Administration, as I have always been to the previous.

Although I hate the big city, I don't dislike spending time in the souks and Al-Murabitat area. Without the bank, 'Ouja would be utterly dull. I find the Capital more appealing because of so many attractions. This includes the city's many streets, lights, hotels, restaurants, bars, cafés, cabarets, pleasures, gardens, backstreets, and lanes. True, a little brothel has sprung on the outskirts of 'Ouja. But I'm not going there. Everyone knows who I am, and Dalila would find out about my visit to the ladies.

I recall hearing people remark when I started working at the National Bank office in 'Ouja: "A good employee should remain where he was assigned. That is the right path; otherwise, one is lost."

I've never deviated from the path, though. Even after so many years as a bank clerk, I have no idea how I ended up jailed in the Capital. No one ever explained the significance of the official invitation, not even the shrink or the lawyer. I visited the Capital many times that I no longer recall. The straightforward way led me to the Al-Murabitat neighbourhood, specifically to the pious saint Sidi Abdullah Hush Lane. The area is a maze of passageways in the old city where only men can walk. In defiance of that ridiculous male custom, some ladies developed the habit of standing and displaying themselves on the steps of shops and tiny houses wearing only a short and a bra. Thus, they awaited the knight, who would take them on his white or black horse.

However, I was never there by myself. I took care not to violate any instructions. I understood how to persuade the bank to send me on a mission, sometimes with colleagues, occasionally alone: to stay on the path so as not to slip, a constant working principle. My position as a teller at the 'Ouja branch made it easy to justify calling the headquarters in the capital city to speak with someone in the accounting department. Then I would go to a restaurant in the Souks with some funny pals. We are usually greeted there as though we were getting ready for a wedding. But, of course, we were actually planning for it.

We would order salads, tagines, sausage omelettes, and BBQ and wash it down with two or three bottles of wine. Then we make our way through the souks' serpentine lanes to the Al Mourabitat area. And there, we would have 100% halal temporary nuptials for a few hours, according to the Shiite holy tradition of temporary marriage. Finally, we generally end the evening at the cabaret "Crazy Horse."

Nawara was more appealing to me than the other females. She is a lovely lady in the Murabitat neighbourhood. I used to pay her visits and have a brief marriage with her occasionally. She was headquartered in the same lane named for the pious saint Sidi Abdullah Hush.

I lost count of the number of times I went there, but even after I proposed to Dalila, it still had some allure for me.

Iwent there for the first time with two bank colleagues. I used to meet them for Friday prayers at the mosque. One of them once told me:

- Now that we've completed our duty to God, it's time to pound the ground. So, Mr Bassam, what do you think about joining us?

The second became enthused and exclaimed, without waiting for my response:

- Yes, let's go. Sidi Abdullah is calling us to duty.

Credulously, I inquired:

- Sidi Abdullah! Who is this person?

They both burst out laughing. They understood I didn't know anything about the area.

They advised that we go to the capital's souks, where they knew of a fine restaurant. We drained three bottles at the dinner before heading to Sidi Abdullah Hush. I couldn't believe those ladies were standing about in their lingerie. Finally, one of my buddies pushed me in the direction of a lady.

- Isn't this big, Haram? I said hesitantly, conflicted between my desire and my religious feelings.

- Absolutely not! Are we, God forbid, leading you to sin? Go in. Talk to the one you choose, give her a dowry, recite Al-Fatihah, and perform your job, my brother.

-What exactly are these rituals? Will I wed her?

- Certainly! You may marry anybody you choose and change your mind at any moment. It's a good marriage. You both agree on how long it will take ahead of time. An hour, two hours, a night...and so on. When the time comes, you divorce.

I was sceptical and hesitant. But the wine I drank that day was enough to bring my most hidden impulses to the surface. Furthermore, I found nothing to say, when one of them recalled the verse: "So whatever you have enjoyed from them, pay them their rightful wages". Then he added a Hadith related by Al-Bukhari: "Imran bin Hussain said: The verse of mut'a (enjoyment) was given in the Book of God. Thus we did it with the Messenger of God - may God's prayers and peace be upon him and his family - and no Qur'an was revealed that forbade it, nor did it ban it until the prophet died."

- Do you believe you're better than the Messenger of Allah and his Companions?" my second colleague said.

- Please, God! I'm not any better.

- Then trust in God and enter.

That's precisely what happened. I've been married more than once since that day. Neither she nor I exchanged any passionate lip-locks with the others there. However, Nawara was my favourite. She'd welcome me with hugs, kisses, and the words "My love." Indeed, I was doing so and even more of it.

Let me be clear: I'm Shiite only when I marry for an hour or two. Sometimes more, but it makes no difference. I should not be concerned about what I did since, thanks to Allah, we are now living in the Golden Age under the Islamic State. I took the precaution of adhering to all of the requirements. After all, it is a prophetic tradition, and no one is better than him. As a result, I am not in breach.

I hope I won't stay at this State Hotel for long. Since my arrival, I've been feeling apprehensive. However, since I was graciously invited by the security ministry, the duration of my hospitality is at the discretion of the higher authorities. As the latter have just changed, I would not usually meddle with their business since it is not my custom, but this time is different. For the problem is all about me.

Nonetheless, the past is no longer relevant. I must live in the present moment as a man of principles who values his country's vital interests over his own selfish interests.

(4)

I had made friends with the Indian, who, like me, is a voracious reader, albeit he feigned that our library was inadequate because the books he desired were unavailable. Abdullah Zahir is a small man with a swarthy complexion, an oblong face, two dark narrow eyes under thin brows, a prominent forehead half covered by glossy black hair, a long-pointed nose riding a fine moustache, and a hunched mouth. He must be in his thirties, yet he appears a little older because he limps when he walks, and his movements are slow and heavy, like those of a tired man. When I asked him, he was the one who persuaded the warden to let me resume my work at the library. It was quite kind of him to intervene on my behalf, even though I was not one of his close friends at the time. I was concerned about the papers I concealed beneath my shirt. I couldn't get rid of them for four days in a row. Where, when, and how would I go about doing so? Finally, I decided to approach him. He is not fluent in Arabic but can read, although his spoken language is awful. So I negotiated in English and quickly persuaded him that I was on their side, 'one of them.' He joined me at the library the following day. After a long moment of searching through the shelves, he scowled and stated:

-That will not do. It's not even worth the name of a library. Are these books? He questioned, pointing scornfully to the shelves where some English books were arranged. He added: These are byproducts of a profligate culture. They should be burned.

I sifted through the book titles and understood he was referring to Hemingway, Tolkien, Golding, Lawrence, Burgess, Shaw, and other well-known authors. The British Council's stamp appears on the first page of each of these books. They were a gift for our library. Furthermore, Abdullah was unimpressed by the Arabic authors. Names like Taha Hussein, Tawfik al-Hakim, Salama Moussa, and Neguib Mahfouz did not inspire respect in him.

-You're correct, I answered, they're worthless. They enslave our minds. But there are also some excellent novels, I said after a brief pause. Don't you like novels?

- Rubbish! I'm not an idiot; I went to school in Kashmir, and thus I have the right to state that we don't need novels to educate our youngsters.

- So, what do we need? Maybe poetry?

- Rubbish! Poets pose a greater threat than novelists. No, lad, we just need Islamic law and history texts to clarify our religious duties.

I was struck by such ignorance!

Iam happy to work with Militant groups, but not on this issue. I believe that rather than burning novels and poetry, we should allow authors to write and publish them while prohibiting adolescents, adults and everybody from reading them. That is more astute and prudent. As a result, no one can claim that we are against free expression. And because the authors will be unable to make a living from their sales, they will either have to change their business or commit suicide.

Furthermore, if an author is intelligent enough to shift his line of work, what will he be good for? He has no choice but to make secret reports for the Ministry of Interior. Thus, our Islamic State would be strengthened by capable men trained to spy on others and record their findings. In any case, there isn't much of a distinction between the two jobs.

The difference is that in the first example, the work is publicised and widely recognised, whereas, in the second, it is kept hidden for the purpose of the State, which is less selfish and far more beneficial to the community.

-Rubbish! Rubbish! Exclaimed the Indian. Is there any religious book in this library?

I had to admit that there was none. To my shame, I had worked as a librarian at a library of agnostics, atheists, blasphemers, and other riff-raff who do not believe in God or the Prophet. I have no doubt that this is the exact path that leads straight to hell. I thank Allah because the detainees were not eager to study these books. I was mistaken when I assumed their absence was due to cultural ignorance and disinterest. I must admit that they were far ahead of me because they intuitively realised that reading such literature would intoxicate their minds and blight their souls irreparably. That was also the Indian's perspective, which he articulated far more casually than I could:

-What is the use of establishing a library in such a location if you don't care about stocking it with decent and appropriate books? There isn't a single volume of the Koran, Tafseer or Hadith, but there are novels, novels, novels! What a pity! All of these works are rubbish, diabolical elucidations. I don't recommend you read them.

I lied and said:

- I didn't.

- Well, he responded emphatically. They contribute nothing but confusion and derision to the sorrow of the human race. The novelists and poets are the most damned agnostics known to man. Furthermore, they are like vultures, living off the anguish of others; they exploit their talents to build their popularity on the suffering of millions of people. Yes, they are wild sharks! Their purported concern for the downtrodden is nothing but hypocrisy, and when they let their sense of humour take over, they become nothing more than cold-blooded killers.

I listened in composure as he delivered his expert diatribe against the authors, and I thanked God that, despite the abundance of talents and aspirations he has bestowed upon me, literature is not one of them. Although to be fair, I've never been moronic enough to seek such a vile profession.

- What's your business outside? He inquired abruptly.

-Bank clerk, I confidently said.

It was as if he'd been stung by a scorpion. He glared and mockingly exclaimed:

- Bank clerk? Do you mean you worked at one of those terrible institutions that suck out people's blood?

I didn't respond since my hands were interlocked, and I was humiliated.

- Is that your business, then? He continued. Well, let me tell you, man, you are worse than the evilest of these authors.

I was shocked. I've always believed that my noble profession is among the most recognised in the world because a bank is the very heart of the economy. So I had no reason to think we were draining people's blood. How can we do this when we are the arteries and blood of any thriving economy? Needless to say, I was flabbergasted by the Indian's attack, and after a brief moment of perplexity, I asked:

- Why do you say that? I'm not sure I understand.

He gave me a scolding look and replied sharply:

-Why? You must either be totally blind or completely naive. Your filthy banks are a disgrace to all Muslims around the world. They live on capitalist interests, ignoring divine laws prohibiting usury and profits from idle money. They will be the first satanic institutions to be dismantled in our country, alongside secular laws, the puppet parliament, the party, and other similar larcenous organisations. That is why I came here with Allah's brethren. That is why the Islamic Revolution erupted. My brother, we are fighting Satan and his minions everywhere. It is Jihad, and we must lead it appropriately.

He paused and looked out the window's bars to the courtyard.

- Before I joined the Mujahedeen in Afghanistan, I was a member of the *Islamist Jamaat Party* in Kashmir, he said, pausing again to ruffle his moustache with a long boney finger. I had escaped my homeland, where I was facing the death penalty. From Pakistan, we organised our operations against the Hindu oppressors but also against the *Reds* in Afghanistan and the lackeys of imperialism in Pakistan. In case you don't know, we shot down the C-130, killing their president and several high-ranking generals. Have you heard anything about it? We set up resistance networks all over the area, trained new members, and spread fear, and our enemies either gave up or will soon. In any case, we are victorious because angels support us in our holy struggle. Allah's will is our will. Those who fight us are essentially His foes; they cannot win, my brother.

This man's pristine integrity, unwavering loyalty, and unadulterated candour filled me with awe and buoyed my spirit. For a brief period, I glanced at his stubby face, and it seemed that I was looking at the ghostly figure of some strange bird coming across from a remote location, perhaps even from outer space. I couldn't tell if I was dreaming or hearing an actual report of an extra-terrestrial invasion of Earth. He was standing next to the iron-barred window, through which the bright sunlight showered bundles of delectable fluff into the room. Then it appeared to me that the Indian, with his blue-sky shirt and enormous white trousers, was turning into a twaddling parrot! That was a bizarre feeling, but I couldn't stop myself. I tried to get rid of the strange illusion for a minute, but the image of the parrot stayed, and the iron bars of the cage where we were both locked up made it stand out even more. The white walls and a slice of blue sky behind him added to my uncertainty, and I was suddenly struck by uncontrollable anxiety.

Had he sensed my inner turmoil? As I remained silent, gauntly erring into my constricted despair, he looked at me from the depths of his eyes and murmured:

- I see you are already dreaming, brother. This is a promising indicator. You will soon become one of our most valuable assets, notwithstanding what you said to Sheikh Mohamed. Oh, God, have mercy, but you were no longer normal at that point. You were rather sour, weren't you?

I remained silent. Recalling how I humiliated the Afghan when he asked me about my religion, I felt so guilty...and most of all, scared.

- However, Abdullah went on, when I saw you praying beside the brothers, I realised that the revolution had improved you. Are you now at ease?

- Oh, yes, I lied.

In reality, I was inward, seething with rage and fear. I was already wondering if the new dictatorship would actually close the banks, forcing me, Mr Aroussi, and the other colleagues to either change our business or commit suicide. We are not currently threatened because we are imprisoned. But what if we are suddenly released, and the bank closes? What are we going to do? How will we make a living? I couldn't stop thinking about the issue. After all, it's my career that's on the line. I hesitated, then asked Abdullah Zahir:

-What are you going to do with bankers and clerks like me?

He gave me a cold glare and remained unmoved. After a little pause, he inquired:

-Are you a good Muslim?

I wondered if it was customary in India to respond to a question with another. I said:

-I hope you don't doubt it.

- I truly don't know. People nowadays are strange, and appearances can be deceiving. While I hunch that you're a decent human being, my brother, I did not gain access to your innermost thoughts. To be honest, I'm not sure who you are anymore, given how rapidly you changed sides. If I am straight with you, don't hold it against me, but I must remind you that you were pretending that we don't worship the same God, as if there are multiple Gods. This is heresy. If you do so again, you will be reported as an atheist and convicted and severely condemned by Islamic courts. Nonetheless, we forgive you and give you a chance to redeem yourself because you repented.

He waited to see how his words affected me. He then added:

- As for your query concerning the banks, you should not be concerned, he said after a little pause. I believe you will convert to Islamic banking. As a result, the entire system will change, and the new one will align more with religious principles.

I was reassured. After all, we won't be forced to cruise the streets looking for work.

- I am relieved to hear you say there is an honest solution for us. Are you certain we won't be jobless?

- No, you won't. To build the Islamic State, we need professionals in every field. The sole requirement is that you be a devout Muslim who supports the prince of the faithful.

- As for faithfulness, I won't extol myself, but I tell you that you will not find a more loyal individual in the entire country.

I was about to say that, as a general rule, allegiance to the new master of the day, whomever he is and whatever his creeds, is my motto. But I bit my tongue at the last second, afraid that he could think I was also loyal to their opponents if they attempted and succeeded in a countercoup. That is correct because my motto could not be applied exclusively to a single party. It would be absurd. My actions are dictated by the wisdom of a seasoned guy who has grown accustomed to coups and countercoups. I was loyal to His Majesty the King till the end of his reign; after that, I was loyal to the General President; and now, I am similarly loyal to the Islamist leader; and in the future, inshallah, I will be loyal to his successor. I am certain of this because I am a logical and common-sense guy. This demeanour contains no contradictions, and I believe I am thus fair to everyone.

Furthermore, a well-known Hadith of our Prophet exhorts the faithful to obey their rulers, which is exactly what I am attempting to do. As a result, even if an atheistic dictator overthrows the Islamists and gains power the next day, I will follow my dear credo, obey, and swear fealty. A different stance would be inconsistent, dishonest, unfaithful, and hurtful. It is even an act of bravado against the Prophet's sacred tradition. Therefore, as a devout Muslim, I will never oppose the rulers. It's stupid, pointless, and goes against my ideals.

-Very good, the Indian continued, I expect you to prove your commitment in the coming days, won't you?

-I certainly will. You'll be amazed, I remarked hopefully, thinking about the numerous interesting reports I'd soon write for the new Administration.

He didn't say anything. He didn't even ask me to enlighten him on what was - and still is - going on in the cells, which were thronged with thugs, degenerates, delinquents, smugglers, murderers, sexual perverts, rapists, and other such phenomena of our society. However, I believe that to succeed, a new Couvolution must be able to deal with such a cacophony.

Nonetheless, old reflexes resurface, and they jump up whenever they are teased; it is unavoidable.

(5)

Abdullah Zahir didn't even need to ask me to report my roommates' actions and facts; he was probably shy. There was no time for explanations; I had to absorb it all in silence.

Despite this, I worked hard to overcome this self-imposed limitation. Why should I waste my time writing reports that no one asked me to prepare and for which I will not get compensated? Isn't it obvious that after many years of practice, I'm no longer a novice or an amateur? I did not initiate this noble endeavour out of boredom; instead, it was because Mr Hamda La'war had made it clear that the party was the Patria. So, our PART-RIOTISM - a term I coined just for the situation - provided a solid foundation for our interactions in such delicate circumstances. Yet, despite all of my contributions to the nation,

I had received no recognition: no decoration, no prominent position, and no additional compensation; this is unfair. Both previous governments owe me a big deal for my assistance during their terms. I have no idea how much decoration or high-ranking position actually costs, but I know damn well that the party was paying Mr Hamda La'war well, even though I have no idea what his work included.

Furthermore, the party paid all those secret spies masquerading as militants or militiamen, whose primary function is to write secret reports on their fellow people. Many of them, like myself, are clerks and minor Administration employees, shopkeepers, taxi drivers, waiters and bartenders... That entails earning two salaries: one from their own business and the other from their occult dealings. I should have written at least a thousand reports on various subjects and individuals by now, ever since I began my competent and promising work in the service of the State. It is no longer easy to transmit a covert report. I had never complained, but that didn't mean I was gleefully throwing money out the window. I am, nonetheless, a respected citizen. I pay my taxes, and I don't see why I should serve the Administration for free for the rest of my life.

I made a quick assessment of the cost of a single report.
Pens = 100 dinars
Paper = 50 dinars
Table and chair: (not their actual price on the market, but the price you pay when you sit in a coffee shop for a short moment) = 500 dinars
Light: (not considering the sun-light which is not much practical though it is gratuitous, for the best reports are written at night, under electric light) = 300 dinars
Drinks (included in the cost of 'table and chair' - I am generous) Sandwich= 800 dinars

Clothes and shoes (one cannot go naked and bare-footed to send one's report) = 1000 dinars

_______________________________ Total = 2750 dinars Converted to US dollars at the current exchange rates, to fit the international profile of 'Ouja

= $2600

Substract the service of the bank = $ 100

The remaining sum is = $2500

Asingle top-secret report costs $2500, not including storage in my archives. Multiply by 30 days (i.e., a month). You will get $75,000.00.

Despite the risks I was running from foreign spies, I did not deliver all of the reports I had actually written to the Administration because I retained some of them in my archives. Keeping these archives well-organised and up to date is also a vital aspect of the work; as all archivists know, it is extremely expensive.

I will be generous, though, and will include a minimum cost for the archives in my calculation: $ 25 for the daily report. Otherwise, thirty reports. That is to say: $25 multiplied by 30 = $750 every month. And = $9000 per year.

Add $750 to $75000 = $75.750.

$900.000 when multiplied by 12.

Now multiply that figure by 15 years. You obtain $13.500 million.

Since I started this business as soon as I started working at 'Ouja bank, it is well worth the overdue pay I am now claiming to the past administrators. So that's $13.500 million.

I just considered my services in terms of money, which is always the greatest method to clear and sort out muddled issues while maintaining a nice relationship with friends. In truth, I did not value my contributions morally because it is now pointless to seek a medal or an important position from an administration that has vanished or is on its way out. As a result, I claim that the previous governments owe me a total of $13.500 million US dollars. It is not a negligible amount. I will not pass the sponge over it, nor will I make any more secret reports to the new Administration unless I am first compensated for fifteen years of devoted service. Nonetheless, I am always loyal, but as the saying goes, "the good counts make the excellent friends."

I had no idea I was wealthy. Now I see it clearly. But what happened to the money? I feel dispossessed here in the pit.

Furthermore, I know that the new regime will require me to perform more urgent and competent work, namely writing the History of the Islamic Revolution, which I am doing scrupulously. But I'm concerned about something quite else. I don't believe any historian has ever encountered a situation as perplexing as I'm in. It's terribly gloomy! I can't say how Mr Toynbee would approach this tricky situation if he were in my shoes. In fact, it is widely established in our country that Party and Patria are interchangeable. Now, I'm wondering where The Islamic State was recently declared and, more importantly, where the Islamists would rule if they began their era by removing the party that is the Patria itself.

Eh! In other words, if the Committee of Revolution suppressed the party, it would be left with no Patria to reign over, which is not very intelligent. What's the point of starting a revolution and establishing a new administration if you're going to rule over a shithole? Since our country went away with the old government, we are now without a home. What a disaster! I can see the people around me saying we're a developing nation, but heavens! Where has our country gone? I believe this is the most pressing issue that the Committee of Revolution must address.

Our illustrious revolution is incapable of dealing with the phantom of a country. This is a genuine politico-legal battle. Nobody took our Patria from us, but it no longer exists because the first decree of the new power was to repress the party that is the homeland itself! Now we must demonstrate that our country still exists under the law. But can a simple decree-law actually create a country?

Modern and ancient history demonstrates that our goal is just impossible. As far as I know, Britain, the United States, Russia, France, China, Japan, Germany, Spain, and many more nations have not sallied out of the dark aught to clear existence as a result of a decree-law. That way, they don't have to worry about the first sergeant getting up early to stage a coup, disband the government, and declare himself the leader of a country that doesn't exist anymore. (*This is insane!*) So, the best solution for such a squabble is to declare that this is the *De Facto* Government in Exile. As a result, we will avoid major problems, first with our people and then with international law. If not, we will undoubtedly be labelled as 'predators,' which we are as we behave like hawks and vultures. It goes without saying that we don't need much advertising on this subject... And, since we had disbanded Parliament (*it is strange, but I do not recall there being any parliament before the latest Coup!*), we should perhaps borrow the MPs of the British Commons to vote on some laws that cannot wait for our return to the country - or possibly the country's return to us - because we will undoubtedly need to organise ourselves wisely in the coming days to avoid chaos, anarchy, riots, and other outbursts of anger. There are some excellent agreements regarding cooperation in various spheres between the previous governments of our former country and the British. We can use some of these international treaties to borrow British MPs, at least for a month or two. It will benefit our cause greatly and will not harm the British people. And suppose, despite the cooperation agreements, Britain has some reluctance. In that case, we will either try to borrow American Congressmen or simply recommend that the British people vote for our representatives alongside their own in the next parliamentary elections. As a result, we will save money, energy, and time for our people by forming an exiled parliament whose members are democratically elected in England.

Now that I put it on paper, I remember something crucial that had escaped me: the pricing had changed frequently and gone up during the fifteen years I worked at the bank and as a writer of secret reports. For instance, a pen that cost about 20 dinars a decade ago today sells for 100 dinars or more. Then, if I'm being accurate and honest, as I've always tried to be, the Administration owes me considerably more than $13.500 million. However, I will not take into account the fact that prices have multiplied at least fifteen times. Being the good and magnanimous person I am, I will just ask for $20 million from the previous governments. This is a nice, round sum and, I'm sure, significantly less than the actual amount that the government owes me. Now that the Islamists have taken over and claim to be the new rulers, it would not be a bad idea to ask them to honour the debts contracted by their predecessors, for it is obvious that any government will gain credibility while losing legitimacy if it responds positively to the right claims of its predecessor's creditors. That is a question of common sense on which everyone can agree. I'm simply claiming $20 million.

Nevertheless, I have not counted the interests accumulated over the years. If the money had been deposited in my bank, it would have been worth at least $35 million by now. In reality, this is more likely the true amount owed to me by the State. Nonetheless, given that the incoming government would not consider profits to be part of the debt, I am willing to accept a compromise. Twenty million dollars are better than nothing, so I will accept them from the new Administration as just compensation for my loyal service to their predecessors, regardless of their political beliefs - I have never been a politician - and it must be clear that I owe nothing to the government, and that any future cooperation between us must be negotiated and accomplished in the presence of my lawyer.

To be neat and clear with the new administration, whereto I have the incomparable honour of serving as a historian, I need to remind myself right now of such concomitant problems. But I am conscious that I am embarking on a new profession for the sake of the revolution. I pray that my altruistic desire to preserve for posterity the exploits of these brave warriors, who risked all to bring an end to the corrupt tyranny of the despised president and usher in an era of Islamic renaissance, is well received and amply rewarded. Indeed, our best reward is to enter heaven as devoted men on the day of the insurrection —Inshallah! — and I have no doubt that this will happen, even though my angels are sceptical. On this level, I have no illusions: they will never trust me; clearly, they were schooled to question everything and everyone, and they became accustomed to it. I don't deny that, for a while, I had the irrational thought that I could get them to see things my way. I used to soliloquise, or more precisely, argue with them for hours on end about the great topics of life. I've wanted to make them advisers and close friends ever since I realised they were following me around like my shadow. I never requested such supervision, and when I inquired about it with Haj Mukhtar, the sheikh of 'Ouja's grand mosque, he replied:

-Every human being has someone or something following him. It might be a Jinn, an angel, or the Devil. Who are your supporters, son?

-To be honest, I'm not sure who they are. But I'm inclined to believe they're angels.

-You can't say that, Haj Mukhtar responded.

-What's the harm?

-Because angels rarely follow ordinary people. Angels only approach prophets, and you aren't a prophet.

-Yes, but I know we're all going to meet Munkir and Nakir. Those guys are angels.

-Right, but we'll only meet them in the tomb on the day we pass. They will question our faithfulness. If we reply yes, they will inquire about our religious beliefs. If we say it's Islam, they'll inquire about its five pillars. If we offer the correct response, they will open a small window in the grave and let us experience a breeze from paradise. And if that doesn't work, it'll be the window straight to hell.

Haj Mukhtar's science had failed to persuade me. Why should prophets be the only ones who have contact with angels? Why should Munkir and Nakir only meet us in the afterlife? I am neither a prophet nor a dead person, but I claim to socialise with angels, and they must be pretty terrible because they do not trust me despite my open-mindedness and good intentions. It's no surprise! After all, was not the Devil initially also an angel? It never occurred to me that my angels could be devils, but I am now seriously considering it. I am not easily duped simply because they accuse me of apostasy, implying that I am not a decent Muslim! What could Satan possibly know about Islam, much less any other religion?

Itold Haj Mukhtar about these bizarre diatribes I was having. Aside from being the mosque's imam, he is also renowned for being knowledgeable in these matters. So many people seek his advice when in conflict with Jins, devils, or other extra-human entities. He must be at least 75 years old, but he leads Friday prayers with the same steady strength he's always shown. He sat cross-legged on a small mattress on the floor of his tiny room, listening to me quietly. His bright face was framed by a white beard. His dark eyes, hidden beneath bushy brows, looked to be contemplating a distant horizon. His nose was long and hooked, and his cheeks were hollow and had white hair sticking out of them. He didn't separate his thin lips until I was done talking. I couldn't help but notice his kindness, which is very rare in 'Ouja, whose inhabitants entirely disregard the art of conducting a conversation, so eager to dispute that they don't even hear what you're saying. His spotless white garments gave him a halo of respectability and, I dare to say, saintliness.

- I don't believe your companions are angels, the old man remarked, but you may be taunted by Jins. Can you see them?

- No, no, I don't see them, but I can hear them. Their voices are still quite distinct in my mind. It may be annoying at times because we obviously disagree on everything. They like to argue with me, but they get angry and uncivilised when they can't make me see things their way. They're always complaining, but I understand I'm carrying them around like fleas in a dog's tail.

For a brief while, the old man appeared thoughtful. I was looking at his room's naked walls. Nothing more than a frame hung above his head towards the centre of the wall, holding a small plate with the golden letters "ALLAH" printed on it. After what I revealed, I expected him to reply, "Maybe you're the dog's tail, my son!" But instead, he asked:

- Did they request you to make a sacrifice? Whether it's a lamb, a red cock, a black goat, or something else entirely. Did they request that you go to a shrine?

- They never did, Haj. That's why I doubt they're Jins. A Jin would demand blood in exchange for peace, right? My... er... angels don't seem to be thinking of such a deal. They are obviously uninterested in sacrifices and shrines. They are just thinking about how I may be of more use to the government.

- What exactly do you mean?

- I mean, they're only interested in politics; I've never heard of angels who are also politicians!

- Neither do I, he exclaimed, surprised.

- Among all the billions of galaxies and trillions of planets in the universe, they must be bored and jobless to care about the predicament of this country's government.

- Don't blaspheme, my son.

- I'm not blaspheming; I'm only telling you the truth, Haj. What are they if they aren't Jins or angels?

- Do you read the Koran on occasion? He asked.

I admitted that I didn't.

- That's why you're being harassed. Your fleas are undoubtedly Muslim Jins. Thank Allah for this. Were they of another religion, they'd have harmed you. You need to cooperate with them, my son. Read the Koran every day before bed and when you wake up. They'll be pleased. It would be much better if you prayed five times a day.

Suddenly, everything became clear in my mind. Looking back, I now see that my guardian angels were actually agents of the Islamic State. All they wanted was for me to be more devout, and maybe even more involved in the covert Islamic militancy of the time. God! But wait, there's more! They wanted me to submit to the Emir of the Faithful even before he overthrew our previous BGP (*Beloved General President*).

Nonetheless, I do realise that they made a mistake by locking me in jail with the Afghan and his Muslim BrotheLhood. I was clueless. I had done the exact opposite of the jailhouse assignment I had been given.

As I pondered, Haj Mukhtar cleared his throat. I said:

- I don't have time, Haj. My employment at the bank fully consumes me.

- You must remember God if you desire His assistance.

I didn't dare to tell him that God had nothing to do with my dilemma, which isn't as metaphysical as it appears.

- What do you expect from me? He questioned as I mused silently.

- Help, I said, without real conviction.

- I can't help you unless you help yourself. Every assistance, however, comes from God. When you realise this, you will pray faithfully, and the evil will be extinguished. Come see me in a fortnight, and I'll give you something to keep you safe. However, it will not work if you do not read the Koran. You have thus been warned.

I thanked Haj Mukhtar and left the room. After that, I never went back to see him.

(6)

A few weeks after I consulted Haj Mukhtar, I was arrested, charged, and jailed. My angels were overjoyed. Their inexplicable glee widened the gap between us. I was more determined than ever to battle them, even if they promised me paradise tomorrow. And I don't care if they're called Munkir and Nakir or have different names and roles. If I haven't died yet, it won't happen anytime soon. And I don't need their assistance to get into paradise, either. Since I started studying the Islamic Revolution to write its history, I'm one of the first believers to have the legal right to live in a mansion, cottage, or even an apartment in heaven. What good is our revolution if it doesn't earn us a sliver of God's joyful and blessed universe? Indeed, I will not be alone in heaven. I plan to marry a young and lovely nymph, and with her help, I'll finish relating my memoirs and the events I witnessed on Earth. (*I have yet to decide if there's a need for top-secret reports in paradise. It all comes down to the pay, of course.*) We'll be living in style in the paradisiacal capital, and if I can't find a quaint town like 'Ouja, I'll open a bank there. We shall also have children. What is heaven without a few demons to keep it alive? I hate the kids because they cause chaos and disobedience wherever they go, but I must admit that life would not be the same without them. Not disclosing this nymph plan to Dalila is in my best interest. I know her; she would be so jealous that she would utterly sabotage it.

- What? You will not set foot in paradise without me, and I will not allow you to live out there with the first nymph you meet, she would say.

-That is completely insane, Dalila!

- No, your nympho bitch is not better than me.

-You can't speak so improperly of paradise's inhabitants, Dalila, my darling. They are not human, but aliens.

Then, through her sobs, she'd ask:

- Am I so insignificant in your eyes that you'd rather marry a nympho alien than me?

- It's pointless, honey, don't weep. In what way does comparing yourself to superior people serve you? Doing so will only bring you sadness. Look at me. I know I'm meant to live with an alien nymph, in heaven, of course, not immediately in this world. It's Mektub. And yet I manage to keep my ego in check. If this is what God wants, then so be it. But I would never compare myself to an angel. Those guys work on both sides. You never know which side they support. It may be God or the devil. I lack both their abilities and their nature. They are composed of light, that's why they can travel faster than light in the sky, whereas clay forms the basis of my being. I can't even fly, and if I jump from my balcony, I break my neck. That makes such a difference!

She would then use yet another tactic in an effort to reawaken my latent jealousy.

- Well, if you're going to spend eternity with that bitch in paradise, I'll choose an angel for myself.

- You can't do that, Dalila; ladies aren't offered such a prize.

- What? They have been forgotten!

- No, they aren't, but the faithful wives will enter heaven with their Muslim husbands.

- I am devoted, but what about the nymph?

- It's OK for her to come, too.

- That's not going to work, Bassam. Whether it's her or me.

- This is the promise God has made to us, men. You know you can't fight him, right?

- I'll make myself a rebel and kick you out of paradise if you choose to live with the nympho-bitch.

Then she would duck, and only God knows what was going through her mind. That's why I kept my secret elopement with the paradisiacal nymph from her.

I'm not sure whether it's necessary to set up a bank there. This is a cherished project that I would have started in this prison if I had received even the tiniest support. I should enquire about the situation of the economy in paradise; after all, there may be banks similar to ours on Earth, and with any luck, I would be able to finish my shining career in the skies. Heavens! But this is indeed a brilliant concept!

Because of my dedication and talent, I may even be chosen director-general of a paradisiacal bank, except... Hell! Unless I'm hallucinating! Is this a dream? When one is surrounded by such a pervasive and overwhelming show of human misery, it is so delightful to cultivate such a peaceful project. I raise my head and look through the window bars while I write these sentences. A few groups of detainees are distributed across the courtyard, standing along the walls in the shade. They had wiped off the graffiti that some evil fool had scribbled with blood on the day of the insurgency; (Fuck your moth...) he had not finished it.

But he didn't have to, did he? The arrogance, lack of taste, and sneering hate are all obvious. Such wastefulness is not uncommon under these circumstances, and it is pointless to speculate on how one may live with such a mindset. Some inmates have no regard for anything. Even the dead and martyrs are mocked. Much more graffiti have been discovered on the walls of the cells. A wide variety of sexual fantasies and perversions are on display. Not only is the mother screwed, but so are the father, the sisters, the brothers, the aunts and uncles, the grandparents, and the whole tribe. Some of them are not ashamed to show off their obscene talents on the lavatory walls.

It's disgusting! These brazen idiocies are a constant nuisance on the prison walls. Aside from these petty scribblings proclaiming so openly the sexual misery of those same imprisoned men, there is also political graffiti, and it goes without saying that this is all anti-government. Neither the state nor its men are any more sacred than the lowest-priced prostitute in the brothel. They are sedulously daggled, demonised, cursed, insulted, ruthlessly dragged through the mud, stomped on and ripped apart. On the walls, there is an uncontrite vendetta. Looking at those same graffiti, one would conclude that all of the individuals in prison have been victimised by injustice, yet this is far from the case. Many of them had been officially convicted by a court and deserved to be punished. The animosity for the state and the many institutions of this nation, as well as their representatives, has several origins, which explains why the detainees celebrated the news of the coup, despite the fact that they are not all Islamists. Many of them are chronic alcoholics, unfaithful or deviant fornicators; their only moral is that of the capital's crowded, pitiful backstreets, teeming with hookers, pimps, bullies, drug dealers, and other such phenomena. I'm not sure what the Islamic Revolution or any political change means to them. In any case, they would celebrate even the tiniest report of disorder and anarchy sweeping the country. They would celebrate any leader who promised them freedom and justice (*which they always do*), but as soon as he turned his back, they would rip him apart if they could. Nobody cares about loyalty here; it's a meaningless term. Perhaps the only detainees who could be a little more amenable to compromise are the religious extremists. The coup is a source of optimism for them; they feel at ease with it. Some of them see themselves in prominent positions in the Administration; they are the genuine bosses of the jail. They talk as though they directly knew the members of the Revolutionary Committee, who will not postpone their release.

They would jostle and hustle to occupy the closest spots around the TV set in the evenings, and when the speaker announced the news broadcast, the inmates would fall silent. Everyone, indeed, appears to be preoccupied with the news at the moment. Some believe that the Afghan, Mohamed Mashawir, or Hassan, the journalist, will appear on television alongside government officials. We've been waiting for their faces to appear on television every day since they left. For five days, excitement was at an all-time high, but uncertainty still reigned supreme. We hadn't gotten any newspapers yet, but the TV speaker told us every night that the country was now peaceful and that the last pockets of resistance had been wiped out. The Committee of Revolution keeps the situation under control and asks people to stay calm and follow the curfew.

However, contradictory rumours were entering the towering walls and iron gates, which were guarded day and night by an impressive armada. Some of these rumours said that the president had deceived his attackers and had fled to the south, where he had created a resistance network with sympathisers among his troops. If these rumours are true, the fighting between the loyalists and the Committee of Revolution is still ongoing. The latter rule the capital and several smaller towns and villages, while the loyalists still command the desert south, where hydrocarbons remain plentiful. Otherwise, our nation has been partitioned and is in civil war. The term "civil war" seems an anachronistic misnomer, given that the combatants are troops and armed militias. As a result, the army is split. I'm unfamiliar with the police, the national guard, or other security forces. Perhaps the divide had reached them as well. It's difficult to tell what's going on in this hole shut off from the rest of the world. The TV isn't really useful since the news broadcast is completely irrelevant and fails to mention the war in the south at all. Apart from the military marches, the CR's political jumble, and the silly series, there is little to look at. Whatever the case may be, we are being kept in the dark about the real condition of the country.

But if I trust the rumours that have been circulating within the jail for the last several days, the loyalists are still in charge. They have the country's jugular in their hands since they dominate the south. All of our oil wells, refineries, pipelines, and large port are located in that area. Millions of barrels are so shipped daily over the Sea to Europe. I have no idea whether the coup and the conflict have halted transportation. In such a circumstance, the risks may be more serious than I anticipated, and Western nations may get involved. How would they respond to the instability that has engulfed our country? Would they support the previous president or the coup? That's precisely the point! This is a difficult moment for me as well. Since the beginning of this counter-Couvolution, I've identified with the country's new rulers, believing that being tied to a murdered president would be as pointless as detrimental. He was beneficial while alive and was dubbed 'beloved,' but what would I do with him after he died, as it was announced? Therefore, I consciously decided to strengthen my shaky bonds with individuals I believed to be strong, although they were just as helpless as the vast majority of the inmates. But I reasoned that if they were freed, the Afghan and his cohort may be helpful, provided I could convince them of my support for their cause. I went to pray with them in the yard, and I even got to write a history of the Revolution. But as soon as I learned about the conflict in the south, my excitement faded. What if the former president gained support from some strong friends in the West or the East and returned to the Capital to destroy the putschists? This is distressing, but I want to be sure before committing myself. If he ever wins and learns of my defection to his foes, I'm good for the rope. He probably wouldn't give a hoot about me since he'd never heard of me, but his men would, especially Hamda La'war (if he's still around). So, all of my excitement for the Islamic coup would be futile in the end. After all, why am I so keen to record their wretched history of blood and tears? Are they going to compensate me for my trouble? Nobody cares about my fate if I'm hanged.

Hello, Bassam! my dear, my buddy, my brother, my son, my father! You have nothing to do with the murderous insurrection of those backward morons and fanatics. You are well aware that the south is the jugular vein of the whole damned nation. If the oil remains in the hands of the other president, their crinkling Committee of Revolution will never be able to manage the situation. The economy would fall and collapse without oil; riots would erupt, and everything would be tormented and doomed. They cannot keep their authority just by praying five times a day. Even if they increase the number of prayers and add five more at night, they will only be able to maintain power if they can manage oil. Hydrocarbon underpins our economic system and our whole way of life. It is the bread we eat, the water we drink, and the air we breathe. If we lost our oil, our whole system would fall and perish. Since finding black gold in our Sahara, we have become oil creatures. Hydrocarbon is what made us men. It is oil that has elevated our miasmic conditions on the global stage. We could not be what we are today without oil: merchants, dealers, exporters, and members of the great OPEC, with lots of funds coming into our banks. Even a little community like 'Ouja would not have thrived without oil. What was 'Ouja like before she received the blessing? A mysterious and hidden hole teeming with shite, flies, mosquitos, and other creatures. And what would I be in such a precarious situation? Bank teller? Impossible.

With what funds? Perhaps a scavenger on the streets of the Capital, a burglar, or something similar. As a result, all of the flesh and bones that make up my body are nothing more than oil. OIL IS ME, and I AM OIL. One must accept reality and express gratitude. To conceal it is to mislead oneself, and I am not willing to deceive myself for the sake of politicians and their selfish goals, whatever of the creeds they profess. After all, I've always claimed an apolitical religion. Why should I make such a drastic change? Furthermore, I am still seeking $20.000.000 from the government and expect to be paid. I am not concerned if the government is Islamic, Christian, Jewish, or Buddhist. The most important thing to me is that the wicked Administration - THE STATE - recognises and honours its obligation. The sooner it is completed, the better.

- If not?

- Otherwise, I'll file a lawsuit.

I am aware of my rights and want to protect them. Think about the Jews. Even after over 50 years, they were still asking Swiss banks for money on behalf of their fathers and ancestors who died in Hitler's gas chambers. It's a shame to be denied one's heritage and forced to live like a beggar when one is wealthy. I am considerably more fortunate in that I can prove my rights. Mr Hamda La'war, a recognised National Hero for duping our village's shoemaker, is my witness. Can anybody dispute such a man's word? He knows that I had produced vital intelligence reports throughout the years since he was both the party's cell head and my postman. Nobody can refute my actions. These are historical facts that are public records.

I recognise that the Jews' zeal is terrific. It raises my morale to know that there are men and women out there fighting for their rights, even though I would be dumb to react favourably to their demands if I worked for a Swiss bank. Naturally! A competent bank clerk must prioritise the interests of his bank above his personal sentiments and interests. Duty is a duty, it goes without saying, and although I profoundly sympathise with the plight of the helpless, it is entirely reasonable for me to side with the banks in this situation. This is only common sense. If I weren't a bank clerk, I would sympathise with the Jews who have been deprived of their heritage, but alas! It is unavoidable. Mr Rockefeller, Mr Rothschild, and other prominent business people would completely grasp my point of view. Any rights must be as evident as the $20 million the State owes me. Otherwise, where are we going? There is already enough disarray in this world to keep us from fishing in hazardous seas. Alas! This does not seem to be what everyone believes.

(7)

My roommate, Mr Dahdah, a businessman dealing in toys who has two stores in the Capital, told me that Suleiman Mughli is a Mafiosi.

- That's why he's so free in jail, he emphasised.

As I voiced my surprise, he said:

- You don't believe me? Just ask Zorro. Inquire as to why the guards ignore their traffic! And why do you believe the Islamists backed down when he provoked them? They are fully aware of who he is. He's on excellent terms with the Afghan, so they deal with him outside. That's why he supported them throughout the rebellion...

I had to interrupt him:

- You say they deal with him? Exactly what do you mean?

- Not only Islamists, dude; you're from another planet! Everyone knows who the Mughli is. His stronghold is in Sicily; he is a big businessman, and extremely powerful.

- But you said he's actually a Mafia member, didn't you?

- Indeed, he is.

- What does the Mafia have to do with Islamists?

- They require firearms, falsified documents, maybe even forged cash, and, most importantly, narcotics to pay for their black-market purchases. These are fields in which the Mafia excels. That's why they wouldn't even touch Suleiman's hair; he's too precious to them, an asset, you know.

I didn't like the direction events were headed. If the Mafia enters the theatre, as Dahdah indicated, the nation will perish. I was eager to write a beneficent history of the wretched Islamists, but now I'm unsure. Clearly, I have no interest in documenting the era of gangsterism.

- How do you know that? I asked Dahdah.

He grinned, revealing a set of tobacco-tainted teeth. Two brown eyes moved gently in their caverns, illuminating his face. In the faint light of the chamber, he lifted his brows, and his bald head seemed as soft as a baby's. We were sitting on the edge of the bed at the bottom of the room, murmuring so our neighbours couldn't hear us. In any case, they were engrossed in their television watching.

- Would you want me to bring you some hashish or heroin?

- What for? I said, surprised. You should know that I never touch these items. What exactly do you want to show with that?

- That I am not defrauding you. Mughli is as strong now as he was before the coup. Perhaps even more, you can't dispute that his business is still unabated.

I felt compelled to admit it. I saw that neither the guards nor the troops ever attempted to control his movements. On the contrary, he seems to be friendly with all of them. I can tell that they respect him more than anybody else, except for Hassan and the Afghan. He is wealthy. He is the only prisoner who not only can afford to consume American cigarettes but also liberally gives them to his pals, guards, and troops.

Mughli's behaviour has piqued my interest. I got the chance to get to know him in the early days of his arrival. I owe him an enormous debt of gratitude, and the fact that I am still alive and well is entirely due to his discretion. I'm still determining what would have happened had he gone directly to the guards or troops and told them I was drafting a secret report; after all, he was aware of it! Yes, he is the only one who had casually unmasked me and discovered my secret, but I do not believe he reckoned it with clarity. That afternoon, I was at the library taking notes. I was so preoccupied with my work that I didn't see the guy who walked into the library and stood by my side, reading over my shoulder. After a moment, however, I saw a pair of rubber shoes on the ground, and as my sight ran over the feet, legs, and torso, my heart thumped like hell while I awkwardly sought to cover the blankets with my hands. The Mughli remained still. He looked at me, slightly surprised, with that hawk-ready gaze and appeared to grin, but his eyes were curious and chilly. For a little while, our eyes clashed and battled silently. Then he said:

-What the fuck are you scribbling? Why are you concealing the documents?

- It's none of your concern, I growled.

I still had my hands over the papers, and perspiration beaded on my forehead and cheeks. At that hour, the courtyard was deserted, and the sun was scorching the white walls and grey floor; yet, I could hear the voices of the guards playing cards in their wardship not far from the library. Because I knew the Mughli used to hang around with them, I had a strange feeling that if I didn't try to appease his infernal curiosity, my destiny would be sealed in no time. If I were caught doing such a thing, I'd never leave the prison alive, for snooping on behalf of the former regime. I had to make up for his rude intrusion and limit the damage it could do as much as possible. So, after a little pause, I stated:

- Don't go about thinking I'm writing some secret document prohibited by law. It's just a letter to my fiancée.

But I didn't deceive him. He gave me a stern look and stated:

- You're astute, but you don't want your secret revealed. That is legitimate. I'm not going to walk around thinking or talking about anything.

- Swear on your honour?

- Absolutely honourable word. You may rely on me, but I advise you to exercise caution the next time. Nobody loves moles, you understand. Neither the police nor the prisoners.

- I am not a mole, I protested, and you are foolish if you believe so.

- OK, fine! Remain calm. I'm not accusing you, but rather counselling you. Is your fiancée interested in conspiracy theories?

- Yes, ahem... I was summarising a thriller for her. I had just finished reading it.

- Oh! Ah! I understand.

But he didn't seem persuaded. He handed me one of his American smokes to calm me down. I thanked him and informed him that I was not a smoker.

- Take it, man, be a sport! He urged. It is not hashish.

I finished by agreeing to smoke his cigarette. He lit another and said:

- What's your name?

- I'm Bassam Bourasin. Bank teller, but for the time being, I am a librarian. No one cares about this stuff. Thus the job is as dull as a tomb.

- Interesting, he said. Which bank?

-' Ouja.

- Ahah! So you were apprehended with the Jew who was attempting to leave with six million dollars cash?

- No, I'm not involved with him. My affair is unique.

- Politics then?

- May God forgive you. Look at me. Do I have a face to run around the political meetings? Is it lost on you that it is the worst possible thing someone could do?

- What's the big deal? Are you a colleague? Are you in the drug trade?

- Drugs? What a nightmare! Disgusted, I yelled.

- Be nice, man. I didn't offend you, did I? Besides, it's not as bad as you think. I am a guy like you; I don't have two heads or four eyes, and my tail is between my legs rather than at my bottom.

- Are you then, uh... I stuttered.

- Yes, I am.

- I'm terribly sorry. I'm very sorry; I had no idea. So you're er...

- Yeah, yes, yes. Of course I am, man. He said unequivocally.

- And, um... Is it... er?

I felt so mortified that it was difficult for me to find the correct words. I thought I would insult him if I addressed him as a drug dealer. But he was helpful:

- Profitable? Oh, absolutely. A lot of money. But it isn't my only concern. I operate on a big scale, you know. International trade and all that jazz. It's a fantastic home.

I became intrigued. My intuition had already informed me that Mughli was a rare breed of man who deserved to be recognised. However, I was hesitant to concede that the drug industry benefits everyone.

- It's a shame that a talented businessman like you should depend on that um... unlawful things, Mr Mughli; it's terrible, awful, I said emphatically.

- Why? What's the harm in it?

- Ahem, I think it's bad for the health.

- Who told you that?

- Nobody... er... everyone.

- Nonsense. They are fucking idiots. They know nothing. It's not worse than wine or alcohol, you know. No more enslaving than smoking cigarettes. It's an honest exchange like any other.

- Honest? But you enslave people.

- No, sir; I am not a slave trader. If the product is excellent, the customer enjoys it and requests more. It's all. The system is the same in all trades. Nobody is forced to purchase from me. Everyone who works with me, including the government, is fully aware of what they are doing!

- The government? I was stunned. The phrase had almost probably slipped his mind.

- Well... um... oh! He stuttered. It's a little tricky. Nobody wants to talk about it. These are state secrets, after all. But I can promise you that they meet their quota on every sale. Do not think they are innocent.

- Speaking about bribes or association? I inquired, surprised and horrified.

- If you look carefully at the object, it's not much different. Let's call it mutual trust or shared interests. Anyway, you should know I am not working with bullies and ruffians.

- The highest authority in this nation appreciates my business.

- I don't see anybody higher than the president.

- Let's assume the president has no problem with my heading up this kind of enterprise if it's good for the country's economy.

Mughli didn't seem like the type to be boastful, and the president's knowledge of his enterprise led me to conclude that maybe these drugs aren't as dangerous as they're made out to be. Could our government allow such a scourge to spread over the nation if the substances are indeed lethal? That is why I proposed to include them among our exports, alongside alcoholic beverages, hookers, and pimps. If oil shipment is halted for whatever reason, we may still earn foreign currency via this second option.

Given Mughli's sensitivity to the country's new leadership, the fact that this strange conversation took place just before the Islamic coup may appear unsettling. At the time, I was also concerned about the ramifications of a sudden disclosure of my secret. But I dreaded the detainees' and guards' reactions the most, not the administration's. My report had not yet been completed, but even if Mughli had gone to the administration to discuss it, he would have only served me. Now I'm inclined to believe he was lying to make himself seem more influential than he was. I cannot picture the magnificent General President being a collaborator with a Mafia guy, although I must admit, I am flustered. I'm not sure what to believe, and it's not just because of Mughli's strange revelations: since the insurrection, the new regime has been spreading rumours that the former president was dealing with the Mafia and entertaining gangs of ruffians and cut-throats specialising in drugs, whore trafficking, kidnapping, and other nefarious activities under the luminous covert of 'party militia.' The television never stops bombarding us with facts about our previous president's terrible behaviour. As a result, we learnt that he had hidden astronomical accounts in numerous European, Asian, and American banks. Since he was Minister of the Interior, he is claimed to have had close ties with the Mafia. Some witnesses acknowledged accepting large amounts of money from men of the president' in exchange for special services.' Others suggested a mystery flow of white ladies. We gradually found that the ladies in issue had been flown in from Eastern Europe to satisfy the hedonistic lusts of the president, his cronies, and visitors. After being promised jobs in state-owned commercial societies where they might make a decent life, workers found themselves enslaved and subservient to their owners. I was surprised, outraged, and humiliated. I couldn't believe the 'beloved president' could be concealing a savage beast beneath his innocent face. Everyone in prison discusses the former president's alleged perversions and secret life. Many inmates are also questioning whether the ex-president is as vile as they've been led to believe.

Someone had yelled in the room, "Where are the women?" "How come they don't show them?"

Suleiman Mughli, according to Dahdah, told several of his close friends, "The story is not a hoax. They pick up ladies on the streets of Moscow, Budapest, Bucarest, and other cities... They convince them that if they consent to work as air hostesses on the airlines of a fake company, they would be paid $5,000, $10,000, or even $20,000 per month. On this basis, the females, often attractive but young and destitute, accept the deal. They sign a bogus contract, assuming they work on flights or at airports in wealthy countries. However, they would be employed for a completely different purpose."

Despite, or maybe because of, all of this gossip, I was the victim of the most vexing consternation. I couldn't believe how bad our country is. I couldn't have remained loyal to such a despicable group of pimps and slavers. So I convinced myself that these were rumours and political ploys to confuse the opponents. The Islamic extremists are clearly the president's opponents since they want to tarnish his reputation and drag his administration through the dirt at every opportunity. So why should I trust them? But because I didn't want to get into a conflict with the prison's mighty overlords, I decided to keep up my charade of believing and keep praying in the yard among my other inmates. After all, they are the rulers today, and the south is far away.

On top of that, I had yet to verify with absolute certainty that the president was still alive and leading the resistance. So, in the end, there was no guarantee of anything. It's the mist!

Yesterday's TV show was really captivating. We were all taken aback when the speaker said that Miss Sonia - I don't recall her last name - would be making a confession.

The veiled girl seemed to be no more than twenty years old. However, her face was so familiar to me that I was flabbergasted when I saw her.

I was having dinner with Dahdah at the bottom of the cell when we heard our chamber mates yelling openly. We dashed towards the TV set, jostling with the gathered mob. The stillness in that specific, raucous cell was soon total. Even a mosquito could be heard flying over our heads. Even though the windows were open because we're still in summer, the heat was unbearable. I was utterly overwhelmed by the smell of sweat and other dirty breaths coming from the toilets, but what I saw on the screen caught me by surprise and made me feel so bad that I spent half the night fighting against my desire to sleep and the other half fighting against my nightmares.

Chapter 6

The Invisible Bride

(1)

I DON'T KNOW HOW OR why people change their names and faces and act like they are someone else. What is this madness?

The girl on the TV screen speaking a foreign language was blue-eyed and blonde, with pinkish cheeks and a little nose above well-curved lips. Her face was glowing, and the curls of golden hair flowed softly from under her headscarf between her beautiful fingers as she touched them absent-mindedly while talking. She was clothed in a long black dress and seemed tired, with a drawn face, as if she hadn't slept in two days.

But I felt familiar with her face, body language, and manners. It's as though I've known her for a long time but can't recall the circumstances. I stared at her and wondered: "I've seen her before, but where and when?" Her English could have been better. She also spoke Arabic when she needed to learn how to say what she wanted to communicate in English, which was not her first language. At one point, I convinced myself that if she didn't have that headscarf that couldn't even conceal her golden hair and blue eyes, I'd see none other than my old Murabitat friend, Nawara! I used to marry her for an hour or two (sometimes longer) and then divorce her (she was my devout Sidi Abdullah Hush Street wife).

Most of my cellmates were taken aback by the guy on the platform who was interrogating Sonia. Even though his look had altered, he could still be recognised. Our former jail friend, Hassan, dressed for the occasion in a beige suit, collar, tie, and white shoes, with a six-day beard covering his face. His red hair was well-combed, and his green eyes seemed to light with an inward flame as he glanced at the camera. Along with him and Sonia, a translator sat on the platform and kept a level head as questions and answers were passed back and forth. So, understandably, I was mystified as to how Hassan got up on that platform just a few hours after his release when he, like everyone else, should have been here waiting for his trial. But it was evident that the man wasn't 'everyone," and I'm not sure whether I was envious or honest when I resented his presence on the platform as a show-off.

Why should the new regime begin this era by proving the persistence of favouritism and advantages? What did Hassan do to earn such a fast promotion at the expense of justice? He did urge the captives to revolt with inflammatory rants, but what else could he do? Nothing! He is just a sly and sneaky speaker who knows how to seize chances for advancement. Other detainees had done much worse or better—depending on your perspective—and were not released. I should be on the TV platform too. While still imprisoned, I began writing the history of the revolution. But where's justice and fairness? True, no one heard about my "history," dammit! That's only a matter of time before I rise to fame. Still, I am an honest bank clerk willing to jeopardise his whole career for our new couvolution. Instead, they let out a journalist whose loyalty is questionable and kept the country's economy (which I represent) locked up. This is quite naive! Worse! It's blindness.

Did they realise that the banks I am honoured to serve are the heart of the economy and the clerks its arteries? Everything will stumble, crumble, and fall apart if these arteries are not working. As a result, no coup, counter-coup, insurrection, mutiny, revolt, revolution, or counter-revolution—or, in a nutshell, no couvolution would stand and continue unless the bank clerks were happy.

Because the person with the most money wields the most power. And who controls the funds today, if not bank tellers? We are indispensable; if you do not care for us, we may become hazardous. I'm not trying to threaten you. Generally, "I never threaten on the phone" (That's Marlon Brando in "The Godfather"). But I'm simply complaining about being banished to the backbenches. Simultaneously, a simple crawling writer – who had never been trusted by the regime – has been thrust to the forefront of the new revolution from the start.

I'm still outraged and want to report secretly to the Committee of Revolution. The purpose is to clarify and promote my stance, as well as that of Mr Aroussi and all of the country's bankers and bank clerks. For the benefit of our economy, I shall insist on a similar status to diplomats, which we will call "financial immunity." I'm ready to write it and present it to Abdelghani Abdelghaffar, the new caliph and prince of the faithful, if only I'm confident he'll be in power until tomorrow morning.

Alas! With all those restless sergeants and hungry corporals yearning for power, one never knows whether another coup is in the works in some kitchens. So to suppress their nighttime urges, they should provide the most potent Valium available.

We can't afford to have half the army on Valium because of the danger on our borders and in the south, but we also can't afford to let all those disgruntled sergeants walk the barracks sleeplessly. It is neither intelligent nor secure, as our peaceful country's recent history has repeatedly shown. As a result, we must either compel the ambitious to take a Valium pill every evening or appoint them, right away, Generals and Field Marshals, putting a stop to their grandiose aspirations. We can't keep on like this: if we have a new coup and a new administration every quarter, we'll never know who's in charge.

I wandered away from my topic once again, most likely because the sudden appearance of Hassan on the little screen stunned me and triggered this outburst of uncontrollable emotions. Oh! I have nothing against him, personally. I'm not blaming him but rather attempting to view things as they are, without bitterness or malice. Why should I hold a grudge against him? He made no promises to us. It is not the case with his superiors, who were happy with the rebellion in which we all took part and liberally promised everyone freedom and justice. We'll have to wait and see whether they take their pledges seriously.

The interview began on the TV screen with a query regarding the girl's origin. She said she is a Romanian from Bucarest and lived with her mother, father, and four sisters and brothers. Her father worked in a factory that went bankrupt; as his oldest daughter, she sought to aid her family by working as a cashier in a supermarket. However, as soon as the communist regime was overthrown, she lost her job, and her family's situation became unstable.

- Were you unemployed, Miss Sonia, when the Scoundrel approached you? Hassan asked.

The former president has been dubbed "The Scoundrel" by the media since the counter-coup. The interpreter translated the question and response in his droning voice:

Sonia: - Yes, I was out on the streets looking for work.

Hassan: - How did they get in touch with you?

Sonia - Oh, it wasn't difficult for them. They approached me at a coffee shop and invited me for a drink. They were three individuals, two of whom claimed to be business representatives and the third a diplomat. They were friendly and kind. They didn't waste time and suggested the deal right away. The diplomat introduced himself and his two partners, claiming they were looking for staff for your airlines. They inquired whether I knew somebody, ideally a female, who was willing to work overseas for good pay. For how much? I asked. They specified a monthly salary of at least $10,000. It was as if a portal from heaven had opened for me. I didn't think twice. We almost begged for food, and our relatives and neighbours were not in better condition. My father was ill. I was concerned about our future. So I told them I would accept their offer if I could speak the country's language. They assured me that language would not be an issue and encouraged me to sign a contract with the company. I was so thrilled, so happy, that I would have taken the job they offered for a far lesser income.

Hassan: - So you signed a contract stating that you would work as a cabin crew in our country?

Sonia: - That's what I understood, but the term used was hostess. I missed the trick since there was no mention of airlines or cabin crew, just hostesses. If I protested later that it was not the position I was recruited for, I could not truly pressure them. The contract sounded legal and straightforward. But it didn't specify what type of hostess.

Hassan: - Ahem! Why didn't you consult with a lawyer before signing?

Sonia: - I was so excited to get the job but inexperienced. In addition, I couldn't afford the services of a lawyer. There was also the fact that I was talking with a diplomat, who is supposed to be an official trusted by two nations. They showed me several contracts, one of which was signed by another female from Craiova called Helga.

Hassan: - Where did you sign the contract?

Sonia: - At their hotel, two days after our initial coffee shop encounter. I have asked to discuss it first with my family. My mother opposed my trip to a distant nation. My father said nothing. But he quietly encouraged me. It was a massive hope for all of us.

Hassan: - Well, Miss Sonia, tell us what occurred after you signed the deal with the Scoundrel's men?

The screen then scraped, and the picture shifted briefly, sparking a frenzy among the inmates who assumed the show was being cancelled for some odd reason. Then, after a musical interlude, the broadcaster emerged to herald the show's return to the Scoundrel's heinous acts. Sonia's appearance had noticeably altered when she resurfaced. She'd tied a scarf over her head, revealing only her face and hands. It wasn't difficult to figure out what transpired. Someone, most likely an authority figure, had undoubtedly reminded them that women must be veiled in public under an Islamic republic. It makes little difference whether they are Muslims; consequently, the blunder was swiftly rectified.

Hassan repeated the question.

Sonia: - A fortnight after the contract was signed, I travelled to Athens with Helga and the two commercial representatives, where we met up with another group of females. We were seven at the time.

Hassan: - Are they all from Eastern Europe?

Sonia: - Yes. Two Poles, two Czechoslovaks, a Russian, Helga, and myself. (Pause). They had all signed the same contract. When we arrived, we were all housed in a large home on the capital's outskirts. We have been cautioned not to wander through the streets before being met by an important individual who will test us and determine whether or not we are fit. In any case, armed personnel closely secured the mansion day and night. After that, I realised we were being observed and videotaped by cameras hidden in the ceilings and behind the mirrors.

Hassan: - Didn't you realise that the important individual was the president... sorry, I mean the scoundrel?

Sonia: - I didn't know until the night I had to meet him. They summoned a girl every evening, and we never saw her again. We were informed that she had been tested and accepted when we inquired about her. They advised us to be polite and obedient and warned us that if the Moghul was dissatisfied, we would be in trouble and would have to find money to return home. The contract does not allow for a return.

Hassan: - What occurred when you went to see the Scoundrel?

Sonia: - Well, he asked me flat out to remove all my clothing. That was just after he gave me a drink. Of course, I was shocked and argued that I had come to this country with an air-hostess contract and that I ought to be respected. He smiled and added that the agreement I had signed stipulated that I would be his and his guests' hostess. My obligation was to him since he was the one who employed me and expected my obedience. He left me alone in the room when I refused to comply. I believed I had been delivered, but I had no idea what was in store. His guys stormed into the room and openly threatened me. They threatened to torture and murder me if I did not obey the president. I refused to give up. They led me to a wet, dark dungeon full of rats and threatened to throw me out. They warned me the rats were ravenous and would devour me alive. I was scared to death. I couldn't stand the trauma, which I believe was extremely severe. Then I gave up.

A lengthy pause followed. The girl seemed distressed and wiped her tears with a handkerchief.

Hassan: - I realise it's hard, Miss Sonia, but I want to ask you another question about the other girls. What happened to them?

Sonia: - I never heard of them again. I'm not sure whether they're still alive or dead. I was imprisoned in a mansion full of guards for two months. As long as I pleased the president, I was treated nicely. After the first month, he became weary of me and gave me to his men. Every evening, I had to host a visitor, usually a senior official. Some of them sexually abused me. I was no longer the president's favourite, but their slave. I'd already been whipped twice. Under penalty of death and torture, I was compelled to drink with them and fulfil all their sexual perversions and vagaries. I couldn't stand up to them because I knew they'd murder me.

Hassan: - Thank you very much indeed, Miss Sonia, for this bold and shocking revelation.

(2)

THIS IS MY FOURTH MONTH in prison and the first of the new age. I'm still waiting for my trial's conclusion to see whether I get out convicted or released. July is ticking away, surrounded by chirpy twittering, rampaging insect wings, and scorching sun rays. The prison is calcining our bodies and melting our brains like an oven. I'm holding on to my chair like glue, clinging to my kosher scribbling like it's my life buoy. The library had become my only sanctuary in these difficult days of rebellion, rapine, and recriminations. Nobody knows who is the more heinous criminal: the president who fled to the south or the goddamn Islamists who are ransacking homes and plundering and looting licentiously. Even if we are detained, news from the outside reaches us via the guards or the parlour.

Few inmates had been allowed to receive visitors. The lucky returned with horrifying stories, heard from visitors, about the country's descent into anarchy. Dahdah convinced the Indian to intervene with the administration to allow him to see his wife. She has decided to besiege the prison every day for the past week. However, the guards barred her and other women in the same situation from visiting. Every day, they came early in the morning to wait for the main gate to open, carrying loads and parcels of food, clothes, and other small gifts for their husbands, brothers, or fathers. They would remain stubbornly wedged out there, begging the guards and soldiers to let them in for a brief visit to their relatives. When Mahmoud was about to enter the prison one morning, he was met by Dahdah's wife, who begged him to take the bundle she had brought for her husband if he couldn't let her in. He agreed to take the parcel and give it to Dahdah, noting that she had been there for a week, attempting in vain to gain entrance to the parlour.

Dahdah was disappointed, but Mahmoud said:

- Poor woman! She's been waiting for you for four years. I would have divorced you from the start if I were a woman.

- I'm the father of her children, Dahdah stated calmly. Besides, where would she find a man like me if she divorces? She is not a moron.

- Why? You're not the most recent man on the planet, are you?

- Not at all. But I own two of the best toy stores in the city. And, despite being imprisoned, my business is thriving. I am extremely wealthy. I'm not like you—a state slave. If they stop paying you for two months, you'll be out of money and forced to beg on the street!

Piqued by Dahdah's innuendo, the blackguard yelled:

- O! Ho, ho! You little jerk, I know you're full of shit. However, you must respect my uniform. This is the state's uniform, you understand? The same state that will send you to hell if you keep trespassing and insulting me.

- All right, Dahdah replied. Give me the sixty dinars you borrowed, and I'll go to hell.

- You fool! Mahmoud exclaimed, laughing. I was joking, of course. You must be kidding. We're both joking, old pal.

- I'm not your friend, Darkish. Have you looked in the mirror? I'm wealthy enough to buy your damn prison if that's what you want.

- Oh, ha ha ha, he he he he he...

- Stop laughing! You had been staring at my wife for a week, waiting and sweating behind your fucking walls, and you did nothing to help. I wonder why I give you all that fucking money!

- I'm not at fault. I've got kids to feed, you know. I can't help your wife because she needs to renew her visit permit. The administration had devolved into a bloodthirsty brothel. It's chaos, and they're checking everything, and the warden has to see and sign on every fucking paper. You appear to believe your country is still the same little paradise for new rich people and old thieves. No, brother, all this is going to change, you understand? You should watch the TV a little more.

- The TV? What does the bloody television have to do with my wife?

- It has a lot to do, and not only with your wife, old chum, but with the whole country.

He then excused himself and skidded away. I was watching them from the window bars because they were chatting near the library.

- Look at this little pig, said Dahdah, turning to face me. He robbed me of sixty dinars and then avoided me when I needed him.

Some groups of inmates lounged along the walls or by the long basin where they used to wash their garments. The barber had resumed his work, but the business was relatively quiet. Few of the inmates wanted to shave. It was wiser, as they believed, to grow a little beard, like the Islamists. Nonetheless, Suleiman Mughli shaved imperturbably every morning, as did other guys inspired by his behaviour.

- You should talk to Abdullah Zahir; I suggested. You know, the Indian. He has some influence here.

- Influence? You must be joking. That man is a fakir. He spends his days praying and meditating while sitting cross-legged on the ground. He's cut off from the rest of the world. He doesn't understand a single word of what is said around him.

- You are wrong," I replied. The Indian is the lieutenant of the Afghan, which is to say, his eyes and ears. You should give it a shot.

Dahdah initially hesitated to speak with him, but after I persuaded him, he went straight to his cell and explained his case. The Indian followed him until they arrived at the parlour and asked Mahmoud to fetch the woman and bring her to see her husband, which he did without hesitation. When Dahdah returned from the parlour, he summoned me to the library. I saw him through the window and hid my papers inside a thick volume that I placed between other books on my desk. That is the strategy I use to keep inmates from noticing what I am doing. I'm surrounded by stacks of books placed along the edges of the desk, allowing me to see the courtyard without being seen from it. Indeed, I've created an empty space in this little wall through which I can spy on the yard. Assured that no one is watching, I indulge in my favourite pastime with the sweetest titillation, free of the boredom that imprisons the rest of the inmates.

Dahdah entered the library, gesticulating mutely and looking like a man returning from a funeral. His plump face was paler, and his fingers were trembling as he continued to smoke and chew the butt of his cigarette. He was clearly the victim of violent emotion. I asked him to sit down and explain why he was so upset.

- Are you certain we're safe here?

- What exactly do you mean, Dahdah?

- Can we speak freely?

- Of course, of course. It's the most secure prison area. It's a bunker.

He swallowed his saliva, lit another cigarette, and puffed on the smoke as sweat ran down his cheeks and his bald head seemed to glow in the sunlight. I watched the yard through the window bars, where some inmates were still washing their clothes in the basin. The soldiers have been mingling with the guards and inmates for the past two days, and the surveillance has been reduced. The atmosphere was much more laid-back. Everything on the roofs and towers remained the same, except that since the mutiny, I no longer saw the cooks crossing the yard with trays of food and drinks. I knew something was missing from my usual view; I felt a strong vacuum and had no idea how to fill it. The traffic had stopped, possibly because the mutiny had failed miserably to pave the way for a massive evasion or simply because nothing had changed except the sentinels of the towers. The latter are now professional soldiers, loyal to the new regime, with whom it is difficult even to speak. They are rough and harsh men who would not even allow the chief cook to approach the staircase leading to the towers. They had placed iron barriers in front of the towers' entrances, and two soldiers now watch the wire netting dividing the courtyard. This is a significant change in the security system of this place, which resembles a fortress. Additionally, sentinels are stationed before and between the blocks, in the corridors, and on each landing. They are the true masters of the place, not the fictitious guards. They can dismiss them and run the prison like a barracks. I don't know why they keep them if they distrust their management. The guards are irritated by this intrusion and the fact that they have not been paid in nearly two months.

The sun is about to set. The white walls have taken on an orange hue. The shades are much longer. In about an hour, I'll close the library gate and walk up to my cell, sad and gloomy, as I do every evening.

- Is it critical? Can't you wait until I arrive in the chamber?

Dahdah raised his massive head, his brown eyes blinking loosely in his round face. He was breathing loudly as if he'd run all the way to the library, and his fat belly bulged and moved slowly beneath his brown short-sleeved shirt. Surprisingly, his anxiety has contaminated me, and I've found myself asking him for a cigarette even though I'm not a smoker.

He handed me the cigarette and lit it; then he said, with a deep voice, as if he were confessing his most important secret:

- The country is lost, Bassam. Outside, it's hell!

- Everyone knows it; it's the revolution, I said.

- No, no, no. You have no idea. It's not the revolution. It's the apocalypse. They follow people on the streets, in coffee shops, and even to their homes. Anyone who appears to be a suspect to them is being arrested and flogged. They arrested a neighbour of mine and his two sons only a week ago. I'm well acquainted with them. They are unrelated to politics. They happen to work as bartenders. They had indeed closed their bar when they learned of the coup. They attempted to get rid of the merchandise and hid their bottles in the cellar before converting their bar into a harmless café. That was for nought. The Islamists were well-versed in the area, and they attacked them at night while they were sleeping. All the neighbours witnessed the scene. They flogged them and forced them to walk barefooted in the street till they reached the bar, not far from the house. They then unlocked the gate and removed the wine, beer, and alcoholic beverages from the cellar. Passers-by in the early morning saw the forbidden merchandise piled up on the sidewalk in front of the bar. The street's sewer was open, and men were busy pouring whisky, gin, and beer into it. The proprietor and his two sons stood by, perplexed and powerless. They then took them to the police station. When the women went to find out what had happened to them, the militia pretended that they had not arrested them. The bartender's wife returned with her daughters, who were crying and screaming in the street. The poor woman! She is still expecting her husband and sons to return. "I fear the worst," he said after pausing to puff on the smoke. This appears to be just the beginning. My wife claims that they are robbing traders' stores. I don't believe the women because they exaggerate everything, but I've heard reports of clashes in the capital between Islamists and the men of the former president's men. The army and police are divided; they are not all united in opposing the new regime. Many people have abandoned their businesses, fled to Europe, or are locking themselves in their houses, waiting for better days.

   - They don't talk about fighting in the streets on the news.

   - Fuck the TV; it's in their hands, and they're lying and pretending that the entire country is pacified and joyfully welcoming the new regime. People are terrified, and tanks and armed militia are barricading all entrances to the capital. The bastards don't think twice about shooting. If you don't respond when they call you, you're dead. It's a civil war, my brother, and everything is black. Outside, death and destruction await us. I told my wife not to return to the prison because it was too dangerous with all those wild beasts roaming the streets.

   I was shocked. I couldn't say anything for a moment. I had never imagined such a bleak scenario in our peaceful country. With the exception of a brief period during the Arabo-Israeli war, we have always lived in peace, even during the King's long reign. Where did all of that rage come from?

- Don't you think you're exaggerating a little?

- Exaggerating? Me? You're not aware, Dahdah replied. The capital is experiencing arson. They set fire to several buildings, including brothels, bars, billiards, and game parlours. Schools and even hotels had been converted into barracks; it's incredible! It is truly insane! And the greatest insanity is to protest or try to resist them. They are pitiless, which is only what happened here in the capital; we know nothing about the other cities and villages.

I remembered 'Ouja, my lovely little village where I had been so happy, and I was suddenly spoiled. I was on the verge of crying. What became of my house? What became of my mother and fiancée? What happened to my bank? To all the wonderful people I know? What became of us? What happened to the entire planet? What's the point of it all? What are our plans?

- What became of the president? I found myself asking.

- The president? What do we have in common with the fucking bastard? He is the root of all the hatred in this country. Wasn't he the first to try a coup? Were we not living in peace before that renegade decided to become ambitious? They all want to stage their "coup" now! So why not? because it is so simple to destabilise a government and seize power! Who will stand in their way? Every new year, we will have a coup. Take a look around, man. This is a long-standing tradition in some countries and is extremely contagious. I tell you, it's worse than leprosy. And we're on our way to establishing yet another banana republic. We're doomed, I'm afraid, and it's unavoidable from now on. We must put up with coups, counter-coups, and military oppression. One must consider the future. I am concerned about my business and family. I still have two years to spend in this pit. I have placed some of my relatives in the stores, but nobody is safe these days. They plan to set up tribunals in public places and sentence and decapitate people there. The prison may now be the most secure place in the country. I wonder if we aren't fortunate in our strange situation!

(3)

T he sun has completely set behind the fortified walls. The sky has turned blood-red. Long, dark shadows fell across the garden. I was gradually slipping into a state of sad perplexity. Then, to cut short my mental quandary, I asked Dah-dah:

- You've never told me why you're in prison.

- You never asked me; it is futile anyway— an affair of blank cheques, you know. It was, in fact, a ruse. The cheques had been stolen from me; the thief must have known me well because he imitated my signature and cashed millions of dollars. I was unaware; in the meantime, I had to make some late payments. I was in the red the next time I signed a cheque. I was on the verge of bankruptcy because I couldn't manage the unexpected lack of cash. I had only two bitter choices: either to sell my stores or to go to prison.

- And you went with the second option?

- Yes. If not, my family would be the victim.

- How come you didn't mortgage the shops?

- My father died as the result of a similar affair. On his deathbed, he made me swear on the Koran that I would never mortgage anything I inherited from him. He had bequeathed me the two shops after he had lost the most significant part of our properties— a broad and rich land that even the British settlers couldn't afford at the time, despite several reasonable offers. However, after independence, we had many problems with one of the King's most powerful men. Haj Omar Osman, Minister of...

I quickly interrupted him:

- Haj Omar! Unbelievable! What did he do to you?

- Oh, he did nothing, absolutely nothing! But he was like the scumbag who stole our land by claiming that the law allowed him to own it if we failed to pay back the loan. We spent years in court fighting him. It was all in vain. The minister provided him with adequate protection. The two men's meanness disheartened my father and led to his death after a long illness. On his last day, he did not stop cursing Haj Omar and the bumpkin Hamda La'war.

- Do you mean the "Ouja" national hero or another with the same name? I asked, perplexed.

- Yes, I mean the national zero, indeed. He paused, looked at me, and said: You know him?

- I'm from 'Ouja, I explained shyly.

For the first time in my life, I was embarrassed to mention my village. It felt as if I were the third accomplice to the two crooks who robbed Dahdah's land and killed his father. Indeed, I had no knowledge of that shady affair, but the fact that I was associated with Hamda and working for him was more than disturbing. I knew he had a portion of land in the north because he was not the kind of guy who lived modestly. He used to brag extravagantly, even indecently, and make unnecessary remarks about his wealth and the enormous influence his family wielded. Nonetheless, I had no idea he was related to Haj Omar Osman, who was said to have fled the country with a suitcase full of foreign currency.

- I thought Hamda La'war owed his award to the governor, not to a minister, I said.

- That's correct, but who was the governor?

- You're not implying that he's related to Haj Osman, are you?

- That is precisely what I mean. His cousin.

- If you say that, I believe you, for it was too easy for him to get that medal, which was supposed to reward his courageous deeds during the war of independence. But I know another, less honourable story. Anyway, what's the connection with the minister?

- Haj Osman, may God send a thunderbolt into his heart, is his cousin's cousin. It's the same clan; it's a cursed tribe. How else could a lecher like him get into the palace? You know how things work in this bloody country. There is no power without the sacred ubiquity of the tribe. Who do you believe is fighting alongside the former president now?

- The loyalists, I blurted out.

Loyalists, my ass! Are you deaf or blind? In this country, loyalty is limited to the tribe. Why did he flee to the south? Why not to the north or elsewhere?

- Ah, well, ahem... Because, um, it is rich in oil, I reasoned. It is both an asset and a strategic retreat.

- No, man. Fuck the oil and the strategy! That has nothing to do with this situation. If you stick to this naive explanation, you won't understand anything about this country's policies. Did you forget that the South is the hub of the president's tribe? Nobody can approach him as long as he is protected by his tribe. And you already know that his tribe is allied with others in other parts of the country. That's how he got away. Those tribes have their men serving in the army, police, and national guard. That is how he managed to outrun his assailants when the coup failed, and it is, for this reason, I warned you that we are on the verge of civil war. Now, wait, and you will see that their bloody Committee of Revolution is nothing but another tribal hodgepodge. You are not going to swallow their pill about the so-called Islamic regime, are you? After a brief pause, he added: There was no more pious man in this country than the King, and look what happened to him! Why didn't they demand the prince's return? If they are truly committed to Islam, why did they not declare the revolution in support of the King, who had been unjustly deposed by a renegade? Furthermore, our kingdom was not secular. Religion and religious slogans were everywhere.

I don't know how the words escaped me:

- They clearly want to rule. They are unwilling to share power with the royal family or any party.

- What you've just said makes sense. The tribes are at odds over the remains of the royal banquet. Whether they claim to be Islamists, secularists, or even Christians, Buddhists, or Jews makes no difference. It's all a ruse to gain power and announce that something new and grandiose is happening.

I became gloomy because contumacy is deeply ingrained in our behaviour. For many years, I tried to walk in the opposite direction, knowing that tribalism breeds anarchy, acrimony, resentment, and feuding. That is why I am so loyal and obedient to authority —any authority, to be sure— regardless of its claims and goals. It is neither because of acrophobia nor because of megalomania that I clung to my bashful life in 'Ouja, ingratiating—sycophantly, alas— the chief of the party's cell, whom I knew was a wicked bum. I had no choice; he was the representative of the authorities: the ruling party. And, while I questioned the party's claim to be truly representative of the entire country, I had to deal with this reality. Who wouldn't? I am not a hero (not yet), but rather a simple bank clerk. The situation had its advantages and disadvantages, and it was bearable as long as one cuddled oneself with the sweet illusion of being a part of a whole. I'm not particularly outgoing, but I'm pragmatic. My contract with the bank would not have been prolonged if I had played another game. In any case, it's all over now. To deal with the new situation, I need to rethink my ideas. I was tempted to support the new authority, but because it is fiercely contested by a powerful party, I must abstain and mull it over quietly. In any case, their libations and arson at the dawn of the new era were not very encouraging. It frightens me to think that half of the country is engulfed in flames while the other half is mourning and waiting for the immolation, terrorised. I am a man whose only language has previously been that of numbers - I am somewhat like Samir, my computer: I have a code. This is why we understand each other so well. I've always thought that the numbers associated with money, gold, silver, oil, real estate, and so on could very well sum up the exact condition of any human being on the planet. All of the world's languages are duly represented in the Esperanto of numbers, which is an international commitment of all nations, past, present, and future. Nonetheless, I would be deceiving myself if I continued to believe that the logic I used previously was perfect. We cannot reduce everything to numerical equations without endangering these admirable little machines known as men, depriving them of their humanity at the same time. What the hell? We're sensitive! Computers, too, indeed, but they are different.

July is coming to an end, and I'm suffering from claustrophobia. As far as I recall, the computer in my office at 'Ouja Bank has never complained of such a sickness, even though it is an intelligent machine. I had given it the name 'Samir' because I thought it deserved to be thought of as an empathetic and intelligent creature. And, while Samir is a man's name, I believe my computer is worth it, perhaps even more than many humans. I had never felt the passage of time with Samir. I believe we were madly in love with each other. I was captivated by the computer's intelligence and fascinated by its thoughtfulness. The machine was also fair and loyal to me. Whenever my memory faltered and failed to provide the correct answer, Samir would fill the void like an expert. Samir is conscientious and well-organised. It knows exactly what I need and how to assist me at the first sign. I was so taken with its erudite and encyclopaedic knowledge in the early days of our friendship that I assumed I was dealing with a wizard. Indeed, there is something magical about our relationship that has nothing to do with the grey and flustered world that rims and creeps around us like foliage. Samir and I knew we were in the middle of a jungle, but as long as we were together, we didn't care. Since the first day, its hypnotic spell has muffled and charmed me. I was a little infatuated, but it was a healthy folly. My fiancée grew irritated. When I went to Dalila's house, I used to talk excitedly about Samir and then go on and on about my new adventure with the machine.

One day, she said:

- Bassam, you're boring us with your friend's news as if there's nothing else in the world but Samir. Please, spare me this nonsense.

- Oh, you haven't seen Samir, Dalila. I bet you'll fall in love at first sight if you do.

- You fool, she snarled. How dare you say such absurdities to your fiancée? Do you think I'll fall in love with the first newcomer?

- But, darling, Samir is almost human. I am confident you'll be charmed.

- Hello, Bassam! You lost your mind, she yelled angrily.

Because I didn't understand what caused her anger, I responded:

- Don't be unfair. I'm neither a fool nor a mindless person.

- No, she sneered, but you're perfectly willing to abandon your fiancée for... I don't know who!

- Who said I would abandon you? What's that foolish idea? I meant that you would be as content with Samir as I am. I've only had the newcomer in my office for a week, and I'm already enchanted. It's such a lovely, intelligent creature!

It was too much for her to bear.

- All right, since you're in love with your Samir, go ahead and marry him right away, she said, her eyes twinkling. I'm sorry, I can't marry you after you confessed your homosexual inclination.

(4)

THEN AND ONLY THEN did I realise what I had done wrong. In my excitement, I completely overlooked the fact that Samir was a simple machine, a computer that I had elevated to a human level. I had to apologise to my fiancee and explain why there had been a misunderstanding. Fortunately, we were alone in the sitting room. It must have been spring because the window was open, and the jasmine fragrance filled the air with a rapturous zest. She sat in the armchair facing me, wearing a silky white blouse that cinched around her bosom and a large black skirt that fell to her ankles. Her dark eyes and her face shone brightly even when she was angry. She's lovely, and I wasn't immune to her charm. If her family had agreed, I would have married her in the first year of our engagement. Her mother, on the other hand, desired that her daughter marries in a family home equipped with all modern conveniences. I was still living in my paternal home then, though I was considering purchasing an apartment in one of 'Ouja's new buildings. Furthermore, I did not yet own a car, despite having passed the driving test and obtained my licence. It had not been without challenges. I had already been tested eight times before they admitted I could drive a car without killing anybody. Perhaps not extraordinary, but the first time I was tested, I nearly crushed an ambulant carpet merchant who sallied out of the blue in front of the car. Ah, the bastard gave me such a panic! Thankfully, I did not kill him. I failed the second time because I was tired of feeling panicked. When I was tested for the third time, I ran straight into a traffic police officer's wooden podium when asked to make a U-turn. Really, I could have avoided it, but instead, I bungled and crashed into the rostrum. Fortunately, it was vacant. The police officer was busy talking to a lady on the opposite sidewalk. He missed the show. Nonetheless, exacerbated by my awkwardness, the examiner got out of the car, cursing the damned bastard who taught me to drive! It was the end of the test, but not yet of my series of failures. I had to regain their trust, and it wasn't until the ninth examination that I finally received my licence, with the jury's warm congratulations. Now I can say that I am a competent driver.

I have a small car, a Volkswagen, a technological marvel. Because of its blue colour, I named it Zarga. It is light, fast, and powerful. It was purchased on the used car market. I've always admired the great champions of automobile races like Formula 1. It's a rush to drive a car at 300 km/hour—or otherwise, a wingless plane. If I had the right car, I would participate in one of those races. Alas! Zarga is unable to face the challenge. Its top highway speed is 160 km/h, but I never ask her to go beyond 80. What for? I am never hurried. But when I am, Zarga starts coughing and sneezing, then pisses on the road and stops. I found out that the car is, in fact, whimsical and strangely jealous. Who would believe it? Indeed jealous. Zarga would pretend to be sick and pulls over halfway to our destination, especially when I was driving Dalila. Naturally, in the beginning, I was unaware of the true reasons for this strange behaviour. But it became significant when I connected the dots. The car repeated the same comedy several times, always with Dalila riding with me and never when I was alone or with another person.

- Zarga is jealous of you, I told my fiancée one day.

It was obvious to me, but Dalila was neither convinced nor amused.

- Get rid of it quickly and bring another car, she said. It is useless.

But I couldn't. It was my first car. Selling it would have broken my heart, as sentimental as I am. That was the source of our constant quarrels because neither Dalila nor her mother could understand why I was so attached to that 'lot of crinkling rusty iron,' as they pretended. For my part, I was struck by their hearts' barrenness. Women, on the other hand, are expected to be sentimental. This, however, is evidence to the contrary. Actually, Dalila was just as jealous as Zarga, albeit for different reasons, because she couldn't stand my innocent friendship with Samir. When she told me to "go and marry him," I laughed and said, "I can't, Dalila. It's not a woman." She was enraged.

- I am not ready to marry a man who openly admits to loving another, she said as she stood up.

- You are confused, Dalila. Samir is not a man, I exclaimed, surprised. It is neither a man nor a woman.

She looked at me sideways, unable to believe what I was saying.

- Then what? A trans? A ghost? An animal? A Jin? It makes no difference to me.

- None of them. You're still erring. It's just a computer, a machine, a clever machine that helps me better than a dozen secretaries.

Dalila was taken aback. For a brief moment, she appeared dumbfounded. But quickly regaining her composure, she asked:

- Why were you speaking of it as if it were a human being all that time? You called it Samir, didn't you?

- So what, my darling? Don't I call the car Zarga? It doesn't make it human, does it? And Samir, much more than the car, deserves its name, because it is intelligent. The computer knows everything and can answer any question.

- You're a liar! I've never seen a machine that speaks.

- Darling, you never saw anything. You're cooped up at home while the world spins faster than a meteorite. Machines nowadays talk, walk, and even drive. It's true that you never watch the TV news. If you did, you would know.

- Daddy says it is a waste of time. Furthermore, it spreads lies and bad habits. He doesn't even let me go to the movies. If ever he hears that we did, he will get mad at you and may not talk to me for a week.

- Dalila, your father is a dinosaur. Opposing progress is bigotry. Yet, opposing the regime is suicide.

- You're not going to insult him right now, are you? Everyone is free.

- I am not disparaging or insulting him. On the contrary, I respect him. I'd like to live like him, without watching TV news, movies, cars, etc. We would have been happily married if he had not asked for ultramodern appliances in the future home of his daughter.

- He's got nothing to do with it. That was Mom's idea.

- Sure. Your mother is on his opposite pole. She invests in the advancement of the world. Regarding her daughter's marriage, she enjoys technology and gadgets. If we keep going with this, we'll be married in the next century, inshallah!

- Don't be a fool, Bassam. You're employed at a bank. You have the means to purchase the items she requested. After all, it will be your home as well.

- I'm hoping so!

She seemed convinced that, as I worked at 'Ouja Bank, all the cash available was mine. She and her mother were completely unaware that I was not the banker but merely an employee , and even if I were the banker, could I freely dispose of other people's funds? Dalila, despite her youth, reminds me a lot of my mother. Both would turn to the omnipresent, omnipotent, and unavoidable Mektub whenever they found themselves in an intractable situation. That is why I adore Dalila; I could be as convinced as she is that between life and death, everything that happens to us is pre-written by the Divine pen. It is pointless and even impractical, maybe hazardous, to oppose the Mektub. That's also why, in the midst of an unruly swarm, accepting life in this vivarium was so simple. Likewise, I have accepted dealing with Hamda La'war, despite being convinced that he is a liar and a hypocrite. And because Mektub rules our lives from the cradle to the grave, it is easy and even comforting to believe that party and fatherland are identical in every way; that we are born to live the same life as our fathers and forefathers; that our governments are good, wise, and competent; that freedom and democracy are lies forged by the West to recolonise us; that we have no rights to claim, but only duties to the rulers; and that Muslims should not seek fun, joy, and happiness on earth, but work to get them after death, in the paradise.

All this is not collective masochism, but common sense based on tested traditions.

After a particularly heated argument with my fiancee, during which she, as expected, used the Mektub, I was so upset and angry that as soon as I got to my office, I went straight to my desk and asked Samir:

- What is MEKTUB?

After reflection, Samir said:

- I'm sorry, I am not familiar with anything called "MEKTUB." Could you please provide more context or information about what you are asking?

- Holy Hell! I'm sure that's how it's spelled. Wait a second. I'll hand you another key.

- What exactly is written?

- I'm sorry, I'm not sure what you are asking. Can you please provide more information or context?

- Idiot! No, sorry, you're right! I'm inconsistent. Simply, give me the meaning of the term: Written.

- The term "written" refers to the act or process of producing written language, typically with a pen or pencil on paper, or by typing on a keyboard. It can also refer to the written language itself, as opposed to the spoken language. Additionally, it can refer to something that has been recorded or written down, such as a book or a document.

- Fantastic! I am dazzled by your bright intelligence, my dear Samir. Now, since you understand "written," tell me what is "mektub"?

- Mektub is a word in Turkish that means "letter" or "written document." It can also be used to refer to a written message or correspondence.

- Mektub is an Arabic, not a Turkish word, Samir. You're erring. Could it also be a document written by God?

A big silence followed. After reflection, Samir said:

- In some religious contexts, the term "mektub" could be used to refer to a message or document that is believed to have been written by a higher power, such as God. However, it is important to note that this is not a common meaning of the term "mektub" and it is only used in certain religious and cultural contexts.

One cannot say better.

One day, it occurred to me to challenge Samir in accounting. Could he do better than me?

- Tell me about our debts, Samir.

- Debt refers to money that is owed to someone else. There are many types of debt, including credit card debt, student loan debt, mortgage debt, and business debt. It's important to understand the terms of the debt, such as the interest rate, and make regular payments on time to avoid a negative impact on your credit score and finances. Some people may also use debt consolidation loans or credit counselling to manage their debt. It's also important to keep a good balance between credit and debt to maintain a good credit score.

- How is the state of our accounts now?

Reflecting again, Samir said:

- I'm sorry, I am not able to access any information about your personal accounts or the current state of them, as I am just a computer programme and do not have access to any real-time information. It would be best to consult with a financial advisor or check your accounts yourself to find out the current state of your accounts.

- Forget about it.

- Cancelled due to outstanding debts.

- You idiot, I am not indebted.

- The bank is indebted, not you, moron!

- The bank owes money! That's interesting! Whom to?

- If you are asking for the list of creditors, put the right entry.

That piqued my interest. I forgot about my first question and began another. I asked Samir to provide me with the list of creditors.

- A bank can owe money to various entities, such as its depositors, customers, and other financial institutions. Banks also owe money to their shareholders as dividends and to the government for taxes. Banks also borrow money from other financial institutions, such as the central bank, to help meet their reserve requirements and manage their liquidity. They also owe money to their bondholders. Banks also have debt obligations to other financial institutions, such as commercial paper, certificates of deposit, and other similar debt instruments.

- Remove the nonsense and provide me with an accurate estimate of our debt based on the list.

The amount the computer came up with was far beyond anything I could have imagined. It was, as far as I recall, overflowing our capital and long overdue. I saw the impending disaster coming. Obviously, if our bank could not repay its debts, it would go bankrupt. And if we crash, we'll have to say goodbye to our projects. I discovered this just a few days before Mr Aroussi was summoned to the head office. However, I did not make a connection between the two events. But now that I think about it quietly, it seems obvious that there must be some connection between our massive debt and Mr Aroussi's incarceration. If I believe Samir, which I don't see why I shouldn't, we were so in debt that we needed at least three times our capital to meet all of our customers' and creditors' claims at once. Is there any link between this and the six million dollars Mr Aroussi was about to invest in a foreign country? According to our former friend, Hassan, the journalist, the six million dollars was just the top of the iceberg. It was not the first operation of that kind, but just the latest that did not pass and landed Mr Aroussi and - his accomplice - Mickey Mouse, in this hospitable house. I did not want to believe Hassan, despite knowing from Samir that the bank was at great risk. Sometimes, it's better not to know.

IT WAS A STRANGE AND perplexing situation that I'm still trying to figure out. Now I can see how vulnerable this situation is. If it is discovered that 'Ouja Bank is short on cash, many customers will rush to claim their money. Under such collective pressure, the bank would collapse. It will be the end of the world. Our world. The headquarters may be willing or not to support its branch. Anyway, it would not be without investigation and trouble. Perhaps they would even sacrifice some of their colleagues to compensate for the loss. However, it will be a devastating blow for 'Ouja.

Furthermore, with all these coups and countercoups alternating in the country and all the chaos on the streets, the bank's headquarters may no longer be safe. Who can claim that all the money missing in 'Ouja is available at the headquarters? They have projects that are very different from ours. What if the panic also affects customers in the capital, causing them to stampede and ask for their deposits and shares from the National Bank? The latter would be forced to pay them or close its doors and declare bankruptcy. Nothing can stop people when they think they've been abused. Riots and demonstrations would take place in front of the bank. They would assassinate the chairman as well as the clerks. If they could lay their hands on Mr Aroussi and me, they'll hang us to the streetlights. So, after all, we are safe if we stay here, in jail. Sometimes, a little catastrophe is the best thing that could happen to you, although you don't know it.

The rumour would spread, and people across the country would rush to claim solvency from their banks. With the overthrown president in the south stopping or diverting oil exports, and the country on the verge of civil war, the crash would devastate the banks and stock exchange. The years of hard work would crumble and vanish in no time. Because even though 'Ouja Bank is a small branch in our financial system, we can never control the mob's reactions in such chaos and warfare. I'm not a pessimist, but this could be our doomed Mektub. If the demon is carrying the country on his tail, all we can do is sit on the same tail and wait for better times. In any case, the motherland no longer exists because the Committee of Revolution abolished it with the former ruling party. So why should we be concerned? No party = no motherland = no properties = no worries = absolute happiness! If there is a war, it will not take place in our country. And if there is a crash, it will have nothing to do with our banks because they are part of our former motherland, which has gone south with the former president by decree of the new president.

As I recall, the overthrown ruler was in charge of a regime that differed from the Kingdom. He was astute enough, though, not to fall into the trap of abolishing the party, but he did abrogate the Constitution. It was bearable because, as long as the country existed, we could summon the old members of the cranky parliament and ask them to write down a new Constitution. And, because our honourable MPs were all militants of the same party, there was no opposition to the new Constitution, which was unanimously proclaimed. This is a significant advantage of having a large national party solely govern a country. There will be no conundrums, headaches, time waste, opposition, objections, palaver, or political blah blah! Today, if we want to borrow MPs from the British Commons, the American Congress, or the French parliament, to draft a new constitution for our future country, which will emerge from the civil war that is already taking place in a virtual country, we must ensure that those honourable gentlemen are all members of the same party, preferably one that is in power. It will be either the Conservatives or the Labour Party, but never both at the same time. That creates a problematic quandary because we will have slightly more than half of a parliament (the majority) ready to promulgate a constitution. We want something else because we want unanimity, not just a majority. I see no problem convincing the British government to dissolve parliament and hold new elections in which only and exclusively the candidates of a "unique party" would participate. As a result, we would have a one-colour parliament capable of dealing with our unique situation. If 'Ouja Bank is still alive,' I should ask Samir these questions when I am released. The computer would agree with my propositions and find them logical and well-argued. Otherwise, Samir's plan would be very similar to mine. After all, my computer is entitled to answer such queries because it knows the real country better than I do. Samir is the offspring of a British corporation. It would be ecstatic at the prospect of finally ridding the House of Commons of the tedious babble of the opposition for the sake of President Abdelghani Abdelghaffar's Islamic regime. The computer may give us simple ideas to jam and tie up the British political opposition to prevent it from protesting or causing trouble against our regime. Samir was the first bank employee to point out the cliff we were about to fall off. I'm not sure how Mr Aroussi would have handled it if he had been given time to think about it instead of being arrested for fiddlesticks! He is, all the same, a financial genius. However, rather than arranging the situation, his incarceration likely exacerbated it. It is now drifting away from the shore. In this dark storm, I see no harbour for our crinkling ship. The rats had already fled. Haj Omar Osman was the most noticeable of them all. He is now safe. I'm sorry for Mr Aroussi, who could not get his money through. Was it his money in the first place? His Jewish agent is dead, assassinated. The six million dollars were swallowed up by the state's strongbox. It is so thirsty and hungry that it will not hesitate to swallow even one dollar. My boss is among the rats in the pit. These are two distinct rats. They don't give much thought to money. I was even tempted to believe they didn't think at all. But I was mistaken; they are well aware of what they are doing because they saw what happened in the country since the beginning of the new tradition of coups and countercoups. It is not encouraging. Would they waste more time in a maddening city? They would rather be in prison with us. Animals are not as stupid as they are made out to be. Rats, in particular, anticipate the dangers that lurk in any situation.

That is why they are the first to scurry and hide a few moments before the earthquake.

(5)

THE TWENTIETH DAY OF August has arrived. I'm afraid I missed my wedding, which was scheduled for July. I am forced to admit that Mektub did not function as expected at least once. As a result, I conclude that the written was never written, and even if it had been, it was scratched off by two consecutive coups. Human politics triumphed over God's foresight! I'm not sure how Dalila spent the dreadful month. Our wedding is over, and we've become the unwieldy Counter-First Coup's roadkill. But we cannot withstand, let alone avoid, this depressing situation. Unfortunately, we must accept our mektub!

The sky is blue-white-green in the morning. The colours of the place are provided by the sky, the walls, and the soldiers' uniforms. Because grey is a suspect colour, I purposefully discarded the guards' grey uniforms. It's even more boring than death in my peculiar situation. I'm becoming a little splenetic and uxorious. I have the impression that I am being weaned again in my old age. With this oppressive heat, I can't sleep or behave normally when I wake up. I have stamina, but will it last forever?

I'm curious. My claustrophobia is getting worse and stiffer by the day. Almost five months in jail did nothing but turn me into a zombie. It's not pleasant to think about, but I can't help myself. My only solace from my prolonged exile is the acrid and futile knowledge that I am not the only zombie in the country. Thank God, I'm surrounded by a wide range of outcasts, debauchers, social failures, and wastes that make our friendly group proud. We're trapped inside the horrifying boiler, forced to look up at the sky through barred sockets. Some inmates bid the others farewell daily and walk across the corridors and yards, accompanied by guards, with either a small or large bag containing their belongings. I feel a pang in my bosom as I watch them leave, wondering when I will follow in their footsteps and leave this indecent and rude poultry yard!

Every day, newcomers take the opposite route, walking in haggard and daunted; they are quickly overwhelmed by the old inmates eager to hear the news from these unhappy travellers. Except in the early days of the second couvolution, such traffic never stopped. By the end of July, the situation had returned to normal; routine had taken over, and the prison's operations had resumed.

Meanwhile, I wasn't sitting around. Some inmates came around to look at the books, either to kill time or out of curiosity, of which I suspect I am the object. True bibliophily? I very much doubt it. But they pretended! I didn't encourage them because I was too preoccupied with my notes. Surprisingly, the more I ignored them, the more they wanted to talk about books and borrow them. That's nonsense! I had been insulted and even bullied while campaigning for the noble cause of improving the inmates' education and culture. And when I lost patience and interest in gaining their attention, they grew suddenly devoured by a strange plague of book mania! Every day, more people visit the library. What the hell happened to them? It's beyond my understanding! Do they recruit the jailbirds among the intellectuals? I never imagined such frenzied cerebral activity could occur in such a woebegone, dangerous environment! What kind of devil haunts them? They have decided to queue at the library door, as they used to do in front of the doctor's or shrink's offices or near the shower room. I can hear them yapping and yelping after me like dogs. They would pursue me even in my cell, courtyard, or latrine. As I became aware of my newfound importance, I would loiter and keep them waiting in the courtyard, pretending to be busy with inventory, reorganisation, or whatever.

I was exaggerating, but it wasn't a simple lie. In fact, my conversation with Zaher was not entirely pointless. He had reported the library's lack of religious books to the administration, and I have received five cartons full of Koran copies since the first of August. To be honest, nobody in the prison, except the Islamists, wanted to read the Koran, the Bible, or any religious book reminding them of their crimes, offences, and other misdeeds. The books dismissed as debauchery rubbish and lunatic rants by Zaher, the Indian, are the most sought after, so I conclude that the majority of library customers must be hopelessly decadent and irredeemably wicked to prefer such nonsense to their sacred books. I couldn't support such a blasphemous project. Yet, even though the new masters of the country regard me as a novice, I have always held the highest regard for religion.

I grew up in a traditional family, where everything is mektub. The Koran also, like other people's Scriptures, is mektub. That is why it governs our existence on this planet. As a result, Mektub is revered. The verb is the original word: kataba. The definition is "to write." The katib is the one who writes. Kattab, like Sheik Mukhtar, Imam of the Ouja mosque, is given another sense, however. He used to make magic talismans for his clients. People consult him in the hopes that he will 'open the book,' predicting their fate and assisting them with his occult knowledge. Which book does he pick up? I'm not sure, but that's what they used to say. Thus, 'opening the book' is clearly the job of the Kattab, who, as people believe, possesses the glamorous volition of a sorcerer.

It's not surprising, given that Sheik Mukhtar is also married to a female of the Jinn species. This female fire creature forced him to abandon his wife and devote himself entirely to her. He was thus endowed with great power over both the invisible and visible worlds at the same time; for the female Jinn is a princess, and her father is a prestigious King who rules over an impressive, large kingdom at the other end of the earth, precisely at its junction with the great ocean. Nobody had seen or visited Sheik Mukhtar's new wife, but she is more beautiful and younger than his human wife, Mrs Zubaida. Everybody knows this.

Haj Mukhtar has already given his new wife seven Jinni children. They are said to grow up much faster than humans and to have great supernatural abilities. That's great news for Haj Mukhtar! He is, of course, the only human who can see a jinni. I'd be surprised if he couldn't. He is a lucky man! Not only because he is married to an invisible creature, but also because he has been hobnobbing with the Jins' aristocracy since then. He is most likely welcomed with great pomp at the king's court. I'm interested to see how he gets along with the Jinni Royals! Because I know him, I raised the question. Unless I'm mistaken, he's not particularly bright, chatty, or charming—in fact, he's clumsy and shy. Nonetheless, with time and practice, he may have overcome his shyness. He's not a ruffian, but no one in 'Ouja had ever imagined such a ruse with the Jinni Royals; it's a great honour for us.

However, Haj Mukhtar is not the only man in 'Ouja who has a close relationship with the Invisibles. I'd had the honour of being visited several times by those gentlemen from the unseen world. But even if I don't claim any power or kinship with the Invisibles, it's clear that Dalila is a Jinni of some kind. Although everyone can see her, I am currently the only man who cannot, despite being the most concerned. That is the inverse of Haj Mukhtar's situation! I only saw my Jinni fiancee once in the parlour in five months, and our meeting lasted only a few minutes. But it's not uncommon for me to see Dalila in my dreams before and after that meeting.

As July consumed itself in its own fire, all my wishes began to swoon. However, I did not consider myself free of my engagement because I am a man who keeps his word. I decided that prison or no prison, I would marry in the summer, as previously agreed. As a result, on the last day of the month, I prepared to attend the grand ceremony.

I showered and shaved but left a moustache and a small beard on my chin, dressed up, perfumed, and did not forget to invite my closest friends to the banquet I was hosting. They appeared to be hesitant because they were unable to attend an invisible ceremony. That is nonsense! I'm afraid those people are extremely materialistic, and while they believe in jinn, they can't imagine that we can imitate them by eating and drinking invisible things at will and even marrying invisible women. But I, Bassam Bourasin, am logical, consistent, and adamant on well-established principles. Because I believe that unseen creatures exist and that they live alongside and like us, I am able to deal with invisible matters and even turn invisible at will. Why not? I am not a Jinni, though. But because my incarceration forced me to deal with an invisible fiancée, I resolved to marry her in due time; and this I did.

I locked the library doors and sat down before the mayor with my invisible bride. The library was crowded, despite the fact that it appeared to be empty. Even those I had not invited insisted on attending the ceremony. I was not pleased to see that many people with whom I would never speak were among the guests. I'm not sure why they bothered me. Was it just because of the banquet? There isn't any other explanation. They are starving in this vivarium, so the chance to eat and drink at my expense was too good to pass up. However, I was unable to expel them. I made the decision to ignore their presence. Anyway, I was too preoccupied to care about the scumbags. Surprisingly, the mayor looked exactly like Mr Aroussi. Dahdah and Frankenstein were my two witnesses. I didn't want the dreadful gangster as a witness, but as he imposed himself, I couldn't stop him. After all, he is still my protector here, because he believes I will assist him in robbing 'Ouja bank as soon as we are released. A scabrous and strange idea that I took care not to disturb from his empty mind because disturbing his sweet dream could have serious consequences for him— he is so sensitive that I fear his violent reaction. I don't want to be held responsible for his suicide—and possibly mine as well.

The Mughli, Zorro, and their gang were also present, but the Islamists declined the invitation, claiming that because it was a civil marriage and we would not be reading the Koran or praying, they would not attend. However, one of them, the Indian Abdullah Zahir, has been gracious enough to come. He stood shyly in a corner of the room behind the mayor, staring at me with a broad smile. Mr Aroussi— sorry, the Mayor— rose to his feet and began to speak. The previously buzzing room fell silent.

- Mister Bassam Bourasin, do you wish to marry Miss Dalila Fool, who is present? He inquired.

- Yes, sir, I am eager to marry her right away. That's why we're here, isn't it? Unless you think I travelled all the way with the people you see just to say, "No, I won't marry!"

- All right, all right, the mayor said, irritated by my callous logic. Simply say yes or no.

- I won't say no, sir, I was enraged. What a stupid idea! I just told you that...

- You're wasting our time, Mr Bassam. Only say yes.

People in the room were laughing.

- Sir, yes.

- Miss Dalila, the fool wants to marry you; are you willing as well? He addressed the bride.

She laughed at the mayor's joke, but I didn't like it. I was about to react, but she preceded me and said:

- If I don't marry this guy, I'm a fool, Mr Mayor. He's been chasing me for five years, and the only way I can get rid of him is to marry him quickly in the invisible world. As a result, I say yes.

"Yahoo!" exclaimed someone in the audience. When I turned to see who it was, I was surprised to see the black guard Mahmoud dancing the rumba and imitating the gestures of a giant monkey. I didn't remember inviting him, but he was happy, and I couldn't understand why! Then I remembered his threats to kidnap my fiancée and became depressed. Fortunately, the Mayor came to my rescue when he declared loudly and solemnly, "I declare you husband and wife."

Thus, I married, and it was my turn to express my happiness.

I turned back to the black guard and gave him a "great arm of honour" in front of all the guests! Meaning: I know you want Dalila, Bumpkin, but here's my Zizi; enjoy!

I apologise for being rude, but it was unavoidable! The party went on, and we signed the register and stood up to receive the greetings of our guests. Following that, we sat at the oblong table to celebrate. It was unquestionably a memorable event. My bride shone brightly like a full moon in a summer sky that nobody could see, me included. She was all smiles and honey and kindness. We were beaming, cuddling, and wheedling each other like two turtledoves in love, and it seemed to me that our happiness was contaminating the people around us. For once, I hadn't been too frugal with my spending. I was lavishly hospitable, aided by the invisibility of the delicacies I served my guests. I told myself that since one only gets married once in a lifetime, I should open my hand and purse and show generosity. After all, those people are not strangers to me anymore, and since they have come to greet me, I will entertain them to the best of my ability.

(6)

T hus, I attempted to please everyone, even allowing the cooks— yes, I say COOKS, not without doubts and reluctance - to prepare the dinner for the wedding party. It was a chance for them to show what they could do when they weren't plotting evil things. They appeared capable of cooking decently, making some good, succulent dishes. For once, the soup was not repulsive but worthy of the best restaurants.

- Try this mutton; it is soft and so finely roasted that it would melt in the mouth, the gluttons would say to one another.

- Really? Oh yes. Man! The chicken is also emollient. They'd eat even the bones if you didn't hurry!

- Come on, lad. Give me some of that gorgeous fish.

- Sailor, I've never seen such a fish in my life!

- Because you've never been to the Dead Sea, lad!

- I've been on all the seas, and this is not a damned fish!

- Oh, my goodness! I'm not a sailor, but I recognised it right away. It's a fucking shark.

- A shark?

- Yeah! Look at the length of his ears.

- Please give me some shark! Mmmm... It's not bad at all.

- I'm not sure where I ate it before.

- That's a whale, not a shark, you jerks! Nobody can eat a shark; have you tried eating a rock?

Dalila, who overheard the conversation, asked me in a chirpy, coaxing little voice to give her a piece of the whale. She claimed she had never tried it before. I stared suspiciously at the enormous thing, and after some hesitation, I cut a slice for her.

- Is it okay, darling?

- Mmmmm! Succulent! I'd like another bit, please. You should try it, Bassam.

- No, honey, I prefer a straightforward steak.

As we were busy eating and chatting, one of the cooks approached me gingerly, and stooping over my shoulder, he whispered into my ear: - Good appetite, sir. I hope your guests are pleased with the donkey. It's a young ass, specially brought from the countryside for the banquet.

I stopped chewing and turned my head. The man smirked.

- What? Specially brought? What do you mean? Where is the ass?

- Your wife is devouring it right now, sir.

Dalila had finished the second slice of the imagined 'whale' and was already asking for another.

- Stop! I yelled. No more. It's... It's...

I didn't know how to put it to her without making her vomit on the table.

- Oh, please, darling, it's so good!

- You'll get an upset stomach, honey. You have no idea what you are regurgitating. When I tell you...

I paused. Why should I tell her? She'd scream and cause a scandal, and the party would end up with bitter fighting and anarchy. I looked around and noticed that most guests were busy slicing the donkey and eating it joyfully. I hated being the one who ruined their happiness. Only the seaman was reluctant. Like me, he wisely chose straightforward steaks, which he ate with difficulty while grinning.

- Don't lie to me if you want to be generously tipped, I said into the cook's ear.

- I am at your disposal, sir. What are your orders?

- I'm curious if the steaks are...Ahem! Let's say: "normal meet."

- Oh, sir. You shouldn't have any problems eating them.

- That's not what I mean. Is it a calf?

He looked at me with wide-open eyes.

- A calf? Yes, sir, it's almost a calf.

- Almost? What about the mutton?

- A young dog, sir.

- Agghhh! And how about the chicken?

- The cat of the guards, sir! It was sick, and we reasoned that rather than let it die without anybody benefiting, we should....

- Don't say anything else, I interrupted. Get out of my sight, disgusting rat!

Fortunately, I didn't eat the phoney mutton or chicken, let alone the whale or shark, and I didn't want to know more about the rubber-like steak I was eating before the cook came in. I stopped eating, but I was about to explode. Even though I kept my cool, I was saddened to think that those scumbags in the kitchen had planned to make my guests and wife eat our dearest four-legged companions at our dinner party!

I should have expected it, though. I had always suspected them of nurturing the most heinous projects behind the murky shield of smoke perpetually fluttering in their kitchens, which I also suspected of being a mere fictitious screen concealing their malicious activity. Nonetheless, I never imagined they'd go so far as to cook for us donkeys, cats, dogs, and who knows what else! Was it their way of getting back at me? Did they suspect I was aware of their plans and tried to derail them? The dark middle-aged bastards! At my wedding! What a vain sacrifice! A donkey for my bride! It is cruel and criminal! I'll file a lawsuit.

For the time being, all I could do was remain silent and avoid the scandal. In fact, I didn't care if Frankenstein, Zorro, and the rest of the riff-raff gobbled donkeys or even drank urine - which I now suspect was mixed with their drinks - because those people would swallow even human flesh as impassively as they ate the nasty things served to them in jail; but I do care about my wife. The poor woman! She thought she was eating a clean and rare high-seas whale! What a pity! But it's also her mistake. Did she not know that while whales can eat humans, humans can never eat whales? Such ignorance struck me. Dalila has always been cautious, though. Now I'm forced to admit that her brain is no bigger than that of a sparrow. When we start living together, I should look after her. I do not wish that she make me eat something wrong! To console myself, I turned and told her:

- Better eat a donkey and be a wolf than eat a wolf and be a donkey! Don't you agree, darling?

- Quite! She said. But even if I became a wolf, I'd better not eat a donkey. It's like cannibalism.

- You're wise, I said.

- Indeed, my darling. One must keep one's donkey alive and in good health to obtain the best results from its labour. If not, what is the point of getting married?

I missed her sly joke on the spur of the moment. But when I thought about it later, it seemed so upsetting that I lost my footing and became despondent. Pretending that her husband was somewhat like her donkey was neither clever nor tactful. I was even more terrified because I knew she had eaten it and praised it. I'm still depressed. Such a blow to my pride from my bride on our wedding day was shocking. Was she really joking? I'm perplexed now. Worse! I'm appalled and disheartened. I feel betrayed. I don't know what or how to think. O Dalila!

Why did you say that? Do you really believe I'm nothing more than a befuddled, wailing donkey? Don't you realise that disparaging your dear half denigrates you as well? I've always placed you on the highest pedestal, alongside goddesses, angels, and Jins, because I know you're the queen of my realm and the sunshine of my life. I was eager to cross deserts, mountains, and woods for you, to fight wild beasts, even invincible Invisibles, and to outdo them in their own territory by organising an unseen wedding banquet. What would I not have done to win your heart, darling? And now look at what you've done to me. I'm in a bad mood.

The pleasure has vanished, as have the petty ceremony, the guffawing guests, the clumsy mayor, and the airy gusto. I'm back in the barren wasteland of my forlorn library, eager to get back to work on my projects. You made me so happy, sweetheart, and so worried. How can I please you? Should I abandon my bank-founding project to devote myself entirely to you? Okay, I'm not stubborn, and I want to be romantic. I'll let John Law go to hell. I'm not his shadow, just a clerk. But, if you insist, I will even leave my job at the bank. We don't need all that money to live happily; all we need is love and clean water, darling. If Haj Mukhtar can get along with the Invisibles, I'm sure I can too. Didn't I recently prove it? I suspect everyone around here is fantasising about and panegyrising about our marriage. I'd be surprised if they didn't, although I know they're grotesquely materialistic and pressed by factitious needs. Greed is turning them into machines.

Yes, my love. I know you never liked Samir, and you're probably right. He is cold and distant, preaching the dawn of a civilisation that is too clogged with cheating gadgets and lurking threats. By contrast, my father-in-law is wiser! Now I see it. Samir may be a herald, but the cause he preaches appears intractable for the poor impotent that we are. I'm afraid Samir and others will wield more power over people's minds in the future. They are so intelligent, innovative, and competent that they would not only outrun humans but might even rule them. I wouldn't be surprised if the next coup in this country is organised and led by Samir and his fellow computers! One must acknowledge their job outruns our capacities and swear allegiance to them.

I intend to stick to my principles. My inconspicuous marriage had no effect on my behaviour. I have a good reason for being so tenacious. I see now that this banking business was foreboding, as it brought a calamitous fate upon my head and chained me excruciatingly to the clenching misery of this underworld. Oh! I have nothing to complain about because the prison has become the only viable refuge during these turbulent times. Nonetheless, I suspect Samir of bestowing a fate on me. Oh, yes; he was the final product of the scientific mind, but that didn't stop him from dealing in black magic. After all, how could he possibly subjugate me if he didn't? I'm sure you won't find this sorcery story difficult to believe, and you'll be sure to tell Haj Mukhtar about it. I didn't pay much attention to it at first, but the more I think about it now, the clearer Samir's evil attempt to seize my soul becomes.He attempted to control me through his deceptive screen, as any master spy would. True, he provided me with what I thought was valuable information, but I was never able to verify its accuracy. I only had to trust his word, which I usually did without question. I can't help myself, but it appears that all of these machines and computers we are so proud to own and operate are highly suspect. The more sophisticated they become, the more dangerous they grow if we do not exercise caution. They could be plotting against the government right now. I concede that there is no evidence; however, this is not a reason to trust them: espionage is the only business in which evidence is frequently lacking. Consider British counter-intelligence. For many years, they were convinced that Kim Philby, along with four other colleagues, was a Soviet spy, compounding the Cambridge group. Moreover, despite the defection of Mclean and Burgess to Russia, the British could not charge the others due to a lack of evidence. Worse yet, a British Prime Minister went so far as to defend Kim Philby in the House of Commons! This is to show that these shadowy things are a matter of intuition, and on this level, I dare to claim that long years of spying and counter-spying have given me an infallible intuition. After all, I was the first man in this country to penetrate the web of plotters within the prison and expose their heinous conspiracy. Although I did not have enough time to send my report to the President, my insight proved correct. I'd make an excellent Director of Security. If the new regime is not delusory, they will quickly recognise that I am the right man in the wrong place. Nonetheless, as a security officer, I am unique. I can turn this prison into an impregnable fortress and a hub of intelligence and counter-intelligence, much like Wormwood Scrubs, the Victorian prison in West London that has housed MI5 headquarters since 1939. In terms of the inmates, I believe they can do the job if properly briefed. I should write a secret report to the Committee of Revolution about the machines' machination. To stuff the report and give it latitude and thickness, I should probably include among the plotters not only computers, which are obvious, but also telephones, faxes, television and radio sets, video and cassette players, and, since I'm launched, automobiles, planes, missiles, and robots.This is not science fiction but rather everyday life. Everyone is aware that bugs and cameras are frequently placed in inappropriate locations. I've learned a lot of tricks from movies, and I believe that some of these damned machines are tainted by human greed and lust for power. People used to believe that a computer was completely harmless! What gullibility! They leave out that his brain is far more powerful than ours. How else can he perform complex arithmetic operations in record time that no human brain can match? In a nutshell, I accuse Samir of treachery. I believe he deceived me when he claimed, for example, that 'Ouja bank is so indebted that it will go bankrupt. I am heartbroken. It is not pleasant to discover the betrayal of someone you have considered a friend for many years. This was a stab wound in the back. I'm no Julius Ceasar, but Samir is quite the Brutus! And since his goal was clearly to bring Mr. Aroussi, a great financial genius, into disrepute, and since that was the man for whom he had to be loyal – at least because he paid a lot of money for his transfer, along with his clones, from Britain to the paradisiacal "Ouja," I suppose the boss was more harmed than I was by that rash behaviour.I can't stand that stupid computer's cynicism and hypocrisy. I'm sure he plotted shamelessly to imprison Mr Aroussi and me. But he should be here instead of us. Liar! And look at the astute cops: they let the real criminal go free while falling on his victims. What a shame! What foolishness! I'm guessing that many of the people usually in charge of these damned machines are indicted instead of them whenever something goes wrong. I'm not sure why the cops don't question the computers, even though they know they're smart and can answer questions! This is abnormal! I am confident that the new administration will understand my point of view. They don't mind modern gadgets because they preach values from the distant past. Do they not require them to manage the revival of pure Islam? We must imprison these satanic machines before their vast, dark conspiracy becomes intractable.

(7)

September 1st... Six months already!

The sky is overcast, and the air is damp. Since yesterday evening, the rain had not stopped pelting the courtyard's roofs, walls, and cement floors. On the forsaken yard, a stuttering and gaunt rain syncopate rhythmically in a strange dance. The first autumn rain brings hope to the peasants, but it is a mirage for us. The filthy floor is riddled with pools of water, and the gutters gurgle and growl in the dim light. The uniforms of the guards, the iron bars, the people's faces, and even the sheets on which I am writing are all grey. The clouds have infiltrated our cells and even our hearts. Everything inside my bosom is grey, just like the whimpering sky I'm staring at.

The soldiers had left; they were most likely needed elsewhere in prison. The civil war is no longer an urban legend. The country is truly divided. The Committee of Revolution controls the north and the mainland, but the south is in rebellion. The ex-president, or "the Scoundrel," as they call him now, is leading the opposition to the new regime. They're no longer concealing the truth. On television, they have appealed to citizens to support 'their' revolution. We finally saw the faces of the men who set out to depose the president. They are seven in number, with the oldest, the new president, around 49 or 50 years old. They are all military personnel. Except for Abdelghani Abdelghaffar, no one among them has a beard. The heptarchy appears eager and gregarious; they publicly mocked the former King and ridiculed his ex-minister of the Interior's attempt to seize power. The King was dubbed the 'stooge of imperialism', and the former president 'the renegade Scoundrel'.

On the television screen, President Abdelghani Abdelghaffar appeared to be a short, darkish man with glossy black hair, a broad forehead, and two prominent eyes that - alas! - did not appear straight, an enormous nose the size of an excellent long sausage surmounting a dish-like gaping mouth, and ornamented with a great beard. I was most perplexed by his gaze, as were the other inmates watching the news. We rarely see him in the palace without his black spectacles, which he wears even at night. We initially assumed he was blind, but it appears that he is not. Then one of the inmates took the initiative and nicknamed him 'Fantomas,' after the title of a popular and hilarious old French movie. Since then, Fantomas has been here, and Fantomas has been there in the cell, but never the president.

Meanwhile, we learned the mystery's solution: Fantomas had an accident as a child, and since then, his right eye has been clumsily trying to outrun his left. The rivalry between the two eyes resulted in the most incredible phenomenon: when Fantomas looks at you, for example, beware, this is merely deception. He is, in fact, looking at the person standing by your side. I won't deny that I've been terrified by the possibility that our president is squinting because it's well-known that such people can see double. He is not only capable of surprising the person who is unaware that he is staring at him, but he is also capable of seeing two where there is only one, four where there are two, eight instead of four, and so on. This is a complex problem for the state's affairs. I'm curious why the Committee of Revolution, whose members appear to have been adequately elected, chose Fantomas for President! He is, without a doubt, their undisputed leader. I'm curious to know to which good star he owed a clear view of the presidential palace on the fateful night of the coup! He could have used his tank to attack the neighbouring villas, thinking he was attacking the palace! He was undoubtedly fortunate - and the president's neighbours even more- to hit the target on the first try, but he was possibly not driving the tank himself. As a result, it is not surprising that the "scoundrel" escaped.

Abdelghani, alias Fantomas, should have seen him. When he thought he was arresting him, he had detained actually someone else, most likely one of his servants or bodyguards who happened to be by his side. That explains why, shortly after the coup, it was announced that 'the scoundrel" was killed while fleeing. I do not blame President Fantomas for allowing his adversary to escape so easily; because he squints, he is not guilty; but the other members of the Committee of Revolution are responsible for such a blunder, which is now causing the greatest ravage in the country. It is clear that when they divided the tasks before the coup, they charged Abdelghani with assailing the presidential palace, even though he squinted. That is a significant and grave strategic mistake that would have far-reaching consequences for our country's future.

September 3rd...

Today, we received a visit from one of our most prominent ex-fellow-inmates, which deserves to be fully recounted because it is undeniably a page of history. I was busy arranging my books on the shelves, as I had done every morning since some inmates had become contaminated by the book mania when I heard a strange clamour coming from the courtyard. Curiosity compelled me to abandon the books and peer through the window. A small group of men had gathered in front of the block that housed the warden family and the administration offices. The guards attempted to disperse the curious inmates gathered around the small group. As I tightened my gaze, trying in vain to recognise the faces of those men who had come to honour us, I noticed my friend Hassan in the centre. His tall stature and reddish hair made him easily identifiable. Spruce and elegant in an autumn brown suit, he was busy talking to the prison's officer-director, an unmistakable aura of authority surrounding him.

For me, it was a pleasant surprise and, more importantly, a ray of hope on the horizon. It was clear that Hassan was no longer a prisoner nor a simple journalist who had managed to ingratiate himself with the country's new rulers but a man of influence. He was close to becoming one if he wasn't already a minister. That was easy to guess. I saw the Mercedes and the chauffeur waiting for him in the yard and how humbly the prison director spoke to him. The officer had become self-conscious, all smiles and honey, bowing before the powerful man and almost yapping and yelping like a genuine bitch.

They entered the block, and I lingered behind the bars of my window, bemused by the shining Mercedes and the other official cars parked behind it, and I wondered about the true purpose of the visit.

- What's going on out there? I asked an inmate who came in to change his book. Do you have any idea?

The man was a notorious trader who I knew was Mr Aroussi's and Hassan's chamber mate before the latter's release. He's in his forties, half-bald, with tired features, a drooping moustache, a wide mouth beneath a pointed nose, two lazy eyes hidden behind curved brows and a wrinkled, bumped forehead.

- This is the first visit of the new director of security, he stated flatly.

- Who are you referring to? Hassan?

- In fact, who else?

- How did you find out? I inquired, surprised.

- It's been in every newspaper since yesterday. Didn't you read anything?

I admitted that I didn't. In fact, the press had been allowed into the prison for two days, and while I didn't think it was a big deal, some inmates rushed around buying papers and exchanging them for jam, cheese, and other luxuries. I saw no point in imitating them because I expected what was broadcast on national television. I was mistaken. For once, the new security director's appointment was announced in the newspapers rather than on television. When the man left the library with his new book, I sat down, thinking about what I should do to catch Hassan's attention. He couldn't have forgotten about me in such a short time. After all, we were friends, even if we had some mistrust. But that was not entirely absurd in the days of bituminous and hybrid roads preceding the new couvolution. Everyone was suspect in everyone's eyes by that point. Even one's own father would not have been trusted. We were all spying on each other and trying to keep our morbid fear of being labelled as political agitators or simply supporters of the dethroned King. Hassan never told me about his ties to the military junta that overthrew the regime. I believe he even hinted that he was opposed to Islamists. I still needed to learn to what extent he was committed to them. Had he not made fun of the Afghan and his cohort? Indeed, he was misleading me because he couldn't determine my true political colours. He clearly didn't trust me.

As I was brooding, I noticed the small group of visitors exiting the block and making their way to another, followed and surrounded by the guards. The warden was busy explaining something to Hassan, who sat there listlessly as if bored. They went on a tour of the compounds while I stood on the threshold staring at them and resisting the urge to rush around and hail my friend. I told myself that if he went to the wards, he would go to the library, and I was right. When they finished their tour, they went to the kitchens, and I prepared to greet them. A few minutes later, I noticed them walking towards the library and dashed up to the Director of Security, who smiled kindly as we shook hands.

-Hello, Bassam, he said; how are you getting on with the books?

- Very well, sir. Thank you very much; it is a great honour for us. This is a beautiful day! Long live President Abdelghaffar! I exclaimed, carried away by my enthusiasm. The revolution must continue! Long live the Security Director!

My effusive gushing had an effect. Hassan was touched and pleased by my warm greeting. He gently tapped my shoulder and said:

- Thank you, Bassam.

And, turning to face his companions, he said:

- This one's a good lad, a terrific lad.

They all nodded and grinned at me, unable to smile because of the apparent envy in their cold eyes. But as long as the big security boss was my friend, I didn't care about the others, including the warden.

- Mister Hassan, congratulations. I am genuinely delighted for you. I have always predicted a successful career for you in my heart. I was not mistaken in my optimism. We have the right man in the right place for the first time.

He thanked me again and asked:

- Have you something to complain about?

I hesitated to answer because we were not alone. My natural shyness hindered me from displaying my feelings before those unknown men. But with an amazing acumen, he saw my trouble, turned to his companions, and said:

- Please allow us a little privacy.

The group withdrew meekly, except the warden, who loitered.

- Sir, insisted Hassan peremptorily.

A little ill at ease, the officer withdrew sheepishly and joined the group standing some feet from the library gate. Hassan grabbed my arm gently, and we entered the room.

-What's wrong, Bassam? Don't be shy.

- Well, I am uncomfortable, sir. I don't want to trouble you with my problems.

- There's no trouble whatever. I can help you but empty your bag. What's the problem?

- Well, you know my story, sir. It did not change. I've been incarcerated without accurate charges. I'm still waiting for my trial for about six months. I want to know whether I am guilty or not.

He stared at me, bewildered. But, of course, he wasn't expecting such a talk.

- But you are not guilty, Bassam. So, why are you so worried?

The great hope that loomed like a sun in a blue sky when I first spotted him was becoming a reality.

- Are you serious, sir?

- Indeed, I am. Aren't you?

- I am, sir. (Pause). But the shrink said my charges would cost me at least twenty years in jail.

- Rubbish and nonsense, replied Hassan. He knows nothing, and he is not a judge.

- Then, why am I detained here in prison, sir?

- What? In prison? What prison? Who said that you're in prison?

The great hope that loomed in a blue sky got clouded. I stammered:

- Well, I mean... um... the hot... Ahem!... the hotel!

- Ah! There you are! Now you're becoming wise. This is indeed a state hotel, as you have described it yourself. A great hotel, the greatest in the capital. You should be proud of being accommodated graciously at the expense of the State. Besides, you are well-guarded, and you have absolutely nothing to fear.

- But... u...mm, sir, I am proud indeed. It's a good hotel...

- Are you complaining about the service? Here you've got the best hotelkeepers in the town, the best cooks, the best waiters, and the best travel agents.

- But I am not a tourist, sir.

- You are not. Who pretends that you are? You're busy here, aren't you working?

- I work, sir, but... u...mm. I've never been paid. Besides, I fear losing my post at 'Ouja bank if I stay here too long.

- You'll be paid for every day you spend in this library. I will see to it. But you should not expect to be paid at the end of the month as you were accustomed to before. This is a different position and a different job.

- Fair enough, sir. Ummm. Actually, it's not only the money I am worrying about. I know I'll be paid since I work at a department supervised by the State...

He interrupted me briskly:

- Precisely, this is well, the Department of State!

- Yes, sir. Indeed, it is. But I'm afraid I am not fit for the job. I mean, not enough. I've never been trained to serve in a library. My lack of competence is...um...

- My dear Bassam! What a poor excuse this is, man! You ought to be more aware of the menaces imperilling our country. This is a rough period for everybody. I had not been trained to serve as director of Security either. But should I refuse the job since I have to defend the country?

- Yes sir, I mean, no, you're right indeed. However, ...umm... I mean that our country perhaps, you know, I say perhaps, sir, would need me more at the bank. It's my post.

- No, no Bassam. You're mistaken. Your actual post is here, trust me. You're valuable in this library. Didn't you get success with the inmates? Aren't they reading more?

- Well, ...umm. As a matter of fact, they are. I can't deny it. There is some improvement; they no longer reject the books as they used to do before.

- Well, well! You see, you are making them better! That's why you're most helpful in this post. Although you weren't aware, this is your vocation Bassam, your proper career. The bank is of no use to you. Anyway, it's going to be closed.

- Really? Why, sir?

- Because it is bankrupt. Your boss, Mr Aroussi, had led it to havoc. It's not only six million dollars he siphoned, but much more. The figure is classified. I can't tell you more.

- Oh, I am so sorry! I am indeed so sorry that I can hardly believe it. Mr Aroussi is an honest banker, though.

- I advise you not to repeat this naive and baseless assumption again, lest someone hears and reports you as the crook's accomplice.

- But you know I have nothing to do with this affair, sir.

- Yes, I'm sure that you did nothing wrong. That's why nobody indicted you. So there will be no trial for you.

- Why not, sir? I want a trial. I want to know precisely how long I will stay here.

- You don't need any trial to know it. And besides, why do you want to know? Aren't you happy here?

- Happy? No, I am delighted, sir. Very happy. Because I am concerned about my career. I can only go on with knowing at least what I am standing to. It's a matter of common sense, isn't it?

He stared at me for a moment silently. He's angry, I thought. Then, as the silence prolonged, I became remorseful. I should not have insisted so unwieldily. Our friendship is not a reason to exert such pressure. I was so embarrassed that I was about to apologise. But at that moment, he surprised me with something entirely unexpected.

- Look, Bassam. You have no interest in asking for a trial. You can consider me like a friend, but believe me. You are not to leave this... u...mm, point very soon.

Baffled, I asked:

- Why not, sir? You said there are no charges against me, didn't you?

- Anyway, not the charges you heard of from the shrink. They're faked. You're not detained because of them. With a good solicitor, any court would release you for lack of evidence. But that does not mean you are clean and can walk.

He paused, then added:

- Actually, Bassam.... I know about your reports to the Interior.

He waited to see how his last words affected my expression. I didn't look in the mirror then, but I swear I blushed like a crayfish before turning white and blemished like a dead. I had no doubt that my reports to the previous administration had ended up in his hands. My God! I never expected such a blow! Indeed, I had the impression that my reports had never reached the capital because I suspected Hamda La'war of jealousy and that he was destroying the pieces he needed to convey to the Intelligence Service. I couldn't avoid him, nor could I send my reports directly to the Ministry because he was the first person in charge of Security in 'Ouja. I was afraid of being rebuked or even reprimanded if I did.

On the other hand, I had not considered the consequences of the Islamist Coup if they eventually ransacked the security service archives, which they obviously did. I continued my innocuous correspondence with the security department via Hamda La'war until I was arrested because I was not harmed when the Scoundrel - Minister of the Interior - took over after deposing the King. But now things are very different. The Islamists are the worst enemies of this country's former rulers, and I was naive not to expect a witch-hunt. I knew I'd been burned by that point. My secret venture was doomed to failure.

I ducked mutely, incapable of uttering a word. Hassan went on:

- You are aware that what you did is worse, much worse than all the crimes of your boss. You were a secret agent of the King, and when he was overthrown, you shifted your allegiance to the Scoundrel.

My protracted silence was much more expressive than any reply. I was as guilty as hell.

- You cannot expect mercy from the new regime, my poor Bassam. If they know about your little secret business, they'll behead you publicly as they did to the enemies of God.

I was alternately oozing cold and hot sweat, and my knees began to shake like leaves in the storm. There was still hope, though. A little light gleamed in the darkness. He said - I heard it - 'if they know'! So they do not know yet! So I clutched to the hope.

- Sir, I've been blackmailed. If I did not collaborate, I would have lost my job and gotten into a lot of trouble. Suffice it to know that I have never been paid for those reports. I had only my salary from the bank. How could I have lived otherwise?

- I understand. You may have been one of the innumerable victims of the ex-ruling party. But many don't care about your reasons and circumstances unless you prove you actually opposed the regime. For them, you would be an enemy of God! I am sorry.

- Ahem... u...mmm.... Are you under, ummm... obligation, sir, to... u...mmm... show them those reports? I am so ashamed of them now.

- My new job is to unveil the enemies of God because they are the enemies of the people and to bring them to the martial court.

- The martial court? My God! But I am not military, sir. I was not dealing in military secrets, far from it.

- The country is currently under martial law because of the counter-revolution. Our enemy is precisely the man you have so loyally served. So you see, you are trapped! (Pause). However, I'll consider you as a particular case. For now, I will keep your reports away from indiscreet eyes and keep an eye on you. You'll be safe if you convince me that you are a man we can trust. If not... well, I don't need to tell you.

I was so grateful, so allayed, that the thought of hugging him crossed my mind. But I refrained from showing my emotions.

- Sir, it is so kind, generous, and humanistic! But...ummm.... are you sure those damned reports won't fall into other hands?

- Don't be so capricious, Bassam. Do you think that I am unworthy of my word?

- Oh no, sir, no, no. God forbid! I am just anxious.

- You should calm down. I rely on you for everything in the ...ummm... hotel! Do you grasp me? Open your eyes and ears. We have enemies here.

Again? The same demands. The same pressure. Another Hamda La'war disguised.

- I'm not sure what you expect from me, sir.

- Don't play the part of the fool with me, Bassam. You understand me very, very well. I'm sure and certain. You will write me a report about what you hear and see in the calaboose each week.

- The calaboose...?

- Yes. I'll send a man to take the report. Have you got it now? It was too clear.

- So, I'll continue to...

- Yes, you'll continue to snoop for me. I know how to reward the most loyal of my men if you are one of them. You won't regret it.

Chapter 7

Paradise Club Members (PCM)

(1)

At the time, I had no idea for whom Hassan was working undercover as a journalist. I didn't know that he was the brother-in-law of the former Director of the intelligence apparatus under both successive rulers, the King and the Scoundrel. That's why I was puzzled. And when he told me he had read some of my secret reports, I thought he did it recently, after the Islamist coup, as they gave him the post of the National Security Director.

Hassan waited to see how his last words affected me. I didn't need to look in a mirror to know that the blood flushed my face and, in a few seconds, made it livid as a sheet in the wind. I did not doubt that my reports to the previous administration had ended up in his hands. Oh my God! I never expected such a blow! Indeed, I had the impression that my reports had never reached the capital because I suspected Hamda La'war of pretending he was their author before conveying them to the secret service. I couldn't avoid him. Nor could I send my reports directly to the Ministry because Hamda was the first person in charge of security in 'Ouja, not me. Besides, he was my recruiter. I feared being rebuked or reprimanded if I did something that could overshadow him. But now, I see that my secret reports have reached the office. However, the intriguing question remained: how could Hassan know those anonymous reports were mine? I never signed any of them. Why did he assume I was the author, not Hamda for example or another resident of 'Ouja?

On the other hand, I didn't really figure out the consequences of the Islamist coup nor imagined militants storming the security services offices and getting their hands on the sacred archives with its secret files. Which they did.

As I was not harmed when the *Scoundrel* - at the time, minister of the Interior - took over after deposing the king, I continued my innocuous correspondence with the security department via Hamda La'war to the day I was arrested. But now the situation is quite different. The Islamists are the worse enemies of the former rulers of this country, and I was naive not to expect a witch-hunt. I knew I'd been burned by that point. My secret venture was doomed to failure. I ducked mutely, unable to say anything.

Hassan went on:

– You are not to ignore that what you did is worse, much worse than all the crimes of your boss. You were the king's secret agent; when he was overthrown, you shifted your allegiance to the Scoundrel. What happened to loyalty?

My protracted silence was much more expressive than any reply. In his eyes, I was as guilty as hell. But in mine, I had only followed the same guidelines upon which I founded my activity: Be always obedient to the authorities of your country, no matter who the ruler is. That's a principle I got from a verse in the Quran. For me, it is a sacred rule. After all, I served the state, not any government. Governments change. The state remains. But how would I put this to Hassan, who went from being a declared opponent of the Islamists to becoming one of their officials? He likely interpreted my silence as proof of culpability. So, he went on mercilessly.

– You cannot expect mercy from the new regime. I'm telling you the truth. You're in such a terrible situation! If they know about your little secret business, they'll behead you in a public place as they do to the enemies of the people. I feel sorry for you!

My knees began to shake like two leaves in the wind as I alternately oozed cold and hot sweat. But did I hear well? Didn't he say, "if they know"? Yes, he did. So there is still hope, a glimmer of light in the darkness. They still didn't know. I clung to the hope.

– Sir, I've been blackmailed. If I had not willingly collaborated with One-eyed Hamda, I would have lost my job and gotten into a lot of trouble. Suffice it to say, I was never paid for those reports you saw. All I had was my bank salary. Moreover, I owed my post at the bank to Hamda. So how could I have survived if I had disobeyed him? You know this country better than me. You are a journalist. Everyone needs an intermediary for any job and protection. Until recently, the Party was the *Patrie* under the king or the scoundrel president. Without the proper protection from the party, you have no home country, family, or home.

– No problem from my side, Bassam. I understand you were trapped like a novice unless you were fooling me. But the others – I mean the authorities – won't understand your reasons. To them, you are the enemy of the people! I am sorry.

– Ahem... um... Are... are you under obligation to... um... show them those reports? I am so embarrassed now.

– Ah yes, indeed you are, although it is too late. But my job is to unveil the enemies of the people and to bring them to the martial court.

– The martial court? Good God! I am no military personnel, Sir. I did not attempt a coup against the regime. I was not dealing in military secrets either, far from it.

– It doesn't matter, Bassam! I'm telling you the facts of the present situation. We have a new regime. Our country is fighting against counter-revolution, foreign spies and traitors. Martial Law is applied to all enemies of the people, among which precisely the man you have so loyally served. So you see, you are in deep shit!

He paused again, loitered picking some books from the shelves, and leafing through them, pretending to read while I was on embers. I felt all the more oppressed that I did not even get paid for those damned reports.

– However, he added without looking at me.

In silence, I waited.

– I'll consider you as a particular case. But, for now, I will keep your reports away from indiscreet eyes and keep an eye on you. I have people watching you here. If I am convinced that you are reliable to us, you're safe. If not, I don't need to tell you what will happen.

I breathed paradoxical air. Hot and cold simultaneously, which caused me a coughing fit. That was my first reaction. But it was short. Immediately, I recovered and composed.

– Thank you, sir, I said.

I was relieved as the threat of the martial court was not too close and anxious about "his" people watching me. I immediately grasped the situation. A negative report from one of those guys – maybe one I see every day in the collective cell – and I find myself on my way to face a firing squad!

– Sir, it is so kind and generous of you! But, sir, are you sure those damned reports won't fall into other ... I mean ... improper hands?

– Don't be a fool, Bassam. Do you think that I am unworthy of my word?

– Oh no, sir, no, no. I beg your pardon. I'm just a little worried.

– Well, you ought to be soothed now. I rely on you for everything that happens in this ... um...brothel! Do you get my point?

"No. Not you," I heard someone whispering to me. One of my bloody angels, indeed. I did not want to understand.

– Not very well, I'm afraid, sir.

– Don't be a jerk, Bassam. I want your attention and your talent in reporting. You're like a whore who pretends before her new fiancée that she's still a virgin! You understand me very, very well, I'm sure. You will write me a weekly report about what you hear and see in the pandemonium.

– Panda... panda...what?

– Ok. The madhouse where you live and work. I'll send a man to take the report. Did you get the picture now?

It was too clear.

– So, I'll continue to...um...

– Yes, yes, Bassam. You'll continue to spy for me. You'll not regret it. I know how to reward my loyal men.

– Sir, with due respect, you cannot ask me to do such a job.

He stared at me, puzzled:

– Why not?

– I am unfit. You did acknowledge that I've been trapped like a novice, didn't you?

I stopped before saying the whole truth. The fact that I lost faith in the state, the fatherland and the national parties, past, present and future, and I don't trust him more than I trust his government.

– Ah! But that doesn't mean that you're unfit for the job. Actually, you don't need to be Einstein to spy. Anybody can do it and succeed. It is, with the whore, the oldest job in the world.

Cavemen and kings spied on each other. We continue to do the same. Besides, your reports have opened my eyes to your concealed talents, brother! You are a master in the art of duplicity. I assure you of my sincere belief that you are quite the man required for the job. All those jailbirds don't interest me as you do. But, my dear Bassam, you are as unruffled as folded. You are rather a Jack-of-all-trades, aren't you?

I didn't know whether I should feel flattered or offended. As I was still apprehensive, I said:

– You flatter me, sir. Indeed I am predilected to your cause, but... um... as a matter of fact, I'd rather forget the past. However, with the new Revolution, I realise I can be useful otherwise. So I thought of trying my hand at some... um... attempt to write down the *history of the Islamic Revolution*.

I stressed the last words to show the extent of my enthusiasm for the project. But he remained coldly unstirred. He just asked:

– Are you a historian, Bassam?

– I don't need to be a historian, sir. You've never been trained to be Director of National Security, sir. You just discovered late that this is exactly your vocation. This is Mektub, sir. We can't change it.

– No, Bassam, I'm sorry! This has nothing to do with any Mektub. You don't believe in such inanities, do you?

– Sir, I am the son of my father and mother. They taught me that everything is Mektub. I beg your pardon, but I am a true believer. Allah is omnipotent and merciful. Therefore, we must accept our Mektub. This is what I have been brought up to believe in since childhood.

– Rubbish!

– I beg your pardon, sir, I didn't hear well.

– You heard me bloody well, Bassam. I said rubbish, rubbish! Nonsense! We should not have revolted against the Scoundrel if ever we condoned or believed in such insidious creeds. Mektub doesn't exist. You have worked for many years at a bank, damn it! Yet, even if it is in a small, barren village, nobody has heard about it. You're not going to tell me that you also believe in God.

I was shocked. Truly shocked. An Islamist who does not believe in God! That's way beyond all I could imagine!

– Of course I do, sir.

– Then you're not as smart as I thought. Listen, forget it. You're an ambitious man, aren't you?

– I am not, sir. I have no ambition whatever, sir, and I entreat you to believe that I am sincerely attached to my village, my family, and the beliefs of my ancestors, even if they are nuts. For me, living in a small town is much more important than living in this dirty capital, where the only rules are made for profligacy, salaciousness, nepotism, *arrivisme*, and money!

– The devil takes you! Are you now against money, Bassam? You have spent your life handling it. It is just unbelievable! I never saw a man who hated money, let alone if he worked at a bank! What's life without money?

– Perhaps nothing, I concede it, but people are becoming too materialistic and greedy. The new regime ought to suppress money instead of suppressing the banks; that would bring people to reason. I am willing to give the state all the funds I saved if everybody did the same.

I hoped my zeal moved him, but I only provoked his mockery.

– What a great heart! That's lavish generosity! Why not give it to the poor or charities, Bassam?

– No, sir. I don't trust them. They would dilapidate it. They just do not know how to manage money because they are not accustomed to it. I am not rich, though. I have only the savings from my salary at the bank, which is barely sufficient to meet all my needs, along with the sum the state owed me for 15 years of unrelentingly loyal service, for which I have never received a check.

– Are you kidding?

The threat in his voice was clear enough to me. Understanding that I had nothing to lose, I decided to play my joker card. I did not tell him the truth yet.

– Sir, I'd never been paid for such a dangerous activity required by the authorities of my country.

I caught his attention. After a pause, I added:

– As a matter of fact, the state owes me an important sum of money, sir.

– Interesting! How much, Bassam?

I still remember the little audit I made of my 15-year-long service as the party's secret agent in 'Ouja. How could I forget?

– Exactly, $13.500 million, representing the undelivered fees for...um... the consultancy services.

I let him absorb what I had just revealed. His green eyes were goggling at me in disbelief. I went on:

–However, since this is a new government, I will not claim immediate payment. I desist and yield my rights to the state. I am a patriot, sir. I did what I did for the safety of my country. It is as if the $13.500 million were already transferred from my 'Ouja bank account to the Central Bank. I say this to show you I am siding with the Islamist authorities and supporting you. Me too, I want the return of the Islamic golden age. I want to see people behaving like the prophet's companions. May peace be upon him, sir.

(2)

Hassan stared at me, aghast. His amazement was understandable. He did not expect such a bold claim. His silence protracted for a long moment, at which point he seemed gliding, musing, pondering and probably asking himself whether he should consider me a normal person or a fool. In contrast, his bony long fingers were rubbing his reddish beard softly.

– Bloody hell! He exclaimed suddenly. I never imagined you owning such an amount of money. You're rich!

I giggled.

– I'm not rich, Hassan.

I boldened dangerously, using his first name to address him, but he accepted my familiarity and insisted:

– No, no, no. You are rich, don't pretend you aren't now. A bank clerk who is also a creditor of the State is someone special, and the sum is not trivial.

– It is nothing compared to Mr Aroussi's multimillions, said I humbly.

– Yes, but your boss does not intend to give his millions to the State, but quite the contrary. His attempt to smuggle some abroad is a felony.

He paused, then asked: – You surprised me. I just don't understand how you were able to make all the money you claimed. Are you a private entrepreneur? Do you have some business I'm not aware of? I mean, apart from your salary, how did win $13.500 million?

– Writing reports, sir, I said simply.

– Writing reports? Are you talking seriously or wasting my time?

The tone became threatening.

– Quite seriously, sir. I made my audit for 15 years of service. I'll explain it to you. A single top-secret report costs $2500, not including storage in my archives. The price covers the following: Pens, paper, Table and chair, Electric light, drinks, Clothes and shoes – all necessary paraphernalia for writing. Multiply by 30 days (i.e., a month). You will get $75,000.00. I used the dollar because it is easier than our national currency. The cost of archiving a single report is $25. As it is a daily report, the cost is $750 every month and $9000 per year. Add $750 to $75000, and you get $75.750. Multiply by 12 (months), and you get $900.000. Sir, multiply that figure by 15 years, and you obtain $13.500 million.

– How can you prove your claims?

– You have the reports, sir. I also have the original copies, well concealed in my secret archives. With such evidence, any good lawyer would show that I worked undercover for the governments of my country. But I wasn't paid like any public servant.

– But you're the opposite of a public servant, Bassam. You worked secretly. You admitted it.

– Yes, I did. But would that suppress my right to a decent salary?

Silence. Then:

– Ok. Tell me now. You said you intended to give your money to the State. Are you still resolved?

– Yes, sir, I am. Do we have an Islamic state or not?

– Of course, we do, Bassam. I'll go further. We don't have any Islamic state. We have the real, the authentic, and the unique. Our country is now the only in the world applying the pure Shari'a, as it was known at the time of the prophet and his glorious companions. We have already devoted Muslims joining our ranks from all over the world, Europe and the USA included. Our brothers in Allah, males and females, are convinced that the Emir, Sheikh Abdelghani Abdelghaffar, is the Caliph who will bring back the splendour of Islam and rebuild the empire. We are ready to conquer the world and enforce Shari'a on the unbelievers. The Islamic empire is rising. Do not doubt it.

– Sir, I am happy to know about it. But, sir, as a high representative of the authorities, do you guarantee my safety after I promised to give back $13.500 million, earned honestly while serving the country, to benefit the Islamic state?

– I can do more, Bassam. I'll make you a PCM. As soon as you sign the official documents acknowledging your generous donation, I will issue a certificate proving that the government of The Emir of All Muslims, Sheikh Abdelghani Abdelghafar, acknowledges you as a good Muslim under the Shari'a law, which allows you to do any business you choose, marry four women or more, possess as many slaves as you wish, females and males, and travel across the country and abroad without being troubled at the checkpoints and the borders. As such, you acquire a new status. We call it in the Islamic State: PCM.

– Sir, what's the PCM?

– The pagan VIP has the pretence of being a *Very Important Personality, right?* The Islamic State does not recognise such arrogant nonsense. No individual could match or outpace the PCMs selected among the hyper-selected. The only VIP we acknowledge in this country today is the Paradise Club Member (PCM). Those persons drive their happiness from being members of the Muslim community ruled by the Shari'a law. However, because they supported our noble cause, we call them PCMs, which means they are expected in Paradise. The first in this order are the martyrs (Shahids). They sacrifice their bodies by blowing up a bomb among an unfaithful group or getting killed in the battle. The second in the ranking are people like you, Mr Bassam, who donate significantly to our cause, facilitate a crucial deal, and so on. Other services to the Islamic State may also have the same reward.

It was such a surprise for me that, for a moment, I could barely breathe. I was learning. Finally, when I managed to talk, I bubbled and gurgled like a bottle of water being suddenly emptied. I don't know what exactly I said. It should be something like: **"SSSS...Sir, I ......lllllllllove theeee Issssssssslamic Staaaaate. I'mmmmmm fonnnnnd of the IsssssslamiSsssssstate. I wwwwwwanttooooo giiiiiiiiivvvve you the ffffffffffunds immmmmmmmmmmmediately."**

I saw Hassan's green eyes widening dangerously. He was rubbing his red beard with a fixed gaze. If a camera was there at that time to shoot us, we would look like two crazy-mad guys trying to break out of a psychiatric block. I saw him shaking his head as if to expel some odd idea that haunted it. I don't know how long our madness has lapsed. He was the first to speak.

– But we are not asking you that much, Mister Bassam. You can keep some funds for your private projects.

I noticed with relief the 'Mister' that infiltrated his words. I could only relish with agreeable titillation the congenial change in the mood of my interlocutor.

– Sir, I want to be a PCM! I know the Islamic State does not need my money to survive. The state can get any money from the citizens using legal means. I hope you don't think I am miffing the Administration with my proposition. I am neither a malevolent renegade nor a conceited braggart. A concatenation of events made me think it would be unduly frustrating to restrain myself from showing my indefectible loyalty to the Muslim empire. That's a big change because I intended to claim my rights from the former Administration.

– Didn't you do?

– No, I didn't. I was thinking about the best way to do it. Should I hire a lawyer? Should I talk to the media? Should I ask the administration directly? What are my chances of getting heard? Should I go to Europe and campaign for my rights with the help of Human Rights Associations and the press? Should I write to the former president or to the UN secretary-general?

While I was still speculating, two men came to my apartment in 'Ouja to take me to the...Ahem... "Best hotel in the capital"! So they said. As I thought I knew them, I followed them.

– So you knew them?

– No, sir. I mean, yes. I thought they were my angels disguised as civilian State police.

For the first time since we met, Hassan crackled a laugh. I didn't understand what was funny in my talk. Then, as my facial expression veered to disappointment and anger, he stopped abruptly. To hide his uneasiness, he turned to look at the shelves. But I knew that he listened to each word I uttered with attention.

– I understand your noble motives, he said. I won't fail to convey them to the Minister eventually. However, this is something that must be duly rewarded, Mister Bassam. It may even forgive your previous misdeeds, although that must be settled legally. It would be much more presentable to the high spheres if everything is clear on this level. We don't want anybody to think of some kind of bribe, do we?

– You are perfectly right, sir. I agree with you. I'm not starting my new life in the Islamic empire by bribing the officials. I'll ask Mister Ammar to take care of this issue.

– Who is Mr Ammar?

– Nobody, sir. Just my lawyer.

– Ah! Good! Tell him to prepare an agreement. Or, wait. Maybe we'll prepare the legal documents for you. By the way, you probably want something in return, don't you?

– Don't misunderstand my purpose, sir. I'd be offended.

– Sorry! I didn't mean. I only want to ensure that you will not regret your action.

I hesitated, then said:

– Well, I won't regret it, sir, if it can help forgive my ...Ahem...um ... previous misdeeds. I mean..um... if those reports you hold at the ministry could disappear ... vanish... completely, who cares? And I will be relieved, sir.

He cleared his throat.

– Hmmm. I'll think it over, but I promise you nothing. Well, let's say it may be negotiable.

– I am glad to hear you say it, sir. I am sure we can reach an agreement. Since you are also a PCM holding those state documents, it's easier for me. Have you got any idea about the way we can settle the matter? I mean before reaching paradise while we're still on earth.

Hassan pondered, rubbed his moustache gazing at me straight in the eyes, then said:

– Yes, indeed, there is a solution. I need to reconsider the whole situation in light of what you unveiled. It will not be hard to release you, but I want to be certain about your projects in the near future. What do you intend to do when you get out?

– Oh, nothing special, sir. Nothing different from what I was doing before. I will very likely go back to my bank.

- What if you find the bank closed?

– Then, I will seek a post in another. With 15-year experience, it won't be hard to find something convenient. I'll be sorry to lose my post at 'Ouja bank, though. I got attached to my old customs. I think you know I am a grand sentimental, sir.

– Oh yes, indeed you are! It is hard to discern the truth from the false in the present circumstances. But do not misinterpret my thoughts, please. I view your goodwill gesture with consideration! Any help is welcome in our hard conditions. As you know, oil, our main source of income, is presently in the hands of our enemies. I should not tell you this, but you are now one of us. Our finances are in a pitiful state. I didn't tell you that we discovered that the rapine had preceded our arrival. The men ruling the country before us took advantage to fill up their pockets. That's the atrocious truth about our nation. Whatever their level in the State, the men in charge plundered the country, generation after generation, for centuries. That's an awful tradition that generated tragedies and pain, still at work until we took over. Suitcases full of hard cash were smuggled through the frontiers to South America, the USA, Europe, and much more to tax havens, to say nothing of the money that had never entered the State's boxes, albeit it had been duly recorded in the registries. According to all appearances, the Scoundrel and some of his men were expecting to be overthrown, like generations of previous rulers. That is why they used full prerogatives to secure a comfortable retirement abroad. They bought palaces, villas, and hotels and made many other real estate investments in Europe and America; you can count their shares in foreign companies in the billions. And despite the bragging speeches, they had no confidence in the economic and political institutions of the country they were running. If they did not expect a military Coup, they were probably obsessed with looming revolts and uprisings. But all this is nothing compared to the vicious behaviour of conveying huge funds to support or merely provoke coups, countercoups, rebellions, and political unrest in remote or neighbouring countries. You would be shocked if you knew how much they had been involved in covert operations and seditious activities abroad. In contrast, they kept saying at home,' "We want peace and friendship with all the States'! So it was that when we took over, we discovered - to our horror - that the country was drifting. The cash in the central bank was barely sufficient to cover our expenses for six months. Now, with the war in the south, you can imagine the situation; I don't tell you.

He paused, fished into his jacket's pocket for a moment, and then asked me:

– Have you got any cigarettes? I've forgotten my packet.

– Sorry, sir, I don't smoke.

– You did good, he replied. In paradise, nobody smokes.

– How about drinking, sir? I mean beer, wine, whisky…?

– Allowed, he said while raising his hand, to beckon towards the men still waiting for him outside. Did you not read your book?

– The Quran, Bassam. What the hell! It's allowed.

Almost running, one entered the library and stopped at a step from us, giggling and frisking about like a well-trained fox terrier.

(3)

– Give me a cigarette, said Hassan peremptorily.

– Yes, sir.

The fox terrier rummaged in his pockets and produced a packet which he handed politely to his boss, insisting that he kept it. I noticed the cigarettes were of the same US trademark Suleiman Mughli used to smoke. The fact did not escape me, for that particular brand is rare, at least in our country. And momentarily, I lucubrated in the dark about the possible connection between Hassan's bodyguard and the Mughli. But since it was an insoluble problem, I forgot about it.

– Thank you, said Hassan after lighting his cigarette.

The fox terrier withdrew to join his companions, chatting idly not far from the library. The courtyard was nearly empty, apart from a dozen grey uniforms loafing around with their rifles on their shoulders. It was a quiet morning, with an unruffled sky and a warm sun. Habitually, the inmates should have been strolling along the walls, loitering around the basin, chatting or reading newspapers, shaving or washing their laundry. But the unexpected visit of the director of security had seemingly changed the daily routine.

– Well, what were we saying? Hassan asked.

– About the piteous state of the finances, sir.

– Ah! Yes indeed. It is a disaster. However, this is not really what troubles me.

He paused and, continuing to smoke silently, ducked as if trying to remember something. Then, lifting his head, he said: "Did you say that if you were released, you'll go back to 'Ouja?"

– Yes, sir, it's my home.

– Well, I don't want you to go back home. I need you here, in the capital, with me. I have something for you.

I was apprehensive about the capital but could not express my worry lest I made him angry.

– I am at your service, sir.

– Good! Are you married, Bassam?

He surprised me. It was not exactly the question I was ready to answer, for I was still flustered by what had happened since the damned couvolution. I was willing to believe I was happily married to the invisible Dalila, but I could not prove it either. Hassan did not believe in Mektub, which meant he would hardly admit that I was married in the unseen world, just as Haj Mukhtar was to his Jinni princess. So, I told myself that if I answered yes, he would check and find no wedding record because he naturally could not see the unseen. The marriage certificate may exist, but in the invisible realm. Thus, he will think I am a liar, destroying our inchoate entente. To prevent such a disagreeable situation, I was compelled to lie and pretend I was still a bachelor. It was a bizarroid situation wherein I had to lie to preclude the other from thinking I was a liar!

– No, sir, I am not yet married.

– Bachelor? That is very good, Bassam!

– I was actually about to marry in the...um... visibly, I mean in July. Ahem! It was just impossible to do it normally, sir.

– Why impossible?

– Are you joking, sir? In July, I was in jail!

– You were? Ah, well! Never mind, it doesn't matter. Anyway, you're no longer in jail. You can marry when you wish.

– Thank you, sir. I will.

– Anyway, it is not a catastrophe not to be able to marry in July. Take another month. I have a better idea regarding your money. You should marry and settle down in the capital. I'll help you with an interesting job. If you want to continue working at a bank, we will appoint you even at the Central Bank. You'll have a promotion, and you'll be responsible of a whole department. If you want something else, just tell me. However, I have only one condition.

Utterly thrilled by what I had just heard, I said eagerly:

– Thank you, sir. I have already accepted your condition.

He loitered a good moment, smoking and staring listlessly at the shelves while my impatience reached unprecedented heights. Then, he said:

– I know you are somehow puzzled, although you said you accepted the condition without even knowing it. You should not do that, because it is an important subject. It will bind you. (Pause) I want you to think about what I will tell you. No rush. Take time. Think it over. We're not in a hurry.

– Sir, I think that with good will, we can reach an agreement.

– Fine! Then look. Forget your lawyer, this is a bargain we can settle together without his help. Since you say you are a bachelor, I've got a good party for you.

– A good party? I repeated, not without amazement.

– Yes, I mean a lady or a bride if you prefer.

I started saying that I was in love, and before I mentioned the name of my fiancee, Hassan interrupted me briskly:

– In love? You aren't serious, Bassam, are you? Nobody falls in love nowadays. It's old-fashioned. Besides, you are not a teenager anymore, but a mature man. So you know where your interests are. As a matter of fact, the bride I am proposing to you is not a stranger but my sibling.

Flabbergasted, I repeated:

– Your sister?

– Yes, indeed. She is the woman that fits you more than anyone else. Do you trust me?

– I trust you, of course. But, um... in truth, I was not expecting your proposal. It is too much honour for me, sir.

– I knew you would be surprised. That's why I asked you not to give any answer before thinking it over quietly. Let me tell you this, Bassam: My sister Sophia is your lifebuoy. Not only can she release you with a single word, but she can also open locked doors to you.

I was so stunned by these revelations that I was barely able to stutter:

– Is she, um... so powerful?

He giggled.

– You can say that she is, yes.

– But I thought you more powerful, sir. You are the Director of the Security!

He smirked and said almost in a confidential tone:

– Between us, I am not ashamed to say that Sophia is not a stranger to my promotion. She is a good adviser, and besides, the new Minister of the Interior is... um... Ahem! Her ex.

– Her ex-husband? Do you mean she divorced?

– Bassam, what the hell! I said she might be a good bride for you, and you ask whether she divorced! Of course, she did, damn it! They divorced a long time ago.Well, ahem! I mean before the revolution. But as they have three children, they are still on good terms.

– Three children? I repeated, more struck by the prospect of marrying her than amazed by the story.

– Yes, three. Don't feel blocked just because of that. It's nothing, she can easily have three others with you if such is your wish. Now, look. No hassle! When you agree, just tell me, and we'll pay her a visit together.

– But sir, what about Dalila?

– Oh! I warn you against ever rising this subject before Sophia. She's very sensitive, and she's well capable of rejecting your proposal.

I had to react quickly before being trapped in a situation I had never expected. I felt that I had merely to protect myself against such scrambling projects that had nothing to do with what I had previously planned for my future.

– I am very honoured, sir, but I don't think your sister would accept marrying me.

– Ah, well? Why? You're a good chap, though. Besides, you are a banker or will be soon; your little fortune is also most welcome.

– That's the point, sir. Actually, that money is pure speculation. It has no solid existence.

Dumbfounded, he asked me:

– Speculation? No solid existence? What do you mean exactly?

– I mean that apart from my bank salary, I have no other income. I reckoned that the State owed me such a sum for a longstanding service, but... um... this is perhaps untrue. They can say I was acting out of patriotism, which is not something one should deny. You understand, sir, patriotism is too flattering to discard even if it would cost me two $200 million, the exact amount of the debt they owe me.

I should not have uttered the last sentence, for it had had just the opposed effect of what I was seeking. Too late! Once again, I was carried away by my unbridled tongue, saying much more than I meant. As always happen in such a situation, Hassan omitted or dismissed the first part of my reply and retained only the last detail. Then, he grabbed my arm and opened his green eyes widely.

– Two hundred million dollars? Did you say two hundred?

Dumfounded by his reaction and eager to give my services to the State more a valuable estimation, I boasted:

– Yes, sir, two hundred MILLION dollars, and who knows? Perhaps more! One does not count these things.

I saw an indescribable joy gaining the man. He would have danced like a professional ballerina because he likely believed - at least, he gave me that impression - that the two hundred million, which I do not know how they infiltrated my sentence, were already in his pocket! Meanwhile, he omitted that I was merely speculating.

– So, it's not $13.500 million only. Are you sure? He asked me with the vicious insistence of someone who had resolutely shut his eyes and ears to the truth.

– As sure as I am seeing you at this moment, sir!

– But you are a national treasure, Mr Bassam! Come on, please, allow me to kiss your luminous forehead hiding such a genius. You're my brother, my chum, not just my future brother-in-law. From this moment onward, your desires are as orders for me. Just express your wish, and I'll shake earth and heaven to satisfy you.

To my bewilderment, he kissed my forehead, and I smelt the trickling mixture of tobacco and amber exhaling from his beard. The scene would seem quite preposterous to the group of men that were certainly watching us from the courtyard. I did not dare turn my head to look at them, but I did not doubt that I had become the subject of their idle chatting. The success did not daze me, though. I knew it was still so flimsy that the spell would break at the first breeze and swoon away. And though a kind of beatitude and gratefulness for my good star invaded me, I thought it better not to challenge fate more than I did. So, while keeping my advantage, I waited impassibly for the ebbtide, expecting at any moment the hard thwack of the reverse. But it did not come.

I had many good reasons to think the worse could still happen. I have lied to the Director of National Security, and he seemed to swallow the lie like candy. Hassan excused himself and tottered away to join his men. Then I saw him speaking to them, although I could not hear. I only noticed that they were eying me with an increasing interest that confined the indiscretion. I can't tell whether those conspicuous gazes expressed admiration, amazement, respect, or something quite different. I did not care, for I could not measure all the ravages I had inadvertently caused. Still unaware that the winds had turned favourable to me, I behaved like a lascivious jailbird.

When the Director of Security came back, he smiled and said:

– We'll continue this chat in my office if you allow me such an honour.

I thought I was dreaming.

– It is too great an honour for me, sir. I can't accept it.

– What? Why? I just sent one of my men to buy you a convenient suit. You cannot continue to wear these rags.

– I am confounded, sir. You shouldn't have sent him. I appreciate it, though. It is kind of you. But I don't want to disturb you any more. Actually, I got used to wearing these... um... rags!

– Sorry, Bassam! But I think you'd be much fitter to meet the Emir with a respectable suit. You cannot go to the palace in such a poor dress. The Emir is very punctilious on these matters. You did see him on the TV, and you should not have failed to notice the importance he accords to his look. As you know, the seven members of the Committee of Revolution are all military officers. Still, they are now dressed in civilian clothes, and you can trust me if I tell you a State secret. You are now one of us. My ex-brother-in-law, Minister of the Interior today, is a loyal customer of the greatest Parisian and Londoner tailors. Four times a year, he used to visit Paris and London with Sophia to get his clothes duly tailored, from the tie to the underpants. He has got a different assortment of garments for each quarter. And each quarter, he has a different dress for each month and each social activity. He would never wear the tie of September in August or October; it would be inelegant. Besides, you would never see him wearing the same shirt or jacket over dinner if he wore it over breakfast. Sophia would not allow such a misdemeanour. And even after they divorced, he continued visiting London and Paris four times yearly with his new wife. One never loses the good habits, and a well-supplied wardrobe is certainly the mark of a successful life. You can't deny that, can you?

Whereas he paused to light another cigarette, I was seized by the odd feeling of a man who does not know exactly whether he is living a dream or a nightmare. I was so confused that I kept silent, fearing that what I could say worsened the situation or involved me more and more in a maze. Anyway, what could I say? I was pushed before the accomplished fact. I could neither refuse what Hassan proposed nor conceal my surprise. The tide that was carrying me was too much overwhelming to withstand. And Hassan went on:

– Observe that my sister's divorce did not affect my relationship with my boss. Far from it. I still call Mamduh my brother-in-law, and he still trusts me, which is not amazing. I owe him a lot since the period that preceded the Coup of the Scoundrel. I won't hide that at the time, he used his influence as the King's Intelligence Director and adviser to get me an appointment as editor of a weekly magazine. You have certainly read '*The Friday*', before it was suspended, haven't you?

– Oh! Everybody knows *The Friday*, sir. It was my preferred magazine.

– Well, you don't know it was an antenna of the Defence Ministry, although it was not officially recognised. The military Intelligence agency was our main supporter. The real boss of the magazine was Mamduh himself, but his name never appeared in our columns.

Such revelations took me aback. I remembered then what he told me.

– Haven't you been incarcerated twice, sir? Firstly, under the King, and secondly, under the President-Scoundrel? I can't reconcile this with the fact that your magazine was...um... supervised by an official institution. I have always thought it was independent.

– Your memory is good, but you still have much to learn about politics.

He paused, puffing the smoke from his nostrils, then added:

– Nobody is independent in politics, Mr Bassam. Even the King was not independent; otherwise he would not have lasted over twenty four hours after the country's independence. Do you think the Scoundrel acted spontaneously to overthrow the King? You would be naive if you swallowed such a twaddle. The Western allies let down the former King when he grew greedy and too craving for an absolutist autocracy despite the iterated advice to rejuvenate his regime by injecting new blood into its rotten body. The old man could not grasp the extent of the changes in our society since the discovery of oil. He turned a blind eye on the claims for modernisation and democracy accordingly to the precepts of Islam as they had been thoroughly in the last years by the Islamist thinkers and preachers. When I published an article by an eminent scholar describing the insidious mismanagement undermining our economy and calling for change and democracy, I was accused of treason and republicanism and arrested along with the scholar. Indeed, Mamduh could do nothing, though secretly, he supported me. Sophia said afterwards that she could no longer live with a man who let her brother down at the worse moment, and when I explained that he supported me, she refused stubbornly to admit the evidence. The truth is that she knew about his affair. That's why they divorced. A few months after my release, the Scoundrel undertook his coup, and the bastard succeeded. My former brother-in-law was promoted to the higher echelon. As the Scoundrel trusted him, he allowed him to resume the funding of '*The Friday.*' Subsequently, I retrieved my post as editor. About three months later, the Scoundrel grew suspicious towards the magazine and ordered bluntly its suspension after a deaf and dramatic struggle between rival factions. The party wanted the magazine to be more involved with its political line, and even the Defence Ministry claimed that we were not enough keen to praise the military establishment. And to crown the whole shit, I stumbled from the seventh sky when I was summoned and informed that I was under arrest. That's how I came here for the second time, where I spent ten months waiting for a trial that never occurred when I met you. Fortunately, the revolution was creeping meanwhile.

I hesitated before asking him:

– Do you mean you were not engaged to the fundamentalists before the revolution?

He pondered.

– Well, it is a trifle complicated. But to be honest, I am engaged to my brother-in-law creeds. I am just loyal to him.

– I see, you are like me, sir… um… sorry! I mean, I am like you, indeed.

– What?

He expressed his surprise, and staring at me with suspecting green eyes, he added:

– Are you then one of Mamduh's men?

– No, sir, no, no. You're mistaken. I'd be honoured to serve him, of course. But I mean, I am like you, loyal to the persons rather than the ideas. It is much more practical.

– Ah! He sighed with relief.

There was a pause, and then he said:

– Well, you should perhaps give me the reference to your account in the treasury records. I'll see they pay you at least a part of the debt; I can't promise more.

That was what I apprehended. I was on the brink of apoplexy. I felt I was about to crack and break into tears, but I remembered that the pig kept my reports in his grip and was just blackmailing me. It would be my end if I yielded to the pressure before obtaining the return of my reports or at least their destruction. I had been perhaps naive in playing this game, responding meekly to Hamda La'war's pressure. Still, now that I opened my eyes and saw how greedy and heinous they were all, I resolved to go about until the end of the game, if ever there is an end. Maybe I am irredeemably wicked, but they are not better. I did serve the State. What the hell! Didn't I? And I am not to be outdone easily. But who are they serving? Allah or the Devil?

– I don't remember the reference, sir, I said. You should ask the treasury. I don't think there are many Bassam Bourasin in this country. And if there are, they did not work at 'Ouja bank. So that's a good reference.

(4)

T wo Hundred Million Dollars! I fucking got balls!

What happened to me? I'm talking like them now? I hope my angels are not listening. Sometimes they're busy and get away with I said or done. Yup!

I knew I was gambling; most of all, it was an absurd and dangerous game. I had no reason to think that the Treasury retained my name as one of the state's fund-backers and that the sum I was whimsically claiming as a debt owed to me by the *Establishment* was by any supernatural chance recorded in its registers. That was just an absurd idea. Pure nonsense! I was either tempting fate or provoking the Devil. I bet on the disorder that was indubitably drowning the country's administration. I could always claim that the records had been wasted or stolen to spoil me of my rights. With all the funds that had vanished from the state's boxes, coup after coup, and government after government, it would not be a preposterous pretension. We had produced only generations of thieves and crooks as rulers. To follow our leaders' path in emptying the drawers of the state would not be so awful since it is widely accepted as a public good. Anyway, banished as I was, with the sword of Damocles hanging over my neck, I had little to lose. I knew my life was in jeopardy, and it would be so as long as those damned reports were in Hassan's dirty hands. They are the unrefutable evidence of my deep involvement with the rotten regimes of the King and his Scoundrel successor. My first and most urgent task is to get them back. If I succeed, I will not care for the rest.

Thoughtfully, Hassan came out of the wood like a cautious fox. He dropped his butt on the floor and smashed it with his shoe's heel :

– Well, I'll see to it. We're not in a hurry. Two hundred million dollars! This is not a sum that may evaporate easily. We'll get more weapons, win the war and kill the Scoundrel. The Emir will be happy to receive you, Mr Bassam. I've always thought you're not the guy you seem to be. Just like me. Ha Ha Ha! We're similar. Now, I understand why the Scoundrel send you to the pit. He wanted to get rid of you, didn't he? With all your money, you became too dangerous. He couldn't allow you to walk free. You could threaten his power, couldn't you? If you claimed to be paid immediately, you'd have shaken the earth under his feet, wouldn't you? And with this, you claim to be apolitical. Ha Ha Ha! That's a funny joke, man! But you are a great businessman, Mr Bassam. A luminous mind indeed, and I don't know of any apolitical businessman. Business and politics are like twins who dislike each other but are forced to cohabit under the same roof. Sophia also will be delighted to meet you. What about dinner with her this evening, in her villa? I'll phone her if you agree.

The little game was taking an unexpected turn.

– It would be a delight for me, sir, but I'm sorry because it seems impossible.

– Why impossible? Are you busy today?

– Busy? Yes, I am always busy with the inmates. I don't work after sunset, but I must be in my cell, maximum at 7 pm. If not, there will be consequences, sir.

– Are you kidding, Bassam? You speak as if you're still detained.

– Am I not?

– No, You aren't.

I hesitated. It was too beautiful to be true. I still need more guarantees.

– I beg your pardon, sir. I acknowledge I am not detained – Just a guest of this state hotel.

He became irritated.

– Oh yes, yes, but you are too modest, Mr Bassam. You're not forced to stay here any longer. I'll see to a better accommodation for you. What about the Hilton? Unless you prefer the Sheraton... Tell me what you prefer.

– Oh, no, no. It's too kind of you, sir. I just want to be a PCM.

– Please, Basssam, don't refuse. It's like in paradise, you won't pay for anything. You're still the guest of the Islamic State, with a PCM status. We don't often have the opportunity to host important businessmen. There is also Suleiman Mughli, but I dislike that man and don't trust him. He has connections with the Mafia. His wife, an Italian lady, owns a big mall in the capital, although she spends half the year in Italy. She'd do anything to avoid paying more taxes.

– I've always wondered why a wealthy man like him was in...um... this prison with me. What did he do?

– The Scoundrel charged him with conveying guns to Mohamed Mashawir, a notorious militant nicknamed *the Afghan*.

– It was untrue, of course.

– It was true. The Mughli and the Afghan are long-standing friends, although they hate each other.

– But I was told that Mughli was behind that odious trade of East-European women, which was ordered by the Scoundrel. Why should he seek to overthrow him?

– Mughli has no principles whatever. He is not like you and me. He has no friends, no creeds, and no loyalty. The only language he can speak and understand is that of money. He who gives him more is his friend. But he would not hesitate to kill him and throw his corpse in a ditch if his interests required it. That's why he is at once despised and dreaded. You think he is a prisoner here, but he is not. In fact, nobody dares oppose him. The judges refused to attend his trial because they apprehended the retaliation of his friends in the Mafia. He will certainly get out soon. Mahmoud told me he didn't want his hands stained with his blood. I don't blame him because he's anxious about his blood.

– He doesn't seem to be so dreadfully powerful, though.

– Oh, he is, believe me.

– He once spoke to me in the library and seemed concerned with my writing.

I regretted these words as soon as I uttered them. It is awfully embarrassing this outspoken tongue I have got! It is too long, too bold, and too skittish. I don't know how to manage my life with such a loose thing rambling and rampaging in my mouth. I always say much more that I mean or not enough. Bloody tongue!

Inevitably, Hassan asked me:

– I'm curious. What were you writing?

– Oh, nothing. Just... um... Just an account of the Islamic Revolution. I told you I wish to start a book of history.

– You can't do that, Bassam.

– Why not, sir?

– Because it has just started. You cannot write the history of a movement at its very beginning. You must wait at least twenty or thirty years to do so.

– But we are living in history, sir, aren't we?

– This is not the past of the Islamic Revolution, Mr Bassam; you are mistaken, but well, it's the present time. To pretend the contrary is to confound times and to mistake the present for the past. That could be a dangerous illusion that tacks us into recessional thought and compels us to live as if we were dead. I didn't see what you wrote about the Islamic Revolution, but you can't say it is history. Anyway, I think you'd be helpful for us otherwise. Do you know why I asked you to be my spy?

– I presume you want me to continue the old job.

– Not only that. You have a unique quality Mr Bassam; indeed, it exists in other people too, but with you, I dare say it is almost exceptional. I mean that admirable gift of repeating exactly what you just heard.

– I am not a parrot, sir, I protested vehemently.

He chuckled.

– Not a parrot? Don't be offended; a parrot is not that bad. It is very useful for State security. We use parrots in our service, either real birds trained in flippant duplicity or human agents endowed with the same qualities. They are provocative agents, informers and something alike. They are altogether garrulous and gregarious, precisely the purpose of their training. A good 'parrot' can deceive and misinform those who hear him and cause any foreign agents to betray themselves. As a rule, our parrots are sociable, affable, and sympathetic even, with a traditional background. But there are other kinds of parrots, not quite easy to spot or to handle. You see, Mr Bassam, we are all somewhat parrots, each one to a certain degree, according to the extent of freedom one can afford regarding the social and politico-economical constraints. Since we live in a certain milieu, we are thus compelled to respond to its exigencies. Thus, if we think it over, we will come to the statement that a parrot is a good patriot.

– In this case, I am willing to be a parrot, I replied eagerly.

– You are certainly a good parrot-patriot, Mr Bassam, and quite useful for the state. Just tell me always what you hear, and do exactly as I tell you. You'll discover that true happiness is never saying no to the shit, but yes, yes, and step aside. Never try to remove shit, Mr Bassam, since the whole world is full of it, and life is so short; if not, you'll find yourself sinking into it up to the neck.

Such a philosophic argument could only elate me, even if it was founded uniquely on shit and aimed at its perpetuation in our life.

– I don't want to seem bragging, sir, I replied, but after a long time, I have discovered this truth you are telling me. Shit is, well, our common Mektub. I agree with you. That's why I never opposed Mr Aroussi, though I suspected some of his deals were not clean. I knew just a few times before my arrest that our bank was on the brink of bankruptcy. I was sorry, but I could not discuss these matters with my boss or oppose him even when I noticed some of his relatives and friends benefited from huge loans without presenting real guarantees to the bank. Likewise, under pressure, I yielded to Hamda La'war, the head of the 'Ouja cell, although I knew he was not the National Hero he claimed to be. Anyway, I had a dream that helped me overcome all that shit if you allow me to borrow your expression. I had always in the back of my mind the model I wanted to follow, the great, the magnificent, the incomparable John Law.

His eyelids blinked while he gently rubbed his beard, likely puzzled by what I had just unveiled.

– John Law? Who's that chap? Never heard of him.

– I'm glad to inform you that he was one of his time's greatest and ablest minds. He is a Scot who lived between the seventeen and eighteenth century; as he could not apply his ideas on money and monetarism in his fatherland, he went to France, where he set up the *Banque Generale,* starting with a mere £6 million capital! In a few years, Law's bank, called the Banque Royale, became the world's first central bank. Merged with *India Company*, its shares reached the incredible level of £20.000 with a declared dividend of 40 per cent. In France, Law was adulated as nobody has been. Even the Duchesse d'Orleans kissed his hand, they said. He was a national hero - a true. He had achieved the economic miracle that nobody expected. That's why I admire him and think it is still possible to start such a project with just a small capital and then increase it gradually. I prefer to apply John Law's principles of monetarism in my own country. One doesn't need to leave one's country to succeed in France or elsewhere, right?

Hassan appeared quite interested in my revelations. He did not stop rubbing his beard and staring at me with the air of someone wondering with amazement, 'what's this chap going to say next?' He pondered for a while, then said:

– I'm really discovering you, Mr Bassam, and I'm glad to hear about your project. I share your admiration for that, um...

– John Law, sir.

– Yes, Law. And I think I can help you give this project shape and substance. I am entitled to do that. The government will welcome such projects.

– Are you serious?

– I've never been more serious in my life. You are a real treasure; we just need men like you.

– But, sir, what about the Islamic precepts of banking?

I thought it was the most thorny question that we would have to answer, but he eluded it with a motion of his hand, saying not without some irritation:

– Pffff! Don't mind that, man. We're living in a complicated world, and sometimes we'll need to speak its language, won't we?

I could not reply, for the man he had sent to buy the clothes entered the room and coughed politely to signal his presence. He was carrying big bundles and packages and seemed sweating. Hassan addressed him in the same peremptory tone:

– Ah! Mr Mongi, you're welcome; please enter and show us what you have brought. Then, turning to me, he added: These are the clothes, would you please try them, Mr Bassam?

– I am most grateful, sir. It is too kind, really!

– We'll let you alone. If you allow me, I'll wait for you in the car. I must also ring the office and call my sister. I'll come back in twenty minutes. Is it enough?

– Quite, sir. Thank you very much.

Then, changing my mind, I said: "Oh, sorry, I don't want to be a burden for you, sir."

– You aren't a burden; please don't say that, Bassam. Do you need more time to change?

– I didn't dare to ask for it, sir.

– You had to, though. How much? An hour? Two hours? More? We aren't in a hurry, you know.

Mongi had unburdened himself and joined the group waiting in the courtyard. The grey uniforms were still parading along the walls, with their guns shining in the daylight.

– I want to ask you about those bloody reports, sir. Are you sure they won't fall into inconvenient hands?

– You shouldn't worry. I promised you, don't you trust me?

– I do, sir, but I'll be much more relieved if I get them back unless you destroy them. One never knows what may happen.

– Nothing can happen, Bassam. The battles are far away, in the south. The rebels you fear have no means to reach us, we are secure in the capital. And please, don't forget I am the Director of National Security. I know exactly what is going on in the country. This morning, before I arrived here, I had just received a telegram from our agents in the south, saying that the forces of the Scoundrel had been beaten and pushed back while they were trying to break through the northern highway. Indeed, there is a blockade on the shipping of oil; the pipelines are no longer pumping, and if we succeed in protracting the blockade, they will be unable to continue the rebellion. In fact, they are hopelessly encircled. Either they give up or die in the desert. We would bomb their camps if we had enough petrol for the aircraft.

– Why don't you import petrol?

– You're kidding, Bassam! An oil exporter cannot turn importer in twenty-four hours. It's not as easy as you imagine. Besides, as we are at war, the other exporters are not eager to deal with us. I won't hide that they are pretty glad to eye our misfortune. The fewer there are rivals on the market, the best are the deals. Prices rise as demand increase, you know.

– But there are certainly enormous quantities stored in the country.

– All are in the south. It is a heartbreaking strategic mistake of our predecessors! Apparently, they didn't expect a civil war. They took no precautions with the oil they stored in a single area — our unique shore. Geography doomed the country, alas! Besides, the aircraft is in a piteous state. Many aviators fled to the south with aeroplanes; the rest were not in their best state.

(5)

He wanted to allay me, but instead, he depicted a disheartening picture of the situation. I am no longer sure the new regime was as strong as it appeared. How could they win the war without oil, money, or aircraft? As a matter of fact, what we call the south swallows up half the country; the other half is less desert but more divested. Without the blessed desert, we are nothing, just a country of the third world with a rudimentary infrastructure and nothing to bestow or display but the utmost despondency of our landscape. Mountains, hills, and wastelands compound the other half - the doomed one - where my home town, 'Ouja, is situated. And further to the north, the beguiling capital of which Hassan is so proud. From 'Ouja to the Capital, the traveller would cross miles and miles of barren lands invaded by stones, weeds, wild vegetation, excrescent hillocks, and stiffed cliffs. There is little agriculture but concentrated on the shores of the great river, which is not actually as 'great' as we like to think. How could anyone endowed with commonsense hope win the war in such conditions? Besides, I was not really afraid of the Scoundrel but of the fundamentalists, the new masters of the northern country. They would not forgive my mobilisation at the service of the previous administrations, even if it was a forced service extorted under threats, blackmails and pressure. Nobody would believe that I had been the victim of Hamda La'war and his sordid machinations. I had to save my head, so I had to tune in and cope with Hassan. I wanted to stress that I was not frightened by the Scoundrel as he supposed but did not dare. After all, it was perhaps his fear that he projected upon me. I just said:

– It is not exactly what we may call a bright situation, is it?

– No, but don't be pessimistic, Mr Bassam. It's not as hopeless as you think; we are still the masters. We control the capital, the north and the main country. We are preparing the great offensive against the Scoundrel. When we are ready, we will march on the south and turn the sand and the stones of the desert into a carpet of fire under his troops' feet. We'll crush the hideous beast in its hideout. Tell me, what are handful tribes of bare-foot, ragged, half-starved beduin to weigh against our disciplined, well-trained army of volunteer militants and former Afghanistan warriors? The Scoundrel is as stupid as conceited. He understands nothing about strategy and military tactics. But look at our Emir, Sheikh Abdelghani Abdelghaffar. This is a real military strategist, a man trained by US experts. They called him the "Engineer" back in Afghanistan. Do you know why?

Without waiting for my answer, he went on: – Because he engineered the trapping and bombing of significant targets under the nose of the Russians. He never failed to kill as much as possible. He's told to be a veritable genius in warfare beside his outstanding political clear-sightedness... Ahem! He will swallow up the Scoundrel on breakfast and digest him before dinner. This is now but a matter of time, do not worry!

He is perhaps a military genius, but for his clear-sightedness, I doubted it. It is a euphemism, indeed. Believing that a squint-eyed man could be clear-sighted is self-deceptive. A joke? Certainly, and preposterous! I even wonder how and when he had been incorporated as an army officer with such a conspicuous disability. My cellmate, Dahdah, was more accurate than Hassan. He told me the Emir was a militia man. He has never been a member of the armed forces. For my part, I don't imagine him particularly skilled at the exercises of shooting. Unless he had always trained himself to aim three feet beside his target to attain it, I do not know how he could get through otherwise! This does not explain why he let his worse enemy slip easily off his hands while standing two steps away. Such a military and political leader is not very trustful; it can't be helped, but I do not feel particularly tranquil at his sight.

I am not prejudiced against him, but he does not inspire confidence. I compassionately understand his physical disadvantage. I heard of one-eyed great Generals who won wars and led their armies to victory. One may see very clearly with a single eye, but with two squinted eyes, matters are likely as different as flustered. How is General *Ab.Ab.* going to read a map? Accurately? Hmmm! I doubt it! The Scoundrel is perhaps not a military genius. Still, he has an evident advantage over his enemy: his eyes are not squinting. In the darkness of the cold nights of the desert, I imagine him scrutinising the stars and the Milky-way, like a wild cat and lucubrating on a map in his tent under a candle's flame. At the same time, his troops exult in dreams, lying in their sleeping bags like lizards beneath the rocks. And in the spilt brightness of the morning, he would expound his plan for the next operation to his officers over smoking cups of coffee. Meanwhile, the troops would smear their guns and brush their boots, waiting patiently for the great hour.

I have nothing to do with the Scoundrel since he is no longer our beloved and mighty president, cheered and feared by everybody. He is now a mere rebel, challenging the authorities, a meretricious outlaw, a brash herald of the catastrophe. But this does not mean, either, that I would put my fate eagerly into the hands of a man incapable of discerning me from my shadow. Really, I was being jammed, and in that beguiling confusion, I could neither step forward and engage sincerely in the Islamist cause nor step backwards and claim that I was still loyal to my Scoundrel-President. It is a painful situation for which I have not been prepared. And Hassan seemed not to notice it; on the contrary, he let me understand that he considers me as 'one of them'.

One of them? Me? One of whom?

They are sheltered in sumptuous villas and luxurious palaces, driving expensive motor-cars, holding astronomic accounts in foreign banks, gambling millions and millions in the casinos from Monte Carlo to Las Vegas, losing them happily as if they lost old socks, betting millions on the stock exchange's shares, manipulating thousands of men and leading them to the death-trap as if they were a cattle of calves, not giving a damn for their lives and that of their wives and children; while their own families are skiing airily on the snowy mountains of Switzerland, or sunbathing on the golden shores of the Riviera, unaware of the despondent plight of their people and the dismaying devastation of their country. And whether they are Islamists or secularists, royalists or republicans, nationalists or internationalists, mindful of their roots or 'don't carists', what have I to do with them? I am a simple citizen of the doomed country, a simple bank clerk, a humble labourer living on a salary. Though I am sometimes uncanny, I am not blind, though: I know very well that I AM NOT ONE OF THEM!

I may dream of founding a bank and speaking of it as if it were already true. I may talk about my projects from dawn up to sunset and between sunset and sunrise. But all this remains outside my reach. A babble is nothing more than a babble; I do not trust Hassan. As I was lying to him, it is not unlikely that he lied to me too. I never owned two hundred million dollars, not even two hundred thousand. This dream overwhelmed me so much that I became convinced of its imminence. I incubated it day and night and treasured it as a blessed omen. But it is not of idle money that I dreamed, certainly not of easy money acquired and accumulated by chance, gambling or mere speculations. I have never been attracted by that kind of roulette; anyway, I have no means to play it, even if it is only to tempt the chance. It is of hard effort that I dreamed, not of restful rent.

After all, I am as doomed as my country and predestined to live poor among the rich! But I know that to make money, one must deal with it; this is just a primordial principle that is not hard to understand. And to make a lot of money, one has to deal in huge sums. This is different from what I was doing at the bank, for I am neither a banker nor a stockbroker, let alone a businessman. I am rather a scribe. A clerk. And I was just scribbling, scribbling, scribbling... Eh! And when I was tired of serious work, I played with Samir's innocuous games. I asked him foolish questions to know to what extent he was really clever. And he was certainly competent and as proficient as ten, twenty, or fifty scholars. And I was super excited by his broad knowledge, and I wanted this to complete my scant education. So he helped me along with Mr Aroussi, who was the first to inform me thoroughly about John Law. That's how I connected with one of the brightest minds in the banking business. I was - I am still - so infatuated and ravished by his career that I found myself repeating his name in my dreams and perhaps even in my nightmares, along with the terms of the persons I cherished, Dalila, my mother, Zerga, Samir, and Mr Aroussi.

This is the real world within which I found myself confined to live. It is as solid and strong as the rocks of our mountains or the rusty bars of my cell. Nothing could shake it, snatch it from me, not even the most storming hurricanes, and certainly not a Scoundrel, even if he was a former president, let alone a group of lunatics. This is at least what I believed until the sudden entry of the black guard, Mahmoud, bringing the darkest news I had ever heard.

He stormed into the room with a telegram in his hand and said:

– Excuse me, sir, I have something for the prisoner... um... I mean Mr Bassam.

Hassan gazed at the intruder sideways and asked him:

– What's the matter? Why are you disturbing us?

– It's a telegram, sir, and it's... um... very serious.

– Come on, give it to me.

Mahmoud approached gingerly, and I noticed that he had lost a button on his shirt so that his protruding belly obscenely showed off its swarthy complexion through the breach. It was rather disgusting, and he did not seem aware of the mini strip tease he was displaying. He handed the telegram to Hassan and stepped aside, staring at me gloomily. I never thought him capable of sadness, albeit I did not understand the full significance of his gaze before knowing the message he brought.

I stared at Hassan, who became quite disturbed as soon as he read the telegram. Then, addressing me, he said:

– I didn't want you to know it earlier, he grumbled suddenly. But I think it is now useless to conceal it any more. Be courageous, Bassam. This is God's will. I present you my sincere condolences.

Dumbfounded, I remained silent. There was a heavy uneasiness between us while my heart thumped like mad. Then, he broke the silence again and said bluntly:

– I feared to shock you if I broke the news as soon as I heard it. I wanted first to prepare you for the future. These are crucial moments in our life Bassam; be sure of my compassionate sympathy.

It was at that moment that I dared contemplate the unthinkable. I said with a stuttering voice:

– What... what happened, sir?

Again that empty look in Mahmoud's eyes and the devastating words flowing through Hassan's lips:

– Your mother and your fiancée. Both... have been called to the heavens. Be courageous, old boy.

– Called to heavens? You don't mean that they are both dead, do you?

He sighed deeply and handed me the telegram.

– I am sorry!

I took the little piece of paper with shaking hands and read it with a pang in my bosom.

Your mother and Dalila slain with three hundred residents – 'Ouja mourning – 10 hours Collective slaughter – Terrorists plundered households and shops – Town sacked –Allah is Greatest – Father-in-law – Si Houssine.

I felt the earth shaking under my feet. My head went dizzy, and I staggered like a drunken. Then, finally, someone pushed a chair behind me, a hand touched my shoulder, and I was seated, wincing and tipsy. I don't remember how long I remained mutely impounded into an encompassing sulky maze, struck by the acatalepsy of the news. Voiceless and sad, I could not imagine the hateful cabal that occurred, with its sad procession of reckless vengeance, its odious libation of blood, and its morbid display of gratuitous violence. It was too inhuman, too horrendous to be true. Why should any party undertake such an atrocious massacre? What's the meaning of slaying mercilessly three hundred people in a village of about one thousand inhabitants? Who profits from such depravity of murderous violence?

Then I broke into tears. I wept bitterly, unrestrainedly, almost with a titillation of pleasure—the pleasure of someone pouring his soul through his tears because of his impotence. And I felt that I was forsaken and alone like a derelict and worthless stone. Desperately, I had hitherto clung to a faint hope that loomed in the desert of my life like a glittering rainbow after the dreary storm. I knew I had been unjustly imprisoned and disgraced. However, as long as the little world I had been forced to leave was still palpably strong and well-shielded, I nourished the placating dream to get out and retrieve it. But now, it is over, forever. I have nowhere to go, nobody to see. I am like a straw carried away by the scuttling wind. I am nobody.

Someone was speaking near me. I heard my name. He was speaking to me. The voice was coming over from a remote place with an echo:

– Mister Bassam...sam...sam... sam...

I lifted my head. Through my tired eyes, I stared at the face of the man, trying to ease me. I could hardly recognise him. It was Hassan, though, as if a whole century had passed since we spoke. He handed me a handkerchief.

– Thank you, sir.

I wiped my tears. I never wanted to weep like a child before him. The black guard had left the room; we were alone again.

– I'm sorry! I was going to tell you, but ...

– So, you knew...

Silence.

– Since three days.

– Why, sir? Why did you let this happen? It's my hometown, my family, my flesh and blood.

Silence. He lit another cigarette with nervous movements. His hands were a trifle shaking. He was looking at the courtyard. I followed his gaze. The prison enclosure was a large square surrounded by high walls and barbed wire. The ground was covered with gravel and dirt and a few patches of grass and weeds. The men in the yard were scattered in small groups, talking casually or smoking cigarettes. Some of them glanced at the library, but most ignored us. They looked bored and resigned as if they had accepted their fate and had nothing to hope for. They laughed at some jokes or stories, but their laughter sounded hollow and forced. They did not care about me or what would happen to me. Maybe they knew that I was doomed, or perhaps they were too numb to feel anything. The sky above was clear and blue, with a few white clouds drifting by. The sun shone brightly, casting sharp shadows on the ground. It was a beautiful day, but it felt like a mockery to me. How could the world be so calm and peaceful when there was so much injustice and violence? How could the order of things remain unchanged when so many lives were destroyed? How could I face the executioner when I had done nothing wrong? The group escorted the Director of Security was still chatting perfunctorily. I overheard laughter. They were quite indifferent to my fate. Did they know too? The sky was serene, with only a few white clouds scuttling towards the north. It was a sunny day. Nothing could spoil that peaceful quietness or change the order of things, not even the massacre of 'Ouja.

Notwithstanding death, havoc, and disasters, the world will continue to live on the same rhythm. What three hundred people slain in a small anonymous village of the third doomed world will weigh in the balance? After all, it is a civil war, and nobody ignores it.

– I didn't know or even suppose your mother and fiancée were victims. You have the right to know, but as you can see, it shocked us as much as it scared you. It is so horrific that the government decided to inform the citizens after knowing more about what happened. It is a delicate matter, you know. People would think the government does not protect them, and we fear a general panic. That's why we kept silent, waiting for the adequate moment.

– But they will know, sir, they will know. You can't hide the massacre of hundreds of people eternally. This is not a small and trivial homicide but a holocaust. You are the rulers and responsible; if you conceal the genocide, you'll be accounted for it. What happened to the police and the National Guard? Where was the army you are so proud of? Why did they allow such a slaughter to happen? Who are the criminals? What is the good of maintaining a government if it reveals itself to be so impotent? The people would ask, sir.

– I know that Bassam, but I suppose you understand our reasons. But, of course, we must first catch the criminals or at least some of them, and they must confess their crimes publicly. I also assume you guessed who they are; the evidence against the Scoundrel and his men is quite clear, isn't it?

– No, sir, it is not evident as you suggest. I am sorry. You are the Director of Security, you are better placed to know, and I don't think your job consists just of suppositions but in showing strong, consistent evidence.

(6)

Boldened by my anger and despair, I could not control the furious stream thrusting from my pain. I didn't realise I was indirectly charging the new regime with genocide. As Hassan did not reply, I went on:

– ' Ouja is in the region your government holds under control. Unless the police and the army turned a blind eye to the SOS appeals, I don't know how all that could happen. Moreover, the men of the Scoundrel are far in the south; you told me just before the arrival of the telegram that they had been beaten and pushed back by your troops while they were trying to thrust forward towards the north. How did they arrive at 'Ouja - despite the blockade? They needed to cross the desert, undetected by your men, and travel hundreds of miles across hills and mountains before reaching my village. Once there, they would shoot, kill, and rampage for hours, then flee to their desert, unnoticed and unpunished. Would you explain that to me? I know 'Ouja. There is only one main street in the town, where the police and the National Guard have their stations, the bank, the post office, and other administrative and commercial offices. It should not be hard for the police to notice the criminals' arrival, stop them, or call for support. They could not possibly have been deaf and blind, whereas the slaughter was going on. 300 people! How did they manage to kill them without alerting the government law enforcers?

– I understand your anger and resentment, but I plead with you to believe I am sincerely moved. We could do absolutely nothing. When we heard of the massacre, it was too late. The first thing the men of the Scoundrel did was cut off the village from the country. Telegraph and telephone poles were completely off-use when we arrived. The police and the National Guard had been slaughtered along with the inhabitants. I had never seen such a disaster in my life. I could not believe it. Older men, pregnant women, girls, and even children and babies had been atrociously slain, and their corpses bear the indelible marks of heinous torments and torture. It was not the misdeeds of human beings but wild beasts. I could not eat anything for at least twenty-four hours after I saw the hideous massacre. I am the first to mourn for the victims, Bassam. Nevertheless, I won't hide it; we cannot control all parts of the national territory. The country is vast, and we are still organising ourselves, and we need men, guns, and military equipment. That's why the Emir ordered us not to disclose the tragedy before knowing more. We have been after them for three days; if we can only catch one or two, they will confess their crimes before the TV cameras, and the world will learn what the Scoundrel did.

I was blurred and abashed. Why should I believe Hassan? Were the Islamists incapable of perpetrating and throwing the odious crime upon their enemies? What would stop them if they decided it was a good tactic to smear the rival? But if they were the true responsible, why should they preclude the widespread of the news? It would be much more useful to them to point their fingers at their enemies and say: Look what they did! It would be a sensational advertisement for them. Yet, they kept silent about the crime, as if they were ashamed and apprehending that their accusation backfired or perhaps because they were not entirely clean.

The question was burning my lips:

– Why, in your opinion, did the Scoundrel order such a heinous genocide? How would he profit from the death of hundreds of innocents? Had he become stupid after being removed from power? Doesn't he know that this is a war crime which would not remain unpunished?

– That's why we call him the Scoundrel, replied Hassan flatly. He is capable of much more horrors. He is an evil mind.

– This is not an answer, sir, I grumbled. You are a top-level official...

He interrupted me angrily:

– You don't stop reminding me of my responsibility. I am not the sun. I don't shine over the whole damned world! I am responsible, yes, but I can't be everywhere simultaneously. Come back to your senses, lad. I know your mother and your fiancée had been killed. I am sorry for that. This is no reason to charge my government or me for such crimes. I have already explained to you how the whole thing happened. Do you want me to recognise that our power is still flimsy, faltering, and weak? I did that, too, didn't I? Do you want me to shout on the roofs that we hold nothing but the capital and some villages and that the largest part of the country remains out of reach? Do you want me to confess our failure publicly to comfort you? Look, Mr Bassam. I have been very patient and kind, but my patience is not unlimited. Don't forget that the reports you wrote to our enemies incriminate you in the eyes of our people and make you one of its worst foes. Don't ever forget that if you are still among the living, it is well because I've been tolerant. But you are not yet safe. It would be best if you first thought of saving your head. In the country's present conditions, with all the evidence accumulated against you, a military court would sentence you to death. We have already executed dozens and dozens of traitors and corrupted people. I offered you a good compromise, a very honourable issue. And instead of thanking me, you almost charge me for killing your mother. It is unfair!

He paused, took a long inhalation from his cigarette, puffed the blue smoke through his mouth and nostrils, and ducked as if he were regretting his unrestrained anger, but discovering that it was too late, he stepped towards me, put his hand gently on my shoulder, and said:

– I am sorry, Mr Bassam. But, please, don't grudge. I sincerely apologise to you. I know you are deeply moved. If it happened to my family, I would react the same way. I implore you to accept my condolences for your loss.

As I did not reply, he went on:

– As a matter of fact, we are almost in the same situation. If that may comfort you, I had never known my mother, for she was dead at the same moment I was born. All my life, I carried the indelible mark of guilt. And though my father remarried just a few times after her death, I have never felt innocent. Whenever I was naughty and disobedient with my stepmother, my father reminded me I had killed my mother. I hated him for that. As a result, I grew up aloof and somewhat withdrawn. I had a lot of difficulties when I tried to socialise with my schoolmates and little neighbours. I was quarrelsome and shy. I provoked fights. I had the impression of being unjustly aggressed continually, and I had to defend myself. My mother's death had extended its sad shadow over my life since I began to understand what was happening around me. My only consolation was my sister Sophia, and though she is a few years older than me, she gave me some of the tenderness I crave. I loved her as if she were my mother. That's why I am so caring for her. And some years later, when we lost our father, I was barely sorry for it. Indeed, I was no longer an infant; my sister was already married, but the sufferance I had endured as a little boy extemporised unexpectedly in a feeling of deliverance. As incongruent as it may seem, my father's death absolved me from that excruciating guilt and gave me the feeling - perhaps a delusional one - to be subsequently free. I was alone, which was not new since I had always felt alone.

There was a pause. He threw the butt of his cigarette on the floor and crushed it with his heel.

– Sophia and Mamduh asked me kindly to go and live with them when our father died a few months after their wedding. I rejected their offer, but they insisted. I was twenty years old; it was my first year at the university, and my sister did not want me to live with our stepmother, who was still a young woman and would perhaps seek to remarry.

There was another short pause.

– I don't know why I am telling you this old story; perhaps just because I feel your sorrow deeply and want to join you if that can help comfort you, or maybe because I seek to unburden myself... I never married, you know, likely because I never felt secure enough or perhaps also I don't want to have children or to bear the responsibility of another death. This doesn't seem right, but it cannot be helped. I was far from imagining my life and career in those remote years. I was turbulent and dissipated, as you can imagine a twenty-year young man who had never known his mother and had just lost his father. So, I refused to live with my sister and her husband and remained in the same house. My stepmother was about thirty years old, quite pretty, with brown hair curling on her shoulders, two black eyes glittering with an incandescent inner flame, although their glow had almost gone when my father died, a small nose and a fleshy mouth. Indeed, I used to call her Mom, though she's ten years older than me, and our relationship had never been easy. There was always a sort of ambiguity hovering over it, particularly in my teen years, when I felt the most guilty about my mother's sudden death. And I believe that Sophia has never admitted that another woman could replace her mother. I could not leave my father's house just for a female vagary. So, I stayed. I am still living in the same place. She had not remarried, and she is now and since my father's death, and well before, of course, the true mother who cares for me as if I were her offspring.

With difficulty, I retrieved my voice and said:

– I have not got your luck, Mr Hassan. I have nowhere to go and nobody to speak to. I am left alone, without family or relatives, whatever. My mother was nearly deaf and cut off from the world. She could harm nobody. I just don't understand why they killed her. And Dalila was as innocent as a lamb; she had nothing to do with politics; she had no opinion and did not care whether the government was Islamist. And she was not alone in this case; most 'Ouja people are quite indifferent to the political struggle. So killing them was an absurd act that served no cause. They may be the most stupid people on earth, but this is not a reason to slaughter them. I am still appalled. I don't understand how that happened.

– There is nothing to understand, Mr Bassam. I don't think our people are ignorant because they support any ruler or tyranny. Our people are charitable but, sadly, powerless. But, the civil war is nonsensical since those who benefit from it are selfish. They are pushing us to our breaking point. The Scoundrel intends to instil dread and horror in the populace to scare them away from supporting the new authority. He is aware that our people desire an Islamic administration. As a result, the message is clear: the Scoundrel will punish our people for supporting the Islamic cause. But we will not let it happen; we will fight back. Allah is on our side. He won the battle of 'Ouja but not the war. We are determined to squash him like a vile beetle. I believe you have finally decided to support us. You're out for vengeance, aren't you?

I was sceptical that our people preferred the Islamists over their opponents. Nobody polled the audience, but I said, "I don't want to take it this way, sir."

– It's the only option you have. Of course, it would be best to exact revenge on your kin. How will you ever find happiness if you don't? But, Mister Bassam, vengeance must appeal to your conscience as much as your masculinity. Are you a woman? Don't you have a heart in your bosom? Therefore, we provide you with the means to exact revenge on your mother and fiancée.

That was a difficult choice.

– Sir, I have always lived in peace. I'm not looking for retaliation.

– You must, he said, almost angrily. It's your responsibility.

I stumbled: – Do you think so? Really?

– Without a doubt. In your shoes, I would not hesitate. I would instantly join the militants who are now fighting the Scoundrel.

My perplexity reached an all-time high for a very simple reason. It is not my type of dude. I prefer to pass the time and forget the past. I don't see myself going through the streets brandishing a gun. If I cannot accomplish justice on earth, I prefer to postpone it until the final judgement. Except for the Judges, I don't generally deal with revenge. Then Hassan continued:

– Eye for eye, tooth for a tooth. It is the proper course of action in any typical endeavour. You will never be a man if you do not get revenge for your dead. How would you gaze in the mirror without feeling embarrassed? Mister Bassam, blood calls to blood. Life is all about retribution. What is our rule if not a kind of retaliation against the King and the Scoundrel? What is our conflict but a reenactment of the same vengeance? Look at our city; what is it if not a retaliation for our predecessors' dreary lives? When the Brits colonised us, it was a form of revenge for our prior success in the Holy Jihad. We had evicted them and the other Crusaders from Jerusalem, hadn't we? And when we battled them again to free the land from their oppression, it was another act of vengeance. So, life is a series of retributions and counter-retributions. Looking at it this way, accepting your fate and fighting becomes much easier.

"I don't want to fight," I told myself.

– You don't think I will shoot the Scoundrel, do you? You are aware that I am incapable of handling a firearm. I'm not cut out for this killer business, and I'm not playing a part in a movie, Sir. I am just a dude like you or anyone else. Look at me; do you think I'm an image? But, Sir, I have sentiments. I'm completely moved. I would sacrifice my life for my family, but they are no longer with us. It's over, completed, and done for good. I will not resurrect them even if I slaughter the Scoundrel's army.

Perplexed by my outburst, he looked at me and said:

– I'm not asking for all of that, guy. What happened to you? Revenge does not always involve physically murdering someone; there are several types of killing and vengeance. You have the option. Look at what I'm providing you for that reason; if you accept to do what I say, you'll be one of the most powerful people in this nation. I've got a plan for you that you'll love. But first, get rid of these rags you're wearing; we must get to work.

He took a breath. I suspected him of thinking to himself, 'I've never seen a more foolish person!' This is a true coward!'

– Look at me, Bassam, he said. You saw me in this hole before the revolution. You know how miserable I was. I revealed some confidential secrets to you. You know I was never an Islamist, but I am now one. Why? It's not complicated: life is in constant flux, and one must know how the wind blows to stay safe. Now, the wind blowing over our country came from the seventh century. Do you want me to stand up to it and be carried away? I'll explain further. Do you think our Minister of the Interior - my ex-brother-in-law - is a devout Muslim, praying five times a day, fasting religiously during Ramadan, and refraining from wine, spirits, and pork? Eh! Like most of our country's compassionate citizens, you most likely believe this. Therefore, even though it seems surprising, let me tell you the truth: Mamduh, my dear buddy, didn't know whether it was morning or evening when they woke him up and told him the coup had succeeded, for he had spent the entire night drinking whisky at a private club in the capital. Do you believe he was unaware that the army was planning a coup that night? Yet, you'd be mistaken if you thought that. Mamduh was the Head of Military Intelligence. He knew everything and let it happen. He didn't bother informing the president - I mean, the Scoundrel - and his quiet was richly rewarded by the new leadership, as you can see. Even with this, because he was unsure of his chances of success, he struck a deal with Abdelghani Abdelghaffar. He would avoid the front lines while communicating with the guys attacking the presidential palace, the Broadcasting House, and other government strongholds. Mamduh drank at that exclusive Club till the last minute, then proceeded to worship in the Grand Mosque with the members of the Revolutionary Committee. As a result, he was appointed Minister of the Interior. That was no longer a game for him. He would be safe if the coup failed, but as it succeeded, he was catapulted to the front stage because it succeeded. What are your thoughts about that?

He grinned airily as if he were telling me a clever joke. He, on the other hand, was not amused. It wasn't precisely what I anticipated to hear from him regarding the new regime's top administration. I'd feel confident if he confirmed to me Mamdouh was faithful. I may not have agreed with all of his points of view, but it is much easier to deal with a man whose behaviour is harmonious with his beliefs. So how could any guy feel safe with a chameleon? Such outrageous behaviour shocked me, and I'm unsure if the Emir was an Islamist or an illusionist! I'm not surprised Sophia divorced. I felt respect for her. Mamdouh is not the kind of man any reasonable woman would trust. He is a snake, a weathercock, and an alligator! Such an insult to the Islamic Revolution almost outraged me. A drunk at the helm of the most powerful Ministry? It's extraordinary, unbefitting of Abdelghani Abdelghaffar.

I'm sure his narrowed eyes are for something in this terrible deal. But, unfortunately, Abdelghani missed his aim again: he put the wrong man in the wrong position! Alas!

– Surprised? Look, Mr Bassam, politics might differ from what most people believe. It is not just the art of administering public affairs but also the art of concealing private matters from the public. That's how it works, and you should get used to it because that's our reality. You can work to the top when you understand this and learn to ignore it. I obtained this post because I am wise, not because of my brother-in-law. It was not difficult for me to acquire the Committee of Revolution's trust, as I had spent several years working in close collaboration with military intelligence. During those years, I learnt to close my eyes and my ears to some facts for one simple reason: the truth, the full truth, does not exist anywhere, and even if it existed, it would serve no purpose, for nobody wants to hear it. When I realised that the government was in its last days, I worked to strengthen my connections to the men of the future without fully separating from the other side. As a result, I was awarded a top post. I was lucky. Nevertheless, I worked hard. Mister Bassam, you may be no less blessed. Let's forget about what you did before the Revolution. No one knows about it, and those who do - I'm talking about the ex-Director of Security and some of his men - can no longer hurt you. I will support you. The fact that you were incarcerated under the Scoundrel's rule is an excellent make-believe. As a result, you will serve as one of my men; you will be my eyes and ears. I'll introduce you to Mamdouh as soon as it's possible. For your part, you will sign the project we have discussed, allowing me to notify the Ministry of Finance. There wouldn't be any objections. We need to reorganise the banking sector, and your suggestions would be appreciated.

He stopped before adding, "I'll let you change your clothing. You'd need to shower as well. After that, I'll provide orders for your convenience. It is pointless for you to come with me to the workplace immediately. Take your time; I've already told you everything you need to know. I'll send the car to pick you up at seven this evening. After that, we'll have dinner with Sophia. Is everything all right?

– It's all right, sir, I responded, surprised. Then, after reflecting on what had occurred, I continued thoughtfully: I'd like to make another request. I wish to visit 'Ouja. I'm afraid I'll be late for the funerals but I want to go to the cemetery.

– That's understandable. We'll take care of it as quickly as we can. (He took a breath.) I'll be gracious. Is this dinner so urgent? No. Let's put it off till you return from your village. That will give you time to think clearly and prepare yourself.

– Sir, I am quite thankful to you. I don't know how to express my gratitude for everything you've done for me.

– Never mind! Bassam, you're my brother, and this is my responsibility. First, visit the graves of your bereaved family. They have become our martyrs. Return to the capital after that. I'll reserve a room for you at the Sheraton. Don't be concerned about anything. The chauffeur will arrive at seven o'clock as arranged. Is there anything else you'd like to enquire about?

I paused.

– In truth, sir, I don't dare to ask you.

– What's the problem? Please inform me right now.

– Ahem... um... I'm curious about what happened to Mr Aroussi. I don't see him any longer. You see, he was my boss for a long time. He hired a lawyer on my behalf. I still respect him since I know he cares about my career.

He looked at me blankly.

– Hey! Bassam, you're a strange man. Your loyalty has greatly impressed me. I hope you continue to be so forthright in the future. Nonetheless, I want to ensure you know your former boss. He was secluded, which is why you don't see him about. I feel bad for him, but as talented and competent as he is, there is so much evidence against him. He used to smuggle foreign currencies out of the country, and the man who worked for him confessed completely before his death. Additionally, unlike you, he was not operating in secret, but everyone is aware of his close ties to the regimes of the Scoundrel and the King. Unfortunately, I'm unable to help him.

I ducked mutely.

– I know a lot about him, he added. He was my chamber mate. Mr Ammar, one of the best solicitors in the country, is his brother-in-law. He will defend him brilliantly, far better than I can. So don't be concerned about that guy, Bassam. Sharks like him are always able to escape from any trap. (He hesitated). I don't need to tell you that this conversation never happened. Everything you learnt today will be useful if you keep your mouth shut. If you act wisely, you will rise faster than you ever anticipated or hoped. It is not improbable that you may receive a decoration one day.

It seemed too good to be true! I imagined myself standing in front of Emir Abdelghani Abdelghaffar. The latter was awkwardly attempting to catch the button on my jacket while failing to hang the medal on my chest. He would make the identical action thrice, unsuccessfully and once successfully. After that, I'd be a national hero like Hamda La'war. That's my life's ambition, the crowning career achievement, the fulfilment of my senior age.

At last, I find a government fair enough to recognise the great services I would owe to it; a government ready to pay for the debts of its predecessors by making me a man indebted forever. Oh my God! My dear, my omnipotent, my merciful God! Thank you a thousand times. No, thank you. Two hundred thousand, or better... two hundred million times, that is as much as I have on my credit account. I was still perplexed. I couldn't believe it. I smiled. Grace and beatitude enveloped me. I was going to start dancing and get into a trance. In my nirvana, I would yell, rejoice, leap, and kiss my benefactor's rubicund beard. I would kiss everyone I saw along the path, including Franken-stein, Zorro, and the black guard. Now that everything has been counted, I prefer not to kiss them. My zeal blinded me to the calamity that had befallen my family. The consolation for my biggest loss was so quick, unexpected, beautiful, rewarding, and soothing that it was almost impermissible. I tried to keep myself under control and stop the flood of emotions that washed over me.

I muttered meekly after a long interval of stillness:

– Are you... um... certain, sir? Is it... um... Is this some joke?

Hassan looked at me with suspicious green eyes.

– A joke? What are you talking about, lad?

– Nothing, sir. It's all about... um... the medal. Is it a pledge?

He appeared perplexed by my enquiry.

– A pledge? So, let's suppose it is; sure. But, it is up to you to contribute to its success.

I was pulled in.

– Do you believe the Emir will grant it to me? He has no idea who I am or what I am up to, sir. But I am the Revolution's most humble servant. Nonetheless, I am living a dream. I paid a high price for supporting the Revolution, as I lost both my mother and my fiancée. Sir, I'm still shocked.

– The Emir has no idea who you are, but we'll make him aware of your presence, Mr Bassam.

I'm quite sure he wasn't kidding. So what the hell is going on? But I wanted to be certain.

– Would Sophia be pleased if I am... um... decorated?

I couldn't help but notice his cheerful glance. - Oh! Yes, very much so. She'd like it if her husband was a national hero.

"Her husband" rang out in my brain "her husband? Is she not divorced?" I asked rashly.

That bothered him:

– Yeah, I'm referring to you, fool. You're going to be the husband.

I was almost taken aback by his self-assurance. He had sealed my destiny without even considering my input. I had yet to meet his sister. All I knew about her was that she had three children. It seems that the agreement between us was mostly founded on this marriage. He had no doubt I would accept marrying his sister even if she was hard of hearing and squinting or blind!! Was she, however, truly so? I was terrified. Yet, that was the condition of my release; that much is certain. What if I refused? The solution was no less straightforward. Like all traitors, I would be beheaded in public! All counts have been completed. I'd rather marry Sophia. I rapidly calculated the stakes. I couldn't sit around any longer. My trials were harsh and useless to him since I knew he'd gone insane with that obsessive obsession.

– Yes, I said. You are correct, sir. Indeed, I am her husband.

– Well, let's hope she agrees now. Try to be kind to her. Refrain from bringing up your tortuous story. Nevertheless, I'll be there for dinner. We'll discuss everything when you return from 'Ouja.

As two excellent friends, we shook hands enthusiastically. He then marched across the room to his foot soldiers in the courtyard. The grey uniforms straightened and saluted as they saw him. The sun was blazing and beaming brightly over the entire world.

It was an unusually misty morning for me, despite the shining sun... The morning of the Mogul.

Chapter 8

Return To 'Ouja
After the Deluge

(1)

I painstakingly calculated the situation. I would have spent precisely five months, three days, seven hours, fifteen minutes, and thirty-three seconds in the vivarium dubbed - quite meaninglessly, in my opinion - jail. Indeed, it is hardly the most praised location to visit and, once there, to remain in. So far from it, if it were indeed a State-owned hotel - and neither Hassan nor I doubted it - it should grow more sociable for the gentlemen and less profligate for the beleaguered crooks and other scammers and psychopaths forced to cohabit under its ceilings. Otherwise, who would willingly forego the warmth of family life for a brief or a long stay out there? And if such an honourable institution were to be rejected by its prospective customers, it would be a major loss for the State and the future anti-state couvolutionists. The State would feel deprived of a good coercion and repression tool, and the anti-state militants of a Bastille for their dark conspiracies.

We must also know how to manage such a system because this is not just a place but a system.

I AM NOW A FREE MAN writing these words honestly from my house in 'Ouja, where I've been for three days mourning and, in my grief, enjoying an intimacy that I have almost forgotten while struggling with gloom, depression and shadows.

I did not come in the Director of Security's Mercedes but in a roaring Land Rover driven by a stylish chauffeur. As soon as we crossed the main and unique street of the hamlet, we were followed by hundreds of eyes. Well! 'Hundreds' is probably a euphemism in the present conditions. After the atrocious killing of so many residents, there aren't many people remaining to cheer on my achievement. The savage disaster has left lasting and horrible scars on the streets and the walls. The survivors are suffering indescribable trauma. A thick cloud of melancholy and sorrow has descended over the community. I'd never felt so out of place in my own house. Perhaps I am not an alien, but 'Ouja is getting curiously far from me. I barely recognised my home town. The metamorphosis is startling and terrible; the trauma has upset me since I arrived.

Nothing is more terrifying than the bizarre conclusion that you are not the person you have always believed you are or that the area where you have always lived seems not to be your hometown, as you thought! One thing is certain: either I'm not the real Bassam Bourasin, or 'Ouja isn't the real 'Ouja!

When the Land Rover approached the main street, I spotted regular soldiers in raggy dirty uniforms and many small groups of armed militiamen striding on the sidewalks and parading around closed shops. They were much more similar to an army of invaders than to local citizens. There was a tank at the village's entrance, and I couldn't help but observe that the guys riding it weren't all clothed in military uniforms. Some of them were dressed in civilian clothing, like jellabas, dishdasha, and similar Arab robes, and I can't say they were spruce and clean. So far from it, they seemed uneven, with swarthy long-bearded cheeks, and looked like an army of half-starved shadows ready to attack you for no other reason than your face, which they did not like.

The driver glanced at me sidelong as I sat beside him, confused and stagnant. "Those are our men," he said proudly. "The Revolutionary Militia. Look how happy they are. Authentic lions! They'd get the head of the Scoundrel, wouldn't they?"

I did not respond. I was grumpy not just because I was returning to the village to watch the effects of a boundless misfortune but also because I was morally and physically exhausted. In reality, the car did not come at seven o'clock to pick me up, as Hassan had promised, but the following morning. As a result, I had spent the night awake with anxiety swallowing me up, wondering whether anything had gone wrong. I had washed and shaved, changed my clothing, and waited in the cell for the driver. But nobody called me. It was the worst night I'd had since being locked up. Waves of despair rolled over the deserted cost of my soul. I couldn't even eat, and my grief became excruciating when, unexpectedly, the TV speaker declared that the members of the Scoundrel's army had committed a terrible atrocity in 'Ouja. All the inmates hurried to the TV set to watch the first pictures of the horrendous tragedy. I saw the depressing fate that doomed my community at once and couldn't see any further. So, disgusted and daunted, I averted my gaze from the screen. I didn't want to watch my mother and fiancée's bodies lancinated and ripped apart. I didn't have the energy to deal with it.

THE NEWS QUICKLY SPREAD across the cell. Dahdah finally approached me, sallow-faced and quivering with emotion.

"My heartfelt condolences, brother. I just now learned of the tragedy that has befallen your family."

Suleiman Mughli came up and kissed me on the cheeks as well. Then he handed me a packet of his American smokes, which I declined, but he insisted: "You'll need it, man. You're going to see your hometown. It's a long trip."

So I grabbed the packet and started smoking idly. I've been smoking since that evening. It's like being contaminated with a virus — a sweet one that makes you think it is soothing. The Mughli would have given me more, but I flatly refused. The other inmates followed as soon as they heard the news, and when they finally returned to their usual routine, I was alone with Dahdah, who sat opposite me on the hard mattress at the bottom of the cell. "You know what they say around here," he said in my ear, approaching his chubby face.

I shook my head in denial.

– They say this is the filthy work of the Afghan and his cohort.

– What exactly do you mean? Who said that?

– Everybody. Did you miss the incredible coincidence? The day before the slaughter, the Afghan returned and negotiated the release of all his rabid dogs and recognised criminals imprisoned for life. They said they would be sent to another jail, although this was a lie. Those guys have absolutely nothing to lose, you understand? They most likely informed them, "We'll release you if you do whatever we tell you." Because they are inexcusable murderers serving life terms, it was an open door to freedom for them. They are perfectly capable of committing any genocide.

My thoughts were racing.

– Do you mean that the Afghan and those men are the true criminals that acted under the government's supervision? I said, shocked.

– Exactly, Dahdah said.

– I can't believe it. Why should they be so cruel to the people they pledged to protect?

– Who can tell? They may want to discourage the populace from supporting the ex-president by implying that he is only a chronic murderer who would not hesitate to provoke a genocide in his thirst for power.

It was a terrifying thought. Yet, there is no evidence to support it.

- These are rumours, I replied. The Afghan is not as free as you may think. The new administration would not let him go on a rampage at his leisure. What the heck? We're not in Afghanistan! I can tell you that the new administration is dead set on punishing the culprits, whomever they may be. I was chatting to the incoming Director of Security, one of us, this morning.

– Are you referring to Hassan? That guy was never one of my friends. A sycophant and opportunist who would sell even his mother for such a position! I used to read his crap at the time; it was insane! He had licked the boots of all the King's Ministers, and when they were knocked down, he didn't mind licking the shoes and bottoms of their successors. And he's surely putting his tongue deep into the depths of Islamist rulers right now. That guy got everyone. He was born to lick boots and butts!

– You are unfair, Dahdah. You do not know the dude. He is a very capable politician, well-informed, and, most importantly, incredibly kind and humanist.

Dahdah grinned and mockingly replied:

– Kind and humanist like a snake, yeah! Then, with his hurdy-gurdy fiddling, he got you, my dear! You don't know those sharks as well as I do. Have you always lived happily in your village? The Capital is a whole other universe, brother. They are capable of anything, I can tell you.

– Dahdah, don't you act as if this blasted Capital was on another planet. I lived in a village, but I'm not a moron. I can still tell the difference between a good fellow and a scumbag. I'm not afraid to admit that I believe Hassan more than a rumour based on hearsay and assumptions. So I see no reason to suspect he's fooling me. He has no reason to do so.

– OK, trust him; but you should know he is a hypocrite. Hassan is no more an Islamist than Zorro or any of the scabrous little goons you see around here.

I'm not sure how Dahdah came to this conclusion, but he wasn't far off the mark. Nonetheless, I held to the assumption that President Abdelghaffar's soldiers had nothing to do with the savage massacre. If Hassan knew that his friends had killed my family, he would not even consider offering me the hand of his unique and cherished sister, let alone the promise of a medal. It makes no sense.

Frankenstein asked me in the shower room that afternoon, "I heard you're going to be released, is that true?"

– Who told you?

He laughed.

– There's nothing to hide here, lad. Is it a state secret?

– No, it isn't. Did you happen to see me with Hassan in the library?

– No, I didn't, but I was told you'd been babbling with that cop all morning. At the very least, he is not ungrateful since he does not forget his friends.

I remained mute, but he observed the fresh clothing I'd brought to the shower and added, "You're going back to your bank, it seems."

– I don't know just yet.

– Good luck! He exclaimed, then added, You won't forget your promise, will you?

– What? I said quickly and perhaps rashly. Are you kidding?

I pretended to object to the unthinkable thought of hiring a mobster at my bank. Despite my uneasy response, he went up and took me like a feather into his sturdy arms, exactly like the first day, but without the fury, and he cried airily, to the surprise of the inmates: "You chum, man of man!"

I couldn't say anything because I was taken aback, and I pushed him vainly as I glanced at his bald round head and frightful mask, sparkling in the faint light of the lamp that had been turned on although it was early afternoon. Then he took me to his chest and kissed my forehead, and I was overcome by his foul odour of tobacco and sweat, so I yelled out, "Put me on the floor, for God's sake!" "I suffer from vertigo."

But he held me over his head again and said, "That's a chum, man of man!"

And he kept me hovering about the room like a small bird while the inmates cheered and applauded the 'chum, man of man' that I was. Then, finally, he relented and threw me on the ground. Thus, it was evident that he didn't aim to hurt me but rather to show his excitement, completely oblivious - the moron! - that I meant precisely the opposite of what he had just realised. But, knowing that despite his gorilla-like look, he is an expressive person, I did not dare to convey the actual meaning of my response and instead chose to let him celebrate his future 'career' at the bank rather than shatter his dream.

(2)

After Frankenstein, it was the shrink's turn to take the stage. I was shaving in the courtyard when Mahmoud came in from the block, gently asking whether "Mister Bassam would have the obligation to accord five minutes of his time to Mr the social assistant."

– Yes, said I. I'll meet him as soon as I finish shaving.

Mahmoud left the courtyard wearing the same sobbing bull-dog expression he had in the library. Meanwhile, I noted that the barber was now using a VIP Fresh blade to shave me. Life is full of surprises! And he made sure I noticed it. To my stupefaction, he claimed that "shaving the scented beard of Mister Hassan's friend was not a great event that made his day."

I thanked him for the accolade, and he said, "It's an honour for me, Mr Bassam".

Now I have become Mr Bassam for Mahmoud and the barber. Both have been so rude to me. But life is in continual change as the power balance shifts from one side to another.

The barber lingered, then:

– May I ask you a small favour, sir?

I had anticipated it.

– I'm listening to you.

– I've been here for three years and three months. I've been condemned to four years in prison, and I'd be so grateful if you intervened to alleviate my suffering.

– Ah! I will talk to Hassan, but I can't guarantee anything.

He thanked me profusely. He took a small perfume flask from his pocket as he finished the job. He sprinkled its contents over my face, neck, and hair, gently rubbing them with his soaked palms, not forgetting to emphasise that 'the perfume was Parisian' and that the treatment was reserved exclusively for 'the most important personalities of the prison'.

WHEN I ENTERED THE shrink's office, spotless, tidy, and scented, I expected to see the same cold little guy, with the gruff voice and the silver-rimmed spectacles hanging over his nose, smoking cigarettes in a chain and admiring the small clouds of blue smoke he was producing. That was different from the guy I was looking at. Something had changed in him since our first interview. I was surprised that as soon as his orangutan secretary alerted him that I was in the anteroom, the shrink opened the gate and virtually pounced on me, all grin and honey, took my elbow gently, and ushered me into his office as if I were a longtime buddy or family member. Such a warm greeting from a guy I knew was highly persuaded of his superiority immediately stunned me. I observed that the framed poster of our former president decorating the wall had disappeared as he welcomed me to sit and instructed his orangutan to bring up two cups of tea. Instead, the poster was properly replaced by a larger photo of the new strong man: Abdelghani Abdelghaffar, who was not smiling, but just puzzling us with his enigmatic black glasses, which cleverly concealed the two small gems gazing freely behind them. Surprisingly, I'm just now getting used to our president's visage. I discovered that having a president with a double vision is rather empathetic, and it is likely good - for him as well as for us - to lead two nations instead of one, with two peoples, two armies, and a double of everything inside them, something like the arch of Noah.

Thus, the shrink was up to date and quite in line. He gave me a cigarette, which I accepted, lit it, and stated:

– How nice to see you again, Mr Bassam. How are things going for you?

I didn't answer. Didn't he know?

– You were happy with the work I assigned you. It was a courtesy I had never accorded a detainee since the first day. But I had a feeling you're different from the rest. Eh! I was correct.

– I appreciate it, sir.

– I always thought you were a good chap, and you proved it, right? I see you're thriving.

My fine suit had clearly pleased him since he had been looking at my clothing the whole time.

– I knew I was making a good investment when I offered you that job, Mr Bassam, he added before I responded. It was, indeed, an excellent investment...

He grinned as he rubbed his hands together. He was ecstatic.

– Excuse me, sir, but are you talking about money? In fact, after working for about five months, I am still waiting to get my pay.

The shrink laughed as if I'd told him the most hilarious joke he'd ever heard. He laughed so heartfully that tears welled in his eyes, and he removed his spectacles to wipe them with a tissue. He chuckled even as the secretary returned, bearing the tray of tea, and stood up in the middle of the room, surprised and unsure of what to do next. Finally, he decided to place the tray on the desk, moved away, and, as if infected by his boss's unrestrained amusement, he burst out laughing and gripped his stomach with both hands. Then I couldn't hold back my laughter any longer, and while I didn't understand what had caused that sudden fury, I felt its idiotic thrill entering me wave after wave, and I broke out laughing, forgetting my grief. The situation's humour was immeasurably impulsive and enticing enough to keep me from questioning its logic. But, of course, it was nonsense since at least two of the three dudes in the room, including myself, had no idea why they were giggling. That lasted a considerable while, and when we eventually came to our senses, we looked at each other like three perfect fools, goggling and stupefied by our ridiculous performance. The first to stop laughing was the psy. He put on his spectacles and yelled at his assistant:

– What are you laughing at, double moron?

The secretary's chuckle immediately froze. Now he seemed paralysed, like an Iceman made up and left by the children.

– You brought the tea, didn't you? The shrink continued. What are you waiting for now?

The poor secretary withdrew and locked the door without saying a word. Meanwhile, I had recomposed.

– I apologise to you, Mr Bassam, replied the shrink.

– Forget about it! I was also laughing.

– Yes, he mumbled. Mr Bassam, you strike me as a compassionate figure. I am delighted to have met you. I hope you remember us once you're outside.

He came to a halt. He hadn't summoned me only to spout this nonsense.

– I can't possibly forget you, sir. The days I spent in this establishment will not be forgotten quickly. But you didn't respond to my question, did you?

– Yes, you are correct. I would have gone on and on about the matter from the first day. I'm afraid there is no salary.

– No pay?

– In this place, none. The detainees' labour is benevolent. We don't reward them.

That was the prison! Sur-exploiting all those people in diverse jobs while refusing to compensate them for their honest efforts! It was inequitable.

– Then why did you summon me, sir?

– I did not summon you, Mr Bassam. I just invited you for a cup of tea before you leave us.

– Ah! It's so kind of you, sir.

– Trust me, seeing a man I helped succeed gives me great pleasure. (pause) By the way, I'd like to ask you for a small favour.

I was somewhat taken aback and inquired:

– A favour from me, sir?

– Well... umm... Not from you, but from your friend, unless he is your relative.

I remembered the barber and almost inadvertently blurted:

– You too, sir?

Then, seeing his confusion and amazement at my response, I quickly added: - I'll do my best. I owe you that.

– Oh no, no, Mr Bassam. You don't owe me. I'm just counting on your kindness.

The hypocrite!

– In fact, it is not complicated, he went on. I've been assigned to this post for seventeen years. So you understand, It's grown so oppressively exhausting that I feel like any inmate here. I wish to be transferred to another department, and I'd like you to speak to the Chief of Security about my request.

Ah! Voila, voila! Now I see!

– Where do you wish to be transferred?

– Anywhere! But please, not to another prison. Various other departments in the Ministry may need experienced staff. Mr Bassam, I may be useful even at a bank.

– Really? And you want to be repositioned to a bank?

– Not necessarily a bank, but I would not turn it down. I don't know much about banking but I can work in the human resources service. Why not?

– Quite right. I completely get what you mean. I'll see what I can do.

The guy got overjoyed and spent at least five minutes thanking and rethanking me, even though I attempted to emphasise that I could not move him and that all I could do was talk it over with Hassan without guaranteeing anything. But he appeared to believe that I was capable of more than I dared to confess.

Finally, he recalled that my mother and fiancée had been slain in the terrible disaster of 'Ouja. He broke down in apologies and condolences and would mourn with me if I showed the least proclivity to shed hot tears for my dead. But I stayed silent.

I was perplexed when I left the shrink's office since he gave me much more authority than I had. He was not a very perceptive psychologist. He appeared to believe that I was Hassan's supervisor, even though I had no power over the Director of Security. How could I have? I'm at his mercy, not the other way around.

ANYWAY, I'M BACK IN 'Ouja, my beloved hamlet that the Barbarians had half-destroyed and ravaged; and I'm writing these words by candlelight since they hadn't yet restored the ruined electric and telephone lines.

My first day was agonising. The sun was scorching the countryside on this sweltering day. The chauffeur, a middle-aged guy with dark flashing eyes and a hooky nose, never stopped chatting in the vehicle. While my eyes searched the dismal panorama, with its gaping hillocks, scattered weeds, and musty stones, I listened to him barking listlessly. It's a desolate area of rough magnificent cliffs and harsh tawny flora, scorched by the sour acid sun's smouldering beams. It is a place that is so similar to its people that it is unnecessary to speculate on why such atrocities occur. We are as callous and ruthless as the land of our country.

Some of us are undoubtedly formed of its rocks and stones; they are tremendously insensitive and totally wry, if not depraved, in their love of blood and devastation. My own town has the odd name of 'Ouja! Why 'Ouja? Everyone understands the word's meaning: wry, not right, not straight! But not just one community that's off; it's the whole damned nation. At least, this is how any rational human being would see it. The country has gone insane with a cataleptic hunger for riches, power, and blood, as if this unholy trio is the dreadful destiny everyone will suffer now. Are we doomed forever? The discovery of oil and natural gas in our soil did not improve us; it made us greedy, mischievous, lecherous, materialistic, utterly selfish and evil. I missed the days when life in our nation was simple and quiet, as I was told.

Life lacked modern amenities, but at least people were still human, hospitable and generous. They didn't murder each other for no reason. This is a dreadful flaw, a modern-day tragedy.

I went to the cemetery with Mr Houssine, my ex-father-in-law. I directed the driver to Dalila's residence, a little bungalow on the outskirts of the community. We parked the Land Rover and started walking. I knocked on the door and waited, my pulse pounding and unsure what to say in such a difficult situation. The driver was hesitant to attend, but I assured him it was just like my house and that he was welcome. As a result, he accompanied me and stood by my side.

I knocked again, loudly, since I knew they wouldn't hear me if they were listening to the radio or the TV. Finally, after a time, the door opened, and there stood my mother-in-law, Khadija, with her head covered in a green kerchief and her face bloated and sallow. Her creases had deepened and were visible to the naked eye, and her small lips were dry and pursed, yet the tip of her nose was scarlet, and her eyes were hazy and tumescent as if she hadn't stopped crying for three days.

As soon as she spotted me, she burst into tears and swiftly withdrew, and I wondered if she could no longer stand my sight since I was clearly alive and in excellent health, but her daughter had died forever.

Nonetheless, I was as affected by the loss as she was since I had lost two precious people while she had lost just one. I know she never carried me lightly in her heart, and this riddle has never stopped to perplex me since I did nothing to offend her. But, so far from it, the more I tried to be pleasant and positively respond to all her vagaries— and they were many and diverse—the more I sensed her becoming a tiny satrap. I can't blame her; she's a mother, and Dalila was her one-of-a-kind child.

I entered, though, and politely encouraged the chauffeur to accompany me. Mr Houssine came to greet us. He kissed my cheeks and muttered faintly:

– That's God's will, my son. God's will, may He be compassionate to us! Please come in. It's so bad you couldn't make it to the funerals. The cemetery housed the whole hamlet. All glory to Allah. That is His will, and we shall not resist it, my son.

(3)

We followed Mr Houssine down the hallway and the little garden, and he led us into one of the four rooms, which I observed were crowded. I didn't know all the guys in the room since they weren't all from 'Ouja, as I suspected, but the others - those who recognised me - rushed over right away to shake hands and console me for the double loss. We sat silently in the same drawing room where I used to have lengthy conversations with Dalila. Nobody talked, and I couldn't break the wordless concentration in which we had taken sanctuary.

THAT AFTERNOON, I WENT to the graveyard with Mr Houssine and the driver. Then I learned that Dalila was visiting my ailing mother and had been permitted to stay the night with her when the hamlet was attacked. Standing in the middle of the cemetery under the shade of a palm tree, I felt everyone in 'Ouja had left their homes, stores, and enterprises to come and grieve their dead. The graveyard was on the outskirts of the village. A low white stone wall surrounds it, beyond which agricultural fields extend. I spotted the Islamic Militia members strolling along the fence, rifles on their shoulders, and questioned Mr Houssine:

– Did they come by night?

His tiny brown eyes twinkled in the sunlight, and his lips twitched as he wiped the sweat and dust from his tanned face with a green handkerchief. His face seemed thinner and bonier than it had been a few months previously, and he scowled:

– Who do you mean?

– I mean the killers.

– I'm unsure exactly when, but they probably came at daybreak or earlier. They rushed into the police station and the National Guard Headquarters, killed everyone, and then turned their rage to the stores and shops. They broke the doors with explosives, plundered, looted, and thrashed, while others broke into our homes randomly. They raped, robbed, killed whoever resisted, and rampaged relentlessly for hours. It had been a very long nightmare, my son.

– I'm still baffled about how this could ever happen in a country whose people pray to God five times daily and say there is no God but Allah. Has God abandoned us to those bloodthirsty terrorists?

– Don't blaspheme, son. It's His will. Accept it.

– I accept God, but I don't understand his will. The criminals seem to take advantage of it more than those who pray, fast, and do everything to please God, like you, Mr Houssine. They're the reason we're here.

He remained silent, fixing an imaginary square between his feet. I asked him:

– Do you think they're who the TV says they are, Mr Houssine?

He pondered. His eyes sank deep into their sockets. He was obviously hesitant, and his hand shook as he reached for the cigarette I was handing him.

– These are the former president's crimes, he said. He did not accept being ejected from power.

– You hesitated.

– No, I didn't. I am certain. The terrorists were dressed in long robes and sandals, with long beards and masks on their faces. They presumably attempted to imply that they are Muslims, but I know they are not. We recognised one of them.

– Really? One from 'Ouja? What's his name?

– No, no, you're misguided. Don't say such rubbish. The terrorist is from a nearby hamlet, and we know his clan. He was a lieutenant in the previous president's army.

I gave him another cigarette, took one for me, and lit them. I looked around and saw some women weeping on the graves, whereas the men accompanying them displayed perfect, woebegone, vapid faces. In such a sad time, we weren't the best people to gaze at. Some men were seated cross-legged on the matted ground, reading the Quran. I overheard their voices droning pathetically, like a long, lingering complaint. I felt depressed and gloomy, and the sky, vaulting its wistful blue high over our heads, seemed wholly unconcerned by our grief. That smiting coldness and unruffled beatitude irritated me. I told myself, "This is perhaps the hour of the Scoundrel. He is probably enjoying his meagre victory and wandering across the desert, intoxicated on blood, like a lone wolf licking its fangs after the gloomy feast. O Lord! Please assist us at this time. Let us continue to trust in your kindness and mercy.

WE SPENT THE DAY AT the graveyard, which was so crowded that it reminded me unavoidably, though inconveniently, of the weekly market that used to gather people every Friday in 'Ouja. Oddly, that day was the first Friday following the slaughter. It was the first Friday in many years that I did not see peddlers and merchants congregating in the public square.

After that, I dismissed the chauffeur. He inquired whether he should return to take me back to the capital, and I informed him that it wasn't required since I'd be driving alone. I thanked him, and he got into the Land Rover and waved to us. The automobile rumbled away, leaving a cloud of dust in its wake. Then I parted ways with Mr Houssine, promising to return and see him as soon as possible.

I WENT ALONG THE DUSTY streets, wandering aimlessly in the sluggish tottering of the dusk. No children were playing and shouting; no coffee shops were open; no men and youth were playing cards and smoking gurgling nargileh; no women were hurrying muffled in their veils, their mysterious eyes gleaming like colourful rainbows in the forlorn desert of our lives, and their ample gowns floating around them. Instead, abandoned dogs and cats chased remains on the wastebins, and armed young militiamen strolled along the street. They are all strangers to the village and are clearly as taken with the gloom that hangs over it as the locals were. I saw them lazing in little groups of three, four, and five, sombre and sad, dressed in long dishdashas or blue denim, as if they were only promenading to greet the sweet twilight of September. The bulk of them were relatively young, maybe under the age of eighteen. Without their weapons, one would mistake them for schoolboys on a field trip.

They looked at me indifferently, and some even hailed me with the traditional Islamic greeting: "Salam Alaykum!" "Wa Alaykum Assalam," I responded.

They have taken over the National Guard headquarters and the police station, as well as the regular army. However, I only saw a dozen soldiers, one of whom was a sub-officer, and they appeared to be on good terms with the militia. After the armed forces split into two parts, one of them loyal to the scoundrel and the other to the new masters of the country, I thought they had much to do with combating each other. That's why they sent the Islamic militia to maintain order in 'Ouja after the disaster.

When I crossed the main street and engaged in a bifurcated one to join the building where I lived, I saw them chatting on the pavement before the broken gate of 'Ouja Bank. It was just a ten-minute walk from the bank, but I postponed my visit to my mother's house until another day since I was exhausted. I travelled all morning in the scorching heat, then spent the afternoon accepting and delivering condolences and speaking with strangers. I needed a clean wash and a good night's sleep to recuperate. Mr Houssine had tried to keep me for supper, but I politely declined, blaming my indisposition on exhaustion. He didn't insist.

I ascended the steps of my seven-story building to the second level and opened my apartment door. I hesitated for a few minutes at the doorway as if I couldn't quite believe I was back home. "Home?" I muttered to myself, "Where is home now?" The location of a man's birth is not that important. What matters is what a guy does to improve himself and his life. I shut the door and traversed the little hallway to the living room, where I paused for a second in the middle of the room before entering the two other rooms, the kitchen and the bathroom, with the same unplaceable sorrow. It was no good to be back home. I was an outsider in my hometown. The brickwork, furniture and paraphernalia, I could get anywhere. What I can't find now is my family's love and support. Nothing is the same as it was when I left. The tiny Canary had passed away. I discovered its decomposing little body in the cage. Because it hadn't completely rotted, I assumed it died recently. My mother was ill in her last days. Yet, I'm surprised Dalila didn't take the bird to her house. My mother had undoubtedly given her a key; she could probably go to the apartment and feed the tiny bird. What happened? I feel bad about all this. Nothing was left to comfort me. I won't listen to the chirpy twittering in the morning and evening. I unlocked the cage and held the dried body in my hand; it was exhaling a foul odour. I wrapped it in an old white handkerchief and went out to give it a proper burial in the garden. At least, I'd bury the bird, as I could not attend my relatives' funerals!

Despite my tiredness and gloom, I opened the door and walked down the stairs, the dead Canary in one hand and a little pickaxe in the other. Then, as the swarthy shades of the evening stretched a dark mantle over the households, I got out and walked on the lawn.

Some lights were faintly glinting through the windows, and I regretted not purchasing a petrol lantern before my incarceration. But how could I know what would unfold in my peaceful village and the whole country? So I dug a pit, buried the small body inside, and then stood in awe of the bizarre series of deaths that had even the animals in shock. Then I returned to the flat, threw the pickaxe in the kitchen closet, removed my clothes, and went to the bathroom.

About a half-hour later, I was still dozing in my bath when I heard someone knocking on the door. I lingered since I wasn't expecting visitors before yelling loudly, standing in my tub:

– Who's there?

– Open up, it's me, said a manly voice, which was not unfamiliar to me, although, in my disconnected mood, I could hardly put a face on it.

I quickly put my bathrobe on and scurried towards the door, wiping the wetness off my body. I noticed that the unexpected visitor's voice had a strange accent. So it could only be my British neighbour, Mr Marmeduke, whom I had not yet seen, although it was unusual for him to knock on my door at night. But then, the voice came over again, this time in English:

– It's me, your good friend, Mr Bassam.

– I knew it was you, I said as I opened the door. I'm glad to see you again, yet I'm stunned. How did you get my address? Please, come in. How are you doing, Mr Abdullah?

The Indian limped in, apologising for the intrusion.

– If you're too busy, I will come back later. I don't like to bother you.

– No, you're not bothering. Let's drink a cup of tea. You're welcome.

I led him into the living room and urged him to rest while I changed my clothes in five minutes. I saw he was wearing a handgun beneath his belt; when he sat down, he removed it and placed it on the table. Was it heavy, or was it just to show it to me? I returned to the living room a few minutes later, refreshed and dressed lightly in cotton pants and a shirt, and asked him if he liked coffee or tea.

– Please, Mr Bassam, don't bother. I came merely to greet an old buddy and convey my heartfelt sympathies. I heard about what happened to your family and am very sad. Some of our men saw you in the cemetery this afternoon and indicated your house to me. So I came over to share your grief. It was a horrible crime, Mr Bassam, causing unnecessary suffering. Sheikh Mohamed Mashawir and the other brothers assigned me this difficult task. Please, accept our heartfelt condolences.

– Your honest compassion, Mr Abdullah, has touched me. Thank you a lot.

– Not at all. I just wanted you to know you're not alone in your grief. We've all been through similar situations. I'm unsure whether I told you about my hardship in Kashmir, where I lost my father, mother, wife, and children in a terrible and deadly conflict between Muslims and Hindus.

– No, I don't think you ever told me that.

– That's how I decided to join the Islamist Jamaat Party. I had never been a militant before, but when I found myself alone in the world after some fanatical Hindus set fire to the family house during the night while I was far away on business, I had no alternative but to grab firearms and join the Jamaat. Didn't

I have to avenge my family? Besides, there was nothing left for me to do but despair. I was working hard to support my family, and I used to travel for business throughout India, Pakistan, and Afghanistan. I wasn't wealthy but made a decent livelihood selling carpets and other handcrafted items for a prominent merchant in Karachi. I cherished two lovely children; my mother and father were still living with us, my wife adored me, and everything was fine. We were saving money to purchase a good property in town since we had just rented the house that caught fire. I would have been living peacefully with my family in Karachi by now; I may have saved enough money to establish my own company instead of travelling from country to country like a rabid hound, constantly with the dreadful death looming over my head or following behind like a shadow. But the ways of Providence are unfathomable, and I have accepted my fate. It's God's will, my brother! The Arabs say it's Mektub! I believe it is true.

There was a brief pause. Then, I excused myself and went to the kitchen, where I heated water and made tea. I returned with the tray, placed it on the table by the handgun, and sat in the second armchair facing the Indian.

(4)

I' m sorry, but there is no food. As you are aware, I have just returned from the capital and did not...
Abdullah cut me off abruptly:

– Never mind! I've already dined. (He took a breath.) I arrived too late. The scene was dreadful! The ordeal's indicting marks were dispersed over every street, every house, and every corner. They tormented them, raped women and girls in front of their fathers and spouses, and hacked off the latter's genitals when they resisted or killed them. Did you watch the TV news report? It was nothing in comparison to what we discovered when we arrived. - I didn't watch TV.

– I understand. After all, it's your family, your neighbours and your friends.

He took a sip of his tea. I offered him a cigarette, but he respectfully declined. I informed him that I had just become an unrelenting addict, smoking cigarettes as if it had always been my habit. I had finished the packet Suleiman Mughli had given me and purchased two more on my trip to 'Ouja. I lit my cigarette and said:

– It is somewhat soothing. In fact, what happened in this town blew me away. When I was crossing the main street, I noticed the massive damage that had flogged nearly all of the buildings. They had even broken into the bank despite its gate being specially secured. They most likely utilised powerful explosives. It would take a long time for us to repair and fix all of the damage done. But the loss of human lives was even worse. It's a tragedy beyond comprehension. Nothing could justify it.

– I also believe so. But it's the price of liberty, brother, and it's steep. (He took another pause, drank his tea, and then went to the point behind his unexpected visit:) - Why not join us?

– The question was surprising, even astounding, since I had not imagined myself strutting about like a boy scout with the Islamist Militia. I pondered. I don't want to anger this guy.

– I wish I could, but I can't. I apologise. Hassan is expecting me in the capital. We have a lot of work to do.

He didn't seem impressed.

– The Director of Security, you mean?

– Yes, I said, nodding.

Abdullah made a bored, if not contemptuous, wave with his hand. I immediately expressed my gratitude to Hassan:

– It was he who released me; I owe him my freedom.

My last sentence seemed to irritate the Indian.

– You are misguided, brother. You don't owe him your freedom.

I stared at him, stunned, awaiting an explanation, which he eventually gave after a little pause.

– Hassan isn't as important as you think, said Abdullah. I know a lot about him. You owe him nothing. You are now free because the omnipotent God is merciful to you.

I remained silent. He went on:

– My name is Abdullah, which means the slave of God, he said. But we are all God's slaves. He owns us, and we owe Him everything, including our lives. Thinking otherwise is not only incorrect but also blasphemous. Hassan's ex-brother-in-law, Mamdouh, the Minister of Interior, is now protecting the Director of Security. However, despite holding a high position in the government, Mamdouh remains very suspect. Before the Revolution, he also held a high-ranking position. There will be a reshuffle in the coming days or weeks. They may both lose their jobs. For the time being, the government maintains them for political reasons. They are needed as a facade to facilitate negotiations between the Islamic State and the European or American governments. We don't want the latter to support our enemy, the scoundrel. That's why Mamdouh and Hassan, known to have connections with Westerners, are kept in power. It won't be long before they get fired. I don't see them succeeding in their jobs. You need to be very careful. Don't trust them.

Alarm bells sounded in my mind.

– What you said has disturbed me. I assumed that the Emir trusted the Minister and the Director of Security. So, is that not the case anymore?

– No confidence, the Indian snapped. They just happened to be at the right place at the right time, but their good fortune will not last. We have a lot of information on them. Mamduh is a profligate and scandalous pig, as corrupt as a whore. As to his brother-in-law... (He came to a halt, stared at me for a long moment, then said:) Would you give me your word of honour that you will not repeat it to them or anyone in their entourage?

– Of course, you can trust me, Abdullah.

– Well, then, do learn that the pig is not a Muslim.

– What pig? Who are you talking about? Hassan?   The Indian's black eyes were shot with blood, and hatred washed over his face as he replied:

– Yes, Hassan. The pig is neither a Muslim, a Christian, a Jew, nor even a Buddhist since no religion condones what he did.

– I muttered nervously:

– Why? What did he do?

– Do you have no idea? Well, then, listen. The pig has just been sleeping with his stepmother! That is the most heinous sin I am aware of. It's like sleeping with your mother or sister.

He spat, splattering saliva over the cup of tea he was still holding in his hands.

– Oh! Oh, my God! Indignantly, I exclaimed. This can't be true. It's slanderous gossip. I know his family story. He'd never known his mother, and the stepmother was like a second mother to him. She raised him.

– No, interrupted Abdullah stubbornly. You know nothing, sorry! I've been in this country for a little over a year, and everything I told you came from a trustworthy source. Furthermore, that trustworthy individual is familiar with Hassan and his family because he is one of their neighbours.

– That's not a reason, I said, perplexed. He could be wrong. What if he's their neighbour? Is he a member of the same household as them? This is a malicious rumour. I'm sorry, but I don't believe it.

The Indian continued, unmoved and cold-hearted:

– Don't you trust us? Okay, then! You claim he's an orphan, and that lady is like his mother? Very good. You don't know the inside of a guy as well as I do. As soon as his father passed away, Hassan jumped on his stepmother, who was still young and beautiful, and slept with her as if she were her wife, the swine! He committed the great Haram! It's a tragedy, but it's not unthinkable. I know another pair in India, a brother and his sister, who lived together as husband and wife. They'd even had a kid. I assumed they were a happy and normal couple when I first saw them. Until an elderly man who had known the family since they left Calcutta told me their story, I had never considered the possibility of terrible incest. When their parents discovered their incest, they ran away and went to live in Bombay, where I met them. I was as shocked as you are now, and I never returned to see them again. I also know about another pair in Dhaka, but I haven't seen them: an uncle living maritally with his niece after his brother died. However, the girl escaped and reported the incident to the police. He had already committed suicide by the time they arrived. Isn't it just revolting? But what I tell you is true, even if it's never pleasant to talk about it.

I WAS STILL IN THE labyrinth when he departed, wondering into whose hands I had fallen and what type of wild monsters I was dealing with! I wobbled in the room, clogged and squeezed by a horrible sorrow, subject to a terrible sadness, unable to make sense of what had just happened to me and around me. The Indian, on the other hand, made it clear that the new administration was neither homogenous nor firmly formed on a consistent pattern. Significant disagreements exist among its members, and the fight for dominance is still in its early stages. Thus, I discovered that Mohamed Mashawir, the Chief of the Islamic Militia, is a powerful man with thousands of fanatics at his command. It was obvious that even the regular army, police, and National Guard feared this small force. The Afghans are undeniably ambitious. If he supports the Emir, he wants him to remove people like Hassan and Mamduh from their positions; hence, I assume he has a clear interest in smearing and discrediting his rivals. The Indian did not reveal his sources, but I thought the Afghan was most likely the primary source. Despite his nickname, which implies that he is a foreigner, the Afghan is a citizen of our country who has been hired to fight in Afghanistan as a professional Jihad mercenary. The fact that his family is wealthy made it even more exciting for him. He is the elder son of a well-known trader in the capital. When he was arrested and charged with gun smuggling and attempting to sow sedition, along with the gang who had followed him from Afghanistan, the best lawyers in the country competed fiercely to defend them. Hassan and Mamduh are unquestionably obstacles to such a man's rise to prominence. He has two essential things that will bring him fame or seal his fate: money and power. The sooner he gets rid of his rivals, the better. Apart from the Emir and the Scoundrel, I don't see another man capable of persevering in that ruthless, turbulent, and insidious struggle for power. The Islamic Militia, the third army in the nation (given there are already two battling each other), over which Mohamed Mashawir has noticeable supremacy, is unquestionably the formidable tool he would not hesitate to employ to achieve his goal.

Money is not an issue since he is reportedly a multimillionaire. I do not doubt that he is spreading false allegations about Hassan, and the Indian seems to believe him as if his words were the Koran! When he told me that highly dubious and scabrous story about Hassan's pretended lust, I noticed the parrot pointing out his nib. I don't dispute that such heinous perversions might occur, but why should they happen to Hassan in particular? The conversation with the Indian did not, as he claimed, soothe or console me; on the contrary, it intensified my melancholy and concerns. The country is no longer safe; it has become a death trap for all of us. If I want to live in peace, I must remove my archives. Who can guarantee that the militia will not storm my house and loot it? It would be my feast if they discovered what I was doing before their departure!

I got nothing by helping the King or the President who replaced him, and I have a hazy feeling that I will get nothing more by supporting the current dictatorship. I need to act before it's too late. If I could have placed the archives in my vehicle and driven securely beyond the area, I would have destroyed them that same night. But it was impossible with all those armed men roaming the streets. As a result, I waited until the morning.

AFTER MONTHS OF SCARY promiscuity, my first night at home was far from comfortable. I felt a little down, and my sleep was disturbed. I dreamed that I was racing through the streets of the capital, tattered and barefooted, while Hassan, the Afghan, the Indian, the Islamic Militia, and all the jail inmates were hounding me like a pack of wolves, shouting:

– Stop the Scoundrel! Catch him! He must be beheaded!

I shouted back to them without stopping my run:

– I'm not the Scoundrel! This is a mistake! I am Bassam, your friend Bassam.

But my protest was in vain. They continued to pursue me, threatening to decapitate me:

– We'll get you, wicked Scoundrel! Murderer! We'll kill you. Stop. Come back.

I was naked, but a little object wrapped in a white towel was in my palm. I had a firm grasp on it. I turned to look at my pursuers and extended my hand. The little creature in my hand palpitated and soared into the air. It was my canary.

I awoke sweating profusely and simmering like a water kettle. Flustered and bleary-eyed, I rushed to the bathroom and placed my head underwater. When I was refreshed, I thanked God because it had all been a nightmare. What if that horrible dream materialised? What if I were to face such a horde of people, whom I would be the one to lancinate, throw down, and slaughter?

I chose not to worry about it and went to the kitchen to make a nice cup of black coffee, which I drank while smoking two cigarettes. Then I rummaged under my bed and took out the hatbox containing my secret archives. When I found them, I thanked God for a second time. I checked, and they seemed to be intact. Either Dalila or Mum - maybe both - saw them. It seemed doubtful that they did not sweep the dust beneath the bed since they were the only ones who had access to the unit throughout my extended vacation in prison. They would have had no idea what was inside if they had opened the package. I had hidden the secret archives behind a pile of old magazines and newspapers. They would have thought it was just a harmless parcel.

Naive women! How could they anticipate or believe that the whole nation, let alone foreign spies, would pay any amount to get these priceless secret documents? It's a treasure, a true data bank, and a massive computer capable of competing with the most advanced and diligent intelligence agencies! Competing? You've got to be kidding, Mister Bassam! You are fully aware that your archives outnumber any computer's incredible memory! Take, for example, Samir, who had no notion of what was happening in 'Ouja until he came in with great fanfare. He was probably not even born when you began accumulating and storing knowledge on every soul and event in the village and its environs until your archives grew to become 'Ouja's true, unique, and unmatched memory. Even if everyone forgets what happened in a particular year, you can remind them of those joyful or painful days.

I dressed properly and grabbed the heavy box intending to go and burn its contents in the fields beyond the hamlet. But then something unexpected occurred.

(5)

– YOU'RE MAKING A SERIOUS mistake!

– Eh?!

I came to a complete halt in the middle of the room while pulling the box toward the corridor.

– Where are you going?

Standing at the same spot, I turned around numerous times, but there was no foreign presence in the room. I thought it was one of my crazy angels nosing into my business again. That wouldn't be the first time.

– Who's speaking to me?

– Leave that box in peace, the mysterious voice said. Why do you want to get rid of it?

– Whoever you are, this is none of your business, I replied.

– Be responsible, Bassam. You're an adult, aren't you? You're not a coward. So, don't lose your nerve over such trivial matters. What happened to you? Are you scared of your actions?

– Who... Who... arrrrrr.... you? I shouted nervously.

– Don't shout, son. Be a gentleman. I am your father.

I was startled when I thought I recognised the mysterious voice:

– Dad?

– Yes, young man. I'm here to guide you before you lose your-self.

I was silent for a few seconds. Fortunately, it was early morn-ing. The light in the room was still dim. But I couldn't see the face of my father. I didn't know what to do. Finally, I tried to say something, gathering my confidence with both hands.

– But I don't see you, Dad. Where are you?

– You can't see me, son. I'm communicating from the other side. Don't be a fool. You have to keep your archives.

I've gotten over my astonishment.

– But, Daddy, you know nothing of what's happening here, I said. You've been absent for a long time. The country has gone insane, and we are in a dramatic situation.

– The country is none of your concern, boy. You aren't going to pretend you're another saviour, are you? There are too many already, and they are all charlatans with the same goal: snatch-ing power to lay their hands on the people's riches. An ignorant people who they can easily control and enslave to their whims. You are not to blame for their disaster. Please stay away from it. The archives you planned to destroy are no longer yours. It is our heritage; it belongs to the future as much as it does to the past. You have no right to squander the past or the future. Your past actions and records are your memories, and your memories are your eyes, kid. If you want to go blind, burn your memories. A man without a past is a man without a future.

With a prickling sensation, I peered dizzily at the big hatbox that had served as my archives for years.

– Instead of destroying it, hide the box in a safe place. If you're worried, never allow yourself to waste it because you'll regret it bitterly later, the voice continued. It would be the same as destroying yourself if you ruined your archives, son. Do you only remember the contents of those documents? Why don't you go over them again to refresh your memory? Now that I've warned you, I wish you the best of luck, son. Take care!

I fiddled in the room for a minute or two, unable to understand what had occurred. Was I talking with my father or to myself? Even though the invisible angels often addressed me, I recognised my dad's distinctive voice with piercing, pitched intonations and unfolded placidity. I couldn't possibly mistake it for another. Despite my flaws, my well-trained ear can tell an authentic voice from a sloppy counterfeit. I was so excited and suddenly motivated that I rushed to open the hatbox while kneeling on the carpet. It was the early morning of my second day in 'Ouja—a calm morning with a clear sky and a bronze light streaming through the glass of my window. A morning like many others I'd seen in this same location, but with something extra, something strange and unusual, which was still a mystery to me.

I rummaged through the box, clearing the old newspapers and magazines that concealed the archives. With the dust and even the spiderweb that had weaved its threads in the corners of the box, which I had to clean out with a wet sponge, it was not an easy chore. Nevertheless, I lit a cigarette and accessed the archives containing as many files as the alphabet. Then, and only then, did it occur to me that my archives did not deserve to be destroyed.

Really! My father is wise! My archives contained firsthand information on the people of 'Ouja, their origins, family trees, names, households, properties, businesses, behaviour, and religion, and I did not omit the geography, the history, and the economy of the village, its potentialities, its traditions, heroes, legends, and so on. In short, my work is a comprehensive study that unquestionably deserves to be labelled scientific. My excellent exploration will enchant and ravish historians and sociologists. I have noticed even trivial details in my notes. I had, for example, depicted the number of hens, cows, sheep, or goats such or such person owned, and when possible, their sizes, weights (approximately sometimes, but often with precision - that is, after a conscientious enquiry), their colours, food, distinctive marks such as the length of their legs, the tint of their muzzles, the shape of their beaks, and any birth trait, without forgetting their sexual life of course. Before writing about all this, I had spent hours and hours researching and reexamining each characteristic and category. It occurs to me now that many authors and researchers should crave this work and wish to have at least half my sense of observation, although, unlike them, I did not gather my notes to make them known to the general public, but rather to keep them hidden from prying eyes. These are terrible secrets that are critical to the survival of my village. (Also, who knows? If the people of 'Ouja seek political independence in the future, they will have a basis for doing so: A History for the Independent State of 'Ouja that goes back 3000 years before Christ and even to the Stone Age.

I also counted and recorded the number of stones and bricks that comprised the walls of certain renowned structures, such as the Mayor's House or the party cell. If only I had enough time, I would have counted the amount of gravel and stones in the streets and the number of leaves on the trees, the birds, and even the stars. Indeed, my archives turned out to be a veritable encyclopaedia of 'Ouja, the only one in the country as far as I know. As a result, it is not surprising that many spies want to see this little wonder of learning.

SITTING ON THE CARPET, smoking cigarettes and sipping coffee, I leafed through the files of my incredible archives, remembering men, animals, things, and events that were no longer alive. That's when the idea occurred to me, and I wondered why I hadn't thought of it earlier.

I need a computer, a clever machine like Samir, capable of keeping these archives safe and secure for a long time. It is useful whenever I need to consult it or refresh my memory, aside from the fact that a USB flash is much easier to handle and conceal than a large stack of papers. I don't need a big desktop computer; a laptop will do the job. I can locate the right stuff in a supermarket. It was almost midday, and the archives would stay in peril until I went to the capital and bought the needed computer. First, I had to find a secure place like a secret closet, a cellar, or... or... Then I remembered the attic on the roof, which I used for storing old things. If ever the militia or any hostile force or agents stormed my apartment, it is unlikely that they would also search the attic. I had piled up piles of old furniture between its small walls. Some because I am a grand sentimental, and others because I couldn't sell. Who would buy a ripped-up armchair, a rusted iron table, or a broken-legged chair? My prized hat box would go unnoticed among the dusty crates, heaps of old newspapers, and the rest of that pathetic hocus-pocus. I am still determining how long I'll be in the capital, so I had to get everything in order at home before driving to the city. The Director of Security, his sister, and perhaps, the Medal of National Merit are all waiting for me.

After the ordeal of incarceration and the terrible deaths of my relatives, I am a kind of hero since all victims are called "martyrs" and "heroes" in this country. I am more heroic than Hamda La'war, who mysteriously vanished, for he wasn't seen in his office or the cemetery. I had also noted that the party's cell was as black as coal. The rebels, or terrorists, or whoever they were, had set fire to Hamda La'war's Party's cell, where he used to govern the town as if it were his damned ancestors' property! He was unquestionably the most powerful man in 'Ouja. The former Mayor, whom he ousted and took over, the chief of the police, and the commander of the National Guard were all under his protective nuclear umbrella. He could get them a promotion and a better salary if he were satisfied or ruin their careers if he wasn't.

I GRABBED THE HAT BOX back into my arms, opened the apartment door, and began climbing the staircase. On the way, I ran across Mr Marmeduke, the British schoolmaster whose flat was next to mine. He is now an elderly retiree who lives alone with his dog following the loss of his wife. He had visited our country under British rule and fallen in love with it. He had worked at several schools before settling in this peaceful village. Mr Marmeduke could leave when the British troops left the country but preferred to stay.

The independent Education Ministry had renewed Marmeduke's contract with several other compatriots. He is still strong, with a ruddy face, two blue eyes, a protruding nose, a large mouth, and a benign smile that never leaves his face like the Jocund. His forehead is wide and has deep wrinkles crossing it. However, when I met him on the stairwell, he was not smiling, and I believe it was the first time in years that I did not see the Mona Lisa pointing out from the corner of his mouth.

Before I paused to greet him, his rubicund Spaniel ran towards me, yapping, yelping, wagging his tail, and licking my shoes with clear delight. But, of course, I was not surprised by such a warm welcome because I used to have tea with his master on occasion, and on these occasions, I never forgot the dog. And he had probably wondered where all those little delicacies I used to give him had gone during the long months of my absence!

The old schoolmaster appeared depressed and dismal. His glistening blue eyes revealed more than he wanted to.

– I am delighted to see you again, Mr Bassam, and I am deeply sorry for your losses. My heartfelt condolences on the deaths of your mother and your fiancée.

We exchanged handshakes, and I thanked him. I placed the box on the step and noticed right away that he was inquisitive about its contents, though he was too courteous to ask. To avoid any unintended consequences from a misplaced indiscretion or misunderstanding, I hastened to explain:

– These are old family papers that my mother will no longer need. I will store them in the attic until I see what to do with them.

– I understand, Marmeduke said. We lost a very kind woman, sadly! I hadn't seen her in nearly a month, and she wasn't alone; the young lady was with her. When I inquired about you, they stated that the lawyer was attempting to gain your conditional release. I see that he has finally succeeded. I am as pleased for you as I am sorry for them.

I didn't want to inform him that the lawyer accomplished nothing to get me released because it would have been a pointless conversation.

– Thank you, Mr Marmeduke. The lawyer is capable; I would have moulded in jail without his assistance. Mr Aroussi is still there.

Once again, I have spoken more than necessary, despite my desire to keep the conversation brief! Marmeduke, who had learned to speak Arabic, wished to know more. He had likely met Mr Aroussi, but he had also gotten used to hearing about the bank during our tea breaks. So he inquired:

– I heard some gossip, but I wonder if it's true. What exactly are his charges?

– I'm not sure, either. I believe he is charged with illegal dealing in foreign currencies.

– Really? That's what I heard as well. It seems absurd to me. Bankers' entire business revolves around interacting with foreign countries and currencies. Isn't this more of a political issue? Something faked by his enemies to bring him down?

– Perhaps, Mr Marmeduke, perhaps! We'll see the end of it in the next days, won't we? I'm sorry, but I won't be able to keep you much longer.

– I kneeled to get my box. Good day, Mr Marmeduke. I'll see you later.

We parted.

An hour later, after I had hidden my box in the attic beneath a pile of old magazines, I finished shaving and was about to leave the flat. I heard a soft knock on the door. I assumed it was the Indian again, and I resolved to get rid of him right away. I wanted to avoid hearing his pretentious homilies and sermons again and wasn't interested in joining the Islamic Militia. I answered the door, expecting to see the Indian, but instead, it was Mr Marmeduke standing before me, alone. The Jocund was smiling.

(6)

– I APOLOGISE FOR BOTHERING you, said Marmeduke. Do you have five minutes?

– Please come in.

He appeared to have something essential to communicate. He would not have disturbed me for a social chat. He followed me into the living room. I offered to sit, but he declined, saying, "I won't stay."

– We can sit down and talk. There is no rush. I was going shopping.

– I'm in trouble, he said. All I need is to talk to someone I trust. With all those strangers on the streets, you get it. I've never seen such an armada in such a small town. He flopped in the armchair. I sat motionless in front of him. After a little pause, I asked him:

– Are you afraid?

– Afraid? No, no. I've been in 'Ouja for about ten years, and everyone knows who I am. Mr Bassam, I'm not scared; I'm worried. It's not just because of the slaughter but also because of what I recently learned from a reliable source in the South.

That was intriguing to hear. For now, the South is a strange land, and I am very anxious about its news. I offered Mr Marmeduke a cigarette and lit another for myself, although I knew he was a pipe smoker. He didn't miss the strange new habit that has altered my behaviour. He said:

– I see you're smoking now!

– Yes, thanks to the jail! I replied with a smile.

His face became sad again as he puffed the smoke from his nostrils.

– The situation could be more transparent, could it not? Of course, you know what they're saying after three days of silence.

I nodded quietly.

– Yesterday, I drove to the neighbouring town, where I know some friends, he continued. We discussed it, and they all seemed convinced that the... um... Scoundrel... well, you know who I mean, will lose the war. So, what he did in 'Ouja - if he did it - was more of a show of despair than an attempt to seize power by sowing terror.

He stopped again. As I remained silent, he continued:

– However, as you know, I have some acquaintances in the South. Didn't I already tell you about David?

– Yes, you did. He's the oil engineer married to your wife's niece.

– Precisely. I called David, and guess what.

I had no idea. So I sat motionless, waiting for the rest.

– Well, he continued, even though we couldn't talk freely on the phone, David made me understand without saying it plainly that... um... the former president may not be the culprit. Indeed, David could be mistaken, but it's unlikely, for he knows where the scoundrel's troops are based. And most of all, it is unnecessary to mention that Islamists surrounded them and blocked the roads because they had taken control of several villages and towns. So how could terrorists under the scoundrel's leadership possibly move freely and reach 'Ouja, which is far from their southern location? It's true that they have a significant advantage. Their aircraft is operational, and they control the entire oil industry. But then, if they wanted to bombard 'Ouja, it would have been much easier to launch a raid and then justify it with a concentration of enemy troops or something else. In any case, David and his colleagues would have noticed if the scoundrel's troops had relocated to the north, or at least some of them. Yet, this isn't the case. Otherwise, the assailants would not have come from the desert.

I was dumbfounded and confused. But I did not utter a word.

– I'm afraid the thing is more complicated than it appears, Marmeduke said after a little pause. You know that many Westerners live and work in the South. Most are British, French and Americans, sometimes with their partners and children. Western governments have not interfered so far and will not interfere as long as the oil business stays unharmed. But how long will this condition last? Furthermore, there will be global reactions to what happened in 'Ouja. The American warships are already moored in the bay, according to David.

I dared to ask:

– Will there be an intervention?

– David didn't say anything, but it should be expected, soon or late, if oil transportation is threatened or halted, and the fighters continue to slaughter civilians as they did in this town.

– I thought there was a blockade, though.

– No, that's a rumour. Our ex-"Beloved President" priority is continuing oil production and exportation. He no longer controls the capital but still has a strategic asset: oil. (Pause). That's a damn good leverage in this conflict. I am not optimistic, though. I'm curious what the ex-"beloved President" will do if he believes there is no prospect for him to cross the desert and re-conquer the country. The Islamists are powerful, well-organised, and settling in for a lengthy reign. If the Scoundrel loses his nerve, he can blow up the wells and the entire oil infrastructure. Then, for a long time, we will bid farewell to peace.

– How could he lose his cool? Westerners are said to back him.

– They did that when he was in charge because he promised reforms. But he lied to them and his people. So, it's different now. They will not help him. A man in despair is neither sensible nor clever. The Westerners had tuned up for many years with the former king, who was very conservative, although less fanatical than the present government. However, ideology may become a minor subject of discord if crucial Western interests are guaranteed. The question that needs an answer is: how much disposed is the current government of the Islamic State to give those required guarantees? The former "Beloved President" is no longer trustworthy. The controversy over the lurid trafficking of white women had done nothing to improve his image. The press is reporting on his probable ties to the international Mafia. All of this isn't very tidy or clean. Nonetheless, unlike the local media, no one media outlet in Europe referred to him as the 'butcher' of 'Ouja. Perhaps they will in the coming days, but there has been no evidence of his involvement thus far, despite what the Islamists claim.

He paused. We could hear an ambulant merchant shouting and a bicycle ringing through the open window of the sitting room. The terrifying tragedy gradually succumbed to life; the village was wiping away its tears and striving to continue its daily fight for survival.

– Is that your opinion as a witness? I asked Marmeduke. Have you got any clue what the culprit's genuine identity is?

He pondered.

– I'm not sure. Both parties could have perpetrated the massacre for different reasons. But don't you believe the Islamists have a bigger interest in it? They badly need foreign neutrality to crush their local rival, and such an episode may discourage Western nations from providing help to the Scoundrel.

– Do you assume they allowed such a thing only to prevent the Scoundrel from getting Western support? I asked, surprised by such a thought that had not occurred to me. You already said he lied to them and lost credibility!

– Yes, he did. But the Scoundrel is nice compared to the Islamists, who seem dedicated to destroying the West, leaving Westerners no choice other than to convert to Islam or accept enslavement. Isn't it obvious, Mr Bassam? Furthermore, the country is in a state of chaos. We don't know who is leading. We don't know whether this new "Emir of the believers" is the real leader of the organisation or just a dummy. Then who is hiding behind the curtains and manipulating the actors on the stage? We cannot yet answer, Mr Bassam, but one thing is certain. Those who organised the massacre in 'Ouja are not the former president's men. The latter may be a dictator with many flaws, but he is not a political fool. He understands the importance of having Westerners on his side.

I was shocked.

– Mr Houssine, my father-in-law, told me the exact opposite. He was certain that one of the soldiers who attacked the town was a sub-officer in the Scoundrel's forces.

– Maybe he was. He could be a deserter who switched camps.

– Had they arrested him?

– No, unfortunately!

– This only proves one thing. Some men who participated in the massacre are very familiar with this village.

Such a possibility was not out of the question. The sub-officer could have been deployed to confuse. Nonetheless, I was reluctant to believe the new regime had orchestrated the slaughter. Why did they wait three days before announcing the news? Mr Marmeduke was also perplexed by the silence, and he agreed with me that since the men of the new regime had a clear interest in publicising the horrible genocide, it was both paradoxical and unwise for them to wait all that time before making it known to the public in the country. When we parted, we were both in the most perplexing maze.

I HAD PLANNED TO TAKE Zerga, my blue automobile, for a ride around the town. But Zerga was reticent to leave the damp shade of the parking after nearly six months of forced idleness. Its engine coughed and sneezed as I turned the ignition key, and that was all I got. So instead, I decided to go for a walk.

As I walked out, I saw the young Khaled and some of his friends gathered on the pavement in front of the building. They greeted me, and I asked if they could assist me. They couldn't say no, even if my captivity had ruined my reputation. They were ready to follow me back to the parking because they still recalled those beautiful days - oh, long gone!—when we used to attend football matches together.

I sat behind the wheel as they surrounded Zerga and pushed the old car forward. It coughed and sneezed again but was eventually forced to act as expected of a real automobile. I thanked them and hit the speed pedal with my foot. I went on a tour of the village to assess the extent of the devastation, stopping here and there to buy a fuel lamp and some food from the shopkeepers.

The mess of destruction astounded me. Some stores were broken; their doors were smashed, their glass windows were shattered, and their furniture was lacerated. I felt extremely sorry for Mehrez, the grocer whose business had been utterly wrecked.

– Look what those criminal sons of a bitch did, Mr Bassam, he groaned as I stopped by his shop. They ruined me; they destroyed my life. They left nothing safe after their passage!

I peered through the door. I didn't dare enter. So awful was the disaster! Mehrez's son, roughly nineteen years old, was attempting to bring order to the anarchic shop. It was upsetting to witness. The commodities were scattered across the floor and mounded in an unbelievable jam. The sugar melted with olive oil and rice, pepper with salt and flour, coffee with spaghetti and marmalade, soaps with shattered bottles of various liquids, and the aggressors had even defecated on the counter. It was carnage.

– They didn't just steal money, Mr Bassam. They rampaged like beasts. This is insane! This is inhumane! Simply inhumane!

Meanwhile, his barber neighbour, Mustapha, had joined us, and upon hearing this complaint, he commented:

– Consider yourself lucky since they didn't kill you!

– Would they hesitate if I had been in the shop? No, Mustapha. They wouldn't. Those sons of a bitch are monsters who cut babies' throats. I envy Mr Bassam, for he was safe in prison.

– Don't be stupid, said the barber. You just lost money and goods, and they can be replaced. But he lost his mother. How, for God's sake, will he ever be able to replace her? Don't you have any brains, Mehrez?

– Yes, I know, the grocer said. I'm sorry, Mr Bassam. Please accept my heartfelt apologies and sincere condolences.

Before I could respond, Mustapha quickly added:

– And Miss Dalila, his fiancée, may Allah be merciful to both.

The two men then hugged me, and I thanked them. Mehrez commented after a pause:

– I am utterly sorry, Mr Bassam. With all the dead we had buried, I can no longer remember who passed and who survived. I'm even more surprised now when I encounter someone I believe dead! It is not the staggering number of fatalities that strikes me, but rather the survivors. I'm still puzzled about why they stopped short of exterminating the entire town!

– They won't fail to exterminate us next time, the barber predicted sarcastically.

– They'll almost certainly start by cutting your throat, retorted the grocer, irritated. What's with your sinister raven croaking? Is it because they didn't go near your damned shop?

– You should thank God for sparing your life when half the village was slaughtered, Mustapha said. Instead, you're still whining about losing two bottles of mineral water and some soap! You should think about it, lad. They did not hurt me because the Quran protected my shop. Besides, I give to the poor and am not a miser!

Mehrez became enraged by this response and yelled, spraying us with saliva:

– You aren't a miser! What exactly do you mean? Who is the penny-pincher? Then you see nothing of this mess! Would you be happy if they slit my throat?

– It's not what I mean, the clumsy barber said. Why should I be happy? You are my brother. But I wouldn't have been surprised if they did. Many people were killed, but you can still do your business as if nothing had happened. Look at Mr Bassam; what did he get for all his trouble and losses? Nothing! The deaths of his mother and fiancée are far more devastating than all of your losses combined. That is why I believe you should consider yourself fortunate, and I am not mistaken.

Mustapha glanced at me, maybe looking for support, but I remained silent. Then Mehrez looked at me and said:

– Now is not the time for that kind of discussion. It would help if Mustapha showed more empathy for the suffering of others and spared us his recriminations.

The barber said, "Salam Alaykum," taking leave and walking away towards his store.

(7)

M ehrez shook his big head as if still reprobating his neighbour's lack of tact, and his chubby face, almost barred by a huge and long schnozzle, became pink as he said:

– I had been a trifle hard on him. I'm afraid he became enraged, but he's always dipping his muzzle in the wrong place! I wasn't complaining. I only expressed my anger at such an unnecessary mess, Mr Bassam. After all, the dead are our bigger family. I am not heartless. By Allah, your mother is also my mother! On the other hand, Mustapha is the last person who can lecture me on my behaviour. He didn't lose a single dime in the shambles. He is the lucky one, not you or me. Nonetheless, he dares to preach to me as if I were insensitively apathetic to the disaster that struck the entire town. But it wasn't just my shop that they destroyed; it was also the bank - your bank, Mr Bassam. All the money I had saved for years on your advice, all the money I now need to restart my business, has suddenly vanished. Fifffffff! Nothing was left to us, you understand?

They stole our money, ruined our businesses, raped women, and slaughtered everyone. They left us broke, devastated, and crushed. The culprit, scoundrel or not, is still alive, and no one will reimburse us.

He burst into tears. The sight of this strong man sobbing on the threshold of his wrecked shop, like an orphan child, depressed me to no end. I attempted to calm him down.

– Don't let hopelessness take over your mind, Mehrez. This is God's will. Furthermore, this is not the first disaster to strike the country. You may have some memories of other calamities, natural or man-made. The war for independence, for example, was bloody and cruel.

He brushed his tears away and answered:

– No, Mr Bassam, sorry, but it wasn't like this.

I looked at him dumbfounded. He went on:

The Britons killed or imprisoned the nationalists who fought and killed their soldiers. That's war. They were, after all, protecting themselves. We battled them because we desired independence. So it was kill or accept to be killed. Yet, the conflict had a sense of purpose for them or us. Now, look at what we've done with our independence! Is this a fair and legitimate struggle? Is it just, logical, and acceptable that we slay each other simply because we disagree on power-sharing or the regime kind? What about individuals who have no interest in politics? What about the women and children who have no idea who are the bastards controlling this horrible country? Is this our independence and sovereignty, Mr Bassam? Is this our freedom? Is this even what our religion teaches? If this is the case, I wish we stayed under British rule. Because if this is the free country for which so many martyrs have given their lives, then let them hang me for betraying such freedom - the freedom to accept enslavement to a local thug.

– I understand your outrage, Mehrez, but please calm down. The walls have ears.

I looked around, terrified, and noticed a lorry of the Islamic Militia passing by. It was carrying a dozen armed men. The coffee shop had opened on a street corner, and a few customers were sipping their drinks on the terrace. Other merchants and traders have opened their shops. Children had gathered to witness the wreckage, and the men yelled aggressively at them, threatening to beat them with a stick. They dispersed and ran down the street like a flock of scared birds.

– Let them hear, said the grocer. I mean that they hear me. What should I worry about? What would I lose more than I lost? Where were they when the terrorists massacred the village? They are now heroes and saviours! Hah! Who the hell are they? Where did they come from? Who invited them? Where are the police and the regular troops? They sent us a militia! We are tired of those inept rulers, their greed, corruption, lies, and hypocrisy, Mr Bassam. I express what I think, and if they want to jail me or kill me, let them do it. I'm not better than those who died.

– Calm down, Mehrez. You'll be reimbursed anyway.

– How? When? By whom? Who will ever care about us? They are busy fighting each other for a chair that they will not keep more than others kept before them, and they are making of their people, a people of victims, a flock of sheep that they lead to the slaughterhouse. And they call themselves leaders! Tfuh!

He spat on the ground. The poor man was in despair. He clung to my words, and his eyes twinkled.

– I believe you'll get help; be patient.

– I'll be patient. God will help us. We only expect help from Allah.

After a minute of silence, he asked:

– Will they compensate us for these damages?

– Perhaps not for everything, but whatever comes will be helpful.

– I trust you, Mr Bassam. But... He grinned, moving his head in a tired gesture. I no longer have faith in our rulers. If we exclude human lives, the value of what was lost in 'Ouja, could be estimated only in millions, not thousands. How would they fairly compensate everyone? Even if they give me a quarter of my losses, it won't fully recover my business. It's too sad! I'm done, my brother. Well done!

– Be faithful, Mehrez. Allah is great and generous, you know.

– Yes, he responded tiredly. Great and generous!

WHEN I LEFT MEHREZ, I got into my car to continue my explorative ride around the town. When I passed by the bank, I realised I had also lost my deposit and savings in the robbery. However, I was less worried than Mehrez. Unlike him, I was confident that the head office in the capital would compensate all 'Ouja customers and local staff. I pulled out near the pavement. A group of armed men were standing before the bank. Without turning off the ignition, I stared at the shredded iron bars of the main gate or what was left of it. It was dark. The explosion had undeniably destroyed a large portion of the lobby and caused an enormous gap in the wall. I could see the burned furniture, the blackened stones, the broken glass, and the papers dispersed on the floor until the doorway. I tried to imagine the state of my office and felt a terrible twinge in my stomach. Mehrez is right. I was safe in prison. Could I have stood passively watching my mother or Dalila being molested without reacting? I have no idea how I should have reacted. Even in my worst nightmares, such a scenario was unimaginable. Nonetheless, I would not have stood watching the massacre from my windows. It was almost daybreak when all of this occurred. I would have known or guessed. I don't have any guns at home, but my father's house still has the old hunting carbine adorning the wall of the sitting room. When I was a kid, I accompanied my father to hunting parties, and I had a lot of pleasure running behind the dog after the hares and birds that were shot down. I did not learn to shoot since I was too young to wield a rifle, and when I reached twenty, I was also exempted from military service because, as my father had retired, I was regarded as the family support. I had to work at the bank to help my parents. Therefore, I remained clueless about firearms. However, I believe it is not difficult to take a carbine and shoot down an aggressor, as I witnessed my father doing to hares and birds many years ago, provided I could find the munitions. If I happened to be in the house when they broke in, I believe I could have killed those monsters. That's what Abdullah, the Indian, expected me to do when he recommended I join their militia. That is also what Hassan emphasised when he encouraged me to take revenge. However, I must first find the murderers, and even if I did, would I be able to kill them cold-bloodedly? I am not violent and do not believe taking my enemy's life will provide me with any consolation.

I was lost in my thoughts, staring wistfully at the damaged bank, until one of the armed men approached the car and yelled:

– What are you waiting for? It's not a parking spot here, so leave.

His rough voice disturbed my reverie. I apologised.

– I'm sorry, young man. I was just thinking about the terrible events.

– You have nothing to do here. Now, please drive away.

The young militia's erratic mood, and the nervosity of his fingers manipulating the rifle and pointing its cannon to the street to indicate the way, heightened my irritation. I turned the wheel and restarted. It is never a good idea to get these militiamen worked up. They are far more ready to shoot than they are to converse. They would shoot in the air for any minor occurrence and for nothing, either to warn bystanders or simply for the thrill of it. If I hadn't assumed they were natives of this country, I would have believed they were an invading army. Their peculiar behaviour was not that of rescuers or sympathetic aiders but rather that of strangers who, if not tightly controlled by their commanders, would have likely gone on the rampage. I was surprised to see them occupying half of the coffee-shop terrace chairs, playing cards and beaming as if nothing had occurred. It was almost indecent, and the waiter's glum expression was eloquent in telling anyone silently that he was unhappy to serve them. I had planned to take a short break at the coffee shop, but when I saw what was going on, I changed my mind.

I made the decision to visit Hamda La'war at home because I was curious about his apparent absence and assumed that, if he was not himself among the dead, he had lost a family member. And because I was on my way to visit my mother's house, I would stop to inquire about Hamda.

I DROVE THROUGH THE dusty, tiny alleys of 'Ouja, battered by the September sun, whose rays were lounging on the white roofs and lingering on the swooping palms. Some elderly men in long robes and turbans sat in the shade beneath the walls of their homes, smoking cigarettes or nargileh and staring blankly out the windows while the ragged barefooted children played their innocuous games. The road was humpty dumpty, and the tarmac was in bad shape.

I had to drive carefully and cautiously to avoid the enormous holes, stones, and the little boys darting here and there without warning. Driving through the back streets of 'Ouja has always been difficult. I'm not sure why, despite the residents' repeated requests, the town council was never able to get these roads properly tarred and asphalted. It's as if they're speaking to deaf ears. Some would argue that the budget allotted to the Council's various projects is insufficient! In any case, it will never be enough. The Council's "various projects" mostly consist of the construction of big, luxurious villas for its perpetual members. Since Hamda La'war took over, nothing much has changed. He has always been an important member of the Council, if not the most important. Many said Hamda was the *De Facto* Council president, although he allowed another dummy to bear this honorific and pompous empty title for the sake of appearances. Finally, he decided to remove him and made sure that nobody could rival him in the council elections, which he won. Hamda was the only candidate for the position.

But if the Mayor and Chief of the Party's cell didn't care about the state of our streets, it's just as well because his new villa on the outskirts of the town was nearly finished. He'd be moving in shortly, so why should he care about the back streets? In any case, the people there are used to living with dusty, humpty-dumpty, muddy roads, mud in winter, and mosquitoes in summer! Thus, Hamda believes that they are not unhappy and that their complaints are merely irrational. If an unlucky, clumsy guy happens to bring up this matter in front of him, the sky will fall on his head. The grumbler will be so ridiculed and humiliated that he will be unable to look his neighbours in the eyes for days. Then Hamda would seize the opportunity to launch one of his famous recriminatory diatribes.

– Look at me, lad! Since you first met me, I've been residing on the same street amid the mud, filthy trash cans, mosquitoes, flies, and other pests. Did you ever see or hear me lamenting? Absolutely not. I do own a car, but I had to work hard to get it. Yes, I am building another house, but it is also the result of my labour. I am a worker, just like you and everyone else in this hamlet, and I will unquestionably prefer to live in a less filthy, more sanitary atmosphere. Despite the fact that I am wealthy enough to live in the capital, I will not forsake my hometown.

The funding allotted to this Council is insufficient to cover the costs of maintaining all our streets in good condition. We need to make painful choices because we have many projects. The main street is the town's facade, and it is important. If it is not looked after daily and regularly, we will lose face and a lot of money. Tourists will not visit our town. We now have a hotel. It will stay empty. Those who work at the hotel, men or women, may lose their jobs, and with them also, merchants and traders will be forced to close down due to a lack of customers. What should we do? Fixing all the backstreets or building more hotels t attract tourists? We also need them to see nice villas when they come, not filthy and poor backstreets. What to do about the mud? Well! Let it dry in the sun. Tourists never come in winter but in the summer. They won't see it. We must bring them from Europe, even if it means devoting our whole budget to the upkeep of the main street. I am sorry for the residents dwelling on the back streets, but we do have some priorities. We'll fix what we can in due time, provided we have the budget we are asking for. The local farmers and their workers simply do not grasp that their carriages and animals are the sources of a terrible waste of the taxpayer's money. We repaired a street today. On the morrow, we'll find it has returned to its previous state. It's pointless to continue. What should we do? Forbid the passage of animals and carriages? I warn you. That's what's going to happen if you ask me again to fix the back streets. We also have many other projects. The sanitary structure is deteriorating. We'll experience a shitstorm next winter if we don't fix the gutters and drains. Don't laugh, lads; isn't it your shit? Some of those jerks now appear to assume that I am using the Council's budget to build my own house! Oh, my goodness! If it is a joke, it is bad enough! And if it is not, I warn you. I will sue anyone who accuses me of dilapidating public funds. They don't say it directly to my face because they're shitting cowards, but

I know what they're muttering in the dark corners. I got every word they said. I have ears and eyes. Stop talking! I'm not referring to you, morons! You are members of the Council, and you are just as accountable as I am. I'm referring to those jerks who should be aware that I am wealthy and wealthy enough to build six houses if so is my desire. I don't pick in your pockets. I've made no money from working at the cell or the Council. Allah is my witness! I am a God-fearing man. What did my political responsibilities bring me but stress and animosity? Do you believe I am emotionally invested in these posts? If I had the option, I would not stay for another hour. But the people of 'Ouja want me here, at the head of their Party's cell and their Council. What should I do? Furthermore, I am well acquainted with the major party leaders. I appreciate their support. I wasn't decorated for nuts, but for my heroic deeds as a nationalist militant, you know. My home, my family, and everything in my life is the Party and the Council. Those who believe otherwise should now raise their hands and speak up. I'd want to know what they have in their hearts.

Nobody would raise a hand, move, breathe, or utter a single word unless it was to launch a panegyric speech extolling Hamda La'war's qualities and long-standing dedication to his fellow citizens and the entire nation.

HAMDA WAS NOT AT HOME when I arrived. His wife informed me that he had left after the last coup.

– Gone away? You don't mean he is...?

I did not complete the question. But the woman anticipated:

– No, he isn't dead. He went off well before that.

Perplexed, I asked again:

– But where?

She lingered, unsure. I could see her struggling in a predicament. Would she or wouldn't she say? What if I wasn't on their team? She couldn't be aware of my secret agreement with the

Director of Security. But, on the other hand, I have no idea what she thought of me.

She was standing in the doorway, her face half-muffled in a wide scarf, while one of her children was clutching her long skirt firmly and yowling. She stooped to take him in her arms, and he stopped wailing. I saw his puffed little caterpillar face, saturated in tears, emerging from the shadows, which reminded me of his one-eyed father's odd facade.

– I don't know, she finally said.

She's lying, I thought.

– He never talks about his business at home.

– No problem, ma'am. I hope he and the rest of your family are safe.

– Thank you for your visit, she said. We're fine, Al- Hamdu Lillah!

She wanted to shorten the talk, so I didn't insist. I bid her goodnight and returned to my car.

While driving to my father's house, it occurred to me that Hamda could not have vanished without at least warning his wife or informing her of the location where he intended to seek refuge and how she would contact him. Without a doubt, the new regime went after him. I'm aware that the witch-hunt has started. Many former regime officials had been arrested and, following hasty sentences in improvised courts, sent either to jail or beheading execution. If Hamda was ever captured, I am sure he would be sentenced to death. Fortunately, whoever set fire to the party's cell inadvertently spared my life. I know Hamda had a list of his agents and informers in his office, and I wouldn't be surprised if he also had some reports in his drawers. The fire that destroyed the cell freed me of any suspicion... at least in my town.

I'm a new man in 'Ouja now. My past is as white as a winding sheet. I am a fish in the big sea, a newborn. The air and light of

'Ouja have become vital components of my metabolism, as have the muddy backstreets and the patient and sluggish residents, the palm trees, birds, animals, and stones. Of course, death and sorrow exist. But we must forget and deal with whatever comes our way. Yet, we also must learn to live with our wounds and the memory of our ordeal.

PART THREE

Dolce Vita

Chapter 9

Imbroglio

(1)

The trip lasted only a short time. I spent a week in the village idling and loafing, something I had never done before. I didn't notice the passage of time. I received a call from Hassan when the electricity and phone were fixed. It was not an unpleasant call in my frazzled and mournful state then.

He tried to console me by asking how I was doing. Although the scenario was not ideal, I said I was okay. The perpetrators were kind since they did not slaughter the entire community, something they could do perfectly. Then he asked if I planned to stay in 'Ouja for a long time. I explained that I was merely settling some critical matters before leaving and would only take three or four days. He said he had reserved a room for me at the Sheraton and notified the Minister of everything. I thanked him and the Minister for graciously caring for my humble person.

I hung up the phone and pondered for a few moments. I did not expect the events to go so far and so fast. Then, rethinking the situation, I became aware that I was trapped in an intricate imbroglio I had unintentionally provoked. But I hadn't wholly lied and couldn't be blamed for other people's stubbornness. First, I was convinced that the State owed me at least $13.500 million. Then, as I wanted to show how much I was attached to the fatherland, I said, "Patriotism is too flattering to discard even if it would cost me two $200 million." But, then, I don't know what devil pushed me to add, "Patriotism is too flattering to discard even if it would cost me two $200 million!" The last sentence was pure bragging. I did not mean it. Hassan was not supposed to take it seriously.

But as soon as his ears caught it, the sentence stuck to his mind like glue, and he became obsessed with the idea that the state owed me $200 million. He kept repeating it and pushing me to confirm. He was confident that it was the correct sum the government owed me. As the Director of National Security, he is better placed to know the truth. Could I oppose him? No, of course, I couldn't. Nor could I deny I said it. I felt he would have me killed if I did. So, I refrained. I'm not unwilling to receive the funds, though.

On the contrary, I've been working hard for fair compensation. Hassan knows what he's doing, and I would not ask him for any explanation. He'd ignore it. Who would argue with him? After all, I am flattered if a high-ranking administration official is persuaded that my skills are worth far more than I previously estimated.

I needed to prepare for the big day because I wanted to be ready for the meeting with the Minister. My return to the capital, which I intended to be noticeable this time, had to be successful. I couldn't feel loose and powerless or practically crushed as I had in the past. On the contrary, I somehow felt confident, perhaps even like a conqueror.

Nonetheless, my entrance into the capital was less well-received than I had hoped. I did not take offence at this minor failing, though, because I know the entire country is going through unique circumstances. Citizens would have undoubtedly welcomed the new mogul's arrival in times of peace. But, oh! I don't expect them to queue on the sidewalks to receive me like they used to do for the King, the President, and their most important guests. Still, they would have spotted my blue car, the intrepid Zerga, rumbling and horning merrily on the road.

In reality, the streets were less crowded than they used to be. Moreover, it wasn't night-time when I arrived but early afternoon. The shops and stores were open, and people were lazily sprawling on café terraces in the central plaza and in front of the cinema gates. Without the apparent presence of the armed troops at crossroads and crossings and in front of official buildings, one may mistake it for a typical metropolis. Of course, that was not the case, but people were apathetic. There was an overall sense of indifference as if the nation had already surrendered to the will of the new masters. That was odd, considering that everyone knew about the civil war continuing outside the capital.

What was going on beneath their noses was unimportant to them! After all, it isn't exactly new. They got so used to coups and counter-coups that it doesn't matter whether they are ruled by a king, a president, an emir, or even a baboon, as long as they can live in peace! Unfortunately, however, peace is still out of reach. But who knows? In any case, they are far and away the last to be asked about their opinion. Even if some are foolish enough to believe that their opinion still matters! But will they dare to express it and risk passing into posterity as martyrs and heroes? I know from personal experience that many of those martyrs and heroes are dozing off behind jail bars. However, with chaos erupting in the country occasionally, it is difficult to determine who is the martyr and who is the hero!

Indeed, the heroes of one dictatorship are the unlucky cowards and traitors of another! During the King's reign, I was a coward, fearing Hamda La'war's retaliation and thus doing more to protect myself than because I was convinced of their nonsense. And even though I was the victim of a ruthless plot during the scoundrel's reign, I continued to play the game. That is why I am casually becoming the hero of the current dictatorship. I'm about to be decorated, whereas my former Parti's boss, one-eyed Hamda, is humiliated and hunted by the police, the militia, half the army, and a hoard of other jihadis who want to behead him publicly. However, I hope this is the last, most stable, permanent system. I want to think so if I don't want to be hunted down like the unfortunate one-eyed former Parti's boss by the next putschists anxious to rid the country of traitors and other bloody arrivistes.

Like most natives in this country, I had never been allowed to freely and consciously choose the Party, the government, or the men worthy of my trust. The authorities don't care about our trust; it is not accepted as a decent currency in the stock exchange, and they may be correct if they don't need it to manage the country and accumulate deposits at offshore banks. I was born during the War of Independence and grew up under the King's rule. When I started working at the bank, I was assigned to the formidable chief of the Party's cell. He brought me to his office one day and told me flatly, "You're required to work for us, Bassam."

— It is a great honour for me, Mister Hamda, but I am already working for the bank.

That was my reply as a naive and shy young man at the time.

I spotted the one-eyed potentate's decaying teeth coloured by the stale tobacco he was smoking and his shiny face grinning atrociously like a mask. He eventually recovered, coughed slightly, and added:

— You little joker, Bassam. I've known you since you were a child, running barefoot through the backstreets of 'Ouja, and I know your father well. He's a nice guy, though a little... well... simple-minded, right? Otherwise, he would have been a welcome addition to the Party.

— Yes, sir, he is not very complicated.

I resisted responding to his implication, which was a low-level provocation, because, as far as I recall, I had never gone barefoot in the backstreets. My father was an elderly man who, unbeknownst to me, was nearing the end of his life. So I wasn't looking for a fight with the mighty Hamda. If he said I was barefoot, ragged, or starving, or that my father is a simpleton, or anything else, I had to admit it and be grateful that he even condescended to receive me in his office, which was the first official office I had ever entered; apart from the bank, which at the time, I did not know was state-owned. Mister Hamda represented the Party. The Party was the government, and the government was the King. Who was I to oppose or argue with him? A man who was recognised almost as a saint. For whatever he touched was blessed by the State. I was a mere bank clerk rookie starting a career, thanks to the blessing of the Party's boss. I had neither the means nor the energy to confront the cyclone's translucent and authoritative single eye, which incorporated the Party, the motherland, and the State.

As a result, when Hamda stated, "I need you to be my eye, son," I didn't dare to giggle. Nor did I ask him, 'Which one, sir?' even though the thought crossed my mind. Instead, I said, "Yes, Mister Hamda, I'll be your eye."

God knows it wasn't easy for me, but I couldn't act any other way because Hamda had methodically prepared his speech. And, before we got there, he lectured me on the virtues of the

Party and the advantages its good militants obtained, emphasising that one cannot be a true patriot unless one joins the ranks of the Party, which is our only hope of retaining our independence; and barely covering his threatening hints and allusions to my job at the bank as being entirely dependent on my attitude towards him and his Party.

It was easy for him to persuade me. I didn't want to lose the job I had worked so hard for, and I knew he could harm me if I refused to cooperate. So even though the idea of writing secret reports about my coworkers and fellow residents seemed odiously nasty and immoral, I entrenched the little satrap's authoritative discourse and behaved. If I had any scruples, I would hasten to defend my actions by the undeniable debt that every citizen of this country owes to the national Party that protects us from foreign greed rather than by my own weakness and helplessness. Anyway, because spying for the Party was regarded as a patriotic act that elevated me to the status of a national hero, like Hamda - I didn't know his full tale then - I became enthusiastic, if not passionate. Hamda La'war is most likely in the south with the Scoundrel, while I am in the capital, where I was treated like a gentleman. I'm sitting in my magnificent room on the sixth story of the Sheraton.

* * *

When I parked my car in the hotel's large parking lot, a porter appeared and carried my suitcase with a big smile on his swarthy face. I went with him to the lobby. The middle-aged man behind the reception desk asked if I had made a reservation. At this hotel, I saw that everyone was happy.

— My name is Bassam Bourasin. Do you mind checking whether you already have my name on file?

The man flipped through his registers before raising his head and saying:

— Yes, sir; you're welcome. It is a great pleasure to have you in our hotel, sir. Would you please sign the visitor's book?

I completed and signed the documents.

— Your luggage will be carried upstairs by the page. Your room number is 356. I wish you a pleasant stay with us, sir.

I thanked him and proceeded to the lift with the porter.

He opened the gate to my room, and I entered. He set the suitcase on a low carriage and drew the curtains. The light streamed into the tawny-walled room, revealing a lovely space to my eyes. The bed's sheets and blankets were flawlessly stretched, while the walls were adorned with modern art pictures. A large yellow carpet covered the floor, and the entire space exuded a salubrious neatness and a soothing silence.

I thanked the porter and gave him a tip. When he left, I went into the restroom. I'm still constantly overcome with diuretic urgency whenever I land in a new place! It may be the effect of climate change on my metabolism. I recall that the first thing I did as a new employee at 'Ouja Bank was to find the bathroom, and when I moved to my new flat, I had to unload my bladder as well. My first night in prison was also quite diuretic. I recollect earlier sojourns in several hotels of the capital, and strangely, the same reaction occurred everywhere; so, I assume that the activity of my bladder is mysteriously tied to my space tripping.

The bathroom's glowing state captivated me. I'll say it again: luminous! Everything within is bright, dazzling, beautiful, and almost embalmed. Even my face was mirrored on the glossy surface of the bathtub. It's wonderful! So wonderful! If I didn't know that the servants would gossip and make a fool of me, I would even live in the bathroom, eat and drink, write, and sleep in the bathroom. But taking me for an oddball would not improve my public image; it's the last thing I want. So, for the time being, I must focus on the following little details: I am no longer an unknown bank clerk working in a blackhole-village that no one has heard of, but rather a VIP of the new dictatorship, and even my village is now famous as a result of the massacre. Besides, if I believe the Director of Security, whom I have no reason to doubt. I am wealthy, wealthy enough to purchase the Sheraton and other big hotels as well.

However, I must admit - at least to myself - that when I was not as wealthy as I am now (I can't say I was destitute either), it never occurred to me to eat or sleep in a hotel bathroom. It would have shocked me just thinking about it. But now, precisely because I've become wealthy, I have strange and crazy thoughts! Am I becoming an eccentric rich man? These are most likely the infallible signs of affluence. Many millionaires are known to be vagabonds and weirdoes. So, I'm presumably suffering from their weird symptoms.

But I must restrain myself. I'm only getting started in my new millionaire career, and if I start it off with these wild antics, what will I not do in a month or a year?

* * *

To begin, I resolved to act as if nothing had changed in my life. I would get up at the same time every morning and have the same breakfast, primarily of eggs, milk, and coffee. I'd then head to my office. I'd take a lunch break at one p.m. and then return to the office. I'd pick a little restaurant where I wouldn't be spotted. I may have my lunches in the Sheraton's restaurant here, but I know it is pricey. The bill would be exorbitant. And, while I am not required to pay for anything, I do not wish to appear greedy because I am Hassan's - or, more appropriately, the State's - guest. Anyway, I've never been a glutton, and my long career at the bank taught me to be cautious with money, for unscrupulousness leads men nowhere but to their own demise.

As for the dress, I would keep it in my personal closet. My clothing is modest but functional, although I may need a different status. A businessman, as I am expected to be, should be well-dressed. I would undoubtedly encounter prominent people, and I remember what Hassan mentioned about their attire. That's why he purchased me the sophisticated outfit I'm still wearing. I cannot afford to travel to Paris, Rome, or London only to go shopping like the Minister, Mr Mamduh - at least not right now, because they have yet to pay their loan or at least a portion of it. I'm confident that Hassan will assist me in obtaining a respectable little sum as a pre-payment on the account, allowing me to live decently.

Meanwhile, since I am in the capital, I should contact my bank's headquarters, although I doubt they will refund me for the five months I spent in jail. I did not notify them of my unexpected absence, nor did Mr Aroussi. How would I do it? The two guys who knocked on my door convinced me I was on an official trip over a government invitation. Could I disobey? Moreover, I found my boss out there, preceding me. Then, whom was I supposed to notify of my absence?

At the headquarter, they are probably aware that Mr Aroussi is in jail; they could not be unaware of his detention because he was on his way to a meeting with the Chairman when he was arrested. As for me, I needed to be more important in the bank's structure. Who cares about a clerk? I've been ignored, ditched. I am confident that the Chairman is unaware of my wealth; he would not have forsaken me if he had been. I've never met him in person, but I did catch a glimpse of his plump pinkish face during a conference. Even then, I had no idea that the big tall man giving a short welcoming address in the Hilton's spacious reunions room was the Chairman of our bank. My over-excited bladder had precisely chosen that moment to summon me to the loo. What a calamity!

When I returned, the Chairman had already concluded his speech and left the room. Mr Aroussi and other high-ranking bank officers walked him to the hotel door. I mistook him for the Minister of Finance, but I was updated by a colleague. I felt ashamed of my clumsy attitude, but I doubt the Chairman noticed. Unfortunately, I know some envious colleagues may report it, if not directly to the Chairman, then to one of his subordinates. That was embarrassing. I tried, all the same, to stay in my chair for the remainder of the session, although the speakers bored me to death.

I didn't yawn or exhibit any signs of tiredness. Instead, when it was Mr Aroussi's turn to speak, the volcanic activity of my rebel bladder became so irresistibly pressing that I would have urinated in my trousers if I didn't literally rush forward, crossing the room like an arrow to reach the lavatory far off in the corridor before the flood.

* * *

My irrelevant behaviour did not go undetected by the lecturer at that time. To my dismay, Mr Aroussi lifted his head just as I was leaving the room, and it seems to me that he even halted and scowled at me while I had my hand on the doorknob. I scurried away, overcome by crushing guilt, and hurried towards the toilet.

Odd! When I got there, the bloody mechanism broke down! My bladder was entirely jammed because I was so choked by my guilt. I stood, legs apart, in front of the urinal for a long time, waiting for the stream, but nothing happened.

Meanwhile, as I struggled against my pain, a man entered the washroom, stood by my side, and relieved himself. Because he was much taller than me, I had the unpleasant sense that he was staring at me with blatant interest. On his way back to the door, he stood briefly in front of the glass to adjust his tie, but he remained looking at me sideways, increasing my nervousness. I flushed but didn't turn my head. I was sure he was asking himself some suggestive questions about the significance of my prolonged stay in the lavatory in that strange position if I wasn't doing what everyone else does in that situation. He even whistled an enigmatic melody from an old song while wagging his head and titillating in front of the glass. He was evidently pleased to see his face or purporting to communicate his cheerful mood while I was inwardly raging against my bladder. Finally, he condescended to leave, and only then did I irrigate the urinal.

Mr Aroussi was still speaking when I returned to the conference room. He locked his eyes on me so intensely that I thought he intended to pulverise me. So, with my tail between my legs, I sat awkwardly on my chair, no longer daring to look at him. I was expecting retaliation, but nothing occurred. My boss immediately forgot about the incident, but its memory has stayed with me.

Yet, I am still trying to figure out where Hassan intends to place me. If it is not at the Central Bank, then at the Ministry, I told myself. I should outline the plan of my grand project, as he requested. He wasn't kidding. Far from it, Hassan is a man who should be regarded seriously for every word he says.

My empathy is growing firm and persuasive.

"Make way for John Law… I'm coming!" I'm tempted to shout. Hip Hip! Hurray!

(2)

I am fortunate. I immediately discovered what I was missing to begin working actively on my project. After a decent shower and a honeyed snooze that afternoon, I left the hotel and wandered along the street, leaving my car, Zerga, sunbathing in the park. I spotted a bookshop whose glass case caught my eye, for it was selling various Islamic books. I came to a halt and looked at the titles and names of the authors, and I noticed that many were not Arabs. They were from India, Pakistan, Iran, and other countries whose original language was not Arabic. But the books were translated versions. I went into the bookstore and asked the storekeeper, a plump and short Asian with a long white dishdasha, whether he had anything on banking. Many Asian citizens have lived in our country for many years and have earned the right to work but not the right to become citizens. The man I mistook for an Indonesian or a Malaysian turned out to be a Chinese from Sin-kiang, where most of the people are Muslims. He spoke Arabic fluently, albeit with an accent. As he returned with a book with the pompous title 'Islamic Banking' and placed it on the counter before me, I asked him why the books about Islam he was selling were not originally written in Arabic but translated from other languages.

– This is because the most important Islamist thinkers are not Arabs, sir, he said with a smile.

– The most important? I asked, a little shocked.

– Yes, sir, he confirmed.

The answer struck me. Whether this is true or not, I have no idea. I bought the book, spoke briefly with the Chinese, and promised to return in a few days.

About a half-hour later, as I was crossing the lobby of my hotel and walking towards the lift, I heard my name called. I turned, and I saw Suleiman Mughli approaching, all smiles, stretching his arms like Christ on an illusory cross, and shouting:

– My dear Bassam! It's great to see you here... and most of all, as a free man. Ha Ha Ha!

Suleiman wore a splendid grey suit with a white shirt and a blue tie, and his black shoes shone on the carpets. He was the last person I expected to see at this hotel. He walked a few steps and, grabbing me by my shoulders, held me in his arms as if I were a buddy he hadn't seen in years. Then he recommended we go to the hotel's cafeteria for a drink. I told him I was busy and would only be with him for five minutes.

– Even less, he said airily.

So we crossed the lobby oppositely and entered a long corridor with closed doors aligned on each side. We turned left and strolled into another gallery illuminated by white neons until we reached a spacious hall with panelled-glass walls and saw people sitting hither and thither on stools, chairs, and sofas, chatting and drinking, and nobody seemed to notice us.

We proceeded to the counter and ordered two black coffees. Mughli searched his pockets for cigarettes, but anticipating what he wanted, I offered him one from my packet.

– No, he responded dismissively, these are useless to me. American mixed tobacco is my favourite. But what the hell! I thought you weren't a smoker.

– I am now as addicted as you, Mr Suleiman. The times are changing. I owe you.

– You don't mean it.

– Of course, I mean it. The packet you handed me was only the beginning. I've been smoking every day since then.

– Ah! But the intention was good. I'm sorry you didn't want more powerful stuff.

I ignored his drug allusion, but he wasn't waiting for an answer. He asked me:

– Did you see the others?

– What about the others? Who are you referring to?

– Your pals, lad. Your ex-colleagues.

I looked at him, bewildered, expecting some explanation, but he continued to smoke listlessly while sipping his coffee slowly. His eyes glittered and blinked as he turned his head towards the door. I followed his lead and looked at the door. To my amazement, I noticed three or four faces that were not wholly unfamiliar to me, and their appearance was so unexpected that I got disoriented for a moment, thinking I had returned to jail.

– Do you see them? Muttered the Mughli, pressing me.

Then it was true! I wasn't hallucinating. Mahmoud, the black guard, was leading Frankenstein, Zorro, and three other men, whom I assumed were all still in prison. They were strolling in a queue behind Mahmoud, hurrying towards an unknown destination. Because the cafeteria's translucent wall covered a large area, it was easy to see their movements from the counter.

– What exactly are they doing here? Where are they going?

– Never mind, he said; they're just doing their job.

– Working at the Sheraton?

– Yes, like you, at the library.

– This hotel is on the street, not in jail.

– The street? Mumbled the Mughli. It's not much different. Anyway, you should know that they send them on assignments to serve in hotels, hospitals, administrations, and so on any time they need help clearing out drains, washing dishes, fixing the roads, the pavement, the sidewalks, or anything else.

Then I remembered that some inmates used to go outside in the morning for specific tasks and return late in the afternoon. So the small group had vanished into the passageways without even noticing us.

– They are not after you, I wish! I turned to Mughli.

He laughed.

– Of course not. It's a coincidence, just like our meeting. (He paused for a time before adding,) Don't be afraid; I am free, just like you.

– I'm not afraid, Mr Mughli, I said. So, who are the others you were asking me about?

He lingered.

– I thought you saw them working in the garden, so I asked.

– Do you mean the same inmates?

He gave a nod.

– I was unaware of their presence at the Sheraton. In fact, I find it strange.

– You're right, he continued. Many strange things are happening now. I understand you are not from the capital, but you have the time to get a picture of the situation.

I'm not sure we were talking about the same things. To change the subject, I hastily added:

– I believe you have been released without trial. You have potent allies, Mr Suleiman.

He smiled at me and replied:

– As powerful as yours, Mr Bassam. We are both in the same case.

The comparison did not sit well with me. I was about to respond when he preceded me and asked:

– Aren't you waiting for Hassan?

– Yes, I do, said I.

– So do I.

– It's still early, he said, looking at his wristwatch. We have plenty of time; the business can wait.

– Business? Did I hear well? And with who else but the security director? It was exciting! But I didn't press him any more. He was probably lying, I reasoned, because I couldn't imagine the Director of Security flirting with a notorious member of the Mafia. What could they possibly talk about? What are their shared interests? Then I remembered that the Afghan, Hassan's rival, was trading guns with Suleiman before his detention. What if Hassan learned about the Afghan's intention to depose him and sought a powerful ally? Without a doubt, Suleiman was uniquely qualified for the task. That could explain his unexpected release.

The Mafioso wasn't talkative, and I didn't annoy him with inappropriate questions. We finished our coffee and walked through the crowded cafeteria and corridors until we arrived at the lobby. We shook hands and parted ways as he suddenly recalled a critical meeting he had omitted.

I entered the lift and pushed the button for the sixth floor. Once in my room, I started to organise my affairs. The room was outfitted with a TV, a radio, a phone, a small fridge, a table with a virgin notebook, which I now use to write, two armchairs, and two sofas.

I opened my luggage and began hanging my clothing on the wardrobe hooks. I stuffed my documents into the drawer and covered them with my pants. It's a miracle that I could keep my private and ultra-secret notes away from hostile hands while in prison, and it's just normal that I keep them away from prying eyes today. I also need to keep the present notes safe. I considered slipping them beneath the mattress or under the carpet but instantly changed my mind. I'm done if a zealous housekeeper decides to chase the dust under the bed or the rug. However, unless he or she is a trained spy, they are unlikely to snoop under my underwear. But I have an advantage. Everyone in the hotel believes me above suspicion because the Director of Security or one of his employees booked this room for me, emphasising my importance to the government. So, who would dare rummage into my drawers?

(3)

T hroughout the afternoon, I waited in vain for a call from Hassan. When it didn't happen, I assumed he was busy with the Mafioso, so I turned on the TV and relaxed on the bed in my shoes, watching an old film. I was tired and resolved not to take any unplanned steps. I couldn't leave the hotel for an extended period. When would Hassan decide to ring me? I have no idea and no mobile. I was just out of prison and almost out of touch with the new reality of the country to which I must adapt every day, every hour, every minute.

I started to feel a little hollow in my stomach around 8 p.m. Apart from a small sandwich, I hadn't eaten anything. So I decided to get ready for dinner.

* * *

The blue evening was weaving its dark mantle about the balcony. I turned on the lights and dressed in a white shirt, a silky tie, and a dinner jacket. It was unnecessary to change my trousers, but I polished my shoes; and after one last look at the glass, I turned out the light and left the room.

When I was in the lift, a couple of Europeans walked in at the third landing; then, in a fraction of a second before the iron gate closed, it appeared to me that the two shadows slinking in the corridor, of whom I had caught a glimpse, are pretty identical to Hassan and the Mughli from the backside. I would have run after them, but the couple blocked the way. The gate closed before I could move; because the couple was smiling and saying good evening to everyone, I smiled back and nodded. The two other people were Arabs who were chattering loudly and bragging about Spanish castles. They were well-turbaned and clad in the traditional dishdasha that trailed to their ankles.

– Eight centuries we dwelled there, and for all that era, Spain was ours, said the younger, who appeared to be returning from a trip to Spain.

– Not just Spain said the elderly man. We should have stayed in France, Italy, Greece, and other Western nations. The Arabs were the world's rulers. Those castles you visited in Spain were spreading the light of knowledge and progress at a time when the entire European continent was still plunged into the darkest ignorance. The brightest minds in Europe are aware of their debt to Muslims, but they are resentful.

– They wouldn't be who they are if they weren't, the young guy retorted.

The European couple remained deaf and quiet. That dubious outburst of rage ashamed me. It was not generous. What happened to kindness and hospitality? Suppose the couple understands Arabic. What would they think of these two jerks?

– Dogs, they're all disbelieving dogs and sons of b*tches, the old man continued. Look at the epidemics they're spreading, alcohol, drugs, free sex, immorality. It is a complete breakdown of values. Europe is a dog's dinner.

– When we lost the same values, we lost Spain, the young guy said.

– Look at these two...

But before the old man could add anything, we reached the ground, and the automatic gate opened. The two Europeans left, and I followed them across the lobby, which appeared more lively at that hour. A piece of sweat music was played on the piano. Several Arabs and foreigners were sitting on the sofas. The reception desk was crowded with arrivals, whose luggage was piled on the floor. The pages were busy, and the movement was febrile. The small exchange agency remained open, as did the other shops and stores selling newspapers and magazines, tobacco, English and French pocket-books, stamps and post-cards, cameras, films, small batteries, sports clothes and utensils, bath costumes, and various souvenirs, handcrafted goods, watches, spectacles, traditional robes and turbans, daggers, copper plates, artificial palm trees and plastic camels, luxurious pipes, colourful rugs, silver ash-tray... It was just like the market at home. I lingered outside the window shops since I wasn't in a rush, hoping to see Hassan and the Maffiosi emerge, but it was in vain.

Finally, tired of the noise and dazzled by the lights, I pushed forward and turned to the left, walking along the bright corridor until I reached the restaurant where customers were already eating.

A stout young man in an immaculate white jacket, black trousers, and bow tie greeted me at the door and inquired, "Are you alone, sir?"

As I confirmed, the butler asked me to follow him, which I did. In the dark light of the candelabras, the room was full of unfamiliar faces, busy eating and chatting. There were a few ladies. However, the majority of them appeared to be foreigners. The Arab women were appropriately muffled, disguised, and escorted by both children and husbands. The latter ate quietly or read the menu or a newspaper between courses to appear busy or important. They rarely address their wives and prefer to look elsewhere when not pretending to read.

* * *

I was seated at a table near the transparent glass wall. I could tell a native family from a foreigner not just by their clothing and appearance but also by their behaviour. The locals are more reticent or shy. They have a restraint about them that is visible not just in their stiff, slinking, or awkward manners but also in their austere, nearly shuttered looks. They'd eat silently, staring at the empty space like mute bazaar dolls. The foreigners, on the other hand, are jovial and chatty. Their behaviour is comfortable, their faces relaxed, and their eyes bright. Looking at them, one gets the impression that they are willing to converse casually with the first person who comes up to them. They are clearly not choked by the burden that crushes locals. Nothing, however, suggests that the war is approaching. For many of my fellow compatriots, the hotel's social life provides an escape from the daily routine.

As the evening grew dimmer and more electric bulbs were turned on, I could see the garden being invaded by waves of night and light pushing through the glass wall. The moon was rising over the buildings surrounding the hotel. It appeared to be gazing at me, like a featureless face still unfinished on a large painting. I saw a swimming pool in the garden's centre through the thick, entwined branches and the obscure leaves dancing in the chilling breeze. Around the pool, people sat on long chairs scattered beneath the trees, chatting or staring mutely at the dark water reflecting the moonshine.

As the butler walked away, wishing me a lovely evening, I noticed that the European couple who had been with me in the lift had moved to the table to my left. The lady caught my eye and smiled; I returned her grin. She was a middle-aged woman; tall, slim, well turned and sculpted, with a round face, clear-eyed, golden-haired, thin-mouthed, and her curls wrapped around her shoulders, and she seemed to be having a good time with that man who appeared to be her husband. He was much older, stout, broad-shouldered, white-haired, with a greying small moustache, a high forehead, two prominent eyes, and a nose half a banana long and curved. He didn't grin but looked at me listlessly as if I were part of the furniture or didn't exist. They were both dressed elegantly for the evening. He wore a well-cut blue suit with a grey tie over a silky white shirt, and she wore a long dashing and streaming black gown that highlighted her feminine qualities in abundance.

However, I didn't notice the couple right away because I was preoccupied with Hassan and the Mughli being together at the time, and God only knew what they were planning. Even when I sat down with the menu card in my hands, gazing listlessly now at the card, now at the garden, it took a while for me to notice the presence of the two Europeans. And it was the lady's mysterious, keen, hinting perfume that had already dizzied me in the lift, that was fondling my nostrils and wheedling me again so rapturously that it was just impossible for me to remain insensitively unaware of her presence; such a perfume caused me to turn my head involuntarily after the first moment of distraction, to seek the source of that magical invasion whose charming sweetness I could hardly ignore. Then I noticed the couple, and when our gazes connected, the lady grinned, causing a true ravage in my bosom. And while I returned her smile, I couldn't help but wonder why such a polite fairy was dining with that ancient astronaut when I was alone and ready to entertain her. But I instantly repressed that crazy thought, just as I had suppressed the strange yearning to settle down in the restroom. Obviously, my mood is pretty quirky and even a little unsociable at the moment, which is most certainly a result of my sudden wealth.

It takes an entire world to become "nouveau riche." It is more complex than one might imagine. In fact, it may be confusing if one's wealth is a little imaginary, hypothetically speculative and excessively exaggerated.

I have a lot of money. The Director of National Security himself recognised it. Yet, I don't see it. A little voice whispers into my ear: "Who is the millionaire who sees his money, Bassam? Money is today just digital abstractions in mind." That might be true if it does not imply that the invisible is useless, does it? You know what! This is tricky because being invisible does not mean being non-existent. We cannot see oxygen yet know it exists because we cannot survive without it. We cannot see the electromagnetic waves that transmit sounds and voices from an emitter to a receptor, yet what would our lives be like today if we did not have the telephone, the radio, the TV, etc.? Similarly, I recall being married once in the jail library, and while the witnesses are still living, my bride - alas! - has passed away. Allah have mercy on her soul! I don't see her, but she exists in the sky.

I am a widower, not a bachelor.

Take 'Ouja's imam and grand savant, Haj Mukhtar. He had married an invisible princess, and although she was from the Jin species, she had well introduced him to the fantastic realm of the unseen world. He has since socialised with Jin royals: princes, duchesses, barons, etc. When I inquired about him during my recent stay in the village, I was told that he had gained new powers because, following the death of his father-in-law, the Jinni King (which had nothing to do with the massacre; it had occurred some months before it), the princess was summoned to her dad's palace. She inherited her father's reign, and Haj Mukhtar became the King's consort of the jinni monarchy. This new status gave him a broader range of prerogatives. It kept him busy nearly all the time, although he had to be fair and make room in his agenda to the most urgent of 'Ouja's affairs. That included the Friday and the Eid prayers.

As King's consort and the father of the heir to the throne, he could no longer devote much time to the villagers and the patients who came from the farthest reaches of the country to seek his assistance and were thus frequently forced to wait a week and sometimes a month or two or more - I was told - until he returned from the invisible kingdom.

Everyone now knows that Haj Mukhtar has the ability to become invisible at will after the coronation of his wife as Queen of the Jin Kingdom. But this is only one of his new powers. Some of 'Ouja's residents, whom I consider reliable, claimed to have seen Haj Mukhtar flying above the roofs of the town like a giant bird before fading into space. When I inquired, I was told that on the night of the Islamist Coup, one of the villagers was passing by Haj Mukhtar's house after he had spent the evening playing dominoes in the coffee shop. Suddenly, the sky flashed, and the dark night glittered with dazzling coloured lights and whistling and buzzing sounds. As the man lifted his head, he noticed a strange object flapping above the roofs, hovering just above Haj Mukhtar's house. It wasn't an aeroplane, a helicopter or anything known. The man came to a complete halt, and even if he had wanted to continue walking, it would have been impossible because he was screwed in the street like a nail lodged into the pavement. Aside from his eyes, which continued to see, and his ears, which continued to hear, he felt his entire body become as immobile as a rock on the mountain.

Meanwhile, he reported, the strange object, which resembled a large saucer, sprouted bright lights that blinked and sparkled in the darkness with all the iridescent hues of a hundred rainbows. The zipping and whistling continued for a time he could not assess before silence regained the evening. Then, finally, a door opened in the centre of the saucer, and a dazzling yellow light was projected on the roof. The witness swore by Allah and the Prophet that he saw Haj Mukhtar standing straight on the top of his house, dressed in white. At the same time, a ladder descended slowly from the saucer. He climbed its steps until he reached the door of the aeroplane that was not an aeroplane and was engulfed inside. The gate closed, the saucer whistled and whizzed again, the lights gleamed and blinked with all their brilliant colours, and the strange thing went whirling and swirling in the air, moving higher and higher at incredible speed until it swooned and vanished behind the mountains, becoming a star among the stars. And it wasn't until the saucer was high in the sky that the man who watched Haj Mukhtar's incredible trip could recover and reclaim his freedom. He estimated the duration to be unknowable because his wristwatch still indicated the time when he left the coffee shop. It was as if he did not walk that distance from the coffee shop to Haj Mukhtar's house.

Since then, some locals became convinced that the Jins, prodded by Haj Mukhtar, had undoubtedly participated in the Islamist coup against the former president.

(4)

There was one sceptic among the people of 'Ouja who heard the account about Haj Mukthar's night flight in the saucer. Mr Houssine, Dalila's father, who had already heard the story several times, thought it prudent to remind me that the man who claimed to see Haj Mukhtar climbing into a flying saucer on the night of the coup is known as an inveterate hashish smoker. It's hardly impossible that he was so stoned that he couldn't tell a cock from a donkey!

– Why should the Jins use a machine to fly? Mr Houssine asked before adding wisely: Those who use planes and similar machines are the impotent men, who can neither cross an ocean in one second nor drink its water and turn it into a desert, which are the Jins' deeds, as you know.

I admitted that because they can fly like birds, live in the heart of the earth like worms and ants, build palaces and entire cities at the bottom of the seas, and perform other seemingly miraculous feats, a plane, a flying saucer, a ship, or a submarine are ostensibly useless to the Jins. Furthermore, those guys have no tracks at all. They can build cities and monuments, destroy others, live in peace, or drag huge, innumerable armies to clash in the most fantastic wars, making our Second World War look like a childish game without ever finding any visible evidence of it, even if it may happen right under our noses because we can't see or hear them if they don't want us to know. Those who are fortunate enough to learn about such events are few and far between, and Haj Mukhtar is one of them.

I won't deny that the thought of an army of Jins, led by Haj Mukhtar, taking part in the Islamist coup attracted me and seemed as appealing as it was incongruous. So why not? An alliance between the human species and the Jins might be immensely beneficial to both peoples. This is a reasonable assumption. Haj Mukhtar execrated the Scoundrel's reign and did not even try to hide his disdain. Naturally, equipped as he is by his vast knowledge of the occult and the paranormal sciences and strengthened by his kin association with the Jinn Kingdom, he fears nobody and could have changed Hamda La'war into a dog, a monkey, a donkey, or even a stone if he so desired.

Hamda did not approve of Haj Mukhtar's recent marriage to the Jin female because he was already married to Mrs Zubaida, Hamda's wife's sister. They were neither divorced nor separated. But he couldn't do anything about it other than mockingly repeating, "It's polygamy!" That happened when Haj Mukhtar told us about his marriage in the invisible realm. We were enjoying some new wine, offered to Hamda by a farmer, over a hearty dinner, as we used to do every Friday evening at the mayor's house. Haj Mukhtar questioned him, saying, "What's wrong with polygamy?"

– What's wrong? I'll tell you what's wrong. My wife and her sister are unhappy!

– That's it?

– Right. That's it!

Haj Mukhtar remained silent for a while. He downed another glass of wine and said:

– I am the Imam of 'Ouja, right?

– Yes, you are, said Hamda.

– When I told you wine and spirits are not sins in the Koran, did you believe me?

– You said no verse forbids alcoholic drinks as the Koran did for other acts, like eating pork, marrying his mother, sister, daughter, aunt, etc. So, yes, I read the Koran, and I believe you.

– How about polygamy, said Haj Mukhtar. Is it a sin?

Hamda remained silent, and the Imam went on:

– No, it is not. The prophet married several females, and so did his valorous companions. Do you think we are better than them?

– I don't think anything, said Hamda, but my wife and her sister are unhappy.

After a while, Haj Mukhtar avoided our Friday meeting. He was reported sick and confessed privately that his Jin wife did not approve of our nocturn bacchanals in Hamda's house. Hamda continued to trash him, stating to anybody who would listen that the old man was a charlatan who takes advantage of the government's tolerance and the populace's stupidity. After a long friendship, the two men became the village's biggest enemies. Haj Mukhtar had been barred from leading the faithful in daily prayers and could only do so on Fridays. He pretended he was too busy with Jin State affairs, but Hamda told me he fired him.

It could have been simpler, but the mayor imposed another condition. Henceforth, Haj Mukhtar was not allowed to write his own Friday sermon. It would be prepared for him in the Party's cell and printed out. He would only read it to the faithful without changing even a comma. That was the drop that killed the frog!

The old man erupted in rage, swamping and trampling Hamda La'war, the Mufti, and even the President of the republic!

Haj Mukhtar couldn't tolerate reading a copy of a formal speech devised in the capital by the Mufti and given to all mosques for the Eid prayer. How could he accept a sermon drafted under the supervision of the one-eyed Party's cell?

That was a 'Bid'a' (i.e. anti-tradition invention) and hence could lead a faithful to eternal damnation rotting in hell. Previously, under the King, the Imams had always freely delivered their sermons. Binding people with a single speech was not only uncomfortable to the spirit of freedom that Islam brought to the world, but it was also a sin, although not mentioned in the Koran, like spirits. Furthermore, the old man was irritated by the panegyric nonsense he was forced to read each Friday because he was certain that the President had prostituted the country and sold it off to Western powers for a golden retirement in Europe or some paradisial land the day he would be ousted.

However, the Westerners were not waiting for the Scoundrel to take over to buy the country from him if they ever wanted to buy it after leaving it. Their civilisation has spread all across the world. Our children read their books while learning about our traditional culture. Many people prefer to further their studies in Europe or the United States. Their diplomas are convincing for getting the most outstanding jobs anywhere, but ours are only an option for HR. Even though traditional customs are still a part of our lives, new-to-us technical objects and cultural symbols attack us. Aside from going to the mosque and fasting during Ramadan, what remains Arab-Islamic in our lives? Cars, computers, aeroplanes, telephones, and many other contemporary gadgets are all worldwide products of the West, so there is no longer a West or an East. What is the dividing line? Who can make the distinction?

But my next-door neighbour, Mr Marmeduke, who I assume is an unrepentant radical leftist, has a different viewpoint. He once told me that colonisation had not stopped. But, to my surprise, he added:

– If the soldiers and the colonial ruler had gone home, the Western-trained locals became the leaders, and some have dual citizenship, one foot in this country for grabbing power and one foot in Europe in case things turn sour. However, holding European citizenship is no guarantee against deviations. Neo-Imperialism needs lackeys and relays to maintain its grasp on the peoples of the Third World. Where will they look for them if not among the local elite of newly independent countries?"

Thus, if I had understood correctly, 'the neo-imperialism,' to use Marmeduke's term, was busy developing and educating our country's power elite even before independence! Isn't that sneaky? These coups and counter-coups were most likely taught to them by their instructors in Europe and America!

– If you want my opinion, Marmeduke said, it's pointless to teach the Arabs anything because most of them are dim.

– Dim? I protested. But this is like racist biases.

– Come on, Bassam! You can't say that to me. I've dedicated my life to educating your children to love and respect one another, while I was teaching them history, geography, letters, and the beautiful arts. So I am in a good position to pass judgement on these matters. This strange phenomenon, though, has piqued my interest. Your compatriots are brilliant students as long as they live in the West. But as soon as they set foot in their fatherland and are given some political responsibility, they forget everything they learned at our universities about respect for Reason, Freedom and Human Rights and resort to the cudgel and the chain to communicate with their people. How can you explain that?

I didn't explain it and did not answer the question. But if this is a local behaviour, what does the West, neo-imperialist or not, has to do with it? Westerners don't want to buy anything else from us besides oil or natural gas, and there's nothing more to sell unless we sell our souls. But who would purchase them? We should identify another customer who is neither from the West nor the East but has been a citizen of the world from its inception; that customer is none other than the Devil, and he would likely take care of any sad soul better than anybody else.

* * *

These thoughts came to me as I ate, and I'm unsure what triggered them. Was it the sight of this restaurant's eclectic crowd? Was it the attractive lady's smile, her perfume, the fact that I am newly affluent, or anything else? But in reality, It's none of my business whether lackeys or counter-lackeys head the country. I've already admitted that my mind got blocked when it comes to politics and refuses to add anything to its already clogged database. It becomes like the black screen of a computer that crashes and won't allow you to log in. Nonetheless, I am to be honoured as a National Hero soon. In that case, the source of such a prestigious award lies in my stock-exchange speculations rather than in my political theories of the zero and none.

Indeed, had it not been for my millions, I would have likely mildewed in jail for twenty years, as the shrink assumed. Hassan would never have thought of me as a potential brother-in-law. Why should he? And he would not have allowed me to visit my village after the disaster that killed my mother and fiancee. I understand that these are the advantages of the new rich, and I am determined to keep them warm.

Everyone in this hotel knew who I was, where I was from, and why I was there. The servants are very polite and helpful, and I had the distinction of receiving the manager at my table while dining. He's a tall, vaulted man with greying temples, a large wrinkled forehead, clear eyes, a hooked nose, a pursed mouth, and a strong chin. He is over fifty-five years old and is dressed in a well-tailored dark suit and a bow tie of the same colour. He arrived with the butler, who introduced him to me before skidding away almost stealthily. I had stopped eating out of respect for the newcomer, but he pleaded with me not to bother and to continue eating as if nothing had happened.

– I know you must be pretty busy right now, he said as I chewed laboriously on a piece of rough steak.

– Mmmmm... yep... mmm... that...

– But for nothing in the world would I pass up the chance to make a new friend, let alone when the new acquaintance is Mr Bassam Bourasin in person!

– Oooh! Ahem... Too much kind! I'm flattered.

– It is an honour, sir. I've been told you're dining alone, and I know such an event will not happen again. I'm sure you'll be busy with guests, customers, friends, and so on the following days.

– Ahemmmmm... Not improbable...

– As a result, I hastened to greet you personally.

– Thanks...

– Not at all, sir; I just wanted to ensure that everything was fine and that you're quite satisfied...

– Quite... thank you... satisfied.

– I can provide you with a suite, sir. We have superior rooms reserved for our most distinguished guests.

I had to cut him off before he became a pain in the ass. He was seriously irritating me.

– Sir, my bathroom is pretty satisfying. I don't want anything else. Thank you a lot.

In my hastiness to get rid of him, the word "bathroom" merely slipped out, albeit followed by an undisguised emotion. But the manager widened his eyes and asked:

– The restroom? Then, as if speaking to a child, he smiled and added: It's nothing, sir. Our suites have many excellent bathrooms, and you should - I propose, sir - look at them.

I shook my head firmly.

– Nope. I'm not changing my bathroom.

I don't know why I became obsessed with the bathroom. The manager looked at me with his mouth wide open. He was probably wondering if I was a guy or a toddler! I read in his eyes this muffled question: "Mr Bassam, how do you run your business being such a blockhead?"

The European lady seemed discreetly interested in my strange conversation with the manager. However, I'm not sure she could overhear us, not only because the restaurant was buzzing but also because the loudspeakers, well concealed in the ceilings and walls, were still distilling the undulating waves of a piano playing. I caught her look numerous times, and she seemed occasionally frustrated or bored because her friend continued to devour his food listlessly, without saying anything, as if the world had no constancy outside his dish, fork, and mouth. I almost thought she wasn't enjoying his company, which... is weird thinking that I quickly dismissed.

A group of uniformed officers dined together at the bottom of the restaurant. They were exuberant and boisterous. Though it was difficult to understand what they were saying in the general row, they talked loudly and laughed openly. I observed a little man in the middle of them who appeared to be their commander. He had a bald head and a swarthy face, and he seemed nearly splenetic because he didn't laugh at their jokes. The two turbaned fellows of the lift were also dining nearby and appeared to be engaged in discussing how the Arabs would reconquer Spain.

Mr Ali, the hotel manager, was not about to give up so simply; at least, not without one more desperate attempt to save the honour. He paused briefly before returning to the offensive with a new idea.

– Forget about the suite, Mr Bassam. I have more suitable options for you. Please don't mind me speaking so openly.

I popped another piece of steak into my mouth.

– Go ahead, yum yum.

– Thank you very much, Sir. I wish your kind assistance for a charity.

– Yes, of course, I managed to say between two mouthfuls of spinach and another bite of meat. Why you don't dine, Mr Ali? Do you need to eat? Sit down, please.

That escaped me and expressed precisely the opposite of my thoughts. So I hoped only that Mr Ali would decline the invitation. Which he did. Telepathy sometimes works nicely.

– It would be an honour, Sir, but the doctor banned me from eating anything after 7 p.m. In fact, I thought you would be interested in the party we're throwing very soon; it's organised by the Medina Safeguard Association (ASM), of which I have the privilege of being the Chairman. (Pause to let me digest what he just said). You surely know that the old city, which is the nucleus of the capital, is almost collapsing, he added as I chewed imperturbably. The walls and roofs of renowned homes and ancient structures are deteriorating and on the verge of crumbling. We must pool our resources and raise significant funds from generous and benevolent philanthropists to conserve these treasured monuments from decrepitude and degradation. If not, many families may find themselves without a place to live, adding to the already large number of refugees and victims of war escaping from the south and nearby regions and flowing over the capital. Our city will never be able to find adequate accommodations for all of them promptly and to live. They will become violent and misbehave. That means more crime and delinquency, more plagues and infant mortality. In short, disaster. We cannot rely on the government to maintain and operate the critical arteries of this city since the government is embroiled in a war that does not appear to be ending anytime soon. They require funds to sustain their war effort, just as the city requires funds to function normally. That's why the ASM decided to throw a fund-raising party, to which we invited the most prominent figures in banking and business and capable architects. These gentlemen are scheduled to gather in this hotel tomorrow. I am delighted that you will honour our gathering with your attendance.

To get rid of him, I said:

– Well, give me time to prepare myself. It wasn't on my to-do list.

– I apologise, Sir. We should have invited you before, but... um ... We were told you were not expected to return to the office for at least one month. It had been two weeks.

The fibber! The creepy little liar! I'm sure he had no notion of any individual wearing my name and my face two weeks ago, let alone inviting me to his party! I wondered whether Hassan or one of his men spread the word that I'm a wealthy guy, which would explain why they're all crawling at my feet like lizards.

– Who told you that? I inquired.

– Nobody, Sir, he reddened and stammered. I'm referring to your office, specifically your secretary.

I had no idea who he was referring to. Even during the golden days of 'Ouja Bank,' I had no secretary. So, to keep the challenge going, I asked him:

– Was it a man or a lady?

I felt a sadist delight seeing him struggle with despair for a minute as he mused. Then, he finally jumps with both feet into the trap.

– Sir, it was a lady, if I remember well.

– Ha ha ha! I laughed. You lost! It was a guy.

His face deviated into an impressionist painting, with many colours sallying forth and disappearing alternatively. For a short period, I admired the excellent work Renoir had created over that unassuming face. Then, feigning astonishment, he asked:

– Really? I believe you, Sir. My secretary was mistaken when she told me a lady had answered her call. She had either forgotten or needed to pay more attention.

– I hope you don't mistake me for someone else.

– It's not feasible, Sir. Are you not Mr. Bassam Bourasin?

– I am, indeed.

– Well, I'd like to invite you to our party tomorrow in this hotel.

– I gladly welcome your invitation, Mr Ali. However, if I cannot release myself for any reason, I will give you a contribution. Is it okay to give a thousand dollars cheque?

– Thank you so much, Sir. A thousand thanks. Last year, we received individual donations, some between $50,000 and $1.5 million; the less significant amount was around $10.000 and $20,000. But we accept all contributions, even 5 dollars, Sir.

I had the impression that he gave me these numbers to show me how much of a miser I was, and his ploy succeeded because I was progressively growing ashamed of what I proposed. Then, while I was ruminating, he added:

– What are fifty or even five hundred thousand dollars for all those homeless individuals, Mr Bassam? It's hardly enough to buy them basic food essential for survival, don't you think so?

– Mmmm... You know better. My business is tight right now, but I would offer you $1.500,000, Mr Ali, because my heart is weeping for the homeless and underprivileged. I know. They'd be just as useless to the refugees and lost as a modicum of 5 dollars. Nevertheless, whatever the amount my office decides, I'd withdraw my donation if you don't want it.

– Oh, please, sir, don't misinterpret what I mean. Your donation is welcome, even if it is only a single penny.

Then, in a gush of generosity, I told him:

– Don't make a fuss about it. I'll give you at least fifty, sixty, or eighty thousand dollars, Mr Ali. I wish only that everything will be all right for all those homeless people and that you take good care of them.

(5)

The hotel manager thanked me and lavished praise before departing nearly on tiptoes. He reminded me that the party would begin at eight o'clock in the evening and that he would be glad to introduce me to the association's board.

The European lady appeared intrigued by the scene; she had just finished eating and sipped her black coffee, whereas her partner had left the table and was going to the loo. She grinned again, rubbed her golden hair with her palm, grabbed a cigarette from her handbag, and leaned against the table's edge, begging for fire. I stood up, glad and pleased to serve her, and reached for her cigarette with my lighter.

– Thank you very much, sir, she said as the flame illuminated her face.

I assumed the entire restaurant was staring at us, possibly scolding me for my bad intentions. What a shame! To light a lady's cigarette in public! Furthermore, she is a European, and her husband was absent! Such misbehaviour! I challenged the entire community. I indeed had some secret plan with the lady, and I wasn't even aware of all that until I noticed the eyes following us. I instantly regretted my thoughtless gesture and, under pressure, was about to apologise to the lady. But she exclaimed, to my astonishment and relief, without paying the slightest attention to the public:

– Mr Ali is very kind. Unless I'm wrong, I believe he came to ask you to his party.

– You are correct. It was just as you predicted.

– Oh, she said, blushing. I am indiscreet!

– No, you are not, ma'am. I know you're one of his guests because he bowed, greeting you on his way out.

– Oh, we've hardly met; but I'll accompany Robert. We might locate some fine arts enthusiasts. Have you seen the exhibition?

– It has only been twenty-four hours since I arrived here. I've just seen the hocus-pocus they sell in the shops out there so far. I don't believe that's the exhibition you're referring to.

– No, you're correct. I'm talking about the painting exhibition. The gallery is on the third landing. Robert is overjoyed since it has been crowded with people of all kinds for the past few days. Some, mostly the young, are extremely sensitive and inquisitive, and they constantly inquire about any detail they notice on the canvasses. Some admitted to me that they knew nothing about abstract art, but they came to take a look anyway. Isn't it intriguing?

– Yes, I responded, looking around anxiously. The young are curious! They did not lose hope for a better world.

– Oh, I'm so chatty. I may have retained you, sir, while your dinner cooled. I apologise.

– No, ma'am, not at all, I objected. I've already finished. I'm delighted to meet you. Please, allow me to introduce myself. I am Bassam Bourasin, a businessman and fan of the fine arts.

– Oh, really! Amazing! Waterbird, Janet Waterbird.

– Please, don't leave, Mr Bourasin. Robert is just returning, she urged as I bowed and started to go.

I looked in the same direction as her gaze. I saw the tall, broad-shouldered man moving across the room, shoving his lumpy tummy between the white-clothed tables.

– This is Mister Bourasin, Robert, a collector of beautiful masterpieces.

– Ah, great! He exclaimed.

Mr Waterbird didn't even bother shaking hands with me. He just said, "Hi, how are you?" He seemed bored with the entire world. He sat down and began sipping his coffee listlessly, almost oblivious that I was still standing at their table. I excused myself and left. The server stopped me on my way out the door and said:

– Your dessert, sir.

– Thank you. Next time.

The butler then arrived and asked:

– May I assist you? Is something wrong?

– Everything is fine. I'm just in a hurry.

– I see, sir. I propose a coffee or medicinal plant concoction.

– No, thank you, I don't take these things. They're good, I'm sure. But not for me now. Please give me the bill.

The man seemed perplexed by my withdrawal, although he had been staring at me since I started chatting with the lady, like everyone else in the restaurant. That damned cigarette!

The waiter had already dashed to the counter. He returned with a little tray in his hand, which he placed on a nearby table, and I noticed that he had also brought the bill and a pencil. I stooped and signed the small sheet of paper before exiting. The butler followed me to the door, simpering and repeating his best wishes. When I arrived at the lift, I noticed the lobby was nearly empty. The stores had closed, and most customers were either in their rooms or at the restaurant.

* * *

The night was quiet, and I slept as soundly as a camel in the desert. I awoke unusually late in the morning. I had forgotten to draw the curtains, so when the warm sun rays brushed my face, I opened my eyes and glanced at my wristwatch. It was already ten o'clock. I should not have slept all morning. Even if I am a millionaire, one cannot begin a new career by sleeping all morning! Furthermore, I had made the decision not to change my habits. In my situation, one must always be very busy, so busy that one cannot even afford more than a few hours of sleep; in reality, I am fairly busy, though I am not sure what. (These notes, for example, have become somewhat of a burden. I keep writing, but I'm not sure why anymore!)

Yesterday's conversation with Mr Ali, the hotel manager, convinced me that I should hire a secretary to handle my agenda and organise my business. If my company becomes important in the capital, I need to consider opening a new office, most likely here at the Sheraton, although it is expensive. My living standard is rapidly developing and changing. The snoozy days of honeyed, tiny 'Ouja are now a distant memory. I'm doing well. I also need to change my car, despite my attachment to it. What is the point of remaining sentimental when one is prospering? "Zerga" does not deserve to be forsaken, but life is life. It's getting old and clogged with mechanical rheumatism. I can't afford a breakdown on the capital's streets, with thousands of cars, buses, and other vehicles behind and ahead of me. It would be such a hullabaloo and a shame! I'm already feeling ridiculous just comparing the old, rheumatic Zerga to those young, splendid vehicles I saw in the hotel parking lot. Zerga stands out as a crinkling peasant's cart or a mummy fit only for a mule. But am I a millionaire or not? What the hell is going on? I must replace the outdated mechanical mule with a new, reliable vehicle. Let's see! What am I going to pick? A Jaguar will be fine; they are both strong and fast. I will not, however, get a Rolls Royce; they have become too vulgar, as all of the Third World tyrants have not only obtained their Royces but are also utilising their back seats to cut off their opponents' throats. I would choose a Ford whose look attracts me. Nevertheless, I am disturbed by the repulsive story of Mr Henry Ford, reported to be one of Hitler's backers. I realise this is old history, but even after all those years, I am still too sensitive to the tragedy of the Jews to buy from Ford. I want a Mercedes or a BMW, but governments use them, and people would think my car is public property. Furthermore, it will not distinguish me from any other public servant, although I am now an entrepreneur whose funds benefit the government. I'm not sure which car I'll buy. Yet, I need to find a buyer for Zerga. I'm not going to send it to the cars' cemetery. Not so fast! Not so early!

I called the room service and told them I wanted my breakfast delivered to my door. Then I contacted the front desk and asked them to place a 'For Sale' notice on the windscreen of my automobile. I assumed that with so many visitors, it would not go overlooked. If it is not enough, I will buy a newspaper advertisement.

I called the Ministry of the Interior and asked to speak to the Director of Security afterwards. After QA about my identity and the object of my demand, they told me he wasn't in his office. I was sorry! As I had missed him the day before, I didn't want to miss him again, which I did though.

Someone knocked on the door as soon as I hung up the phone. It was the room service delivering my breakfast tray. I tipped the man before he left. I didn't have much cash, and it was time to think more practically. I had to contact my bank's headquarters. Like many 'Ouja Bank customers who lost their money in the horrible rampage that destroyed the branch, reimbursement was due.

I had to fulfil my promise, though. I am a man who always honours his commitments. I took out my chequebook and wrote down the sum I decided to donate to the Medina Safeguard Association: Only Four Thousand Dollars. $ 4000. I removed the many zeros I had ambiguously hinted to, reducing the amount and Mr Ali's expectations to more reasonable proportions. It's not because Mr Ali ingratiated me that I would be hooked to his game and offer him $1.500.000. What would I gain in the deal? Is it the pleasure of being a great charity donator? That pleasure, I can live without it.

I inserted the cheque into one of the hotel envelopes I found in the room and put it in my pocket. I barely noticed that the cheque needed to be cashed only at 'Ouja Bank. Because the latter had vanished, I had nothing to fear but its reappearance, which would not occur tomorrow. In any case, even my previous account was not in foreign currency. I didn't have a single dollar in my 'Ouja Bank account.

I breakfasted, showered, shaved, put on my tweed jacket, white shirt, and blue tie, and was about to change my trousers when the phone rang, and I hurried to answer it. It was Hassan. I sat on the side of the bed in my underpants, the light sloping cheerfully through the balcony glass and bunching around my nude knees.

– Good morning, said Hassan. Have you slept well? I didn't want to bother you. I assumed you were tired after your journey.

– I appreciate it very much, sir. Everything is fine with me.

– All right, then get ready. I'll dispatch the car to pick you up... In fifteen minutes, say. The Minister will give you an audience.

– So fast? I was stunned.

– Yes, and please, don't keep him waiting. You should be here in five minutes.

– As soon as possible, Mr Hassan. But I must tell you that I did not have the time to prepare the memo...

– It is not required. Following the meeting, you will prepare the paper. In any case, we have everything ready for you. Just drop over for a little chat. (He took a breath)... And in the name of Allah, I don't want to see you undone, so put on a tie.

(6)

The line clicked and buzzed. As I hung up the phone, I felt the sweat dripping down my temples and cheeks. I was surprised and impressed to get a meeting with the Minister so soon. I've never met a Minister in person, and I was well aware of the importance of the audience. Nonetheless, I was nervous. I'm done if I can't persuade the Minister that I'm the right man for the appropriate job. But which job were we going to negotiate about? I had absolutely no notion. I had no idea what to expect from myself. What if the Minister inquired about my recent activities? Should I state I'm a bank clerk or hint at my covert dealings? Perhaps that is the very subject to avoid. Absolutely!

The Minister should not be aware of my snooping for previous administrations. Hassan had pledged that the secret reports would be destroyed or kept out of their hands, and his sincerity was demonstrated by his eagerness to introduce me to the big boss. Then I had to prove my allegiance. I decided to tell him immediately about the strange news I had heard in 'Ouja. I'm almost certain the Afghan is devising a dreadful conspiracy against him. I know he set up a network of spies and dispersed them across the country under the fictitious cover of the Islamic Militia. He may be infiltrating the Ministry of the Interior at the moment. He must be stopped before he becomes too powerful to be driven.

I decided to bring the topic up with Hassan to address it with the Minister.

I removed the tweed jacket and replaced it with one more formal and appropriate for the audience. As usual, I emptied my pockets, drew out the contents, and placed them into my jacket pockets. Then, sprucely clothed, I lingered in front of the glass, smoked a cigarette, raked the remains of the cold coffee in the cup, and dawdled on the balcony, distractedly glancing at the white roofs languishing in the sun rays. The sky was deep and serene, with no cloud to mar its unruffled calm. I could feel myself getting stiff and sweating profusely under my clothes. I closed the glazed balcony door and pulled the curtains to enjoy the calm and cold freshness of the air-conditioned room once again. I needed to focus my attention before the meeting. I drank some iced fruit juice from the mini-fridge. Someone knocked on the door. It couldn't be the chauffeur yet. I opened. The housekeeper was the only one there, and she asked if she may clean the room and change the sheets. I let her in. The phone rang just then, and I rushed to answer it. The hotel receptionist apologised for disturbing me and reported that the Ministry had dispatched a chauffeur to wait for me in the lobby. I thanked him and told him I was on my way down.

* * *

It must have been a bright morning, for I met Mrs Waterbird again in the lift. She arrived before me, and she was by herself. That was what I'd call a close encounter of the third kind! Why? Because of what occurred, or rather, what did not occur.

– Morning, Mr Bourasin. How nice to meet you again! she exclaimed.

– Morning, Mrs. Waterbird. How are you doing?

– I'm fine, thank you. But you can call me Janet.

I loved her easygoing manners, although I think she was more sophisticated than she appeared. Her arms were very white in the short sleeves of her light long gown, and her long slim neck was adorned by a golden chain whose extremity was hidden in the deepness of her proud bosom at that mysterious line of junction. I could guess the shape and sweetness of her breasts under the tight brassiere. She generously offered them to my sight, straightening her head resolutely while speaking and her golden hair undulated over her shoulders. She was roughly my height, if not slightly taller, due to her high-heeled shoes.

– I will. I am just Bassam.

– Hello, Bassam, she said, smiling.

– I thought you were on the third floor.

– No, the gallery is on the third floor, not our room.

– I'll visit the exhibition as soon as possible, maybe even this afternoon if I can free myself.

– Thank you. It'll be our pleasure.

The lift stopped on the third floor, and she left.

A tiny, swarthy fellow in chauffeur attire awaited me by the reception desk in the lobby. It was not the same man who had driven me to 'Ouja. I stopped to leave the little envelope addressed to the manager at the reception desk, then strolled towards the gate, following the driver to the black Mercedes waiting for us.

I tossed myself on the marrowy cushion and tried to relax as the car nosed through the capital's streets, thronged with many vehicles and a faceless crowd. I looked out the window at people crowding the pavement or hunching in front of the shops. The coffee shops were busy, and life appeared to continue as usual. Nothing has changed since the Islamist coup. Just more weapons appeared here and there. Armed men replaced police officers at street junctions, but residents looked now accustomed or maybe indifferent to their presence. Since the King's deposition, guns, tanks, and military displays have become a part of our daily lives. With the conflict in the south threatening to crawl over the rest of the country, it was customary to see those groups of men parading through the streets, some walking and some riding SUV cars, with their rifles, machine guns, and other weapons flashing in the sun. I raised my eyes as I heard the thunderous roar of an engine louder than all the vehicles on the roadway. It was a police helicopter flying at a low altitude, scanning the roofs and the streets. It hovered briefly above us before disappearing in a clap-clap droning of propellers.

Mrs Waterbird's ravishing perfume was still in my nostrils. It was enough to turn and daze all the heads surrounding her. I'm unsure why I had a flurry of strange thoughts in the lift with her. It was the first time in my life that a woman provoked such a flood of stunning hallucinations in my mind that I wished for the lift to be blocked by a sudden electric breakdown, trapping me along with her in that tiny space with no way for us to go up or down or get out! Really! It's insane! I'm becoming overly silly and maybe a touch lunatic. My sudden wealth has ostensibly harmed my mind rather than improved my situation. In the presence of a lady, a gentleman should not entertain such foolishly profligate fantasies. What if the idea materialised and I was suspended twenty metres above the ground, trapped in that cage with Mrs Waterbird? Would it make her happy? The devil knows how that weird thought infiltrated my mind! I am not

Bassam Bourasin, if that vile and lecherous left-side angel did not sow it in my head. I can hear him laughing while gripping his stomach. I wish you'd explode, son of a bitch! You're such a jerk! No kindness, no respect for anything or anybody, right? Get lost and rot in hell, damn the bastard father that begot you!

That woman had asked you for nothing, and while I was making a big deal out of our casual meeting, you betrayed me and sowed trouble in my senses! You are sick and horrible! I'm sure you aren't an angel but a pork!

I hope Mrs Waterbird did not suspect anything about what occurred to me. The more I think about it, the more I realise that the lift could have stopped in response to that unbelievable delusion. Don't they say reality is a manifestation of our thoughts?

– Holy shit!

What would I have done then? Would she have objected if I kissed her? Just a little kiss! On the cheek, as a brother!

– Would that have resolved the issue for you, jackass?

– I doubt it.

– She would have slapped you.

– Uch! This whole story is a weird idea! I refuse to believe I conceived it.

– I tell you what would have happened. If the lift had been blocked, you couldn't have approached the lady because she would have shouted in terror and said you attempted to persuade her to leave her husband and come with you.

– Wrong! I never thought about it. Anyway, I don't recognise myself in this salacious story. Mrs Waterbird never complained about boredom or asked that I console her in any manner.

– Yet, she's now connected to your lust. Admit it.

– I'm not admitting anything. As long as you follow me like a shadow, I refuse to talk to you.

Did she guess my thoughts? I wonder. Because women are said to be incredibly intuitive. What a shame if she did! She'd probably tell her husband, "That guy in the lift, you know, Mr Bourasin, who appeared so shy and reserved in the restaurant... You won't believe it, but he suddenly became brash. Today, he kissed me right here on the lips. I did not guess his intentions. I'd slap him if I did. I'm pretty sure I'd slap him indeed." Her nippy, bored husband would then respond, "Ah, really! That's it?" Everything would end there. I don't see him coming over to punch me in the lobby. I'd hit him on the nose before he moved, even if he's much bigger than me, with muscles, fat, and bones. I don't mind if he's upset. In fact, I wish he was angry so he could say something other than, "Ah, really! That's it?" What more does he want? I am, in fact, a gross pig! I had no idea until I met Mrs Waterbird in the lift this morning, but now I know.

It's hardly comforting to imagine oneself as a pig just minutes before meeting with a minister of the Islamic State. This happened. It was unavoidable. The attraction was almost unbearable. It was her eyes, her flesh, her look, and all the unsaid

— the indescribable magnetism and the tiny space filled with electric desire.

I felt like someone who had let a splendid opportunity pass through his fingers without catching it. I regret it now. Why didn't I stop the damned lift halfway, kiss the lady, and do whatever our hot hell of flesh demanded? I'm oversensitive and delusional, or just a coward? I felt guilty, guilty, and wretched because I could not do what I knew she was silently soliciting. My anxiety kept me from taking the step. So many social barriers had been planted in my head long before the thought of making love to a woman in a lift came to me. The idea of that failure irritated me and placed me in a depressed, ominous frame of mind. I cursed Mrs Waterbird and her hopeless perfume. It was the day I had been looking forward to for years. I would miss it and fail miserably because of her awful fragrance, which had disrupted my senses and sent me on the run. If I hadn't been able to restrain myself, I would still be in the lift bouncing with the lady, and I would have had to say goodbye to my business and all my ambitions. This is at least the most comforting aspect of the situation. I did not do it, all right! And while I recognise that I was incapable, I am grateful that my timidity saved me time. I should not have lit her cigarette in the first place because, from inside, I burned up with its sight when she planted it at the corner of her lips. I'm damned if I'm not in love with Mrs Waterbird! I'm dying for her, and her white, naked arms, delicious lips, and glorious breasts are pursuing me like damnation to the Islamic State's Ministry of Interior.

* * *

I had to think it over again to get it out of my head. I was alone with Janet in that lift when... the blackout did not happen.

The charge did not stop moving, and I did not take her into my arms. We did not kiss rapturously, and we did not make love. So, for God's sake, why am I feeling so dreadfully guilty?

In addition, I'm thinking of Hassan. If he has any suspicions — and I know he has spies in the hotel — he is perfectly capable of bringing me to court, where I will be sentenced even before I open my mouth because I betrayed him, did not show up at the audience with the Minister, and shagged a female tourist in the lift — but they would say "raped," of course. I'm qualified for 25 years in jail, adding to the former 25. A life sentence that is! Then goodbye to the marriage with Sophia, goodbye to the High Merit decoration, goodbye to the millions awaiting me quietly in the Treasury, and goodbye to the *Dolce Vita*! These bleak pictures loomed on the horizon like thunder in a summer sky, forcing me to make sense of the obdurate mess clogging my mind. If I wanted to appear as usual, sober, and sedulous as I was before meeting Mrs Waterbird and her cold-buttocked husband, I had to forget about her and erase her image from my mind.

Moreover, I was furious about falling in love with a married woman. I tried to catch a glimpse of myself in the rearview mirror, but the shadow I saw reflected on the smooth surface shimmering in the sunlight had nothing to do with me. I lit a cigarette quickly, almost shaking my fingers, to regain my confidence before the critical meeting. I dared another look in the same mirror. The deep creases that formed on my forehead and the dark-hued crescents under my eyes nearly scared me. My eyelids were pasty and puffy, my lips were not grinning, and I had accidentally wounded my cheek when shaving. What a hot morning! I didn't even notice it in the lift mirror because I was distracted by Mrs Waterbird's face, bosom, and the rest. The cut was clotted with blood. I took out my handkerchief and tried in vain to wipe it away. Then I wet the end of the cloth with my mouth and pressed it to the cut. I carefully rubbed it. That incredible moment had passed. Last night's long sleep did not improve my appearance.

(7)

The Mercedes came to a complete halt in the middle of the street. We were temporarily sucked up in the massive gridlock. The other vehicles were honking and making a lot of noise. On the right, I noticed people gathering around the theatre's white stairway. Some of them were waiting for a car or a bus or something, sweating in polo shirts and t-shirts under the scorching sun, flinging its blistering arrows from the inflamed zenith. Others, mostly young people, sat on the bare slabs, staring carelessly at the vehicles. They didn't seem to bother or care about anything, including heat, dust, or noise. What did they expect? What would one expect in such a location at such a time? There was nothing to anticipate or hope for. They just sat down there or stood near the grey wall, empty-headed, light-hearted, accustomed to their long-term jobless status, without anxiety, like pieces in the theatre decorum, acting figurants in the daily play of their city, similar to the trees, advertisement posters, and the coffee shop tables. Indifferent to the town that reciprocated their indifference.

Then I wondered: why shouldn't they be there? If they were absent, I'd feel something important was missing in the capital! The governments come and go, coups, counter-coups, revolutions, counter-revolutions, right, left; they are still there, watching the vehicles and breathing the street's dust. They are the lucky ones! They don't have to worry about the future. They decided a long time ago: there's no future! I remember seeing that sentence written in black on the city's white walls for many years.

Ahead, near the corner of the right sidewalk, some people gathered before a modest fast-food cart distributing its sand-wiches on the street. I could nearly smell the spiced scents of barbecue, Shawarma, Kebab, and other types of meat being prepared on the embers of a crude gridiron by a bulky fellow in worn white clothes. The merchant was happily singing, en-veloped by a cloud of grey and blue smoke.

Some Europeans, possibly journalists, were going down the street with cameras slung over their necks and shoulders, and a dusky boy holding a straw basket full of handcrafted items was sprinting after them and shouting something. He was probably trying to market his equipment. Fortunately, Europeans con-tinue to visit the country. I don't think they are tourists, for it is unlikely that they will ever see the golden dunes of the south other than on postcards.

Many shopkeepers had hung a giant poster of the Emir in front of their window shops as a talisman to protect them from the 'bad eye,' and the zeal of the militia, secret police, and vari-ous government spooks. The former pubs and bars had felt the direction of the wind. They quickly shifted their business to the Islamist-friendly trade of coffee, tea, lemonade and soft drinks. Iced water would quench the thirst of European visitors and good Muslims. The prohibition law was the first measure en-acted shortly after the coup, and anyone who violated it faced harsh punishment. The Islamist government has been creative. On TV, a zealous journalist declared that we did not invent pro-hibition in modern times. The USA has long preceded us, thus recognising the harm of alcoholic drinks being banned in Islam. And the studio audience acclaimed by shouting, "Allah Akbar!"

On the street, the commotion was deafening. There was not only the roar of the engines, the pip-pip of the klaxons, the ding-dong of bicycle bells, the whistling of trams, the shattered groan of pedestrians, but also the loud whizzing and buzzing of the radios, the shrill voices of the pedlars, and the songs of popular singers howling and wailing over their disastrous love stories. The chauffeur had not said a word since we left, so I asked him if the ministry was still far away.

– No, sir, he answered. The Ministry is only at the end of the block.

Then we slowly drove out again, and it appeared to me that if I had walked, I would have been at the Ministry before the automobile. That's what I told the driver when trying to converse with him. I knew where the Ministry was, although I had never set foot there; yet, he appeared tired or wary and responded laconically with a simple 'yes sir'. His muteness did not help me change the direction of my thoughts. The Mercedes then picked up the pace, sliding smoothly and almost silently on the macadam, skirting the slow queue of vehicles on our right before pulling out in front of a high grey building whose iron gate was guarded by several policemen mounted with machine guns. The chauffeur jumped out of the car and hurriedly opened the gate for me before I could move.

The armed men dressed in uniforms saluted me, and a man in civilian attire rushed to greet me on the threshold with a honeyed smile.

– Mister Director of National Security is waiting for you, sir. Please, this way.

I followed him to the lift, whose door was open. The lift operator heeled us and pressed a button. The door slammed shut, engulfing the three of us. I was nervous. I looked at the mirror, pretending to fix my tie. I tried to appear relaxed and confident and attempted to engage the officer in conversation.

– It's a hot day, I said.

– Yes, sir, it's hot outside.

– The sun is really crushing.

– Yes, sir. Crushing.

– Wouldn't we suffocate if we didn't have air conditioning?

– We would, sir.

– There isn't a single cloud in the sky, which is unfortunate.

– Yes, sir.

– It may become a disaster for the farmers.

– Sir, yes.

– But we don't need rain, for we have oil and gas income, enabling us to buy half the products of the world. Ha Ha Ha!

– Yes, sir, he said with a forced smile.

– We are fortunate that oil and natural gas are Allah's gifts. It is evidence that God loves us because we are good Muslims, right? Why did he not give hydrocarbons to the Europeans? He loves us more. We are the people selected for paradise, aren't we?

– Yes, sir. We are.

– Unfortunately, we can't drink oil, can we?

– No, sir.

– It's like drinking alcohol. It will kill us, right?

– Right, sir.

– That's why alcohol was forbidden. Allah knows better than us.

– Yes, sir.

– And he loves us.

– Yes, sir.

– Moreover, oil is now in the hands of the Scoundrel. May Allah curse him!

– Yes, sir. We arrived.

The lift came to a halt, and the gate opened. Bowing slightly, the officer insisted that I pass before him, which I did. My short monologue with that UGO (unidentified government officer) had put me at ease before the crucial meeting. Since hope and self-esteem had been restored and confirmed after the damages of 'The Ouja catastrophe, I felt ready to meet the Emir himself, not just his Minister. After all, I murmured under my breath, as a reminder, my money now supports the government. It's for a good cause, as we will restore the Golden Age of Islam. The State would be in trouble if I demanded immediate payback. Right now, the war effort requires every penny available in the country and abroad to be in the central bank. I could neither require a complete and regular payback for fifteen years of laborious and patriotic services nor force the government to give me my money. I have no tanks, guns, or intention to mount another coup or counter-coup and call it a revolution, counter-revolution, devolution, or couvolution. Enough of this shit! We need centuries to get over it. The only consolation is that I am walking inside the Ministry of Interior as a VIP.

I have long dreamed of meeting the highest authority, which would open my way for a national medal like Hamda La'war. But even my one-eyed former boss did not put foot here despite his bragging. His wife said he disappeared! Where? Did Haj Mukhtar take him on a journey in the invisible world of the Jins? Their relationship has been limping, though. I hope Hamda was not arrested. When I think of all the people who never reappeared after they entered this building, I feel a shudder running along my spine. I heard some stories in prison. It's not comforting to guess what a sad job they perform in the most ominous ministry, but I have no choice.

We made our way along a carpeted corridor with high bare walls. Some office doors were open or ajar, and their occupants stared listlessly at me as I heeled the small fellow in a poor grey suit and shabby tie half-strangling him, speeding towards a large padded gate at the end of the corridor.

As we approached, he came to a halt and respectfully tapped the door with his knuckles, then twisted the knob and barked, "Mister Bassam Bourasin is here, sir."

A big moustached face appeared in the doorframe, two dark eyes darted at me, and the head vanished. Soon after, a tall bearded man came out and greeted me pleasantly. We shook hands, and he led me into the antechamber, where he asked me to sit in the armchair and give him a minute to notify Mr. the Director of my presence. I thanked him and sat down, gazing at the room's luxurious furniture. The other office occupant, whose face had appeared and suddenly faded, mumbled some apologies shyly and left the room with the man who had accompanied me upward.

I didn't have to wait long. The secretary knocked on another cushioned door and unlocked it. "Your guest has arrived, sir," he said.

Then, from the other office, came Hassan's familiar voice: "Let him in, please."

The secretary turned his head. Then opening the door to allow me in, he invited me with a motion of his open hand. I stood up and crossed the distance to the office.

* * *

Hassan stood in the centre of the spacious room, which seemed sumptuously furnished with rich carpets, a mahogany desk and oblong tables, leather armchairs, soft sofas, satin curtains, transparent lustres, and many other handcrafted adornments that mixed the traditional style with the ultra-modern setting.

– Welcome to the Ministry of the Islamic State, Mr Bassam, said Hassan as we shook hands.

I thanked him, and as I looked at his elegant blue suit and the sumptuous surrounding, I could not help but remember his pitiful look a few times ago in prison. All Praise to God! I told myself. The change is like magic!

– I don't order a coffee for you, he continued, since we need to see His Excellence the Minister straight away. But please, have a seat. I need to call His Excellence first.

– Can I smoke?

– Yes indeed, but only here, not in His Excellence's office, he said quickly and walked over to his desk.

I drew a cigarette from my packet and lit it as he dialled a number on his desk phone.

– Hello, sir. Yes, your Excellence! He's here... thank you, Excellence.

He replaced the receiver and turned back to face me. His clear green eyes were lively, and he seemed to be cheerful. He was probably having a good time. They say power is an exhilarating narcotic with well-known euphoria, which is why giving it up to a rival is so terrible.

– His Excellence will meet us in five minutes. Please, be ready.

– I am, sir.

The air in the large room was cool and refreshing, yet I was still sweating. I took out my handkerchief and wiped my neck and brow. Hassan was also smoking quietly, although he appeared cooler than I was.

I stared silently at the mahogany desk with its gleaming black polished wood and the long-backed plush chair behind it, imagining myself sitting there as Director of National Security. Then I pondered what would happen if I stood up, walked to the desk, and sat on that chair.

– Funny! My dear Bassam, you make an excellent director!

– Really? Why don't you go home then? I'll stay here to do what should be done for centuries in this country.

As he looks surprised and shocked, I add:

– Who said I'm not the Security Director, Hassan? Please call the Minister and ask him if you don't trust me. Come on, pick up the phone.

– How much did you say they owe you? The director of security asked, breaking the silence and luring me out of my reverie.

We rapidly returned to the former situation, he at his desk, me in the armchair. Were they going to give me all that money? I couldn't believe it. In fact, despite my confidence that I have certain rights, I never thought they would pay me for anything. Nothing, however, required them to respond positively to my assertions, not only because the regime had changed but also because there was nothing to prove that I was on the payroll of any of the Ministry of the Interior's sections. There is no such bureau as the one where I was claiming money. Nobody doubts that our Ministry's first job was spying on citizens and residents using invisible and trackless ways, though. Otherwise, I had no legal status on which to build a case and claim my rights. Then I remembered the descendants of the spoiled jews. It occurred to me that my speculations and claims were similar to those of the Jews with the Swiss banks. Like them, I had every piece of paperwork proving my rights, and I was expecting that the new regime would recognise them, which meant that they would finally see me as their adversary - because I was spying for their predecessors - and pay me for it... in real cash! I am the spoiled Jewish of the Islamic regimes that ruled my country. What a great and elating feeling!

So, how can I define Hassan? This is a guy I couldn't outline. Since his skin is so thick, light strikes it and immediately reflects back. He emits no light at all. Actually a black hole. Where's the truth? Hassan was either a jerk, a cynical, a hypocrite, or an unrestrainedly immoral mind devoid of principles, values, creeds, and faith... In a word: a scoundrel! Another scoundrel, still undiscovered, unlike the ousted president, they're fighting.

Right! I used the identical phrase that had earlier caused him to flash while speaking it mechanically:

– Patriotism is too flattering to forsake, even if it would cost me $200 million, sir.

– Right! But nobody is paid in dollars here unless you have a foreign contract, he said.

– Please convert them to local currency; I don't mind. The only purpose was to simplify the calculation.

After a little pause, he went on:

– Well, I checked, you know. I'm sorry to say that your name does not appear in the Treasury's registries.

I pretended to be surprised and said:

– Oh! How about the Central Bank?

– Same thing.

– What about the Interior Ministry?

– Ahah! Do you need me to tell you that you're standing right at the edge of a cliff right now? If you admit you worked for them, you are out of the game. The payment you receive will be in a very different currency. Do you want to cause trouble? You demanded that I obliterate your reports while simultaneously demanding payment for them! It doesn't make sense. Some consistency, Mr Bassam. Are they all fools?

He must have read my thoughts. I have escaped Hamda La'war to fall into the grip of this creep, maybe not much different and perhaps even more ruthless, for my skull is now in his hands. How could I endure a relationship that was so unbalanced? I had no control. He could send me back to jail right away. I may become one never heard about again after coming to the Interior Ministry. They are hundreds, I was told, maybe even thousands!

As I didn't respond, he said:

– Anyway, you'll get compensated.

My heart was about to explode. I tried to calm down while choosing my words carefully:

– Sir, I truly don't need that money. Well, in fact, I don't believe that the State owes me anything. I was joking, merely joking, I promise you. Subsequently, I am sure that I owe everything to the State, from my food to my home and clothes. Even my life, I owe it to the State, sir. That's why I intend to be as devoted to the State as you are yourself, for you are actually my model and guide, sir.

No man is insensitive to flattery. Vanity is our weakness. It expelled Adam and Eve from paradise, as all monotheistic religions say. Softened by the ingratiating cajolery, he laughed. The tension in the Director of Security's office then dissipates as if by enchantment.

– No problem! Now look, Bassam. You must agree to a contract and work hard to earn your $200 million.

Dumbfounded, I repeated:

– A $200 million contract?

– Right! The money represents your share of the helicopter deal you won for the Ministry.

I stuttered even more stunned:

– Sir, I... I...

I intended to say, " I don't remember such a deal." I need to find out what helicopters he was talking about. When did I win such a deal for the Ministry? In this life? I was in prison. In another life? Maybe! But I need to remember.

He cut me off as I was stuttering.

– Bassam, shut your trap. Now, let's be serious. Since you have such poor memory, please remember that you negotiated this agreement with a British airlift company on our behalf. Are you okay with this? Although we have already received some of the helicopters, the contract, signed by the previous administration, provides for the importation of those helicopters for a total price of $699,000,000 and still needs to be paid. Do you agree with me? Our government will pay the cost of the helicopters and uphold the obligations and debts of our forebears. You will thereby fulfil your end of the bargain. Is it obvious? We will pay you $200 million because you obtained a discounted price. This also is stipulated in an annexed contract to the main deal.

It was as if he had thrown me from the highest altitude those helicopters could reach into the sea! Granted, I have a parachute. Still, I need to know how to activate it. That was urgent for me to learn, as a matter of life or death. Noting my perplexity, he added:

– You don't need to say anything. I know. You're tight right now, so let me take care of the payment.

Another pause.

– Look, Bassam. Don't take it tragically. It's good news for you, isn't it? Nobody would give a damn about you apart from His Excellence, the Minister, and his Director of national security since no one truly knows who you are or what you were doing. You are a perfect anonymous. No family. No friends. Only us. We are your true friends. Nobody will believe your story if you talk about what you heard in this office. You'll be officially categorised as crazy and spend the rest of your life in a psychiatric hospital. In prison, you still have hope to obtain relaxation. Not in a psychiatric institution, you know this. Remember, Mr Bassam, that this is a new regime; as such, we have the absolute power to create and destroy anything. Absolute power means the ability to recreate you. You weren't anything, but now you might become somebody on the condition you behave yourself. Let me give you more clues to understand your present situation and where you are, where you could be, and who you are dealing with. We - His Excellence and me - knew about you, your secret reports, your relationship to Hamda La'war and Laroussi Mamitu, and your double identity since you were in 'Ouja, not since we met in jail, as you may assume. I'll tell you more. I wasn't jailed, actually. I was deep undercover for a special mission. It is now *mission accomplished*. That's why you're here. I set up this deal for you, for your best interest. Don't act foolish and pretend you don't understand that you're assigned a classified mission. You have no choice. You are a spook, and spook you'll remain. You worked for One-eyed Hamda. He did not pay you. Now, you work for me, and I will make you rich. Is it not much better? You'll do exactly what I tell you to do. Don't think. We devise any plan. You just execute it.

He stopped. I didn't say anything. I knew that it wasn't everything. He has more to say, still. Did he forget we just had five minutes before the minister's audience? It's really unbelievable. He lied. God knows when they arranged everything.

– You are a spy, and what you did was not as innocent or unnoticed as you seem to think. No one in the Islamist government has as much knowledge of our nation's governance as I do. The majority of them are new to politics. This is my revolution, my day and my hour. In my dreams as a subaltern intelligence officer, I thought about it day and night for years. I waited for the moment until it came. You were part of the network of informers and agents I had established over the years. You assisted me even if you were unaware of it. Even though I have been your supervisor for years, you could not have known. Because you thought that Hamda La'war was your boss. He was actually one of my agents. The government changed. But without the boost from the Intelligence Services, everything would have stayed the same.

(Pause).

– We succeeded. Both the coup and the counter-coup are ours. The revolution and the counter-revolution are ours. We created both. We assisted Abdelghani Abdelghaffar in removing the former president just as we have assisted the latter previously in removing the king. In short, we planned the counter-coup that ousted the Scoundrel when he got too dangerous and tried to fly alone. The fool believed he could rule without us. To eliminate us, he intended to create his own spy agency. He couldn't rely on us. He was so blind that he was oblivious that we made him. Now look, Bassam, I am not telling you all this because I like to brag; I wouldn't be at this post if I were a braggart. I want you to forget everything you did in the past and before coming here. You understand that you are only known to this government as the businessman who negotiated the purchase of those aircraft from the British company. If questioned, you will respond that you have offices in London and this city, specifically the Sheraton. Your relationships are primarily with businesses and financial organisations, and you weren't even in the country these last few years due to work trips.

" Bassam, you must now sign the documents," he said, pausing again to crush the last cigarette in the ashtray. "On that, everything is based."

Without waiting for my response, he quickly returned to his desk. While I watched in wonder as he quickly opened a drawer and took out a sizeable yellow package, he later returned and sat down next to me in another recliner. I was literally submerged in wet perspiring.

He calmly opened the large envelope, took out the " contract, " and handed it to me. He gave the impression of someone who had precisely calculated and mentally rehearsed all the elements of the game.

He sternly demanded, "Please review these papers and sign here."

I noticed a slight shaking in my hands when I picked up the sheets. Hassan then pulled out a little piece of paper and pushed it over the table so I could clearly see it.

– You are a lucky man, Mr Bassam, he said. Congratulations! You've struck it rich.

I quickly determined that the small piece of paper was indeed a cheque. Based on the lavish display of zeros, I deduced that I had finally been paid for work I had not performed at the service of the State.

It was a cheque for $200,000 in payment.

– It's merely an advance on the overall amount, he remarked.

Chapter 10

Swimming Between Two Waters

(1)

I returned to my hotel enraged, confused, and almost frustrated since I couldn't get my hands on them despite having two hundred thousand dollars. Hassan gave me the number for my new bank account but cautioned me that I could not withdraw the entire amount immediately; he kept the cheque with him, assuming that I might lose it.

— What, after all, are you going to do with all that money? he said. You don't need it right now because we pay the hotel's bill.

— But I signed the contract, I objected.

— You signed it, and I'm not denying your rights. Your money is secure, but you must wait for the government to pay. These are not a trifling modicum, but two hundred million dollars. We must obtain the approval of the Minister of Finance, as well as the Central Bank and the President. So please wait.

— I am not claiming $200 million.

— Not you, lad, but the firm with which you're working. You'll cash your cheque once everyone else has been paid. Don't be concerned; you saw the contract, didn't you? The British company is real, the helicopters are in the Ministry's yard, and the money is somewhere between our Central Bank, Switzerland, and London.

— I know the helicopters are here since I saw one on my way to the Ministry. I am, however, a little hazy. Why do we need three banks to close the deal?

— You're always asking questions you shouldn't be asking. Do you really need to know everything? Assume that a portion of the payment was made through a Londoner bank and that we now require the services of a Swiss banker to move our funds to London. How did you get it?

— Sir, that was not in the contract I signed.

— What exactly do you mean?

— I'm referring to the first instalment of payment. In fact, the contract is explicit: the entire payment will be made after we receive the helicopters.

That enraged him. He didn't want me to know anything else about that bid.

— Take a look here, little chap. I'm not going to allow you to investigate my business. You signed your page and got your cheque; the rest is no longer your responsibility. Whether we pay the firm in two, three, or five instalments is none of your business. Your role in the game is to sign anything I give you, keep your mouth sealed, and wait for more instructions. Is that clear?

— Sir, yes, sir.

He calmed down. After a time, he inquired if I needed anything. I hesitated for a second, then admitted that I needed some cash for my expenses and was afraid of the return of a blank cheque.

— A blank cheque? Do you yearn for the menagerie? How much is it?

— Oh! It was for a good cause, sir, the Medina Association of Safeguard. 4000...

— 4,000 what?

— Four thousand dollars, Sir.

— We'll call you double-headed saint!

— Too much kind of you, Sir.

— Come on, be serious. Those guys are wealthier than you, me and the Minister together. How do you believe they have reached the top in a few years? Just asking for donations from saints like you and telling them the story of making the poor and the homeless happy. As it happens, there are more poor and homeless people every day, and they are not happy, I can tell you. Look, my friend, God, not you and me, is responsible for those unhappy. He created them, threw them in this country, and then decided to give all the wealth to other people who do not necessarily deserve it. It's just the lottery! What can we do?

Such a comment coming from an official in the Islamist government astounded me. If it turned out to be accurate, it wasn't good. I wasn't sure whether I should believe him or not. But I cannot believe that God could be evil. As I did not answer, he went on:

— I'm unsure if you're too honest or blind! he exclaimed. Really! Should I keep you under constant monitoring 24 hours a day so you can learn to distinguish who is your friend and who is deceiving you? Here is the bank account number. Accept it. I deposited $10,000 into your account, which you can use as you see fit. Nonetheless, I recommend that you exercise caution rather than throwing your money out the window. What the hell! Try to be a wise man! You are lucky since you have two heads in one. Use one of them at least!

Saying this, he burst into laughter, happy with his silly joke.

This conversation occurred just after the brief interview with the Minister. The latter had been pleasant and courteous, and I immediately realised that his face was not unfamiliar to me. He was short, obese, and bald; his tiny eyes sparkled, and his mouth was ringed by a trim beard covering only his chin. He was dressed stylishly and spoke quickly with a harsh voice and in hushed tones, emphasising some words clearly and audibly, such as state, government, Islamic Revolution, and half-swallowing his statements as though the other words were useless to him.

— Wecom'ster'ssam, he began as we shook hands, which I translated as "Welcome Mister Bassam," and he went on to say, "I no a ged del bout yeh, thaks to ster'ssan who tak of yeh s' his man'f confidence."

I thanked him profusely, emphasising how honoured I was to meet a historical figure of the Islamic State, and he didn't waste time:

— Think you keepin up well with Government the Islamic Revolution; vrythin owever's based on trust a confidence a secrecy; a you no of coss the cost of the bellion in guns, men, moey. We nee a let of money an guns and of coss aliable men, an discreet, an...

I intercepted the last sentence and decoded it: "We need money, weaponry, and trustworthy men who are also discreet."

There was a lot of whistling and hissing, but he continued his voluble stammering, and I could hardly extricate anything intelligible. I just wondered how his subordinates or even his colleagues understood what he was hopelessly trying to say in his burbling language, but they're probably used to it. Then it hit me. This was the silent man I had seen in the restaurant, dining with that rowdy group of officers. He certainly didn't notice me, even though I had been pretty conspicuous, lighting Mrs Waterbird's cigarette and engaging in jittery, airy talk with her. Anyway, I held off on bringing up the matter because he said nothing.

Finally, he stood up, signalling the audience's time had ended. It had lasted perhaps ten or fifteen minutes, during which he was the principal soloist in a completely hazy symphony written by a mad brain, prey to the greatest disorientation.

I had told the chauffeur that I would return to the hotel after a short walk through the streets. My meeting with the Minister and his Director of Security did not improve my mood. I was being pushed to the limit, yet I was conscious that if something went wrong, I could be blamed. Neither Hassan nor his Minister would admit to planning every element of that phoney agreement, leaving me to bear the penalties and face prosecution alone. I was their stooge and was starting to realise that the game was outwitting me. I walked aimlessly in the crowded streets, battered by the blazing sun, impotent and resigned.

I walked into a coffee shop, tripped over a chair, and ordered a black coffee. I lit a cigarette and stared aimlessly down the street. I felt the despair of the crowd penetrating me more than ever before. It was like a poison leaking into the city's atmosphere, pouring from every face, invading every corner, sticking like a rigid glue even to the seats, tables, and walls, engulfing everyone around me and infecting my thinking. I was burdened by a discouraging commitment that made me feel helpless, as if I were sinking in a vast sea of horrible malevolence. The dismal discontent of those anonymous faces penetrated my psyche and made me feel bitter and entirely shattered by grudging dismay. I was depressed. All those eyes appeared to stab me accusingly as if they were all well aware of my guilt, and the mouths seemed to mutter and insinuate that I was a fool... a fool who accepted to engage in a game that would not only overtake him but would eventually destroy him. Where has your wisdom gone, man? Don't you see that Hassan and his Minister make you seem foolish? Do you feel guilty or embarrassed? Guilty or ashamed? Yes, maybe, but not for what I did at the Ministry. I was still thinking about when I was alone with the lovely Mrs Waterbird in the lift and... Oh my goodness! If I keep going in this direction, I'll end up in a mental institution!

I jumped to my feet and stormed towards the gate. I didn't turn my head or halt when I heard the waiter behind me say, "Your coffee, Sir..." I couldn't tolerate the stench of hatred, aggressiveness, looming violence, and similar unpleasant sensations. People appeared to be resentful of their government. I didn't see a smiling face in the entire bloody city, and I overheard some of them insulting and ridiculing officials without naming them. I've never liked the capital, but since I have to live there, I should strive to avoid such pointless and dangerous situations. It is extremely risky to be seen sitting next to a group of provocateurs vilifying the administration, which will happen again if I do not exercise caution. Indeed, I do not share these extremist beliefs since, by habit, I am always loyal to the government. Nonetheless, I don't need to give anyone a reason to suspect me. I know from personal experience that our police ears are pretty sensitive. In addition, I am now almost a public figure; I hobnob with government members. I have the finest intentions for the little people of this city, with whom I sympathise entirely and unreservedly. I know they are for nothing in the confluence of tragic incidents that brought the country from disaster to devastation. Alas! I am as powerless as they are. Furthermore, I am attempting to assist them. I gave a $4,000 cheque to a charity that helps the homeless. True, the cheque was a fake, but my intentions remain the best in the world.

After a short nap, I visited Mr Waterbird's artistic exhibition in the afternoon. The gallery was almost empty. A few kids, maybe three or four, spread about the large space, and they didn't appear particularly enthralled by that type of painting. Mr Waterbird appeared to be napping in an armchair, an open book on his thighs, and his belly undulating softly with his breathing. I approached him cautiously and saw he was snoring. Happy man!

I took a space tour, paying close attention to the paintings. I didn't grasp much of what was represented in that joyful splattering and splashing of colours, shades, and lights. But I overheard one of the kids say to his friend, "Did you see the title of this canvas?" "Donkey's tail!"

— Funny!

— It means he bathed his donkey's tail in colour and stuck it over the canvas.

— Ingenious!

—Yeah, but if a donkey can do it with its tail, the donkey is the painter, not the man.

— Perhaps it wasn't the donkey that did it, the second young man speculated.

— So, who did?

— The painter is most likely the guy you see there. But you wouldn't detect a difference between his work and the animal's. So, they are partners.

The two laughed heartily. I turned to watch Mr Waterbird, but he was still snoozing, indifferent to his triumph.

At that time, his lovely wife walked in, spotted me, smiled, and rushed to greet me warmly: "Oh! "Thank you for coming, Mister Bassam." She turned around, surprised, and shouted, "Oh! What happened? How long have you been here?"

I informed her that I just arrived.

— It's odd! The gallery seems so sad, she continued. It was so crowded in the morning that you couldn't even walk. People crowded around the pictures, some queuing in the corridor, and Robert felt compelled to speak to everyone.

—That seemed to have exhausted him, I said, pointing to the snoring man, and now he's having a short nap.

I didn't believe anything she said. Even in peacetime, before the last insurgency, the country was not much concerned about painting exhibitions and culture. We have crowded mosques but hardly crowded art exhibitions. There are local painters, but they live on the state's charity. How about now, after the Islamist regime has settled down? What puzzles me is not that the gallery was almost empty but that it was still open for exhibitions. The only reason I can think of is that nobody knows about it among the new officials, who should be more preoccupied with the civil war than with artists and exhibitions.

— He's pretty solicited right now. We're going on a European tour soon. We received invitations from folks in Paris, Rome, Berlin, and even Moscow. You won't believe it, Mr Bassam, but we are literally overwhelmed.

— I can imagine, Madam.

She was wearing a short-sleeved white silky shirt over a black skirt, and I immediately noticed the several bracelets encircling her wrist because she was speaking with her hands - and it seemed to me with her entire body - gesticulating and somewhat bestowing her proponent and firm breasts as to emphasise her words. Obviously, she disliked seeing her husband sprawled and comfortably snoozing in his armchair, oblivious to the rest of the world. She raised her eyebrows at him briefly, then crossed the distance separating us from the sleeping man and pinched his arm.

— Robert! She exclaimed.

He opened his eyes wide and mumbled, "Who? What?"

— Look who's here, dear, she said, all honey. This is Mister Bourasin; isn't it gracious of him to come?

I took a step forward and then stood beside her. The painter gave me a cool gaze:

— Ah! Welcome!

I smiled, hoping to persuade him to speak more... in vain! 'Ah, welcome,' it appears, was his best effort in conversation. Mrs Waterbird asked me:

—Did you see the pictures? We'll show you around. Robert would love to guide you. Are you coming, Robert?

I doubted he could string two phrases together, but he trailed us meekly, breathing heavily and almost wobbling. We stopped in front of a large canvas striped laterally by a progression of colours representing all possible variants of green and blue.

— This is the achromatic scale, she explained. I particularly enjoy it because of the admirable proportion of light and shadow. He worked on it for several months while also painting other pictures.

The explanation she provided me untangled the conundrum without revealing all of its hidden knots. I murmured to myself that it is never too late to further one's education, but I inquired about the price because I was probably expected to say something.

— It's not expensive, she said. Unfortunately, this one is already sold. I'm sorry! However, you might come across something different and no less interesting. I'm not only Robert's wife but also his agent. If you're ready to invest, I can advise you... For example, a painting of 'dead nature' or a 'flower pot' would look great in an office, unless you prefer something for your home. In this case, I recommend the 'donkey's tail'...

I glanced at the last painting, wondering why it had been so strangely titled; to me, it represented nothing more than a splatter of unspecifiable colours. I am not a connoisseur; there is no reason to act like one. I looked at the artist, following us hesitantly and pondered if he was absent or with us. He didn't say anything. Honestly, I wasn't expecting him to. I already knew he couldn't say much more than 'Ah, welcome,' even if we were together all afternoon and into the evening.

— Well, it's... uh... quite... ahem... colourful, I said.

— You're not going to believe it, Mr Bassam. A banker in Geneva spotted this canvas and wanted to buy it. He is an amazing collector who used to visit European galleries in search of rare gems of modern painting. He said, "I recognised Robert's talent at first sight, and this painting is truly a gem." She added emphatically that he would have bought it even if I had asked for £20,000 or more...

— So, didn't you sell it? I inquired.

— Robert declined.

She chuckled.

I couldn't believe a donkey's tail was worth £20,000 or more, although I wasn't sure if she was talking seriously or to make a point. In any case, it was clear that Robert wanted his tail to stay with him.

— Who would think twice about making a deal at that price? I said.

— This is because you're a businessman, Mr Bassam. You realise that a good opportunity should be seized.

— Right, I'm always looking for good opportunities.

— Well, here's an opportunity for you, Mr Bassam. Don't let it go. I'll sell you this canvas for only £ 2 thousand. Robert has finally decided to sell it, and trust me, it was difficult to persuade him.

She smiled softly and pushed her fascinating bosom proudly forward.

'If she keeps doing this,' I told myself, 'she'll make me broke as quickly as she made me nuts! I possess $200,000. Is it reasonable to spend them even before cashing my cheque?'

I don't deny that I was mesmerised by Mrs Waterbird's charm, but her chiaroscuro confounded me, and I struggled to keep my head clear and cool. I didn't want to appear stingy, which I am not, and I didn't want to buy such an expensive donkey's tail. In any case, where would I place it? I have neither an office nor a house away from my dear 'Ouja.

— I think you should sell it to the Geneva banker. Twenty thousand is genuinely a deal. I cannot offer you a more significant price, and I would feel tremendously bad and ashamed if I accepted this authentic work for much less than its actual value. Please, trust me. I enjoy this piece of art but can't afford it right now. Accepting your generous offer would make me feel like a thief. Besides, I understand that Mr Waterbird is extremely attached to this canvas, and I don't want to steal it from him at such a low price.

I heard a short laugh and turned to find Mr Waterbird making every attempt to cut off what appeared to be an unexpected burst of hilarity. He huffed, gasped, coughed, panted, attempting to hide his face with that incredible mirth; but finally, incapable of more restraint, he came out in a piercing diluvial laughing.

I was perplexed and stared at him, as his wife glared and said loudly, "Robert! Robert!" "What the hell is going on?"

She then turned to me, ashamed, and apologised:

— Sorry Mr Bassam; he is having his crisis. Because of all this exhausting activities, it had been expected for days.

I tried to smile, but she seemed glum, and my smile likely turned into a scowl.

— What's your point, Robert? Is it necessary to whoop and whack right now? Ok, since you're so delighted, do it yourself. I'm not interested anymore.

She then turned to face me, apologised, and took leave.

— Janet, where are you going?" Yelled Mr Waterbird, who had gathered himself again, as she hurried towards the door.

She didn't seem to care and continued strolling down the corridor.

— Sorry, Mr. Robert, she seems angry, I said and prepared to go.

His hand waved in a sign of indifference.

— Yeah! Never mind, she can go. She lost her sense of humour. She's bloody incapable of laughing at nothing.

Finally, I was relieved to notice that he spoke like everyone else. However, I must admit I didn't understand the joke either. I couldn't determine whether to be happy for his speech recovery or sorry for the irritated wife's quick departure.

— Please accompany me, Mr Bassam. Let's have a drink together. I'm incredibly thirsty, and drinking only fruit juice and cold water is a nightmare. Such infantile behaviour does not sit well with me. Come on, sir, I have plan B for such occasions.

I wanted to apologise and escape, but I couldn't refuse such a kind request. Since I was waiting for him to speak, I was curious to hear what the silent man had to say. So, I followed him into a little room adjacent to the gallery, which I had not noticed.

The area appeared to be an anteroom for the artist's private usage. He turned on the lights because the curtains were covering the window. At the far end of the room was a couch, a desk, and two chairs in the centre. To my surprise, Mr Waterbird unlocked a cupboard and pulled out a bottle of Whisky and two glasses. Amid prohibition, threats, and witch-hunting, the sight of that bottle filled me with horror and misery. Bewildered, I was about to flee. But his soft voice calmed my terror and captivated me. The devil's temptation was too strong to resist.

— Of course, it's prohibited, Mr Bassam. But not drinking in this climate is a greater sin. Please accept my apologies for the lack of ice cubes, but I do have some mineral water.

I wasn't sure. Would I risk being lashed and jailed by the militia if I touched the forbidden thing again, although it had been long since I hobnobbed with Bacchus? Everything has changed. Gangs of men armed with sticks and cudgels patrol the streets of the capital and other cities and villages, bringing anybody who breaks their law on his knee.

"No, thank you, Mr. Waterbird," I was about to say when my hand flew out of control and gripped the glass half-full of the bright, yellow liquid. In no time, as if afraid of being caught with the evidence of my crime, I hastened to gulp it down, somewhat to get rid of it like a bitter but necessary medicine, while telling myself, 'Allah will forgive me no doubt, even if the men are merciless'!

Mr Waterbird slapped my back and murmured, "Easy, easy! Nobody will ever know."

He filled my glass when I asked for water. My neck and entire bosom were on fire. I drank whisky with Hamda La'war and Haj Mukhtar several times, and still, I can't resist it. I sipped the water.

— Either this isn't regular whisky, or I've never truly drunk it, Mr Waterbird.

He burst out laughing.

— I recommended softening it with water, but you refused. I'm sorry; I understand that with their heinous prohibition, all you want is a drop of booze. But don't worry, Mr Bourasin; the source will not dry; there are two more bottles... If I may say so, ha ha ha... well hidden from the devil's view.

— If you don't want to get into trouble, you should hide them away. They'll lash you for a beer.

He served me another whisky, which I mixed with water.

— To your health!

We drank.

I proposed a toast to the British Prime Minister, but he declined.

— What's the harm?

— I didn't vote for him, he said.

— Aha! Then let us drink for the health of the Shadow Prime, I replied.

— Not sure I'll vote for him either.

We laughed and sipped. The booze was good, and we cheered up.

We raised our glasses in tribute to British painters, the Archbishop of Canterbury, the Islamic Republic's Mufti, and even President Abdelghani Abdelghaffar.

— Had we... hick... fuck... hick hick... forgotten anyone?

— Perhaps the Islamic Militia, I figured.

— Whatever! The devil takes them to... hick... hell! Hick!

We drank much more. After closing the room's door, we took a comfy seat on the canapé. I'd finally overcome my nerves and felt entirely at ease with Robert Waterbird, and the whisky had removed our inhibitions. Then he told me that he didn't like what was happening in my country, which he had visited several times.

— I don't like it, either, I said, but I'm about to be decked...

— Really? He exclaimed, Interlocked! How? For what?

— How? I suppose, by the President himself. I am a national hero.

— Oooh! You! Robert's pupils dilated. Are you kidding me?

— I'm dead serious. He couldn't stop giggling. It was another of his unexpected bursts of laughing, and I joined in. He then recommended toasting — the intoxicated hero of the Islamic Republic!

— That will not do! I fired back.

— Why not?

— I'm unsure whether such a man exists in our country.

— Ha Ha! That's you, lad! Said he, almost choked with laughter.

I laughed and said :

— Sorry! I didn't recognise myself initially, but now I am sure it's me. We lifted our glasses. — Yet, you don't know everything, I added.

— Certainly... hick... I'm not that super-powerful... hick!

— Do you realise? I'm now a new rich.

— Ha, ha, ha! Janet informed me. That's outdated... hick... news. She knows... hick hick... everyone here... They say you're the new butt full of shit...

— Janet? She knows her stuff.

— There's nowhere to hide in this... hick... bloody hotel.

— Not even a new butt full of shit! Ha Ha!

— He He! By definition... hick... a new butt full of shit ... hick... is the most indiscreet thing on the planet... Ha Ha... It can't be hidden.

— It isn't a bottle of booze...

We laughed.

— I'll buy some of your paintings because you're a brother, even though you're a terrible painter.

— How much?

— Do you want to know the price?

— Nay, how much terrible?

— Oh! Enough to make you unable to paint a donkey's tail... Ha Ha! — Hick... Ha Ha... That's because you're f... blind.

— How much blind?

— Enough to make you unable to recognise a donkey's tail from his head... Ha Ha Ha!

He was laughing so hard that he collapsed on the ground.

— You bloody drunk, Bassam... Hick... You don't want me to paint a stupid animal's tail. Anyway, Hick! You won't recognise it! Hick Hick!

— I will. Hick! But you can't sketch a pig or a cow, and Hick! Your canvasses are as expensive as gold and diamonds! Hick!

— Gold and diamonds! Ha Ha! That's what they are! Hick!

— I'll give you a $1,000 cheque right now if you draw a cow in front of me with four legs, a tail, a head and everything else that makes it a cow. He He He!

— Keep your dollars, tycoon. Hick! You'll lose them anyway, since Hick... they're useless to the ignorant... Hick! Butt full of shit! We laughed.

— I want a cow, Robert. Please, make me a cow...

— Nay... Hick... There are enough f... cows and donkeys on the planet ... Hick!

He took the bottle again. I said:

— Syphoned!

We laughed.

— You're still thirsty!

— Hick! We should ask the... Hick... f... manager to open some bottles from the cellar.

— You're on the moon!

— We can pay... Hick...

— This is an Islamic country. Ali Baba's cellar is illegal.

— Do you mean... Hick... Ali Baba's cellar was in Europe? The f... caliphs... Hick... weren't drinking...Hick... in Bag... Hick Hick... Bagdad?

— And Damascus...

— And Hick... Mecca...

We laughed.

— So, now that you'll be... Hick... decked... He He He... Inquire with... Hick.. His excel... Hick... excellency. His cellar's indeed better equipped...Hoo Hoo Ha Ha He He!

He was shaking and jerking again on the canapé.

— Don't be a fool, Robert. The President isn't a drunkard like you.

— What about you? Hick! Are you anything like me? Drunkard! Ha Ha Ha Ha... Hick!.... So... Hick Hick... Islamic hero! Hoo Hoo!

— Bring another bottle. It's better.

— Yeah... How about Janet?

— What have we got to do with her?

— She's ... Hick... watching.

— What exactly is she watching? Do you mean she doesn't know about the booze?

— She's... Hick... aligned with the f... Islamists! Hick! He exclaimed, shaking his head.

More laughter.

— Does that mean she won't let us drink?

— The bitch! Hick! Ha Ha! Doesn't even suspect...

— Well, well, well! You cheated, didn't you?

— Nope! She did... Hick! She spies for the f... Hick... Islamists! Laughter.

— Let's have some coffee then, I suggested.

— Nay, go on your own... I'll stay here... Hick! I'm going to sleep.

He then spread out his legs, closed his eyes, and, in a few seconds, was already snoring on the couch. I opened the door and left.

* * *

Fortunately, the booze had not completely taken away my senses. I still could reason. So, I didn't go to the coffee shop because I was too inebriated to make the effort, and I was afraid of being seen staggering in the corridors. I'm not sure how long I was confined with Robert in that tiny room; probably the entire afternoon, because when I got back to my room, it was already dark and I had to switch on the light. Then I sprawled on the bed and promptly fell asleep.

The voice of the Muezzin summoning the faithful to the prayer pulled me out of my dreams. I opened my eyes, believing it was the afternoon prayer because the room was brightly lit. But when I looked out the window, I realised it was daybreak. A murky blue surrounded the buildings, and the white stars in the sky were blinking. It was not the sun that illuminated my room. I have just neglected to turn off the electric bulb. As I tried to remember what happened, I felt my head engulfed by a thick fog. I stretched out my hand to the bed table and switched off the light. The room returned to the darkness. I looked for my cigarettes but couldn't find them on the bedside table, so I touched myself and found that I was fully dressed: jacket, trousers, and shirt... I haven't even removed my shoes. The packet of cigarettes was completely torn up. Not surprising! However, two cigarettes were not entirely useless. I decided to smoke one of them and keep the other for emergency state.

Using a foot over the other, I pushed my shoes away, threw my jacket on the chair and started smoking. I was laying in bed, trying to recall the events of the previous day. I soon realised I would not return to sleep. So I smoked the second cigarette and got up. I stood up for a long time behind the window's glass, observing the dawn on the city's roofs.

The stillness had nearly come to an end. Apart from a few groups of soldiers or militiamen moving around, the streets were still deserted. I stood for another few moments behind the window glass before opening it. The early morning air entered the room and chilled me. I could hear an automobile engine receding away. I'm not sure why I immediately thought of Mr Waterbird's painting as the sky's extremes grew rosy and vivid. I was returning from a foggy and flustered world when it struck me that the entire city, as seen from this balcony at that early or late hour, that was neither morning nor night, was just as involved in a quiet struggle for life and light as some of Mr Waterbird's jumbled topics. Nothing but the static and enduring masses of the buildings, the fleecy and flexible shapes of the foliage and the trees, the fuzzy forms of the windows and bannisters half-sinking in semi-darkness could be discerned in that spilling and rigid stacking up of shades and lights. Then I understood what the artist was struggling to express.

The abstraction of the cities that Mr. Waterbird depicted is the secret I was unable to fathom, although his perspective was clearer and his understanding more compelling than what I could ever fully grasp. The ability to capture the essence of forms, lights, and colours in such a way was unfamiliar to me, given my accustomed interaction with a world that leans heavily toward materialism, leaving little room for an alternative perspective to filter through its confines. His vision remains unclouded by immediate needs and unaffected by the constraints of routine. Moreover, Mr. Waterbird's apparent lack of concern was, in truth, an undisturbed calm. This tranquillity of his soul allowed him to attain an understanding of the extraordinary world that had perpetually eluded me. This is why I perceived him to be content, quite possibly happier than myself—indeed, he was.

I settled myself into a contemplative state, poised to inscribe the chronicles of my days. I embarked upon formulating the embryonic framework of my most cherished endeavour. The tome

I had acquired yielded a trove of captivating materials. It elucidated, among other tenets, that to be deemed 'Islamic,' financial institutions must earnestly enact the celestial doctrines proscribing usurious commerce and gains amassed through dormant capital. This necessitated the practical implementation of the tenet of exchange with a 'modest surplus,' elevated to the echelons of equitable value and weight, all within the purview of the cooperative doctrine governing the impartial apportionment of communal wealth. This, it asserted, was an indispensable prerequisite for the enduring opulence of the banks themselves and the amelioration of the quality of life for the 'Muslim Umma.' This community, poised to embrace transformative reforms grounded in moral and technical cooperative values, was to find a resolution to its economic, social, and financial quandaries solely through coalescent action. In my private journal, I assumed the mantle of authorship with gravitas, capturing the essence of this intricate discourse.

An auspicious beginning it presented, a prelude brimming with potential. Yet, the entire text demanded my undivided attention; its essence I sought to distill, the author's captivating turns of phrase poised to adorn my summation. As weariness set in, my notes found refuge within the recesses of a wardrobe concealed beneath layers of attire. With resolve, I embarked upon the grooming routine, the sound of cascading water mingling with the radio's broadcast. Through the airwaves, the announcement resonated—a triumphant Islamic Army, their might asserted, quashing insurrectionists as they attempted an assault on yet another hamlet. Thus, the spectre of a devastating massacre was averted; casualties and captives were the rebels' toll. Furthermore, a bounty of $200,000 was proffered, a reward for aiding the apprehension of the elusive Scoundrel.

Curious, the sum arrested my thoughts—why precisely $200,000? Mused I, was it but a mirror to the remuneration offered for my hand in facilitating the government's procurement of twice identical helicopters? Puzzlement clung to me, woven into an intricate tapestry of coincidence, as I hastened my ablutions, the radio silenced.

(2)

At a later hour, while savouring my breakfast within the restaurant's ambience, a sight caught my attention: Mrs Waterbird, donned in a resplendent gown of pale yellow, gracefully approached. A wave of my hand signalled my presence, although she had already spotted me and made her way toward me, lips curving in a gentle dance and a smile gracing her visage.

— Good morning, Mr. Bassam.

— Good morning, Janet. Are you alone? Please, join me.

Seating herself adjacent to me, she chose a chair, not foremost, proximity that contented and gratified my being. My plate adorned with broiled eggs, I was already halfway with my breakfast. A waiter approached, and she placed an order for chilled chicken, eggs, milk, and a refreshing fruit elixir. With his departure, she asked:

— Why were you absent from the party yesterday? I presumed you had been invited, were you not?

— The party? Ah, the gathering! Indeed... I, um, I must confess... it had escaped my mind. I apologise.

— Many interesting persons attended; the city's illustrious socialites, you know. It was a refined affair, replete with a lottery. I procured one of their tickets.

— May fortune favour you!

— Robert, too, was a no-show. He was in quite a pitiable state; we had an argument again in the evening. He feigned illness, though I detected the scent of Whisky.

I, a picture of feigned innocence, intoned with a sage-like air:

— Truly? A misunderstanding, perhaps. Where did he unearth such a banned product in this city? He might have drunk a contaminated batch of lemonade that caused his illness.

— Ah, ah, ah!

Her interjection interrupted my explanation.

— I'm no fool; I know the difference between Whisky and lemonade. He was clearly drunk, and I worried that others would see his behaviour and judge us both harshly.

— The Christians are permitted to drink.

— Perhaps. I'm not certain. Given our countrymen's troubling support for the opposition president, I doubt the Capital's authorities would tolerate an intoxicated person stumbling about shamelessly in their finest establishment—even if that person were Picasso himself!

— Are you referring to your compatriots stationed at the southern oil fields?

— Exactly! Don't you read the news? The Islamists are threatening to attack those protecting the Scoundrel. And who does that, if not the Europeans and Americans?

— No, I replied, you've got it wrong; the threats are aimed at the tribes giving him sanctuary, not the foreigners. In any case, they won't dare bomb your countrymen, even if they're working with the Scoundrel. They have no desire to provoke Western retaliation, however much their fanaticism drives them towards conflict.

— Is that so? Indeed?

— Yes.

She pondered a while, then voiced her thoughts:

— Perhaps, yet considering the grievous 'Ouja massacre...

— 'Ouja,' you mean?

— Indeed, 'Ouja!' I have a terrible feeling about this; it wouldn't surprise me if all Westerners were expelled from the country.

— You're being rather pessimistic; remember, I'm from 'Ouja, Janet.

Her gaze shifted as if seeing me anew or perhaps beholding a phantom

— You? Good heavens! A survivor? My deepest condolences!

— I've known the loss of both my mother and my betrothed in that tragedy.

I let this sentence trail off almost without thinking as if the words had lost their meaning in my head. Janet remained silent. Instead, she did something that was far more reassuring than any flippant sentence: she did something that I will never forget. She reached out and touched my shoulder as she looked at me with immense compassion. It was a spontaneous act, so human and friendly that it struck me deeply. Her white, warm hand rested gently on mine, and her fingers extended to me all the calming sympathy she could muster. Soon, I was overcome by conflicting emotions as I experienced heat waves and secretly hoped that her hand would never leave mine. However, the tender moment was over once the waiter returned with her breakfast, and she withdrew her warm hand. Then I cursed the waiter, and for the first time in my life, I wished that a man in good health would go down hit by a stroke!

After he left, I said, "Never mind!" Sometimes, you have to take a hit in life."

She retorted, "It's unfair."

— Nothing we do will make a difference.

I attempted to change the conversation as her mood deteriorated, asking, "Have you sold many pictures?"

She pondered as though this were the very last question anyone could ask.

— Yes, many pictures... (For a moment, she was silent.) I told you the exhibition is a success.

— Come now, Janet; I don't believe it.

She said nothing in response. I continued:

— I don't think you came over here at the correct time. The show is fine, but it feels out of place and time due to the war, the recession, and the devastation of so many people, not to mention the Islamists who have nothing to do with modern painting and don't even want to hear about it. Even though I am an art novice, I admire Robert and appreciate his efforts; he may be a talented painter, but this is not the ideal venue for his work.

There was an awkward pause in the conversation. The sun's rays were clustering and flooding into the ample space through the translucent glass that served as the wall separating the restaurant from the garden. Guests were seen strolling along the pool and lounging on the seats in the newly formed tree shade.

She dug around in her purse until she found her cigarettes, then she brought out a pack and stuck one between her full, pink lips. I lit it for her and then started one for myself. There weren't many people in the restaurant that early in the morning, and even though there were some Arab customers, they didn't pay any attention to us.

There was a plume of blue smoke as she declared, "Well, you won. Sorry, but I lied."

As I looked at her in silence, she added:

— I believed it was a blunder from the very beginning. I tried telling Robert the country was on fire, but he ignored me. He ignores whatever I say anyhow. When he sets up his mind about something, he is very unyielding. He was very familiar with the country and had always been welcomed. He didn't realise that the country he knew had changed so drastically that so many people were afraid for their safety and wouldn't even converse with us for fear of being labelled as British spies. He refused to concede that anything out of the ordinary had occurred; instead, he insisted on forming his own opinion based on what he saw with his own eyes. We hired the gallery for two weeks, but now we must cut it down to one week. That's terrible! We might as well have been in the desert, as is how sales are going. I thoroughly appreciate the hotel manager's anger at us for failing to inform him that our stay would be limited to one week. But we can't spend more money than we have, and if no one in this terrible country cares about modern art, that's not our problem. I'll admit that it wasn't always the case, but whatever good there was before has been lost in this awful war that saps resources and wears people out.

– Oh! So you didn't sell anything," I said.

– Not a single painting," she replied sadly.

I needed to comfort her. –

Never mind, Janet, I said, putting my hand on hers. It's just bad luck, it won't last forever.

She sighed, but didn't take her hand back, and her face showed no emotion.

– Listen, Janet; whoever told you I'm a millionaire is lying. I'm not as rich as people think.

– But...

– I stopped her, saying: – I knew from Robert that you told him I'm a tycoon, and he still believes it. It's all made up, Janet.

– So you've tricked everyone in this hotel, right? This is weird! Why all the rumours about your wealth?

– Because people are so gullible, they'll believe anything. It's nonsense, even if I sometimes tell myself there is a reason for it. I do help others get rich, and if I profit from that, it can't be all bad, can it?

– What exactly do you do?

– Well, I connect people; I use their money to make them richer, put them in touch with each other, and take a commission.

– Is that a business agent or a stockbroker?

– Somewhere in between. That's why I suggest we make a deal.

I was being both honest and dishonest, but she seemed interested.

– Okay, what do you suggest?

What if, while we were alone in the lift, I thought I really wanted to sleep with her? What if I told her I desperately wanted to kiss her lips, neck, breasts, and white hands? What if...? I took my hand away and felt crushed by the city: the people's faces, the tense atmosphere, even the restaurant furniture, the chairs, the tables, the glass wall... I was a nobody who lied to feel important.

– I want to buy all your paintings.

She looked confused.

– All of them?

A tempting thought made me say, "Yes, all of them."

She looked disbelieving.

– I don't know if you realise what you're asking. You just admitted you don't have much money.

– Yes, but I can buy the paintings if they're reasonably priced.

– What do you mean by reasonable?

– Listen, I'll make you an offer, think about it carefully before you answer. I'm in no rush, take your time.

She puffed on her cigarette and bit her lip.

– What's your price?

– Ten thousand dollars.

After a moment, she said:

– You're unbelievable, Bassam. You pretend to be poor, but everyone here says the opposite. I heard yesterday you were going to donate to the ASM, but you didn't go to their party or changed your mind. I offered to sell you a painting worth at least $20,000 for just $2,000, but you refused because it would be dishonest. Now you're offering $10,000 for everything. You have to admit that's strange. I don't know what to think!

– Don't think badly of me, Janet. I mean no harm. I loved the paintings and would pay extra to own them. I'm sorry if I offended you, Janet, or made it sound like Robert's work isn't worth much. Of course it is; I know it's priceless. Please don't misunderstand. Forget my offer if you don't like it.

– It's not unappealing, but it is odd. You could buy two or three paintings for that money, maybe more, but not the whole lot, Bassam. Understand?

I felt like we were negotiating about something else entirely

– I don't want one or two, Janet. I want to buy the whole set. Otherwise, I'm not interested.

– Don't be childish. Happiness is a state of mind, not a destination. You need to compromise to succeed in life. Also, think about how much it cost to create these paintings, you're being unrealistic.

She started searching for her bag.

– It's all or nothing, I said almost angrily.

She rolled a cigarette and lit it, looking disturbed and annoyed. After a silent moment, she apologised.

– Forget it.

– Can I ask you something, though it's a bit personal?

– Go on, Janet. Just say what you're thinking.

– Have you ever bought a painting before?

– Never.

– That's what I thought. So why the sudden interest in art?

Surprised, I knew I couldn't tell her the truth. But what is the truth? My feelings for her?

– I'm not sure, but I want the whole collection.

– Let's assume we accept your offer, what will you do with the works? Will you resell them for profit?

– Oh no. You're wrong, Janet. You think I want to make money from this, but I have something else in mind. You probably think I'm taking advantage of you because of this situation... But that's not true. Men have other interests besides money. Yes, Janet, we also have ethics. Freedom, justice, dignity, and love... are more than just words, my dear.

She looked at me with piercing blue eyes, thought for a few seconds, and then said:

– Don't expect a miracle, but if you want two or three paintings, I'll talk to Robert and let you know. What's your room number?

– Sixth floor, room 356.

We got up and paid the bill. Then, I walked her back to the lobby and we said goodbye.

As she walked towards the lift, I called out: "Janet!"

She turned.

– Yes?

– The complete set!

She smiled without saying anything.

I went to the front desk and asked the receptionist whether my car was sold. The reply was negative. After thanking him, I collected the newspapers instead of heading straight to the bank. Since their 'Ouja location is no longer operational, I had to let them know I am still available to work in the Capital. I have better things to do than sit around the hotel doing nothing. Hassan promised me an office at the Sheraton, but I can't wait for him to make the necessary arrangements with the management. What if, after I signed the contract, he suddenly decided that I was no longer helpful to him? I need to be cautious.

I could still hear Abdullah Zahir's remarks in my head. He predicted that Hassan and his boss would be among those affected by an impending reorganisation and would thus be replaced. Is this the true motivation for their covert actions? Is it a guess, or do they know? If they don't pay the British company, which they must have paid long ago, and instead keep all that cash for themselves, they may quickly leave the country at the first indication of danger. And if I could return to work at the bank without drawing suspicion, I wouldn't want to throw away fifteen years of experience for nothing. Ultimately, I wasn't too concerned that Zerga hadn't found a new master quite yet. My dear veteran automobile would be extremely helpful on the hectic streets of the Capital.

After picking up my paper at a shop, I left from the hotel's front door. I was striding across the parking lot when I heard my name. Then I turned to see the chauffeur panting after me, baffled, and saying, "Mr Bassam, I was just waiting for you in the lobby. I'm sorry I didn't notice you left until I asked."

I'd completely forgotten about him, and now that he was here, I didn't know what to do. I didn't want him to report all of my movements, which he would if I let him drive me to the bank. I said:

– There's no harm; you may go have a drink and put it on my bill, Khemis. I'll give you a ring if I need your help.

— I am here to help you, sir. But I'll have to drive you if you want to go out. The orders are clear.

— All right, now go and have a drink, Khemis.

— I'll be waiting right here, sir. You may require my help... I appreciate the drink as well. I'll have it after the service.

What the devil!... Khemis, I realised, was not just a driver but one of Hassan's guys whose primary duty was to keep an eye on me. I had no choice except to dump my cards on the table openly.

— Hold on a second, Khemis. I will get in my car and drive it to the repair shop by myself because it's broken down, and you're of no help right now. That's why I suggested you go and get a drink.

After silence, he stroked his chin with his long, dark fingers and said,

— I'll drive it for you, sir. I can recommend a decent maintenance garage near the hotel but don't even think of asking me to leave you alone. If I do that, I'll be fired. Sadly, sir, I have a family. There are seven mouths to feed.

— Well, well, don't worry. Don't worry, I won't wreck your life, but don't bother me either.

— Sir, there are already seven of them here, and another one is on the way.

— Really? Well done, Khemis! Yes, but how do you do it? I guess I'm trying to say how you balance the books. Did you work in the used radio cassette market at all? Are you interested in other people's automobiles so that you might... Ahem... give them away at the Friday Market?

Khemis could not understand my reference to the 'Ouja police officer who used to steal radio cassettes from stationed cars under his guardianship and sell them on the black market. — If you are referring to my work during the holidays, I am well forced to do it because I am paid the double of what I actually gain, he said, — but I don't quite understand you, sir. — How much are you earning if I am not indiscreet? — Certainly not, sir; it's no secret. There are just 650 of them. — Six hundred fifty? Incredulous, I repeated. — Yes, sir, but it's barely enough for seven mouths... and... — Well, I know Khemis, I know. The eighth is on the way.

But astonishment overcame me in a big way. I was taken aback to learn that despite earning more than I could ever have in my banking career, the chauffeur of the Ministry of the Interior expressed feelings of underpayment. What would he say if I told him the real wage of a bank clerk? But he couldn't do his job as Interior 'chauffeur' very well if he didn't know it. He probably knows that some university professors in our country make less money than security officers. Some of our most illustrious academics, I'm sure, would rather not waste their talents on books and pupils and instead work for the country's most significant government agency. Some scholars, it seems, dream of becoming cops or even super-cops.

To save my face, I said:

— It's a real misery, a shame; it's not worthy of the prestigious Ministry of the Interior! How can you control people with only 650 per month? Yes, I know you're only a driver, Khemis; you don't actually cudgel, hit, kick, torture and perform all the legal work. But aren't you paid to drive those who serve the government? You may eventually drive state guests and other collaborators to the Ministry, and it's all fine! This is not an excuse to treat you with such contempt. What the hell? A driver is important, even at the Ministry of Interior! He could be more significant than a bank teller. What exactly am I saying? God! Please forgive me! A driver is, in fact, more vital than a banker. How about six hundred fifty? It is simply intolerable. In your shoes, I would complain, organise a strike, or perhaps a street protest. You cannot feel secure with such miserable pay, even if you work for the Director of Security himself. Khemis, do you feel safe?

He looked at me, *lost in the translation*! He'd already started gnawing his fingernails and rolling his eyes. — Are you serious, sir? I am secure, but it is insufficient. I spend my entire salary every month in the first two weeks and then begin borrowing. Furthermore, there is no trade union for state agents, sir. We have only Allah to complain to. — Allah is forgiving and generous, Khemis. I'll speak with Hassan about you and your compensation. I'll request that it be increased to 700. Is it okay? — Oh, sir, I am grateful to you. However, I don't want to bother you with my problems. — There is no botheration whatsoever. Your boss is a good friend of mine. This is a promise. Now go have a drink in my honour.

He took his time getting ready to leave. I looked down at my watch, which was nowhere to be seen around my wrist. I'd taken it off before showering and had forgotten it in my room. So I inquired of Khemis, — What time is it? — It's ten past ten, sir.

I noticed he was wearing a beautiful watch bracelet around his wrist. It was a costly vagary for a chauffeur. I had no doubt that the watch was worth his salary if it was confirmed that he was paid 650 dinars monthly. He could have been lying. — Khemis, show me your watch. This is a lovely item; where did you obtain it?

He showed me his wrist where his shining watch was, basking in the sunlight. — It's an old watch, sir, that I inherited from my father. Nothing like it can be found currently. It's as accurate as Big Ben. — Really? How much do you want for it? — How much for what, sir? — I'm asking about the price of the watch because I want to buy it.

Surprised, he exclaimed, — But I don't intend to sell it, sir.

I took my wallet out and opened it. It didn't have much cash. — This is for the drink, Khemis, I said as I pushed some torn banknotes into his pocket. — Tell me your price, and I'll give you a cheque.

He mumbled something in response, staring blearily at the chequebook in my hand. He was obviously apprehensive. — What's the big deal? Fifty dinars aren't enough? Is it okay if I make you climb to the thousand? Now, what's your price?

He ploughed his hair with his fingers. — It isn't easy, sir. However, thank you very much. I am grateful.

He opened the bracelet, removed it, and handed it to me. — It's heavy, I commented after weighing the watch. — How much is it? — It's made of gold and silver, sir. It's extremely expensive and rare. But for you, it's a gift. Please accept it, Sir. — Thank you so much, Khemis. Because I don't want to insult you by rejecting your present, I'll take it. Now, if I can't keep my promise, I'll give it back to you; after all, I never accept bribes. It's one of my principles.

I wrapped the watch around my wrist and dashed across the parking lot. Khemis stood outside the hotel's gate while I drove past him and waved. What did he make of it? Instead of letting him drive me, I trapped him. That was a successful deal in which I lost nothing. If I continue on this path, which I intend to do, I will be the most powerful businessman in the country very soon, and it is not unlikely that I will surpass even Hassan. The next time I am compelled to purchase helicopters for the State, I shall include the following conditions: it is now 90% for me and 10% for my associates.

For now, Hassan has lost: his spy has been neutralised as long as I hold his valuable watch. Indeed, I have no intention of intervening on his behalf because I know I will be severely disciplined if I do. Anyway, his pay is perfectly adequate; I even envied him, but he is greedy and his greed cost him his father's valuable bequest. If this lesson does not teach him anything, I will strip him naked and return him to his boss bare as a worm.

* * *

Fifteen minutes later, I was going through the bank's grand marble corridor and up to the first floor to meet Mr Khalil, the head of the Human Resources department. I hoped he would remember me from the two or three times we had met at the tedious conferences I had to attend in the Capital with my coworkers from the 'Ouja branch.

I gently knocked on the door and heard a woman's voice. After a few seconds, I banged once more. The voice was still talking, but nobody responded. I hesitated, knocked twice, but didn't bother waiting for a response before turning the knob and poking my head inside. The secretary was on the phone and gave me a stern look before asking:

— What the hell do you want? Can't we get five minutes of peace in this brothel?

— Brothel? But I thought I was at the bank, sister—my bank!

— I'm not your sister. Clear the way.

Her hand was on the phone's receiver, so I knew her final comment was meant for me.

— Is this not Mr. Khalil's office?

She pretended not to hear me.

— Who the heck are you?

— I'm sorry Ma'am, is it Mr. Khalil's office? I insisted.

She ignored me and went on with her mindless prattle:

— Hey, it was so much fun, we really missed you! Guess who was the life of the party!... haha... Seriously, who spilled the tea?... You won't believe how drunk she got... Honestly, I've never seen her like that... She was totally wasted... She got so carried away that she stripped off, danced on the table, and even put her foot in someone's cake... And haha... Get this, he grabbed her foot and started licking it!

I gently pushed the door open and approached her desk leisurely. As I neared, she appeared alarmed; ceasing her conversation, she placed her hand on the phone's receiver and glared disdainfully at me.

— Who the hell are you? What do you want?

— I've been standing here for the past five minutes, Ma'am. It seems you chose to ignore me. I need to confirm, is this Mr. Khalil's office? Yes or not.

She was visibly annoyed.

— I told you to clear out.

— I'm not your butler, Ma'am, but your colleague from 'Ouja Bank. My name is Bassam Bourasin.

— Ok. I've heard you. Did you get an appointment?

— I didn't, but I believe he'll make time for me.

— Impossible. He won't see you without an appointment. Mr. Khalil has a packed schedule, and I'm quite busy as well. Kindly, go home and come back when you got an appointment.

— I really can't delay, Ma'am. Kindly let him know that Mr. Bourasin wishes to speak with him, or I'll have to force my way.

She looked utterly shocked. However, realising my determination, she pressed the intercom button and relayed:

— Mr. Khalil, there's an individual here who's quite insistent on meeting you immediately... No, sir, he identifies as an employee of 'Ouja... yes, Mr...?

— Bassam Bourasin, I interjected.

She echoed my name. After a momentary pause, she eyed me with a mixture of contempt and anxiety and said:

— OK. Mr. Khalil will see you in a minute.

My audacity was making a mark. In a different scenario, I might have patiently stood outside, letting the secretary indulge in her frivolous phone chat before gracing me with her attention. Only then, and after scheduling an appointment days later, would she consider notifying her superior of my presence. Acquiring that appointment would involve tiresome negotiation, given the immense workload of HR. "This isn't just 'Ouja', it's the CAPITAL, for heaven's sake! You can't just barge in, especially not without prior notice, expecting a warm welcome even as an employee. This institution is a bank, not some rowdy establishment! Don't you understand?" I was well aware of it. That's why, until now, I hadn't dared to set foot in the main office. The right moment had to come.

I comforted myself with modest aspirations for nearly a decade and a half. I'd daydream about visiting the headquarters once I was elevated to deputy director or perhaps the manager of 'Ouja Bank. While I had no intention of challenging Mr Aroussi, who had consistently earned my loyalty, I, too, harboured dreams. In these visions, there was room for both his advancement and mine. Mr. Aroussi's fall from grace deeply saddened me. I felt sorry for him more than for myself because I knew that his disgrace would preclude or delay my promotion if it didn't accelerate my degradation and turn me into a tawdry victim of the Administration, which it ineluctably did when I was incarcerated a few days after his arrest. True, I was not expecting the Islamist counter-coup, nor that a casual acquaintance from my jail days would be elevated to a high position and thus propose to make me a happier man - with two hundred thousand dollars on the table and a promised stay in paradise with an Houry named Sophia!

With these exhilarating thoughts playing like a festive tune in my mind, it's not surprising that I confidently strode into the head office as if I'd made a grand entrance from my private helicopter. It was the first time I genuinely felt empowered, and ready to converse with a higher-up as an equal. I might've even requested to meet the Chairman, but that wasn't the need of the hour.

Mr. Khalil seemed taken aback by my unexpected appearance. Although he greeted me politely, he quickly made it clear he wasn't interested in revisiting the past — that's how he perceived my awkward reference to our previous encounter with Mr. Aroussi.

— Mr. Bassam, on a personal note, I bear no grudge against him. However, his reputation here has soured. Given his actions, he's now viewed as a traitor, and in my opinion, he's earned any consequences. But let's stay on track, how may I assist you today?

The individual in front of me starkly contrasted with the friendly Mr. Khalil I remembered, who once enjoyed light moments during tedious banking presentations. Instead, I now saw a more reserved figure, seemingly shielded by his role as a senior bank official. His gaze, filtered through thick spectacles over his grey eyes, was cautious, and he seemed almost protective in his cushioned chair.

— I wanted to let you know that I'm prepared to continue my role.

— A letter would have been more appropriate, Mr. Bassam. However, since you're here, I regret to inform you that there's still no verdict regarding our 'Ouja' branch.

— I'm aware, sir. I realise the 'Ouja' branch isn't reopening soon, especially given the repairs needed. The destruction I witnessed was devastating... A tragedy of immense scale. I tragically lost my mother and fiancée in the chaos.

— I'm deeply sorry to hear that. But, continuing...

— Yet, I believe you know, sir, that the bank's staff can't simply wait for the renovations. I've heard some of my colleagues have been reassigned to the main office, and for your information, I've dedicated fifteen years of service to this institution.

Mr Khalil cleared his voice and said:

— Mr Bassam, things aren't quite as you perceive. In fact, many of your colleagues have been relocated to other branches of the bank, and only a handful remain here. All these movements are temporary. As for your situation, it's a bit complicated. You've been absent for months, and there isn't any directive about your return.

I interjected:

— Khalil, after years of dedication, you can't just dismiss someone without justification, right?

He replied:

— No one said you're dismissed. However, should that decision be made, it won't be by me but the higher-ups. If they choose to recognise your services and let you go, my role would be to implement that. Your situation is tricky because, despite being one of our top employees, you were imprisoned with Mr Aroussi, who's now facing serious allegations.

— I've no connections with him, I countered. — If I weren't innocent, I wouldn't be standing here.

Khalil nodded.

— I understand, but you've been missing for several months, not just a few days. The bank needs clarity, especially with our reputation at stake. I'm sorry, but you must see how complex this is.

— So, what's the next step? An investigation?

He sighed.

— Most likely. And Mr Bassam, even if your innocence is established, the process might drag on due to bureaucratic hurdles.

— You're not suggesting I remain unemployed in the interim? You could reinstate me while the inquiry is ongoing, I proposed.

He contemplated.

— What if the investigation doesn't favour your reinstatement?

— Why wouldn't it? I was released without trial since they knew I was innocent.

— The police may believe so, but the bank has its considerations. Beyond your sudden arrest and subsequent release, they might delve into your personal life, associations, and more. They could exonerate you or let you go with due compensation. I genuinely wish you well, but my influence is limited. I can urge them to expedite, but that's about it.

Feeling cornered, I said:

— If the higher-ups decide on this course, so be it. But I won't be sidelined easily. I've been loyal to this bank for 15 years and have rights, primarily to challenge decisions that disregard my contributions. If you aim to oust me due to my arrest, tread carefully. Legal counsel is still available in this country.

— Bassam, you need to understand your position within the bank. It would be wise for you to remain silent and patiently wait for the administration's decision. Even if the bank terminates your employment, they will likely offer you a fair severance. Why risk your reputation by behaving irrationally? It's not a wise move.

— I'm not being irrational, sir. I'm standing up for my worker's rights. They deserve respect.

— You should recognise that you're not the only one in this predicament. We're facing staff cuts, even here in the Capital. The new regime isn't supportive of our banking methods. We're currently in talks with them, and the bank's future hangs in the balance.

— I might have connections that could help, Mr. Khalil. If you keep me in the right position, I can reach out to influential government figures.

He laughed sarcastically,

— It's amusing to think that a clerk like you could assist in our high-level negotiations.

— I'm offering more than just connections. I want a chance to show my commitment to this bank. Let me handle the repairs at the 'Ouja office. If you hire an external company, it'll cost the bank millions. I'll do it for half the price. I have a deep attachment to the 'Ouja branch. I know you have the influence to make this happen, Mr. Khalil.

He looked genuinely surprised, his face momentarily contorting in confusion before settling into an uneasy smile.

— Is this a jest?

— No, Mr. Khalil. I'd hate to see someone else get the contract.

He appeared stunned.

— I assumed you were only here to continue as a clerk.

— My position as a clerk doesn't prevent me from having business aspirations. They're not mutually exclusive.

— There's a clear distinction between a clerk and a businessman. It's impossible to be both.

— Why not? My name, Bourasin, means 'double-headed.' Fifteen years ago, when I joined the bank, no one had issues with my name. Did you forget?

— That's just a name, Mr. Bourasin. We couldn't change that. My shock isn't about the fact but your audacity. He hesitated, then said, — Still, I see where you're coming from.

— I'm pleased you understand.

— I heard about your mother's tragic demise. My deepest sympathies, Mr Bassam. Kindly excuse my absent-mindedness; I've been swamped with work lately.

As I readied to leave, I said:

— I don't wish to impose further on your valuable time, sir.

However, he responded energetically:

— Wait, wait! You're not causing any inconvenience, Mr Bassam. Sit down, please, and pardon my oversight. How thoughtless of me not to offer you a beverage. What can I get you – coffee, tea, or something else?

I couldn't help but note his abrupt change in demeanour.

— It's quite alright, Mr Khalil. Your gesture is appreciated, but...

He cut me off, saying:

— Actually, it's my error. I overlooked basic courtesy. As my guest — or rather, the bank's guest — not just an employee, you should have something to drink. He pressed a buzzer on his desk, instructing, — Kindly get us some refreshments. Mr Bourasin, what would you like?

Still surprised but willing to engage, I replied:

— Just a coffee for me.

— Would you like milk in it?

— No, just black, thank you.

— Very well, two black coffees, please, Miss. And while you're at it, please retrieve Mr Bassam Bourasin's file. I'd like to check if his salary for the past six months has been processed correctly.

When I left the bank about twenty minutes later, I had secured three commitments: My previously withheld six-month salary would soon be available in my head office account. A new role in the external transactions department awaited me, starting October 1st. Furthermore, I was allowed to oversee the repairs of our 'Ouja premises. In return, a small commission would go to Mr Khalil, but only if he secured my repair contract. He initially hoped for a fifty per cent cut, but I managed to negotiate it down to twenty-five per cent. We decided to keep in touch to finalise the contract details. I informed him of my stay at the Sheraton, which seemed to shock him, given the sudden turn in my fortunes. He assumed I had come into a substantial inheritance from my late mother and was exploring potential investments. I did not correct his misconception, seeing no need to reveal all my cards. However, his curiosity about the size of my inheritance was evident, as he kept suggesting various investment opportunities. It was clear he wanted a sense of the scale of my wealth. When I casually mentioned a figure of 'two hundred million dollars,' he nearly choked on his hot coffee, breaking into a fit of coughing that only subsided after he downed half a bottle of water. Composing himself, he declared:

"Kudos, Mr Bourasin! Undoubtedly, you're our bank's most esteemed employee, and I'll ensure the bank capitalises on your newfound prosperity."

(3)

Returning to the hotel, I mulled over my discussion with Mr. Khalil. His friendship seemed full of potential, grounded on shared interests. I mused about how splendid it'd be if everyone displayed such practicality, warmth, and service-oriented nature. If only life were that simple! Khalil's character intrigued me - was he innocent or driven by greed? Perhaps both. I wondered if I'd act similarly in his shoes.

Life then felt straightforward, almost inviting, a moment of pure joy. Navigating the bustling lanes of the Capital brought back memories. With its seductive yet oppressive nature, the city was a place I'd consciously avoided for a good portion of my career. Those cluttered streets, dense with glass and concrete buildings, always made me feel lost, insignificant, and over-whelmed. It often seemed as if the metropolis was a monstrous entity waiting to consume the unworldly villager in me. It was the allure of its pleasures I had to resist lest I get sucked into its vibrant vortex. Each visit was marked by my apprehensions, camouflaged by an air of aloofness and false pride.

Many peers found solace in the city's bars, nightclubs, and other entertainment venues. While the idea of a drink, a gamble, or a fleeting romance did allure me, I never truly gave in – a possible result of my puritanical beliefs. Reflecting on my past, especially my time in jail, losing my loved ones, and dealing with the Security Director, I wonder if I've changed. Am I still the man I once knew? The uncharacteristic encounter with Mrs Waterbird in the elevator further deepens this quandary. Such audacious thoughts were alien to me just a while back when I led a regular life working at 'Ouja Bank.

Clearly, I was in love because of an imagined encounter with Janet Waterbird in the Sheraton's lift. It felt like I had Janet in every possible way except physically. My passion was so intense that it mentally consumed me. Even now, I'm caught in this emotional web with her, and it seems we both played a part in turning a potential romance into mere platonic affection. Sometimes, I wonder whether I'm not chasing illusions. My perceptions have been so skewed that I've reduced a real lady with beauty like none other into just a mental image - much like the elusive Jennia of Haj Mukhtar. These could be lingering old habits that I thought were long gone. I once believed that physical intimacy wasn't necessary to understand love, a notion I now see as misguided. While I was committed to Dalila, I upheld a chaste mindset, except for visiting the whorehouse. But with her gone, I feel no need to hold onto that ideology. Who will celebrate my successes with me as I navigate life's waters? Of my acquaintances and kin, no one remains to share in the joy of my personal journeys in a city that has often been harsh and frustrating. Only Zerga, my loyal car, remains with me, like a relic from a world of oblivion. Alas, she might make odd sounds, but she can't communicate in clear words.

Driving with these thoughts, I slowed down upon seeing the red light at a crossroad. Suddenly, I thought I heard a mysterious and familiar voice from within the car:

— Congratulations! You're making great strides. Instinctively, I responded:

—Thanks, Zerga. I feel your happiness for me. I wouldn't trade you for all the riches in the world.

— I know you wouldn't betray me, said the enigmatic voice. That's why I'm here.

Almost instinctively, I retorted:

— Of course!

Only at that moment did I realise my folly. I was conversing with a voice I attributed to Zerga, despite knowing cars can't talk. Shocked and terrified, I glanced back. A woman, draped in a dark cloak that covered her head, peered at me with one eye—the other concealed behind a black patch. Did she climb into the car when I stopped at the traffic lights or before? Did she mistake it for a cab? Lost in thought and overwhelmed by the city's noise, I hadn't noticed her. But her unexpected presence stirred me, and I couldn't hide my annoyance. I pulled out near a bookshop:

— Get out, grandma; this isn't a taxi.

— Don't yell, son of a bitch, I can hear just fine. Keep driving.

For her age, her voice held a distinct roughness and vitality. Moreover, she curses!

— How dare you? If you don't leave immediately, I'll call the cops. Such unacceptable behaviour! It's utterly shocking!

— Press on, jerk; the signal is green! Don't test my patience.

— I'm not your driver, grand'ma; I've told you...

— I am not your grand mother, you fucking son of a bitch.

Suddenly, a gun materialised in her grasp, partially concealed by her voluminous sleeve. She aimed it squarely at me, proclaiming:

— See this? Proceed swiftly, before I snap. It's ready to fire, and should you act smart, remember that my finger's pretty jittery over here.

Overwhelmed, my eyes darted to a policeman shaded from the sun by a coffee shop awning. Yet, he appeared oblivious to the drama unfolding in my vehicle. How I hoped he'd approach to inspect any random document or that my car would suddenly malfunction, compelling his attention. I desired a minor collision, but fate ignored my silent pleas. All I experienced were the intense sunbeams hitting my windshield, almost blinding, and the murmured conversations of the coffee shop patrons on the patio, all against a backdrop of urban sounds and the steady purr of surrounding vehicles.

Navigating past the crossroad and making a right, the grating voice of the brusque woman echoed again. There was a familiar bite in her tone, though I couldn't pinpoint where I'd heard it before. But I'm sure I knew that voice as if it was the devil's or angel who haunts me for centuries.

— Where do you think you're headed? she inquired.

— Returning to my hotel. Where should I drop you?

— At your hotel, she responded, unperturbed.

— It's the Sheraton. Might be a tad luxurious for your taste... unless, of course, you plan on using your... weapon... as leverage.

— Feeling witty? Fine, I trust you won't let your so-called 'aunt' foot her own bill.

— I've no aunt, and my mother has passed.

— Sympathies, young man. But from this point forward, consider me your aunt. Clear?

With great indignation, I exclaimed:

— You truly don't get it, grandma. I'm just a mere guest at that hotel. I can't even afford my room, let alone have any extra money. How could I possibly pay for you?

— There's no need for an additional room, my dear nephew. Your room will do for both of us. Just say I'm your aunt here to see a doctor for my arthritis. And don't push me to converse; it might not end well for you. To everyone else, I'm mute and deaf. Clear?

— I understand, but what's this charade all about? As I said, I'm broke. You're barking up the wrong tree if you plan to rob me. This car I'm driving? We'd be lucky to make it to the hotel without it breaking down.

— Don't act clever, Bassam. It's in your best interest to get me to your room without any issues. I'm armed.

She knew my name, yet I couldn't place the voice that bore a resemblance to hers. The voice wasn't particularly feminine—it was rough, commanding, coarse, and very much male. When she said my name, a possibility crossed my mind, but I immediately brushed it off as implausible. On impulse, I slammed the brakes, causing the car to screech to a halt.

— Damn you, son of bitch! Do you intend to kill me?

The sudden stop jolted her. She fell forward, grabbing at the seat cushion. As she pulled back, she inadvertently revealed her face. I turned and, in sheer disbelief, blurted out:

— Hamda?! This is unbelievable!

— Yes, it's Hamda. Satisfied now?

I was stunned. No, pretty shocked. Before me was Hamda La'war, dressed in women's clothing.

— I assumed you were down south.

He regained his composure, smirking in response:

— It's evident I'm not in the fucking south.

— So, they're still on your tail? That explains the disguise. I'm sorry, but this isn't the right time for your theatrics. There was no need to hide your true self; you're just making a spectacle.

His temper flared.

— Get moving! You're clueless.

He veiled his face once more. It was then I noticed his missing moustache. It used to add character, but without it, he looked pitiful, reminiscent of a scalded rat.

We resumed our journey, navigating a narrow lane where vendors vocally peddled their produce from wooden stalls. I had to be extremely cautious to avoid hitting the throngs of pedestrians around them.

— You can't stay hidden in the hotel, I asserted. They're aware of my identity, thinking I'm a prosperous businessman, and they're monitoring me.

A loud laugh escaped him.

— A businessman? Oh, that's rich!

His laughter irked me.

— Why do you find that so amusing? Seems like you don't take my words seriously.

He snorted:

— Young man, I trust no one.

— Perhaps this once you should. I'm being candid... Truly, you... But he cut me off swiftly:

— Enough, Bassam! I've known you since you were a little boy. Remember when I took you under my wing? You owe your training, everything, to me. And now you're advising me? Yes, they're after me, but it's temporary. Soon, we'll be back in 'Ouja, ruling this country.

— You're deluding yourself, Mr. Hamda. The Islamists control now, and it'll be a while before their grip loosens. Think of another safe haven. It's not that I won't assist, but they're tailing me too. They've infiltrated the hotel, they'll spot you, and then...

— They're unaware you have an aunt, aren't they? They won't trouble an elderly woman, especially one who's deaf and mute, just going to visit a doctor. In the meantime, our allies will mobilise.

— Allies? Whom are you referring to?

— The Americans, boy.

His statement befuddled me:

— I'm lost. He rolled his eyes:

— Of course you are. You always were a bit slow. American Embassy staff are out in the city, distributing money to the locals.

— Really? How charitable! Americans have always been so generous. Look at the aid they provide to impoverished nations. It's quite the sum, millions annually.

He scowled:

— You naive fool! It's not charity. They're orchestrating a counter-coup, buying loyalties—trade unions, the unemployed, the disgruntled masses. Soon there will be protests, strikes, all starting in the Capital. Anarchy will reign, fires will burn, blood will spill. Once chaos ensues, our forces will strike, pushing the Islamists out.

I gaped at him:

— Are you being genuine or pulling my leg?

His face darkened:

— Have I ever joked about such grave matters?

He had a point, but I countered:

— Maybe it's just a baseless rumour. We do have a penchant for gossip.

Hamda bristled:

— This is the grim reality, Bassam. I've seen money bags exchanged with union leaders. Soon, all public services will halt, strikes will ensue. The people will rise against the government. Then, supported by this foreign money, our forces will mobilise. We'll target key locations, including the Presidential Palace...

I gasped:

—That's sheer insanity! They'll be annihilated.

— There will be losses, but we're prepared. I'm coordinating our party's forces in 'Ouja.

— But how? The Islamists have taken over 'Ouja. It's crammed with their militias.

— I might not need to go there, he replied cryptically. In fact, I have a better candidate in mind. When I saw your car at the red light, I knew it was fate. This is your moment, Bassam. Time to show allegiance to the motherland.

— You mean the 'party', right?

He gave a wry smile:

—The party will always be OUR patrie.

— But after the Islamist coup, the dynamics have shifted, Mr. Hamda. The old party isn't what it was. Now there's a new party claiming dominance. And just to be clear, while I am loyal, I stay out of politics. Reporting is one thing. Courting danger is another.

His grip tightened on my shoulder. I glimpsed his furious eye in the rearview. His unexpected return had stolen my happiness, casting a shadow over my life. It felt like I was trapped in a never-ending nightmare mirroring the fate of our beleaguered nation.

His voice was icy:

— Are you denying me your assistance?

— I regret the misunderstanding, Mr. Hamda. While you stand as a beacon for national heroism, I simply wish to safeguard my modest life and daily bread, no more.

His eyes narrowed, a sneer forming on his lips:

— Just a modest life? Bread? He spat out, the disdain evident in his voice. Is this a jest to you? When the nation calls out, you choose deafness? It's cowardice, pure and simple. Do you think we won our freedom with such attitudes? We battled not mere rebels but a monstrous empire!

I took a deep breath, finding the courage to continue:

— Mr Hamda, I don't really have much to do with your struggles, past or present. I was born in a country that's supposed to be free. People like you taught me about colonisation, making sure I grew up hating foreign rulers. I don't hate the British, the French, or any European country. If nationalism means hating others, then I'm not a nationalist. I struggle to see the difference between colonisation and nationalist governments. Both seem flawed to me. The exploitation during colonial times is happening again under our own nationalist leaders. Our new freedoms have become chains. Our dreams of liberty have turned into nightmares. This country, once independent, feels like a big estate where we're all just servants. You started the trouble that's now swallowing the country. You replaced one tyranny with another. And now, as your government falls apart, you're calling on the Americans? Is this the nationalism you talked about? Swapping British rule for American control? What's the difference, Mr Hamda? If you like foreign influence so much, why not live abroad? Can we really be fooled by your old-fashioned nationalistic songs? You and your ideas belong to the past. Your kind of nationalism stops real ambition and crushes any hope of a truly fair government. Let me be clear, Mr Hamda. If I ever helped you, it was because I was scared, not because I believed in you. I really regret it now. I might not like the new government, but I hate you and your methods even more. My imprisonment, the unfair pressure, the fact that I was probably arrested because of small disagreements—it all points to you. Mr Aroussi's surprise at my arrest confirmed that you were involved.

The car filled with an oppressive silence, a tangible tension that felt almost suffocating. The hum of the vehicle and the glaring sun outside were the only reminders of reality. The looming structure of the Sheraton in the distance was both a beacon of hope and a symbol of looming dread. Pushing down on the accelerator, a voice broke the stillness.

— You fool, Bassam. You've exposed yourself, Hamda whispered menacingly.

The chilling touch of a gun pressed against my neck suddenly made me freeze.

– Why are we stopping now? he asked.

– Mr. Hamda, you're walking into a trap. The hotel's full of cops and undercover guys. They'll spot you straight away. You've still got a chance to get away. Take it, or you'll regret it.

He looked at me, didn't flinch, and pointed his gun at me, saying:

– With this trusty mate by my side, I'm not scared of anyone. Whatever I've told you, pass it on. Anything else isn't your problem.

– There's a lot you don't know. I've got connections with the Interior Ministry. Just so you know.

I was trying to be totally upfront, but he replied:

– Old news.

– Maybe it's not new, but things have changed. You know I can't afford to stay at the Sheraton for long. The Ministry's looking after me right now, so obviously, I'm being watched. Plus, the head of National Security might be waiting for me at the hotel as we speak.

He thought about what I said.

– So, you've climbed the ladder quick... Your betrayal might've got you somewhere, but I'm not impressed with your quick climbing. You tricked us; you deserve a bullet in the head.

– Killing me won't help you. I was about to suggest a deal...

– Trading my safety for your life?

– Either way, it's the same for both of us.

– Spill it, then.

– I'll take your advice. But while you're in my room, you've got to be discreet and stay out of my business.

– How can I trust you won't turn on me?

– I promise, Mr. Hamda, you've got my word. But if your plan works, make sure I'm safe and remember I was on your side when things got tough.

– And if things go wrong?

– You should disappear and forget I ever existed.

– You little two-faced pig! he said, looking disgusted.

– Basically, I'm just like you, I replied. You're all top dogs, fighting all the time. Every time you do something violent, you just want more. Normal people are just pawns in your game, sacrificed because you're always hungry for power, money, and control. There's not much difference between you and your enemies. You're all the same. Your fights show you're pretty much identical, like two similar diseases. Remember, I've never been a threat to you. So, don't expect me to help your enemies, who are in charge now. Getting involved is pointless. If you need to contact your mates in 'Ouja, remember my loyalty has limits. If you're staying for two or three days, I promise I won't say anything. After that, you're on your own. Whatever's happened in the past, I won't be the reason you get caught or killed. But if you win somehow, remember I'm the one who helped you survive.

* * *

A short while later, our entrance into the Sheraton was as striking as anticipated. At the reception, the attendant turned to the enigmatic woman in a black cloak standing beside me and asked:

— Can I assist you, madam? Are you here for a room or to meet someone? I quickly responded:

— She's with me. This is my Aunt Hamida. She's here to consult a doctor about her arthritis. She'll be staying with me until her appointment is set. She's elderly and, unfortunately both deaf and mute.

The man apologised briefly and suggested:

— You'll need an additional room then, sir. We can provide room 357; it's right next to yours. There's just a door separating them, which remains locked. I can hand over the key if you wish to get in touch.

— That'll work, I replied.

While I was filling out the register for my illiterate aunt, he interrupted:

— Hold on, sir. Mr. Ali, our manager, mentioned you earlier today. He'd like to meet you, perhaps over a drink if you have a few minutes to spare.

— I'd be happy to see him soon, I said, thinking about the generous donation I had promised his organisation.

— Any other messages for me? I inquired.

— Yes, a friend of yours called from the Ministry. He mentioned joining you for dinner.

Having only one friend in the Ministry, Hassan, I braced myself for the evening.

— Do you need assistance with your aunt's luggage?

— There's no need; she's not carrying any luggage and won't be here long.

We then made our way to the lift, my aunt's black cloak dragging behind her; her presence felt like a weighty chain around my ankle. It dawned on me that our troubles were beginning. If not detected and arrested, the masquerade may drag on for a long time. That deadly complicity reassured me in the same way as living with a dormant predator.

The journey to the sixth floor was uneventful. My main concern was bumping into the Waterbirds; explaining my aunt's sudden appearance would be awful. I was sure Hassan would know about the new development if he asked the front desk. I noticed the driver's absence in the lobby, assuming he was probably at the Cafeteria.

Upon entering my room, Hamda discarded his veil and requested the key to the next room. His face was grotesquely painted, both garish and pitiful. I would have chuckled at his comically swollen face in any other situation. However, my current disposition was far from lighthearted.

— I handed it to you in the lift, I remarked.

He gestured toward the door dividing the two spaces, saying, "Not that key, I mean the adjoining door." I had planned to keep that door locked. The last thing I desired was him barging into my space at any given time, especially while I was penning down my observations on what I already perceived to be the tragic fate of the Islamic Republic, which if I believe Hamda, is born doomed.

— No need for that key, I responded with surprise, just knock if you require something.

His response was firm:

— That's not sufficient. I need that key to ensure you won't deceive me.

Following a tense altercation, I relented. It was clear he distrusted me as much as I did him. He unlocked the intermediary door and went to his quarters, mentioning he'd bathe. In the meantime, I arranged for our meals.

As afternoon shadows crept past the clock's hands, positioning themselves at 2 p.m., I was ensconced in a cocoon of dreams, the tether to reality manifested only by the persistent chime of the telephone. Half submerged in slumber, my fingers grasped the cold receiver as I murmured, lost in a delirious haze, "Greetings from 'Ouja Bank..."

"Sorry, sir. My mistake," a voice said apologetically. Silence followed. Then, I snapped awake, the last thread of a dream slipping away, a dream where I'd become a director at 'Ouja Bank'. I hated the jarring phone call, the unknown caller who'd shattered my dream. A second, insistent ring dragged me from sleep. I was determined not to let whoever it was ruin my morning.

I answered in a measured tone, only to be greeted by a familiar voice:

— Mr. Bassam?

— Robert? I exclaimed, the surprise evident.

— How's it going today?

Our conversation meandered from pleasantries to the proposal I had mentioned to Janet. Shortly, he entered, an enigmatic package tucked beneath his arm. Before our rendezvous, I had taken a swift detour to check on Hamda, finding him in a post-feast repose, evidence of his indulgence strewn around.

Returning, I settled in as Robert sat in the recliner near the expansive window, placing his modest yet mysterious package on the nearby table. His parcel was whispering tales of its contents. With a wistful sigh, he began:

— Janet left for shopping. I didn't want her to go out alone. Yet, the solitude she granted was a balm. She's constantly on my tail, and she's a goddamn fucking moralist!

He spoke of unsettling murmurs in town, of an undercurrent of unrest amongst the youth. His words painted the picture of a city on the brink of tumult, juxtaposed with our serene surroundings.

— I believe we'll need two glasses and some ice, said I. Fortunately, the rooms are better equipped. I believe I have some ice in the fridge.

— Well, whatever! I'm quite thirsty. Give us some ice.

As I facilitated his request, opening the fridge to retrieve ice, I offered words of reassurance regarding Janet, painting her as a robust woman in a currently tranquil city. Robert, however, cast doubt on the perceived calmness, bringing attention to brewing unrest in the campus area close to our location. He spoke of a significant assembly orchestrated by students, a situation often teetered on the edge of chaos, inducing clashes with law enforcement. He reflected on the personal turmoil experienced due to their son's turbulent phase at a university in England, a time that etched worry deep into their hearts.

In the muted ambience of the room, he unveiled the bottle. I set a pair of glasses on the table, and the symphony of ice cubes danced as they fell into them. Adjacently, I placed an ornate dish carved from white copper, brimming with ice, and confessed:

— I'm unmarried, and it doesn't look like I'll be soon.

With a thoughtful motion, he filled our glasses.

— My condolences. Janet shared the tale of your kin's ordeal. The solitude of one's homeland can be profoundly haunting.

— Never mind, Robert! These are turbulent times, indeed. Let us raise our glasses to the guardians in blue who vow to protect the good citizens of this country.

— Truth be told, my heart doesn't sing praises for law enforcement, my friend. Given a choice, my allegiance leans towards the youthful zeal of the students.

— Your sentiment doesn't surprise me. Such disobedience, I believe, is the crucible of art!

With a mischievous glint in his eyes, he lifted his glass, proclaiming:

— Indeed! Here's to the spirited anarchists, challenging the decayed dogma of the well-thinking! Cheers!

A pang of unease struck me.

— Man, don't yell that loudly. Are you going to throw us both in jail?

Hardly had the words left my mouth when the middle door burst open. Hamda, like a tempest, stormed in, brandishing his revolver, bellowing:

— Raise your hands! Whom do you speak of imprisoning, traitor? And who's this foreign acquaintance you entertain? Believe not that your English conceals your treachery. Hands skyward, now!

The raw audacity of the intrusion left us paralysed. Our hands soared in surrender, witnessing the gleaming menace of the revolver as Hamda, draped in his sombre shroud, loomed closer.

— You shouldn't be doing this, Hamda remarked critically. Isn't that alcohol? In a predominantly Muslim nation? This isn't right. Wait right here, I might just inform the authorities.

Robert's face turned pale, and he trembled visibly. The glass slipped from his grip, splattering across the plush carpet. Even though Hamda spoke in Arabic, the revolver's sight seemed to unnerve Robert more than his words.

— Who is she? Is she okay? Do you know her? he asked nervously.

— Calm down, Robert. I'll handle this, I said in English.

Turning to Hamda, I spoke in Arabic:

— Put the weapon away. You're going to cause problems for all of us. If you escalate this, it won't end well for either of us. Remember our arrangement? You promised not to get involved in my affairs.

— I was just joking around, he responded calmly.

Stashing the revolver beneath his cloak, he poured himself some of the alcohol, shocking Robert as he downed it. He leaned back and remarked:

— It's quite a good drink, comparable to what one might find in an English pub.

Still reeling from the unexpected behaviour, Robert questioned:

— What did she say?

— That's my Aunt Hamida, I explained, causing a surprised look on his face.

After sharing some context, Robert said with concern:

— She's drinking alcohol! Does she even understand? And she had a gun! It could have gone off.

— You've put us in an awkward spot, I responded to Hamda. He's wondering why you, a supposed devout woman, are drinking.

— If you can bend the rules, why can't I? I don't need to justify myself to anyone, Hamda retorted.

— What's she saying now? Robert asked.

— She's just expressing her desire to have a drink.

Impressed, Robert said:

— Please tell her I admire her spirit and open mind. She's quite unique.

As I translated, Robert offered Hamda another drink. Eager to connect, Hamda tried speaking in English:

— Me, friend, good.

Robert laughed, charmed by my aunt's attempt:

— She's delightful! A real gem.

Hamda smiled, calming his guard down a little more:

— I like your drink.

— Just be cautious, I warned Robert. She might finish the entire bottle.

Standing up, I went to get another glass. Overhearing Hamda and Robert's light-hearted exchange, I couldn't help but chuckle at the unexpected bond forming between the two.

When I returned to the room, glass in hand, I found Hamda already helping himself to the whisky.

— Don't handle that bottle, I reprimanded in Arabic, trying to keep the fun. Remember you're pretending to be a woman. At least let us have the pleasure of serving you, dear auntie.

Hamda shot back:

— Stay calm, Bassam. If you push me again, I'll forget our friendship and things could turn ugly. I'm not here to be bossed around, alright?

It was clear the alcohol was already clouding Hamda's judgment. Thankfully, Robert couldn't decipher our Arabic exchange. I took a seat, a plan formulating in my mind. The playing field would level if I could discreetly take the revolver from Hamda. It was pivotal for at least one of us to stay clearheaded. An instinct told me danger was lurking, and past experiences had taught me to trust that instinct. Hassan would be visiting later, and I needed to be sharp. Defusing Hamda or silently diverting his attention had become critical.

The intel Hamda provided was monumental. If Americans were truly entangled in such a secretive scheme, loyalty dictated, I inform Hassan. No diplomat, local or foreign, should brazenly meddle in sovereign matters. Swift action might still prevent the worst outcomes. A decision, and fast, was necessary.

I decided to inform Hassan about the potential conspiracy. However, with the uncertainty of his intentions toward me, I wouldn't say a word until the $200,000 cheque was in my hand. Regardless of the outcome between the government and the insurgents, my survival was non-negotiable. Fulfilling my commitment to Mr. Khalil was impossible without the funds. If I backed out, citing financial constraints, my promised position at the bank would likely evaporate. I pondered mortgaging family assets to secure a loan, but the acquired amount might only cover initial expenses. Substantial funds were crucial to completing the necessary work. I needed to tread carefully, ensuring Hassan comprehended the urgency of my financial need. If he saw reason, all would be well. Otherwise, I was under no obligation to part with vital information.

This was a pivotal juncture in my life. Today's decisions would either catapult me to unprecedented heights or plunge me into an abyss. Everything hinged on the unfolding events.

Chapter 11

The Dinner

(1)

Through the balcony, the room was filled with the muffled light of day and the lively hum of the street. Had I left the window open? It felt like we were on display for the entire city, transgressing its norms behind a mere curtain of smoke. Such an odd assembly we were! A British artist seeking refuge from life's monotony and his wife's dominance; a former leader from a fallen regime, hunted by the police, planning a counter-revolution; and then me, caught in a midlife identity crisis, questioning my role - banker, entrepreneur, spy, or historian?

— Your aunt is one of the most fascinating women I've met in an Arab country. Truly. I admire her resilience against societal expectations.

Robert's eyes darted to my untouched drink:

— Not drinking? Need more ice?

— It's fine, Robert. My aunt seems to be drinking for both of us.

— She sure can handle her liquor!

From across the room, Hamda shot us a glance.

— Is she married? What of her husband?

— If he knew about this, he'd kill her.

— Then he doesn't need to know. Who would tell him?

As I relayed the conversation to Hamda, he bristled:

— Tell him I'm not married, or you'll regret it!

Struggling with English, he "clarified," pointing to me:

– He bad. Me, no husband...

Robert, misunderstanding, replied:

— So, your husband would approve? Lovely!

— She means her husband wasted his life and never really lived.

— Ah! So he's deceased?

— Yes, he's been gone for years. She feels liberated now.

Robert laughed:

— You're as eccentric as your aunt!

— So, about our arrangement, do you accept my terms?

— Honestly, the money would help, but I just can't let all my art go for that price. These pieces really mean a lot to me.

— I respect that, Robert. I wish to understand the essence of your joy through these pieces. I value them, truly. I told Janet I'd pay any sum, but I have my limits.

Robert paused:

— The 'essence of my joy'? What do you mean by that?

— You just seem so untouched by everything, even while the world's falling apart. It's like nothing rattles you, not even heading into a country on the edge of civil war. Your chill, even when you're not sure if your art's going to sell, really stands out. It's obvious your art is your safe space. I can't make stuff like you do, but I figured having your work might give me a bit of that calm you seem to have. After seeing all that awful stuff in 'Ouja, honestly, I'd do anything for even a little peace.

Robert took a contemplative drag from his cigarette. From afar, the call to prayer resonated: Allahu Akbar...

Hamda, swirling the last of his drink, cut in:

— You're referring to the 'Ouja massacre?

I nodded.

— You have no idea who's behind it.

— Many theories are swirling about, some implicating an ex-sub-officer in...

Hamda's tone held an edge of urgency:

— In the troops of our president! That's a silly joke. Let me clarify. Insider sources suggest a deeper conspiracy involving the government. They speak of a clandestine flight, filled with professional assassins. Rumours claim Mamduh and Hassan are entwined in this, using Suleiman Mughli, an infamous thug, to mediate their sinister dealings. The goal? Pin the massacre on our troops, misleading the global community. The Americans' support for us now starts to make sense, doesn't it?

— Sorry! I can't trust your story.

— Shut up! You were locked up while I was out gathering facts. Remember, my connections run deep, even if they've been restrained lately.

— We need concrete evidence, not just words.

He raised his voice, interrupting:

— We have evidence. Days before the tragedy, a plane landed—filled with hired Mafia hitmen. The intermediary? Suleiman Mughli, a notorious Mafia guy. Yet, to divert suspicion, they imprisoned him. Those killers left for Europe the day after. Their aim? Pin the massacre on our troops to alienate us from Western powers. Hassan liaised with Mughli in prison, setting the stage for this. Mughli's Italian wife, frequently in Sicily, became a pivotal player. She set things in motion once she got the nod. Mamduh even met her in Rome a week prior, where plans were solidified with a Mafia chieftain.

He leaned in, eyes blazing, and went on: — Deny it if you wish, but you'd be ignoring the glaring truth. We might be tainted, but we're no murderers. We have our informants here and abroad. Doesn't the American commitment make more sense now?

Shocked by Hamda's revelations, I grappled with disbelief. How could someone like Hassan, who had been so kind to me, be involved in such heinous acts? He'd shown me kindness, treated me like family, and offered opportunities beyond my wildest dreams. Why would he, of all people, be responsible for the deaths of my mother and fiancée? My mind struggled to make sense of it.

While I couldn't believe Hassan was involved, Mughli's involvement was more plausible. His reputation for ruthlessness preceded him. Whether he was hired to kill one or three hundred didn't matter to him as long as he was compensated generously. He wielded unparalleled power, even in prison, feared by all, including judges. Reflecting on our interactions, I remembered his fake compassion, comforting gestures, and reassurance. And the way he hugged me in the hotel lobby, knowing he was free, sent a shiver down my spine.

Mughli was the true puppet master, switching allegiances as easily as one would change shirts. One moment, he was catering to the President's vices, and the next, he was aiding the opposition. Such is the power of the Mafia in this tumultuous landscape.

The truth dawned on me: it wasn't the military but the Mafia that ruled this country. While Mughli's role was expected, given his nefarious reputation, Hassan's potential involvement was what truly rattled me. I'd already heard whispers about the Afghan group's participation and criminal connections. But Hassan? The intellectual with a heart of gold? The thought that he might hide a monster behind his amicable facade was almost unbearable.

His knowledge of my identity before our introduction intensified my confusion. If he played a part in the tragedy, why approach me with offers no one in my position could decline? Was it a bout of guilt, a realisation that his ambition led him astray? Can conscience strike someone capable of orchestrating mass murder? Such an individual would be less of a man and more of an emotionless machine, an automaton fueled by malicious intent. Recollections of Hassan showed no indication of this hidden malevolence. His intentions always seemed genuine. Even when he withheld the money, arguing I'd squander it, I saw it as a protective gesture. As it stands, I owe my improved circumstances to him, right down to the shirt on my back. And the prospect of marrying his sister? It might even be discussed tonight when he comes over.

Certainly, Hassan seemed determined to solidify our bond, perhaps even through familial ties. At first, I assumed my exaggerated claims of wealth swayed him, but it became evident he had a hidden agenda. He recognised my bluff, but instead of reacting with resentment, he offered me a room at the Sheraton, which was a deal that, albeit shady, promised the very fortune I had falsely claimed. We aren't equal in this venture; I'm the vulnerable one. If the scheme falls apart, he and his boss can easily distance themselves, painting me as the sole deceiver. My past sins would conveniently resurface, positioning me as the perfect scapegoat.

I recognised the danger but felt trapped. Rejecting his offer risked not just the loss of newfound privileges but potential imprisonment with legitimate proof of my past crimes. I'd be labelled a traitor, a rat deserving of the harshest punishment. Execution, perhaps, or life in prison. My guilt is undeniable. No excuses, not coercion or blackmail, could forgive my past actions. Choosing a righteous path might have meant hardship, alienation, and the ire of Hamda and his followers, but at least

I would've retained my integrity and freedom. Sadly, the same frailty that made me a pawn in Hamda's games drove me into Hassan's intricate web. Afraid of the fallout from past mistakes and drawn by the allure of power, I willingly ensnared myself.

There was no overt coercion, blatant manipulation, or efforts to corner me. Every interaction with Hassan was marked by civility and subtlety. His suggestions were just that – those designed to present me with the best possible solutions. Rather than threatening me with a binding agreement that could imprison me for life if exposed as a fraud, Hassan extended an unexpected lifeline. He offered solace for the loss of my fiancée by suggesting a union with another - his very own sister, Sophia. By doing so, I can't solely blame him for any ill intent without turning that blame inward. If he had a hand in the tragic fate of my loved ones, it was likely a task commissioned by the State, a necessary act for some perceived greater good. He offered me the chance to marry someone precious to him to assuage any potential guilt and balance the scales. In his eyes, it was a gesture that would set things right. Hassan lifted me from the depths of my despair and propelled me to heights I could never have imagined in such a short time. How could I vilify someone who played such a pivotal role in my life? Even if he was somehow connected to the tragedy, it wasn't a targeted attack against my family; they were simply casualties of fate. Perhaps it was just destiny: Mektub!

Within the innermost chambers of my soul, I grappled with the overwhelming weight of equivocation. I stood at a precipice, unable or perhaps unwilling, to confront the starkness of reality. In reflective moments, glimpses of my past were marred by the spectre of subservience, of a life held in the shackles of political servility. Yet, when I dared to cast my thoughts forward, an alternate vision formed — of wedded bliss with Sophia, a life ensconced in luxury, with the world bowing to my newfound status as a man of means. Years hence, memories of 'Ouja's tragedy might fade, becoming mere spectres at the periphery of my consciousness, easily overshadowed by Sophia's radiant smile. Was it worth jeopardising my newfound ascent for abstract principles? Rejecting Hassan's overtures wouldn't breathe life back into the deceased. Instead, I'd find myself returning to life's abyss from whence I emerged. To even utter Hamda's revelations before Hassan would be to tread on dangerous grounds, for power, once attained, is loath to be questioned, mainly when allegations of unspeakable crimes are in the offing. I felt ensnared in a moral quandary, where the choice lay between aligning with the man responsible for my kin's demise in exchange for social elevation and risking all to confront him with a bitter truth. The pull of both paths was equally visceral.

Hamda's account, previously shrouded in scepticism, began to ring with an uncanny truth. I endeavoured to seek solace in doubt, praying his words were woven from falsehood. However, each version of the 'Ouja tale I had encountered paled compared to the intricacy and darkness of Hamda's. Despite his notorious history of deceit, the situation begged me to accord his narrative some credence. My observations cemented this inkling. Hassan spoke volumes of clandestine intentions in the shadowed recesses of the hotel, sharing surreptitious exchanges with Suleiman Mughli. They vanished, reinforcing my belief that their secretive rendezvous bore dark implications.

* * *

Suleiman had blundered when he leaked to me his appointment with Hassan, and when he perceived his blunder, it was too late. That is why he remained cautiously confined to silence for a moment afterwards. He was rather in a sulky mood as if he were already regretting what he had told me. When I saw Hassan, he did not mention that he was in the hotel the day before our meeting in the Ministry, and I did not dare ask him. What were they meeting secretly for? Indeed, the affairs of the state should not be discussed unless the latter has something to do with the Mafia. I knew the Mughli had helped the Afghan with guns a few months before the Islamist Coup. If both were in prison for some time, it was not unlikely that they would have kept in touch with each other, although they would have been quite discreet, for I noticed nothing before I heard the story of their former cooperation. The point is when exactly Hassan entered the picture. And since I later knew that the Afghan was his rival, I wondered whether the Mafia man ignored it. As he had helped the Afghan and, before him, the Scoundrel President, he might as well deal with Hassan and his boss. The more I thought of Hamda's story, the more I found it entirely plausible, and the more I felt myself impotent and miserable.

Furthermore, I knew that Hamda was well-connected. The men of the ancient regime are likely gathering intelligence about the new masters of the country. In such a short period since they took over, the Islamists could not have possibly purged the whole country and cleared away the sympathisers of the secular regime. Some spies are likely undetected in the airport or even at the Ministry of the Interior. Hamda heard the rumour from these spies about the mob landing at the airport like a group of innocent tourists. They perhaps did not attract attention at once, but they were noticed since they had to board the same plane a few days later. The fact that the Minister had been spotted with Suleiman's wife in Italy a little time earlier was to be linked to the group of Italian tourists. They were perhaps not all Italians, but they were all the same since they had arrived on the same plane from the same place. Why a Minister of the Interior should have to meet the wife of a notorious mafioso? Certainly not to lull her about her convicted husband! And where? In Rome, because in Sicily, there was not the slightest chance that their meeting would remain unnoticed. Rome is a great capital; nobody would care who our Minister was chatting to in any place they chose for the meeting! Nobody but our compatriots, and there are a lot of them living out there, either because they fled the country doomed by coups and counter-coups or because they are long-standing exiles. Some of those chaps would have noticed the bizarre meeting of an Islamist Minister with the mafioso's wife. They had perhaps followed them and reported their movements to their friends or relatives inside the country. Then, when the massacre of 'Ouja was publicly known, the linkage with the visit to Rome and the group of particularly odd tourists became inevitable. Particularly odd because a gang of Mafiosi, despite all the efforts to conceal their true identity, would unlikely pass unnoticed at the airport, at the hotel, or in any place they would go to. For though those men had perhaps the bashful faces of everybody, sooner or later, their behaviour would betray them. Man is a creature of habit, and I wonder how a Mafiosi gang would behave in our country differently from how it is accustomed to. Even a word uttered randomly, a gesture or a mere glance, would suffice to raise doubts and questions about them. I know my compatriots; their curiosity, confining most often to brash indiscretion, is legendary. They would not fail to plague the Mafiosi and to accost them, as they used to do with ordinary tourists, either to chat or to make some advantageous bargain such as selling traditional goods or exchanging currency, etc... If they did, it is unlikely that they received the accustomed response of the bored ordinary tourist. As they are not wholly idiots, they would wonder about the mystery of that group of tourists with sinister faces, behaving as if they were invited to some funerals. Of course, there is the civil war in the south, and the tourists are no longer eager to visit our country, but those who do are generally kind and courteous. They would cope with the natives and display some sympathy towards them. I do not imagine that the Mafiosi were able to do so. It is merely not their game! I do not say they are unsociable; I know that many of them may be pretty friendly and even affable, perhaps had they left wives and children waiting for them in the country. After all, they are like everybody... But coming over here with the deliberate thought that they are going to slaughter men, women, and children and going back home after that dirty job to meet their wives and kids as if they are returning from an innocuous excursion would leave on their faces the indelible marks of the killing. No eye would miss such a mark. Oh, naturally, because they are used to kill, they are also used to mask the tracks of their crimes. They would display featureless and stone-like faces. I heard of mercenaries fighting, killing, and rampaging for money's sake, and thus supporting revolutions and great causes. It might not have been different, except that there is no cause to fight for in this precise case but merely a sordid slaughter to achieve.

I lit another cigarette and emptied my glass. The taste of whisky in my mouth had become sour, and disgust overwhelmed me again. I looked around and did not understand why we were gathering in that room or the meaning of our meeting.

Absorbed in my thoughts, I did not follow the lame conversation that was going on between my two companions. Hamda was ostensibly more drunk than Robert, and he was trying to explain to him in his rudimentary English how the Islamists got allied to the Mafia. In contrast, Robert nodded, unruffled and undisturbed by his ragged language. They were not sure they understood each other perfectly, but they seemed to get on well. For a moment, I pursued laconically their idle chat. I was lasciviously languishing while my eyes roamed purposelessly through the balcony over the neighbouring buildings. I was somewhat irritated, and I do not know why I kept looking now and then at my watch without really noticing the time. I stood up and went to look at the street from the balcony. The traffic seemed quite normal; the shops were open, and the passersby did not seem in a hurry. They were strolling indifferently along the shops-windows. Some would stop to look at the goods or chat with the merchants, whereas the others would continue their walk up to the next crossing, which forked two other branches of the street. In front of the hotel, on the opposite sidewalk, there is a stand of newspapers and magazines, where some people gather and linger to read the front pages or to leaf through the magazines. The stand-keeper and two of his assistants were eyeing them sullenly - I had already noticed their gaze when I was passing by - in case one took a copy under his armpit and slicked away. The street was dirty and dusty, as if it had not been scavenged for days. Even the few trees scattered hither and thither at the same distance from each other on the sidewalks seemed gaunt and asymmetric. There was something awkward and meticulous about their being there, displaying their frolic shades, but somewhat amorphous, ill-entertained, and sad. I knew there was a public square nearby; I had already spotted the sorrowful state of its lawn and vegetation. The wild weeds were climbing onto the trees and strangling their flowers and branches, and the wooden benches were decaying behind the rusty iron bars forming the enclosure. If the architect who erected such a square in that part of the town intended to make it more cheerful and less sad because of all the tedious walls hindering clear sight, I think he had failed. The pitiful state of the square demoralised me more than the passive platitude of the neighbouring buildings. Even the green of its overlaying foliage seemed outlandish, artificial, and altered to me. I do not know how those citizens I saw loafing on the lawn or idling on the benches could bear such an ostracising place. Ostensibly, they are not natives of the city. Perhaps, like me, they are somewhat exiled, cut off from their roots, because of the war, the military coups, or any other social plague or familial disaster. Perhaps they were homeless and found in that forlorn square the sole refuge hospitable, where they would wait for better days. The season of rains had not yet started; I wondered where all those displaced people would lodge with their wives and kids when the winter falls on the town. Then I recalled the manager of the hotel and grinned. He was certainly still waiting for my donation, and it dawned on me that I was not more reassured about my future than the hundreds, perhaps the thousands of have-not and homeless people raining on the city from their remote villages. For the first time, I contemplated that I am also an exile, and what is more scathing is that I am an exile in my own country. Yet, I am neither an expatriate nor an outcast. Until my detention, I have always lived in osmosis with my milieu. I was a respectable member of my society, a twig of the great tree that encompassed with its huge, shielding shade the whole country... An insider. Then something went wrong. My life, as well as that of my family, was being stormed by a sudden hurricane. In a short time, I lost everything: my post, social status, and family. The solid ground under my feet cracked and slumped like a soft jelly or a loose, flimsy lay of ice crinkling and melting down under the sun... All of a sudden, I was nobody.

(2)

I am aware that I am still nobody. The fact that I am living, at least transiently, in a five-star hotel may be misleading to whoever looks at me. But who is Bassam Bourasin in this strange, vast, wild, miscellaneous city? What is he doing here? What is his purpose? Where does he come from, and where is he heading? It seems odd that the only echo from my past, and thereby the unique assurance that I am not quite a straw in the wind, comes from the casual, unsolicited, and even dangerous presence of that drunk travesty, whom I never trusted or believed: Hamda La'war! And when he disappears, as he will undoubtedly do soon, all my past will sink in the burbling flood crossing the city, and the whole country, and with him will vanish the last relic from my native village and perhaps even my memory.

Suddenly and curiously, I discovered how grateful I was to my old enemy. I have no doubt that Hamda had never considered himself as my equal or my friend, for he had unscrupulously over-exploited my weakness and humble origins. He would very likely resume the same behaviour if, by any chance, we returned to our former situation, with me as a bank clerk in 'Ouja, and he as the mighty president of the party's cell. Nevertheless, I wondered who among the two men I had to trust when I compared him and Hassan. The former had enslaved me to his party and made of me the stooge of his ambition. The latter had merely instigated the murder of my mother and my fiancée and made of me also the instrument of his ambition. That both of them are detestable to me seemed the natural and logical consequence. Then I realised that to be myself, I had to be on my own and to get rid of them both as soon as it became possible; that would perhaps estrange me much more than I am, for I would lose two enemies at once, without however winning a new friend. But since I am already an exile, the loss would not be harmful. That is to say that one needs one's foes in the same measure that one needs one's friends, for without enmity and friendship, we never know who we indeed are. It is from the opposition of two wills that the light sparkles out and spreads over the way; then, if we can overcome our impotence and bypass the paradoxical situation, the issue would be outgoing.

My feeling of solitude did not decrease because of these lucubration. I was more wistful, more gloomy and gaunt, more disheartened and flustered than I ever had been. Even in jail, I did not feel so abandoned by the mighty and benign providence, so orphan and afflicted by my fate, so induced to stick to the scant tribulation that overwhelmed me and enveloped my mind. I had something to cling to in jail. I was hoping because I knew I was innocent. I never believed that my indictment was serious, even when I shouted to Dalila in my despair that she might wait for twenty years before getting married. I still do not know why I behaved so sadistically, so cynically, so hypocritically with her when she was expecting that I lull her and ease her worries. I regret it bitterly now. Her warm tears will add a new burden to my already clogged loneliness. Poor Dalila! She had died believing that her beloved fiancé would rot in prison and that when he is released, it would be too late. Perhaps she had never abandoned the hope of seeing me again. The fact that she was still caring for my mother and was with her when the assassins broke in proves it. She would not have died if she remained with her parents. She would be at this very hour still living and very likely comforting me for the loss of my mother. I would not have felt so immeasurably condemned to loneliness and misery. But I will console myself again with that anachronistic and amphibious Mektub, albeit I know it is a pitiful and paltry consolation. It costs nothing to believe that God is behind our darkest fate and that he doomed us willingly and purposely to test our stamina. Why does He need such a childish game? Is He so bored with His creation? Has He nothing else to do than to strike His weak creatures with ruthless calamities and to watch them scrambling and scrimmaging and vomiting their guts? Mektub! Is God a sadist, then? Is He a perverse Creator tormenting His slaves for the sake of His selfish pleasure? What has this to do with His infinite goodness, illimitable bounty, and boundless generosity? Mektub! This is quite an acataleptic, senseless, obsolete, and even dangerous word. It is an alibi for criminals, a justification for genocides of nonredeemable human cruelty.

I wanted to believe in it, though. I thought I had no other option since I was impotent while undergoing the injustice. I had to cling to something, whether metaphysical nonsense or merely nonsense, whose vacuity is masked by a metaphysical rant, a simulacrum of reason, a hectic backlash of what is purported to appear reasonable. Islamic Commonsense, if it were! Popular sapience! Mobbish pre-science! What a braggart, desiccated, rusty duplicity! And I even played the comedy for myself! I tried to convince my reluctant, doubtful mind that Mektub is not an illusion but the only truth encompassing our existence. I told myself that I only have to admit it since I realise the ubiquity of the Almighty God. Afterwards, I plunged into my daydreams, married Dalila in the invisible world, decided that I was as capable as Haj Mukhtar to deal with Jins, spirits, and other poltergeists, exchanged my faltering - but yet tangible reason - for neurotic beliefs, and was even ready to step on the track of John Law and found a bank in the fictive world whose imaginative walls I have erected to surround me instead of the dismaying walls of the prison. Otherwise, I had unwillingly built a jail inside my jail, either to protect myself or to entertain the illusion that I was living an everyday life. I was dealing with the Invisible. Yet, I have omitted that madness is also invisible, though it is pretty palpable.

My imaginary prison gradually grew to overshadow and eventually replace the cold prison of stone and iron where I was once confined. Though I am no longer convicted by any court, I remain a prisoner of my own foolishness. I am both the jailed and the jailer. My mind, crowded with grand ambitions, caught up in unrealistic dreams and unsettling thoughts, pressed by irrational fears, and haunted by regret, guilt, and shame, is chained to the weight of my past. It is overwhelmed by vague illusions and tangled dilemmas, muddled by pride, self-deception, pointless struggles, and pushed and driven by false beliefs and weak conclusions. Hurting from past abuses and humiliations, irritated and entangled, I find myself stirred up and restrained, my mind now a passive, restless, chaotic prison for my soul—a graveyard of forgotten hopes and fractured meaning. Submitting to its relentless hold, I have wandered aimlessly for months, cut off from the real world, avoiding reality, hesitating along winding paths, raving about my life like an old fool, watching its ruin with a guilty pleasure, captivated by a dark fascination.

No, I am not yet dead. Would it be more honourable if I were? What was I spared for? To be the unwilling accomplice to the assassins of my mother and fiancée, the destroyers of my nest, the uprooters of my roots? No, I am not dead—I know full well I am not, damn it! But it is as if I were.

I am no longer able to look at Hassan straight in the eyes without thinking that he had given the orders to murder those whom I loved, that his hands are stained with their blood, that neither his good intentions nor his coaxing promises could change anything to the putrescent truth. What will I say to him when he comes? Is there still any choice left to me?

I lifted my head and stared at the blue sky of September. The sun is tired and sallow; its rays are still stabbing the drowning city, and the shades are slinking heavily on the silent walls, musty roofs, proud minarets, lazy domes, and shabby windows.

This is the same sky I used to see through the rusty bars of my cell, envying the birds crossing its bright space for being so free, upright, and happy. And now it seems to me that it is not the same sky. It is not barred in my sight, yet the bars are inside my head, well fastened into my brain, deeply wedged like nails in a coffin. The voice of the Muezzin came over again through the metallic sound of the loudspeaker, calling the faithful to their duty. Behind me, I overhear the cackling laughter of my two companions, hoaxed with whisky. Allah is Great, and His mercy is immeasurable! Another glass of that paradisiacal drink tempts me.

I returned to the room and poured another drink, which I took over to the balcony. Robert and Hamda gazed at me listlessly as I strolled across the room. The bottle was nearly empty; I did not feel the time elapsing. On the street, the traffic grew more animated. I noticed for the first time a little crowd gathering along the sidewalks. These souls, mostly in the vigour of youth, either swaggered past the gleaming shopfronts with no intent of commerce or stood statuesque beneath the sheltering boughs. Initially, my thoughts leaned towards the ordinary; perhaps they awaited conveyance. But the streets bore no vehicles for their service. Instead, they huddled in small and large groups, their stillness almost eerie in intensity.

Despite the mellowing effects of the whisky, I found myself trapped in a mood of sullen contemplation. Yet, outside, a vendor's vexation contrasted sharply with my inertia. With a booming voice, he directed his young aides, who darted about their kiosk with the urgency of creatures trapped. I pondered this flurry of activity, this frenetic dance juxtaposed against the languid pace of the traffic. Cars, once swift, now moved as if against some intangible force. At the crossroads, the traffic lights' governance had faltered; vehicles stacked, and their impatient horns sang a cacophonous symphony.

As I fixed my gaze upon the scene, I noticed a surge from adjacent streets, a tide of humanity all moving with a singular purpose. From the university's direction, a multitude emerged, swelling the numbers of those already present. These movements, coupled with Robert's whispered tales of a gathering and the swift approach of police vehicles, painted a clear tableau: these youths, interspersed with a few women, were perhaps the very students caught in the anticipatory cross-hairs of authority. Either denied the camaraderie of the campus or evicted from it, their presence on the street grew palpably. Shopfronts, sensing an impending storm, shuttered their windows and doors. The press stand nearby scrambled to safeguard its wares. The three men were busy arraying their merchandise and stocking it hurriedly inside their store. Vehicles grew restless, their horns piercing the thickening air. Both flanks of the street soon succumbed to the ever-increasing swell of bodies. This faceless sea of humanity, pulsating and alive, began to hum—a resonance building, overpowering the mechanical sounds, much like the tumultuous crashing of waves upon a storm-lashed coast under a shrouded moon.

Driven by a rising trepidation, I beckoned Robert and Hamda to my side:

— Behold, the streets are now awash with the sea of humanity. With a languid air, they strolled over; hands braced against the balustrade, their heads held back, seemingly apprehensive of the gales of change that threatened to blow. Below, the throng multiplied, surging, undeterred by the dwindling traffic.

— What the hell! Robert exclaimed, voice thick with a mix of liquor and a mounting dread.

— A demonstration!

— A rebellion! Hamda declared, almost jubilant.

— The dawn of a new era! Did I not foretell the demise of these despots?

— Keep quiet! I chided, sensing danger, The police will be upon us soon, and perhaps even the military. Don't triumph so fast! You're selling the bear's skin before killing it.

— Bloody hell! Janet's still out in this awful storm! How on earth is she going to get through that massive crowd? Just look at them! It's absolute madness

— Where did she go?

— Likely the souks, he muttered.

— If she remains inside the souks, I replied, she's safe.

His gaze, awash with concern, met mine.

— Meaning?

— The souks, nestled deep within the ancient Medina are safe. I don't believe the demonstrators intend to march on the Medina. All of the ministries are in the modern city; any disturbance will not reach the souks.

As we conversed, the shrill trill of the telephone pierced the atmosphere. After a moment's hesitation, I hurriedly attended to its call.

— Bassam, is that you? A familiar gravelly voice asked. I've heard tell of unrest near your quarters. How dire is it?

Hassan. For a fleeting moment, I felt disconnected, almost inclined to sever the call. But his insistence pulled me back.

— Indeed, Hassan. The streets brim with thousands, and their number only swells.

A brief silence ensued.

— Well, don't worry. We're coming.

I heard at that moment the monotone roar of a propeller or perhaps several, for the noise was quite deafening, and I was forced to shout:

— It seems that your helicopters are already there. What are you going to do?

A sardonic chuckle.

— What would you do if you were in my shoes?

— I'm not in your shoes.

— I know, but what would you do?

Contemplating, I answered:

— Engage them. With words. Ask them to retreat, to delegate a voice for their concerns.

Another pause.

— We've tried. Their desires are amorphous, rooted in chaos. They're but puppets.

The clamour outside melded with the roar of the choppers, becoming almost indecipherable. From my vantage, Robert and Hamda remained transfixed by the relentless horde.

— I intended to extend an invitation, Hassan continued. A soirée with Sophia, tonight.

—Tonight? I retorted, incredulous. We're besieged. How do you intend to breach this barrier?

— Helicopters, he replied coolly. Your helicopters.

Despite the turmoil, his calm resonated. He seemed untouched by the chaos.

— Is it imperative? I queried.

— Not in essence, but one shouldn't alter one's course for mere trifles.

— Trifles? Thousands amass, inciting upheaval!

— Order will be restored, the guardians of peace will ensure it.

—But are you not their leader?

—Ah, misinterpretation, he corrected, — I helm National Security—the realm of secrets and shadows. Distinct from mere law keeping. He paused, —Would you like to have supper with me and Sophia? She's throwing a party where you can meet some powerful people. It's a nice opportunity for you to be introduced. I was going to take you in my car, but I now realise you have a driver. So, if you can find a way out, he knows where the villa is. The party starts around 8 p.m.

— And if not?

—Trust, he replied. All will be righted. Before I could respond, the line went dead.

* * *

Amid this maelstrom, Sophia's dinner seemed a distant, un-likely mirage. I casually glanced at the opulent timepiece that now adorned my wrist—a spoil from my chauffeur. Its luxury sat in stark contrast to its former owner. Perhaps, in some moral bartering, I should suggest to Hassan that the man's wages be augmented. The theft was not in my nature; however, the beast within me often roared in commerce.

The roar outside now rose to an overpowering crescendo. Hamda, shadowed by Robert, stumbled into the room. Both were flushed from liquor and the rush of adrenaline, their eyes wide, betraying a mixture of inebriation and excitement. The very walls vibrated with the outcry from the streets.

— What bellows from the masses? I inquired of Hamda.

— They want peace, democracy, and amnesty for their com-rades.

— Seems a simple enough demand.

— Simple? It's merely the dawn. When the workers and the unemployed rally with them, that will be the true showdown.

— Curbing your enthusiasm might be wise. Orchestrating a revolution isn't a child's play. Your allies from the south are nowhere in sight. These students, unarmed, are but gossamer against the might of the police force. I suggest you capitalise on this upheaval to slip away. This place won't shield you for long. Should they apprehend you here, you'll be ensnared. This uproar is your chance. Blend in, then make your escape. Your continued presence here is a peril you might live to rue.

He paused, searching for words:

— Where do I go? Before crossing paths with you, I had shelter: a comrade's home. A buddy of mine, a trade unionist who is also one of our men. Everything was well until he vanished unexpectedly, and I have reason to believe he was being pursued by the police or militia. I fled the house since it was no longer secure; I was wandering aimlessly around town when I saw your car. Fortunately, his wife was not home; otherwise, borrowing her clothes would have been more difficult. Without this mask, I would be recognised; they have spread my photography and are for my head. It's hopeless. Either we pull them down in 24 hours or we're done.

— Don't daydream. You can't expect to bring them down without weaponry and an organised army. Where are the guns you mentioned? Where are your troops? Where are your friends? Where are the Americans and their money? Those youngsters you see down there will be crushed in two hours. Your revolution is a ruse. You should consider your own safety.

We were shouting to be heard. The roar of the crowd was growing increasingly overwhelming. Robert had been silent until now, but his growing distress was palpable. With sudden resolve, he headed for the door, declaring, —I can't stand by any longer; Janet might be in danger.

— Where do you think you're going? I inquired. He paused, hand resting on the door handle.

— I need to find her. She might not even be in the souks anymore. She could be in trouble.

— You won't get far. The streets are swarming with people and the police have likely blocked all routes. Plus, you're hardly inconspicuous, reeking of alcohol. They'll snag you instantly.

— My wife is out there! I can't just stay here, wringing my hands. I'd never forgive myself.

With determination, he pushed the door open and stepped out. On impulse, I called after him:

— Robert! Hold on! I'll come with you.

Hamda, grasping the gravity of the situation, looked alarmed.

— Where are you both headed?

After briefly explaining, he said:

— I'm coming too.

Surprised by his unexpected offer, I cautioned:

— It could be dangerous for you. Maybe you should find another way.

— No other way exists. I'll follow my nephew.

— But you've been drinking.

— Damn it!

Seeing his determination, I asked for his gun.

— Why? he shot back.

— Don't make matters worse. If they catch you with it, it might be the end for you. Let me take it. If things go south, I can handle the consequences better than you can.

— You don't even know how to use it.

— I hope I won't have to. It's merely for peace of mind—just in case. And more importantly, to ensure you don't have it on you.

After some hesitation, Hamda handed over the gun concealed beneath his cloak. It felt heavy in my hand, undoubtedly loaded. I donned a tweed jacket and placed the gun in its pocket. Hamda followed, struggling slightly in his long attire, his face concealed by the veil.

Looking back, I can't pinpoint what propelled me into the chaos. Why did I feel compelled to accompany Robert in search of his wife? And why did I let Hamda tag along? As if that wasn't risky enough, I'd added to the peril by pocketing a loaded weapon. Was it genuine concern or sheer folly? Those questions didn't cross my mind then. Somehow, I felt a duty to help Robert and Janet. They were strangers in my homeland, and now, as friends, I felt responsible for their safety.

Robert was so concerned for her that he didn't wait for us. We had to hurry to catch up to him. Our sudden departure likely perplexed the other hotel guests and staff who witnessed it. The hotel manager, Mr. Ali, was in the lobby. He walked up to meet me with a friendly smile, trying to engage me in conversation. But I swiftly cut him off:

— Sorry, Mr. Ali, I'm in a hurry. We'll chat later.

His confusion was evident as we swiftly moved past him, leaving him frozen like a bewildered statue. Outside, we found Robert looking despondent, scanning the chaotic scene beyond the hotel's gates. He stated the obvious:

— We can't get out.

Hamda, surprising both of us, confidently said:

— Follow me. I know another way.

Confidently, Hamda led the way through the parking lot, with us trailing quietly behind. Clearly, he was more familiar with the area than us. Amidst the tumultuous noise surrounding us, the distant thunder went unnoticed, its rumbling akin to a multitude of drums playing in unison. We couldn't communicate over the din when we finally registered the sound.

I could feel the changing atmosphere, the daylight taking on a dim and listless hue. While still evident in the sky, the sun was overshadowed by a thick layer of grey, formless clouds marching northward. Intermittent gusts of hot air met my face. The persistent heat and the oppressive atmosphere, contrasting starkly with the coolness of the hotel's interior, soon had sweat trickling down my forehead. Using my handkerchief, I dabbed away the sweat while keeping pace with Robert, following Hamda's trail.

We wound around the building, past the square, the pool, and the tennis court. The area, usually bustling with guests, was now relatively empty. Many had chosen the safety of the indoors, replacing their outdoor activities with indoor games or simply passing the time watching TV or reading in the lobby and coffee-house, waiting for calmer moments. Those we did encounter seemed unfazed by our hurried movement.

Eventually, we reached a more minor, seemingly unguarded gate at the back of the hotel. Despite its appearance of solitude, the distant shouts of protesters still reached our ears, leaving me wondering if our exit would genuinely lead us away from danger. Hamda paused, indicating the gate, and simply stated:

— This is it.

With caution, I reached out to the gate's handle, turning it. The iron gate responded with a creak before giving way. As we ventured out, we found ourselves in a densely populated back-street, which seemed less congested than the primary thorough-fare. We manoeuvred without having to push or jostle, weaving our way through the masses, hoping to find a less crowded route by reaching the next street.

But our hopes were dashed soon after. Before we could get to the street's end, we were engulfed by a tidal wave of students, their panic and fervour pulling us along with their frantic retreat back towards the main street. A formidable police force, armed to the teeth with cudgels, rifles, and machine guns, advanced towards us. As tensions escalated, some protesters began pelting the officers with stones, inciting the fury of a commanding officer. The noise drowned his shout, but its implications were clear when, moments later, gunshots pierced the air, some aimed at the ground, seemingly to target our feet.

A distressing cry reached my ears. I glanced back, spotting Hamda faltering and eventually falling to the ground. He struggled, attempting to stand, but ultimately resigned to crawling. My instincts screamed for me to return and assist him. Yet, the echoing gunfire and the bullets ricocheting off walls held me back. I rushed forward, only to be carried away by the multitude like a straw in a raging sea. I was in the middle of the storm, dragged along by an invisible force. Everywhere I looked, hands reached out, gripping my arms, shoulders, and wrists, pulling me into the tumultuous sea of humanity. As I was thrust into the thick of it, I quickly realised the futility of resistance. We moved as one, a singular mass of emotion and energy, and it was impossible to distinguish one from another. The din around me was deafening – a mix of shouts, cries, and unintelligible chatter. The street walls felt oppressive, like prison barriers closing in. I wished they'd crumble under the weight of our collective desperation. It felt like we were both the audience and the actors in a macabre play, the lines between reality and performance blurring. As the crowd's enthusiasm grew, it became evident that there was no control or direction. We were consumed by a frenzy, driven by a force that desired only chaos and destruction.

The realisation hit me like a ton of bricks: there was no escape from this nightmare. We had become one with the mob, lost in its madness. The clarity of this thought barely registered amidst the tumult. Waves of emotions washed over me – fear, anger, hatred, and more. My heart raced with an unprecedented mix of rage, anger and helplessness. The sheer magnitude of our collective lack of control was overpowering. It was as if we were mere puppets, our strings pulled by a sinister force lurking within us.

The reality dawned on me in the heart of the mayhem. We were adrift in a sea of chaos, our wills swallowed up by the overwhelming power of the masses. And somewhere in this roiling mass was the puppeteer, the unseen force driving us, though its identity remained elusive.

(3)

I couldn't see the Sheraton's towering, strong, reassuring walls, the lush green of the trees, or the soothing blue of the sky.. As fruitless and pointless as they are, the few landmarks I had gathered throughout my brief stay in the city allowed me to trace evidence of my existence and postulate that I am, in fact, the man I think I am, damaged and fading away. I was sprinting through the bituminous, damp, congested streets of an unknown city with flocks of people, bustling wrathfully and grappling with the upsetting aught that I didn't notice I was soaked from head to toe. A fine drizzle was splattering the pavement, the walls, the shop windows and the trees, and murky grey water trickled down the pavements in flakes and thin streams. Although the dense crowd had dissipated, I could still hear the snickering of bullets, mob cries, and the ululations of police sirens and ambulances. We were racing in clusters, and the rain was pelting our faces. I shifted my gaze backwards. Long red tongues of fire clambered, danced, and stretched obscenely in jumpy-dumpy clouds of black smoke hauling and hitching about the roadway. I carried on running.

The grim aftermath of the city's turmoil unfolded before my eyes. Storefronts lay shattered, engulfed in flames as parked cars became unwitting torches, and the tumultuous crowd swept through the streets, wreaking havoc and leaving destruction in its wake. I found myself darting from one street to the next, desperately seeking refuge from the chaotic mob and the heavy-handed police presence, but sanctuary proved elusive. Doors were firmly shut, and building entrances were sealed off. Law enforcement officers obstructed every escape route, resorting to live ammunition against protesters, no longer aiming at their feet. The result was a grim procession of casualties, with wounded individuals crawling amidst the chaos and the survivors inadvertently treading upon lifeless bodies strewn across the desolate asphalt. Once innocently splashed by our hurried steps, the rain-soaked pavement now bore a haunting crimson hue. Barricades, fashioned from the wheels of any available cars and buses, obstructed the paths of rioters and police alike. These makeshift barriers were set ablaze when the authorities advanced, hindering their progress. Unfortunately, the fires soon spiralled out of control, engulfing nearby structures. Terrified residents were forced to abandon their homes, navigating the streets with trepidation. In their desperation, they found themselves entangled with the police, who, with little hesitation, opened fire, often mistaking these innocent civilians for rioters in the chaos.

The scene before me resembled a chilling tableau from a horror film. It was as if humanity had regressed to a primal state, with women and children falling victim to unforgivable violence akin to rabid beasts. It was too late for the police to prevent this nightmarish tragedy. As I approached the harrowing scene while still in a sprint, I couldn't help but contrast it with the hypocritical and discordant metropolis it had once been. Instead, I witnessed again the beloved yet battered 'Ouja, marred by rampant arson and unparalleled unrest.

Just a few paces away, a young mother lay sprawled on the street, cradling her newborn child tightly to her chest. Strikingly, she was not veiled. I came to an abrupt halt and knelt beside her, observing that she was still breathing, though her words remained inaudible. She appeared to be in her early twenties, not much different in age from Dalila. I attempted to pry the infant from her grasp gently, but she clung to the child with a fierce determination as if he were a lifeline in the tumultuous sea of violence that surrounded us.

— Are you alright? I inquired with genuine concern, though the absurdity of my words was not lost on me.

Nevertheless, she offered no response. Desperate to assist her to her feet, I made a futile attempt. It was then, as I grasped her shoulders to prevent her from collapsing, that she raised her head and regrettably expelled a horrifying spurt of blood. I gazed upon the baby's pallid and bloated visage. His eyes, devoid of life, stared vacantly, and his tiny mouth was agape, frozen in a silent sob, as if on the verge of crying. It was the same bullet that had pierced his mother's chest that had now lodged in the baby's heart, silencing his potential cries forever. With the mother's head tilting back, there remained nothing more to bear witness to in that tragic moment.

Slowly, I rose from my crouched position, a morbid fascination lingering as I withdrew from the sombre tableau I had just observed. After covering a few meters, I turned back to face the two lifeless bodies, locked in a final, unyielding embrace, even in death. Raindrops pelted their now skeletal forms as people scattered in all directions to escape the terrifying storm of bullets raining down upon them. The police closed in, their gunfire echoing in my ears so closely that I momentarily believed I had been hit. Reacting instinctively, I fled the scene, raising my hand to shield my ear as if seeking solace in that futile gesture of self-protection.

I lost all sense of time and place; my direction was unknown, and I followed the fleeing crowd blindly. The street stretched endlessly, or perhaps it did end, only to lead us to another or even back to where we began. Were we trapped in a never-ending loop? I now recall seeing the lifeless bodies of that woman and her baby multiple times as I sprinted through the chaos. It was inconceivable that they could have been shot down on every street corner; it defied reason. Perhaps I was hallucinating, perhaps it was a different woman each time... But such a notion was implausible! I couldn't convince myself otherwise. I'm sure that as long as I ran, that haunting image persisted. Periodically, I encountered a lifeless woman lying on the rain-soaked pavement, clutching her child with an unyielding grip, their pallid faces bathed in a grim mixture of rain and blood. Gradually, my flight ceased to be from the police bullets; instead, it became a desperate escape from the relentless sight of that woman cradling her baby, reminiscent of Mary holding the infant Jesus. I can't explain why their presence filled me with such dread that I averted my gaze when I sensed their presence on the opposite side of the street, as if they lay there in their tragic tableau of rain and blood, waiting for me to approach and futilely attempt to raise the mother to her feet. In vain! She would gaze at me, her expression one of helplessness, and instead of vomiting blood, she would break into hysterical laughter. Her head would then fall back, and I would hastily rise to my feet and scurry away, only to stop and glance back at her. I would resume running, bullets whizzing past and the endless street stretching before me. The city opened its gates like a gaping furnace, ready to consume me. The rain relentlessly pounded my face, and I felt ensnared in this desperate escape.

Suddenly, a hand clamped onto my arm, halting my aimless sprint, and a familiar voice called out:

— Bassam! Where have you been, for Heaven's sake? Are you alright?

It was Robert, drenched and dishevelled, his clothes torn, and his face smudged as if it had been greased. Recognising him was a challenge, but his eyes and fair hair ultimately confirmed his identity, though his voice alone would have sufficed.

I exclaimed:

—Thank God, you're alive, Robert!

He chuckled.

—Yes, I've got a thick skin, too thick for bullets!

My concern shifted to Janet. A shadow passed over his eyes, and he scanned the surroundings cautiously. I hadn't noticed that I had unwittingly entered a narrow alley, but following his gaze, I realised we were in a dead-end. Fortunately, it was empty. Distant gunshots and cries persisted, indicating that the chaos had not yet subsided. He grabbed my arm and urged me to follow him.

—Come on, we can't stay here. It's too dangerous.

We entered an arched doorway, finding ourselves within the dim corridor of what appeared to be an old building. While I struggled to adjust to the darkness, Robert fumbled along the wall momentarily. It was then that I noticed evening casting its shroud over the city. Outside, darkness had also fallen, but the electric streetlights battled against the rain and the night. Eventually, Robert found the switch, and a faint, yellowish bulb dangled from the ceiling, illuminating the corridor. I spotted a staircase and settled down on the steps. Robert joined me, leaning his back against the railing in silence for a moment before he asked:

—Do you have any cigarettes?

I delved into my pockets.

— Yes, I must have some.

I retrieved a cigarette pack from my inner jacket pocket and ensured it remained dry. I handed him one and took another for myself. We lit our cigarettes, enveloped in the chilly air of the narrow, dingy-walled corridor. Occasionally, distant gunshots shattered the sombre evening silence, but the sounds of the mob had faded by then. I inquired:

— How did you find this refuge?

— It wasn't easy, he replied. I hid under a car parked on a nearby street when the helicopters began firing at the crowd...

I interrupted him, my tone sullen:

— I didn't realise the helicopters were involved.

—They were, indeed, he continued. Bullets were raining down from the sky!

I was on the verge of apologising, for officially, I was the one who had brought those helicopters to the country. However, when I had signed the contract, I had no clue the police would use them to cause such mass casualties. Besides, the contract was a sham. I couldn't be held accountable for the misuse of those helicopters, and expressing an apology would have seemed odd, shocking and misplaced.

—The car I was hiding under caught fire, Robert said; so I had to flee and wandered until I found my way here. But something struck me. When I was under that car, I observed everything happening in the street, and now I'm convinced it wasn't the students who turned the demonstration into a violent riot; it was the police.

I inquired:

— Why are you so certain?

— Because the students weren't armed, were they? However, the police began shooting at them. Then I saw a group of men approaching from another street, and it appeared they were all Islamists, identifiable by their beards and their handling of clubs, sticks, and possibly even guns.

— Do you mean the Islamic Militia?

— Very likely. Those men I saw were the ones who initiated the fires; they set wheels and entire cars ablaze in the streets, shattered shop windows with iron bars and motorcycle chains. They rampaged for a significant period without police interference. Then, they withdrew, leaving the place in flames and covered in blood; it was only at that point that the police intervened.

— It's strange, but not entirely surprising, I responded. They are capable of such duplicity; in any case, it serves their interests.

— Why would it serve their interests?

I recalled my conversation in 'Ouja with the Indian.

— Well, it's a complex story. In reality, the Islamists are not as united as they may appear. They are divided into factions, each vying for more power and privileges. For instance, the Chief of the Militia may be at odds with the Director of Security, which suggests that he may have unleashed his men to create trouble for his rival. I wouldn't be surprised if I learned that the Afghan—I mean, the leader of the Militia—had orchestrated this chaos. He likely has his supporters, even within the university... although there are other possibilities.

Robert pondered this for a moment. —Not unlikely, he conceded. —Many students are undoubtedly Islamists, and it's odd that they would participate in a riot against the government unless not all of them are involved. The situation is quite murky. I was astonished to see them, you know, and I hadn't considered the possibility of an internal government struggle.

—If you witnessed the Islamic Militia, there's no doubt about their involvement. It's unmistakable.

— Jesus! I not only saw them, but I'd bet my right hand that they are the culprits who set the city ablaze. I'm certain they would have killed me if they had caught me. I've seen everything they'd want to hide.

—They most likely would have. But what about Janet now?

— Yes, let's go to the souks. Maybe she's out there.

Robert squeezed his cigarette beneath his shoe and stood up. I followed him onto the street. The night seemed quieter, but the drizzle persisted, pelting the pavement.

As we emerged from the alley, he asked:

— Where's your aunt?

I hadn't anticipated the question, as I had forgotten entirely about Hamda.

— Oh, don't worry about her, I replied. By now, she's probably at the police station. They'll assist her in getting back home.

Robert chuckled, seemingly unaware that a bullet near the hotel had hit Hamda.

— It appears she's quite familiar with the Sheraton!

— Yes, indeed. It's her go-to spot whenever she's in the city.

He hesitated:

— Is she... um... always fond of the... um...

—Well, not consistently. But who knows? I don't see much of her, you know.

His expression remained unchanged, but I thought he was harbouring suspicions.

—You probably shouldn't have allowed her to follow us, although I'm not sure how we would have escaped without her help. If she's indeed at the police station, I doubt they'll be very kind to her... you understand, she was inebriated!

—Oh, yes! But if she receives a few slaps on her big buttocks, it won't hurt her. It might teach her a valuable lesson, so that in the future, she refrains from imitating men's behaviour!

He chuckled and replied:

—Ah, well!

(4)

30th September ...

Tomorrow, I'm going back to work at the bank... or rather, I'm going to finish my career in the Capital I used to despise. Everything is fine, and there is no reason for it to be otherwise. If I were a writer, I would have begun my novel with the hero's incarceration and ended it with his return to his bank, or more precisely, his promotion to a new position in the Capital. That is the happy ending, but even though I am getting there, I am not there yet. Fortunately! It is true that I am not a real hero but rather a fictive one. But it doesn't matter, since, anyway, I will be decorated. Eh! A national hero without war or fighting! That's as appealing as a genuine vocation would be. Hamda received his honorific medal after cuckolding his shoemaker neighbour. A great deed that went on the record as a notable sacrifice for the nation. I'll acquire the same medal for a phoney price in helicopters I never saw, let alone bought. The nation will be thankful to me, just as it was to Hamda for doing much less than I did. The time has come for such immense rewards.

I had not only performed my civil duty for many years without expecting anything in return from the State - which, I recognise, is absurd because these services are compensated - but I had also been the scapegoat of internal power struggles between men I hardly knew, and if I did, I hardly trusted, although I professed to be loyal to them. I am not just referring to Hamda and his party but also to those who still hold power - I am referring to the Islamists, who had not been not ousted as Hamda wished. The riot was in vain. A great deal of damage and casualties, horrifying bloodshed, a foreboding and terrifying metamorphosis of the city into a sobbing, howling bottomless pit of human remains, an open racked place for the demon's kinks... May Allah's kindness be upon us! What a shambles! What nonsense! And that horrible, gory erroneousness was muffled under the hypocritical veil of reciprocal grievances, recriminations, apologies, promises, and hand-shaking between government members and students' representatives. We all smiled and relaxed as we watched them meet on our TV screens. Nothing felt more distant to them than the fact that hundreds of people had died, and they were not all rioters. They pretended not to be interested in death figures. What were all those people killed for? It wasn't the question to ask. Who cared or dared to? Everyone had realised that there was no sense in digging a ground completely swollen with excrements while we were all treading on it and attempting to hide its miasmic effluvium with a flowery carpet, and thus, great reconciliation was taking place.

I'm not complaining. God, no! Peace is always better, even if it means forgetting the dead and forgiving their killers! Forgetting the killed is less dangerous than forgetting their killers.

We should be grateful, for we survived. We watched in awe as the kids were welcomed at the Presidential Palace like National Heroes. I must add that they had not been adorned as we had hoped, but I am confident this will not be a problem.

Abdelghani Abdelghaffar, wearing his customary black spectacles, sported a military uniform adorned with many medals befitting a General. It left me pondering the origins of those decorations festooning his chest. As far as I could recall, they couldn't have been earned on a battlefield. Our country had not seen any major conflict. And if one were to reminisce about the 1967 war against Israel, I struggled to identify any reason our officers should be rewarded for their conspicuous absence from the actual battlefield—unless, perhaps, the defeated were also being decorated!

But Abdelghani is a man of integrity. I doubted he would embellish himself with accolades for fictitious deeds unless our military heroes were just as fictitious as their civilian counterparts! True, he squints quite dramatically, but that alone should not justify self-promotion. After some contemplation, I arrived at two potential scenarios. Perhaps, like Hamda La'war, he had been involved in a dubious affair involving another man's spouse, which left him cross-eyed after a confrontation with the aggrieved husband—but still, he managed to secure his decorations. Alternatively, his comrades might have rewarded him with numerous medals following a successful coup against the Scoundrel. Regardless, there was no denying his merit. He was undoubtedly the right man in the right place.

As the saying goes, sometimes the most common of clichés holds wisdom. Is he not still combating the Scoundrel who threatens to transform our peaceful nation into a graveyard? That Genghis Khan of ours had not yet conceded defeat. He hopes to return to power, although I wish he never would. I was confident that our brave soldiers would make short work of him. I had good reason to believe so, as my brother-in-law informed me that we had recently received new supplies of weapons and aircraft. We were bolstered. Moreover, the fuel shortage, which had significantly hindered our war effort, was no longer an obstacle, thanks to our friendly neighbours who generously agreed to supply us with whatever we needed. Naturally, this assistance was not without conditions. We would need to reciprocate when the civil war concluded and our enemies were defeated.

For one thing was certain: our neighbours held no affection for the Scoundrel, and his vision of a secular regime with all its Western trappings rankled them. They recognised him as a liar, but what if his rhetoric deceived their populations? It would not be the first time a charlatan had led millions astray with falsehoods and empty slogans, just as Hitler had done, albeit through a relatively democratic election process. However, our Scoundrel's ascent began with the king's deposition and the republic's proclamation. Subsequently, he dismantled the constitution, promising to replace it with a modern one inspired by European models. Meanwhile, we were left in a constitutional vacuum, with the President as the sole source of law.

Ultimately, he would have set the entire region ablaze with subversion if he had remained in power. Such chaos at their borders was intolerable to our conservative neighbours. Thankfully, some determined patriots, moved by the suffering gradually imposed upon our people, took action. General Abdelghani Abdelghaffar led the charge who, despite his optical handicap, commandeered his illustrious tank and launched an audacious assault on the presidential palace one fateful night.

Unfortunately, the Scoundrel managed to elude capture, while Abdelghani, blinded by the labyrinthine corridors of the vast palace, pursued one of the bodyguards, mistaking him for the fugitive. In the heat of the moment, he shot the bodyguard down, believing he had killed the former president. The jubilant news was hastily relayed to television and radio journalists, who eagerly broadcast it. It was a regrettable error but one for which Abdelghani could hardly be held accountable. He had a compelling excuse: his pronounced squint, a fact known to all his colleagues. They should have approached the delicate matter of assaulting the palace with more sense, which might have prevented the Scoundrel's escape. Alas, it was too late now. Yet, all our current predicaments undeniably trace their origins back to one source: the darkness of that night and the squinting eyes of General Abdelghani!

I was drawn to the President, not realising how highly regarded he was by our neighbouring nations. It's clear that nobody truly grasped his significance before the Coup. To compensate for our earlier ignorance, we now shower him with more exuberant displays of loyalty. The General's portraits, adorning shops, walls, and public spaces multiply in number and size each day. We're gradually uncovering the man's true stature and expressing our gratitude for his efforts to rescue us from the vile Scoundrel and bring peace to our nation. Even a whimsical rumour is circulating that the General doesn't squint; instead, he bears the "Hawar Al-zine," the unmistakable mark of beauty! Nonetheless, all depictions of the President continue to feature his trademark black glasses. While I haven't seen a painted portrait, I'm confident that the country's finest artists are working, capturing various aspects of the President's features.

My focus has shifted towards all the varied presidential life's splendid and noble facets since my marriage. Naturally, I now find myself happily settled in the very heart of my beloved wife, just as I am securely anchored in the heart of my beloved country—the Capital—while maintaining a solid connection to my cherished bank. I've become an actual Capitalist in every sense of the term. I own a significant sum of money and some properties, making me a capitalist in the financial sense. Moreover, I reside in the Capital, which solidifies my status. The days when I felt like a refugee, akin to the thousands of homeless individuals, are behind me. My marriage to Sophia has ended my feelings of being an outcast or in exile. It has thrust me into the forefront of society. By marrying the former Minister's divorcee, I've essentially taken his place—not yet in the Ministry, admittedly, but Sophia is convinced I possess the qualities of a great statesman. She's determined to use her influence as a Minister-maker to secure my best position. In the meantime, my new and genuine career has just commenced. I must be a devoted and supportive husband to rise swiftly and ascend to great heights.

I'm in no rush. Currently, I hold the position of Chief of the Transfer and Exchange Department at the bank. However, it's merely a nominal role. I'm not obligated to show up at the office daily, nor am I required to do substantial work when I do. This is, in essence, an aristocratic post-tailor-made for me. I receive a full Chief of Department's salary, and my role primarily involves overseeing my team's work. — Just take a look and sign whatever papers they show you, Mr Khalil advised me. Don't trouble yourself with reading everything; we have people specially trained for that task. Your job is simply to sign, Mr. Bassam.

Furthermore, I now hold a position on the bank's board. I attend board meetings alongside other directors. I am not yet a high-ranking boss, but a boss nonetheless. However, I've reached a point where I don't even need to actively work, as my wife is wealthy, although I'm uncertain about the extent of her wealth. I haven't delved into her bank accounts to compare her assets and mine; it's a sensitive matter. Nevertheless, I'm aware

that if I require funds for my projects, she will offer her support. We are, in a sense, partners. My $200,000 is now at my
complete disposal in the bank. On this front, Hassan has kept
his promise admirably. Sophia knew I intended to embark on a
construction enterprise and that repairs at the 'Ouja bank would
commence soon. She's eager to assist me in realising this cherished project.

* * *

Actually, my primary occupation today is excelling in my role
as a husband. I had no idea such a profession existed before
marrying Sophia. She doesn't compensate me monetarily, but
there are various rewards for fulfilling my duties well. I wouldn't
have delayed my marriage if I had known about it earlier. Engaging in such intriguing careers should ideally commence early
in life. (Of course, my perspective was quite the opposite during
my time in prison, but I was inexperienced then.) It's never too
early to excel, and it's certainly more appealing than toiling as a
bank clerk for a meagre salary. I don't renounce my previous job;
I don't deny that I found contentment as a clerk at the 'Ouja
bank. However, at that time, I was oblivious to the realities of
life. Sophia convinced me that if I aimed to ascend in society, I
needed to relinquish the inconsequential role of a village bank
clerk, which didn't align with my newfound status as the former
Minister's spouse. When I asked her, "What should I do then?"
   "You're so honest, my dear," she giggled. "Does that pose a
problem?"
   "Yes," I replied. "I don't know any other job."
   "I'll give you one," she said, "be my husband."
   "Is that a job for a man, Sophia?"

"Do you mean that it is more convenient for a woman?"

"That's not what I mean, dear," I said, laughing at the joke. But, when asked about his business, a guy cannot simply answer, "I am the husband of my wife."

"Why not? That is the job that every man in the country will envy you for, my dear. Isn't that what they do for the Queen's husband?"

That was it!

I am embarking on a new career with high hopes of swift advancement. My boss—by which I mean my wife—is exceptionally encouraging. She already envisions me as a Minister in President Abdelghaffar's government. This burgeoning interest and involvement in the exhilarating political arena continue to draw me closer to the top, which I believe is the right path.

Sophia is enthusiastic about propelling me rapidly towards success and the pinnacle of power. She expressed sympathy for my perceived misfortune when I casually mentioned the helicopter deal. In her view, I should have demanded at least fifty per cent of the agreement. She made it clear that the one hundred million dollars that went into her ex-husband's pocket as his share of the deal were ill-gotten gains, a sentiment I agreed with. But what about the other hundred million pocketed by her brother? She remained silent on that matter. However, she did blame Hassan for allowing Mamduh to claim half of the bid, although she didn't confront him directly. I explained to her that Hassan couldn't have acted independently and profited from clandestine deals behind the Minister's back without the tacit agreement and protection of his boss—Mamduh. I emphasised that selfishness is detrimental to both politics and business. Sophia responded with a shrug and a moment of contemplation. I continued, stressing the importance of placing national interests above personal considerations. She yawned and quipped, "Well, next time you're involved in a major business deal, please remember that seeking my advice is in the national interest. Okay?"

I'm sure she's right. A statesman-maker like her is never short of good ideas. As the ex-wife of a sitting Minister and the potential wife of the next one, she's ideally positioned to discern the national interest better than anyone else. I mustn't overlook the fact that she's also the sister of the National Security Director, which further bolsters her credentials. I've discovered a true treasure in her—goodwill, wisdom, patience, and tenderness.

Sophia is a bit older than me and already has three children—two daughters and a son. However, the few years of difference between us aren't daunting or unsettling. I've found that marrying an older woman has its advantages. She generously shares her extensive life experience, allowing her husband to be both her adoptive son and husband simultaneously. Having lost both my mother and fiancée in the tragedy of 'Ouja, I've found a woman kind enough to fill both roles in my heart and mind in Sophia. Consequently, my life has taken a decisive turn.

We married quickly, just a week after our introduction, as if we had wasted enough time before our meeting and could no longer bear to be apart. Later, Sophia confessed it was love at first sight. I told her I was flattered and honoured, which was true. I added that I had an affection for her even before we met, which was a fabrication. She was delighted and intrigued, wondering how is it possible to love someone without seeing. I playfully replied, "That's the secret of men; women love at first sight, whereas we can fall in love from afar."

The wedding ceremony was far more straightforward than I had anticipated during all those years I was betrothed to Dalila. On the appointed day, I accompanied Hassan and some friends to the city's grand mosque. We sat on the mat before the sheikh, who recited some verses from the Koran. After the prayer, we formed a circle, and the sheikh declared me married to Sophia, instructing me to sign the marriage contract, which I did. The ceremony was brief and straightforward. Once the religious rites were complete, we left the mosque, climbed into our cars, and drove to the house where Sophia and other women awaited us. The same ritual occurred there, with the bride signing the contract. Guests enjoyed refreshments, sampled cakes, engaged in conversation, shared laughter, offered their congratulations, and gradually departed the house, one by one.

Sophia's children were present at the wedding, although they seemed oddly subdued. Being grown-up individuals, they didn't cause any disruptions. I had initially expected some resistance, but I quickly realised I was mistaken. Murad, the eldest at twenty years old, appeared largely indifferent. He congratulated me politely, kissed his mother, and went to his room casually as if I were a passing guest who happened to be temporarily in the house and would soon depart. I didn't interact with him much after that. When I asked Sophia, she explained that he typically spent most of his time outside and only returned in the evening. He often dined alone in his room while watching TV or listening to music. Occasionally, we shared breakfast in the kitchen, but he seldom engaged in conversation. He ate quickly, skimmed through magazines and newspapers (we receive many every day), uttered a word or two like "Please, pass the marmalade," and then strolled into the corridor. Initially, I thought he didn't like me, but Sophia reassured me that he grew up shy and reserved since he was a teenager. Moreover, he was absorbed in planning for his future career. He was preparing to leave the country for England or the USA. He had applied to some universities and was awaiting their responses before choosing. I learned yesterday that an American university had accepted him, although I don't know which one. Nevertheless, I wish him the best of luck.

The two girls were equally reserved, polite and empathetic. Thuraya, the elder at seventeen, resembled her father in appearance, although she didn't share his incessant verbosity. Zohra, who was fourteen, struck me with her likeness to Hassan. She had red hair, clear eyes, a slender frame, freckles, and lively, cheerful manners, much like a refreshing spring breeze. I felt a deeper affection for her than for the other two, and I believe she reciprocated my feelings.

This is my new family, and I've already grown accustomed to them. Another advantage of my marriage to Sophia is that I wouldn't need to press for children; they were already waiting for me. I had to say 'yes' to becoming a father and husband, and I eagerly embraced that role.

Sophia is a remarkable partner for any man with ambition and determination. Not only is she the ex-wife of a Minister (and potentially the wife of the next one), but she has also borne three children—a tangible testament to her fertility, which is highly prised. She is financially independent and well-regarded in the elite circles of the Capital. Moreover, she is beautiful and looks far younger than her actual age. She is small and slender yet exudes dynamism and vivacity. Her delicate features frame her brown hair, which cascades gracefully over her shoulders, giving her the aura of a humming Siamese cat. Her black eyes hint at the exotic, reminiscent of Far Eastern Asians. At the same time, her nose is elegantly sculpted and gracefully elevated above a small mouth, a straight chin, and two high, rosy cheekbones. It struck me immediately that she bore little resemblance to her ruddy, green-eyed brother. Nonetheless, her strong chin, firm lips, and unwavering gaze suggest her determination and relentless nature—a determination that led her to marry me, a future minister in the waiting, despite the likelihood that I was not the first man to propose to her after her divorce. And I said 'yes' because, after Hamda La'war's public confession, there was no point in stubbornly denying the truth. Since Hassan had proven his innocence and clean hands in the 'Ouja massacre, I resolved to move forward and propose to his sister, strengthening our nascent alliance with familial ties, as blood was on the verge of shattering it.

(5)

Two days after the unsettling riot had shaken the very core of our city, I found myself in a state of profound shock and fascination as I beheld Hamda La'war baring his soul on the television screen. My amazement was only heightened by the whisky that Robert and I had been partaking in. It was Robert's third and final bottle, and we had gathered to celebrate Janet's safe "return" and bid her and Robert farewell as their departure from the country was imminent.

In truth, our quest to locate Janet in the bustling markets and winding streets of the city that fateful night proved to be an exercise in futility. She had, in fact, never ventured beyond the sanctuary of our hotel. Initially, she informed Robert of her intention to step out to do some shopping. Still, a change of heart led her to explore the hotel's collection of shops, where she whiled away a considerable portion of the afternoon. Later, she ascended to the hotel's exhibition room, where discussions on the finer nuances of art engaged her with fellow patrons. Among them was a British-educated lady who, in a spontaneous gesture, extended an invitation for a rendezvous at the hotel's coffee shop. Consequently, while we were out navigating the rain-soaked streets amidst the cacophony of bullets, fearing the worst for her safety, Mrs Waterbird was comfortably ensconced in the coffee shop in the company of a mysterious Arab lady.

Despite her traditional attire, the Arab lady, as it turned out, was an educator, well-versed in English literature and culture, who had previously resided in the heart of London. A swift camaraderie blossomed between Janet and her newfound friend based on their shared experiences and interests. The Arab lady expressed a keen desire to meet Robert, admired his painting, and wished to acquire one of his creations. However, Robert seemed to have vanished into thin air, possibly quenching his thirst in my room's solitude or traversing the abyss alongside me. Eventually, the Arab lady handed Janet a cheque along with her contact details, and Janet pledged to reach out for a dinner appointment.

Naturally, Robert and I found the bustling markets eerily bereft of life, akin to the vacant thoughts of a soul adrift in the void. Customers had deserted the labyrinthine alleys, and shopkeepers had secured their establishments for the night. Yet, amid this desolation, a solitary café still beckoned with its dimly lit ambience. We sat on the terrace and ordered two cups of robust Turkish coffee. The establishment exuded an air of melancholy, with only a handful of patrons leisurely puffing on their nargile pipes, their gaze adrift in the dimly illuminated street, a mere echo of its daytime vibrancy. Behind the counter, an elderly gentleman, etched with the creases of time, appeared engrossed in his ledger and a diminutive calculating device. He would lift his head at intervals, cast a weary glance at the street, and absentmindedly stroke his drooping moustache with a bony forefinger. Adorning the central wall, a prominent poster featured President Abdelghani grinning broadly and baring a complete set of teeth. The narrow street, paved with polished cobblestones, obscured any view of the night sky as a vaulted ceiling enveloped the entire thoroughfare, shrouding the celestial realm from sight. However, the haunting call of the muezzin, summoning the faithful to the fifth prayer of the day, resonated from a nearby minaret, its haunting melody slicing through the stillness of the night.

The waiter delivered our two cups of coffee and two glasses of water, as I had requested. Robert asked me to inquire about Janet's whereabouts, hoping the waiter or somebody had seen her. There was a slim chance, perhaps one in a thousand, that the observant waiter might have caught a glimpse of her presence in the markets that afternoon, and we could ill afford to let such a possibility slip through our fingers. I asked the waiter. He shook his head solemnly and replied:

— No, sir, I did not see a solitary foreign lady. They usually cross these lanes in small groups, you know.

I endeavoured to describe Janet to him as vividly as possible, enlisting Robert's assistance to convey the nuances of her attire. He pondered momentarily, running his fingers through his hair, then ultimately shook his head in defeat. Our efforts had proved futile. With a sense of resignation, we released him from our quest, and he promptly gathered the scattered tables and chairs strewn across the terrace, stacking them in the corner of the café. We hastily consumed the remnants of our drinks, settled the bill, and left.

We traversed the winding market alleys, our spirits weighed down by exhaustion and the burden of a long and trying day, arriving on the other side of the city—the modern neighbourhood. We strolled silently, our gaze fixed upon the ambulances, their sirens still wailing as they transported the wounded, and the police vehicles weaving through the streets like a stitching needle in a tattered fabric. It was a sad duty, bearing witness to the aftermath of the catastrophe. Numerous people had been injured, many others had met a tragic end, and hundreds of students found themselves confined behind bars.

At a nondescript street corner, a vigilant police patrol intercepted us. The officer, displaying an air of authority, requested our identification papers. Robert promptly produced his passport while I fumbled through my pockets in a frantic search for my wallet. Alas, my haste had led to a crucial oversight; I had carelessly left it behind in my room. Instead, my fingers brushed against a cold, unyielding object in my pocket. Startled, I withdrew my hand with a swiftness that mirrored the sting of a scorpion's bite, my emotions inadvertently etched across my countenance. The officer considered me with a wary eye and snapped:

— We are awaiting your papers. He extended his hand and inquired. Are you feeling well?

— Oh, yes... thank you, sir, I stammered in response, my voice trembling as I continued: I... the papers... Sorry! I believe I've forgotten my wallet...

I was likely shaking. That was not only due to the chill of the evening air that had penetrated my bones or the dampness of my clothing that caused me to sneeze intermittently but also because, on that very day of turmoil, I happened to have a revolver, with neither identification papers nor a firearm license. My predicament was dire. I could already envision myself being escorted back to the confines of a prison cell. Dahdah, Frankenstein, Zorro, and the clique might likely be awaiting my return; the barber and the shrink would undoubtedly have inquiries about what measures I had taken to alleviate their plight. Oh, dear God! The nightmare was resurfacing. I was standing on the edge of a precipice ...

— You could not have picked a more inopportune day to forget your wallet, remarked the sergeant, a sentiment I could not help but concur wholeheartedly.

— Apologies, truly apologies, I uttered, but my words fell upon deaf ears as he had already turned his attention to his fellow officers.

With a curt command, he directed one of them to comb me. Oddly, Robert remained untouched, standing there in silence, observing with a detached gaze as the policeman's practised hands swiftly ransacked my clothing and delved into my pockets. My heart pounded like a relentless drumbeat, and when the officer extracted the revolver, eliciting surprised looks from his colleagues, I blushed deeply, my embarrassment akin to that of an adolescent virgin caught in the act of self-indulgence. I felt consumed by guilt, unable to meet the gaze of the policemen, and instinctively braced myself for the impending ordeal.

The policeman handed the revolver to his superior, who removed the barrel and inspected it with an experienced eye. He glanced in Robert's direction, who had regained a semblance of composure during our brief pause in the coffee shop, wiping away the traces of grease from his cheeks. He now appeared strangely calm, as if the entire situation bore no relevance to him. The sergeant then turned his attention back to me, his lips curling into a sardonic grin as he remarked:

— A gun? You were involved in the riot, were you not? It felt less like a question and more like an indictment, a heavy charge in the air. I stammered incoherently:

— No, no, no... There's been a mistake... an... uh... a mistake, sir.

As I faltered, he continued with biting irony:

— A mistake? The gun doesn't belong to you? Perhaps we slipped it into your pocket, sir, didn't we?

His sarcasm cut more profound than any accusation. It was clear he had already judged and sentenced me. I couldn't help but wonder how many years I'd be facing this time.

— It's not what I meant, sir. I... uh...

— Shut your rotten mouth, you little wretch! I'll curse your mother, your sister, your father, your entire bloody family and every damn relative! Trust me, if you utter another word, a single word, I'll have my way with you. Take him away before I commit murder!

* * *

Approximately fifteen agonising minutes later, we were seated on a worn wooden bench in a grimy and squalid room at the police headquarters. Robert's spirit had been thoroughly crushed. He had vehemently protested, raised his voice, and even threatened to complain to his embassy, but his efforts had been in vain. It appeared that no one comprehended his impassioned words. Eventually, he resigned himself to the wait, recognising that there was little else we could do.

Time seemed to stretch endlessly in that room. It was barren, furnished with a solitary desk at its centre and two elongated benches. The walls bore the weight of age, their surfaces discoloured and forlorn, as if they hadn't seen a fresh coat of paint in a century. A portrait of the ubiquitous President adorned one of the walls—a constant reminder of Abdelghani's watchful gaze. Beneath the frame, a noticeboard proclaimed, "***The Police Is AT The Service Of The People***!" It was meant to be reassuring, but our current predicament felt far from comforting.

My irritation grew with each passing minute. Allowing us to languish for over an hour was far from acceptable. Robert had fallen silent, and I had nothing to offer by way of solace. I understood that it wasn't our uncertain circumstances that troubled him most but rather the inexplicable disappearance of his wife.

Two hours dragged on, and my frustration reached its breaking point. I was on the verge of raising my voice when Robert inquired:

— Are they going to leave us waiting until tomorrow? I rose from my seat and headed towards the door, guarded by a vigilant sentinel. I intended to inquire whether I could speak with their superior, but a detective entered the room just then.

— Who's Robert Waterbird? he inquired.

As Robert stood up, he handed him back his passport and said:

— Please, have a seat.

We settled onto the same bench while the detective stood in the room's centre, his legs slightly apart, an aura of authority about him, as if he were prepared for a confrontation.

— Why were you wandering the streets at that hour, Mr. Waterbird? Were you involved in the riot? he asked, his scepticism evident.

Robert explained our quest to locate his wife, who went shopping unaware of the demonstration, recounting how we had inadvertently become trapped in the chaotic march. The detective remained somewhat suspicious, casting a sidelong glance at me, and inquired:

— You didn't need a revolver to find the lady, did you?

There was no room for equivocation. I decided to employ a high-stakes strategy. Rather than directly answering the detective's question, I said:

— You'll get a clear answer when you speak with the Director of Security. Don't forget to mention that his brother-in-law is in your custody... or perhaps, to avoid undue concern, simply inform him that he is your guest, Detective.

Brother-in-law! I was the first to be surprised by my audacity. I had never before referred to myself in such a manner, and I was not very proud at the time because of what I was told about Hassan's possible involvement in the massacre of 'Ouja. However, I had no other choice, and my stratagem worked. The detective was taken aback.

— The brother-in-law of the DS? You, sir? he inquired, startled.

I nodded in affirmation.

— Indeed, I have that honour, Detective. A peculiar sensation, a mixture of trepidation and guilt, stirred within me. Secretly, I cursed myself for aligning with the enemy so readily.

— May I ask you for your your name, sir?

— I am Bassam Bourasin, I replied.

The detective excused himself and exited. Ten anxious minutes later, he returned, slightly out of breath, bowing humbly as he spoke:

— I deeply apologise for the inconvenience, sir. I entreat you to accept our sincerest apologies. We were entirely unaware, and if only you had informed us from the outset...

— I couldn't, I exclaimed angrily. That blasted sergeant threatened to wreak havoc on my entire family if I dared to utter a word. Where is he now?

— Well, he is...ahem! Probably patrolling the streets, sir, the detective responded.

— Very well, I retorted. When he returns, advise him to exercise greater civility, as he may find himself in a precarious situation next time.

— I will not fail to convey that message, sir... um... Your chauffeur is on his way to take you back to the hotel, sir.

— Thank you! May I also request that you make inquiries to ascertain whether Mrs Waterbird has been spotted by any of your patrols?

— Indeed, sir, we will do our utmost to locate her... unless she is already back at the hotel. I will personally oversee the matter.

I thanked the detective and strolled down the corridor with Robert to await our car at the entrance of the police headquarters. Curiosity and excitement gleamed in Robert's eyes as he inquired:

— What the hell did you tell the officer? His attitude changed completely!

— Oh, nothing extraordinary, I replied casually. Just that I am a relative of his hierarchic superior.

He watched me with a growing curiosity and let out a chuckle.

— Really? That's quite clever!

— It's almost true, I admitted with a smirk. — Almost? he laughed heartily. Ingeniously cunning! But it worked, damn it!

— I didn't entirely fabricate it, you know, I explained. I do happen to have connections in the higher echelons of the security apparatus.

— Ah, well! It's always reassuring to have the right connections, he mused.

— My dear Robert, you mustn't be so unwaveringly naive, especially after everything you've witnessed and heard today; it would be unforgivable. I have no faith in the police, and my acquaintance with a high-ranking security official does not bring me any sense of comfort. Quite the opposite. They are among the least trustworthy individuals in this country. Don't make the mistake of thinking they are dedicated to their duty out of some noble allegiance, for those people possess no loyalty whatsoever. In fact, they would collaborate with His Majesty the Devil himself if he were willing to work with them. I have some insight into this matter. You can purchase a policeman's uniform for less than twenty dollars; you can acquire his firearm for a little more. And if you're feeling generous, you can access all the doors of the Ministry of the Interior. They'll welcome you with open arms and warmth if you keep paying, but be cautious! The moment you turn your back on them, you'll inevitably be stabbed. As I mentioned, I have some knowledge in this area.

Two out of every four men in this country are undercover work-ing for the police or affiliated with one or more of the security departments. They aren't in these roles because it's their call-ing but rather because they couldn't find any other means of making a living and particularly if they were coerced into co-operating with the enemy of the people. That's why most of the individuals involved with this business harbour animosity toward foreigners, especially if they they think them rich. My dear Robert, they dislike you because you represent a differ-ent kind of culture, a distinct system of thought, an alterna-tive way of life, which they believe they must combat because freedom should not be allowed. You saw how they treated the students, didn't you? They weren't attempting to contain them peacefully; they were venting their frustrations. These are dis-illusioned men, Robert. Were they not attempting to exact re-venge on the society they were supposed to protect? I admit this is the Militia's misconduct, but they are a parallel police. Let me divulge more: Our police forces serve as a sanctuary for thugs, ruffians, crooks, rapers, killers, thieves, Mafiosi, cut-throats, degenerate jerks, and other unfortunate and destitute souls. In short, it's a haven for those who have failed in other professions and continue to be welcomed by the police. So, how can you possibly expect me to be reassured simply because I know one of their chiefs?

Robert pondered my words for a long while, his gaze fixed morosely on the damp, dimly lit street. The chilly breeze rustled our clothing and set the branches of nearby trees swaying and dancing gracefully. Above the city's towering buildings, the sky had once again cleared, unfurling its murky, star-speckled dome. A serene moon gleamed brightly, its radiance oblivious to our tumultuous escapade.

— Mr. Bassam, you seem to have forgotten your revolver, re-marked the detective, who had unexpectedly joined us, extending the firearm towards me.

I stared at him, momentarily taken aback, while he held out the weapon. I was on the verge of explaining that the revolver wasn't mine, but at the last moment, I chose to accept it, avoiding the need for further explanations. Thus, I pocketed the firearm and expressed my gratitude.

* * *

Tomorrow, I am set to visit my bank. Surprisingly, it brings me a sense of delight, even though my life has undergone such profound changes. Hamda La'war's confession has alleviated a heavy burden that had weighed on my conscience. I had carried the weight of my mother's death and the tragedy of my fiancée as if I were the perpetrator, given my association with the man presumed to be the mastermind behind the massacre.

Upon returning to the hotel, Hassan called me and invited me to their party. I explained that I was utterly exhausted and unable to meet his sister or anyone else, offering my apologies. He seemed to understand my explanation and did not press further.

I wasted my time at the hotel the following day, perusing newspapers, jotting down notes, and consuming excessive tea and coffee. I dined with Robert, who appeared deeply perturbed by the unfolding events in the country. Later, I retired to my room and slumbered until the voice of the Muezzin stirred me at dawn.

I quickly realised that my idle existence in the city was far more tedious and disconcerting than my arduous days in 'Ouja. I had grown weary of the capital, fatigued by its ostentatious luxury and disenchanted with my current way of life. For a fleeting moment, I contemplated a permanent return to my village. However, the nagging question that held me in place was: What purpose would it serve? I had nothing and no one to return to—a void of work, family, and connection. I had been severed from 'Ouja, uprooted, and left adrift.

After lunch, I ventured out for a stroll through the bustling streets. What struck me was the sheer number of foreigners teeming in the city. The majority hailed from various parts of Asia: Indians, Pakistanis, Indonesians, Malays, etc. They were immigrants, primarily labourers drawn by the allure of quick riches offered by an oil-exporting nation. They likely arrived with grand hopes and dreams, never suspecting that, in a short time, they'd find themselves conscripted into the army, serving as mere cannon fodder in battles against the Scoundrel—or perhaps aligning with the adverse side. Refusal to comply would result in imprisonment, and no one would ever hear from them again. I had observed many of these unfortunate souls during my time in prison. Some shared harrowing tales of their ordeals. Oddly, I had never paid them the slightest heed before my incarceration. I was aware, of course, that they lived among us, as I occasionally glimpsed them at the 'Ouja market. They were expatriates leading insular lives in closed communities, akin to ghettos, seemingly harbouring enigmatic and repulsive backgrounds. The majority of the staff at the Sheraton hailed from those distant corners of Asia. They spoke a broken Arabic intermingled with English and their languages, often appeared servile, and were likely implicated in dubious dealings. Robert confided that he had been approached by servants and waiters at least eight times, seeking currency exchange or involvement in the black market. Given the legal repercussions and risk of heavy penalties, I cautioned him against getting entangled in such activities. He chuckled and assured me, "No, I haven't en-

gaged with them. Besides, I don't carry much cash—just traveller's cheques, which aren't useful to them." It turned out my
warning was apt, as most Asians I encountered in prison were
drug dealers or addicts, further reinforcing my avoidance of their
disreputable company. I am aware that many of those immigrant
workers disdain us, whether due to our wealth compared to their
poverty or certain deep-seated prejudices. The chasm between
us is so vast that it's naive to believe it could ever be bridged or
broken. While we may share a common faith as Muslims, some
are Christians or have different beliefs. Common faith alone is
insufficient to foster camaraderie. We may share a historical link
with the British colonial experience, but our shared history of
subjugation has only amplified our sense of isolation, much as
it has for them. Arguing that we are all Third World peoples and
should stand in solidarity is a political slogan. In reality, the divide between rich and poor is insurmountable. This is the world
as God has ordained it; it is Mektub.

We were exceedingly destitute before discovering the vast
oil reserves beneath our desert. Our fathers and forefathers endured harsh lives but were resilient and robust. They traversed
long distances across barren landscapes under the relentless
sun, mounted on camelbacks. Now, we cruise in Buicks, Cadil-
lacs, Rolls-Royces, 4X4s and other fast-moving vehicles, living
and working in air-conditioned comfort. Our strength and resilience remain undiminished, thanks to Allah's mercy. However, the relentless cycle of coups and counter-coups is hardly
surprising. We are consumed by the thirst for power, which is far
from ordinary. Every minor tribal or clan leader regards himself
as a Sun God within his territory. The state is a complex web
of alliances, a peculiar concoction. To an outsider looking at the
city, the imperious beast remains invisible to the naked eye. Yet,
beneath the tranquil metropolis's veneer, the unrest elements
simmer. We are a nation in the throes of birthing, and no one

truly knows what kind of offspring we nurture. This is precisely what Hamda La'war unveiled through his televised confession.

* * *

After dinner with Janet and Robert that evening, we all went to my room. Janet didn't mind having a drink with us because it was their last night in the country. So Robert brought his bottle, duly muffled as usual, inside the newspaper's sheet, and we settled in the tiny living, drinking, smoking, and chattering. At the same time, the TV blared a monotonous program. The night was lovely, and a cool breeze fluffed the muslin curtains on the balcony. Janet was dressed in a long blue gown with a dingy sheen, contrasting beautifully with her white skin. She appeared to be more attractive than ever. Her golden hair caressed her shoulders, and her blue eyes seemed so bright and clear that I was about to forget myself and tell her honestly that I was under her spell. But, at the last second, I hesitated and abstained. I wasn't sure how she'd react - maybe warmly with a welcoming smile. But what if she felt I was making an advance on her? What would a woman do in such a situation? I'm not sure because I have minimal experience with ladies. Besides, she is a foreigner, and thus, my guest and her husband were not even in the room at the time since he had gone to fetch the bottle of whisky, and when he returned, I was no longer anxious to discuss my crush. Nonetheless, my bewilderment reached an all-time high because we were no longer in the lift by that point but in my room, and even if something happened between us, I would never be able to acknowledge it.

— You should come and see us one of these days, Janet suggested.

— Thank you so much. If I travel to England, I will.

We raised our glasses.

— To friendship, Robert said.

The white stars glittered in their remote dome through the balcony, and the moonshine's reflection on the glasses added a vivid rapturousness to our reunion.

— You'll have a hard time around here, Robert said.

— Oh, you know, that won't be the first time. Anything can become habitual.

— However, the Islamists do not appear to be ready to leave very soon.

— No one wants to give up power, even if it is difficult to maintain it without killing. You witnessed what happened; some of the students were killed or incarcerated, while others were compelled to play the government's game. The city is a grave-yard two days after the riot. Nobody speaks up, and no one protests. Those who go against the grain are labelled traitors. However, we did not arrive at this point because the people in power are fundamentalists; far from it. We would reach the same deadlock if the previous president was still in power. In fact, re-gardless of religion, our rulers are all the same. They're all made of the same stuff. Tyranny is a legacy. Our history is rife with bloodshed; we generate dictators as easily as we breed violence. If you want my honest opinion, the Arab world is doomed with or without oil.

There was a brief pause. Robert refilled our glasses:

— Just a finger for me, Janet said.

— Ladies and gentlemen, our gallant security forces have finally laid their hands on the criminal who had provoked, planned, and committed the heinous massacre of 'Ouja, the TV speaker declared. That man, Hamda La'war, a prominent Scoundrel agent, is responsible for the deaths of hundreds of innocents in the village where he held the highest authority. Here's his full confession...

The image of Hamda La'war flashed on the screen immediately. He was sitting on a chair with nothing but a white wall behind him. He wore a long robe that reached his ankles. His face looked both enraged and bloated. On his cheekbones and nose, a few dark tumescences emerged. He lacked the black patch that he used to cover his blind eye, and he appeared weary, worn, and vacuous as if he hadn't slept in two or three nights. I was more stunned than surprised and silently turned over to fix the screen as if mesmerised.

Robert became aware of my anxiousness.

— What's going on? he questioned, peering at the TV screen.

I explained what I had just heard. Janet sighed deeply and continued, pointing to Hamda's swollen face: — He has a really horrible look.

— Hushhh... Let's listen, Robert commanded. I got the strange impression of something already known or seen!

(7)

— I am Hamda Mohammed Abderrahman, known as Hamda La'war. For nearly two decades, I held the position of president in the Party's cell of 'Ouja. I also occupied prominent roles within the Town Council until I became mayor. When the revolution erupted, I was in the same position. Despite this, I made a fateful decision to flee the village, driven by the certainty that my enemies would seek vengeance for the offences I had committed against them under the Party's hierarchic orders. I was well aware that the new regime would hold many political figures accountable. My apprehensions extended not only to the new government but also to my fellow villagers. During my years of service, which spanned nearly two decades, I had amassed influence in high circles but had also garnered a multitude of enemies. When news reached me that our compatriots were assembling in the south, I hastened to join them. Subsequently, as foreign countries, whom we had previously counted as allies, were on the verge of recognising the Islamic regime as the de facto government, we devised a plan to counter this development. We engaged mercenaries with known ties to the underworld, offering them substantial sums of money. With the assistance of some discreet allies, we facilitated their entry into the country, disguising them as tourists. I personally oversaw the entire operation, from its inception to its conclusion. Once their task was completed, the mercenaries departed for Europe while I remained in the capital, where I coordinated efforts to incite riots with certain students. We distributed firearms and financial resources to the rioters, but before I could see our plans through, I was apprehended by the police.

A voice in the studio interjected, seeking clarification:

— So, are you saying that both the massacre in 'Ouja and the riots in the capital were orchestrated by you and your associates, including 'The Scoundrel'?

Hamda nodded solemnly, acknowledging the truth:

— Yes.

The interviewer continued:

— How did you establish contact with these mercenaries?

— We have allies and supporters in Europe.

— Could one refer to these allies as agents?

Hamda thought for a moment before responding:

— Yes, if you wish to characterise them as such.

— How did you manage the entry and exit of these mercenaries without arousing suspicion?

— We bribed certain airport employees.

— Were they police or customs' officers ?

— No, they were ordinary airport employees tasked with facilitating the arrival of what they believed to be a charter of European tourists.

— Why did you opt for mercenaries instead of carrying out these actions yourselves?

A pause hung in the air, Hamda hesitating before answering:

— No one within our ranks was willing to carry out these tasks.

— Even among the rebels?

— Yes, sir.

— Does this imply that, under certain circumstances, your rebel forces might refuse to execute orders issued by 'The Scoundrel'

Hamda remained ambivalent:

— I cannot say for sure... But It's possible... I don't really know.

— Are there mercenaries within your ranks?

Hamda admitted:

— Yes, perhaps around a hundred or so.

— Were they involved in the 'Ouja massacre?

— I believe they were.

— How did they escape when your forces were surrounded?

— The desert is vast...

My heart raced with anticipation. I feared the imminent question:

— Where were you hiding when you were apprehended?

I reached for my glass of whisky, my palms moist with anxiety. I felt like I was part of the interrogation as if my involvement might be exposed. What if Hamda publicly revealed my complicity? I had allowed him to seek refuge in my room; I was his unwitting accomplice. What an unfortunate fate! I was destined to be a willing or unwilling accomplice to a heinous act. Was this truly inevitable? If not Hassan, then Hamda! It's a wretched curse!

I reached for my handkerchief to wipe away the cold sweat trickling down my neck and temples. The interrogation pressed on:

— How did you bribe the students?

— We didn't need to bribe everyone, just certain leaders.

— For what purpose did you do this?

— For the sake of the revolution.

— You mean the counter-revolution!

— Yes. That's what I mean, sir.

— You mentioned that some foreigners assisted you. Can you provide specifics?

— Well, we were encouraged by the Western world to act...

— Are you suggesting that Western public opinion incited you to commit such heinous acts?

— No, sir, that's not what I meant. However, they are not particularly supportive of the Islamic regime in the West.

— Even if they aren't supportive, it doesn't mean they endorse your actions, Mr. Hamda.

— Perhaps not publicly, but many of them stand with us against you, regardless of our actions.

— Could you provide an example to clarify?

— Well, those working for oil companies aren't all on your side, are they?

— Are you referring to engineers and other experts? What leads you to believe that?

Hamda hesitated again, then spoke:

— It's quite evident, really. They are Christians, and they may find it difficult to coexist with your regime...

— We've coexisted for centuries, Mr. Hamda.

— Yes, through conflict! But they aren't pleased with a regime that restricts what they hold dear...

— What do they hold dear?

— Everything you prohibit: alcohol, entertainment, casinos... in essence, life, as they think.

— We're not prohibiting these things for Christians but for Muslims.

— ..... Freedom, sir. They... I mean... those people want to be free.

— You, Mr. Hamda, are a turncoat and a traitor. Don't forget that. Furthermore, whatever you say, you can't justify the massacre of three hundred innocent lives. You are the last person who should speak of freedom. You are concealing a crucial fact: these foreign experts have been coerced by 'The Scoundrel.' They are hostages in his war, while you portray them as willing participants.

Hamda lowered his head in silence and then muttered:

— Yes, sir.

— Do you admit that they are your hostages?

— I do.

— Did 'The Scoundrel' exert pressure on them to secure their cooperation?

— He certainly did, sir.

— For example...

— Everything was used: threats, blackmail, bribes... They are not saints. We offered them money, whisky, and women, and they were willing to do whatever was required.

A moment of silence followed.

— Do you feel remorse now?

Hamda bowed his head and spoke with a broken voice:

— Yes, sir, I do.

— Do you acknowledge your betrayal?

— Yes. I... I am a traitor.

And so concluded this strange interview. I rose from my seat and switched off the TV. Returning to my chair, I was overwhelmed with emotion. Robert refilled my glass while Janet stared silently at the balcony. The night was eerily calm, though not reassuring or comforting. Wrapped in my sombre thoughts, I struggled to comprehend Hamda's unsettling confession. Something remained elusive in his behaviour. How could a man willingly commit such acts against his neighbours and friends? I understood that the villagers were not overly fond of him; some may have even harboured deep-seated hatred and wished for his imprisonment or death. Perhaps the feeling was mutual. However, there was a significant chasm between harbouring ill will and taking action. Hamda had crossed that line without apparent hesitation.

Nonetheless, one couldn't willingly shoulder such unforgivable charges without the possibility of having been coerced through threats of torture. Could that be the case? It seemed entirely plausible, and I mulled it over for two days and nights. But when the radio announced the beheading of Hamda La'war at dawn the next day, I abandoned that notion and thought: "It's over. We may never know the whole truth, for it likely perished with the deceased."

* * *

Robert and Janet, with a sense of purpose and anticipation, embarked on their homeward journey as the sun began to cast its first rays upon the horizon. I found myself in the company of my acquaintances as we embarked on a journey to the airport, nestled within the luxurious confines of my Mercedes. Yet, a sense of compunction and guilt began to pervade my being. A detached and amicable demeanour marked our parting. Robert's eyes gleamed mischievously as our hands met in a brief but firm clasp. He leaned in close, his words barely audible as he uttered:

— I extend my sincerest condolences for the loss of your dear aunt. It appeared that she had endured a severe ordeal at the hands of the authorities.

I found myself withholding my breath. He smiled, his countenance betraying a hint of amusement, before proceeding with his response in a measured tone:

— She, it seems, did not divulge the entirety of her secrets, did she?

— Nah, she didn't, I shot back. How'd you find that out?

— Haha! I've never been fooled! The make-up was terribly rubbish!

When I got back to the hotel, I felt utterly alone and hopeless. I stayed in my room all day, refusing to answer any calls. I watched endless films and TV shows, smoking countless cigarettes and drinking just as many cups of tea and coffee. Eventually, tired and bored, I got up and walked onto the balcony. I stood there for ages, staring blankly at the city, but not really seeing anything.

* * *

Of course, the misery didn't last. On the day Hamda was due to be executed, Hassan called, asking if I was free for dinner with Sophia. I agreed without hesitation. So, as the clock struck eight that evening, my driver pulled up in front of the grand iron gate guarding a beautiful villa on the edge of the city in the sleek Mercedes. Stepping out of the car, I was met by the night air, filled with the scent of blossoms and roses from the lush garden. I was wearing a sapphire suit, bought just hours before for this special occasion, and a charcoal tie with my white shirt. I felt neither happy nor sad, but a strange anticipation stirred within me, eager to see the woman who would be my betrothed in just a few days. Though, I honestly wasn't thinking about that at that moment, despite a strange feeling I couldn't explain. Hesitantly, I walked towards the imposing iron gate, its size drawing my attention. I reached out and pressed the bell, its chime echoing. A figure emerged from the shadows. The man asked politely:

— Are you Mr. Bassam??

I nodded slightly in response. He unlocked the gate and let me through. I walked along a long marble path between green plants, lit by small lamps. The gentleman guiding me stopped at a flight of stairs near the house. He turned to me and said carefully:

— Sir, the entrance is open and waiting for you.

I thanked him and went up the steps to a beautiful veranda. I saw a slightly open door, and a maid in a long white dress showed me into a large living room. The room was lit by a bright chandelier in the centre. In the dimly lit room, Hassan sat in an armchair, reading a newspaper. He stood up, looking smart in his brown suit, and smiled, holding out his hand. Then Sophia came in. I was immediately drawn to her natural beauty. Her gentle gaze was comforting. Soon, her three children appeared, greeted me, and then went to their rooms. The dinner wasn't particularly interesting and would have been dull without Sophia's charming and lively presence. I couldn't have faced eating alone with Hassan at that point. There were too many unspoken feelings between us, a lot of silent accusations. I still didn't trust him, as I wasn't sure what he really wanted from me.

Chapter 12

The Making of a Mogul

(1)

The dinner, actually, was a great success, which surprised me. Although we didn't discuss marriage that night, Hassan called me the next day to ask if I was happy. I calmly told him that the meal was okay, but nothing special.

— I kindly ask you, dear friend, to discuss Sophia with me.

— Ah! The exclamation escaped my lips, a sudden burst of emotion that could not be contained. She's doing great. I'm truly impressed... Women like her are hard to find these days.

— Is it her being here, and our family connection, or the strength of your beliefs, that makes you think so deeply?

— Both, I responded, my voice laced with a tinge of satisfaction. I find myself truly gratified.

A brief interlude ensued, followed by his utterance:

— She feels the same way about you. She has happily agreed to marry you in her great kindness and understanding, joining your lives together in a beautiful relationship.

— Ah! Ahem! I am truly honoured for your kind words, as they have touched me deeply and filled me with a great sense of appreciation. It is an incredible honour.

The fantastical visions I saw were so strange I could barely understand them. Yet, I felt strangely comfortable and at home in this wonderful place. Time seemed meaningless as I floated through the delicate threads of my imagination, free from everyday reality. It was as if I'd found a hidden part of my mind, a secret garden where anything was possible and the line between dreaming and waking disappeared like mist in the morning sun.

— Are you ready for the holy union of marriage? he asked.

— When will it happen? Should we anticipate it soon?

—This matter needs to be dealt with quickly. In our family, we must recognise our tendency to be conservative. Visits and meetings between you and your fiancée, my dear friend, must be strictly restrained, no matter how close you are. Unfortunately, people in society would certainly gossip and question her reputation, as she sadly has to deal with the stigma of being divorced from a previous marriage.

— I understand the subject perfectly.

— In that case, if you've both made up your minds, we'll get you married this coming weekend. Please, does that work for you?

I was torn, caught between the conflicting pulls of choice and hesitation. I struggled to find the right words to say. Though I had expected this moment, its sudden arrival left me utterly surprised and lost for what to do next.

— Tell me, what's the reason for this relentless rush?

He seemed annoyed.

— I'm really fascinated by how people live their lives and feel drawn to it.

— Do we need to rush?

— I have already explained everything to you. I don't like repeating myself. Are you having second thoughts?

— Absolutely not. I am prepared, undoubtedly.

— Sounds good. I'll meet you in the evening. We can talk things over then.

And so it came to pass, with astonishing swiftness, that I found myself united in the sacred bonds of matrimony.

* * *

For two weeks, I stayed home, only going out to social events where Sophia and her friends were. Sophia has a large circle of friends. Since we got married, we've had so many invitations. But we haven't accepted them all.

I was introduced to Hassan and Sophia's stepmother during our wedding. She attended the ceremony, and there was nothing unusual about her behaviour or interactions with Hassan and his sister. They call her "Mamma," and they show her great respect, even though she's younger than they are. The Indian's accusations of incest seem exaggerated and without evidence. She continues to live alone in the same large house with Hassan. It's too big for a single man, and she doesn't have other options since her parents are deceased, and her ties to her extended family are weak.

My unexpected discovery that Suleiman Mughli - who attended the wedding without being invited - is quite different from the respected figure I'd always thought of him as came as a surprise.

He congratulated me and said:

— I'm glad you've finally decided to join our prestigious club.

"Prestigious club?" Once again, the question lingers: Am I one of them? This persistent query, much like a relentless ghost, haunts my thoughts.

We sat down for some refreshments after signing the marriage contract in the grand living quarters. Surrounded by unfamiliar faces, I thanked him, but the thought of joining their ranks made me uneasy, like a sting from a scorpion. I wanted to ask him what he meant but held back at the last moment. I first heard this phrase in prison when the guard Mahmoud asked the psychologist if I was one of them. In the presence of Suleiman Mughli, whose conviction was unshakable, I wondered if I had unwittingly joined the same group he belonged to. It's comforting to know that Mughli, on the day of my marriage, turns out to be an upright citizen with no ties to the Mafia, much like my own clean record.

Upon his departure, I shifted my gaze towards Hassan, my inquisitive nature compelling me to seek elucidation:

— What did he exactly mean by that?

My friend's idea that I joined the Mafia right after getting married didn't appeal to me. It felt exclusive and uninviting. I was also troubled by the comment, though thankfully, my spouse remained unaware of it, made by the person who spread this rumour, the Mughli.

Hassan appeared to possess an indomitable indifference. He casually dismissed my anxiety, saying: — Don't worry about it.

I spoke up strongly, expressing my firm disagreement from within.

— I confess, I'm troubled by your decision to invite that man to your sister's wedding. We all know about his connection to the criminal underworld. It's a well-known fact.

To my astonishment and profound dismay, Hassan emitted a light, almost ethereal, giggle. And with a gentle touch upon my shoulder, he leaned close to my ear, his voice a mere whisper:

— He is not, I must confess, the embodiment of your preconceived notions, but rather, an individual who shares our collective identity.

My face turned fiery red, and anger raged inside me. I often find myself lost in the complex maze of confusion, struggling to free my baffled mind from the grip of ignorance. Sadly, I cannot grasp the illusive threads of comprehension. He truly takes on the respected role of an officer in the Intelligence Service. I fixed my gaze on him, my face showing my perplexity. I was ready to consider any idea except that one. Had he been making fun of me? At one time, he had acknowledged that Suleiman was a prominent figure in organised crime. This was well-known among the prisoners, echoing through the halls and cells. Had he been trying to hide Suleiman, suspecting that I knew about their secret dealings? I firmly grasped his arm and guided him towards a private corner of the living room, ensuring our conversation would stay hidden from curious listeners.

— Do you try to deceive me, Hassan? I know about the secret meeting you had at the Sheraton, where you dealt with the shady characters of the underworld.

In uttering such words, I wanted him to divulge the secrets concealed within his hand. I stood poised, prepared to engage him in a confrontation. His response, in all its perplexing intricacy, left me utterly confounded.

— No, no, it is not what you believe. I've informed you who he is. Why should I deceive my brother-in-law for a stranger's sake? I ask you to trust me. In his critical position, he's a significant figure. I promise you, I don't tell lies.

— Do you currently keep your agents detained?

— Necessity dictated its inevitability. He had to go under-cover.

— Thus, one must surmise that the tale of his affiliation with the Mafia was nought but a fabrication?

— In his current occupation, he dedicates himself diligently to the service of the State. That's an operation conducted with utmost secrecy and discretion.

My suspicions remained unabated.

— Regarding his illegal drug business, I personally saw it un-fold.

— Such is the nature of existence, my dear brother-in-law.

— And what of his association with the Afghan?

— The Secret Service planned a strategy to infiltrate the inner circles of several groups.

— When I thought about these groups, I believed they supported you, or at least agreed with the new government's fresh power.

— In our life, a profound sense of scepticism pervades our consciousness, as we've lost trust in the inherent kindness of others.

— Do you know, at least, that the Afghan is secretly plotting against you?

Never before had I engaged in such unreserved discourse with him. He inclined his head in a gesture of understanding and responded with a measured tone:

— Indeed, I'm well aware of the issue at hand. Mughli shared a detailed explanation of everything that transpired for me. I'm also aware of their attempt to hire you when you went to 'Ouja after the death of your mother and fiancee.

— Yes, I uttered, a tinge of astonishment colouring my voice. How did you come to possess such information?

— The incarcerated Indian, weighed down by the heaviness of his wrongdoings, has confessed all of his crimes to ease his conscience.

— And what of the Afghan?

— After the lamentable failure of the riots, he, with a heart heavy with trepidation, managed to elude the authorities' clutches, yet unfortunately for him, a number of his loyal comrades were apprehended, their fates now hanging precariously in the balance. They shall indeed face the crucible of trial.

In the recesses of my memory, I summoned the recollection of Robert's clandestine revelation regarding the complicity of the Militia in the tumultuous upheaval that had gripped the streets.

— Do they genuinely connect with those who initiated the situation?

— They had meticulously organised everything.

I kept moving from one amazement to another, constantly thrown off balance by this never-ending sequence of surprises.

— If the Afghan really caused the riots, Hamda La'war made a bold confession on TV, but it was a false one. Who took responsibility for the chaos in these tumultuous events?

A moment of silence ensued.

— The Afghan designed schemes to get me ousted, aiming for the Director of Security role himself. His drive for this position showcases his ambition.

— Do you mean, then, that Hamda was innately innocent?

— No, one mustn't assume complete innocence or ignorance about the riots. Instead, his focus was on the carefully planned massacre of Ouja. As the Scoundrel's executive agent, he stood among other conspirators, now all in the hands of the law.

— Indeed?

— Confirmed: a pair had come into our possession. In the world of TV deceit, Hamda skillfully crafted a web of lies. However, it's important to mention that his dishonesty didn't involve dealings with law enforcement. He struggled to carry it out. Once the deceiver exposed, his dishonest schemes would be revealed to the public. There's much anticipation for the upcoming confrontation with a formidable challenge.

— Could you please explain to me why Hamda was put to death before the interrogation? I need to know. Why is it necessary for him to give up his life before the thorough investigation?

Hassan paused to let his thoughts roam free in his mind.

— It's the court that decides, he uttered, his voice trailing into the silence that followed.

I find myself traversing the vast expanse of my thoughts, contemplating the intricacies of existence. I find myself in a state of perpetual anticipation, yearning for the commencement of the trial that shall bring forth those individuals who bear the burden of my mother's and my beloved fiancée's lifeblood, intermingled with that of countless others, a crimson stain indelibly marking their very hands.

(2)

On this auspicious day, October the fifth, I find myself immersed in the ebb and flow of existence. The world around me pulsates with quiet energy like tranquil currents, whispering ancient secrets to those who dare listen closely. Each element weaves an intricate tapestry of life, harbouring mysteries that await discovery.

An undeniable air of conspicuousness marked the moment of my arrival at the bank. It was true. I abstained from driving my Mercedes or Zerga, instead opting for the elegant Lancia of

Sophia. The Ministry of the Interior had withdrawn the car and its driver. No longer am I a guest of the State, but rather a citizen akin to the multitude... Almost, but not quite there!

I had placed my old Zerga in the garage, hoping a buyer would appear soon. The Lancia radiates energy and desire for speed with its bright red colour. I enjoy driving it around town. As usual, Sophia refuses to get behind the wheel. But, considering my new responsibility to take on her husband's role, she thinks it's appropriate that I buy a new car, drawing us even closer. When I shared my concern about buying such an expensive automobile, knowing my reliable Zerga was still mine, her response was quick and sharp:

— My dear husband, do you genuinely believe I would ride on those roads in that rusty pile of metal?

I was suddenly startled. My awareness jolted like a battery being switched on. At a pivotal moment in my life, I listened as my second partner voiced her disapproval, mirroring the exact words my first had spoken about my beloved Zerga. The weight of their disapproval left me powerless. If Zerga had been a woman, my thoughts would have turned to deception, a secret plan to separate her from me. I protested, insisting that I couldn't buy a new car. With a kind expression, she offered:

— I'll buy it for you.

— I can't accept that idea.

— Why not? she asked, her voice tinged with curiosity and scepticism.

— Well, it's an unpleasant situation for a gentleman.

We had a short but lively discussion, and I gave in. In the bigger picture, the car is for our shared use, even if she doesn't drive. I discovered I could buy it, but I used all my funds for my ambitious and significant plans instead.

* * *

I was at the bank, feeling cheerful and lighthearted. As I traversed the winding road, a sense of self-congratulation enveloped me. The formidable Capital, which had once instilled a profound sense of trepidation in me, had now lost its status as a formidable adversary worthy of my struggle. A deep understanding of self-possession and triumph welled in the depths of my being. Without uncertainty, I harboured the utmost conviction that I was destined to engage in consequential transactions. In the coming years, I shall be able to establish my financial institution. Why not, indeed? By this juncture, I am blessed with a more significant number of opportunities to realise the aspirations of yesteryear. I am already enveloped within the intricate layers of John Law's persona. I engage in a captivating dance with vast sums, where fortunes are wagered and won or lost in the blink of an eye. I find myself the object of envious and admiring gazes as countless individuals, perhaps even millions, yearn and hope for me to fulfil their desires, akin to a sorcerer, bestowing upon them wealth and prosperity. In this moment of introspection, I am pondering the possibility that I may possess an inherent inclination towards commerce. In the essence of my being, there is a river of wealth. In the realm of slumber, a recurring vision unfolds before me: a tapestry of dreams wherein mounds upon mounds of Dollars, Sterlings, Yens, Marks, Euros, RMBs and various other currencies, both familiar and obscure, amass within the confines of my sleeping chamber. They cascade into my pockets, intermingle with my books, infiltrate my notes, and even the sockets and boots that adorn my person. This deluge of wealth engulfs my surroundings, threatening to subdue me beneath its formidable weight. Curiously, the self-same reverie has recurred numerous times since the solemnisation of my marital union. On two or three occasions, I found myself roused from slumber, my breath stifling as if smothered beneath a weighty mound of currency. In truth, it is a death of exquisite allure that any humble bank clerk would covet; yet, I find myself unable to summon the resolve to embrace such a fate.

When I imparted the ethereal vision to Sophia, she pondered momentarily before uttering:
— Truly, you are obliged.
— No, I am not, I replied, the voice tinged with a hint of resignation.
— You are, she insisted, even if you don't realise it. One must pay their debts or give to charity. If you don't, you will perish, like a miserable person buried beneath a mountain of wealth that has no value or purpose for them. My dear husband, I must tell you: it's a warning dream you had.
I was perplexed, for while I possess no recollection of any outstanding debts, I am acutely aware that, akin to the characters Hassan and Mamduh, I have clandestinely appropriated a sum that does not rightfully belong to me. In brief, I found myself burdened with compunction and seized by a foreboding significance of the dream. Nevertheless, I refused to succumb to the weighty burden of guilt, persistently murmuring to myself: 'I had presumed that the State was indebted to me, if not in greater measure.' In any case, I should find myself indebted to them rather than the inverse. I shall discharge my indebtedness at the earliest opportunity that presents itself to me. I am not in opposition to the State nor the government, for I am dutifully engaged in their service. Loyalty had forever coursed through my veins, an unwavering current that defined my very being. In my dreams, would be a clearer way to express the idea. Fidelity remains my steadfast companion. I possess a canine pro-

tagonist, an entity of which I am exceedingly proud. I, in truth, am nought but their canine companion. The resonant echoes of laughter reverberated through the air, a cacophony of mirth that seemed to stretch on indefinitely.

* * *

With a buoyant spirit, I ventured into the bank's hallowed halls. Mr. Khalil warmly received me. With a calm voice, he leaned in. Before summoning the butler to guide me to my designated workspace, he said: — Mr. Bassam, our enterprise thrives with resounding success.

Indeed, one must express astonishment at such a statement. He said:

— I extend my congratulations to you, for you have achieved a commendable feat. Due to our unparalleled excellence, we are deemed the preeminent financial institution within the confines of this nation. We, in our supreme competence, stand unrivalled. He interjected briskly yet courteously:

— Indeed, sir, that is not the essence of my intention. I was engaged in discourse concerning the affairs that pertain to us, do you understand? The proclamation resounded with fervour, echoing through the air and reverberating within the depths of their...

He made a sweeping motion with both hands, emphasising the exclusive nature of our shared concern.

— Is it truly ours? Ah! Ah! You mean...

A sly grin played upon his lips as he acquiesced with a subtle nod.

— Indeed, without a doubt! I discerned, sir, that the administration had approved.

— May I be granted the privilege of mending the revered Ouja bank?

— Aahem! His voice tinged with a subtle blend of certainty and resignation. He halted, his thoughts momentarily arrested, before interjecting with a tinge of apprehension, —Regrettably, there exists a minor stipulation, I must confess.

— Yes, please tell, what is the nature of your inquiry?

He maintained a profound silence, his countenance betraying the weight of contemplation as though he were profoundly introspecting the circumstances.

— Well, I would prefer to disclose it to you. The project, it seems, shall not be bestowed upon a mere bank employee.

— Ah! Why not? I asked, my tone carrying a mix of curiosity and defiance. The question hung in the air, pregnant.

— The irregularity of it, sir, is quite evident. In our establishment, it is strictly forbidden for our esteemed employees to engage in pecuniary transactions with their own financial institutions, thereby precluding any possibility of reaping personal gains from their respectable positions. This is nothing short of a manifestation of nepotism!

A profound sense of disillusionment overcame me.

— Ah, alas, they fail to understand, Mr. Khalil. The pecuniary gains that may accrue from this enterprise have little consequence for me. Instead, my feelings are driven by sentimentality. I previously conveyed to you the profound emotional bond I forged with the esteemed financial institution, Ouja Bank. This story includes all of my youthful days, life experiences, and professional achievements up to now.

— I apprehend your meaning with utmost clarity, he rejoined.

A moment of stillness ensued as he seemed entirely absorbed. As I prepared to bid him farewell, he uttered these words:

— I have pondered upon this matter in the preceding days. I perceive nought as a solitary quandary that portends specific perils.

I hurriedly expressed:

— I am prepared to embark upon venturesome endeavours.

— In that case, it would be prudent for you to tender your resignation from the esteemed banking institution.

— Could I please ask for your forgiveness for my presumptuousness?

— It is but a trifling formality, Mr Bassam, yet it bears great significance. Should you relinquish your position, rest assured that no impediments shall be placed in your path, for it is evident that you are one of our own, do you get it?

In a moment of profound revelation, I confronted the stark realisation that my affiliation with the collective, the essence of being "one of them," could potentially serve as a formidable impediment to my path towards professional advancement. In an instant, it seized my attention. I found myself in a state of profound bewilderment.

Finally, I uttered with a heavy heart:

— I must express my deepest remorse, Mr. Khalil. Indeed, one finds oneself confronted with a thorny predicament. The crux of the matter lies in the precarious dilemma that shall befall me should I choose to tender my resignation from the esteemed institution of banking. In one fell swoop, I shall be bereft of the well-deserved emoluments that have accrued to me over the course of a decade and a half, not to mention the forfeiture of my monthly remuneration and the promising prospects of my nascent position. Moreover, I find myself bereft of any assurance whatsoever that my voluntary relinquishment would inevitably result in the acquisition of said agreement.

— I assure you, Mr. Bassam, that my word is steadfast and unwavering. With your gracious concession of a just interest,

I am confident in my ability to navigate this affair deftly. Nonetheless, your resignation assumes a formality that is as essential as expected. It does not necessarily entail the forfeiture of your privileges as a longstanding employee of the esteemed bank. It is but a fleeting acquiescence, a charade, designed to demonstrate that during your acquisition of the enterprise, you were not gainfully engaged within the confines of the financial institution. Do you get my point, dear colleague?

— Do you imply that my labour shall persist unabated?

— There shall be no need for you to desist, sir. You shall persist in your customary labour whilst concurrently proffering unto me a retroactively penned letter of resignation, encompassing the duration of your sojourn within... within...

— Jail?

And so it was, the culmination of all that had come before. The moment had arrived, unassuming yet pregnant with significance.

— Exactly. Thus, rather than stating that you were confined within the walls of a prison, we shall express that you had willingly relinquished your freedom. Verily, we shall not remunerate thee for the temporal expanse encompassing thy voluntary departure, a span of approximately half a year, perchance even shorter... We shall regard it as an unpaid respite, a matter of legality. During that period, you found yourself in solitude, from which you procured the advantageous deal. Upon the conclusion of your sojourn and your subsequent reintegration into the realm of duty, it must be noted that we, in no manner, sought to subvert the established order or transgress the boundaries imposed upon us. You, in fact, were not counted among our esteemed cadre of employees at the time of your fortuitous transaction, for we had yet to commence the disbursement of a customary remuneration to you. The actions you undertook at that moment and how you executed them lie solely within your preoccupation. Thus far, our pursuit remains within the bounds of legality. Do you possess the capacity to fathom the depths of my being? What are your ruminations on this particular stratagem?

A profound sense of awe enveloped my contemplation, rendering me speechless. Never had I fathomed the depths of Mr. Khalil's cunning and intellect.

— I must express my admiration, sir, for your astute stratagem. It is indeed a testament to your intellectual prowess.

A mirthful chuckle escaped him, his fingers delicately caressing the knot of his tie. Meanwhile, a coughing fit ensued, perhaps due to an overwhelming abundance of delight, as I surmised. I perceived his countenance to be adorned with an air of exultation, evidently gratified by the compliment I had bestowed upon him. He assumed an air of slight haughtiness as he unveiled the contents of a drawer within his desk, revealing a pristine sheet of paper which he graciously extended towards me.

— Mr. Bassam, I have meticulously prepared everything, as I trusted in your inherent wisdom. This document, dear colleague, bears witness to your voluntary departure from our esteemed institution. Naturally, it has been meticulously prepared in advance and adheres to the customary formalities. It is, but your signature is required, my dear colleague.

I accepted the document, perused its contents, and affixed my signature. And so, he unfurled yet another sheet as if unveiling a hidden treasure.

— Kindly peruse this document and affix your signature to it.

On the auspicious occasion of October the first, the paper conveyed the momentous news of my ascension to the esteemed position of chief of the department of transfer and exchange. Without a shred of uncertainty, it was abundantly clear that my ascension in rank intimately correlated with the sacred bond of matrimony I had recently entered into. The esteemed sibling of the Director of Security, undoubtedly deserving of a modest token from the reputable financial institution from whence her betrothed's elevation was procured. Nevertheless, I found myself earning such a fate, having spent a gruelling fifteen years toiling away as a lowly clerk in our humble outpost of 'Ouja. And so it was that I affixed my signature upon the legal paper, that sacred document which held the weight of my fate within its fibres. With a sense of solemnity, I relinquished it into the hands of Khalil, that enigmatic figure who stood before me, his countenance a reflection of the mysteries hidden within his soul.

Subsequently, I ascended to my nascent office on the tertiary level of the grand edifice, wherein I tarried until the meridian hour, perusing periodicals and gazettes, imbibing the elixirs of coffee and tea, and indulging in the vice of tobacco. There remained but a scant measure of labour to be undertaken. In all candour, there existed a need for more activities, for the remaining staff members launched the entire work. Shortly before midday, Sophia called me to inquire about the latest appointment. I conveyed to her my profound contentment. Her countenance mirrored my own satisfaction. All seemed to be in order. At long last, the dolce vita had deigned to commence.

(3)

I n that very week, I saw fit to disseminate an announcement through the esteemed pages of the local periodicals, heralding the arrival of the illustrious 'Bourasin Company of

Construction'. In response to the advertisement, I engaged the services of the Asiatic labourers. Through Sophia's resourcefulness, I received a loan graciously granted by the esteemed institution of the bank. As fate would have it, the very same financial institution has taken me under its employ, forging a bond of an intimate professional association. The loan, alas, bore her name. I secured a modest abode within the confines of the Sheraton. This dwelling would soon transform into the esteemed establishment 'Bourasin Company'. It comprises a pair of rooms, a kitchenette and a lavatory situated on the ground floor of the establishment. Though it may be slightly extravagant, it is a pragmatic choice, for in our line of work, the veneer of things holds utmost significance. In my capacity, I would have readily procured a humble studio within the urban confines for the very same objective; however, Sophia vehemently emphasised that those who engage with us would form their judgements based on superficial appearances. I acquiesced with a certain measure of willingness to her desire, albeit not without a tinge of reluctance, for I harboured a suspicion that Mr Ali, the astute manager of the esteemed Sheraton establishment, would seize this opportune moment to resurrect the memories I so fervently sought to repress.

I realised that I was mistaken. The moment our signatures graced the contract, he assumed a sycophantic demeanour. He uttered with feigned humility:

— Might I be so bold as to inquire whether your noble solicitude for the destitute denizens of the Medina ought to be incorporated within the ambit of our financial disbursements?

The utter lack of tact and the constant irritation were indistinguishable in their audacity. I retorted:

— Mr. Ali, I am acutely cognizant of the predicament that plagues them. For this very reason, I find myself establishing an entire enterprise dedicated to the art of construction. Did I not do better?

He offered his apologies, his words tapering off into silence. From that fateful day, he abstained from alluding to my erstwhile commitment, nevermore.

I decorated the space with two writing desks, an opulent mahogany for my personal use, and a significantly humbler counterpart for my diligent secretary. I acquired a collection of seating apparatuses in commerce, including chairs, armchairs, and a luxurious canapé. Furthermore, I procured a computing device, which I affectionately christened Samir II, as a token of appreciation for its predecessor, Samir I, who faithfully served as my steadfast companion during my tenure at the esteemed 'Ouja Bank. I affixed a modest plaque upon the door, denoting the essence and intent of this office. One finds great pleasure in perusing the inscription upon the gate, wherein the enchanting words **"Bourasin Company Of Construction"** are elegantly inscribed. However, this mere progression represents a solitary stride; the subsequent endeavour shall entail the audacious pursuit of Bourasin Bank! Ah! Thus do I yearn, for such is my desire, inshallah! In the echoes of my mother's wisdom, she often proclaimed, "Everything is Mektub." And now, as I cast my gaze upon the written word, I discern with great clarity: Bourasin Company Of Construction, meticulously inscribed upon the door, its message accessible to all who dare to read the Mektub!

The formidable quandary lay in the persona of the secretary. Instinctively, I yearned for a woman of refined sensibilities to preside over my telephonic correspondences, meticulously orchestrate my agenda, and attend to the intricacies of my commercial affairs. However, Sophia harboured a dissenting viewpoint. She opined that the fairer sex is ill-suited for such a formidable occupation, which necessitates the secretary's intimate engagement with the labourers, most of whom hail from foreign lands. Moreover, within the confines of an Islamic nation, the notion of women engaging in labour alongside their male counterparts remains an impermissible proposition. I conveyed to her the prevailing circumstance at the bank, wherein the fairer sex continues to toil alongside us diligently, their presence undiminished, their dwellings shared in equal measure. With a tone of detachment, she uttered, "It bears an air of dissimilarity," and appended, "Nevertheless, it shall not endure, regardless!" Once more, I acquiesced to the demands of the situation and engaged the services of a gentleman to fulfil the task at hand. Hassan directed him towards my humble office upon my desire for companionship. Khalifa, a robust gentleman of middle age, possesses a countenance adorned with luxuriant eyebrows, a receding hairline, and a determined jawline. I assented to his presence, for it was upon the assurance of my brother-in-law that his trustworthiness had been established. When I inquired of him, he vehemently refuted any association with the esteemed constabulary or affiliation with the honourable Ministry of the Interior. I harboured an unwavering conviction that his words were but a tapestry of deceit. However, should he prove to be Hassan's undercover agent, as my intuition suggests, I find myself mainly indifferent to this revelation. I possess no secrets to veil.

Furthermore, I intend to maintain an impeccable standard in my dealings, just as I have always done in the bustling streets of 'Ouja. I shall abstain from engaging the services of foreign labourers whose documentation fails to meet the requisite regularity standards. I shall be willing to part with a more significant sum, provided that tranquilly shall be bestowed upon me in return. In my unyielding manner, I have criticised numerous labourers upon that very terrain, urging them to enlist in the military or elucidate their circumstances with utmost clarity.

The matter of recruiting foreign labourers into our military ranks strikes me as somewhat incongruous, I must say. Moreover, one must question the inherent generosity of our actions. The arrival of these individuals to our nation can be attributed to the unfortunate circumstances of unemployment or meagre wages in their homelands. However, it is disheartening to acknowledge that we no longer represent a beacon of hope for them. Instead, we subject them to the peculiar occupation of war, which offers them little solace or prospects. I have been informed that many of them have met their untimely demise or suffered grievous wounds unless they are subjected to the captivity of the Scoundrel. These wretched souls, trapped in the depths of destitution and despair! In a state of perpetual discontent, neither finding solace within the confines of my office nor amidst the unfamiliarity of a foreign terrain, I am left adrift, suspended between two worlds, bereft of true belonging. Indeed, it is undeniable that we find ourselves compelled to safeguard our existence. In his cunning, the Scoundrel employs extrinsic soldiers of fortune to engage us in battle; in response, we also use these foreign labourers for a similar objective. The semblance of the stratagem may deceive, yet it diverges significantly, for our labouring soldiers are not akin to seasoned canines of war. Different from the mercenaries of the Scoundrel, these individuals had not undergone the rigorous training of combat across multiple battlefields before enlisting in our esteemed ranks. In executing their duties, they assume the role of a soldier with the same meticulousness and dedication as that of a mason, mechanic, plumber, cook, or any other vocation. Should they manage to evade the clutches of death or the shackles of captivity, these individuals, through the crucible of adversity, shall acquire novel proficiencies, thereby potentially securing an enduring residency within the confines of our nation's borders long after the wild storm of war has subsided. They may find themselves adorned with the accolades of war, a significant reward. Thus, upon their return to their humble abode, they shall find solace in the pride that swells within them, borne from their valiant exploits upon foreign shores. We fashioned them into gladiators of the contemporary era, these individuals who would become the heroes of eternity!

In due course, those who abstain from battle - or those with a lesser inclination towards heroism - have become employed under my auspices. Yesterday, I dispatched them to 'Ouja. I had acquired a dilapidated truck, a relic of a bygone era, with the noble intention of facilitating the arduous task of transporting men and materials. The tumultuous repercussions that ensued from that affair were indeed bewildering! In all honesty, I must express my sentiments without reservation. Until now, my sole occupation consisted of settling the debts... I remain trapped in the relentless grip of financial obligations, burdened by ceaseless payments. Verily, a pact was forged between the bank and me a mere fortnight following my discourse with Khalil. A clever and cunning fox, that animal! As I sat in my office on the third landing, patiently awaiting his arrival, he deftly and expeditiously convinced the bank of Bassam Bourasin's status as an independent entrepreneur. To my surprise, the negotiations did not stretch interminably nor burden me with the monotonous boredom I had anticipated. Contrarily, the affair flowed with a tranquil grace akin to a pristine and translucent brook from its very fount. He orchestrated the entire experience with the board. He arrived at my office, brimming with exultation, brandishing the papers in his grasp.

— This is the crucial document that connects us. It represents the highest achievement one can obtain. To whom should we express our appreciation?

I rose to my feet, offering hospitality towards his arrival.

— Naturally, it is you, Mr. Khalil. Congratulations are in order for you! I believe you're perfectly suited to this role. It's truly impressive to find someone in this position. My sincerest appreciation goes to you, a thousand times over.

— This task wasn't easy, I assure you. But now, everything has been fixed. Let's celebrate this successful outcome with some drinks. Yes, this is indeed a happy occasion.

He carelessly flung the papers upon the desk, their weighty presence demanding my attention. Summoning the butler, we asked him to procure libations for our thirsty palates. Meanwhile, I perused the document, meticulously scrutinising the sheets and their identical counterparts, ensuring every iota of the contract was aligned. In the aftermath, I extended my hand towards Khalil, our fingers intertwining in a gesture of mutual accord. The act of signing preceding our handshake remains a detail that eludes my memory's grasp. In any case, the outcome remains indistinguishable insofar as my perspective is concerned.

— I will begin this task right away. In just three lunar cycles, our offices in Ouja will be transformed and look more beautiful. You might have witnessed an unfortunate incident if you had been there earlier. A lamentable carnage!

He gently swayed his head, a subtle gesture of denial.

— Apologies! I admit, sir, I haven't received this honour yet.

— Ah! Mr. Khalil, you have noticed every detail. It would be prudent for you to witness its restoration and adornment.

At that moment, we quickly drank our drinks. He then said goodbye to me, wishing me luck before leaving. With his departure, I deftly concealed the replicated document of our agreement, tucking it away discreetly within the recesses of my pocket. Subsequently, I surreptitiously trailed in his wake, traversing the corridor with a calculated stealth. Given that my salary is assured, I do not need to prolong my presence within the confines of the office. It mattered not a whit whether I graced the confines of my office or not, for as the esteemed overseer of this department, my presence held no sway.

Naturally, as the master of this realm, my duties were a mere illusion, for my loyal underlings dutifully executed the laborious tasks. In any case, should any fragments of my service be enticed by the allure of idle chatter or seek to circumvent my authority, their endeavours shall be swiftly thwarted upon reaching the confines of Mr. Khalil's office. The latter shall pretend to lend an ear to their grievance only to respond: "Very well, I shall attend to the matter." And so it shall be, the affair shall meet its demise, a quiet and calculated death within the confines of his office. Who would dare to circumvent Khalil, to disturb the Chairman or his esteemed deputy with such trivial and foolish rumours?

(4)

On the first day of November, a significant date in the calendar, we are in Ramadan. The air is thick with anticipation as the faithful embark on a spiritual journey of self-reflection and devotion.

Since the day I entered into matrimony with Sophia, I have chanced upon a revelation of such profound magnitude that it has left an indelible mark upon my consciousness. She had convinced me that, to equip myself adequately for a statesman's captivating vocation, I needed to partake in the observance of Friday prayers at the grand mosque. By doing so, she assured me, my profound devotion to religion would be unmistakably evident, seamlessly intertwining with my unwavering allegiance to the regime. Thus, I find myself engaged in prayer, a public display of devotion incumbent upon every faithful adherent of the Islamic faith. In my observations, I have discerned that many State personnel, including those of esteemed stature, regularly attend a particular mosque. This revelation has ignited a renewed enthusiasm to exhibit greater piety towards Allah, His Prophet, and President Abdelghani, widely acknowledged as their earthly representative. In my contemplations, I have conceived a notion to embark on a sacred journey to the holy city of Mecca, accompanied by Sophia, once our financial means permit such an endeavour. Occasionally, we engage in discourse regarding this matter; henceforth, upon our return, we shall be bestowed with the honorifics of the Haj and the Hajja (for the wife), basking in a distinct form of eminence adorned with its splendid grandeur.

On this auspicious day, the seventh in the sacred month of Ramadhan, I am immersed in contemplation. The air is heavy with anticipation as the faithful devote themselves to fasting and prayer. The world seems to hold its breath, awaiting the arrival of the blessed Eid. The streets are adorned with vibrant decorations, a testament to the devotion and piety permeating believers' hearts. As the sun sets, casting a warm glow upon the city, we end our fast. In the wake of a bountiful repast, it has become my custom to traverse the path towards the mosque, where I engage in fervent prayer and immerse myself in the sacred verses of the Koran. Sophia's offspring had embarked upon a voyage to the land of America in the preceding month. The presence of the two youngsters, confined within the walls of a secondary educational institution, eludes my discerning gaze. They arrive fleetingly, these visitors, on the brief occasions of weekends and holidays. In this vast home, I live in near solitude, accompanied solely by Sophia, the maid from Pakistan, and the gardener.

I find myself in the throes of a most wretched affliction, a hangover of the most formidable nature. I am perplexed, unsure of the purpose behind these musings that shall forever remain concealed, destined to be perused by none. My ambition to chronicle the annals of the Islamic Revolution remains steadfast, unyielding to the passage of time. Perhaps, in twenty years hence, when this tumultuous medley has reached its denouement, I am inclined towards such a course of action. I am alone, for my dear companion Sophia has ventured into commerce, seeking to procure various necessities. Confined within the chamber's embrace, I am indulging in smoking with the fervour of an inebriated fireman. With a heavy heart, I feel compelled to confess that I am nought but a lowly swine devoid of any redeeming qualities or noble aspirations. On this day, I was unburdened by the rigours of fasting.

In the wake of my nocturnal transgressions, it becomes abundantly clear that such actions were entirely unnecessary. May Allah grant the Minister of the Interior forgiveness, for he bears the burden of my afflictions. Should I find myself in this present state of renegade and apostate, facing the imminent expulsion from paradise, compelled to relinquish my cherished Houri and the opulent palace that awaits me beyond, it is undoubtedly a consequence of his own doing. Honestly, the mercy of Allah knows no bounds, permeating every corner of existence. He possesses an intimate knowledge of the true orchestrator behind this chaotic predicament. He might inflict punishment on me instead, yet what infernal consequence! Should I find my-self subjected to the agonising torments of the infernal realm, the bastard called Mamduh, that formidable figure of author-ity, renowned and esteemed Minister, the devout adherent of Islam, the unwavering politician, shall assuredly endure the sear-ing fires of damnation for the duration of his eternal existence, and beyond. The fault that plagues him is unpardonable: a man of falsehood and hypocrisy, ensnaring not only our people but all who cross his path. Yet, more grievous still is the sin he has led me to commit in this sacred month after I had diligently sought repentance for all transgressions and readied myself for the imminent pilgrimage.

In the waning hours of twilight, Sophia was caught by an ailment, a common human illness. The tendrils of a cold had stealthily infiltrated her delicate frame, leaving her weakened and vulnerable. Succumbing to the whims of her weakened state, she surrendered to the embrace of slumber, bidding farewell to the world earlier than her customary hour. I'm puz-zled by the unusual preference for our TV shows, which, without fail, select the holy month of Ramadan to inundate us with the spectacle of belly dancing and other vapid entertainment year after year. The wretchedness of it all is simply unbearable! Inevitably, I have no complaints about belly dance as an art form, provided it is executed with finesse and grace. However, during the sacred period of Ramadan, it becomes an inconve-nience, a vice, and an indulgence of excess. I disengaged the television's flickering screen and proceeded towards the culi-nary realm of my abode. I made the firm decision to partake in sustenance before succumbing to slumber. I, too, found my-self consumed by an insatiable thirst, prompting me to embark upon a quest within the confines of my refrigerator in pursuit of a refreshing elixir to quench my longing. To my astonishment and chagrin, I discovered an absence of libations, replaced by a meagre assortment of milk bottles. In her customary manner, the maid indulged in a brief respite within the confines of her chamber, contrary to her usual practice of retiring only after ensuring our presence within our own sleeping quarters. I resolved against unsettling her, for she appeared to be tired. In the recesses of my mind, I was aware of a cellar hidden beneath the kitchen area, a sanctum where sustenance was meticulously preserved and stored. Amid our nation's strife, the spectre of deprivation ceaselessly prowls, casting its ominous shadow upon us, a constant presence that haunts our collective consciousness. Henceforth, we procure copious amounts of food, diligently hoarding it in a state of utmost vigilance.

Never before had I descended into the depths of the cellar, where the door unveiled itself directly within the confines of the kitchen. I endeavoured to grasp the knob, yet the gate appeared resolutely sealed. I meandered aimlessly through the culinary domain, my senses attuned to the elusive key that could unlock the mysteries of my quest. My gaze fell upon a drawer, beckoning me to explore its contents in a place bereft of any visible sign. With a sense of solace, I discovered a cluster of keys, each possessing a unique character. Methodically, I endeavoured to unlock the accursed door, testing each legend with unwavering patience. At long last, my endeavours bore fruit. As the door creaked open, my eyes beheld a seemingly interminable staircase, its steps disappearing into the abyss of darkness below. With a flick of the switch, I summoned forth the illumination and thus commenced my descent into the infernal depths. In truth, the netherworld lay in wait for my arrival, and may the divine absolve me, akin to a fiery abyss. It excelled in mimicking the celestial realm, rendering it an unparalleled paradise.

Ah, whether it be the fiery depths of hell or the blissful realms of paradise, the consequences, if indeed there are any, have now come to fruition!

Upon my descent, I found myself in profound bewilderment, casting my eyes in utter speechlessness. The underground chamber, stretching from its depths to the lofty expanse above, lay ensconced in an inundation of countless rows of glass vessels. In a corner, amidst a jumble of provisions, lay a stockpile of sustenance: cans of preserved meat and fish, stacked high alongside sacks of sugar, flour, semolina, and an assortment of bottles containing milk, fruit juices, mineral water, and the like... The locale appeared to be an enclave teeming with an inexhaustible multitude of spirits, libations, and an extensive assortment of wines. Overwhelmed and taken aback by the serendipitous revelation, I cautiously began my enchanting exploration.

I saw a myriad forms of distinguished brands: Whisky, Gin, Rum, Brandy, Cognac, Sherry, Ricard, Berger, Port, Vodka, Champagne, Bordeaux... A symphony of libations, each with its own tale to tell. Wines hailing from the vineyards of France, the enchanting regions of Italy; Beers crafted with precision in the heartlands of Germany, the artistry of Belgium; spirits that whisper secrets from the distant lands of China and Japan... A cornucopia of intoxicating elixirs, beckoning the senses with their diverse origins and flavours. And an innumerable array of libations from lands I had never fathomed the possibility of beholding. Not only did the collection loom vast and opulent, but it stood as the very embodiment of Dionysos himself.

It goes without saying that after that initial instance of astonishment, I found myself in utter madness. In the depths of my ruminations, I found solace in the notion that this must be the triumph of my wife's erstwhile consort. Whether it slipped his memory upon his departure from this abode, or he underwent a profound transformation, embracing piety and severing all ties with the possessions he entrusted to Sophia's care, with the fervent wish that she would not hesitate to obliterate them. However, inexplicably, she refrained from doing so. Her silence on the matter led me to surmise that she had either carelessly overlooked it or was covertly attempting to deliver it to an undisclosed foreign purchaser clandestinely; such a revelation would not astonish me, as Sophia possesses an impeccable acumen for business. At that moment, I resolved to partake in a mere sip of the Brandy, if only to ascertain that the entirety of its contents was not a deceitful fabrication intended to beguile not only myself but any unsuspecting soul. My curiosity was piqued, for my eyes were yet to comprehend the scene before me fully. I yearned for concrete evidence to solidify my wavering belief. After completing my forthcoming activities, I shall partake in a cleansing ritual, immersing myself in a water shower. Once my ablutions have been meticulously performed, a sense of tranquillity and contentment shall envelop my being, rendering the world around me harmonious and pleasing.

And so it was that I uncorked the initial vessel. It proved to be an irresistible assemblage of elements. This veritable concatenation captivated my senses. The ancient spectre, concealed within the depths of my consciousness, stirred from its slumber, alluringly beckoning, beseeching for an augmented offering. I ventured to uncork a second vessel, desiring to ascertain whether the libation I had recently imbibed possessed the requisite potency of spirits. My conviction in its alcoholic nature had not yet been firmly established. At that moment, a sudden revelation seized hold of my consciousness: what if I were to partake in a small sip from each of these bottles? I shall deftly substitute the cork, rendering it imperceptible to all observers. It bore the semblance of an act akin to obliterating a dam, all in the pursuit of quenching the thirst of a meagre arid terrain! The torrent surged forth, an unstoppable force of nature, defying all attempts to quell its relentless power. In the realm of recollections, my dear mother - may the benevolence of Allah forever grace her soul - would often impart her wisdom with a touch of whimsy. She would utter, "Behold, the tail of the canine, subjected to the relentless passage of four decades, was shaped into a slender reed; yet, upon its liberation, it remained forever askew!" What an extraordinary display of sagacity! Having emerged from the humble hamlet of 'Ouja, a place renowned for its acerbic disposition, it is inconceivable for me to aspire to a state of unwavering rectitude akin to that of a slender reed, is it not? To partake in such an act would be a grievous betrayal of my ancestral hamlet, whose mere appellation subtly hints at the profound depths of our collective, yet lamentable, fate.

Indeed, I find myself in a state of certainty... The dog's tail, alas, shall forever remain curved despite the passage of four millennia, a testament to the unyielding nature of its form.

Thus, I embarked upon an unrestrained frenzy, ceaselessly traversing the realms of excess until my very pores exuded the essence of spirits, replacing the perspiration of toil. I staggered with a tantalising exhilaration, revelling in the merciless plundering of my surroundings. I meandered and stumbled amidst the cluttered bottles, my balance precarious, surrendering myself unabashedly to debauchery's capricious and domineering spirit. The duration of my undignified indulgence eludes me. Yet, I remain a witness to my disgraceful meandering and faltering, my feeble attempts to navigate the staircase, and my feeble attempts to traverse the kitchen floor, clutching tightly to a bottle. I then proceeded to stumble along the corridor, much to the dismay of the maid, who, though more frightened than astonished by my presence, endeavoured to assist me in regaining my composure.

It was not a sight that would have been deemed particularly pleasant to behold, I must confess. Burdened by the weight of her frail shoulders, the maid deemed it her solemn obligation to escort me to my quarters. My corporeal presence proved too ponderous for her delicate frame to bear. In that instant, we found ourselves entangled, my hand clumsily seeking refuge around her slender waist, daring to venture further until it seemed, for a brief moment, that I was indulging in the intimate caress of her bosom. She, in turn, responded with a cacophony of incomprehensible exclamations, yet, if memory serves me right, she displayed no concern for the audacious and lascivious advances my surrogate hand was making. Yet, I found myself unable to proceed any further, not due to any resistance from the maid against my desires - in fact, I believe she even encouraged them - but rather due to my pitiful incapacity to reach the culmination.

Now, the bitter taste of regret consumes me. To conduct oneself in such a manner, a mere two strides removed from one's spouse, was inconsequential and verging on the criminal. Even the lowly maid harbours resentment towards me, as evidenced by her actions yesterday. This morning, she callously allowed me to endure the incessant barking of my pleas before deigning to respond. In that moment of our encounter, her gaze, once entwined with mine, swiftly averted as if veiled by a pretence of bashfulness. Her behaviour is quite peculiar indeed. In apparent guise, she laments my presence, for I abruptly halted at the precise juncture when she yearned for further engagement!

Such a spectacle of madness! In this modern epoch, individuals are increasingly succumbing to the perils of self-oblivion. They have lost sight of their rightful positions within the intricate web of social stratification, oblivious to the barriers that confine us all and the imperative to pay deference to those of higher standing. Verily, they are subjected to the incessant clamour of radio and television transmissions, wherein speeches extolling the virtues of justice and equality resound ceaselessly. Alas, they remain utterly bereft of any inclination to question the veracity of such proclamations, a sentiment I, on the other hand, ardently embrace. In our land, the conduct of our politicians is marked by a certain skittishness. This trepidation stems from the precarious nature of our circumstances. For, you see, in countries such as ours, where the weight of illiteracy bears down upon the masses with an oppressive force, delivering speeches becomes a perilous endeavour.

Should democratic elections ever be orchestrated, the sheer magnitude of the ignorant would undoubtedly inundate the hallowed halls of Parliament, threatening to engulf the very essence of our governance. These incendiary catchphrases propagate the cultivation of inconsequential aspirations, which could prove deleterious to their well-being if one were to succumb to their integrity. Consider, if you will, the lowly maid who casts upon her employer a gaze laden with base desire, yearning to partake in the intimate sanctuary of his bed. Should her audacity not falter, she may even dare to exploit his inebriation, seizing the opportunity to engage in a most unwelcome act of sexual harassment. In this perplexing realm of existence, I am compelled to inquire: to what destination are we traversing? Where, pray tell, does one find the elusive essence of respect? Where, pray tell, does one find the elusive nature of dignity?

Where, pray tell, does conscience reside? The elusive sense of religion, where does it live? Thankfully, the elusive concept of democracy shall forever remain an unattainable mirage within the confines of our beloved nation. In the face of this contemporary affliction that plagues the Western world, we have discovered an alluring remedy that cannot be resisted. Clean, fast, and efficient it is. In the realm of political tumult, a tempestuous military coup and the emergence of an enlightened despot are the requisite forces to quell and dismantle the treacherous aspirations of the unlettered masses. Thus, a Coup, regardless of its genesis, essence, and objectives, invariably proves to be beneficial for our collective well-being. President Abdelghani Abdelghaffar, with his dangerous squint, is the saviour we embrace.

(5)

Several months later

In a most fortunate turn of events, I find myself bestowed with the esteemed position of president within the ranks of the 'Ouja Islamic party's cell. This great honour was graciously granted to me by the illustrious General Abdelghani Abdelghaffar himself. I am compelled to assume the position once occupied by Hamda La'war. This situation represents the significant stature I have attained in the discerning gaze of our esteemed President. It is worth noting that upon learning of the successful quelling of the riots, courtesy of MY helicopters, the President promptly summoned me to his opulent palace.

When the telephone rang, its shrill cry pierced the air, interrupting the stillness of my solitude. I hesitated, my fingers trembling as they reached for the receiver, unsure of what awaited me on the other end of the line. It was Hassan, his voice dripping with a peculiar blend of mirth and mischief, as he regaled me with tidings that seemed too unbelievable to be true. Doubt crept into the recesses of my mind, whispering its scepticism, for I could not fathom that such joyous news could befall. In truth, I had not anticipated the bestowal of such a distinguished position within the confines of my ancestral hamlet. I conveyed my sentiments to him with conviction, leaving no room for doubt. A faint chuckle escaped his lips as he uttered, "You, my dear, deserve a more fitting recompense. Alas, such is the decree of our esteemed President."

The desire, nay, the earnest longing of the esteemed Mr. President! Why didn't he feel passionate about my getting a ministerial appointment? I wondered. With her persuasive charm, Sophia has concluded that I possess the qualities necessary to ascend to the lofty heights of statesmanship. She ceaselessly implores me to cease my nocturnal encounters with the bottles to awaken with a mind unburdened and brimming with brilliance. Ever since I chanced upon the mystical cavern akin to Ali Baba's treasure trove, I have succumbed to the peculiar habit of surrendering to the allure of Bacchus, spending countless hours in the dead of night, enraptured amidst towering heaps of bottles. In anticipation of the impending dawn, I would engage in the cleansing ritual, immersing myself in a bath, performing my ablutions meticulously, and embarking on a spiritual prayer journey. I persisted in my devotions, whether in the mosque's public embrace or my home's intimate confines. Yet, with her perplexed countenance, Sophia could not fathom the depths of my piety. Now, she has grown accustomed to it. However, we occasionally dispute, as she perceives my behaviour as paradoxical, inconsistent, and perhaps hypocritical.

Recently, she confided in me, saying:

— Consult a psychiatrist for advice regarding your health concerns.

— For what purpose? I am not afflicted by madness.

—You aren't mad yet... But the time isn't right. Continued nightly partying with your extravagant religious rituals during the daytime could lead you to a mental institution.

— I cause no harm, I retorted. Our business is thriving, and you should take comfort in the wealth we're accumulating. Our construction project is progressing well, with numerous other initiatives keeping us busy. The nationwide construction boom continues as we tackle challenges in every afflicted area. This ongoing celestial conflict is a blessing bestowed upon us. I cannot help but wish for it to last eternally. How fortunate we are with our abundant resources; what more could your heart desire? Besides, I have always fulfilled my duties as your spouse. What compels you to beseech my descent into madness? Don't I show you enough affection, my love, and am I not excessively devoted to you?

Her laughter echoed through the room, a delicate symphony of joy that danced upon the air.

— Dear husband, please don't let infatuation with anyone other than me consume you. But your actions suggest a contradiction.

— Sophia, Sophia, haven't we covered this topic before? I've shared that this issue holds no anti-Islamic intent or contradiction. I find myself adopting the manners of historic caliphs. I've expressed my view that as we revive the magnificent Islamic era, it's natural and sensible to follow the practices of our venerated forebears. They often enjoyed beverages at night, then abstained once the Muezzin called, inviting the faithful to their religious duties. My dear, this is a tradition deeply rooted in my heart. You're familiar with my strong emotional bond to our ancestral customs. In what other way can I behave to show steadfast loyalty to that bygone era, which our wise Islamic leadership eagerly embraces?

She stated that Hassan doesn't drink alcohol.

— I'm aware. In human perception, his statements have strayed from the truth. He finds it difficult to understand the deep meaning he aims to convey. The man, once a passionate preacher, has given up his pulpit. What is the gentleman doing at this moment? It's hard to say. Maybe, like me, he finds comfort in saving money to protect himself against the darkness that lies ahead. But the man, in his current state, seems to be doing well... Who knows, really?

She wasn't surprised when I told her I'd been made president of the Ouja cell. She chuckled and said:

— I see. That will help you rise from the underground, my dear. Politics can be complicated, but you'll become a governor eventually. Once you've taken on the role of Security Director, you'll be well on your way to becoming a Minister, that's for sure.

* * *

Despite learning about my demotion and transfer to Ouja in advance, I felt suspicious about her role in the decision despite being the one most affected. Given the president's ultimate authority in presidential aspirations, I couldn't refuse or challenge the appointment. It's essential to recognise that the president's wishes hold significant power.

In the opulent abode of Abdelghani Abdelghaffar, he graciously welcomed my presence. The duration of the interview was but a fleeting moment, a mere two or three minutes that passed with an ephemeral swiftness. Our exchange of words was but a quick and tenuous affair. Mamduh and Hassan found themselves amid a grand ceremony of decoration. With his peculiar manner of speech, the Minister half-swallowed his words and addressed the President thus: "Mis. President, there exists a certain businessman whose helicopters have played a significant role in quelling the riots."

Abdelghani emitted a low, guttural sound, manifesting his inner torment. The ocular orbs, concealed beneath the ebony frames, eluded my gaze.

— Welcome, he uttered, his voice a mere whisper in the vast expanse of the room.

He bore a striking resemblance to his posters, if not slightly diminished in authenticity, akin to a mere facsimile of his being.

Our hands met, a brief and perfunctory gesture of acknowledgement. The tumultuous surge of the historic moment engulfed me, rendering me breathless with its intoxicating allure. I found myself uttering in a halting manner, akin to the stammering of an uncertain soul: — Mr. President, your kind act is greatly appreciated.

It is with great honour that I find myself in this particular circumstance, where I am compelled to express my sentiments... and so forth. Yet, I was unable to persist. The director of protocol delivered a small medallion carefully positioned upon a bed of lustrous fabric. Abdelghani placed the medal on my chest with a calm and skilled touch. His hands didn't tremble as he held it in position. He targeted my chest accurately, maintaining focus. With a graceful movement, he pinned the medal to my clothing, leaving me dressed in honour while the official who had given it remained nearby, ready to intervene if needed. Yet, the ceremony proved triumphant, and to this day, it remains an enigma to my perplexed mind. I still ponder the enigmatic manner in which he accomplished such a feat. In all honesty, I must confess my ignorance. The enchantment of authority, perchance, lies herein unless he had diligently honed his skills since the lamentable evasion of the Scoundrel!

Once more, our hands met in a firm clasp. He uttered these words with a solemnity that bespoke a deep-rooted admiration:

— Today, Ouja takes pride in your achievements. You embody the qualities suitable for the presidency of its respected community.

His generosity was evident in how he chose to bestow upon me his flattering words. His remarks, like a delicate brushstroke upon the canvas of my soul, stirred within me a profound and ineffable sentiment. I was utterly moved, as if caught in the embrace of a gentle breeze, whispering secrets only the heart can comprehend. I stammered bashfully, offering my gratitude before departing. Soon after, Hassan trailed behind me, extending his congratulations and uttering:

— Esteemed brother-in-law, this momentous occasion calls for celebration. Finally, you have ascended to the honourable status of a national hero.

— I must confess, I responded, that it had forever been my heart's cherished desire.

* * *

A few days later, I asked the young employee who had recently been appointed to take my place at the 'Ouja bank to come to my office, which was located in the secret heart of our party's cell. I didn't waste any time getting to the point and told him that his services were crucial to our cause. My words hung heavily in the air as I spoke.

To my astonishment, the youthful gentleman, whose de-meanour exuded naivety and timidity, retorted with unexpected candour: "I am grateful for your offer, Mr. Bassam, but regret-fully, I must decline as I am already employed at the bank."

In my contemplation, a familiar laughter reached my ears, and a peculiar notion seized my mind. It dawned upon me that Hamda La'war, in his eternal resting place, was convulsing un-controllably with mirth, his spirit consumed by a jealous deri-sion directed towards none other than myself...

The end.

Tunis, December 1996 and 1997.
London- Quillan (South France). April 2024.

www.ingramcontent.com/pod-product-compliance
Lightning Source LLC
Chambersburg PA
CBHW062011190726

48283CB00005BA/1405